Eileen Ramsay lives in Angus but grew up in Dumfriesshire. After studying in Edinburgh she went to teach in the United States, where she remained for twenty years. She returned to Scotland with her Scottish husband and their sons because she missed primroses.

By Eileen Ramsay

THE BROKEN GATE
THE DOMINIE'S LASSIE
BUTTERFLIES IN DECEMBER
WALNUT SHELL DAYS
THE QUALITY OF MERCY

EILEEN RAMSAY OMNIBUS

Butterflies in December
Walnut Shell Days

EILEEN RAMSAY

WARNER BOOKS

A *Warner* Book

This omnibus edition first published in Great Britain by Warner Books in 2001

Eileen Ramsay Omnibus Copyright © Eileen Ramsay 2001

Previously published separately:

Butterflies in December
First published in Great Britain by Little, Brown and Company in 1995
Published by Warner Books in 1996

Copyright © Eileen Ramsay 1995

Walnut Shell Days
First published in Great Britain in 1997 by Little, Brown and Company
Published by Warner Books in 1998

Copyright © Eileen Ramsay 1997

'Dreamers' by Siegfried Sassoon is reproduced by kind permission of
Mr George Sassoon

The moral right of the author has been asserted.

A CIP catalogue record for this book
is available from the British Library.

ISBN 0 7515 3171 5

Printed and bound in Great Britain by Clays Ltd, St Ives plc

Warner Books
A Division of
Little, Brown and Company (UK)
Brettenham House
Lancaster Place
London WC2E 7EN

www.littlebrown.co.uk

Butterflies in December

For
Mr and Mrs James Harrison McGlothlin
from No. 4

Acknowledgements

With thanks to: Fiona Scharlau, Archivist; Ian Flett, Archivist; L. Ball of the Commonwealth War Graves Commission; Robert F. Newell, Director General of the Royal Overseas League; Dr Gary Colner; Dr Jim Inglis; Dundee and Angus Librarians; Mrs Jo Currie, Special Collections, Edinburgh University Library.

1

Washington DC 1888

THAT YEAR THERE was a particularly fine Indian summer. For those foreign residents of this capital city who had alternately burned and sweated profusely during July and August and who could not afford to leave for cool cottages on Cape Cod, it was doubly welcome. Mind you, here in the old colonial city of Georgetown with its splendid trees, relief from the usual breathless days could be obtained. Lucy Graham lay back in the swing beside the man she loved more than anybody or anything in this whole world and idly watched the blue sky appear and disappear behind leaves. Just round the corner the Bliss Estate with its friendly name, Dumbarton Oaks, ran from high ground all the way down to the waters of Rock Creek. A bridge from the Dumbarton Oaks side straddled the clear waters of the creek and gave access to Virginia: home of fine horses, gracious living and, of course, several presidents starting with George Washington.

'Maybe I should have put Washington first,' thought Lucy idly, 'before the horses.'

She spoke for the first time in several somnolent moments. 'Have you ever met anyone who was born and bred in this city, Father?'

Colonel Sir John Graham lay back in the garden seat beside his daughter and considered the question.

'No,' he finally said. 'Can't say I have. Everyone at the Embassy is a foreigner. All the politicians, too, come from other states.'

With his heel he set the swing in motion again, and father and daughter drifted back and forward under the massive trees watching the sun chasing its beams in and out of the leaves above them. They revelled in the time that they could be alone together. Beside them, Amos, Lady Graham's general factotum, finished sweeping the afternoon's drift of leaves while he listened to their gentle well-bred Scottish voices. He loved the sound and paid little attention to the content, unless it was directed at him. It would never have occurred to him to say, 'Look at me, Colonel, sir. I been born here, and my daddy and my daddy's daddy.'

'Not many more days of sitting outside, Lucy.'

It was September and already chill winds were blowing down from the north.

'Mother will be pleased. She finds swinging with one's own father a complete and utter waste of time.'

They laughed together.

'Not that I agree with her,' Lucy went on lazily. 'Poor mother. To be stuck with a bean-pole for a daughter.'

'A delightful bean-pole.' Colonel Graham stopped the swing and looked measuringly at his daughter. 'You have my height, Lucy, but your mother's looks and her grace. I can't understand why this garden isn't swarming with teenage boys sporting boating blazers and carrying tennis rackets. There are enough of them in the diplomatic community.'

'I inherited your brains too,' said Lucy flatly. 'I cannot simper.'

'You refuse to simper.'

'I cannot chatter.'

'You refuse to chatter.'

'Would you have me different?'

'Not me, my darling child. A woman like you, Lucy, is rare as a butterfly in December.'

A butterfly in December. How sweet he was, and how poetic for a soldier. She looked at his clear-cut profile.

'We must look for a collector of rare butterflies,' she said lightly and watched him laugh.

'Auguste Arvizo-Medina?'

Lucy started up from the swing in mock horror. She was enjoying this repartee, knowing perfectly well that they could not speak so boldly and openly if Lady Graham were present. 'Good heavens, no. Would you have me mother of at least five fat babies in as many stultifying years?'

'He says he is fascinated by you.'

'I would bore him to distraction when I refused to turn into a brood mare. I should have been a man, Father, and then I could have, could have . . .'

'Followed me to Military College?' The Colonel spoke the words lightly, rather as though he and his daughter shared some absurd joke.

'Rather to Oxford.'

There, she had said it. Lucy looked at him from under her eyelashes, but there was no shock on his face.

'It's not the way of our world, my dear. Don't despair.'

'American women go to college, Father.'

'My dear child. I will not have my only daughter labelled a blue-stocking and besides, there is something so unfeminine about the college girls we have been obliged to meet.'

'Perhaps because they have had to fight like men

for a place they should have by rights, although you must agree that Americans have been so much more modern in their thinking than we Scots. It's perfectly acceptable for well-bred American girls to be educated. Mount Holyoke Female Seminary must have been in existence for almost fifty years – and there's Vassar Female College, and Wellesley, and Smith.'

'You're remarkably knowledgeable, Lucy,' said Sir John drily and decided to change the direction of the conversation; he was a brilliant strategist. 'You can still use that not inconsiderable brain.'

'How?' Lucy almost jumped from the swing and he registered, with appreciation, the compelling picture she made as she walked about the garden. 'By deciding how much chicken feeds two hundred guests, or how much cream is needed to pour over those peaches Amos gathered this morning? Women have brains, Father, and I have been luckier than most. Because of Kier, I am as qualified as any man to enter a university.'

She sat down again beside him and he set the swing into gentle motion. They did not speak but Lucy knew that her father, Colonel Sir John Graham, Military Attaché to her Britannic Majesty's Embassy in Washington DC, had to be thinking, like her, of the son of their neighbour in Scotland. Kier Anderson-Howard had been Lucy's friend since early childhood. Having had a bad riding accident when he was twelve years old, for nearly five years he had been unable to continue his education in the public school system. Because his parents did not want him to be educated alone, they had invited their neighbours, Sir John and Lady Graham, to send along their daughter to share Kier's tutor.

A new world had opened for Lucy: Latin, Greek,

Mechanics, German, Philosophy, Mathematics, a world away from the History (abridged), French, English literature (censored), and Drawing, which was the bulk of what Miss Bulwark had been able to teach her.

'That prissy girls' school where you were enrolled would have collapsed from shock at your ignorance if you had ever joined them, Lucy,' Kier had teased after their first morning together in Herr Colner's classroom.

'I'm glad dear Mr Colner did not,' Lucy had said seriously and had gone on to astound herself, her friend, and their tutor with the remarkable agility of her mind. By the time Kier was pronounced strong enough to return to Fettes to take the entrance examinations for the university, Lucy was as ready and as able as her schoolmate. But in 1886, no one considered sending young ladies to university with their brothers.

She had joined her father in his appointment to Washington, where she received long interesting letters from Kier who did not try to spare her maidenly blushes – knowing she had none – and told her about everything he experienced, first at Fettes and later at Oxford University.

'What of Kier, then?' asked the Colonel into his daughter's silence. 'You will come out next winter and then . . .' He did not add that his daughter, even at sixteen, should be thinking of a future with a good husband.

'Kier is my best friend,' said Lucy, and then, because he was her father and she had always known that she could tell him absolutely everything and anything and never be judged, she poured out her feelings. 'I love him desperately. I think I always have . . . even before the accident, I mean. That

changed everything. Not just my education but . . .
my relationship with Kier. That first year when he
couldn't move, I did so much for him. I saw him in
so many moods, dealing with pain, with fear, being
sick. There's little romance left when someone has
wiped up your vomit.'

She lost herself in her memories and her father
looked at her in wonder. His sheltered, protected
daughter cleaning up vomit! Her mother would faint
at the very idea.

'I read to him in the afternoons sometimes when
Herr Colner would rest. He was ill too, you know,
some wasting sickness from years of privation: the
Jews have never been well treated, have they? I wonder why that is? I hardly think God chooses to punish
them for eternity for denying Christ.' Lucy shook
away that thought impatiently. 'Anyway, Father,' she
went on, 'Kier could not bear his mother about him
– she fussed so, and wept constantly over his broken
bones. It was easier to clean him up and dispose of
his soiled nightshirts than to send for her. I cared
deeply, but somehow I was able to do what had to
be done for him with the minimum of hysteria. Still, I
doubt that he sees me as a delicate flower; a butterfly,
if you will.'

'He will see quite a change when we return home
next Christmas. You will be sixteen; your hair will be
up. Your flashing eyes will devastate him.'

Two years in one of the most sophisticated and
richest cities in the world, albeit one that was still
classed as a hardship post by Her Victorian Majesty's
Government, had had quite an effect on Lucille Graham. Her father could hardly wait to see the effect
she would create in London and Edinburgh salons.

'Sir John, stop filling the child's head with nonsense.' They had not heard Lady Graham glide

elegantly out of the French doors, managing her skirts with a grace that Lucy would always envy. 'Senator du Pay and his son have called. Lucille, I would like you to meet the du Pays. They are very wealthy and, what is more important, very influential.'

'I'd like to meet them, Mamma. Max du Pay is the one with the matched bays.'

Lady Graham threw up her head – almost, thought Lucy wickedly, like one of those self-same horses. 'Not one word about horses.' Elizabeth Graham looked at her daughter, almost 'out', and all that was in her head was books, horses, and books again. Where had she gone wrong? John's influence. Not for the first time she wished that she had been able to give her husband the son they had both wanted. 'Go and tidy yourself, Lucy. Max du Pay is already at Harvard. He is used to sophisticated young women, not hoydenish schoolgirls who can think only of books and horses.'

Lucy went upstairs, but not to her room. She went to the circular landing where she and her father had their favourite indoor retreat. It was no more than an enlarged landing really, and was full of huge, comfortable, but decidedly unfashionable, armchairs, bookcases and dog baskets.

From the huge windows, almost as tall as the room, which flooded the staircase with light in all but the depths of the Washington winter, she could see the street and, more importantly, the horses Max du Pay was driving today. She caught her breath. Oh, such beauty!

'Aren't horses the most beautiful creatures God put on the earth, Digby,' she told the elderly Sealyham who had merely raised one eye by way of greeting. 'If you weren't too old you would adore to chase this pair; they're black as night and they shine like polished jet, like Mamma's mourning beads. Oh!'

She remembered that her mother was waiting for her and without doing a thing to her appearance, ran downstairs. She had time to stop and compose herself before entering the drawing room and, because she was late, the guests were already drinking tea and she had the opportunity to look at them before they saw her. She knew Senator du Pay by sight, but she had never seen his son before. 'What do they feed them on in the South?' she asked herself, for if her father and the American senator were tall, this young man was a giant.

He turned and looked at her and the oddest feelings ran through Lucy.

'Why, here is your little girl, Colonel, sir,' drawled the young man and his eyes, as he looked at Lucy, registered her blush and laughed at her.

She lifted her head and ignored him completely.

'Senator du Pay. How do you do, sir. Father and I were just analysing your dissertation to Congress this week.'

The senator took her hand and tucked it into his arm as he led her to a seat in the window. 'My dear young lady. I can't believe such a beautiful young woman bothers her pretty little head with such dull stuff. Lady Graham, you British mothers are to be congratulated. Beauty, charm, and brains too. Why have I not met this delightful young lady before?'

Lady Graham revelled in the game the senator was playing; he and his son could tell the tale being told by the long hair dancing on Lucy's shoulders and catching the light from the candles already burning on the tables. 'Senator, you know perfectly well our daughter is not yet out.'

He pretended surprise. 'Why, ma'am, she will lay

waste this city with her beauty as her compatriots once wasted it with their bullets.'

Lucy looked at him. She was not unused to such silly talk; it was the way all her parents' elderly friends flirted with her, but the senator's son said nothing and Lucy was intensely aware of him. He was laughing at her. Why? She put her nose – classically straight, thank heaven – even higher in the air.

'I will be too busy to take Washington, sir. Why, Father and I were discussing college this very afternoon.' Not completely true, but she would not have Maximilian du Pay look at her as if she was nothing but a silly schoolgirl allowed for a moment to a grown-ups' party.

'Together with Father's speech.' He laughed down at her, down. Lucy was used to looking into the eyes, if not over the heads of most men.

Why was he teasing her? He made her uncomfortable. Never, ever, had she been so aware of a man. She threw herself into the verbal fray.

'And many, many more important things.'

'Oh, shush, Lucy.' She had gone too far and even Father was angry. But he said nothing; that would come later.

'Lucille, would you go to the kitchen and ask Amos to bring those peaches we picked from the glasshouse this morning? I would like the senator to try them.' Lady Graham was ushering her daughter to the door. 'And then you go straight to your room, young lady,' she whispered as she opened the door.

Lucy almost ran to the kitchens. She was angry and embarrassed and she hated that supercilious, overbearing Maximilian – what a stupid name – du Pay. It was his fault that she had been rude. She would never, ever, ever speak to him again. He would beg but she . . .

From the kitchens came the sound of a crash, a scream, a muffled groan. Lucy picked up her skirts and ran. She opened the door and saw the cause of the commotion. Female, the young black maid, had obviously tipped over a kettle of boiling soup and it had splattered Amos as he was in the act of slicing some of the splendid peaches. The knife had slipped and buried itself, not in a peach but in his hand. Lucy did not even pause to think.

'Stop screaming, Female, and get me some water. Sit down, Amos, and keep your hand up.'

'This ain't no job for you, Miss Lucille,' whispered the old man. 'What will your mamma say?'

Lucy knew perfectly well what her mother would say, but she lied. 'She'd say that we should get you to a hospital as soon as possible. (Hospital: doctor. How did one staunch blood? Should the knife come out or be left embedded in the wound? Tell me, tell me.) 'Female, go to the drawing room and ask Sir John to come down.' She did not wait for the girl's flustered protests: 'The drawing room. I doesn't go in there when there's white folks there,' but calmly went on staunching the blood with a cloth. 'Right now, Female.' The girl threw her apron over her head and ran.

'I hope she doesn't bump her head on something,' she said and in spite of the pain Amos grinned. 'She know her place, Miss Lucille, and it ain't in your mamma's drawing room.'

They could hear the servant girl shrieking out her story and in a minute or two the kitchen was invaded. Lucy ignored the du Pays.

'An accident with a knife, Father. We'll take him to George Washington, or would Georgetown be better?'

The four men, three white, one black, looked at one another, and one of the white faces flushed.

'It don't make no never mind, Colonel, sir,' said Amos gently. 'I can't go to them fine hospitals, Miss Lucille; that's for white folks. I thank you for your help: she didn't swoon or nothing, Colonel, sir. I can take care of it myself now, Miss Lucille. Female can sew it up with the thread she been using to sew up that chicken. The knife ain't cut nothing important, and now she's stopped screaming she'll do a good job. Won't you, daughter?'

Female wiped her tear-stained cheeks and nodded. 'Pappy's learned me lots about wounds, Colonel, sir, Miss Lucille. I'm sorry I yelled so; I just hates the sight of blood. How can you stand it, Miss Lucille? Ain't it indelicate in a young lady – and a white one at that – not to swoon?'

Lucy ignored everyone but her father. She was hardly aware of Maximilian du Pay leaving the room.

'It's bleeding badly. He should see a doctor. I just don't know what to do.' She turned to her father, the soldier. 'You must have dealt with wounds?'

'I got a ointment for bleeding, Miss Lucille,' said Amos before the Colonel could answer. 'You'll see, I'll be fine tomorrow. Female'll go get her mother when she's done sewed me up and Abra will look to everything here.'

The young American came back, his indolence gone. 'I've arranged the carriage, Father. I'll take him to Freedmen's myself, with your permission, of course, Colonel. 13th and V Street, I think? I've never been before.'

Was that a glance of admiration he gave Lucy? She could not be sure. More likely it was surprise, distaste even. Hadn't he heard Female say her behaviour was indelicate? Well, she didn't care. Look at them, look at them just taking over, putting the little woman back in her place. She followed the men out of the kitchen and wearily made her way up to her bedroom to await the tirade that was sure to come. She felt certain that she could write the script herself.

In the end, it was not her mother who came to her room but her father.

'Mother must be furious,' said Lucy lightly when she saw his set face.

'You amazed us both this afternoon, Lucy, and we've talked. Mamma loves you and she wants for you the things she enjoyed – a coming-out, new dresses, parties, dancing. But she is broad-minded enough to see that those treats don't interest you . . .'

'They do, Father, of course they do, but . . . not so much as . . . as doing something really special with my life.'

'I can think of nothing more splendid for a woman, Lucy, than being a good wife and mother,' said Sir John seriously, 'but we've decided – to use a horsey term – to give you your head for a while, till it's out of your system . . .'

A few weeks later, Lucy found herself a very young student at the vey young Smith College for women in Northampton, Massachusetts. She decided not to think of Maximilian du Pay and the extraordinary effect he had had on her, and after a few months she forgot all about him and everything else that kept her from learning, learning.

She loved Smith; she loved New England. She both loved and hated being surrounded by so many people. Lucy had never been to school; her largest class had had one classmate. Here there were dozens of bright, articulate, young women. Classes of five,

ten, twenty girls were uncharted waters for Lucy
and she set sail eagerly. Often, though, she had to
steal away from the laughing, loving companionship
and seek solace and a kind of inner rebirth. For this
she would wander in the grounds among the age-old
trees. At all times of the year, the College was lovely.
In the autumn – the Fall as her American classmates
called it – the grounds were breathtaking. How was
it possible for leaves to turn those colours, and all
with an intensity that she had seen nowhere before?
Yellow, red, brown . . . but yellow, red and brown
that had been ignited by a fire that was only to
be found in these New England states. The trees
burned their way into winter. The leaves crackled
on the branches as they struggled to free themselves
from their tenuous hold on life and they crackled
under Lucy's soft leather boots as she wandered
among them. She wrote long letters, weekly to her
parents and monthly to Kier Anderson-Howard. She
told him of her delight in the formal education for
which Herr Colner had so ably prepared her. She
told him of her pleasure in joining five, ten, fifteen
alert brains in healthy argument and discussion.

I loved being educated with you, Kier, but I have
just realized that because of that education, I have
knowledge but no friends besides yourself and I
did not know what I missed. I would not have it
different, but now I am happy to catch up with
my own sex. Already I have been invited to spend
an exeat weekend with a classmate who lives in
New York City and I have invited another, who
lives in Oregon – which, as you know, is about
as far from Massachusetts as it is possible to go
without falling into the Pacific Ocean – to spend
the Thanksgiving holiday with us in the capital.

What fun to introduce an American to her own historic buildings. Mirabelle, from New York, is to take me to the Opera and to dine in a *restaurant* with her huge family of brothers. How decadent I am become – exactly what Mother feared!

In a later letter she asked him what on earth she could do with the degree she would soon earn. Even to Kier, she could not mention the only real idea she had had, which was growing so strongly that it threatened to blot out everyone and everything. She felt that she was two different people: Miss Graham who lived in Massachusetts, and little Lucy who lived in Washington DC. Little Lucy went home at the holidays and did the things her mother wanted her to do, although the trip to Scotland and the presentation at Court had had to be sacrificed on the voracious altar of further education. On her last Thanksgiving holiday from Smith, Lucy returned home like every other student but, unlike most students, she found herself heading for a recital at the Russian Embassy.

They had almost been late. Female, Amos's daughter, had been announced to be in a *delicate* condition. Female was unmarried and Lucy found herself fascinated and wanted to know the whys and the wherefores. Her unseemly interest in something that had caused friction between her parents – Lady Graham wishing to dismiss the girl and Sir John more interested in keeping excellent servants like Amos and Abra happy – had caused Lady Graham to remember Lucy's own wayward and unfeminine behaviour several years earlier; she had never really mentioned this, no matter how hard it was, but it had gnawed at her occasionally. Now she lapsed from self-imposed virtue a little.

'A girl in your position, with your advantages,

should have nothing to do with such things, Lucille.
I still can't bear to think what the du Pays thought
when they found you alone in the kitchen with a
black male servant . . . I'm quite sure their friendship
cooled a little.'

'Mother, how can you ignore Amos's very presence one minute and the next be so conscious of it?'
Lucy had teased.

'They found you doing what no well-brought-up
young woman should even contemplate doing.'

'Florence Nightingale is a lady, Mother, and she
did a great deal more than bind up a bleeding
wound.'

'One admires Miss Nightingale. One does not
necessarily wish one's only child to emulate her.
Besides, she did it for our soldiers.'

'Oh, and of course none of them was black. I
wonder if it would have made a difference to her.'

The Colonel stirred on his seat. The quarrel
between his wife and his daughter was becoming
a little too heated. 'Lucille, your mother is right to
concern herself with the opinion the world has of
you.' He laid his hand gently on Lucy's satin-covered
knee and she decided to argue no more.

'I'm sorry, Mother, but I'm sure you didn't want
poor Amos to bleed to death. He is, after all, an
invaluable servant.'

'And could have been looked after by other servants: that hysterical daughter of his, for instance,
with the ridiculous name.'

'Feh-ma-lay,' smiled Lucy, drawing out the sylla-
bles the way their servants did. 'It's rather sad, actually, that they couldn't pronounce Female, couldn't
read . . .'

'And where, by the by, was Abra during that
incident?' Lady Graham interrupted, a sense of

injustice gnawing at her. She had been quiet for
too long; she would have a little satisfaction now,
and Lucy had brought it on herself. 'Now that I
think about it, I don't remember giving her time off
mid-week.'

'We did discuss all this, Elizabeth,' the Colonel put
in. 'Remember, my dear, Amos had asked me when
you were with your dressmaker. It seemed only fair;
they do work such very long hours.'

Lady Graham sighed. Her husband would never
learn how to treat servants properly; they would do
exactly as they liked if she didn't keep a firm hand on
the reins.

The carriage drew up at the Embassy and Lady
Graham was considerably cheered when she saw that
her daughter was to be partnered by the very handsome and very wealthy Russian Count Fyodorov. She
smiled complacently. Lucy could make a beautiful
countess, if she so chose.

Lucy well knew what was going through her mother's mind, and because she loved her she decided to
be good and to charm the Count as best she could.
There was another more compelling reason to shine
with the Russian. Almost the first voice she heard
as she entered the Embassy was the low drawl
of Maximilian du Pay and, what was worse, she
found that he was to be seated very near her but,
thankfully, on the other side of the table; she need
not speak to him at all. She nodded stiffly, as if
she vaguely remembered him but could not quite
place him though would never for a moment be
rude . . . and then decided to ignore him as best
she could.

'I wish we were to have dancing after dinner, Miss
Graham, instead of that dreadfully boring, and even
more dreadfully fat, mezzo-soprano. I should insist

that you dance every dance with me but perhaps, while they prepare the salon for the entertainment, we could walk a little on the terrace. It is mild for November, no?'

'It is mild for November, yes,' agreed Lucy. 'If others are strolling on the terrace, Count, then I am sure we may join them.'

'Not a good idea, Miss Lucy. I may claim the privilege of old friendship, may I not?'

Lucy was amazed. She had turned, as custom demanded, to the guest on her right, and had caught Max du Pay's eye. Obviously the odious man had been listening to her conversation. It is one thing to flirt with a handsome Russian, it is quite another to be observed doing it by someone one loathes, and especially when flirting is completely against one's principles. She blushed rosily.

'Charming,' he said. 'I had no idea that empty-headed, rich young women could blush any more.'

Lucy was furious and she forgot all her mother's rules for good behaviour. 'How dare you! You know perfectly well that I am neither wealthy nor empty-headed.'

He laughed. 'And being called empty-headed rankles more, I'll be bound. But as I was saying, Miss Smith College, don't stroll in the moonlight with the Count. He is a most notorious philanderer.'

'I think I'm capable of taking care of myself, Mr du Pay. No one would be invited here who was . . .'

'Not *comme il faut*?'

'Not empty-headed . . . I mean who was empty – oh, stuff!' She heard the ridiculous words as she was speaking them and would have drawn them back if she could. He saw her predicament and laughed.

'You need have no fear to speak your mind around

me, Miss Graham, although usually we Southerners prefer our women meek and mild.'

'How nauseating.' Again that unruly tongue.

'I do believe you are right, Miss Graham.' He laughed and turned away from her.

Since Count Fyodorov was still engaged in conversation Lucy studied the American, safe in the knowledge that, since he was giving an inordinate amount of attention to the very sophisticated but married woman on his right, he could not see her. What had he been doing for the past year? He must be finished at Harvard. She had been to balls at that prestigious college twice during this heady year and had never seen him – had tried, oh, yes, she had, not to look for him. She had forgotten how tall he was and how fair. His hair, which was too long for fashion, was almost bleached by the sun, and his face and hands showed that he spent rather too much time outside in all weathers. She was so busy watching the man she had resolved to ignore that she almost missed the next move in the conversational game of bat and ball.

'I detest Maximilian du Pay and I adore charming Russians,' she said to herself and turned with a glorious smile to her dinner partner.

After dinner she found herself walking with him and several other people towards the glass doors that led to the terrace. Count Fyodorov solicitously wrapped her light voile scarf around her bare shoulders.

'You should wear ermine,' he said.

Lucy smiled. She could just imagine her father's face if she were to ask for an ermine cape. His diplomatic salary made up the sum total of the Graham fortune, and a military attaché's income did not stretch to fur stoles for his daughter.

To her surprise, she found herself whisked behind

an enormous urn and held tightly in a man's
embrace.

'Miss Graham, Lucy, that smile. It tantalizes; how
you are adorable,' he said and, to her amusement,
kissed her ruthlessly.

This was not the first time that Miss Lucy Graham
had been kissed and, really, she chided herself, 'You
ought to be able to handle men better by this time.'
She pushed the Count away and laughed. It worked;
it always did. Nothing deflated an enormous ego
more than laughter. At least, it had always worked
with the college men who haunted the grounds
at Smith.

Count Fyodorov visibly controlled his annoyance.
He bowed. 'Your servant, Miss Graham. May I escort
you back to her ladyship?'

'I'll take her, Count.'

'Not nice, Miss Graham,' said Maximilian du Pay
in an amused voice as they watched the discomfited
Russian walk away.

'You had no business spying on me, Mr du Pay.'

'Max, please, and I wasn't spying. You're lucky the
entire diplomatic party did not witness your petty
triumph.'

Petty triumph! Lucy could not believe it. She had
been assaulted – well, not quite – and a second
arrogant male called it a petty triumph.

'Don't bristle, for I won't say you look charming
when you pout . . .'

'I never pout,' Lucy broke in.

'You led that poor man by the nose all through
dinner, and then you act surprised when he accepts
your invitation.'

Lucy flushed to the roots of her hair. Was there
some honesty in what he said? A gentleman, however, would never have said it.

'I think we have nothing further to say to one another, Mr du Pay.' She would refuse his invitation to make free of his Christian name.

'Au contraire, Miss Lucy,' he smiled, 'but not yet. I decided, and I never go back on my decisions, that when you have grown up a little . . .'

He did not say what he had decided, but he bowed courteously and turned away and Lucy watched him, her mind in a turmoil. He was the rudest, most arrogant man she had ever met. She must make a real effort never to meet him again. She hurried back to the magnificent salon where seats had been arranged for the recital. Her parents had saved a chair for her and if they were surprised to see her unescorted they were unable to say anything.

In the carriage, on the way back to Georgetown, there were no such restrictions and, while her husband sat quietly in a corner, Lady Graham was able to allow a flood of recriminations to fall upon Lucy.

'Two of the most eligible men in Washington beside you at dinner, Lucille, and you throw away the opportunity.'

'Then you would have preferred that I submit to Count Fyodorov, Mother, pretend that I enjoyed his kiss.' She would not ask about Mr du Pay.

'Of course not, girl, but if you had not wanted it then it should never have happened.' Lady Graham sat back in anger and then relaxed. 'Oh, Lucy, you are very young. You know we have nothing but Father's salary. Count Fyodorov is related to the Tsar; his family is extraordinarily wealthy . . .'

'Then they should have spent a little more on his education,' said Lucy quietly.

Lady Graham pretended not to have heard. 'And he specifically asked for you at the dinner.'

'Definitely not a butterfly collector, Lucy,' said Sir

John, and then when he felt rather than saw his wife's growing anger he turned to her and added, 'But you must admit, my dear, that Max du Pay seemed taken with our daughter. We have all been invited to join the Thanksgiving Hunt this year.'

The Thanksgiving Hunt! Lucy had not expected an invitation to one of the social season's most prestigious events. She conveniently forgot how much she detested the Southerner.

'Oh, how wonderful!' She clapped her hands together in excitement like a small child. 'Can we go, Father?'

'You will hill-top with me, Lucy,' Lady Graham answered for her husband.

Hill-topping: following the horses by carriage and watching their progress from the tops of hills. Great fun, but not so much fun as sweeping across the Virginia countryside on the back of a strong, spirited horse.

Lady Graham saw the disappointment in her daughter's face. 'Mrs du Pay has generously invited us to join her in her own carriage, Lucy. Every girl in Washington will be green with envy.'

'Except the ones on horseback,' Lucy mumbled.

Lady Graham sighed and ignored the mumble. 'The du Pays are one of the most important families in the South, and it is a great honour to be asked. And there is the ball, Lucy. She will have to have a new gown, John; it will do for London too.'

'What did you think of Max this time, Lucy?' asked her father. 'Your first meeting had a rather unfortunate ending.' To his surprise Sir John saw his daughter blush.

'I didn't have too much conversation with him, Father.' Lucy was annoyed with herself. Senator du Pay was a personal friend of the Ambassador and a good ally for Her Britannic Majesty's Government, and here was she crossing verbal swords with his son. 'He doesn't look like a . . . a . . . socialite,' finished Lucy for want of a better word.

'Rather unconventional: he's studying animal husbandry, but I think he's interested in art. I thought you would have liked him,' said Sir John. 'Never mind. You can adjust your thinking when you see him in his own setting.'

The rest of the journey passed in silence. Amos, as usual, was at the gates to meet them.

'Nice party, Miss Lucille?' he asked as he handed her down.

Lucy kept his hand in hers. 'Delightful, thank you, Amos, and how are you?'

'Lucille,' scolded Lady Graham when they had gone upstairs to prepare for bed, 'you really must not be so familiar with black servants. You treat Amos just the way you treated Annie at home, and she's been with us since before you were born.'

'I really can't see that his being black is relevant, Mother, and if Annie is part of the family in Scotland, then surely Amos and his family are part of our family here. Besides, I was merely enquiring about his health. Perhaps it's just that I've been away from home so much, but he doesn't seem quite himself. It's odd, Father, but his skin looks a little paler and there's a clammy feel . . .'

'Lucille, I have had quite enough of this unhealthy interest in Amos . . . good heavens, do you realize the man doesn't even have a surname?'

Lucy looked at her mother. How was it possible to love someone and be so annoyed and exasperated by them at the same time? She kissed her parents and went to bed. She would check up on Amos, quietly, in the morning.

The morning brought a posy of flowers from Max du Pay and a magnificent bouquet from the Count. Perhaps even more exciting than the flowers was the note that accompanied the posy:

> Should you care to ride in the hunt, Miss Graham, I should be delighted to provide a mount suitable for a thinking woman.

He was teasing; he had remembered their conversation but had conveniently *forgotten* that she had admitted to being both intelligent and poor. Sir John could not provide his daughter with a riding horse. But Max du Pay's horses . . . Lucy rushed to her mother's bedroom. Lady Graham was sitting up in bed looking delightful and quite young in a froth of pink silk as Lucy handed her the posy and the note.

'Aren't they lovely, Mother? I shall keep them in my bedroom.' She looked at her mother, who was smiling complacently as she read Max's note. 'There's a disgustingly vulgar bouquet from the Count too.' Ah, that shot had gone home.

'Flowers from Count Fyodorov, Lucy. How very sweet.'

'A hothouse full of them. These are in such innate good taste, wouldn't you say, and I may accept the Senator's offer, Mother. The horses must belong to him. Max is only a boy after all . . .'

She stopped at the look of consternation on her mother's face.

'A riding-habit, Lucy? We must get you a new riding-habit.' Lady Graham slipped from the bed, hurried across to her voluminous French wardrobe and began to rifle through the contents.

'Here, darling. We must have this altered.' She

handed a dark blue velvet riding-dress to her daughter and looked at her carefully. 'Oh, Lucy, when are you ever going to . . . fill out?' she finished delicately.

'I'll look better in this than in the ball-gown Petal is making,' said Lucy as she held up the dress in front of her. Yes, dark blue was a very good colour.

'Petal should be working on the dresses now. Run upstairs and beg her to get this finished for Thanksgiving . . . only two days . . . and then you may write Max a note of acceptance, and change your dress. It's possible the Count will call.'

Lucy picked up her posy and rushed upstairs to the attics where Petal, Lady Graham's dressmaker, was doing wonders with yards of pale green silk – not such a good colour as the blue, but better than insipid white. She had hardly had time to make her request when Female followed her upstairs to say that a gentleman had called. Amos usually announced visitors, but Lucy was too excited by flowers and gowns and, oh, yes, a magnificent horse 'suitable for a thinking woman', to wonder why he had not.

The next two days passed in a whirl.

'Why am I so happy?' Lucy asked herself several times a day as she stood in her petticoat while Petal tried somehow to make her look more girl than boy. The riding-habit suited her slim figure. Max would notice. 'I don't care if he notices. I haven't ridden in two years. I am excited by the thought of such horses and galloping, galloping, free of restrictions.' She lowered the green silk over her head.

'A dark Venus rising from the waves,' was Sir John's comment.

'Petal has worked wonders,' agreed Lady Graham, 'and only just in time.' She looked at her watch. It was already Thanksgiving morning. 'We'll have Amos make up a basket for her to take home, and you must find a bonus, John.'

'The others are surely in bed, Elizabeth, and Petal must stay the night. She can't walk through the streets at this time of the morning. Come along, Cinderella, take off that beautiful gown and get some sleep or you'll be too tired to dance away tomorrow evening.' Sir John looked at his daughter, but Lucy was not listening to his banter. She stood, head poised like a deer who senses danger.

'I hear Female,' she said. 'Something's wrong, Father.'

She opened the door. Although it was so late all the lamps were still lit. 'You see,' she said triumphantly, 'Amos is still awake. He never goes to bed before we do.'

But it was Female who stood on the stairs, her voluminous nightgown disguising the bulge at her waistline. It was obvious that she had been crying.

'Ah so sorry not to be dressed, Ladyship, Colonel, sir. Ah been in bed, but Mammy says Pappy jist cain't git moving although he sure done tried.'

'What's wrong, Female?' asked Lucy. 'We must go to their quarters and see, Mother.'

Lady Graham was furious. 'Female! How dare you walk around the public part of the house in your nightwear? Go downstairs and send your mother up here at once.'

Female burst into loud sobs and turned and ran for the servants' stairs.

'I'm sorry, Lucy,' said Lady Graham, looking at her daughter's angry face, 'but we must maintain standards. Please go to bed. Father and I will find out what's wrong and send for a doctor if need be.'

'I'd rather wait, Mother.'

Abra was a tall slender woman, as neat at two in the morning as she would be at two in the afternoon. She came upstairs quickly.

'Amos has taken some kind of a turn, ma'am, Sir John. I'm sorry Female was in a state of undress. There ain't a brain in that girl's head.'

'What kind of turn . . . ?' began Lucy, but her mother was in charge.

'I will come to see Amos, Abra.'

She swept from the room and Lucy and her father sat down. They did not have long to wait, and one look at her mother's face told Lucy that Amos was seriously ill.

'I've sent Female next door to wake John-Joseph. He will bring some of their own people with a cart to take Amos to Freedmen's. I'm afraid he's seriously ill.'

'Surely we can do something. Get Professor Archibald . . . something?'

Professor Archibald was a close neighbour who was also on the staff at the nearby Columbia Hospital, a hospital established for the wives and widows of Union soldiers and sailors.

'At this hour of the morning, Thanksgiving morning, for a negro! You are so young, Lucy,' said her mother disparagingly.

Lucy refused to go to bed and sat in the drawing room and listened for the next-door servants to arrive. She did not notice how cold the room grew around her without the heavy diet of logs with which Amos fed the fire's insatiable appetite. She heard her father's voice and he went out – to do what, she did not know. It was only later that she learned that he had roused the coachman at the stables used by the Grahams, that he had driven to Freedmen's hospital and had sat, one white face in a frame of black ones, while Amos gave up the battle against his exhausted heart.

Sir John had found her in the drawing room, still in her sea-green ball gown. He had shaken her awake gently and told her the news, only half expecting the terrible outpouring of grief.

'But Amos was only a servant, Lucy,' he had hazarded, in an attempt to understand. 'You hardly know . . . knew him.'

'I couldn't help him; I knew nothing, Father.' She lifted her ravaged face to him. 'It could have been you.'

And that, Lucy confessed to herself later when she was safely and anonymously back at Smith, one student among so many, was the real cause of her distress. Had it been her beloved father who had continued to function with the weakness in his arms, the clammy skin, the alternate hot and cool skin, and eventually on that last morning the tightness in his chest – 'not a pain, Miss Lucy, he said he didn't have no pain' – she would have thought that perhaps he had eaten something that had disagreed with him, or that he had over-indulged. She would have sent at last for a doctor, one who would perhaps have come at two o'clock in the morning because Sir John was a fairly important part of the British Legation, and Sir John would have been taken to Georgetown Hospital, and perhaps . . . perhaps, he would have recovered.

'I will not give up the Thanksgiving Hunt at the du Pays for a servant,' said Lady Graham, who had kindly given Amos's family paid leave to bury husband and father, and who would willingly have accepted the hospital costs as one of the necessary expenses incurred by looking after good and valued servants.

There was no need for a family disagreement, however, for when the members of the family finally managed to get to sleep, they slept soundly through the hours of Thanksgiving morning and, in the afternoon, could find little for which to be wholeheartedly thankful.

'I'm sorry, Mother, I just can't go to a ball.'

'I don't feel much like dancing either,' agreed Lady Graham.

'Next year,' said Sir John.

But next year saw Lucille Graham in Edinburgh, Scotland, and there were so many beautiful and talented girls at the du Pays Thanksgiving Ball that hardly anyone missed her, hardly anyone.

2

Dundee 1888

ROSIE SAT SHELLING peas and whistling. The whistling did not help her work but it kept Ma happy. If Rosie was whistling, she couldn't be eating the peas; or so Ma thought. Rosie actually had the eating of fresh young peas while keeping up a piercing chorus of whatever was playing at the Playhouse that week, off to a fine art. Mind you, she had to hold them lodged in her jaw for quite a while before she could take a breath and then swallow them all at once. That rather spoiled the pleasure of eating but it increased the pleasure of winning, and that, for Rosie, was the greater pleasure. Rosie liked to win.

There was a much more important battle on the horizon and Rosie was concentrating on that while her strong young fingers automatically prised open the pods and released the peas. If only it had been done before . . .

If it had been done before, she could talk about it and ask how it had been done. Then, armed with all that information, she could go to Ma and say, say what? Say, 'Ma, I'm not following every other member of this family into the mills, I'm going to get an education: I'm going to be a doctor so that no more bairns up this closie will die because we're poor and we cannae afford the doctor or the medicines.' But doctoring was for men, and universities were for men, and even though some lassies, and especially

Rosie Nesbitt, were cleverer far than any laddie in the class, nobody would teach you Latin and Mathematics for those subjects were suitable only for men, and whoever had come up with a braw notion like that hadn't the sense he was born with. Rosie Nesbitt could read, write, spell, and add, better than any boy in her class. She had won a bursary at the age of ten that allowed her to attend the Harris Academy with all the nice, well-brought-up, well-dressed lassies from the West End of Dundee. One ancient teacher had even been heard to say that he had never come across a brain as gimp as Rosie Nesbitt's. But the powers that be – and all of them, wouldn't you know it, male – would not allow her a real education. Mind you, Scotland, that thought very highly of itself in terms of education, still barred women from its universities, but Rosie did not allow that small point to worry her. Something would happen: for Rosie Nesbitt something always did.

The idea came so suddenly and was so right, so sensible, that Rosie stopped whistling and nearly choked to death on her accumulation of peas. Old Wishy! She thought of the Classics master at the Harris, a bit like a hoodie craw – the children laughed at him in his threadbare old gown – but with a face that didnae fricht a child. At least, not Rosie Nesbitt. She had smiled at him that first day as she passed him on the stair, so pleased was she at being there in that old building, a bona fide pupil among all the toffs frae the West End. He had smiled back at her, a smile of genuine liking and approval, and had said, 'Welcome, my wee lass,' in that nice voice that wasn't a toff's voice but wasn't the sound of Dundee either. It sounded of education. Rosie almost hugged herself with joy at her brilliance. Why hadn't she thought of him before? She would pay him to teach her Latin.

There were plenty of ways of earning a few pence; she would just have to think of a few of them.

Rosie finished the peas and, quiet as the proverbial lamb, went in to help Ma with the rest of the dinner. Some dinner. Potatoes, mostly. Occasionally a bit of minced beef; sometimes fish, if the boys caught it.

'You're awfie quiet, Rosie.' Ma was tuned in to the moods of all her children and perhaps especially to those of this strange child, this cuckoo in the nest. 'Did ye eat too many peas?'

Rosie bristled; there was no way Ma could know. 'Did I stop whistling?' she demanded rashly.

Elsie smiled, a smile that wiped years and strain from her face. 'It's yer grannie thinks that's foolproof. Why did ye think she worked that oot? Was it no me that ate peas years afore you were born, Rosie? Noo, whit's on yer mind, lassie?'

Rosie looked at her mother. How old was Elsie Nesbitt? Well, Frazer was near twenty and so she had to be at least thirty-five. Could you birth a bairn afore the age of fifteen? Elsie, Ma, had to be between thirty-five and forty years of age. She couldnae be more than forty even if she looked, what, fifty? It was too late for Elsie. Rosie's turn. Better just to tell her right out. 'I'm going to be a doctor.'

Elsie Nesbitt sat down hard in a chair and looked almost in awe at her fifth child. It had to be blood. The others weren't like this. Rosie's dad had not been one of her regulars; Rosie had resulted as the outcome of a chance meeting at the docks – a lad who spoke differently, who'd given her a rose instead of the two shillings he had promised. Now here was Rosie, already too big for her boots with a school uniform and a real schoolbag, talking about . . . oh dear God, what kind of a nonsense?

'It's not nonsense, Ma,' said Rosie as if she could

read her mother's thoughts. 'Why should I no be a doctor? I'm clever. I like taking care of folk and I'm good at it. You aye said I was better wi' Grampa than onybody.'

'Och, lassie, that's a long way from getting all the book learning that makes a doctor.' Elsie had no real knowledge of higher education but she knew, as well as she knew the face of the girl in front of her, that the fulfilment of such a dream would take years . . . and money. Where could she ever get the money that was needed? By some strokes of divine providence, Rosie had aye managed to pay her way, and to see her stepping out of the door in the morning with her face washed and her hair brushed and a schoolbag full of exciting books in her hand did her mother's heart good – but doctoring!

'Here, Rosie. Take a penny-halfpenny oot the jar and run doon for a bowl of potted meat; it'll go nice with the peas.' She had meant the money for two nice girdle scones from the bakery at the bottom of the stairs – sometimes the smells rolling up the closie on the wind were almost too good to be borne – but the meat was probably a better buy, more nourishing.

Rosie was already half-way down the stairs. Buying anything from a shop was an adventure. 'Ma's thinking on it,' she told herself. When Elsie changed the subject, it usually meant she was thinking.

She took her place in the queue outside the butcher's and waited, ignoring the other customers, her two sisters playing with their skipping-rope in the middle of the street, and the slabs of raw red meat. They held no interest for her; she had never tasted anything other than mince or boiling beef and her salivary glands agreed with Elsie – 'What you've never had, you'll never miss.'

No need to wrap up the wee bowl for the run

back up the stairs. Rosie's mind kept pace with her steps. 'I've done it, I've done it.' Nothing was settled; nothing had been won; but she had brought her great dream out into the open and now it could grow. After all, it was only when flowers faced the sun that they really began to flourish.

Ma was still in the front room; she had not moved. Was she merely enjoying the unaccustomed peace of an empty room or was she still awed by the pronouncement from her third daughter? She turned from the window as Rosie catapulted into the room.

'I've been thinking on your plan, Rosie.' She moved to the huge oak dresser her grandfather had carved thirty years before and took out a patched but clean tablecloth which she threw over the scratched table top. 'Here, help me set the table; they'll all be in afore we know it – but I've been thinking that there's nae harm in trying for it. I heard a verse frae the pulpit once and it stuck in my mind. "Without vision the people perish." Well, I aye thought it meant a vision of angels and such, but it doesn't. You've got the vision all right, lassie, and we'll have to see aboot it. If I only kent where tae start.'

'With Latin, Ma. I need Latin, and I'll ask old Wishy tae teach me after school.'

'And whit would a bonnie lassie like you need with the Latin?'

With shrieks of joy Rosie and her mother rushed to throw themselves at the tall, windbeaten young man standing in the doorway. Frazer Nesbitt was Elsie's oldest son, and he had been gone over six months on a whaling expedition.

'I must have kent you were coming, laddie. Have I no just sent Rosie for potted meat?' Elsie was laughing and crying as she pulled her first-born into the room and forced him into the one good chair by the fire.

'And fresh peas, Frazer,' cried Rosie who was now perched on her brother's knees.

'Aye, there's whit madam's no eaten. I'll make you a cup of tea, laddie. How long can you stay? You didnae get hurted in ony way, did you?' Elsie's questions rained down on the boy's head like the snows he had been glad to leave in the far north but, goodnaturedly, he tried to answer all of them.

Rosie's grandiose plans sat and simmered like the soup on the back of the fire while Frazer talked and ate and talked again. Such places he'd seen; such people he'd met.

It was only after the others had come home – Lindsay, Leslie, and Murray from Baxter's jute works where they had started as half-timers and were now full-time, and Donaldina and Granta, the wee ones, from their play in the street – and after they had all eaten and heard again and again the wonderful stories, and admired the strange carvings that Frazer had bought for a plug of tobacco from a man he called an Eskimo, that there was time to talk about Rosie again.

'And now, whit's this about Latin, Rosie? What would a wee lassie want with the Latin?'

'I want tae be a doctor, Frazer.'

Frazer did not laugh; neither did any of the other children. Elsie Nesbitt had always insisted that her children get as much education as circumstances would allow. Education was the way out of poverty; everybody knew that. Wasn't there a fellow called Carnegie who had started near as poor as themselves and now had suitcases full of money?

'And for doctoring you need Latin?' asked Frazer.

'Aye. I could easy win a bursary, when I'm big that

is, but I need tae learn Latin and Mathematics and the Harris only teaches them tae boys.'

'You'll need private tuition, then,' said Frazer quietly and in such a matter-of-fact fashion that his mother stared at him, almost in awe. It never occurred to Elsie Nesbitt that it was something in herself that made these children different from the other children in the closie. Frazer had lapped up the learning too in the few years he had had at the school but, unlike Rosie, he had never set himself against circumstances but had gone out, as soon as he was able, to set about earning a living for himself, his mother, and the other children.

'I've a fortune saved, Ma,' he smiled. 'I aye fancied you in a smart new coat for the winter.'

'Ach, Rosie'll keep the hale gang of us in fur coats when she's a doctor – will you no, Rosie?'

Rosie stared at them both. She could say nothing. Words of gratitude were chasing one another around in her head but refused to find the way to her mouth.

'You can take the money to Mr Wishart the morn efter the school, Ma.'

But Elsie could not bring herself to confront a terrifying schoolteacher and, the next day, it was strong young Frazer who met Rosie as, almost sick with excitement, she left her last class.

'Whit if he says no?'

'I've £10 here in my poke,' said Frazer. 'That's near a half-year's wages for a teacher.'

Rosie looked up at him, almost as if she could not understand why the weight of such a vast sum of money had not bent him double.

'And after he says yes, Dr Nesbitt, there's still enough money to take you and Ma and me out for a fish supper and a cup of tea.'

Rosie clutched at his hand to steady herself. Latin tuition *and* a meal in a fisherman's café! She could not take much more. She almost stumbled along the corridor to the classroom of the Classics teacher.

Francis Wishart looked up from his marking when they answered his abrupt, 'Come.'

Whatever he had expected, it was not wee Rose Nesbitt and this tall weatherbeaten, old young man.

'Come in, Rose,' he said courteously. 'And this must be . . .'

'My brother, Frazer, Mr Wishart. He's a whaler,' finished Rose proudly. The teacher held out his hand to the whaler, who shook it in some surprise.

'What can I do for you, Mr Nesbitt?'

'It's Rosie. She wants to be a doctor.' Frazer looked into the older man's face but there was no scorn or derision there, only interest. 'She needs Latin.' He put his hand in the pocket of his rough jacket and pulled out a salt-stained pouch. 'I've saved my wages . . .'

'It was for a coat for Ma,' burst out Rosie and subsided quietly as Frazer looked at her in sudden anger.

'And you want me to tutor Rose for the entrance examination?'

Frazer looked at him in surprise. He was out of his depth now. 'Entrance, tae what? . . . sir,' he added.

'There's a medical school in Edinburgh for women.'

Edinburgh. Rosie and Frazer looked at one another. It might as well be on the moon. Rosie shrugged. Something would come up.

'Aye,' said Rosie. 'I mean, yes, Mr Wishart.'

Wishart looked ahead to the years of commitment.

'You understand what you are proposing, Rose? An hour of tuition one night a week and hours of private study . . . and for the next four years?'

'Yes, sir.'

'Four to five every Thursday. Other nights I have pupil teachers.'

'That will be fine, Mr Wishart.' Frazer gestured with the pouch.

'I'll give you the list of books your sister will need, and I'll update it as required. Buy your mother a coat, lad. I'll have free medical care from Dr Nesbitt when I'm in need of it.' He picked up his pen and dipped it in the inkwell on his desk. Rose and Frazer looked down at his bowed head.

'Till Thursday then,' said Rosie. 'Thank you, Mr Wishart.'

Out in the corridor, she walked to the front door, reserved for teachers and visitors, with her head high as befitted one of Scotland's first woman doctors. No one saw them leave and, rather to her regret, she went unchallenged out into the street.

'He's no going to charge, Frazer. Teachers must be rich.'

'I don't think so, Rosie. That one's good.'

'Oh, aye. Everybody's says he's the best Latin teacher; Greek too.'

Frazer looked down at his young sister sadly and then shrugged. She was very young and had lots of growing-up to do. He wished that he could be around to help her do it.

'Let's get Ma and take her out for her tea. Tomorrow I'll buy her a coat.' He stopped walking and caught Rosie's arm. 'Work hard, Rosie, and never let him regret what he's doing for you.'

'Or you, Frazer. I'll never let you down either.'

'Good lassie.' He gripped her tightly by the arms and stared down into her face as if he could see the woman behind the immature child. 'Doctor Rose Nesbitt. God in heaven, lassie, you've signed your life away and I pray I'm here to see it.'

'Ach, you will be. I'll invite you months before the graduation. Heavens, you'll be an auld man wi' bairns. You can bring them all, but dinnae let them greet and disturb the ceremonies!'

3

Edinburgh 1891

IT WAS AS Lucy had expected. Father would force himself to be supportive. She realized, however, that not so deep down, just below the surface of his habitual control, he would have preferred that she follow the usual route of a young lady of her class. He took her side now, just as he had done three years before when she had stupidly lied to Max du Pay about her plans for going to college.

'Not a bad idea,' he had told his wife as they argued and tried to discuss, rationally, the future of their only child. 'Get all this nonsense out of her head. She'll settle down, you'll see.'

She had not settled down, and then the sudden and tragic death of Amos had made it all worse.

'It's almost as if she blames us,' said Lady Graham.

'Worse, my dear. She blames herself.'

'I was too interested in my new dress,' she had cried, 'and going to the hunt with Max du Pay. If I'd even looked at Amos, really *looked* at him, surely I would have known he was ill.'

'Stuff and nonsense!' said Lady Graham, who had a clear conscience. She had sent for help when her servants told her they needed it. She had not asked Amos to work when he was unwell; he was the one who had said he was just a little seedy.

And here they were two years later listening to Lucy voicing this totally unacceptable idea.

'I should have sent her to school in Bath. It was all those years studying with Kier.'

Perhaps it was, although Lady Graham, of course, had no real knowledge of how intimately her daughter had involved herself in the care of her friend. Nor did she really know how Lucy had felt that night when Amos suffered his last massive heart attack.

'Actually cost about the same as bringing you out, my dear,' Sir John said when he finally believed that his daughter was serious. 'So don't worry about anything. Just as long as you're really sure.'

'Oh, I am. It's been simmering away for years now.'

'It's absolutely ridiculous, John, and why you encourage your only child in such folly I can't imagine.' Lady Graham was not supportive. She tried again. 'Lucy, have you any idea what our people will say? It's totally unsuitable, so unladylike. You'll be cut, Lucy, cut completely by the people who matter. Decent women don't study medicine; everyone knows that. People wil say you're fast or . . . worse. Think, Lucy, think. Do you really wish to become so . . . intimate with the human body, with all its . . . unpleasant functions?' Lady Graham could not find suitable words to clothe the horrors she felt sure were lined up waiting for her cherished, sheltered little girl. A girls' college had been one thing but this, this! 'And it's not as if you need to earn your living. You'll have grandmother's money and everything Father and I have.' Looking at the unhappy young unlined face before her, she wanted to scoop up her child and run away with her to safety. She said the last thing she could think of in support of her position. 'You should be thinking of marrying. Who would want to marry a female physician, a woman who knows so much of . . .

everything impure? Oh, child, please, before you find yourself completely ostracized. There's Kier, or what about Max du Pay? When you're here, he's here. You do like him, don't you?'

Lucy thought of Max, his calm, deep voice like honey on warm toast, his humour so like her own.

'I do like him. Of course I like him.' A sigh of stifled agony surged upwards again. 'He understood my feelings of inadequacy over Amos's death but . . . I haven't seen him very often lately.' She did not add that whenever she had seen Maximilian du Pay he had seemed to be in the company of one of his own Southern belles, and that he was obviously perfectly happy.

'You'll meet him often this autumn. I know his father wants him to work in his office. Now, Lucy, let's be sensible. We have delayed our furlough home so that you need not miss any of your classes at Smith, and I'm perfectly happy about the quality of education you have received there, but after graduation there must be an end to it. We will return to Scotland and you will be presented at Court.'

'If you can arrange it during the summer, I will be happy to comply, but my mind is made up: I'm entering the Edinburgh School of Medicine for Women. Please be happy for me.'

'Happy for you? Happy to see my only child spend her life amongst dirt and disease . . .'

'Eradicating dirt and disease, I hope.'

'You are under age. I refuse my permission.'

Desperately Lucy looked at her father. Well she knew that he was happier confronting an enemy battalion than his wife or daughter, but he did not let her down.

'She has my permission, Elizabeth,' he said sadly.

Lady Graham looked from one unhappy face to

the other. 'As usual, you have conspired together and now submit to me a *fait acompli*.' She moved towards the door, her silk skirts rustling on the polished wooden floor. 'But how am I to explain . . .' She stopped as Lucy half rose. 'No, Lucille, there is nothing more to say.'

Sir John rose to follow his wife from the room. 'Don't fret, Lucy. Mother is a hardened campaigner. Now you feel guilty. Next, Petal and her army of dressmakers will be busy with all the new clothes for our furlough. Dresses to show Kier and sundry other men your charms; dresses to make you think that it might be very pleasant to spend your life ordering more dresses and – what was it you said to me once, "trying to decide how much cream is needed for so many peaches".'

'There are no peaches in Scotland.'

'In the Anderson-Howard succession houses, there undoubtedly are. The next few months will possibly bring your hardest battles, child, and if you can defeat your mother without breaking her heart, then years of medical training should cause little difficulty.' He stopped at the door. 'But what of Kier?' he asked.

She had looked at the white door as it swung gently behind his departing figure. He had his way of campaigning too.

Now, six months later, she was being asked almost the same question, and this time by her mother.

'And Kier? You've been constantly in his company since we returned. What has he to say?'

'I plan to tell him this afternoon. I'm riding over for tea.'

'Let's hope he puts some sense into your head. Please be back in time to dress for dinner.'

Lady Graham stood up and left the room and

Lucy longed to run after her. It would be so easy to capitulate, to throw her arms around her mother and to say, 'I didn't mean it. I'll be a dutiful daughter and find a husband,' but she could not do it.

As always her father, now relaxed and happy in his almost disreputable old country tweeds, read her mind. 'She'll come round, Lucy . . .'

'So you keep saying, Father.'

'I know her. She'll scold and fret and try to argue you from this chosen way, and you must admit it will be a hard life you've chosen, but she'll fight for you and your reputation like a lion. She'll be very proud of you once she's managed to turn her mind around, away from bride clothes and . . . baby clothes,' he finished softly.

'I want those things too, Father, but not yet. I need to be a doctor; I don't need to be a wife and mother . . . not yet. One day, some day.'

'Go and tell Kier.' Colonel Graham held her close for a moment. 'I am so proud of you, Lucille Graham, B.A. I always have been, always will be, no matter what you choose.'

'Poor Father,' thought Lucy as she rode slowly across fields not yet ploughed. 'Deep down he's hoping Kier will change my mind. Am I hoping that too?'

As always she stopped at the rise of the hill to look down on Laverock Rising. Built and extended in the reigns of the Georges, it had been the centre of the huge estate on which the Grahams' more modest house also stood. A hundred years had seen the estate farms sold one by one until now, at nearly the end of the century, less than a thousand acres of owned land surrounded the great house but it still stood, even more beautiful as it settled its foundations yet more firmly into the rich Fifeshire soil. Soft light spilled from its windows, for it was a dull day, and Lucy felt welcomed and quickened her pace.

'You know where to find them, Lucy,' Kier's mother welcomed her, 'and won't I be grateful to you if you can prise them out!'

Kier and his father were in the room always called the estate office, although now only three farms comprised the estate. The room smelled of wood-smoke, tobacco-smoke, dogs, and a further indefinable smell that Lucy put down to a mixture of men and old paper and spilled ink. She loved it.

'How you ever find anything in this mess, I do not know,' she said by way of greeting and since that was how she had announced herself at any time in ten years, Kier's father answered as he always did. 'Why, we know where everything important is. I'll go and find your mother, lad.'

Kier too had stood up as Lucy entered, and as he held the door for his father Lucy wondered aloud at one of the questions that had fascinated her for years.

'You must be near a foot taller than your father, Kier. I wonder why that is.'

'He's pure Celt, Lucy,' said Kier as he cleared a place for her to sit by the simple expedient of swiping several ledgers from an armchair. 'I am a throwback to some rapacious Norseman. Come, sit down and tell me what's bothering you.'

Lucy sat as she was bid. How well he knew her, almost as well as she knew herself.

'I've come to a decision and I wanted you to hear about it first. I've told my parents, of course, but . . . you are my oldest and dearest friend .. . .'

'Good heavens, Lucy! What's wrong? You sound so formal and . . . are you all right? You're not ill or anything?'

'I've never been better. It's just that . . . I want to
be a doctor, and I have already been accepted at the
Edinburgh School of Medicine for Women.'

She looked at him as he received the rather bald
statement, and for the first time felt that she could
not read the emotions that followed one another
across his handsome face. University had changed
him, changed both of them.

'Rather you than me,' he said at last. 'God, Lucy,
you scared me. I thought you were going to become a
missionary or a nun or something. Well done! I didn't
know there were any women doctors.'

'There aren't many. Universities in Scotland don't
admit women. London admitted women to all
degree courses three years ago, and there's now a
medical college for women in Edinburgh. Actually
there was a British lady doctor as early as 1849,
one Elizabeth Blackwell, but she had to qualify in
the United States where educational ideas are more
advanced. Thanks to this college, however, there will
soon be seven female physicians who have qualified
in Edinburgh.'

'And you want to make it eight. Whatever for,
Lucy? I always thought, well, one day . . . aren't you
for presentations at Court, and ball-gowns and parties and too much champagne and "Here comes the
bride", wedding trips to exotic places, and gummy
little people dribbling all over one's best shirt-front?'

As he spoke Lucy saw it all, and she realized how
different her experience was going to be, experiences
instead of . . . no, no, before . . . I want it all, I want
it all, her heart cried.

'Of course I'm interested in all that,' she said
calmly and then added daringly, 'especially the
gummy litle people, if they have the right father
. . . but, not yet. There isn't time for them yet.'

Kier smiled at her and stood up. He held the door open. 'Let's tell the parents. God knows what Mother will think. Not very socially acceptable.' He stopped. 'Gosh, Lady Graham?'

'Yes, her reaction was exactly as you picture it.'

'Oh, poor Lucy, but I can see her point. Besides, won't it take years and years?'

'Yes.'

He stopped walking and she had to stop with him. She looked up into his face.

'Hell, Lucy. Years. Have you thought it all out?'

'I've thought of everything, Kier.'

He smiled, the gentle sweet smile that reminded her of their shared childhood. 'Then I must be your strong supporter and your first patient.'

'You *were* my first patient.'

He laughed. 'And no bedside manner did you have. We must hope for an improvement, Doctor Graham.'

The awkward moment was over. Hand in hand they went to the cosy sea-green drawing room where Lucy had spent so many hours with the ailing Kier.

'Mother,' he announced as they walked in, and Lucy listened to him and thought that perhaps she had never loved him more, 'you will never guess what our frightfully clever Lucy is going to do.'

The evenings arrived early in that part of Scotland. Kier rode back to The Larches with Lucy, for even a girl modern enough to contemplate becoming a doctor could not ride home alone in gathering darkness.

'I have the curious feeling I've lost something very precious,' he said, surprising himself more than Lucy, 'and I can't think what it is.'

Lucy's heart raced and she was glad the twilight

hid the blush she could feel stealing over her cheeks. 'Everything is just the same,' she said calmly. 'We'll always be great friends.'

Kier said no more until they reached the stables. Unlike his own home, where at least ten servants were needed to answer the basic needs of the small family, no stable-boy rushed to unsaddle Lucy's horse and Kier did it for her automatically, just as he had done since she first put up her hair.

'How long will it take, Lucy?' He spoke quietly, but she had a strange feeling that a great deal depended on the answer she was able to give.

'Only a little while, three or four years, perhaps a little more if I want really worthwhile qualifications.' Lucy knew that she was not being quite truthful. 'I really don't know the answer myself,' she thought.

Kier heard her calm, almost deep voice through the darkness. How often had that same quiet, matter-of-fact voice steadied his nerves through the panics of illness and fretfulness? Three or even four years? 'I can wait,' he said and surprised himself, for he was not sure what he hoped for at the end of the wait.

Once she had made her opinion known, Lady Graham threw herself into the process of making years of medical schooling as easy as possible for her only daughter. Before they returned to Washington DC, she had found a good tenant for their beloved little house and had bought a small flat in a good area of Edinburgh.

'Annie will come with us, won't you, Annie, to look after Lucy while we're abroad?' Lady Graham spoke to Annie Bell, their maid of all work who had been with her almost since Lucy's birth. 'The Archibalds want you to stay on here, but I said you were part of the family, not a servant. You will come, won't you?'

And Annie went, although a noisy, dirty city full of smoking chimneys and horse-drawn carriages that bowled past her at . . . well, she wouldn't be surprised if they went as fast as five miles every hour, and horrid little boys with iron hoops that they spun clattering along the cobblestones, was not precisely where she would have liked to be. She made no judgement about Lucy. God had called her to a station in life where she was to look after her mistress and, to the best of her not inconsiderable ability, she would ensure that Lucy had a clean home, three decent meals every day and clean underwear – which she might well need if she were to be knocked down by one of those self-same carriages and taken to the very hospital down Leith walk where she was going to do her practical work.

Lucy had a fair notion of the sacrifice the country-woman was making for her, and although she vowed to take her back to the country whenever possible – had they not an open invitation to stay with Kier's parents? – she realized very quickly that she was exactly where she should be and sacrifices would have to be made, by Annie as well as herself, for the greater good.

From that first morning, when she had walked into the lecture room and been warmly welcomed by her fellow students, she had known this was where she wanted to be. These few women were, she felt sure, the vanguard of an enormous army that one day would take the field against ignorance and prejudice. They were not all young; she was quite sure that the tall bronzed woman who sat so quietly waiting for the first lecture was at least thirty. Good heavens, half her life was over already and she was prepared to start to study. Lucy looked at her with respect and interest. What had brought her here? Perhaps she would never know, but it was enough that they were together.

She had had no idea of the enormous scale of illness and disease in the world. Illness caused by poverty, and there was too much of that; illness caused by accident or neglect; and the more frightening one, illness caused by ignorance. She threw herself wholeheartedly into medical training, everything she learned filling her with an almost unbearable excitement and desire to learn more and to help more. Letters from her parents, once more in the American capital, or from Kier at Oxford, called her back unwillingly from what was to her the real world. She answered them quickly, assuring her mother that Annie's cooking was as tasty and nutritious as ever and that, no, she had not had time to make herself known to Mrs This or Lady That yet, but she would, honestly, just as soon as she had a moment to spare. Her letters to her father and to Kier were different:

I am to have one hundred lectures in Anatomy from a Doctor Dewar, another one hundred lectures in Physiology from Doctor James, and so, academically, you will agree that there is nothing I will not know of the human body. What really interests me, of course, is why the body malfunctions from time to time and, much more important, what I will be able to do to set it back on the right track. I am thrilled to discover from Amy Wood Browne, a fellow student, that we are to enjoy fifty lectures in Practical Pharmacy from Doctor Jex-Blake, yes, *the* Dr Jex-Blake, the pioneer. Shall I sit in such awe of this wonderful woman that I shall be totally incapable of making a single note and shall fail her classes miserably? I am also to have, see how bold my language has become, Father, fifty lectures in Midwifery from this same idol. I think the subject interests me the least of all the wonders in store.

Her first lectures were in Physiology and in Surgery. Physiology was interesting. Her dictionary told her it was the branch of science concerned with the functioning of organisms. Dr James, the lecturer, made it almost holy, for was not the human body a collection of the most interesting and fascinating and yet secretive of all organisms? They went to the hospital down in Leith for their first lectures in Surgery. Amy Wood Browne was among the three students who silently collapsed and were unceremoniously helped from the operating theatre. Did Dr Cathcart even notice them as he continued dissecting? Lucy did not. The human tissue so revealed did not repel her, it engrossed her. She could not learn quickly enough.

She considered remaining in Edinburgh for the winter break. There was so much reading to do; her notes should be read and corrected. Hospitals could be visited. Goodness knows, a pair of hands that had some idea of what they were doing were very welcome, especially in the poorer area. Textbooks and clinical specimens were well and good and they could be examined over and over again at any time of the day or night, but people, real people, suffering people, that was where one really learned.

'I must remember always the person. I must not be so excited by symptoms that I forget the living, breathing body.' Healthy people had to be considered too. Kier's parents, who had renewed their invitation; her own parents, who wanted her to have a rest; and, of course, the most important person that Christmas was Annie, who missed the country and her family.

Lucy packed her suitcases and found space for a few textbooks. When they boarded the train at Waverley she was pleased that she had bought first-class tickets, for it was packed with holiday-makers. She had almost resented the break from what she was coming to consider the real world, but at last she began to feel that delicious sense of growing excitement that had always heralded Christmas.

'Lucy? I don't believe it. What absolute luck,' called a well-loved voice, and she found herself caught up in a strong masculine embrace.

'Put me down at once, you idiot,' she scolded as she tried to wriggle free from Kier's exuberant greeting.

He did not quite release her but looked down into her face. 'Gosh, it's good to see you. I have had the most appalling forty-eight hours. The wine at the Christmas Ball gave me the most unbelievable headache. Did I drink too much, or was it the quality that was dubious?'

'Both,' said Lucy, pushing him away firmly and sitting down to meet Annie's aggrieved look. 'What else happened?' she asked.

'The train was like something out of the Inferno – too hot, and too many people squealing around.'

'Definitely too much to drink,' diagnosed Lucy. 'Does your mother expect you by this train? She said nothing in her letter.'

A wash of colour swept across his face. 'You will never believe, Lucy . . .' He stopped and she waited. 'I was going to a house-party; chap I met at school. They're all coming to me for the New Year. They think Scotland should be fun – "quaint", I think was the word she used. Anyway, his sister ... I took her to the ball, and there she was, behind an urn, wrapped around some chap.'

Lucy, who had once found herself behind an urn, felt a sneaking sympathy for the unknown girl. 'Perhaps she couldn't help herself.'

'My very thought. But when I pushed him away and walloped him, she screamed at me like a little cat.' He glowered at her morosely and then laughed. 'Women,' he said. 'I'm giving them up!'

'I've given you the best guest room, Lucy dear,' said Mrs Anderson-Howard.

They had arrived at Cupar station to be met by Kier's delighted father.

'Welcome home, welcome home. There's a nice hot pig for your feet, Lucy, and a warm rug. Have you snug at home in no time. You sit up here with me, old chap. Fresh air might cure whatever ails you.'

'More likely kill me, sir.'

'Then all the more reason for you to sit up here and blow away the cobwebs and the tobacco smoke. We've had a powdering of snow, just enough to slow me down, but I'll be as quick as safety allows.'

And now here they were home, and Mrs Anderson-Howard had taken Lucy straight upstairs to a delightful bedroom where a coal fire blazed cheerfully. 'Such a surprise that you met Kier; I had not expected him till nearer Christmas. Dinner is ready as soon as you like, my dear, but there's just the four of us so no need to dress.'

Lucy, quite rightly, took this to mean that if she had diamonds she need not wear them, and she washed in the hot water brought up to her, uncoiled her hair and quickly put it back up again, and changed her wool travelling dress for a dark blue silk dinner-gown.

The soft lamplight in the dining room lit up the faces at the dinner table but not the corners of the large room, and Lucy was lulled into feeling that they were the only four people in the world. The talk went from one young person to the other and Lucy told as much of her medical training as she felt the older couple would find interesting, and Kier recounted what Lucy felt must surely be an expurgated account of his activities.

'He tells me things he does not tell his parents,' she realized and had a sudden overwhelming desire that this dinner-party could continue for ever, that she could really belong to the loving circle and not merely be a welcomed guest. 'Have I made a terrible mistake?' she thought sadly. 'Have I pushed him towards all these, no doubt beautiful and eminently suitable, young women he talks about? At least this Cynthia has blotted her copybook.'

But, although Cynthia of the urn did not come for the New Year festivities, it seemed to Lucy that the house echoed always with the laughter of others.

'What do they mean to him?' she asked herself sadly as she watched Kier flirt with each girl in turn, but the only person she could confidently ask about the strange ways of marriageable young men was three thousand miles away.

She returned to Edinburgh early in January. A letter from her mother had reminded her yet again of the visits she was supposed to make in the capital and Annie Bell, who had professed to hate the city, was definitely unhappy away from what she now saw as her own home. When Kier took Lucy to the station to catch the London train, they were both quiet, perhaps restrained by Annie's presence.

'It's been a lovely . . .' They had spoken together and so they laughed, at last at ease.

'Will you come home for the Easter break?'

'No,' said Lucy quietly, 'and I won't come back in the summer either. Leith Hospital is allowing me to do volunteer work in the spring and I'm going to Rouen for the summer, to work in a hospital there.'

'Alone?' Kier was shocked.

'Don't be silly. There will be hundreds of patients and not a few real doctors and nurses.'

'You know perfectly well what I mean, Lucy. Your parents will never allow it. You're a girl, you're young: you need the protection of a brother, or father, or . . . well, a husband.'

The word dropped between them like a stone but Lucy managed to laugh.

'I've had enough trouble getting into training, Kier. A husband would certainly be an encumbrance I can well do without . . . at this point,' she finished softly.

'Damn it all, Lucy,' he said suddenly, and like poor Cynthia behind the urn, Lucy Graham found herself being thoroughly kissed.

'He must mean to marry you,' said Annie comfortably as a slightly dishevelled Lucy watched the young man stride away.

'He's going the wrong way,' she said.

'What did I tell you?' said Annie triumphantly and steered her mistress to the open door of their first-class carriage.

4

Dundee 1892

IN 1892, WHEN Lucy Graham was finishing her first year of study at the Edinburgh School of Medicine for Women, Scottish universities opened their doors to women for the first time.

'There, didn't I tell you?' With frozen fingers Rosie Nesbitt stuffed the newspaper she had been reading inside her schoolbag and hurried home, her thin coat protecting her as best it could from the biting wind. It was all coming together. With the University of St Andrews a mere eleven miles away across the Tay, she need not live away from home. That troubling thought had managed to surface every now and again over the last few years. How was she to live in Edinburgh when she had gained entrance to the women's medical college there? It had never occurred to Miss Nesbitt that she would not win a place. If you were prepared to work, you could do anything in this exciting world. She could hardly wait for the new century. It would see Rose Nesbitt, M.A., M.B., Ch.B., most likely with distinction, for Miss Nesbitt was thorough. She had thrown herself into her Latin studies so well that dear old Wishy had insisted on teaching her Greek too. Rosie could not absorb enough and now, thanks to the generosity and far-sightedness of Sir William Taylor-Thomson who had left the residue of his estate to provide bursaries for students of either sex, and especially so

that females might study medicine, she was working
towards winning such a grant to St Andrews University. She would have to wait until she was nineteen
to study medicine, but at least she could start on an
Arts degree. If she came top in the combined entrance
and bursary examination – and there was no reason
why she should not – she could win an amazing
£20 a year. Then Frazer could afford to marry his
sweetheart, Nancy, who had waited so patiently.
Everything and everyone had willingly sacrificed
themselves to Rosie's driving ambition and as soon
as she found the time, she would tell them so. And,
oh, how she would thank them and make it all up to
them once she had qualified?

She raced up the stairs, for once so excited by the
wonderful news she had to read to Ma that she forgot
to watch out for daft old Tam, the 'flasher'. He had
waited for her, as he did every night, and his sad
genitalia almost withered away as she raced past
without even seeing him. He settled back against
the closie wall to wait for the next woman, and Rosie
banged into the kitchen where Ma was painfully
stirring the stew in the pot over the fire.

'Your back's bad again,' said Rosie, taking the
spoon. 'Sit down and put your feet up. I'll make
you a cup of tea and read you the paper. Where are
the weans?'

'In the street. Mind you, it's that cauld with this
bluidy snaw day after day that they're probably in
somebody's hoose. Did ye no see them?'

Rosie straightened up. 'Ma, I'm so happy I didnae
see old Tam and he must have been there waving
defiance at me.'

They laughed wickedly at one another. In the past
few years they had become more friends than mother
and daughter. Elsie treated Rosie as if she were an

adult and Rosie rewarded her by telling her everything, by sharing her learning, assuming rightly that
her mother, though illiterate, was intelligent. Ma had
even learned a word or two in Latin and Greek, in
German and French.

'Come on then, lassie,' said Ma, gratefully gulp-
ing back the scalding hot brew, 'tell me whit's sae
exciting.'

Rosie pulled out the *Dundee Courier and Advertiser* and unfolded it. Then she smoothed out the
crumpled sheets and read out the article. '"Tuesday,
March 15th 1892. The Senatus Academicus of the
University of St Andrews has agreed to open its doors
in arts, science, and theology to women students
from next session onwards, and, although it rests
with the University Court to make arrangements in
detail, women will henceforward be taught along
with men. Next year the University will receive
the sum of £30,000 to be spent by it in bursaries
open to students of both classes attending the university, one half of this sum being devoted to women
exclusively." There, Ma, what do you think of that?
D'ye see what it means? Instead of waiting till I'm
old enough tae get into the women's college in
Edinburgh, or instead of leaving the country for an
education – and heaven knows how we could have
afforded that – I can bide at hame and take the train
into St Andrews every day. Frazer can marry Nancy
and get their ain bit. Losh, Ma, with just the two of us
and the two weans, we'll be rich and there'll be that
much room we could hae a lodger and you could stop
working in the mill.'

Ma looked around at the shabby room that she had
tried to keep clean and tidy through many years of
bringing up her children on her own. 'A lodger?'

'We should hae done it when Frazer went tae the

whaling or when . . . when pair Lindsay died.' Like too many children in Dundee's crowded tenements, Elsie's oldest daughter had died two years before from tuberculosis. 'Or we should definitely hae done it when Leslie got wed.'

Leslie, the next girl, a mill-worker like her sister Lindsay, had married two months before. She was five months pregnant at the time, but there was no scorn or shame heaped upon their sinful heads for anticipating holy matrimony. It was the way of the world. It was cheaper to live separately and so young couples in love lived with their own families, or what passed for a family circle, until the imminent advent of their first child forced them to marry.

'I cannae think why I never thought on it afore,' Rosie went on, 'but at least now you can start to take things easier. A nice country laddie, we'll get, that's come to work at Cox's or Baxter's. He'll sleep wi' oor Murray when Murray's hame – and this year he's been awa' near as much as Frazer – and you'll probably see the back of him on a Sunday.'

'A nice laddie?' Ma grinned wickedly and, by doing so, looked years younger. 'A click for you, mair like. We'll hae ye marrit, and then where will all your fine plans go?'

Rose Nesbitt was not yet thirteen years of age, but in some ways she was already quite, quite old. 'There's no the braw laddie born that could turn me from my path, Ma, and I'll certainly no throw masel' away on some mill laddie. I've no interest in men, and forbye, how could I tell Frazer and even auld Wishy that I was giving up? Years Nancy's waited for Frazer and years Mr Wishart has spent coaching me. I'll no throw it back in their faces, not for the Prince of Wales himself.'

The thought of her daughter with Edward, Prince

of Wales, was too much for Ma and even Rosie saw the funny side and they began to laugh. They stopped suddenly. Was it not just two months since the sad death of the Prince's oldest son, the young Duke of Clarence, from the fearsome influenza, this killer disease that weeded out both the low and the mighty?

'You're a real joy tae me, Rosie Nesbitt,' said Ma at last. 'I'll think on a lodger; could be grand, but what about your studying? You're aye throwing the weans oot.'

'I'll be a university student, Ma. I'll do my studying at their grand library. Think on it. In nae time at all me, at the University of St Andrews!'

'My mind willnae accept it, lassie. Goodness, I wis thinkin' it wis a' arranged and ye've years at the skill yet.'

'Ach, Ma. Life's like building a wall. Ye pit one brick on top o' the next and ye dinnae think on it falling. Everything's going tae be great.' She stood up suddenly. 'I've had a grand idea. We'll go the first fine Sunday. We'll take the weans and a piece. There's sand there, Ma, and a ruined castle and buildings from books. Then when I'm there, every single day you'll be able to picture me walking through the arches in my grand red goon. Wishy says it's so rich and poor will look alike. Naebody kens that you've only the one skirt if it's aye hidden by a grand red goon.'

'Clever fowk think on everything.' Ma was over-whelmed.

'I'll shout the weans for their tea, Ma. Noo, no a word about the surprise. I'll need tae find the money fer the train first, and the driver'll need to be able to see the way across the bridge through this damned snow.'

As with everything else Miss Nesbitt set her mind

to, the weather began to improve. Rosie did without her lunch piece and so money was available for the train. Never had there been so much excitement in the Nesbitt household and even Nancy, Frazer's fiancée, agreed to join them.

'Whit a lot I'll hae tae tell oor Frazer,' she said as she helped Elsie scrape dripping on the doorstep slices of bread. Nancy sighed a little, for she had popped in to see Leslie before coming into the next closie to join Frazer's mother. Leslie's swelling belly only reminded her that all she ever had of Frazer was kisses.

Elsie understood the sigh and she hugged the girl in a quick gesture of affection. 'It'll be all the better for the waiting, hen. Frazer loves you dear, and soon you'll wed and then you'll no be quite sae jealous o' oor Leslie when it's you having bairns like shelling peas, year after year. Where they come frae, I sometimes wonder.'

'That's what Frazer, well, that's why he says . . . well, he's an awfie guid man, Elsie.'

'You've nae need tae tell me, lassie. Is he no spending a fortune on oor Rosie's education, books, exam fees, but she'll mak it up tae the both of you, and free medical attention for a'body up the closie. So, noo let's get wir pieces ready and off we go like toffs tae St Andrews.'

It was a day none of them would ever forget. Donaldina and Granta, Elsie's two youngest, were unable to talk for the excitement of being on the train but they made up for that as they rushed pell-mell, here and there, over the streets of the beautiful medieval city: Market Street, North Street, South Street, St Regulus' Tower, St Rule's, the castle with its horrifying tales of murder and mayhem and starvation in a bottle dungeon, the sands, the sands,

the sands. Rosie and Elsie were content to touch the
walls, to dream of the thousands of men and women
who down the centuries had walked under these
archways or through those doors or along this very
beach. Nancy thought of her sweetheart somewhere
on the ocean and dreamed of a honeymoon weekend
with him here in this beautiful place that Rosie had
shown her was easy, easy for anyone to reach and to
enjoy. A train from Dundee rattles aross a bridge and
through the kingdom of Fife and in two shakes of a
ram's tail, as Elsie kept saying, they were there.

Never had bread and dripping tasted so good.
Nancy had brought slices of dumpling and Rosie
bought a bottle of lemonade and they all shared
its sour refreshment. No one thought of shared
germs, only of shared fellowship. Silently, in awe,
they walked through the university buildings. Rosie
taught the wee ones to avoid the sacred stones on
which the student martyr, Patrick Hamilton, had
breathed his last in the grip of cruel flame, and
then, since she had scared them so much, she
walked them, clinging tightly to her hands, along
the walk where she told them every Sunday the red-
gowned students would go.

'You can picture me here on a Sunday morning,'
she said.

'How can we when you'll be at hame?' said practical Donaldina.

'I niver get oot o' ma bed on a Sunday, Rosie,'
confessed Granta. Granta was the silliest of all the
silly names Elsie had given her children. Not one
child, as far as she could judge, had the same father as
another, and she punished the fathers by calling their
children after them so that eveyone in the Hilltown
knew who had fathered Elsie Nesbitt's latest bairn.
Elsie had never married. She had kept herself and

her parents alive by selling herself on the crowded streets of her home, and she had raised a large family of clean and healthy children in a remarkably clean home. Elsie Nesbitt had integrity and pride and, as her daughter Rosie knew, she also had brains.

Rosie looked at her mother now. She was a child, a grey-haired, wrinkled, stooping child, and very soon she would be a grandmother, and Rosie vowed that her future would not resemble Elsie's past.

Too soon it was time for the train.

'You'll be back loads of times, Ma,' she said. 'You'll get tae ken St Andrews as weel as you ken the Hilltown.'

'As long as you ken it, Rosie.'

'I'd like fine tae come back wi Frazer, Elsie. Whit a place fir a holiday.'

'Aye, Nancy. Ye ken, oor Rosie gets me that fired up I believe her grand thochts. I wis ready tae believe she wis sterting at the university this year, but she's years tae dae yet. But she will dae whit she says and she will get the grants. Can you imagine somebody geein' money jist sae bairns can learn? There's guid folk in the world or ma name's no Elsie Nesbitt, but whit I wis wantin' tae say is that Frazer'll no need tae worry aboot us and wi' Leslie marrit and Murray an apprentice and awa maist o' the time, I could easy tak a lodger and then, jings, Nancy, I'll be rollin' in it and I'll no need Frazer tae help.'

'You mean?'

'Aye, hen, there's nothing tae stop you and Frazer being wed.'

Nancy lay back in the questionable comfort of the Caledonian Railway's third-class carriages and the little girls fell asleep on the train. When they got out Elsie carried Donaldina and Nancy carried Granta up as far as Reform Street where they almost dropped them.

'That woke ye baith up,' said Rosie, now again as broad in speech as the rest of the family. 'They wis hivin' the pair o' ye on. I'd hae left the baith o' them on the train tae Eberdeen.'

'Come on in by wi' us, Nancy,' suggested Elsie. 'I've a stane o' tatties waiting tae be fried up.'

'No, I'll no come in. I'll awa hame and tell my mither and I'll look in on Leslie. She was having a bit of bother this morning.'

'Oh?' Elsie, who had carried and delivered seven healthy children with the help of a few neighbours, was perfectly ready to see that childbirth was not easy for everyone.

'She's too fat,' said twelve-year-old Rosie unkindly but truthfully. 'Bert brings her sweeties and cakes on his way home from the works and she hasn't washed a dish since the day they got married. He does everything.'

'Frazer'll be like that,' sighed Nancy and went off to see the girl she hoped soon to be her sister-in-law.

When they got home, Rosie and Elsie scrubbed the two small girls in front of the fire. It was a Saturday night and no matter what else happened in the Hilltown on a Saturday night, Elsie Nesbitt's children had a bath and had their hair washed. Then Elsie fried the potatoes which she washed down with beer and the girls with hot strong tea.

'I'm awae tae ma bed tae, Rosie. Dinnae you stay up late wi' books. I don't ken whit it is, but that day in St Andrews has fair tired me oot.'

Rosie agreed with her and so they were both sound asleep when Bert, Elsie's eighteen-year-old son-in-law, came flying up the stairs and knocked furiously on the door with a knock loud enough to wake any of the neighbours who was already asleep.

Leslie had gone into premature labour and there was something wrong.

'Turn yer back, laddie, till I get my drawers on. There's nothing wrong jist acause she's a bit early, and hoo would you twa ken hoo early it is, onyway?'

'There's something wrang, Elsie, even ma mither says so.' Bert's mother was the best midwife in the area.

'I'm coming.'

They looked at the small figure in the big bed.

'You're no practising your doctoring on my wife, Rosie Nesbitt. You're no decent, wanting tae come tae a lyin'-in.'

'I jist want tae help.'

'Stay here and look oot fir the wee wans, Rosie. You're too wee and even had ye book learnin', unborn bairns cannae read and it's them that's in charge.'

Rosie was angry. Here was her first chance to witness a birth at first hand, her own sister, her own nephew or niece, and she was being kept away like a wee lassie.

'I wouldn't be feart,' she told the fire as she sat beside it in her gown and made the first of many pots of tea. She was not conceited or foolish enough to think that she could be of any help, but there were so many things she might have learned. How did the baby get out? She had far too true an idea of how it got in.

She was asleep when an exhausted and heart-broken Elsie let herself into the house.

'Our Leslie's deid,' said Elsie as her daughter sat up in the chair.

Rosie eased her mother into the chair and poured her a cup of the – by now, stewed – tea. Death. She had seen it before when Lindsay had coughed her lungs up in the big box-bed, when neighbours had died of age or infirmity, but death in childbirth? Oh, she heard of it often, too often, but not Leslie with her adoring young husband who gave her too many sweets.

'But how? She was well, she was strong, well-fed; it's two months since she did a day's work. Did ye get the doctor?'

'Oh aye, wan came eventually, along frae the infirmary, a nice laddie, seemed tae ken whit he was daein', though hoo a man kens is beyond me. Tam, Nancy's brither, is oot lookin' for Bert. He went screamin oot o' the hoos like a bogle. They wis jist bairns theresels.'

'Whit went wrang, Ma? Did the doctor ken?'

'Ach, lassie, whit questions. Well, all richt, if ye'll jist get tae yir bed and let me be. A bairn's supposed tae come oot heid first. Well, first a wee leg cam oot and they shoved it back in, and he put his airm in and tried tae turn the bairn, but its wee backside cam next and it wis too big and it ripped my wee lassie awful.' She looked down at her skirt in horror. 'That's my wee lassie's life's-blood. A mammy shouldnae see that. Och lassie, whit noo?'

Poor Elsie. At 3.30 in the morning of Sunday the 22nd of March 1892, she cleaned up Rosie Nesbitt who had been violently ill for the first and last time in her medical career.

There were two tragedies that night. Young Bert, maddened by the screams of his young wife – he had refused to do as every other man in the closie did and seek solace in the pub from the pangs of labour – had run shrieking from her deathbed and thrown himself into the Tay, the river that was often Dundee's life-line and too often the source of death to the town's miserable. Leslie was buried

with her unborn child in the local churchyard and
her husband was buried in unhallowed ground.

'That cannae be right,' thought Rosie, but wisely
said nothing.

She continued cutting her brilliant path through the
Harris Academy and even saw the Rector begin to
consider Latin and Mathematics – in a limited way,
naturally – for brighter girls. Already she had made
a difference.

Frazer never saw her win a combined university
grant and bursary of £20 per year. He never came
back from his last voyage, never saw St Andrews,
never married Nancy. His ship returned from its
long voyage on May 20th 1893 and the Captain had
only letters, wages, and consoling words to give his
mother. Frazer's letters were very different from the
tone of the various articles that appeared in the local
press after the voyage:

Dear Mam,
We left Dundee on September 6th and went south.
We sailed for weeks with nout to do but play
cards and nout to see but the sea and sometimes
other ships.

In three months we reached the Falklands. There's
nout there but sheep.

It's mid December and we have found ice. It's now
bluidy cold. We look for black whales.

No whale but seals. We've killed thousands.
It turned my stomach. They're no feart. They
havenae learnt tae fear and they lie and wait for
the kickey. Their eyes follow me.

The Captain says we are congenially occupied.

We're killing penguins. We laughed at them, like funny wee men from London or grand places. They line up in rows and we walk atween them, whack, whack, whack. They taste good, like yon jugged hare I had one time at Nancy's. You wouldnae believe the ice.

I've been in the Brig. I wouldnae hit nae mair wee birds. If they'd fight us, snap, or bite. I havenae been eating. I couldnae eat penguin. We should sell them in Dundee, says the mate. They cost nout and they taste good, but when I eat, I see them standing waiting tae be killt. I'm rowing the boat because I want tae stay out of the Brig. The money's grand for this voyage. 10/– extra the month. I dinnae like the ice. The sea goes twa roads at the same time and you have tae watch oot for ice slipping past . . .

The Captain gave Elsie her son's letters and his bible; Frazer owned nothing else. He also gave her the full £45 the boy should have earned had he completed the nine-month voyage, and he told her of the accident. The rowing boats had been in a channel where two currents met. Frazer's boat, heading south, had been grazed by an iceberg travelling north at 3 knots per hour. He had fallen overboard and his body had never been recovered.

'He was a good man, Mrs Nesbitt,' said the Captain seriously. 'The men tried desperately to find him.' He did not add that it would have been useless even if they had found him, for he could not have survived in such temperatures.

Nancy waited for him for two years. Every time a whaler came in to the harbour she ran down to the docks and watched the men disembark. In 1895, just as Rosie was preparing for her final year at the Harris

Academy, and just as one Lucille Graham, B.A., was graduating with her first medical qualifications, Nancy emigrated to New Zealand. She travelled with her sister Jean who had married Rosie's other brother, Murray.

'You'll tell him where we are, Elsie. You'll tell him I'll never give up?'

Elsie watched her last young son climb the gangplank. 'I've lost four,' she thought, 'Four,' for when would she ever see Murray again? And there was Nancy. Did that make five?

At least for Elsie there was the dream of Rosie, the dream even Elsie was beginning to believe could come true. For Rosie was now a university student. She jumped out of bed every morning when the milkman arrived at 6.30 and just had time to wash, dress, grab a bap and eat it as she ran like a hare for the 7.10 train which would get her into St Andrews in time for a tutorial class in Maths, a condition of her acceptance, for Rosie, mainly self-taught in mathematics – another unsuitable subject for females – had done badly in the entrance examination. Often she cut her train-catching so fine that she had to be pulled into the luggage van by the guard, who would then proceed to air his views on education versus motherhood as a reward for not allowing her to miss the train.

Rosie was content not to argue with him in her awakening state and, besides, he said the same things every morning.

'What does a braw wee thing like you want with an education? Are you jist looking for a better type man? What good will all that book learning be when you're peeling tatties?'

Rosie knew that his views were only half serious. He just liked having someone to talk to, but his atti-

tude changed when she roused herself one morning
and told him that she would not be content with a
mere degree. She was going to become a doctor.

'A doctor?' His eyes narrowed. 'And you look like
such a nice wee lassie. Well, you can never tell.'

Like countless others, men and women, he had
assumed that she was not a *good* girl because she
wanted to become a doctor. Narrow, narrow minds,
she thought, as she looked at the cold, set face and
vowed to get up before the milkman. She had a feeling that from now on no friendly helping hand would
pull her aboard and she would be left disconsolate on
the platform. Nothing, nothing must keep her from
her classes.

Rosie loved everything about university. She
loved the walk from the station in the morning, in
every weather. She walked around the golf course
and never once wondered what it would be like
to play golf, although someone told her that Mary
Queen of Scots had actually played here on the
ground on which she trod.

Occasionally she, a travelling girl, would meet one
of the town girls, and they would walk together.
There were three types of students at St Andrews.
Those who lived in the University Residences – there
were, as yet, no Residences solely for women – were
top of the social tree. Then there were the town
students who lived in lodgings, and the travelling
students who came in every day by train or bus or
farmer's cart. Attendance at all lectures was compul-
sory and a student could only sit examinations if he,
and now she, could prove by production of a certificate that they had done all the course work. Rosie
could not understand how anyone could contemplate missing one word of the drops of knowledge
that fell so readily from the lips of learned professors.

Constantly she pinched herself to assure herself that, yes, it was true, Rosie Nesbitt was a student at St Andrews University.

Apart from lectures, what she remembered most about her first few years was the singing. Students sang everywhere, not raucous rowdy songs, although many were silly nonsensical ditties, but folk songs, melodies from the theatre.

When a Residence was built for women students, the Warden invited Rosie for tea.

'I'm getting a name for myself, Ma. I'm known at the university, and this Warden wants all the town and travelling girls to come along and have lunch at the Residence. There's no common room, you see. I'm sure she's only worried that we're not having a hot meal.'

'How much?' Practical Elsie.

'9d.'

'A week?'

'A day.'

'My God, does the wumman think we're made o' money? You go and have your tea, but don't let them rich people . . . whit's the word?'

'Patronize.'

'Aye, make you feel cheap.'

'Oh, they won't do that. Thank God for the gown.'

'Will you maybe have to take it aff in the hoos?'

'I'm great at pretending I'm too cold. Ma, don't worry. I'll see what she wants to discuss and I'll not stick my pinky up when I'm drinking my tea.'

Rosie took the train back to St Andrews. 'Poor Ma,' she thought. 'She thinks tea is a meal; she'll be hoping I get sausages.' Rosie had never been particularly interested in food, but she did like a good sausage.

She washed and ironed her *good* frock and washed her hair. She darned her stockings with tiny stitches and cleaned her shoes. 'Hell, hell, hell. I won't ever give a damn what I eat, but I will have leather shoes in all colours of the rainbow and hell, hell, hell' – this last as she looked at her one pair of gloves, too shoddy to take her hands to tea – 'gloves, silk gloves, leather gloves.' Did gloves look right with the gown that hid all other imperfections except the scuffed and well-polished shoes? Ladies always wear gloves. Do they? Do they not?

The Warden of the new Residence for female students was not wearing gloves . . . but then she was inside her house.

Miss Louden, herself a brilliant scholar, was aware of most of the worries besetting Rosie. She recognized the look almost of belligerence that disguised shyness and a fear of being pitied. Only too well she knew that in men and women the gown too often hid inadequate clothing draped on a too-thin body.

'I feel that it is very important that I get to know as many of the travelling girls as I can, Miss Nesbitt. I am aware of all the reasons that many young women have for not living in this Residence.' She saw Rosie's proud head lift and the small nostrils almost flare. 'A natural desire for independence being foremost. Students who live in Residence enjoy a completely different view of university life. I would like all the women of St Andrews to share that fellowship in some way.' She gestured to the table where an exquisitely embroidered cloth made a perfect backdrop for the porcelain plates with their beautifully arranged sandwiches, their delicate and delicious cakes and pastries. 'China or India?' she asked, and looked at Rosie whose mind was a complete blank. Before the silence became embarrassing she realized that Miss Louden meant the tea. My God, what kind of tea? The tea that comes full of stoor in a wooden box from the shop in the Pillars in Dundee. I know no other.

'I'm afraid I'm not a connoisseur, Warden,' said Rosie and could have sworn that a look of genuine liking crossed that austerely beautiful face.

'I like mine hot and wet, and quite frankly rarely notice the flavour, but we'll try China and next time India perhaps. I hope you don't mind if I eat like a ravenous schoolboy, Miss Nesbitt, but I find that there are so many interruptions at luncheon that I very rarely have a chance to finish. Do try the roast beef. I swear Mrs McBride should have been a surgeon. See how thinly she cuts.'

Rosie took a sandwich. Roast beef. 'This is my first ever roast beef. I must remember everything for Ma and I must not like this woman. She wants something from me.'

'You are hoping to do medicine, Miss Nesbitt. I wish you well. Sophia Jex-Blake is a friend of mine. You may have heard of her?'

How had she managed to eat three sandwiches? 'Doctor Jex-Blake. *The* Doctor Jex-Blake?'

'Yes. We fought together for the right of British women to get to university, Miss Nesbitt, not to have to go abroad as she did, and so you will see that the welfare of all female students is very precious to me, for her sake as well as mine.'

Rosie held out her cup, what a beautiful cup, for a second cup of the China tea. 'What do you want from me, Warden?'

'You are very popular with the students, Miss Nesbitt. You look surprised. Are you so involved in your studies that you have not noticed?'

'Yes.'

The Warden laughed, a tinkling musical laugh. Rosie liked the sound.

'You have or could have influence with the travelling girls and the town girls – oh yes, of course

I know the names by which you call yourselves. I would like you . . .' She stopped. She could see Rosie bristle. Silly child, silly child, I will not insult you by offering you a free meal. She pretended that she was checking the silver pot; 'my God,' thought Rosie, 'a silver pot with nothing in it but water.' 'I would like you to come, at least occasionally, for lunch in the winter. If you come, many of the other travelling girls will come, and the town girls. We will give a three-course luncheon, a different selection every day. Fish on Fridays, of course. Are you Catholic?'

Violently Rosie shook her head. 'I don't think we're anything.'

No disapproval. Just acceptance . . .

'We could arrange luncheon recitals, poetry readings, music. We might have guests, like Doctor Jex-Blake, or, who knows, the divinely handsome D'Arcy Thomson from Dundee. You do know about the Marquis of Bute, by the way?'

Rosie could not follow this quicksilver mind. 'The Rector?'

'Yes, my dear. He intends to fund a medical school. He is dedicated to the development of medical and science teaching in St Andrews. But you must know, as a doctor manqué, why we are unable to complete medical training in St Andrews?' She waited for Rosie to acknowledge the correctness of her remark.

Rosie blushed. It had simply never occurred to her that she could not complete medical training at the university; she had been so glad to get a place in the Arts department. Medical training was not allowed for women before the age of nineteen, which would have been three wasted years.

'I was so grateful to have been accepted by the university, Warden.'

Miss Louden nodded. 'There is no hospital within

reach . . . for experience, Miss Nesbitt, clinical training. You must, if you are accepted, finish at Dundee. His Lordship is building a conjoint medical school with the University of Dundee and funding it. £20,000 per year. There will be scholarships, £100 per year. I would imagine you will be one of its first students, Miss Nesbitt, if not its scholarship winners.'

£100 every year. God in heaven! With money like that a body could have a 9d lunch, three courses with fish on a Friday, every day of the week, and have money left over.

The Warden stood up. Between them the plates were nearly empty.

'St Andrews is so beautiful, Warden, that it is a joy to wander the streets during the lunch-hour. But in the winter . . . well, I could imagine that a hot lunch . . . occasionally . . . would tempt me from the wynds or the links.'

'You are a golfer?' Even more interest.

'No, but I love to walk along and smell the sea and see St Andrews rise up . . .' She stopped, embarrassed.

'It casts its spell on all of us, Miss Nesbitt. I will keep you informed of my luncheon programme.'

She offered her hand. It was white and soft, and the fingernails shone without the aid of polish. Rosie grasped it in her short, stubby, rough red hand and was surprised at the strength of the grip. Well, perhaps someone who ate sandwiches like a schoolboy did not notice such stuff as bitten fingernails.

What had that old recipe book said? Half an ounce of pure glycerine in a three-ounce bottle. Fill it up with distilled water and rub it into the hands every time you wash them and before they're quite dry. Easy, easy, to be well groomed.

'And I can at least stop biting my nails,' said Rosie aloud and rushed, exhilarated, to a late tutorial.

5

Edinburgh 1893

IN 1893 HERMANN Dresser introduced a substance called acetylsalicylic acid. For years Lucy called it aspirin. It was a magic potion and doctors loved it. Doctors' lives and, of course, the way of the world changed with other news that Sir John gave his daughter in a letter from Washington that same year. Henry Ford had developed what he called a gasoline buggy.

> They say we will all take to the highways and byways in these noisy smelly contraptions, Lucy, but quite frankly, it will never be as reliable as a horse. I do not intend to buy one – that is, if the man is not a maniac and actually gets the thing into production. Your mother, however, insists on being the first diplomatic wife to have one, not, I would say – but who listens to a poor soldier? – the most diplomatic of manoeuvres.

Lucy laughed. A letter from her father was like a week's holiday, so refreshed did she feel after reading them. It was years since she had seen him. He would have no home leave for another year, and she had used her two long summer holidays in further study. She was reading the letter in Dublin where she was taking a summer class at the famous Rotunda Hospital. Moving from one hospital to another was as much of a holiday as she allowed herself. There was just so much to learn.

The letter continued:

> I have some bad news for Mother's ambitions. I am to be transferred. Actually I am surprised that we have been left here so long. We are to go to Delhi. I was there as a subaltern and enjoyed the life very much. Will you visit? I know your mother will enjoy the social life once she has forgiven the Foreign Office for another hot posting. The good thing about it is, of course, that we will have home leave, and by the time you receive this letter all should be in train for our removal. Shall we take a hotel suite – I do not want to ask the Alexanders to move: they have been excellent tenants – or can your tiny flat accommodate us? What a wonderful Christmas we shall have.
>
> Max du Pay continues to cut a swath through society. We cannot understand why he has not succumbed to the blandishments thrown his way. His mother is one of those fragile women who ask for nothing but always seem to get their own way, and there is a certain Southern belle of her acquaintance . . . !
>
> What shall we bring you from these United States? I regret that we did not travel more here. I should have enjoyed a visit to the west coast.

Lucy read the letter several times and then folded it away. Max du Pay! When his face, a memory of his voice, had pushed itself into the forefront of her mind in these past years, she had ruthlessly thrust the memories away. Once she had thought . . . what had she thought? That she liked him, that he liked her, that perhaps they could be friends. 'When you

have grown up a little,' he had said, but she had
grown up and he had seemed deliberately to ignore
her. There had been no other personal invitations to
the du Pay Thanksgiving Hunt. Her parents seemed
to have dined with the du Pays often, but when they
returned the invitations when Lucy was at home,
Max was always somewhere else . . . tiger-hunting
in India, skiing in Switzerland, trekking in Africa, or
already engaged with one charming Southern belle
after another. And now one of the hunted seemed to
have captured the great white hunter. Good luck to
her. Who cared for Maximilian du Pay? Her parents
were coming, though Father had not said when they
were to leave. She would write immediately to insist
that they stay with her. It would be wonderful.

And so it was. November had been a dreadful month when a tempest swept across Scotland,
destroying property and even life. The beginning of
December too had been windy, with great trees being
blown down in Perthshire. Now, as they approached
Christmas, the winds had settled down and there
were frosts, flutterings of snow and rain, rain, rain.
'Typically Edinburgh,' said Lucy as she clutched at
her skirts and her umbrella.

The flat was warm and welcoming. Lovely smells
came from the kitchen where Annie, delighted to
have all her family together, was singing as she
worked. Sir John lay in an armchair by the fire, his
long legs stretched out to the flames, the *Scotsman*
over his head.

'That is not the way to absorb the news,' said Lucy
as she removed it and kissed his forehead.

'I'm living in a lovely dream, Lucy,' he said.
'Toasting my slippers by the fire, my daughter blowing in from school . . . sorry, College, my wife
bankrupting me buying Christmas presents, steak

and kidney pie, if I'm not mistaken, in the oven, that same daughter pouring me sherry . . .'

Lucy took the hint and filled a crystal glass with amber liquid.

'Join me, my dear.'

'I'll wait for Mother. I have some notes to write before dinner. Why does it always happen that just as I congratulate myself that I have sent all my greetings, two drop through my own letterbox from people I have forgotten about completely?'

Lucy left him and went to her room. Annie had drawn the curtains against the dark and cold, but Lucy opened them again. She loved to look at snow or rain falling against lamplight. She busied herself with her correspondence and after a while heard a horse-drawn cab pull up at the door. Lady Graham stepped out and then reached behind her for her parcels.

'What can be in that huge box?' laughed Lucy and hurried down to help her mother. Annie was there before her and the box had been spirited away.

Lucy felt twelve years old again. 'That in my room, that in the kitchen, that in . . .' The orders went on and on, a beloved part of Christmas past.

'Lucy, my dear. Has Father told you we are going to Fifeshire for New Year? I refused the invitation for Christmas, but there is to be a Hunt Ball and lots of young people and old friends of our own we haven't seen in an age.'

'Where?' asked Lucy but she already knew.

At New Year it would be exactly two years since she had seen Kier, although he still wrote – not so often as before, but every few months.

'Will Kier be at home?' She followed her first unanswered question with another.

'I expect the Ball is to announce his engagement?'

Lady Graham looked at her daughter's stricken face in some surprise. 'Why, Lucy my dear, you don't mind, do you?'

'Of course not.' His letters were full of Cynthias and Alices and Janes. Lucy had never believed they meant anything to him, and now one did and she heard herself tell her mother she did not mind and did not know whether or not she told the truth.

On Christmas morning, the big box revealed a sealskin coat with fur trimming. It was absolutely lovely and Lucy threw it round her shoulders and danced around the small drawing room.

'It is the most beautiful thing,' she said over and over again.

'It will see you through Medical School, darling,' said her mother. 'That wool coat you're wearing is not nearly warm enough for Edinburgh winds.'

'Good gracious. I wore it in Washington,' laughed Lucy as she stood before a mirror admiring the fetching picture she made in the lovely soft grey coat.

'Ah, but Americans know how to heat their houses,' said Lady Graham, and frowned as her husband laughed at the irrelevance of her remark.

Lucy wore the coat on the journey to Fife and was glad to know that she looked her best as Kier handed her down from the train and kissed her with all his usual exuberance.

'I ought to have a sleigh drawn by reindeer to pull you home,' he said. 'I've put my name down for one of these new gasoline carriages though, Sir John. Have you seen one, sir?'

It was as if they had never been apart. It was always like that with Kier. He had been a big part of her life for so long and she could not imagine him belonging to anyone else.

'You have a large party this year, Kier?' she asked.

'Oh, you'll meet them all at sherry,' he said. 'Family, people I knew at Oxford, one or two from the Regiment, their sisters, that sort of thing.'

That sort of thing. Not the remark of a lover. Make a diagnosis, Doctor Graham. Your pulse has been racing all the way from Edinburgh to Leuchars; it races just as fiercely before an examination. Your heart leaped when he kissed you; it did exactly the same when you met your father off the boat train. Diagnosis: you are delighted to see a childhood friend again. Oh, Lucy, be truthful. You are even more delighted that he has not told you about a special Cynthia.

He waited until they were all gathered in the drawing room for sherry before dinner. The room was as Lucy always pictured it: lit by soft lamplight, warmed by blazing logs, the furniture and carpets faded and worn.

'Lucy, I would like you to meet Sally.' He proffered Sally as if she was some rare species of butterfly for Lucy to admire.

'How do you do, Doctor?' The voice was as timid and gentle as the girl herself.

'Good God, she lisps,' thought Lucy. 'Whatever attracted him to a girl who lisps?'

'Hello, Sally,' she said. 'Just call me Lucy, please. I'm not a doctor yet.'

'Ooh, we have all been quite, quite terrified to meet you.'

Lucy looked at Kier, expecting him to laugh with her at the absurdity, but he was gazing down into the tiny face as if he was hearing the words of an oracle.

'So that is love,' thought Lucy. 'I prefer to be rational and sensible, and if and when they have children I shall suggest a good teacher. There is no excuse for the moneyed classes to speak so poorly.'

Brave words, but over the holiday period she did admit to a little pang of what . . . regret, jealousy? All the other young people seemed to be paired off, and the charms of the rather elderly clergyman who was the only unattached male did not appeal to Miss Graham. Several times, had she been vain, she could have made herself believe that Kier sought her out. He partnered her at dinner; he danced as often with her as with the fair Sally; he rode neck and neck with her in the hunt. Sally did not hunt. 'Too, too terrifying, and horses smell so.'

In the treasure hunt she found herself alone with him on the nursery landing, as they crouched behind a dresser and waited for their pursuers to pass by. When it seemed that they were safe, Lucy went to rise from her cramped position but Kier held her down.

'Let's wait awhile, Lucy. I am determined to win the prize. Let's just sit here on the floor for a time. I must stretch my legs or I'll cramp.'

They sat in the half dark side by side on the floor, leaning against the dresser. They had hidden up here so many many times during their childhood, but this time it was different. She was intensely aware of him, the warmth of his arm, the length of his leg, through the thin stuff of her gown

'This is fun,' said Kier quietly.

Lucy nodded. She could not speak.

'Sally would never sit on the floor.'

'Her gowns are finer than mine.'

'Oh, I don't know.'

They sat still, listening to the laughter and the cries from downstairs.

'Not fair, not fair. Kier and Lucy know the house.'

'Lucy?'

There was something in his voice that told her what he was about to say was vitally important. She did not want to hear it; she must not hear it. She moved to get to her feet, but his hand on her wrist held her down.

'Lucy. How many more years?'

She could say, 'I will be a registered physician this year. I will have achieved that much,' but she could not. To throw it all away to marry Kier and follow the drum . . . Part of her longed for it, for the security of a warm, loving relationship, but there would be no Dr Graham in the Regiment. No Doctor Graham. That was the thing, the only thing. 'I am so unfair to Kier. Let him go, Lucy, let him go,' she told herself.

'Three . . . at least. I must do practical work, and there are other courses. I want to take a course at the Rotunda Hospital in Dublin, in midwifery, you know. It is not my favourite subject, but Dr Jex-Blake's lectures were an inspiration, and if I am to set up general practice I must be as well qualified as any man, more qualified.'

'The Regiment's going to India in the summer. Delhi. Isn't that a strange coincidence?'

'Very strange.'

'I'll be gone two years. You would like Delhi; you're used to a soldier's life.'

Her mouth was very dry. 'I plan to visit . . .'

She got no further, for with a stifled moan he had pulled her into his arms. His mouth was on hers, not the brotherly kiss as at the station. This was searching, demanding. Was it the memories of childhood, the warmth of the holiday season, the mulled wine they had drunk in the drawing room just a few minutes before . . . but Lucy answered his kiss. She too was searching, demanding. Her arms were around his neck and somehow they were full length on the floor and her body was on fire and she was desperate for the fire to be extinguished. She came to her senses when his hand found its way inside the low neckline of her dress, and she pulled herself away and stumbled to her feet.

'This is madness.'

'I am the one who is mad, Lucy.' She could see the effort he made to pull himself together. 'Forgive me,' he said and she was back in the sick-room of the fourteen-year-old Kier who had behaved abominably and thrown his medicine and his crutch at her and then begged so sweetly for her forgiveness. 'We must go downstairs,' said the man, Kier. 'I'll go first, give you a chance to . . . There is no excuse for my behaviour.' He half saluted and ran quickly down the stairs and she heard him calling lightly.

'Lucy? No, I have not seen her. Has she found the treasure?'

'Yes, and lost it too,' thought Lucy. Had the treasure been within her grasp? Should she have pulled it to her and kept it safe against all comers? She straightened her dress and smoothed her hair and went back to the party.

Her father came to her room on New Year's Eve as she dressed for the Ball in a made-over gown that Lady Graham would not need in Delhi.

'You look charming, my dear,' said Sir John as he fastened her twenty-first birthday gift of pearls around her neck. 'The announcement is for midnight, Lucy. Are you able to wish him joy?'

'I wish him luck, Father.' She tried to sound light-hearted, even flippant. 'She will bore him to tears in a twelve-month.'

'Not if she gives him a child, Lucy. Kier is ready for fatherhood and will make a doting papa.'

Lucy laughed. 'What an absurd idea! Kier is a child himself.'

'He is twenty-three, two years older than you.

And I have often found that it is more the desire for stability, for a wife and children to return to, that shepherds a soldier into holy matrimony, than deep, passionate love.' He handed her her shawl, another relic of Washington. 'I am glad your heart is not broken. I always hoped you might marry Kier, but if you do not love him . . .'

'Of course I love him. I always have but . . . oh, Father, I don't know. If I marry anyone that will be an end to my dream. I'm so very selfish. I want it all. Isn't that greedy of me? I want Kier . . . or someone . . . to wait until I am ready, and I do not want to marry for another three years. Even after that, I would like to go on to the University for an advanced degree. There is so much to learn and every day there are more and more discoveries. Perhaps I am not meant for a domestic life. I would find it . . . difficult to give up medicine for any man.'

'Then obviously you have not yet met the right man for when you do, Lucy, when you know that this is the man with whom you want to spend your life, nothing, including the practice of medicine, will stand in your way.'

At midnight Mr Anderson-Howard wished the company a very happy New Year, but he looked discomfited, puzzled. Kier was nowhere to be seen and neither was Sally, whose parents looked even more discomfited than Kier's. There was a buzz of speculative talk among the young people and Lucy heard some of it.

'Of course they were going to announce.'

'He never actually asked her, you know.'

'She assumed, we all did . . .'

'He's going to India, for God's sake. No girl in her right mind would want to get engaged and then see her beloved go off to years in India.'

'But where is she?'

'You don't think they've run off, do you?'

Lucy's heart skipped a beat. Run off? She forced herself to kiss her parents, to chat normally to Kier's mother and father.

'You don't know what's happened, Lucy dear?' said Mrs Anderson-Howard. 'We were so sure, you see. He said he was going to ask her; I'm sure he did.'

'Perhaps they decided to wait until after India.'

'That'll be it. She's not like you, Lucy, used to trailing half-way across the world every few years. Oh, do make the musicians play, Archie. This is turning into a funeral tea.'

The musicians played, the waiters poured champagne, the young danced, their elders sipped the wine and talked and tried desperately to avoid the only subject they wanted to discuss.

It was nearly one in the morning before the door opened to reveal a flushed and windblown Kier and Sally.

'So sorry we're late,' said Kier cheerfully. 'We went for a walk and then found ourselves, blondes both, about to become your first foot of the New Year, Mother, so we went around the house tapping on windows till we could find a dark-haired footman to come out and lead us in.'

'The butler was frightfully fierce, Mrs Anderson-Howard,' said Sally. 'He attacked us with a cricket bat.'

'Not really, Mother.' Kier reassured his mother, who had half risen in alarm. 'Bless his fierce old heart, though, he did have it in his hand, ready to beat off the invaders.'

'Rather a strange time to go for a walk, Kier.'

Kier looked at his father. 'We had such a lot to talk about.'

'Snakes and things,' said Sally with another little shudder. 'Oh, Kier darling. Champagne!'

Lucy watched them for a few moments before excusing herself and going off to bed. Sally had recovered from her disappointment at not becoming an engaged woman. 'Snakes and things.' Kier had obviously filled the poor girl's head with a lot of nonsense about living conditions in the outposts of the Empire. But why? Had it anything to do with that wine-induced moment of madness on the nursery stair? And it was wine-induced, wasn't it? He would not have kissed her so had he been completely sober. Lucy looked sternly into her mirror as she brushed her hair. 'If he asked you today, would you leave everything and go off with him to India?'

But Lucy Graham refused to answer the question.

6

Edinburgh 1893

IN THE FORMAL setting of a house-party it was impossible for Lucy to avoid Kier altogether, although she tried. Her mind was in a turmoil. Part of her said that if Kier truly loved Sally he would not have kissed her, Lucy, on the nursery stair. On the other hand she worried that she might just have spoiled poor Sally's romance.

'But she looked happy. She doesn't love him enough. He does not love her enough. I do not . . .' Oh, the permutations were endless. Her racing blood told her that she had wanted more, much more, from Kier on the nursery landing. But was that love, or Christmas spirit, or wine, or frustrated spinsterhood?

'If he loved her, truly loved her, he would not have frightened her with tales of life in India. If she loved him, truly loved . . . if I . . . oh, dear God, why is life so complicated?' She murmured to herself.

'Hello, Lucy. I felt sure I should find you here.'

It was Kier.

Lucy turned from the nursery fire she had kindled herself – had she not done the same so often in the long ago – and looked up at him. He looked tired and pale. The ravages of a New Year holiday, no doubt.

'Sir John says you leave tonight.'

'My classes start soon, and there is so much for

my parents to do. They are considering selling The
Larches, you know. Did your father tell you so?'

'No.'

She did not stand up. He did not kneel down
beside her

'Finance. India will be expensive. The Alexanders
love the house and so it would seem sensible
to sell.'

'Lucy, I love you.'

She continued to look into the flames. 'I know. I
love you too,' she said softly.

He laughed but it was not a laugh, almost a cry
of pain. 'This is where we should fall into each
other's arms.'

What could she say?

'Lucy. I want a home and healthy little children
playing in the orchard and creeping out at night to
feed their ponies extra sugar-lumps. I want a wife . . .
you – I have never ever really wanted anyone else –
at my table, on my arm . . . in my bed.'

She stood up, the firelight throwing her shadow
on the wall.

'In three years' time you will have had a chance
to get all this out of your mind. You should have
fulfilled whatever it is in you that longs for . . . for
. . . what I can't, no man can, give you. I should make
Major about the same time. A perfect time for us to
marry. I won't ask you to become engaged. For one
thing, if you accepted me, it would be a dreadful
humiliation to poor Sally; I'm extremely fond of her,
you see.' He turned away from her and his voice
was very quiet. 'Sometimes it's nice to be admired
by someone who doesn't really know one, bumps
and all as they say. And you know me so well. I have
no secrets from you. But you, Lucy, you have always
kept your counsel. We'll write, shall we? And then in

three years' time, I shall come and all you will have to say is, "Yes, Kier. The time is right."'

She said nothing. The tears were flowing freely and oh so quietly.

'Oh, my love, don't cry. My soul tells me that you are worth waiting for, Lucy Graham.' He bent down and gently kissed her. 'Make it better, Doctor,' he said softly and when she looked up he was gone.

Had the adults, the parents, made a pact? No more was said about Kier's engagement. Nothing was said about the fact that, for the first time ever, he did not see them off at the station. Lucy had her story ready but was not called upon to tell it.

She returned to her medical lectures and her parents eventually sailed to India. Her father sent her a straw hat from Firpo's at Aden which she hung on the wall.

'I shall wear the hat as I sail through the Canal,' she told him in a letter.

But she never went to India. Lady Graham died from dysentery within a few months of arriving in Delhi. Sir John brought his wife's body back to be buried in the graveyard of the wee kirk in Fife where they had been married and, after a few weeks' compassionate leave, returned to India. Lucy worked harder than ever, if that was at all possible. Why had medicine been unable to save her mother? There was so much to learn, so much to do.

The frontiers of medicine were being pushed farther and farther. Doctors all over the world, male doctors, were adding – daily, it seemed – to the understanding of the human body. Halstead explained his operation for mastectomy. Oliver and Schafer discovered the nature of adrenalin and, a year later, Röntgen discovered X-rays. Lucy read of every new discovery and she studied, in Edinburgh, in Dublin, in Rouen. She moved to Dundee and attended lectures given by Professor Geddes, and Professor D'Arcy Thomson. In 1896, when a little Dundee girl called Rosie Nesbitt was entering the hallowed portals of St Andrews University for the first time, and an anti-toxin against diphtheria was being introduced, Lucy Graham at last became a fully qualified doctor. She graduated M.B., C.M. and was among the first woman doctors ever to graduate from a Scottish college. She put Kier Anderson-Howard, who had not been able to attend her graduation, firmly to the back of her mind. He was now in Africa, likely to remain for a while, and while he was there she did not have to think about marriage. And who would want to marry in this wonderful year when the whole world was spread out before her.

She could stay in Edinburgh and run a practice from her home or she could move. She had liked Dundee when she studied there. It was almost home, since Fife and the now sold Larches lay just across the Tay. It was immaterial, she told herself, that Laverock Rising was also just across the river. Quite bluntly she faced the fact that there would still be prejudice against her because she was a woman. The Anderson-Howard patronage would be useful to her, and there was the good-will her own parents had built up in the area.

Sir John smoothed the rocky path which lay ahead of his daughter. 'I think you're right to go to Dundee,' he said. 'If you sell your Edinburgh flat, you should be able to buy the right address. Somewhere at the West End would be best.'

He could not stay long enough to see her settled, but instructed his lawyers to help her in every way possible. A house was to be found in a quiet residential street, preferably quite near the centre of town and the university. The lawyers went to work.

'This house offers excellent accommodation, Miss Graham,' said Mr Dryden, the senior partner in Dryden, MacDonald and Dryden. 'There are four floors, the first of which would be ideal for offices for the practice of medicine.' The distaste in his voice was so palpable that Lucy almost recoiled. 'The second floor makes ideal living accommodation; in fact, so it is with several of the neighbouring houses. Then the attics for servants, and the basement for the usual offices, kitchens, pantries.'

'Why is the house for sale, Mr Dryden?'

'I advised it. The owner lives abroad and has rented out the property for some years. He needs an income and wanted to ask £40 per annum, that is a £5 rise in one year. I could not see the last tenant paying such an ambitious sum. On the other hand, should we sell the property, which needs little in the way of work, £420 invested sensibly brings in a handsome income and with no worries.'

'I should like to see the house.'

He rang a little bell and almost immediately an aged clerk entered in reply to the summons.

'Ask Mr Colin to come in, Herbert.'

Mr Dryden turned to Lucy as the old man shuffled out again. 'My nephew will show you the property, Miss Graham. Ah, Colin. This is Miss Graham and she would like to see No.4.'

Lucy looked up into twinkling brown eyes.

'This is an honour, Doctor Graham,' said Colin Dryden, with a very slight but noticeable stress on the title. 'My aunt, Mrs Dryden, is anxious to become your first patient. I have the keys, Uncle,' he said and held out his hand to help Lucy from the deep leather seat.

'You must be the second Dryden of Dryden, MacDonald and Dryden?' asked Lucy as they walked down the great stone staircase.

'Good heavens, no. That's my Uncle Ian. I appear nowhere at all on the family escutcheon and, if Uncle Alistair has anything to do with it, I never shall.'

'Oh, why not?' asked Lucy. She looked at him carefully as he handed her into a cab that had been waiting patiently, and liked what she saw. Only of middle height, so that she stood eye to eye with him, there was an engaging frankness about his roundish face.

'For one thing, I advocate the rights of women. Uncle Alistair thinks women should be in the . . . kitchen.'

'And your aunt?'

'Stays out of the kitchen . . . and everywhere else, as much as possible. She says, "Yes, dear," regularly and does exactly as she chooses. Seriously, she will make every effort to wear the accolade, *Doctor Graham's first patient*.'

'I have already had hundreds of patients, Mr Dryden,' said Lucy acidly. Medicine was not a joke. She softened, for he was so very anxious to please. 'Is there something wrong with her?'

'My dear Doctor Graham. What has that to do with anything? You are the social event of the season.'

'Are you sure you don't mean pariah?' Lucy interrupted.

The eyes twinkled at her again. 'The old biddies will be lining up in the street. There will be dowagers, young women from the upper echelon of society, female lecturers, students, maids.' The eyes became serious and Mr Dryden frowned. 'The men won't come.'

'Will they let their wives come, their children?'

'Some. Well, what do you think?' They had reached No.4, a tall, narrow white house with wrought-iron railings around the windows on the first floor. There was a slight air of neglect.

'The door needs a lick of paint,' said the young lawyer as if he could read her mind.

They walked up the outside steps and he put the key in the door. Inside, light spilled into the hall from a stained-glass window and danced around the black and white tiled floor.

It was the most extraordinary feeling but Lucy, who had spent most of her life travelling around the world, immediately felt at home. The house welcomed her. Mentally she shook herself, for she did not approve of people who accorded human values to inanimate objects.

She wandered around, seeing her mother's furniture arranged in the living areas, deciding where cabinets and tables and chairs should go in the offices. There was no doubt at all that she would buy the house.

'The kitchen is a joy, is it not? That range is very up-to-the-minute. See, it's an Eagle, and has the latest in flue construction, lifting fire and' – he kept the best till last – 'a reversing damper. Your cook will adore it.'

Lucy, who knew next to nothing about kitchens and even less of the mysteries of ranges, agreed with him but did not award him the satisfaction of telling him so.

'I shall have to see what my housekeeper thinks of it, but I believe we can come to an arrangement about the house, Mr Dryden. The location is certainly excellent, and no doubt the garden is quite pleasant.'

'Do you have a gardener, Doctor? If not, we will be delighted to advertise for you. See, we can go out here

through these French windows and the balcony of the
main bedchamber also looks out over the gardens.'

Lucy looked in dismay at the overgrown flowerbeds and the barely recognizable vegetable garden.
Originally, the gardens had met the needs of a large
family.

'I may not be able to afford a full-time gardener,'
she said with a frankness that almost made Colin
Dryden wish he had the time and talent to care for
it for her. 'Until I build up a practice . . .'

'A few hours each week should keep it under
control. Do you need to see any of the rooms again
today, or shall we return to the office?'

'I would like to show the house to Annie, my
housekeeper. She has been with me almost all my
life and deserves the courtesy.'

He understood. He bowed and, after he had carefully locked up, took her back to the cab.

Annie, who was staying with her sister in her home
village of Cupar, refused to visit the house.

'I really should have given up some time ago,
Miss Lucy, but I can't go on working. I prom-
ised your mother that I would look after you in
Edinburgh . . .'

Lucy looked at the woman who had been with her
for so many years in so many places. She saw a thin,
wrinkled elderly lady: someone who had certainly
earned the right to stop working.

'Oh, Annie, how selfish of me. Of course you must
retire.' Lucy's mind was working feverishly. How
would Annie live? She must see her way to making
her a monthly payment. But from where was this
largesse to come? 'Where will you live?'

'Here, with my sister and her man. I'll still see you,
Miss Lucy, but it's time you got a young woman. I'll

be all right here. I have the £100 your mother left me invested and . . .'

Lucy was about to protest, to say 'That was for your old age,' but this *was* Annie's old age. 'I have taken her toil so much for granted   she thought, 'and my parents. My poor mother . . . She could not bear to think about her mother, who had not even had the satisfaction of seeing her unsatisfactory daughter graduate.

'I'll see that you are all right, Annie,' she said. 'You'll never want for anything.'

She took a fond and tearful farewell of the woman who had laboured conscientiously for years and years, in hot climates and cold, to see that her life ran smoothly. Clothes were soiled: Annie washed them. Food was ready whenever Lucy chose to eat. Not a particle of dust was allowed to lie unchallenged. An evening dress, thrown carelessly over a chair after a night's dancing, was returned, cleaned and pressed, to the wardrobe, ready to be worn again.

Lucy caught the train back to Dundee and her mind went in tandem with the click-clack of the wheels.

'I have no housekeeper: more importantly, I have no patients. My grandmother's money will furnish my office and Mother's money will keep me until Christmas. I must make Annie an allowance. I must get a gardener or my weeds will upset all my neighbours. So first I must place an advertisement in the *Courier and Journal*.'

'An announcement that Doctor Lucille Graham etc. etc. is now practising at 4 Shore Terrace will probably be more helpful in the first instance than a request for a maid-of-all-work.' Colin Dryden made the suggestion as Lucy sat in his book-littered office and drank coffee.

'This cubby-hole, dare I call it an office, reminds me of my childhood,' said Lucy lightly, so at ease with the young solicitor did she feel. 'All it needs is tobacco smoke.'

'Filthy habit,' said Colin Dryden dismissively. 'My father smoked constantly and I'm sure it contributed to his early death. Don't you agree – or are you encouraging me to buy a pipe?'

'I don't know enough about it, but a Professor Potts did find a marked incidence of . . .' – she stopped the word 'scrotal' just in time – '. . . a cancer among chimney sweeps. The carbon, he thought.'

He smiled. 'Well done, a doctor who listens. Usually medical men are so dismissive. Now, shall we send the announcement and the advertisement?'

Lucy decided to ignore his sweeping judgement of the medical profession. 'Yes, please.'

'And will you dine with me this evening? The ladies' dining room of my uncle's club is suitable.'

Lucy had often dined with groups of other students during her years of study, but perhaps because most of the men were too hard up, or perhaps because they were all working too hard, she had not made any intimate friendships. Even when she had gone to a ball or a party with Kier, it had been as part of a group. She felt as nervous as she had done on the day she put her hair up. But it did not occur to her to decline.

'I would like that,' she said simply.

'Good. I shall brave Mrs O'Brien at half-past seven. In the meantime I shall place these advertisements.'

Lucy's thoughts as she walked swiftly back to her boarding-house were not of her career or the size and upkeep of the house she had so rashly bought, but

of what to wear. The late summer evenings were
still warm and so an Indian shawl for her shoulders
would be nice, but which dress? In the end, there
was no decision to make. Most of her clothes were
packed in trunks and the only evening gown she
had with her was a half-mourning gown she had had
made after her mother's death. It was lilac, and she
congratulated herself for the colour suited her. The
neckline was not very . . . not too low.

'If I remove that little satin frill around the neckline
and sew it very neatly . . . and then Mother's little
gold chain with the amethyst teardrop . . .'

Lucy Graham banished Dr Graham and set out to
be frivolous.

What an amusing companion Colin Dryden turned
out to be. He had a fund of stories about his student
days and his early years in his uncle's office. Perhaps
they were so endearing because he was laughing at
himself, never ever at anyone else.

'My aunt, by the way,' he said as they sat in the
lounge waiting for their after-dinner coffee, 'says that
she feels the most dreadful migraines approaching
Dundee from the south-west. They should arrive just
about the time your office opens.'

'Is she as frivolous as you, Mr Dryden?'

'Oh, eminently more so. If she likes you, and I
know she will,' he added with a look that caused
Lucy to turn her head away from the intensity of his
gaze, 'she will have everyone who is anyone rushing
to sign on Doctor Graham's list.'

'I want to take care of the sick, Mr Dryden, not
overfed, underworked matrons who are suffering
from ennui.'

'Oh, they will adore to be cured of ennui. It will be
the disease of the century.'

'A Doctor Rehn in Frankfurt has just sutured a

heart wound. Do you realize what that means?' Lucy
asked him seriously and at once sober and serious he
shook his head.

'Doctors will begin to operate on the heart itself.
The bounds of medicine will soon know no limits.
In Italy they have found that if a substance called
chlorine . . .'

She stopped as he looked puzzled, and blushed
with embarrassment. As always she had the bit
between her teeth. 'I'm sorry. This must be boring
for you.'

'No, not at all. Your face lights up with enthusiasm;
your eyes flash; even your hands speak.' He stopped
as she looked away again. 'Sorry. What is chlorine?
I've never heard of it.'

She laughed and they were at ease again. 'I was
hoping you wouldn't ask that: I'm not too sure
myself. It's a gas, one of the halogens, smells terrible
but if, according to the Italian research, it is added to
water – and don't ask me how – it kills germs. Just
think. Typhoid wiped out all over the world, literally
overnight. What next? Dysentery? Cholera?'

'How good is it at hunger and poverty?'

'So there is more to you than laughter?'

He looked pained. 'Sometimes laughter is the
only pill that works, Doctor.' He reached across
and grasped her hands and she did not pull away.
'There are sick people here in Dundee, Lucy. Don't
think about Germany and Italy; we need you here.'

She decided to ignore his unwarranted use of her
name. He was so young, so sincere, and yes, it was
very pleasant to be admired.

'Your law firm has just sold me a house that cost
me a king's ransom. I must stay in Dundee to pay for
it . . . but I need patients.'

He smiled at her. 'They'll come.'

But they did not come. Day after day Lucy sat in her newly decorated and furnished consulting room and waited. She visited the hospitals and introduced herself to the various heads of department; she was known to many of them already from her years at Dundee Medical School.

'Our patients are sent by their own doctors, Doctor Graham, or they are too poor to afford one. We will recommend . . . should the opportunity arise.'

Opportunity. She found herself almost hoping for an accident in the street so that she could rush to the aid of the injured and thus make herself known. Kier's mother invited her to lunch and to dinner several times and, in this way, she met many prominent and wealthy people, but they did not rush to her rooms.

The attitudes of several of the women she met in this way were interesting and sometimes ambivalent. They thought her terribly clever and brave to have spent so many years fighting her way into the closed world of medicine but, oh no, they could not possibly consult her themselves.

'Why did you want to study medicine, Miss Graham?' was an often asked question, and the answer was always the same.

'I want to help the sick.'

'There is great discussion in Dundee, and I'm sure elsewhere, about the advisablity of having only fully trained nurses in hospitals,' said Mr MacDonald of Dryden, MacDonald and Dryden, who, in this small world of society, was well-known to the Anderson-Howards. 'Is that not women's place in medicine, Doctor?'

At least he awarded her her hard-won title.

'It is a place, Mr MacDonald, but there is a very

special place for a woman doctor, a unique place.
Women bring special skills to medicine . . .'

'To nursing, surely. Their God-given role of nur-
turing, caring?'

'In the field of medicine for women, Mr MacDonald,
a woman is surely better qualified than any man.'
She tried to make her arguments simple, perhaps too
simple. 'Merely by virtue of being a woman, she has
empathy and understanding.'

'A properly qualified and trained physician, Doctor
Graham, will surely have the same understanding of
the more intimate functions of a woman's body as an
unmarried woman.'

There it was again. Unmarried women should be
gentle little flowers. The practice of medicine was
indelicate and robbed them of their femininity.

'You do not have to have experienced childbirth to
understand it, Mr MacDonald.'

'An unmarried woman should know nothing of
these matters, and moreover, Doctor Graham, a
decent woman should not want to know of them.'

There was nothing more to be said but, as luck
would have it, that strange unwritten law that allot-
ted twenty minutes to the partner on either side was
working and Lucy was able to turn her burning face
away from his appalling rudeness. She could hardly
concentrate on the conversation of the young man on
her other side and he was so tongue-tied that he dried
up completely, and each of them sat in misery until
the dessert course was brought in and he, at least,
could seek solace in a chocolate meringue.

That her embarrassment had been witnessed by
others was made obvious by the solicitude with
which Kier's mother poured her coffee.

'My dear,' she breathed sympathetically and moved
on.

'May I sit down, Doctor Graham?' The woman who stood before her was expensively if not fashionably dressed in a pale green silk gown that hung on her too-thin frame.

'I am Mrs MacDonald,' she introduced herself, as if afraid that Lucy would prefer her to sit elsewhere.

'Do please sit down,' said Lucy and smiled at her.

The woman still stood, twisting a silk handkerchief in her long thin fingers. 'Some men find progress . . . difficult, Doctor Graham. Have you found this to be so?'

'Some men, yes,' Lucy agreed.

Mrs MacDonald seemed to gather herself together as if she needed courage. 'It is quite wonderful that you have come to Dundee. I hope you will be very happy and successful,' she said and turning on her heel walked rapidly away.

The party finished early since so many of the guests had to catch the last ferry across the Tay, and Lucy was glad that she had refused the Anderson-Howards' offer of hospitality.

'I hope you will be successful.' Mrs MacDonald's words rang in her ears as she watched the shores of Fife slip away.

'I hope so too, Mrs MacDonald, I hope so too,' she said to herself.

7

Dundee

EXACTLY ONE WEEK after she officially opened her
new consulting rooms, Doctor Lucille Graham found
a housekeeper, a gardener, and her first patient, and
they all came to her through the good offices of Mrs
MacDonald.

The patient came first. The MacDonalds' nursemaid had a backache and her mistress sent her to see
what the new young female doctor would advise.

'The advice is to stop carrying heavy loads,
Mhairi,' said Dr Graham after she had given the
young woman a thorough examination. 'How old
is the baby?'

'Well, Archie's three and then the twins is two and
the baby's six months.'

'No wonder,' thought Lucy, 'that Mrs MacDonald
is so thin and pale and that her overworked nursemaid has an aching back.'

'The twins must be walking?'

'Oh yes, Doctor, but they get jealous if the mistress
is feeding the baby, and they want to be babies, and
then little Archie wants to be a baby and . . .'

'And you give in to them?'

'Well, it saves yelling. They yell, and the master
doesn't like that and the mistress gets upset and
starts to cry, and that's not good for her milk, is
it?'

'No, but neither is it good for you to be carrying

heavy children around, children who are perfectly capable of walking for themselves.'

'The mistress thought maybe . . . you being just qualified . . . you would know of some pill . . .'

Lucy looked at the anxious face. A pill. Everyone was looking for a pill that would cure everything.

'Perhaps, since there are so many small children . . .' She stopped for a moment, remembering Mrs MacDonald's age. 'Are there other, older children?'

'Oh yes, Miss, I mean Doctor. Margaret is eleven and Alice is nine.' Mhairi smiled with pride as if she herself was the mother of so many children. 'I think we're really pleased that the twins are boys . . . three of each, we have now.'

'A fine family,' said Lucy wryly. 'And the girls are in the nursery too. Perhaps a little more help . . . ?'

Mhairi looked quite shocked. 'Oh. The master says his own mother raised eight perfectly healthy children with no help at all.'

Lucy thought rapidly. A five-year gap between the older girls and the next child; that probably meant at least two miscarriages. No wonder Mrs MacDonald was so pale and worn-looking; too many children, one after the other. Before the body had had time to recuperate from the demands of one pregnancy, another child was on the way. How she wished she could do something to regulate that. There were the rather bizarre methods she had heard a little about: vinegar-soaked sponges inserted in the vagina, for one. She could hardly see the fastidious Mrs MacDonald resorting to that. And what of Mr MacDonald's part in all this? He did not like to hear his twin sons yelling. Their crying disturbed him and he got annoyed. Poor Mr MacDonald!

Lucy sighed. Such was the way of the world.

'Try to avoid carrying heavy loads, Mhairi. If

you must lift the children, bend your knees and
don't bend over from the waist to pick them up.
I don't know why that helps but it does. Tell Mrs
MacDonald that hint too. And perhaps . . .' She
stopped, suddenly appallingly aware that she knew
absolutely nothing about the minds of small children,
of any child. 'Perhaps you could make getting up and
down stairs a game for the twins and Archie. A race
to see who is the fastest or perhaps,' she groped
desperately back to her memories of her father in
her own nursery, 'perhaps they could play at being
frogs hopping about . . .'

To her amazement Mhairi's face lit up. 'Or tigers,
Doctor. The mistress read them a tale about a tiger
from foreign parts and they liked it.'

Lucy stood up. 'Yes, that's a good idea. Capture
the imagination.'

'Oh, I will, Doctor. I feel better already.'

Lucy sat for a few minutes looking at the door
which had closed behind her very first patient, a
delighted patient. Would that it would ever be
so! She remembered Annie and a friend from her
childhood. 'What a little blether Miss Sarah is,' Annie
used to say wonderingly as they sat at the nursery
tea-table.

'Well, Annie. I did a bit of blethering myself just
now and I sincerely hope it worked. Sir Ronald Ross
may have identified the cause of malaria and that
would be a great help were I in India, but I'm
not. I wonder how Sir Ronald would deal with
nursemaid's back – my first ailment.'

No patient followed Mhairi through the door.
Doctor Graham wrote up case notes. She almost
blushed to call it a case but no, she chided herself,
the ailment is very real to poor overworked Mhairi.

'Shall I ever be overworked?' she thought as 5

o'clock came and she made her lonely way upstairs to her living quarters. She looked in her pantry and there on the stone shelf, the tried and true method of keeping food cold and fresh, was the piece of beef she had rashly bought for her evening meal. 'I really don't know quite what to do with you,' she told it and reached further along the shelf for the remains of the cheese that she had had for lunch.

That did not look too appetizing, even with the addition of a lovely piece of crusty bread and a rather tired apple.

'I'll melt the cheese,' thought Lucy, 'if this stupid unobliging, terrifically modern up-to-the-minute range with its reversing damper hasn't reversed itself again and gone out.'

The meanest of her patients, had she had any, would have been shocked to see how much cold or undercooked food the wonderful new lady doctor was eating. Doctor Graham was not overburdened with domestic skills.

'Blast!' There was no warmth at all from the great iron monster that took up so much room. Lucy looked at it. Could she bear to try to light it again? Would it stay lit till the morning and thus make a nice hot cup of tea a possibility?

She heard the front door-bell and half sighed as she ran upstairs to answer the summons. It might just be a patient? It was not.

'Doctor Graham. Mrs MacDonald sent me. My name's Isa Murray and I need a job.'

'Come in, won't you, Miss Murray.'

'It's Mrs, Doctor, and I hope that won't make a difference. Mrs MacDonald thought with you it might not.'

Mrs MacDonald? Why was the woman making so much effort? Was it because, as a loyal wife, she could

not straightforwardly apologize for the arrogance of
her husband but would do so in other ways.

'I was in service before my marriage, Doctor, to
Mrs MacDonald's family. I know how to mind fine
furniture and I'm a good plain cook. I've even been
lady's maid and can sew small stitches. But I have a
husband and won't be able to stay nights. We have
a place near the Mill.'

'Your husband is a mill-worker?'

'Was, Doctor. It's done something to his lungs and
he can't work in the mills no more. We wanted to
do farm work up the Carse, but he couldn't manage
like, not full-time, and we'd not get a tied cottage and
we've got a place: only three shillings the week. We
can manage that. I've been doing a bit here and there.
I was doing Mrs MacDonald's silver and she said as
there was an advertisement . . . I would stay really
late when you were entertaining, Doctor.'

Lucy had always thought deeply, and would
always think very hard before she reached an
important decision, but this once she made an
immediate decision and it was one she was never
to regret.

'Mrs Murray, I need someone in the house very
much and I need them right now. The garden needs
attention. You can see from the window here, it is
not too large and has been well planned. The top floor
. . .' She stopped. The floor was a warren of empty
rooms.

'We have our own bits and pieces, Doctor,' put
in Mrs Murray eagerly. 'If that was what you were
wanting, like. Donald's a good man and works hard
when the coughing's not on him.'

'Phthisis,' thought Lucy. 'Or perhaps it is the
effects of inhaling jute hour after hour, day after
day.'

'Has he worked in a garden before, Mrs Murray?'
she asked.

'When he was a lad, like, Doctor. He's from the
Carse, raised in the country. He only came in to
make a better living from the jute and he was a
good worker. He'd do the garden beautiful, but it
would have to be in his own time.'

'I'll show you over the house and then you can go
home and discuss it with Mr Murray.'

To Lucy's everlasting embarrassment, her new retainers turned up with their possessions on a hand-cart
borrowed from a friend who was a carter.

'I should have hired the removal company for you,
Mrs Murray.'

'Oh no, Doctor, we couldn't be beholden. The
neighbours will see we're clean and respectable,
and that's what counts, isn't it? I'm sorry if we've
disgraced you.'

'Clean and respectable.' That was what was important. And that they were not beholden. Very well,
thought Lucy. Let her grand neighbours think what
they liked. 'Let me give you a hand, Mrs Murray.'

The rather austere face softened into a smile of
singular charm. 'That wouldn't be right, Doctor. Off
you, and I'll make us all a nice cup of tea when
we're done.'

There was not much to unload and soon Donald
and his friends were setting up the bed and arranging
the lovingly polished bits of furniture, while Mrs
Murray bustled around in her kitchen, returning
again and again to touch the surface of the magnificent but, to Lucy, frightening range.

'Mrs MacDonald had one of these. So easy, and
it makes bread beautiful, and heats water and the
kitchens.'

Lucy did not confess that she had not found it easy. 'We'll go to Draffens tomorrow, Mrs Murray, and get you a uniform for answering the door. I put some aprons in a drawer in the kitchen. You'll know which ones are which.'

'Oh yes, Doctor, and it's Isa, Doctor. I'd like for you to call me by my name.'

'Very well, Isa, but not in front of patients.'

Isa smiled again. 'That's right and proper, Doctor.'

Lucy went to bed that night after eating the best meal she had yet had in her own new house and the next day, as if Isa's coming had been an omen of good, two new patients turned up at morning consulting. They arrived together, but one had been driven in a private cab and the other had walked up from the steam tram stop.

Isa, in her own old but clean dress and one of Annie's starched white aprons, showed the elder of the two ladies into the consulting room.

'I think you have been expecting me, Doctor Graham. I am Mrs Dryden.'

Mrs Dryden was as engaging as her nephew had painted her.

'How do you do, Mrs Dryden. How may I help you?'

'At my age, Doctor, there are a dozen things going wrong, but nothing that we need worry about.'

Lucy was at a loss. Surely this was not a mere social call?

'Perhaps I should find at least one of the ailments, Mrs Dryden, and see if medicine can do anything to alleviate it.'

Mrs Dryden looked at her measuringly. 'Well, Doctor,' she said at last, 'there's something that has been a bit of a nuisance over the last six months or so, perhaps even since last winter. Sometimes – I hope you don't think I'm stupid – but sometimes when I walk my right knee gives way.'

'Do you fall?'

'Stumble would be a better word. In fact I've taken to holding on to the banisters as I walk downstairs.'

Lucy nodded. 'Is the knee painful . . . or any other joints?'

'Are thumbs joints, Doctor? Sometimes my thumbs ache so much I can't hold a pen. I noticed it when I was writing to my daughter. She lives in Edinburgh,' she added as if that had some relevance. 'But sometimes a pain shoots right up my arm when I lift my heavy silver teapot. I've even spilled tea, once on my best linen cloth.'

Lucy smiled. Ruining the cloth was the tragedy. She held out her hands. 'May I look at your thumbs and then your knee?'

The thumbs were very slightly misshapen and the knee was slightly swollen.

Arthritis: a word that meant simply inflammation of the joints, one of the most common ailments known to man.

'I'm sure it's just normal ageing, Doctor. My mother was just the same and that was what her physician said.'

'Ah, but medical science is rushing breathlessly into a new century, Mrs Dryden. We can make what is natural rather more comfortable. As yet we don't know what causes the various arthritic conditions,' she said, as she felt sure that Mrs Dryden would appreciate complete honesty. 'It may be a bacteria, or some disruption of the body chemistry. Tell me, do you feel more pain when the house is cold and perhaps even damp?'

Mrs Dryden agreed that this was in fact the case.

'You must strive to maintain a uniform body

heat. Don't allow your shoulders to be caught in draughts.'

'Draughts. My dear girl. Have you not yet experienced the winds that blow across the Tay?'

'Uniform body heat, Mrs Dryden, twenty-four hours a day, and I should like you to pay attention to your diet.'

Mrs Dryden looked down at her solid well-fed body in its tight casing of corsets. 'I have the best of everything, I assure you, Doctor.'

'There is some . . . speculation . . . that the best of everything may not be good for us. I have read some interesting studies. Would you, perhaps, agree to monitoring your diet with particular reference to what and how much you eat and drink on days when your aches and pains are particularly severe?'

Mrs Dryden looked sceptical.

'I have heard that potatoes cause distress in some patients, while watercress and even parsley alleviate the condition.'

Mrs Dryden pulled on her gloves and rose to her dignified feet. 'I am to be a medical experiment then, Doctor?'

Lucy felt flustered. Should she just have prescribed some drugs which would certainly ease the pain? 'I'm sorry, Mrs Dryden . . .' she began.

'Not at all, my dear. I am flattered and will send my coachman for a ruled notebook this very instant. Before the month is out, every matron with an aching back will be competing with me to find what triggers our pain.' The old eyes twinkled. 'I should be most unhappy if I should find that my dinner glass of claret affects me adversely.'

Lucy would not be drawn. Medical science might speculate that gout was caused by over-indulgence, but she would not insult this delightful old lady by comparing gout and arthritis, which surely were unconnected in any way.

'Well, Colin was right,' said Mrs Dryden. 'You are going to do very well in Dundee, Doctor Graham. I hope you will join us for luncheon some Sunday? My husband's nephew comes to us on Sundays. He's like my own son, and he admires you very greatly.'

To her dismay, Lucy found herself blushing. She had had dinner twice with Mrs Dryden's nephew and had found him a pleasant companion, no more.

'I'll see you out, Mrs Dryden,' she said, 'and I will come to luncheon one Sunday soon.' She rang the bell and Isa appeared. 'Show Mrs Dryden out, Mrs Murray.'

Isa opened the door for Mrs Dryden and returned a few minutes later with the second caller.

'Miss Bell, Doctor.'

Miss Bell was a tall, slim woman who looked as if she might be forty years of age. In fact, she was not quite thirty.

'I'm just that tired, Doctor,' she said in answer to Lucy's first question. 'Perhaps you know of some new tonic?'

'I might, but first I have to find out why you are so tired, Miss Bell.'

Heather Bell – her parents had thought that a romantic name – was a dressmaker at Draffens, the big department store on the High Street. She lived with her elderly parents who were able to do very little for themselves. After working a full day in the shop she went home to cook and clean and nurse the old people and, if there was any spare time, she earned a little extra by taking sewing home with her. No wonder she was tired.

'My father had the tuberculosis, Doctor, and he was in the fever hospital.'

'King's Cross?'

'Yes, but he's cured, Doctor. We thought them as went into King's Cross never came out, and I'm sure it was the worry of that that brought my mother down so low. Her mind's gone, Doctor, but Father is fine, well as fine as anybody can be who's had the tuberculosis. Wonderful doctors there, and nurses too, most of them, that is.'

'They do sterling work, Miss Bell, and . . .' Lucy had a feeling that Miss Bell herself was terrified that she too would be sent one day to the fever hospital, and set herself to ease the woman's mind. 'You know that all nurses who work in hospitals have to be properly trained now. The standard in Dundee is first class. But I think, before we do anything else, that I should examine you, and perhaps do a blood test.'

'I can't be ill, Doctor, else who would look efter meh fowk.' The broad Dundee dialect fell out by mistake and Miss Bell pushed it back soundly, thinking wrongly that this fine doctor with the high-faluting accent could not possibly understand her. 'Just a tonic, Doctor, if you'll be so good.'

'Let's have a look first,' suggested Lucy and showed her patient to the screen behind which she could modestly shed her outer garments.

Without blood tests she could not be sure, but she was almost positive that exhaustion and worry were her patient's ailments. Worry she could not do much about. Exhaustion? Rest should cure that, if she could persuade Heather Bell to rest.

'Have you any other relatives who would help you with the care of your parents, Miss Bell, if I was able to arrange a little rest for you?'

'A rest?'

'There is a new hospital for women in Dundee. It has just opened and I might be able to get you . . .'

Heather Bell had jumped from the chair in alarm. 'You dinnae understand, Doctor. I need tae work and I need tae look efter the old folk. There's naebody. I have a sister, but she's tied down with six bairns and forbye she lives up the Hilltown – and my brithers, they're deid.'

In the years to follow Lucy was to hear that terrible story again and again: a surviving unmarried daughter, or son, bravely caring for elderly parents in the face of appalling poverty and want. Even Mhairi Johnston, with her several small charges to care for twenty-four hours a day, had good food and a warm bed and surely a little rest when the children slept.

'I'll mix you up a tonic, Miss Bell, but I will approach the hospital authorities to see if there is a chance for even a week's rest for you.'

'I couldnae stop the weekend, Doctor. I'll take the tonic and I'll thank you for your concern, but I couldnae leave them. Mither wanders if you're no watching her, and if he's worrit he sterts coughing.'

Lucy rang her bell.

'Mrs Murray, will you give Miss Bell a cup of tea in the kitchen while I make her up some medicine?'

Later, when the woman clutching her bottle of medicine had gone off to wait for a tram, Lucy stared into the garden and went over and over her day's work. One woman who could afford everything that would help her deal effectively with her medical condition, and one who could not and who would probably drop dead from exhaustion. A welfare service that would help the poor was necessary. But was that something for the politicians? Anyway, she would try to help both women. She would go to the Women's Hospital to see if there was a bed for poor, tired, undernourished Heather Bell. She could not, however, force her to get into it. What to do with the aged parents was the problem.

Doctor Graham, however, had miscalculated the strength of comradeship among the poor.

Two nights later Lucy was discussing with Donald Murray the future, if there was indeed to be a future, of several venerable apple trees along the back wall of her property.

'I wouldnae like tae mislead you, Doctor, but I dinnae really ken onything aboot fruit. My gut tells me never tae tak doon a tree though. I think there's probably some pruning and maybe even some mulching as would help it. I seem to mind on my faither steeping sheep's dung in water and pitting that on his fruit trees. Gin it's right wi' you, I'll cut the affected bits aff these trees and see what happens and, in the meantime, I'll ask them as kens mair.'

'Good idea, Donald,' agreed Lucy, who was a great believer in asking information of those who knew more.

'Sorry to disturb you, Doctor Graham.' Isa had come out without their being aware of it, so engrossed were they in the fate of the trees. 'There's a person to see you, Doctor. I've left her on the step.'

Lucy looked at her in some surprise. Usually Isa showed visitors into one of the waiting rooms, but this 'person' was obviously so disreputable that she had deemed it better to leave her outside the very door of the house.

'I hope she's not ill, Isa.'

'Not unless light fingers is a disease, Doctor. She looks no better than she should, and I told her if she had to see you she could wait till I found if you were available. She's probably gone by now.'

Lucy was annoyed with her maid's officiousness. 'I sincerely hope not, Isa. This house is open to

everyone. Bring her into the morning room and I'll
see her there. Go ahead and do what you think best
with the trees, Donald,' she said and hurried back
into the house.

In a few minutes an unrepentant Isa was showing
in a type of woman with whom her employer was
only too familiar.

'How sheltered does Isa believe medical training
to be?' thought Lucy with an inward laugh and went
forward to put her frightened caller – for she was very
frightened – at ease.

'Do sit down, Mrs . . .' she began.

'It's Miss, Miss. I mean I'm Miss Nesbitt, Doctor.
I'm fine, Doctor, not ill. I've come aboot pair wee
Heather. She telt her sister whae telt me, us being on
the same stair.'

Lucy looked at her in bewilderment for a moment.
Never would she have considered that there might
be a social connection between a woman like Heather
Bell and the sorry woman who stood before her now.
Miss Bell was obviously from the working class, but
in every way she was superior to this Miss Nesbitt.

'Miss Bell?' she asked.

'Aye, and I can see hoo you're wonderin' how me
and Heather even kens one another. It's men, Doctor,
men that's the ruin o' us all. Janet's Heather's wee
sister, and she lives up meh stair. Her man's useless.
Niver worked a day in his life, but he's that bonnie
Janet fell for him, mair fool her. Onyway. E'll look
efter them, the auld ones, while Heather has a bit
rest.' She lifted up a sad face and looked the doctor
directly in the eye. 'You can tell my life history, I've
nae doubt, Doctor, but I'm clean in my person and in
my cooking. I've had my lumps, same as everybody,
but I have time tae help my neighbour if she'll let me.'
The speech had obviously exhausted as much control

over her nerves as Miss Nesbitt had, and she began
to shake and Lucy was stirred with compassion. The
woman's body and dress were, indeed, relatively
clean. Neither met her standards and they obviously
offended Isa's but they were respectable.

'If you can persuade Miss Bell to take up your offer,
Miss Nesbitt, I will do my best to see that she has a
place in the hospital. You are very kind.'

The woman blushed but she was in control again.
'Oh, we all help wir neighbours up the Hilltown.
They'd do the same for me.'

When she had gone, Lucy went back to the garden
and Elsie Nesbitt walked back up the town with a
light step. What a lot she would have to tell Rosie! It
had taken great courage to go to see the aristocratic
young lady doctor in her beautiful house at the West
End, not an area of Dundee that Elsie was in the habit
of frequenting. She was walking to save the tram fare,
but suddenly she decided to splurge. She went into
a café and bought a buster, that delicious supper
of peas and chipped potatoes that the Dundonians
loved. As she walked along eating her chips, there
was a new spring in her step. She had actually seen
the new lady doctor, had sat down in the same room
with her and they had talked. One day, at last she
believed that it was possible. One day soon, Rosie
would be just like her. She wouldn't talk so posh,
but she'd be far prettier; they didn't come much
prettier than Rosie. And would she have a maid, a
frozen-faced woman like that Mrs Murray who had
looked down her nose at Elsie Nesbitt? You bet she
would. But her mother wouldn't see it.

'I'll never embarrass you, Rosie, love, not in places
like that. Now I've seen it, I'll keep it in my mind and
picture you in a gown like that, sitting in a chair like

that, having old sour-face and everybody else call you Doctor.'

Elsie felt good. Might as well earn a few bob since she was all dressed up and nowhere to go. She thought for a minute, finished her buster, and turned off the main street into one of the narrow streets that laced themselves like a spider-web behind the smart face of the town.

8

Dundee 1897

'YOU MUST COME. Just think. A stately home, well almost, but more importantly, Rosie, glorious free food and lots of it.'

Rose Nesbitt had long ago trained her stomach not to expect too much food; she remained unimpressed. 'There's too much work to do.' She gestured towards the pile of books beside her under the tree.

Mary Black arched her back in an almost wanton gesture and held up her pale face to the sun. 'There will always be too much work to do. That's the profession we've chosen.' She sagged back against the trunk of the tree. 'Rosie, there's a man, an older man, just the way you like them.'

'Harmless,' laughed Rosie. 'In his dotage?'

'Gorgeous.'

Rose sighed. She was not interested in men; the only two she had ever liked were Frazer and old Wishy. She never stopped to analyse that she liked them because she felt completely safe with them. Frazer was her brother, and as for old Wishy? He was far too old for any of *that* nonsense. 'Who is this Kier Anderson-Howard?' she asked. 'Already I don't like him.'

'You don't like his name. It's the little hyphen that bothers you.'

'Utter pretension. He should be Anderson or Howard; not both.'

'Don't fight with me, Rosie,' laughed Mary. 'It has something to do with money. Either an Anderson or Howard heiress wouldn't marry unless they got to keep their name.'

'Then I shall marry him,' joked Rosie, 'and insist that Nesbitt be added too. Anderson-Howard-Nesbitt. Nesbitt-Anderson-Howard.' She played with the variations and then, serious again, asked, 'But why are they dispensing largesse to the women students?'

'His parents are rolling in money, absolutely amazingly rich, and his mother is on the Board or something like that. They wanted to have annual garden parties but he got wounded or something; he's a soldier, or was. Now he's on the mend.'

'I've never met a soldier.'

'Then you'll come?'

But Rosie would not be drawn. Graduation with her first degree and matriculation into the medical faculty was so close, so very close that sometimes she woke from an exhausted sleep, terrified that the struggle of the past ten years was all a nightmare and that she was not a student at the world-famous University of St Andrews but Rosie Nesbitt, mill-worker.

As usual Ma was waiting at the station to walk up the road with her, to share the load of books.

'Maybe somebody'll think I can read them,' she had joked and Rosie had laughed with her, but had understood that her mother really would like to have been able to read and understand the material in the heavy old volumes.

'And what did you learn the day, hen?'

'I had only one lecture today, Ma. Mary and I sat under a tree and studied.'

'Aye, you look the better for a wee bit sun. I bet Mary does tae. Awfie pasty-faced, that lassie.'

'She invited me to a party.'

'What like party could Mary Brown have?'

'Well, it's not her exactly, but she lives in, remember, and she hears everything that's going on. Seemingly some rich family near the town is giving a party for this graduating class.'

Elsie knew better than to say outright that Rosie should attend the party. That would make her daughter think of a dozen suitable excuses not to go.

'In their hoos, Rosie, a grand hoos. My, would I love to be invited to a grand hoos.'

'I don't really have much time for parties, Ma.' Rosie was weakening. 'There is so little time left before my finals. Besides, I have nothing to wear. I can hardly go in my gown.'

The red gown had saved the pride of many a St Andrews student through the years. Costly garments and the threadbare were equally hidden by the thick red wool.

Wisely Elsie said no more, but next afternoon she went up and down the Hilltown, stopping first at Gallagher's.

Gallagher was usually happy to have the attentions of someone reasonably clean. 'I've no the notion, Elsie, but I'll be bursting for it the nicht.'

'I'm needing money noo, Sandy.'

'One o' the bairns?'

'Aye.'

'Get yoursel' spayed, Elsie,' said the big man, reaching into his till. 'I'll want full value for that, efter closing time.'

Closing time. She was too old to stay awake till the small hours. Clutching the coins, Elsie went out. If she could find what she needed, then she could sleep all afternoon and thus be ready to fulfil her part of the bargain.

She was at the station when the train from Leuchars pulled in but said nothing about her purchases. It was only after Rosie had eaten the simple supper of skirlie and mashed potatoes that she brought them into the front room.

'Look what I found up the Hilltown,' she said as she saw her daughter put the heavy books on the table when the meal had been cleared away. 'I thocht you might like it for your graduation.' She did not add that the second- or was it third-hand dress would be perfect for a party in a grand house.

Rosie's heart sank. She had innate good taste and everything in her told her that the dress was a disaster. At least it was not a flamboyant red; it was a demi-mourning gown, a lilac silk dress worn by the respectable in that period when good manners decreed that they might leave off their blacks but not return to flattering colour.

'It's a wee bit big and the colour's no' your best, but there's only the one darn in it, Rosie. Heather Bell would take it in for you. The material's bonny.'

And it was. It was pure silk and the feel of it as it caught in her rough hands was sensuous.

'Real silk,' breathed Rosie as she gently laid it aside. 'It's lovely, Ma.' She did not add that the dress was more suitable for her mother's age than her own, and she did not waste time wishing she had skill with a needle for she would certainly not bother her mother's friend Heather. Heather spent six days a week sewing. Leave her her evenings. Rose Nesbitt herself had always been too busy acquiring knowledge to acquire any domestic skills and, goodness knows, Ma had learned few of the arts that turn the simplest house into a welcoming home or a too-big dress into something suitable for a first party. She would go to the party, for it was only too obvious that Elsie needed the second-hand pleasure of hearing about a grand 'hoos'. Anyway, what did it matter? There would be no one at the party whose opinion Rosie valued.

Charabancs were hired to convey the parties of students to Laverock Rising, the house where the party was to be held. It was a fine summer day and the clouds that had hung threateningly over St Andrews all morning obligingly lifted to allow a rather weak sun to warm their spirits. Rosie was small and, pressed into the third row of seats facing the driver's broad green back, she saw very little of the Fife countryside and did not really care to sway so high above the ground. The carriages had stopped before the imposing Georgian front of the house before she was aware that they had reached their destination.

She stood on the gravel carriage sweep, her too-big hat slightly tipped over one eye by the proximity and exuberance of her companions, looking bewildered and, to Kier Anderson-Howard, totally adorable. Every protective instinct, long buried, came rushing to the surface and he hurried over to her as she stood, almost swaying, too close to the hind quarters of the rear horses.

'Stupid brutes, horses,' he said in the voice of one who loved them and accepted all their little foibles. 'They get very nervous when they feel something at their . . . back ends.' He took her arm and quite naturally she clung to it for a moment as the world righted itself.

'I'm sorry,' she said in a soft voice. 'I'm not used to charabancs.'

'They do swing about a bit, don't they? Kier Anderson-Howard,' he introduced himself. 'May I get you some lemonade . . . and you too, of course,' he smiled at Mary who had materialized behind Rosie.

'Mary Black,' said Mary. 'My friend is Miss Nesbitt, Rose Nesbitt.'

'Rose,' he said. 'Of course.'

'He's taken with you, Rosie,' said Mary as their host went off to fetch the lemonade. 'You've landed the biggest fish.'

Rosie shuddered in distaste. For someone who had grown up in a home owned and occupied by her family, Mary was sometimes amazingly coarse.

'You should have told him your name, Rosie,' said Mary. 'You don't mind my saying, do you, but when someone introduces themselves, you tell them your name.'

'Perhaps I didn't want him to know it,' lied Rosie.

Mary smiled. 'You are clever,' she breathed and turned to their returned host. 'Oh, this is lovely,' she said. 'Isn't it, Rosie?'

Rose sipped from the glass and, completely unaware of the power of her eyes, looked at Kier over the brim. 'Thank you,' she said. 'I feel better now.'

'May I show you the gardens, Miss Nesbitt, and you too, Miss Black? I believe my mother is on the front lawn, and tea will be there later. I hope you'll feel like a little something,' he smiled down at Rosie. 'Mother's cook has been baking for days. She is so excited by the thought of all you wonderfully well-educated young women. What are you planning to do with your degree, Miss Nesbitt?'

As Rosie had dared to take a second sip from her glass just as he spoke, she was unable to answer and Mary spoke for them both.

'We're going to be doctors.'

Kier stopped walking. 'By all that's wonderful,' he said. 'Doctors! My best friend is a doctor. Jenny,'

he called to a hurrying maidservant, 'has Doctor
Graham arrived yet?'

'Doctor'll be later, Mister Kier. There's been an
emergency.'

'You see the life you've chosen, ladies. Every
minute at the beck and call of your profession.'

He led them to a garden seat and solicitously
helped Rosie to sit down. He looked down at her
with regret. How he wished she would raise those
eyes to him again. Every atom of his being asked
him to stay with her and to protect her. She was so
small, so vulnerable; her frailty, and the colour and
style of the too-big dress suggested that she was in
mourning, for a father perhaps. Her voice, with the
broad Scots words aching to get out, told him her
social class. 'And yet, she's struggling to become a
doctor,' he thought to himself in admiration.

'I'm afraid I must greet some of our other guests,'
he told the girls, 'but I'll certainly look out for you
both later. You must meet Doctor Graham.'

'We've landed on our feet here, Rosie,' said Mary
as they watched the elegant figure move away. 'The
son of the house for you, and it looks like a man for
me as well.'

'A doctor in his dotage, Mary? You must be desperate.'

'He's not that old: must be early thirties. And just
think how useful a fully qualified doctor could be.'

Rosie frowned. That thought had entered her head.
She pushed it away. 'Come on, Mary. We're doing
this all by ourselves. Rights for women: votes for
women.' She stood up. 'Some tea on the lawn, Doctor
Black?'

Mary laughed. 'How too, too thrilling, dear Doctor
Nesbitt.'

*   *   *

Kier spent the next hour being the perfect host and neither his parents nor any of their excited guests realized that his mind was firmly fixed on a small figure smelling faintly of mothballs. Rose's nose was so full of the smells of the closie and of the jute-filled air of Dundee that she had not noticed the slight odour hanging on her gown.

'Either she is so poor that she had to buy the dress second-hand for her mourning period,' thought Kier, 'or she has been given it by some kindly neighbour.' Never could he have guessed that it had been bought with the sole aim of dazzling him, although poor Elsie had not known for sure but had only hoped that he might exist.

He looked for Rosie as soon as manners decently allowed. She was in the middle and yet somehow slightly apart from a large group of her fellow students, and he had time to admire her small profile. 'She's like a bird,' he thought and looked down at his hands. 'I could circle her waist with these. How can she ever withstand the rigours of medical school . . . the horrors of the wards?'

'Miss Nesbitt.' He drew her aside. 'Doctor Graham has not yet arrived but I should like to introduce you to my parents – and you too, of course, Miss Black.'

Mary at least went with him willingly enough, although Rosie would have preferred to stay safely on the lawn admiring the trees and the beautifully-laid-out and well-stocked flower gardens. She had learned Latin and Greek and Mathematics and for the last three years she had read great literature and history, but no one had ever told her how to speak to someone who owned a house like this one, a house bigger by far than the entire closie where several families lived. Rosie had got into the habit of holding herself slightly apart, listening and saying little and trying, trying hard to learn, stumbling sometimes as she struggled to develop taste. She could argue that such small matters were of little value, and of no value at all to a doctor who was going to work with the poor who would know no better than she, but, she realized as she walked by Kier Anderson-Howard's side on his family's immaculately-cared-for lawn, she wanted to feel at ease here, she wanted to belong. She held her chin up and straightened her spine and so, when she met Kier's parents, she did not look frail and helpless but hard and belligerent.

'How do you do, Miss Nesbitt, Miss Black.'

'How do you do, Mrs Anderson-Howard,' said Mary. 'How very kind of you to have us here.'

Rosie was tongue-tied. 'How do you do' sounded stupid – was that really what you were supposed to reply? – and she could think of nothing to say at all. She watched the easy and perhaps too familiar way in which Mary chatted to Kier's parents and she desperately tried to unlock her jaws. She walked with them to the huge marquee for tea, and here was another insurmountable problem. How do you eat a sandwich and hold a cup and saucer at the same time? She clung to the saucer and prayed that she would not drop it; only once before had she held such fine china. She could not believe that this was what they used in the garden. Rosie was not enjoying her first garden party.

And then she felt Kier stiffen beside her. She looked up at him, saw his eyes shining with joy and turned to see what he was seeing. A small dog-cart was being expertly wheeled in through the gates, and driving the horse was a woman in an incredibly smart bottle-green riding coat. She handed the reins to a groom who had hurried to her and stepped down from the cart. She chatted, laughing, to the groom for a moment and then she picked up her skirt over her arm and hurried towards them. Kier left Rosie and went to meet her and when he reached her he kissed her on the cheek, the gesture of one who had done the same thing a hundred times before. 'Oh, for such serenity,' thought Rose, 'for such ease.'

'Lucy, darling.' Kier's parents had gone forward too to greet the latecomer.

'Miss Nesbitt, Miss Black,' said Kier grandly as one does who is presenting a trophy, 'may I introduce Doctor Graham? Lucy, darling, you will never guess. The first two of our guests I met are medical students.'

There it was again, that odd response. 'How do you do?' This time Rosie was ready. 'How do you do, Doctor Graham,' she said and for the second time in her life was aware of the difference between the hardworking hands of the poor and the hardworked hands of the rich. Dr Graham's hands were beautifully shaped, long and slim and capable, but they were white and soft and the nails, cut short and blunt, were polished. Rosie almost snatched back her rough red hands with the bitten nails. 'Whatever else I have to do without I shall have that glycerine ointment for my hands, and this time I promise that I shall never bite my nails again,' she vowed as the conversation went on around her, Mary gamely holding up Rosie's side as well as her own.

Eventually Kier remembered his duties as a host and, with a look at Rosie that was almost regretful, he took Dr Graham's arm and steered her towards the tea tent.

'You are staying for dinner, Lucy?' Rosie heard him say.

'I'm spoiling myself and staying until Monday,' Dr Graham answered and then, before they drifted too far away for even Rosie's keen hearing she continued,

'Which one of us terrified your young friend, Kier? I do hope it was you and not me.'

Rosie felt herself blushing but no one else seemed to have heard. The Anderson-Howards excused themselves and went off to greet others and Rosie and Mary were left alone.

'I should have known the Doctor Graham was *the* Doctor Graham,' said Mary.

'Why the emphasis?'

'Rosie, where do you hide yourself? Doctor Graham is not only one of the first female doctors in the entire country but she is the only one in Dundee. She has a society practice at the West End. Could be very useful to an up-and-coming Dundonian doctor.'

Rose had heard once before of Doctor Graham but she had forgotten until today. Ma had said she was the one who got poor Heather into the women's hospital. Imagine Heather having the nerve to go to see a woman like that! Still, it proved what she had thought all along. Women needed women doctors. Heather would never have gone to a man to ask for a tonic. Now it suited Rose to ignore the poorer part of Doctor Graham's practice.

'I have no intention of working with the rich, Mary. I want to have a practice in my own street, right up the Hilltown among the tenements.'

Mary looked at her in amazement. 'You are incredibly naïve, Rose Nesbitt. Be so kind as to tell me how you are going to afford it.'

'Something will turn up. It always does if you work hard enough, and besides things will change. Perhaps the Government will help with the medical care of the poor.'

'You shouldn't be out without your keeper. Thank God I am here to look after you. The son of the house is obviously smitten . . .'

'He's in love with Doctor Graham,' interrupted Rose.

'Maybe, but I don't think he knows how much; he's got used to loving her, and she treats him the way I treat my wee brother, hardly lover-like. The "daaalings" all over the place from the toffs don't mean a damn thing. What you should be thinking about, Rosie, is making sure that neither he nor Doctor Graham forget you're around.'

'I can't make friends with someone just so they'll be useful to me.'

'Rosie, you are a marvel; you've worked so hard against all the odds. You should be in a jute-mill, girl, not a world-famous university. Now you're a guest in the home of someone who obviously likes you and who has a friend who just happens to be the only female doctor in the entire area. You'd be mad not to encourage him and her to help you.'

'I've got this far on my own,' began Rosie and then realized that that was not true. There were the sacrifices of Frazer, Frazer who might have been able to marry, to become a father even, had he not given everything he earned to her; Wishy, who had spent hours coaching her; Elsie, who had somehow earned this dress. No, it was not tailored to fit like the green silk Dr Lucille Graham had been wearing, but it was beautiful, beautiful.

'Mr Anderson-hyphen-Howard won't give the likes of me another thought, Mary. Come on. It's almost time for the charabancs and I want to get a better seat this time.'

To give him his due, Kier did not forget Rose. Her pale face swam before his mind's eye quite often and he found more and more reasons for going into St Andrews, business that seemed quite often to take

him near the university. He even went more often to
Dundee for, when he had been able to prise a word
out of the girl, she had told him she was a Dundonian.
Kier, however, had not taken into consideration that
a girl like Rosie would have to work during the long
summer holiday, and he did not look for her in the
Angus berry fields which is where she could easily
have been found.

Lucy Graham did not immediately forget the
frightened young girl in the ghastly dress either.
She had ambivalent feelings about her. The child
had been terrified and Lucy always felt sorry for
things smaller and less able than herself, but Kier
had been unable to hide his interest in the girl. He
had talked of nothing but her courage and ability
and ambition, until not only Lucy but Kier's parents
were heartily sick of the sound of her.

'I have such a stupid prejudice against flower names
for girls,' confessed Mrs Anderson-Howard when she
and Lucy were having a quiet chat together in Kier's
mother's own little sitting room, 'and besides, she
looked to be a really aggressive young woman.'

'No, Auntie, she was terrified, totally out of her
depth. Try to look at the afternoon from her point
of view.'

'How like you and Kier to look out for the
wounded of this world. Those girls will never make
doctors, never. The blonde one couldn't even speak.
And there's my silly son gazing at her as if he had
found the holy grail.'

So Kier's mother had noticed it too. Well, the
afternoon was over and the girl was gone and no
doubt they would never see her again.

'If I had not had all my advantages, perhaps I
would be rather like Rosie Nesbitt, or, more likely,
I would have given up long ago.'

'Given up and married my son! You still can. We really do want grandchildren while we're still young enough to play with them, Lucy. Hasn't Kier asked you lately? Has he got out of the habit?'

'Am I a habit with him? Sometimes I think so, and when I see him looking at someone so young and so lovely . . .'

'Lovely? Lucy, you must be blind, my dear. That dress . . . and the smell . . .'

'That's poverty, Auntie. And Kier saw past it and saw the beauty of her face. He's never really been aware of clothes anyway.'

'Just like his father, my dear. They notice when their horses need new saddles, but I think their womenfolk could walk around in rags and they'd mutter charming, charming, which is all Archie ever seems to say about anything . . . But tell me, Lucy, how would a girl like Miss Nesbitt get into medical school?'

'Brains and hard work and determination and vocation, and endless sacrifices from many people. Exactly the way I did it myself, and every other female doctor, except that I had money to oil the wheels.'

'Oh, Lucy dear, your family was not wealthy.'

'To people like the Nesbitts of the world, Auntie, I must appear to be fabulously wealthy. Rose Nesbitt is a remarkable young woman and I wish her well.'

Mrs Anderson-Howard rose from her chaise-longue as the dressing bell went. 'Go and make yourself beautiful, my dear. If you want him to, Kier will forget all about Miss Nesbitt.'

In her room Lucy slowly undressed and, for the first time in years, critically examined herself in the mirror. Too tall; Rosie Nesbitt was small and dainty. Too thin; Miss Nesbitt was thin too, but her body curved seductively in all the right places. Lucy did not admire her clear, guileless eyes or her firm straight nose; she saw a cloud of yellow curls framing a pretty little face and eyes that glared at everyone but Kier.

'I should have married him when he came back from Africa but no, no, I couldn't. There was poor Mrs Dryden so ill, and Donald's relapse.'

Lucy had received two proposals of marriage within a month of the wounded Kier's return: one from Kier himself. 'A habit, a habit,' her brain told her. The second was from Colin Dryden. Gratitude for the way I looked after his aunt. She had almost said 'Yes' to both proposals, and as she looked at herself in the mirror Lucy wondered why.

'Is it because I am only too aware of the toll that time takes on the female body? Did I merely want a husband? Did I want children? Am I right to wait until one day I find I do not have to ask myself questions about my feelings? Is Auntie right? Can I make Kier forget the lovely little Nesbitt?

Thirty minutes later a sophisticated, elegant woman walked into the drawing room and instinctively responded to the admiration in the eyes of the men there. Not one of them could guess at the turmoil in her heart.

9

St Andrews 1899

MRS ANDERSON-HOWARD WAS quite right: Mary Black never became a doctor. She never returned to St Andrews University, and Rosie had almost forgotten her by the time she learned much later that Mary had died of consumption. It wasn't that Rosie, by now trying hard to drop the diminutive and to be known as Rose, easily dismissed from her heart all those who had been her friends, but that the goal she had set herself was always to the forefront of her mind.

In 1898, at the age of nineteen, she had graduated with Honours in Arts. She had looked down from the podium with her parchment in her hand and seen Elsie crying so hard with love and pride that the tears running down her old face were bringing with them the ghastly make-up that she had worn 'tae look ma best fir ye, hen'.

'I've done it, Ma.' She sent the message silently down to the clown face. 'No, we've done it together, you and me and Frazer and old Wishy. A shame they didn't live to see this day.'

And now nothing and no one would be allowed to interfere with her ambitions. She was going to be a doctor, and none of these super-sarcastic male students who thronged the lecture rooms at St Andrews University and who enjoyed baiting the female students would be allowed to bother her hard-won serenity. Because Rosie was a street fighter, and

when she walked into a room and found herself
the butt of jokes and the object of cat-calls her
first impulse was to scream and kick, just as she
had done on the streets of Dundee in her early
childhood. From the age of ten when she had first
walked all the way to the centre of Dundee to attend
the Harris Academy, she had schooled herself and
she had learned to appear to ignore the disparaging
remarks of wealthier girls, and now she was able
to appear unaware of the frightened malice of her
fellow students.

'That's all it is,' she assured more delicate women
students. 'They're afraid of us and so they say we are
unfeminine. We will show them, ladies, that not only
are we very feminine, but that we are also very, very
clever, and we will win all the prizes.'

The first prize Rose won, she was not allowed to
have, and its winning and subsequent non-award
brought her to the attention of several of the professors including Sir James Donaldson, the Principal
of the University, and earned her admiration and
respect.

There was a bursary of £100 per annum for two
years. Rosie took the examination and won. She
was elated: £100 each year for two years! Properly
invested with a little interest added, and she could
sail through medical school with nothing to worry
about but passing exams, and she had never had to
worry about *that*.

£100! Rose and Elsie walked up from the station
and made shopping lists as they passed the shops.
What could you not buy for £100?

'I cannae see that much siller in my mind, Rosie,'
said Elsie. 'You could eat meat every day o' the week,
twice on a Sunday if ye wantit. You could hae silk
underwear. Look at thae knickers. You could hae a

clean pair every day fer a month. And look at that suite. Whit dae ye think the neighbours would say gin we took that posh furniture up the Hilltown? Goodness, you could get on a train and go . . .' Elsie was at a loss. Where could £100 take her? She herself had only ever been to St Andrews and that had been an adventure. '. . . farther than London,' she finished off, not even sure that there *was* anywhere farther than London.

'It's going in a bank, Ma,' said Rose, ending the insubstantial dreams of silk underwear or upholstered furniture.

'A bank?' Elsie looked at her daughter in awe.

'If I open a bank account, Ma, the money will be safe and it will earn interest. I'll have all I need for textbooks, instruments, even some new knickers when I need them, but not silk,' said the practical Rose.

The grand plans went for nothing though because it seemed that it would take practically an Act of Parliament to award the bursary to a woman. When it had been set up, universities were not open to women, and the wording of the long legal document that talked about the awarding of such a magnificent sum showed that the money had been intended to benefit a poor *man*.

'You do understand, Miss Nesbitt; the grant was set up in a time when there was no thought that women would breach these portals.' (Was there a hint there that he too, sitting so comfortably in his silk gown, would prefer not to think of mere women within his sacred walls? He would not fight for her.) 'We must needs see to the rewording of the documents but, unfortunately, and I mean this sincerely, it will not be in time to aid you. The grant this year must be awarded to a man.'

Rose could taste the disappointment in her mouth. It stayed with her for days and she never forgave the university authorities for the injustice. No matter that the wording was changed so that subsequent female winners could be awarded the prize. In good faith she had been encouraged to enter the bursary competition, and she had won. She should have had the prize.

But now she sat stoically and listened to explanation after explanation, and not one of the Council knew of the turmoil inside.

They stood up and so did she. The interview was at an end.

'Thank you, gentlemen,' she said quietly and they watched her leave the room, her small head held high.

Out in the street she wanted to run; she wanted to cry. But she would do neither of these things. She walked and walked and found herself miles along the beach. Then she turned around to see St Andrews.

'How could they do that to me?' she asked the great towers. She could almost hear Elsie. 'What ye've niver had, ye'll niver miss.'

'Oh, I'll miss it, Ma, but you're the only person who'll hear me moan.'

She went back into the town, for it wouldn't do to miss the train home.

'God disnae make life easy fir the working classes, does he, lassie,' was all Elsie said, visions of silk knickers disappearing for ever.

'They're giving me £30 a year for two years instead, Ma. That's an extra £10.'

'Jist don't let it be a moneyed laddie that gets your bursary,' moaned Elsie.

'Come on, Ma. What you've . . .'

'. . . niver had, you'll niver miss,' finished Elsie

obligingly but without her usual smile. 'God, lassie, do you no care? I'd be wantin' tae tear their hair oot.'

'I'll not give anyone the satisfaction of knowing what I feel, Ma. That's my revenge.'

She almost added, 'It always worked at the Harris,' but managed to stop the words. It would only hurt Elsie to be told that her daughter's poverty had been the object of ridicule. She remembered the Dominie at her primary school: a nice, kind man who had been delighted that she was to attend the Harris Academy.

'My niece Edith is a pupil there, Rosie. She's in the third year. Introduce yourself and she'll take care of you.'

Rose had promised to do so and had plucked up courage one day. She could still hear her quavering voice as she managed to force herself to approach these well-groomed young ladies with their beautiful ribbons in their shining hair.

'Are you Edith Morrison?' she had asked one tall, blonde, haughty beauty.

'No, I'm Queen Alexandra,' the girl had laughed and she and her friends had gone into paroxysms of mirth as Rose walked away, scarlet with embarrassment.

'No, keep your feelings to yourself, Rose,' she had told herself then and she told herself now. She took out her notebook and set herself to reading and memorizing the notes she had made on intermittent claudication. There was no point in worrying over injustice, she could do nothing about that, but she could help to eradicate disease.

She stayed later and later every night and often did not eat before going to the library from the lecture rooms. Elsie met her every night in whatever weather

and walked with her from the station. Rosie found
soup being kept warm on the fire, and for several
years her diet consisted almost entirely of a bread
roll in the morning and a bowl of soup at night, and
tea, tea, and more tea.

Kier Anderson-Howard saw her one afternoon
just before Christmas in her second year of medical
school. Had it not been for the red gown that told
the world her status, he would have thought that the
slight little creature fighting against the wind on the
way up Market Street was a child.

'Good heavens,' he thought delightedly, 'it's that
young student. What was her name? Some flower,
I seem to recall.' He began to hurry after her – he
would not shout in the street to gain her attention
– and when he caught up with her and her startled
eyes looked up into his, he remembered. It could not
be anything else.

'Rose,' he said and lifted his hat. 'I do beg your
pardon, Miss . . . ah, Nesbitt, wasn't it?' and because
she still looked puzzled or startled he added, 'Kier
Anderson-Howard. We met at a garden-party.'

He saw recognition come into her eyes and then,
well, he was not really a conceited man, but was it
pleasure he saw there too?

The look, had it been there at all, was gone. 'Hello,'
she said simply and moved as if to hurry on.

'Wait, Miss Nesbitt. Am I keeping you from some
class?'

'No. I'm hurrying to get out of this wind.'

He laughed. Most of the girls of his acquaintance,
except Lucy of course, would have been simpering
up at him by this time.

'It is a cold one,' he agreed. 'Bringing snow, our
shepherds say.'

She said nothing and he wished he hadn't said

that, but he'd never had to hide his wealth before. Obviously she wanted to get away, to go where she had been going when he stopped her.

'I'll walk with you if I may, Miss Nesbitt, steady you against this wind.'

She stopped then and laughed. 'But you don't know where I'm going.'

He laughed too. 'Oh, heavens, could be a lecture on the most unmentionable of subjects. I was hoping you were going to find a nice hot cup of tea.'

She blushed. Why on earth did she blush? Gosh, he'd done it again. Possibly she couldn't afford to eat in a restaurant. Could anyone be so poor that they could not afford a few shillings for a meal?

'I was,' he lied. He had been on his way to where his carriage waited. 'I was going to have tea; I'm starved. And it would be so pleasant to have some company. Would you join me, Miss Nesbitt, if you're not on your way to a lecture?'

Again he saw some battle in the beautiful eyes. 'I was going to the library, to read.' She blushed again.

How delightful. A woman who can still blush.

'I very rarely read in the library,' he said solemnly. 'Used to get into the most fearful trouble instead. There's a delightful hotel right here on the links, very respectable. Can you spare the time? My mother would love to hear how the first lady graduates are coming along.'

Mrs Anderson-Howard went to regular meetings to hear how the female students were surviving, but cheerfully Kier threw her into the fray. For some reason, he did not want to sever the tenuous connection with this young woman. Why? Why should he care what happened to Rose Nesbitt, who was so obviously from quite another world?

'I can spare the time,' Rose was saying.

'Wonderful,' he said. He tucked his hand under her elbow and fairly bowled her along to the majestic front of the hotel and up the broad stairs into a carpeted and lavishly furnished hall.

A hovering waiter gestured towards Rose's red gown.

'Madam's still a little chilly,' said Kier. 'Perhaps later. We'll have everything,' he added, 'and we'll have it here by the fire.'

The waiter bobbed his head and withdrew and Kier steered Rose, still in her red gown, to two plush seats beside the huge roaring fire. How quiet she was. Was she always quiet, or did he frighten her? Lucy had said that he had frightened her that long-ago summer day. What was it today here in the hotel? The waiter? The fire? Surely not the fire? Kier tried to imagine what it must be like to be cold and poor and to come into this luxury. 'But this is a bit shabby. It can't be the furniture. Is it the fire blazing merrily away in an empty room? Well, it's not empty now. We're here to enjoy it.' So his thoughts ran.

'Have you been shopping?' Rose asked, and he saw that she made an effort, that conversation was difficult for her. 'Christmas shopping, I mean.'

'Quite the reverse. I've been selling. Geese, you know, and hens. We supply one of the local poulterer's.' He tried to look as if he knew all there was to know about breeding poultry, that he had done more than merely agree to terms and sign his name on a piece of paper.

'I always believed . . .' She blushed again and he finished for her.

'That I was a soldier. I was.' His face darkened with sorrow. 'My father died. Fifty-two years old.

Can you imagine? Never sick a day in his life, or so we thought, and then suddenly . . .'

'His heart?'

'No, they said it was a cancer. He was fine till the doctors started poking about. Seems it had been growing for some time . . . Ah, good, here's our tea.'

His face lightened. The waiter had put the heavy silver pots before Rose, who blushed again. Surely she knew she was supposed to pour? 'Shall I pour the first cups, Miss Nesbitt? That pot looks frightfully heavy.'

'Thank you,' she said quietly. 'It does look a big pot for two people.'

The hot tea and the warm scones dripping with butter made conversation easier. He was happy to see that she had a good appetite and he ate much more than he needed or wanted because he felt sure that if he stopped she would stop, and he had no idea when she would have her next meal.

'Are you in a residence, Miss Nesbitt?'

'No, I still live with my family in Dundee.'

'Gosh, that must make life a little difficult,' but she disagreed and made him laugh with her stories of running for the train and of the guard who had helped her until he found out that she was one of these dreadfully modern, unfeminine women who had more interest in the human body than a decent woman should have.

'You are a tonic, Miss Nesbitt,' he said finally when she had told him that now she really had to go because she would miss her train.

'Wait here. My horses are just round the corner and I'll drive you to the station.'

He hurried out of the hotel but he did not go straight to the waiting carriages. He sent the doorman for his phaeton and then ran back along Market

Street to the poulterer where he bought back, at three times the price, a huge goose he had just arranged to sell that afternoon. Rose was waiting at the door, her red gown wrapped tightly around her. Again he felt that surge of protectiveness. He had never, ever experienced the feeling before and he liked it. Lucy had always protected and managed him; all the other girls, even Sally for whom he had really cared and who had married one of his classmates while he was in Africa, had mainly roused desire.

He kept to the other side of the street away from the lamps so that Rose would not see him and then he crossed the road and deposited the goose in the phaeton.

'Here we are,' he called to her. 'Your carriage awaits, madam.'

'I've never been in one of these,' said Rose, almost at ease with him.

'They're not really comfortable but they're fast. I shall certainly get you to the station in time.'

'I could walk to the station in time,' she said and he laughed.

He handed her into the phaeton. 'You are the most refreshing young woman, Miss Nesbitt.'

They waited four minutes for the train. He felt he could not let her go, could not let her just disappear again.

'Where do you live, Miss Nesbitt? Perhaps I could call some time, maybe during the holidays.' He thought swiftly. He dare not invite her to dinner. Whatever his mother thought about his ability to recognize anything other than the needs of his horses, he knew perfectly well that Rose's wardrobe was limited and he would not cause her embarrassment or distress. 'The theatre, perhaps; there are some fine productions in Dundee.'

'I . . . I have a job for the holidays. Here is my train.'
He heard the relief in her voice. 'Thank you for the
tea. It was lovely.'

'Another time, perhaps. I am often in St Andrews.'

She smiled at him then. She really had a lovely
smile. He helped her climb into the train and then
he ran back to the phaeton and lifted the goose.

'Here,' he said to the guard, handing the man the
goose and a guinea.

'Well, thank you, sir,' said the man.

'Give the goose to the young lady who just got into
the carriage. Say, "Merry Christmas from Kier." Go
on, man. The train is about to leave.'

'Not without I tell it, yer honour,' laughed the
guard, who had bitten the guinea to find that it really
was the biggest tip he had ever had in his life.

Kier stepped back from the train and watched it
pull out. He had a quick glimpse of Rose's startled
face as the huge goose was put into her arms, and
then she was swept away from him. He put out
his hand as if to stop the train, for it had suddenly
occurred to him that the goose was heavy and
perhaps her home was miles from the station.

'What must she think of you, you idiot?' he scolded
himself, but his heart was light as he bowled along
the roads to Laverock Rising. It was only later that
he realized that never once had she called him by
his name.

Rose said his name over and over to herself in the
train as she and her huge silent companion clattered
over the new bridge across the Tay.

'Anderson-Howard, Anderson-Howard. Clickety-
clack, Clickety-clack.'

Her second meal in a restaurant! She remembered
how the long-dead Frazer had carefully counted out

the pennies for the fish suppers in the rather dirty
café. Kier Anderson-Howard had not even asked for
the bill but had nonchalantly tossed a coin down on
the table as he hurried for his phaeton – or really, as he
hurried for the goose. She almost hugged the goose to
stop it sliding off her small knees. What would Elsie
say? How would they get it home and what would
they do with it once they got it there?

She pictured her home and saw again in her mind
Laverock Rising, the magnificent Georgian mansion
in which Kier Anderson-Howard lived. She tried to
picture the elegance of her afternoon's escort in the
tiny rooms up the Hilltown. The image in her mind,
the perfectly cut tweeds, the hand-made shoes, the
open friendly face would not transfer itself to the
dingy tenement. Here Rose did Kier a disservice.
Perhaps he did not expect her living conditions to
be quite so poor as they were, but he did know a great
deal about public housing, at least academically.
Was he not on several committees that did practical
work towards the alleviation of poverty?

Was she to say goodbye for ever to the chance
of a friendship with Kier? Rose had enjoyed her
afternoon. After her first cup of tea, as the blaze
from the huge fire had warmed her chilled bones,
she had relaxed. He was so friendly, so warm,
had made her believe that he really was interested in her. She had talked and laughed with
him as she had never talked with anyone in her life
before, except perhaps Elsie, and with Elsie she had
been unable to talk too seriously about her studies
because, try as she might, Elsie did not understand.
If she had enough courage to admit him further into
her life . . . but she did not want him, anyone, in
her life, did she? There was no room for anything
but study.

'A friend would be nice,' a little voice in her head teased.

'If I ever see him again, I'll . . . well, I could agree to meet him at the theatre, say it was easier for me to go straight there from university. Why didn't I say that?' She saw herself arriving at the front of the theatre; she saw that look of . . . what? pleasure, joy, light up Kier's face. How pleasant it was to see such a look.

The train pulled in and she forgot her lost chance when she saw the astonishment on Elsie's face.

'Whar the hell did ye get that?'

Rosie dropped the goose that she had clutched almost to her bosom all the way across the broad sweep of the Tay, and began to laugh, and Elsie lifted it up and began to laugh too as Rose tried to tell the story. She left out the effect that Kier had had on her and she left out the tentative invitation.

'We'll never get that up the Hilltown in one piece, lassie. It's bigger nor you and, onyway, I wouldnae ken where tae begin cooking it.'

They carried the goose between them to the nearest butcher where Elsie sold it for half what Kier had paid for it, plus a pound of best pork sausages – Rose's favourite food.

Despite the large tea she had consumed earlier, Rose was hungry by the time Elsie had the sausages spluttering and squeaking on the iron griddle over the fire. Rose raised her eyes from the book before her on the table and looked around the room. Last night, just last night, this room had looked cosy and friendly. Now she was seeing it with Kier Anderson-Howard's eyes and she did not like what she saw. The table was propped up with old papers to keep it steady, more as a convenience for Rose than for either of the other members of the by now small family. Donaldina, the only other one of the children who still lived at home, lay in exhausted sleep in a chair by the fire. She worked eight hours a day in a jute-mill and spent the time between coming home from work and going to bed dozing in that same chair.

Usually Rose felt pity for her sister, too tired even to go out to dances with the other mill-girls. Tonight she saw her, not as tired but as lazy.

'You'll have to have a word with Donaldina, Ma,' she said now. 'Look at her, night after night, just lying there snoring.'

'Pair wean hasnae the strength for the mill, Rosie. The mills are like that fer some, juist working or sleeping.'

'That's no life. She should make an effort. She's not even clean, and there's no excuse for that.'

'Oh, pardon me for living, Doctor Nesbitt,' snapped the by now awakened Donaldina. 'Are they sausages ready, Ma? Ma belly thinks ma throat's been cut. You'll no mind me haein'a sausage, Your Majesty? It's my wages that bocht them.'

Rose almost recoiled from the venom in her sister's voice. Of course, it must look like that to Donaldina; it must look as if Rose contributed nothing to the family purse. She said nothing, but watched as the girl took a sausage from the griddle and blew on it before stuffing it into her mouth. Then she wiped the back of her hand across her face.

'How often have I seen her do that?' thought Rose. 'And it's never really bothered me but if . . . if . . . *he* saw her. If he came here, what would he think of them and me?'

'I know you're hungry, but could you just wait a minute and I'll clear the table . . .'

'No, I cannae wait a bluidy minute, Lady Muck. Ma and me has wir tea sittin' by the fire every nicht afore yer majesty gets hame.'

Rose said nothing. Every night that she could remember, Elsie had put a cloth on the table, and such dishes and cutlery as they had. She looked now and compared the cups with the one she had used that afternoon.

'Come on, lassies, we'll hae wir tea nice at the table. Come on, Donaldina, Rosie bought these sausages and we've ordered a chicken for Hogmanay. Think on it, the end of the century's coming.'

'So's my patience, Ma, if I dinnae get ma tea.'

Rose said nothing. She had lost her appetite. Oh, to be able to afford to live in Miss Lumsden's beautiful residence.

'I like things to be nice,' she thought, 'and is that so wrong? I want Donaldina to have more respect for herself, to keep herself clean all week and not just when she's going out with her pals. I want us to live like civilized people, not like dogs.'

Again she contemplated the bottomless ravine that stretched between her and the young man she had had tea with that afternoon.

'But he seems to like me. We have met twice and each time he has seemed to like me.'

She forced such thoughts from her mind. There was only one thing in the whole world that was of any importance at all, and that was that she should continue with her studies. Men were a distraction she did not need and besides, look where men had got Elsie.

'There are men in the world like Frazer and old Wishy,' her conscience told her, but she would not listen.

'I'm not hungry, Ma.' She smiled at Elsie. 'I'll go on with this.'

'What is it, hen?'

'Anatomy, Ma. Sort of, how we're put together.'

'You're that clever, lassie.' Satisfied, Elsie went off and sat beside Donaldina at the fire. Rose began to read but she was still conscious of them both sitting there and of the smell of the sausages. When in her life had she ever turned down the offer of a sausage? The words on the page danced in front of her eyes but she could not understand them for, unbidden, unwanted, *he* came into her mind. She did not realize how closely she had marked him. She saw again the way his hair just curled at the nape of his neck, the long fingers with the manicured fingernails. Oh, yes, they were manicured but they were not effeminate. His hands were strong. She pictured them holding the goose. She felt them holding her, caressing her. Her mind fled from the thought, from the feelings aroused.

'Where on earth did the goose come from?' she asked herself and she smiled and, somehow, the symbols on the pages became meaningful and she began to study and did not even notice when Elsie put a mug of hot tea on the table beside her hand.

10

Dundee 1900–1905

THE EARLY YEARS of the century saw great changes in Rose Nesbitt's world and in the wider world around her. She moved to Dundee to finish her first degree and, instead of staying at home, she moved into lodgings nearer the university. She told herself, and Elsie, that it was to make running at all hours to the Dundee Royal Infirmary less of a burden on the family, especially Donaldina who certainly did not need to have her sleep disturbed. Had she not already once fallen asleep at her loom and almost lost her hand and her job?

Elsie seemed to accept her leaving with no apparent regrets, but still Rose found herself trying to justify the decision she had made. She told Elsie of the long hours spent visiting the sick.

'I'm studying midwifery and the diseases of women, Ma. There's this professor, a real smasher.' She decided to have a joke at her mother's expense. 'He had to get married.'

Elsie loved a bit of gossip and she heard constantly of people 'having' to get married. Rose laughed at her mother's expression.

'No, Ma. The university thought it unseemly that he, a bachelor, should be a specialist in women's troubles. We may be in the twentieth century, Ma, but in some ways our minds are still in the Middle Ages.'

'That's a shame, that he didnae have tae, I mean. I'd like fine tae prove that the rich are nae better nor the poor.'

'I'm quite sure they're not, Ma, but I was only joking. What I wanted to explain was that I'm taking cases in the district for practice in midwifery. I'm out at all hours. You know better than anyone about the times babies choose to arrive. Sometimes a qualified doctor goes; he gets £1 if he attends a birth; sometimes a nurse training as a midwife comes with me. The women like them but they like me better. Last night we were out. God, Ma, you kept us in luxury compared to how some exist in this city. Two o'clock in the morning. There's this lassie on a filthy rug on the floor; nothing else in the room but a rickety table and a chair with three legs and the stuffing and springs coming out of the seat. Oh, yes, there's some sacks on the table: that's what she does for a living, sews sacks. Everything is dirty, filthy. A neighbour comes in to help; she's dirtier than the lassie on the floor, so I don't let her touch anything. "Boil some water," I tell her and "Where's her man?" I ask, but she looks funny and says nothing. I cleaned a basin with turpentine and . . .' Rose looked at Elsie and tried to read the expression on her face. Better not to go into the details of the fairly straightforward birth. 'The baby was born and I washed him. Did you know it's thought unlucky for anyone but the doctor to wash a new-born baby? I washed him, wrapped him in newspaper – newspaper, Ma, not a wee frock in the place – and gave him to his mother. Her face, Ma, like there was a candle in her skull. "Is ma bairn a' richt?" she says. You know, Ma, every woman I've ever delivered has said exactly that. "Is ma bairn a' richt?" Then the neighbour made us some tea and I had to drink it for the lassie's talking to me. "Oh,

Doctor," she says, "I couldnae tell the ither doctors but I can tell you a' aboot it." It was her father, Ma: her own father, a drunken sot that abused her from the time she had any memory, and there's nothing I can do.'

Rose fell silent and Elsie looked at this daughter whose experiences she could barely fathom.

'She'll no be the last, lassie. It's a fact o' life. Noo tell me whit else ye get uptae.'

'There's a professor that's a real click, Ma. Professor D'Arcy Thomson. Everyone agrees he's devastatingly handsome.'

'Like one o' they stars in the melodramas,' breathed Elsie.

'Oh, ten times better, Ma. He's tall and broad and has a full beard like a lion. Very friendly but, well, you wouldn't take liberties. Then there's Professor Weymouth Reid. He teaches physiology and his particular interest is the study of insulin.' She stopped. Physiology and insulin were new words to Elsie.

'That's the stuff that controls the glucose in your blood, Ma. Glucose is sugar, and you've got to have just the right amount or you get sick. Well, there is nothing the professor doesn't know about sugar and last week he taught us all how to boil sugar to make sweeties: great fun. One day we'll have a fund-raiser for the new university, but the next time I'm home I'll make some for us . . .' When would she be home again? She thought of the peace and quiet of her room, the plain but unbroken furniture, the clean wallpaper, and admitted to herself but not to her mother that she never ever wanted to live in that room and kitchen again. Elsie's hard work could defeat dirt but it could not defeat poverty. 'When I'm qualified, when I'm qualified I'll make it all up to you, Ma,' she said over and over again inside her head.

'Then on Monday mornings I'm up at the Royal Infirmary to see surgical outpatients: all the cuts and bruises and broken bones from Saturday night. That can be funny sometimes. I had a big bruiser in this week. I doubt his own mother would recognize him, the mess he'd made of his face, but he says, "Aye, lassie, it hurts richt enough, but aw it wis a grand fecht." There's just something about the human spirit. Here, I'll let you have a listen through my stethoscope.'

Elsie wiped her hands down the sides of her dress before she took the instrument and inserted it in her ears. 'I cannae hear nothing.'

Rose waited and then saw the look of incredulity on her mother's face.

'I hear an awfie noise, lassie. Here, have them back. I wouldnae like them spoilt. Whit dae you hear?'

'Oh, I'm beginning to hear, Ma, with my understanding as well as my ears. That's what Professor Stather says we have to do, "listen with understanding". And I can administer chloroform. That's the thing, the anaesthetic, that makes you sleep so you don't have pain during surgery or childbirth. I don't really like doing that; it's scary.'

'Don't do it then, lassie. God meant women tae suffer in childbed.'

'Away you go, Elsie Nesbitt. You sound just like a man.'

It was good to laugh and joke with her mother away from Donaldina's sullen animosity and in the fresh air, as she ran from the university up through the wynds and parks to the infirmary, she was able to see her sister's viewpoint, even though she did not agree with it. Her fellow students, men and women,

ran with her and made her forget everything but
medicine. Together they chanted the Dundee medical students' doggerel. 'Come in, come in, put out
your tongue. Have you got a bottle? Next please.'
   Their tired young voices rang in the clear air.

Rose was so busy that she barely noticed the
announcement of the death of Queen Victoria or
the wave of real grief and nostalgia that washed
the country. She did not know that the new king
had typhlitis and that his coronation had had to be
postponed. She was more interested in applying
for a summer job as an assistant dispenser at
a chemist's shop on the Perth Road. At least
two of the male students had applied for it and
they, like Rose, were well qualified. She did not
know that she got the job because she was a
woman and could be paid less. Rose was thrilled
to be out of the berry fields and earning £1
each week for, it seemed to her, nothing but
measuring out 10 grams of phenacitin into clean
little papers and selling them to headache sufferers
for a penny each.
   She saved the summer money and bought herself
a new costume made of soft golden-brown wool. It
had a straight plain skirt and, the latest fashion, a
three-quarter-length sac coat which just skimmed
her knees. With it she wore a plain brown felt
toreador hat trimmed with a quill. In the fitting
room, she looked at herself in the mirror and liked
what she saw.
   'New shoes and gloves,' she vowed, 'and even
my mother wouldn't recognize me.' She ignored the
glow of pleasure that told her that she was a very
pretty girl.
   The costume, wrapped in a sheet to keep it clean,

hung behind her bedroom door. She was saving it for something special.

The university planned a fund-raising bazaar for October 1903. Rose and her classmates made their mouthwatering sweets and Rose herself worked on their stall. She loved every minute, not only of the camaraderie and fun of the bazaar itself but all the hours of work that she and other exhausted students, not just medical students, had put in before the event. Excitement added some colour to her usually pale face, and that was how Kier and Lucy saw her as they wandered from stall to stall.

Lucy saw Kier's eyes light up and at first she did not recognize the small golden-brown figure laughing and joking behind the table.

'Come on, Lucy, it's little Rose Nesbitt. I haven't seen her in years.' He pulled Lucy along and she went willingly enough.

'Have some of my delicious toffee, sir,' said Rose in her new persona. 'Dental students at the next stall will take care of any damage done – at a reasonable . . . cost,' she finished lamely as she recognized her customer.

He laughed down at her rosy face, now red with embarrassment as well as excitement. 'We'll have a pound of whatever you made yourself, Miss Nesbitt, won't we, Lucy? You remember Miss Nesbitt, don't you, my dear?'

'Of course,' said Lucy, although she had not thought of Rose Nesbitt for years. 'How are you, Miss Nesbitt?'

Miss Nesbitt could feel her new-found confidence ebbing away under the eyes of this elegant, sophisticated woman, and Lucy saw it go and tried to make amends.

'What a wonderful occasion, Miss Nesbitt. I can't

think how you have all managed to do so much. No sleep at all, I should imagine?'

Rose stammered something and Kier stepped in.

'You're right, Lucy, and probably no food either. A puff of wind will blow you away, Miss Nesbitt. We insist that you come and lunch with us, don't we, Lucy?'

If the suggestion was an unwelcome shock to Lucy, she recovered quickly. 'Absolutely,' she said.

Rose hesitated.

'Doctor's orders,' teased Lucy. 'Do come, Miss Nesbitt,' she coaxed. 'I should like to hear how the medical school has responded to the invention of the electro-cardiograph.'

'Oh, yes, Doctor.' Rose was excited again. 'And phenobarbitone . . .'

'Ladies, I refuse to lunch with pills and potions. Next you'll be talking about votes for women, and that I will *not* have.'

'Don't listen to him, Miss Nesbitt. He's a powerful advocate for the rights of women. Are you free for lunch?'

She checked the time on the delicate gold watch on her wrist while Rose looked at her own service-able one.

'I'm free in ten minutes,' she said.

'We'll come back to fetch you,' said Kier and turned away. 'Come along, Lucy. I must just confirm that mother is lunching with Lady Donaldson.'

His voice receded into the distance and Rose looked after him until a bag of toffee, pushed almost into her face by a grubby urchin, recalled her to her duties and she exchanged the sweets for a sticky coin.

'Well, you are a dark horse, Rose,' said Eddie Reid, the third-year student who was manning the stall with her. 'Here's me been trying for weeks to have you come for a buster with me. "You'll get nowhere with Rose," said the other lads. "Keeps herself to herself." That wouldn't be the Lady Donaldson who just happens to be married to the Principal of St Andrews University, would it? No wonder you don't have time for us when you go around in that company. Must help . . . with lots of things.'

'Don't be sillier or nastier than you have to be, Eddie. I don't know Lady Donaldson . . .' Rose stopped. No, she would not justify or defend herself. She had nothing of which to be ashamed. Eddie was very young after all. 'I'm off to have lunch, Eddie. See you at the hospital on Monday.'

She pulled her lovely new brown hat with its jaunty feather down over her yellow curls, picked up her bag and smoothed her first pair of leather gloves over her almost soft hands.

Lucy saw her standing there, small and erect and very lovely. 'Well done, little Nesbitt,' she thought and she smiled and went towards her. 'Miss Nesbitt, what a charming hat. Are you ready? Kier's gone off for a cab. The street is absolutely jammed.'

Rose felt herself almost pulled along by Lucy's personality, and she hurried along and tried to answer the questions that were raining down on her. Not that any of them were personal or difficult. She did not realize that, in a different way, Lucy was as nervous and ill at ease as she was herself, or that she was annoyed to be experiencing that same nervousness.

Was she not the daughter of a diplomat? Had she not been trained from earliest childhood to make people feel at ease? 'I forget the lesson on being at ease myself,' Lucy thought wryly as they reached the doors of the crowded hall.

And there on the pavement was Kier.

'What a mad crush,' he said as he helped first Lucy and then Rose into the cab. 'The university coffers must be overflowing.'

'I was just telling Doctor Graham that we had taken almost seven pounds,' Rose managed to say.

'Gosh, and since you paid £5 for that ghastly clock Mother's been trying to lose for twenty years . . . where is it, by the way?'

'I lost it,' said Lucy and together they dissolved into laughter and Rose watched them and envied the ease of their relationship.

Lucy recovered first. 'How awful you must think us, Miss Nesbitt, but it really was a most ugly clock.'

'And notoriously unreliable,' said Kier. 'Where did you put it?'

'Actually, I gave it to a little girl as a gift for her mother.'

'How unkind of you,' laughed Kier, 'but seriously, I've told the cabbie D.M. Brown's. Does that suit, ladies?'

'Five pounds,' thought Rose. 'More than the price of my costume and my hat, and she can afford to just give it away.'

'D.M. Brown's would be lovely,' she said. 'I believe they have started afternoon teas too.'

It was the new clothes, of course, and the gloves that covered the almost soft hands. They gave her confidence. She was able to smile, to chat, to relax, and Lucy saw her at her best and liked what she saw.

'We should stay for tea, too,' said Lucy. 'Certain people in this world, Miss Nesbitt,' she solemnly gestured towards Kier, 'will always find time for tea but others, like you and I, have to take our food when we find time.'

It was a delightful afternoon. Rose forgot, for once, the huge gulf that she always felt existed between her and people like these two, and she did not realize how hard they both worked to make her feel welcome. They did not speak of her career plans until they were in another cab on their way back along the Perth Road to Rose's lodgings.

'I'll give you my card, Miss Nesbitt,' said Lucy, reaching into her handbag. 'When you are qualified I should be happy to give you some experience in a general practice.'

'General, Doctor Graham? I had thought you had only female patients.'

'At first, yes, and still the bulk of my practice is female, but women have brought their children and now there are even one or two men. I can truthfully say "General Practitioner". Are you interested in general practice?'

'Yes, but I am mainly interested in the health of women, their pre-natal and ante-natal care.'

'Ah well, that is the least interesting part to me. I think, perhaps, I should have gone on to specialize in surgery but there were and are so many closed doors.'

'You are pioneers, Lucy, you and Miss Nesbitt. She will find it easier than you, because at least she has been allowed to enter a university.'

'Pioneers,' said Lucy, and her mind went back to an early autumn afternoon. She could almost hear the swish of Amos's broom against the leaves and a beloved voice: . . . 'butterflies in December'. Was Rose a butterfly too?

'When you graduate, Miss Nesbitt, do call on me. I would love to visit my father, who lives abroad, and a good locum would be worth her weight in gold.'

Kier walked Rose up the steps to the front door of

her lodging house. 'I shall not lose you again, Miss Nesbitt. May I call on you sometime?'

'Yes, Mr Anderson-Howard,' said Rose, aware that it was the first time she had used his name.

He smiled. 'That wasn't too hard, was it? Keep in touch with Doctor Graham. She does mean to help you and help will be necessary. Qualifying, I think, may well be the easiest of the tasks before you.' He surprised Rose by quickly changing the subject. 'Do you enjoy the opera?'

'Yes,' said Rose rashly.

'Good. I'll get some tickets.'

He lifted his hat and was gone and Rose would have liked to watch him drive away, but felt that it would be better just to slip inside without gazing after him like a besotted little fool.

She was about to open the door when she heard someone call her name from the other side of the street, and she turned to see Donaldina running across.

'Eh wisnae sure it wis you, getting oot of a private cab and dressed like a dish o'fish. Nae wonder ye're niver hame wi' a bonnie click like thon.'

'I'm not allowed visitors,' Rose lied. 'What is it you want?'

'E'm no wantin' in yer fancy digs. Eh widnae be here at all if it wisnae fer Ma.'

Rose felt cold suddenly. The beautiful glow caused by the afternoon left and never returned. 'Ma?'

'She's fell sick.'

Rose felt her stomach turn right over. Ma, Elsie, sick. It had never occurred to her that Elsie could be sick. Elsie was indestructible: she had always been there and would always be there, taking care of everyone else.

'Sick,' she said stupidly.

'Are ye deef tae? If ye'd been near us ye'd hiv seen
fir yirsel. Ye've been that busy ye havnae seen her
for months. Are ye comin?' Donaldina looked at her
sister, at the elegant fashionable clothes, the jaunty
hat. 'Ye'd maybe better change. Ye'll get jumped for
that costume, or are all yer claes that guid noo?'

Rose shook her head in answer to that question.
She understood the envy and anger in her sister's
voice. 'How far I have come,' she thought, 'and all
due to Elsie.' Oh to be Lucy Graham, and casually
to order a private cab to take her to her mother.

'Let's hurry. There's a horse-bus due in a minute.'

Donaldina did not sit beside her sister in the bus,
but whether from dislike or embarrassment, Rose
could not tell. They changed buses in the centre
of the city and again Rose sat in solitary state and
saw nothing but visions of Elsie. Elsie telling her to
whistle so that she could not eat the fresh young
peas. Elsie crying her eyes out at her graduation
and making a Greek mask of her face. Elsie listening
in wonder to her own heart through her daughter's
stethoscope.

The house smelled. Never before had Rose been so
aware of the smell of poverty, but with the poverty
there was a smell she knew only too well. It was the
smell of death: a horrifying death from syphilis.

Elsie was lying in the box-bed and for a second
her eyes lit up as the shining daffodil that was her
daughter dispelled the darkness of the ugly room.

'Rosie.' The voice was a croak.

'It's me, Ma. I'm here to take care of you.' She
turned to Donaldina. 'Boil some water. A wash
will make her feel better, and these blankets are
soiled. Could you not have washed them?' And
all the time, against Elsie's feeble protests, she was
probing, examining. 'This disease-ridden hag is not

my mother,' her mind kept saying as the bile rose in her throat.

She turned in time to see her sister slip out of the room, a bundle under her arm.

'Donaldina . . .' she began, but then she turned back to the dying woman on the bed. 'I'm going to get you to the hospital, Ma. I'll make you a wee bit more comfortable and then I'll go for an ambulance.'

There was no response and Rose set to work to get some water to wash her patient. She moistened the dry, cracked lips. 'I'll make us a nice cup of tea, Ma, when I get back with the doctor. Tea you can dance on, all right? Just wait for me, Ma. Don't die.'

She hurried out, her mind still conversing with the woman on the bed. 'You should have gone to the doctor. There's a women's hospital in Dundee. They can cure syphilis, but now there are so many complications. It's not too advanced: you'll get better, Ma. In the hospital with real doctors and real nurses, where it's clean and . . .' She was crying as she ran along, but the tears had dried by the time she had reached the hospital and had arranged for the horse-drawn ambulance to bring her mother back.

'Where are all the neighbours?' she asked herself angrily. 'Ma was always taking care of everyone else. I must find Murray's address. Ma must have it somewhere. Frazer's dead and Lindsay's dead, and God knows where Donaldina's gone.'

Elsie was lying as Rose had left her, But she was dead. Her heart had stopped beating

'She's deid, lassie. Even I can tell that.'

'No. Get her into the ambulance.' Later she would come back and look for addresses. Her children would want to know that Elsie was . . . was in the hospital.

Doctor James Robertson was on duty. If only it had

been anyone else. He looked down physically and mentally on all women, and especially those pushing their way into what he believed to be the rightful place of men.

'There was a football match this afternoon, Miss Nesbitt. We have been busy enough without having to deal with this.'

'She has syphilis, Doctor.'

'An understatement.' He turned to the duty nurse. 'Take it away.'

Anger blazed through the tears in Rose's eyes and he saw it and looked again at the body on the table before him. Very gently he began to examine Elsie.

'I'm sorry, Miss Nesbitt. She's dead. Perhaps if she had come in weeks, even days ago . . . She's lucky. The heart gave up before the worst.' He looked again at the intense young face before him. Good heavens, if she took the death of every patient so hard she would burn herself out before she was even properly qualified. 'We all lose patients. You'll have to face it if you're going to be any good, Miss Nesbitt, and they say you are going to be good, you know, but you're not God. None of us are, although sometimes our patients think so and adulation like that can go to one's head. I'm sure you did everything you could.'

Rose shook her head. 'I did nothing, nothing.'

'Good God, girl, don't be childish. I suppose it's your monthly time that makes you so irrational. Isn't there something in the rule book that says you are supposed to stay off the wards when you are unbalanced?'

Unbalanced! Rose began to laugh. She had almost been ready to like him: he had been so gentle. There had been no distaste on his face as he had dealt with what had been Elsie. Elsie with the hard hands, ready to slap, readier to cuddle and console. And now she was dead. Wishy was dead. Frazer was dead. Elsie should have gone on for ever. And then, unbidden, unwanted, a thought came into Rose's head that she condemned and loathed, and was unable to forget for the rest of her life. 'I'll never have to introduce her to Kier.'

'The patient's name is Elsie Nesbitt, Doctor Robertson. She is my mother and I will take care of her burial.'

Again he surprised her. Did she expect him to look at her differently when he saw the stock from which she had come?

'Nurse,' he said, 'fetch Miss Nesbitt a cup of tea. I'm afraid she's had rather a bad shock.' He turned to Rose. 'Sit down, my dear, while I take care of the paperwork for you. A cup of tea is always the very best medicine.'

11

Dundee 1905–1907

'HIGH TIME YOU got someone to help in the surgery, Doctor Graham.' Isa looked down at the thin slice of rare roast beef on the plate in front of her mistress. 'And when are you going to have a holiday? You've been talking about a holiday all the time I've known you.'

Lucy roused herself. 'Don't take it away, Isa. I'm sure it will be perfectly delicious.'

'No, Doctor. It should be hot, and the gravy, and the vegetables. I'll warm up a plate, and you should have it with a nice glass of wine.'

'No. I'm rather worried about Mrs Dryden. I may be called out.'

'Young Mrs Dryden?'

'No, she's not due for a few weeks yet.'

Isa hurried out with the dishes and almost stomped down to her kitchen where Donald was sitting in his shirt-sleeves, cleaning the silver soup spoons.

'She hasn't eaten again,' he said, looking at the untouched plate.

'She got as far as cutting some meat. She's too tired. On the go all day, and then all night sometimes as well. If she's not going to marry Mr Kier, and God alone knows if she'll ever get round to that, she should at least take a business partner.'

Isa bustled about, arranging the cauliflower, carrots

and potatoes as temptingly as possible around the meat.

'Don't overdo it, Isa. Too much food makes you tired just looking at it when you're already exhausted.'

Isa removed a floret of cauliflower and then, when Donald had turned to the sink with his spoons, popped it back on again, covered it with another plate and slipped it into the warming oven.

'I've been telling her she should take a partner, and it's about time she had a holiday.'

Lovingly Donald polished one of the beautiful spoons. 'She had a few days here and there with Sir John last summer.'

'A jaunt into the country for a picnic is not a holiday. She's been all over the world and never been to Greece, she was saying, or Italy.'

'Wouldn't fancy them foreign places, but the rich are different.'

Isa agreed with her husband and then straightened up from the stove with annoyance as they heard the peal of the front door-bell. She pushed the plate back, whisked off her apron and hurried back upstairs tidying her hair as she did so.

Mr Colin Dryden stood on the doorstep.

'Hello, Isa. Is the doctor in? I'm afraid my aunt has had a turn for the worse.'

'Doctor hasn't eaten yet,' protested Isa, but she knew better than to keep a patient from her employer at any time, day or night. 'Come in, Mr Dryden, sir. She's in the dining room.'

Lucy was sitting at the window that looked out over a garden changed beyond measure from the one the young solicitor had first shown his client, now his friend and his beloved aunt's physician. She rose at once at the sight of Colin's face, papers scattering from her blue silk lap. 'Oh, my dear,' she said. 'I'll get my things and come at once.'

A few minutes later, Isa closed the door behind her mistress and returned to the dining room. She cleared the table of all evidence that dinner had been set there, but she left the papers on the floor. They were probably case notes, and therefore were not to be touched by any hand but the doctor's own.

'At least she died in her own bed. Thank you, Doctor Graham. I will always be grateful for that and, of course, all your care these past years.'

Mr Dryden senior, looked very much as he had always looked, but already the loss of his beloved wife was taking its toll.

'May I act in this instance as *your* physician too, and beg you to get some rest?'

'You're right, of course, my dear, but I would like a few minutes more with her.'

Lucy and Colin withdrew and left the old man with the body of his wife.

'You should go home to Sophie, Colin. I hope she will have gone to sleep, but she cares for your aunt very deeply.'

'Her mother, in fact her parents are with us.' Colin poured himself a brandy and gestured with the decanter.

'No, I must get home. I have to call at the hospital first thing.' He made as if to stand. 'No, Colin, I'll go in a cab. Your wife will need you and I would prefer that you see your uncle to bed. Have Edith give him some warm milk and this powder.'

'She's left a great deal of money to the Women's Hospital, with the stipulation that you become a trustee.'

Lucy could barely speak. 'How very kind. She

was such a good woman.' She set aside her own grief for a moment. Mrs Dryden had been a mother to Colin.

'Oh, my dear, I had forgotten . . .'

'I'll be all right, Lucy. We knew she was dying and it's almost a relief in a way that her suffering is over.' He swallowed painfully. 'We are grateful; no one could have worked harder than you to make her last days comfortable. I'm concerned about my uncle. You see, he always knew she bullied him. I didn't realize until I married Sophie. He said it was the secret of a happy marriage. "If she's a prudent and loving woman, give her her head and pretend that you think you're in control," he said. They would have been married fifty-two years in June.'

'The baby is coming in June, my dear. That will be your uncle's saving.'

'She wanted to hold this baby so much.' He set the glass down very carefully and stood up. 'Come, if you're sure, I'll put you into a cab. You really ought to have a companion, Lucy. You should not be going back to that big house alone.'

There it was again, even after all these years, this unspoken belief that a woman could not possibly manage on her own.

'Isa will have stayed downstairs. She's beginning to fuss as much as your dear aunt did.'

'A servant isn't the same thing.'

'Oh, I don't think of Isa and Donald as servants, Colin. Now, make sure Mr Dryden takes that powder and then you get off home. The next few days will be very stressful.'

They were, and for Lucy too. It threatened to rain on the day of the funeral but by afternoon the skies had cleared.

'She would have hated a dismal day,' said Mr Dryden as the mourners waited in the church garden for their carriages, the horses strutting proudly, their black plumes nodding. It was as if the whole of Dundee had come to bid farewell. 'Lucy, my dear, you will stay with us after tea, for the reading of the will?'

Lucy, who had intended to slip quietly away after the graveside service which she knew many of the family women would not attend, could only nod. Should she have told him that she already knew of Mrs Dryden's generous gift to the hospital? She went in the MacDonald family carriage. Mr MacDonald had not mellowed over the years; his wife would not attend the graveside, but would wait with the other family ladies at the family home. He had, however, given up trying to apply his values to Doctor Graham's life.

'I was once very rude to you, Doctor Graham . . .' He saw the slight smile she tried to hide. 'Perhaps I was rude more than once, but I have meant, often, to apologize. I cannot see that you have done anything a responsible male practitioner could not have done, but the women of our family are certainly happier, if not healthier . . . and who is to know the truth of that? I know Mrs Dryden has asked that you be put on the board of the new Women's Hospital. You will also be asked, soon, to take the Chair of Gynaecology at the university. I believe it is a two-year secondment, and several board members have put forward your name.'

Lucy was glad that they had arrived at the cemetery. And what was she supposed to do with her patients? Had these generous gentlemen, who finally half grudgingly admitted her capabilities, thought what would happen to her patients, to the practice she had laboured night and day to establish? 'Keep your Chair of Gynaecology,' she thought angrily. 'It's absolutely the last subject I would dream of teaching.'

The earth falling on the coffin brought her back shamefacedly to the day.

'Oh, dearest Mrs Dryden, I'll miss your generosity of spirit. I'll miss your humour and I'll miss your warm friendship. The world is a colder place without you, but I would not keep you in such pain as you suffered these last few years. Say I helped, my dear, I pray I helped.'

The minister was praying and the crowd around the grave had bowed their heads. Lucy lifted hers and felt the spring sun warm on her face.

And then suddenly she knew. 'I'm saying goodbye to my own mother,' she thought and she smiled. There had been a memorial service in the wee church in Fife, but Lady Graham lay for ever under the parched dry soil of India, in a cemetery Lucy had never seen. 'At last, at last, goodbye, beloved mother. I hope you're proud of me. Goodbye, dearest Mrs Dryden.'

Lucy's heart was light as she left the cemetery, not heavy as it had been when she stood in the church listening to a list of her patient's virtues. She saw Mr Dryden, eyes clear, back straight. 'Father must have looked like that. Good men, both. I'll write to Father tonight and tell him. I know he'll understand.'

She sat through the interminable tea. Colin did not stay but went home to his wife who, of course, could not be seen in public in her condition.

'And why ever not,' thought Lucy. 'In the midst of life we are in death and surely, surely, in the midst of death we are in life? I hope they have a little girl for Mr Dryden.'

Those mentioned in the will were shepherded into the drawing room, a dark and gloomy room at the best of times since it still wore all the trappings of Victoriana; today it was even more grim as the curtains were drawn against the pleasant early summer sun and black ribbons swagged the family portraits. Lucy felt cold. This room needed Mrs Dryden's cheery voice to warm it.

Mr MacDonald read the will, a straightforward enough document. There were a few sentimental bequests to her husband, the bulk of her jewellery to young Mrs Dryden, legacies to other relatives and to devoted servants, and then *'all monies left to me by my late father and invested for me by my dear husband, I leave to the Women's Hospital of Dundee for the succour of any indigent woman of this place and with the sole stipulation that Dr Lucille Graham be appointed to the executive board of the said hospital for her lifetime.'*

There were no ripples of surprise, no angry or offended glances. Mrs Dryden must surely have discussed her incredible generosity with her extended family. The lawyer was waiting once more for Lucy's attention.

'I read this as she dictated it,' he said. 'She had a most particular sense of humour.'

'I also ask Doctor Graham to choose one of the two paintings that I bought in Paris and to hang it in her consulting rooms so that her patients may, like me, be cheered and fascinated by it. The other is to go to my dearly beloved nephew, Colin, who, like Doctor Graham and unlike the bulk of my very worthy family, is possessed of an open and enquiring mind.'

Lucy saw a smile of genuine merriment cross the face of the elder Mr Dryden. How often had she caught them in loving battle over the two pictures.

'A child could have done them.'

'Don't be ridiculous; you know nothing of modern art.'

'There is nothing to know except that you have been robbed by an unscrupulous charlatan. He saw you coming, my dear.'

'You have an uneducated mind. In twenty years your thrifty Scots soul will be wishing that you had bought Monsieur Dufy's entire collection.'

'At least you need not look at that monstrosity in the peace of your home, Doctor Graham,' consoled the wife of one of Mrs Dryden's many nephews.

Lucy smiled but said nothing.

'I think when I miss her too much, Lucy, I may find myself in your consulting rooms,' said Mr Dryden as she was leaving. 'I still prefer a nice pastoral scene. I'm afraid my mind is quite closed to this so-called modern art, but she loved them and she loved you.'

Lucy knew she did not need to tell him what she felt about his wife.

'You are welcome at any time in my consulting rooms, Mr Dryden.'

'I'm too old to become a patient, my dear.'

'Why should you change from Doctor Bracewell? He is a fine doctor and he forgave me for stealing Mrs Dryden away from him.'

'Together with all the other women in this family.' There was a clatter of frenzied hooves in the street. 'Why, here is Colin . . .'

They both looked at the street where a horse-cab had lunged to a halt and Colin Dryden had almost fallen out on the pavement.

'Lucy, quick, quick, it's time! Oh, Uncle, what a time to intrude but Sophie . . . Lucy, quickly, the baby's coming.'

'Calm down, Colin. I must get my bag. Goodbye,

Mr Dryden. I'm absolutely certain that Mrs Dryden, like young Sophie, is in excellent hands.'

The elderly man and the young doctor smiled at one another in perfect understanding and Lucy turned and led Colin back down to the cab.

'Stop at No. 4 Shore Terrace,' she ordered the driver, 'and see if you can do it without injuring me or this poor horse.'

'Do as the doctor says,' ordered Colin, since the cabbie looked belligerently at Lucy. '4 Shore Terrace first, as safely as you can, and as quickly.'

'Try to calm down, Colin. Your nervousness will frighten your wife. Even if she in labour, and she is two weeks early you know, the baby will take some time.'

'You will make sure she suffers no pain: you have this chloroform?'

'I have it, yes.' She did not tell him that she would ease his wife's labour pains, not sedate her completely.

They fetched Lucy's bag and then drove on to Blackness Avenue where a frightened-looking maid-servant who had obviously been watching for them opened the door.

'Oh, Mr Dryden, sir, the mistress is suffering something awful,' she blurted out with some degree of pleasure.

To Lucy's surprise Colin turned as white as a sheet and, had it not been for her quick grip of his arm, would have fallen.

'My poor darling,' he breathed. 'I must go to her.'

'Oh,' thought Lucy, 'for a nice working-class home where I could set the expectant father to boiling water.'

There was a piteous cry from upstairs and Lucy hurried towards the staircase. 'No, Colin,' she ordered as he made to accompany her. 'Join your father-in-law and keep him from worrying. Sophie's mother and I will manage between us.'

Sophie's beautiful bedroom was at the top of the stairs and, when Lucy reached it, she found her patient lying back against the lace pillows, already exhausted – but more, she was sure, from fear than from effort. Her mother sat by her side holding her hand and attempting to quieten her.

'When did the labour begin?'

'She had a show this morning, Doctor, but the pains didn't begin until this afternoon. They're quite strong now and about ten minutes apart.'

Lucy bent to examine her patient. 'Good girl, Sophie, everything is just fine. You and baby are doing very well.'

She straightened up. 'I think we'll make her more comfortable, Mrs Caird . . .'

'Chloroform?' Sophie's mother looked happily and expectantly at Lucy's open bag.

'No, if you'll help me, we'll change her nightgown. I can't see what I'm doing for all this lace. I know there are some plain cotton gowns in her dresser.'

'I made this gown myself.' Mrs Caird was offended. 'It's her favourite.'

Lucy had found a simple gown. 'Will you help me, please, Mrs Caird?' She ignored the anxious mother's annoyance. 'And if you could fetch a towel? Sophie is sweating, and we'll dry her off and make her much easier, won't we, Sophie dear?'

They worked together quietly, although Lucy could almost feel the resentment coming from the woman at her side. Mrs Caird had often told Lucy that she was not one of these terribly modern women who were rushing to change the established order of things. She had tried to persuade her daughter to stay

with their own family physician, but although Sophie
had been attended by Doctor Bracewell all through
her childhood, she had been delighted to find a lady
doctor when she married.

The change of clothing was effected just in time
for the next contraction. Sophie screamed and her
mother clutched at her hands. 'Oh, my poor baby,'
she cried. 'Give her something, Doctor.'

Lucy waited until the contraction was over and she
had settled her patient back against her pillows, but
lying on her side this time.

'There, Sophie, you will feel much more comfortable on your side. You are experiencing back labour;
it's perfectly normal, and all that is happening is that
the canal is widening so that your baby will soon
be able to make the exciting voyage into the world.
Think of your little baby, striving to reach you. You
must help by being as relaxed as you can and by not
fighting against the contraction but by going with
it.' She straightened up and turned to her patient's
mother. 'Mrs Caird, you are frightening my patient,
and if you can't behave I will have to ask you to leave
the room.'

'You see, darling, you see. She's trying to send
Mamma away. Let me send Papa for dear Doctor
Bracewell who . . .'

Another contraction prevented anyone in the room
from knowing what Doctor Bracewell would have
done. He would certainly, as Lucy well knew, not
have come to the house.

Sophie remained on her side and Lucy exerted
gentle pressure on the small of her back as the
contraction took its course. 'Breathe, Sophie, that's
it, don't hold your breath. There, dear, that's better,
isn't it? Now lie back again and your mother will
moisten your lips.' She gave Mrs Caird a simple task

to do. There was no point in completely alienating the patient's mother, but she would do it if she had to in the interest of her patient.

The evening wore on; the contractions became more severe and at last Lucy decided to administer a little chloroform, enough to dull the pain but not so much that Sophie was unable to help her baby on the greatest and most hazardous journey it would ever undertake. The sickly-sweet odour of the anaesthetic filled the air as Sophie inhaled.

'My husband is the dearest man, Doctor Graham, but Colin and I had to fight him every step of the way over the use of chloroform. He would suffer the pangs of childbirth for Sophie if he could but he is so set in the nineteenth century. "Women are supposed to suffer. It's God's law," he says, but I think he'll change his mind when he sees how you've helped Sophie.'

Lucy said nothing. She had no intention of becoming involved in a moral or philosophical argument, nor had she any intention of making her patient completely unconscious.

'Not long now, Sophie,' she said. 'Relax, relax, keep your strength for your baby. Go with the pain, that's it, that's it.'

'Auntie's dead, isn't she?' Sophie said suddenly.

'Yes.'

'I know she is, but I thought I smelled her perfume . . . it's the chloroform, isn't it? It does funny things to your mind.'

Lucy smiled but did not answer. During births, during deaths, sitting by the side of the very ill, she was often aware, like the patients themselves, of other forces, other presences. If it made Sophie happier to believe she could smell her aunt's perfume, then let her believe so.

Just before midnight, on the day when his great-aunt was buried, John Joseph Dryden slipped easily into the world and set up a bawl that had his father and grandfather, jacketless and tieless, racing one another up the splendid oak staircase.

When she had finished with her patients, Lucy walked slowly down the stairs to the library where a meal was waiting for her. She was too tired to eat, but she sat back in the chair and sipped a glass of wine while she waited for the coffee she had ordered. She was vaguely disappointed. It would have been so perfect if the baby had been the little girl she was sure Mrs Dryden had always wanted. Not that Sophie and Colin were disappointed; they were quietly and emotionally ecstatic over the birth of their little son. Presently Sophie's parents joined her. Mrs Caird had forgiven Lucy for threatening to remove her from her daughter's bedside and sang her praises to her husband.

'Easiest birth I ever saw,' she said. 'Muriel was right about you, Doctor Graham, and I shall tell everyone so. She was right about the baby too.'

Lucy was suddenly alert. 'The baby? She had so many nephews; I always thought she wanted a little girl to spoil.'

'Oh, no, my dear. The greatest tragedy of her life was that she was unable to give Alistair the son she thought he wanted. Colin was the nearest to her, and she would certainly have tried to usurp my place as little John's only grandmother. She would be absolutely thrilled if she knew the baby was a boy.'

'Perhaps she does,' thought Lucy. 'Perhaps she does.'

Not for the first time, Lucy fell asleep in the cab on the short drive home. Isa, watching from the hall, saw the cabbie waiting and went out to wake her mistress and to pay him.

'Mr Kier was here,' she said as she tucked Lucy up in bed. 'He had a young lady with him. He thought you might be upset after Mrs Dryden's funeral and he and Miss . . . Napier was it, thought you might join them for supper. Seemingly they was at the opera. Can't think as how opera, with all those people singing at the tops of their voices, would calm anyone down after a bad day, but the young lady was having her finals . . . did he say orals in all the subjects?' She waited for Lucy's answer and since it did not come, continued. 'The young lady is going to be a doctor. It's the new degree: M.B., Ch.B., and the young lady is lovely, a very gentle manner. I bet she would be wonderful with our older patients and, of course, the younger ones, ones like young Mrs Dryden, would be pleased to have such a pretty young doctor in the practice. I bet she's snapped up right away, if those that know she's graduating don't take advantage and snap her up before it's in the papers. We could have a holiday then. Sir John plans to tour the western states, doesn't he, or we could have that holiday in Italy we always wanted?'

Isa had sown the seeds. She had been married to a gardener long enough to know that the same seeds had to be left to germinate. She turned down the light and left Lucy to sleep.

Lucy lay in a delicious half-awake half-asleep mood. Her mind was once more full of the knowledge of Mrs Dryden's generosity. Mrs Colin Dryden was there too, exhausted, but happier probably than she would ever be again in her life, her first child, her son, held securely in her arms. Lucy saw her face now as she had not seen it when she attended the birth, soft, glowing, vulnerable.

'Will I ever look like that? Will anyone ever look at
me as Colin looked at Sophie? Kier? He was here with
Miss . . . Napier, no, Miss Nesbitt, who is about to
graduate. He came because he felt that I would need
him but he brought Miss Nesbitt. Did I need him? Be
honest, Lucy. It is so important that you are honest
with yourself. No, dearest Kier, I did not need you.
Perhaps, just perhaps, the night Mrs Dryden died, it
would have been . . . nice to share the burden of her
death with someone.'

Lucy thought of Isa who was becoming more and
more motherly, more and more anxious that she eat
well, sleep well, have a holiday. A holiday . . . with
Father? She would think about it later.

Lucy slept and, not too far away, Rose Nesbitt lay
awake. She could not sleep because she had been
kissed and because she had been so careful, all her
life, to make sure that such a thing never happened
to her. Now she had let it happen, and she was not
sure if she was changed or if life could go on the way
that she planned. Perhaps it was the giver of the kiss
who was the problem because Rose felt, correctly,
that Kier Anderson-Howard had kissed quite a few
girls in his time. Did it mean anything or was it just
a gesture of admittance into the inner court, the
women like Dr Graham who could be greeted with
a kiss on the cheek and a 'Hello, darling, how lovely
to see you.' Yes, that was all it meant, and it should
be treated just as nonchalantly. Rose was quite, quite
sure that she had no special feelings for Kier. She had
even become used to having him around, to hearing
his voice which had ceased to thrill her. When had
that happened? When she had first known him, when
she had first, so nervously, accepted an invitation to
the theatre, she had listened to the music of that voice
and been excited and happy and even amazed that it

was directed at her. She had avoided him for months after her mother's death. It had been easy: she had been so busy, so tired. Had she also, unconsciously, been weaning herself farther and farther from the roots that were now well and truly pulled out of the soil that had nourished them? There was very little of Rosie Nesbitt left in the delicate, sophisticated young medical student who ran furiously between university and hospital, and hospital and home. Then in October of 1904 a Students' Union was opened in Dundee. Naturally, the President of the Union was a man, but Rose had been overwhelmingly voted in as Convener of Social Events. Mind you, the women could not go in the main entrance; they went down the basement steps and entered the Union from there, but still they had achieved something.

Rose could hardly believe her first official function. She looked at herself in the mirror, admired the hard-earned pale olive silk suit, the carefully waved hair. 'This can't be real. This can't be me, wee Rosie Nesbitt, arranging a luncheon for Mrs Andrew Carnegie whose husband just happens to be Lord Rector and one of the richest men in the entire world.'

Not only did Lucy arrange the luncheon, she hosted it. Among her guests, besides Mrs Carnegie, were Mrs Woodrow Wilson, wife of a prominent American politician, and Lady Donaldson, wife of the University Principal. It was to be a ladies' luncheon and the men had cheerfully given up all rights to the dining room for the afternoon. They themselves were giving a reception before the luncheon for all the ladies and their powerful husbands.

Rose was immediately aware of the unbelievable personal magnetism of Andrew Carnegie. As she shook his hand and smiled, 'How do you do, sir,' into those compelling eyes, she was aware of nothing and no one but the man himself.

'He has quite an effect, doesn't he?' The voice was one she had vowed would never overawe her, but she was overawed. Kier Anderson-Howard stood at her side, a sherry glass in his hand.

'Miss Nesbitt, I will not complain that you have been deliberately avoiding me if you will allow me to take you to the theatre this evening.'

Rose's hard-won sophistication flew right out of the Union windows and disappeared somewhere beyond the Tay.

'At least you don't deny that you have been avoiding me. Come, Miss Nesbitt, we poor males are not bidden to your hen party. I will admit that Doctor Graham was to accompany me to the theatre, but she has a patient. Doctors always have a patient, Miss Nesbitt. Will you come to the theatre while you have a chance to sit through an entire performance?'

Rose laughed. It was that kind of day. 'Yes,' she said, her sophistication returning, 'to celebrate my meeting with the great man.'

'Oh, more than one, Miss Nesbitt.' He misinterpreted the look she gave him. 'Good heavens, not me. They say we will hear more of Mr Wilson.'

'Rose, Rose, Mrs Carnegie and Lady Donaldson are looking for you.' Sybil Anderson, another student, bustled up. 'I must tear our Rose away, sir,' she added to Kier. 'Quickly, Rose, Sir James has told Mr Carnegie of how wonderfully you behaved when you lost his award. I heard him say it would have to be made up to you.'

Rose stood for a second, unable to move. She wanted to go; she wanted to stay. Too much was happening all at once.

Kier smiled. 'Same address?'

She nodded.

'Seven?'

'Seven.'

And that had been the first of not many but several engagements with Mr Anderson-Howard. He had even asked her to a Christmas Ball at his home, that lovely, lovely house with the lovely, lovely name, Laverock Rising, but there was no money for a suitable gown and no Elsie to buy one in one of the second-hand shops in the Hilltown.

And soon she was to graduate and Kier Anderson-Howard had kissed her, not passionately, but gently on her unrouged lips.

'Next time I see you, you will be Rose Nesbitt, M.B., Ch.B. I shall be terrified to kiss Doctor Nesbitt.'

And then he had asked the question that was also keeping her awake.

'What do you plan to do, Rose?'

12

Dundee 1905

THEY COULD NOT meet. Rose looked in her mirror and hated what she saw. She saw, not a girl who was going to become a doctor in a few weeks' time and who had worked and slaved and sacrificed for the opportunity, but the face of a girl who finally admitted to herself that she was ashamed of her family. For Kier was not the only visitor to the students' lodgings in the West End; Donaldina Nesbitt too had become a common visitor. She came, quite frankly, not because she loved or missed her older sister but because, in her perception, Rose was rich and she was definitely poor and so the balance must be redressed.

Rose had suffered badly when Elsie died. She had castigated herself for the neglect she felt her mother had suffered. 'I could have done more. I could have helped. I should have stayed at home' – there, she still called that two-room flat up the closie, home – 'during the summer holidays and given Ma my money instead of saving for a costume.'

Elsie was dead. Donaldina was alive and Rose tried to help. Donaldina knew about the approaching graduation and she hinted for an invitation.

At least Rose did not try to pretend that Donaldina would be ill at ease in the grand hall where the degrees would be awarded. It was quite simply that she, Rose Nesbitt, did not want her half-sister to meet

Kier Anderson-Howard. For he too had hinted that he would like to attend.

Unlike Donaldina, he had not been subtle but almost direct. 'There's only this half-brother of yours in Australia, Rose . . .' (Rose had given him a carefully edited version of her life story. She had never actually lied about Frazer – Frazer was too good, too noble not to be admitted into her life – but she had never told the whole truth either) '. . . and he'll never manage to come. Unless he's one of these fellows who suddenly finds gold. He's not an Australian millionaire, is he?'

'I doubt it. Murray is my half-brother, Kier. We're not really in touch. Men are notoriously bad correspondents.'

Kier, who had written letters religiously to and from many corners of the globe, did not deny this sweeping statement. 'You can't graduate alone, with no one to cheer madly,' was all he said.

'I'd like you to be there.'

'Good, and what are you doing with this hard-won medical qualification?'

Should she say something? Should she tell him? He could approach Dr Graham. Hadn't Dr Graham promised, hinted even, that she might help?

'I'm not sure yet. There are several possibilities.

In fact Rose could hardly believe, herself, that so far there were no offers of employment. No private doctor, no hospital, was rushing to hire the new female graduates.

'There's a further degree . . .' (my God, I've spent my entire life studying. Now I want to practise . . .) 'I'm not sure,' she finished lamely.

In the months before her graduation, Rose found herself worried more and more about the future. She was unconcerned about whether or not she would pass the examinations. Of course she would; quite simply she was the best. She could not share her fears with Kier. He would speak to Dr Graham, and Rose had decided that she would rather starve than ask Dr Lucille Graham for a helping hand. If Dr Graham wanted Dr Nesbitt, she could jolly well come and ask her. Donaldina Nesbitt became her half-sister's only confidante.

'Whait will ye dae, hen?' Donaldina had asked, with a certain amount of relish as her sister became more and more dejected.

'I don't know. I can't believe it's happening. It's men, always men, with their wee small minds. They're terrified we'll beat them at their own game. Do you know that there are still professors in this very university who believe that if we were decent women we would find ourselves husbands and stay at home having children? Their knowledge has moved forward, but their petty little minds are still rooted in the Middle Ages. The law of the land says they have to educate us, but as yet it doesn't force them to employ us.'

'But the other lassies? Are no some of them getting jobs?'

'Yes, but not in Scotland. I want to stay in Dundee. I want to work right here, to help my own people.'

That much she could do. She could try to deny her own immediate family, but she would not deny her people.

And so the night before her graduation, which should have found her joyously looking forward to a glorious new dawn, found Rose Nesbitt biting her carefully nurtured fingernails and worrying herself sick about the future. She did not even try to sleep. She sat at her bedroom window wrapped in an old coat and went over and over again the interviews, the rejections. It was bizarre. It was insane. It could not be happening . . . but it was. Rose had applied for every opening in every hospital anywhere in Scotland, and had been rejected by every one. She was a woman and this authority and that authority did not hire women. Hospitals did not even want her on gynaecological wards, where one might have supposed there was a special need for a female physician. The other graduates in Rose's situation – that is those who had no money, no connections in the medical world, no fathers or brothers prepared to offer them a chance – were in the same position.

Rose re-read her letters of recommendation from her professors, from the Dean of the university: *'outstanding diagnostic skills . . . eminently qualified . . . first-class honours . . .*

'This prize, that prize . . . this professor says, that professor says . . .' she muttered. But no one wanted to know. If a woman was poor, medicine was still a closed profession.

Rose got up from the window and moved restlessly around the room, her frustration mounting as she walked.

'It's so damned unfair. I'll be a doctor in a few hours and I can't work.'

Donaldina's voice echoed in her aching head.

'They cannae stop you, surely? Just hing a sign oot o' the windae and sharely the fowk'll come flocking.'

Rose stopped. Elsie too would have seen it as simply as that. A sign out of the window: 'Doctor Rose Nesbitt'. Consulting hours . . . any minute of the day or night. Oh, she'd be kept busy all right . . . eventually. Could she do it? What did she need apart from her skills? The list was endless. And how would she live while she waited for the first person who was brave enough or afraid enough to trust her? She looked around the simply furnished little room. She could not practise from here, from her lodgings, could she? The room was clean. One table, wooden. One overstuffed chair. A three-drawer chest. A wardrobe.

She remembered the handleless furniture in Elsie's wee place, the drawers that opened easily enough if a knife was stuck in just so; the curtain, heavily darned but clean, that hid the box-bed where Rosie and Ma slept. Suddenly she could see Elsie with her mug of tea. She was real; she could almost touch her.

'It wouldn't do, Ma,' she told the memory. 'It takes some money to start a practice and the folk up there, the ones I want to treat, couldn't afford to pay me anything. I have to find a job in a hospital or an opening with another doctor who needs a junior.'

As if in a dream, she saw Elsie reach over to put the kettle closer to the fire. 'Well, lassie, you could go on and do that ither fancy degree you wis talkin' aboot.'

Rose felt an almost overwhelming feeling of love and gratitude well up inside her. 'Take still another degree. Don't hurry to pay us back. We were happy to help.' Was Elsie real? Was she a dream?

'I wish you were here, Ma.'

The dream Elsie emptied the cold tea into a bucket beside the fire and made a fresh pot. 'Ach, Rosie lassie. I'm that happy with whit ye've done. Look at yirsel. Nae faither, yer ma nae better than she should hae been.' She held up her hand to still Rose's automatic protest. 'The good Lord kens fine whit I was, Rosie. I wisnae feart tae meet Him wi' ma lassie there no' denying me. Lassie, lassie, yer a doctor. You can save life . . . you can . . . Ach niver mind. I cannae find the words, but I'm the proudest woman in the

Hilltown, in the hale of Dundee. My lassie's a doctor. I'll be at your graduation, and oor Frazer and auld Mr Wishart'll be there tae, never fear.'

Rose shivered. 'Go to bed, Rose, or you'll look dreadful in the morning,' she told herself.

She slept, and the morning brought a huge bouquet of roses from Kier and a telegram from the university authorities. Miss Nesbitt was to be offered a Carnegie Research Fellowship at the instigation of Mr Carnegie himself. She was to become Assistant Professor of Obstetrics and Gynaecology for two years, at the end of which she would be offered the new degree M.D. For Rose Nesbitt, M.B., Ch.B., M.D., there were to be no limits. Did Miss Nesbitt care to accept?

Miss Nesbitt sent a telegramme of acceptance and cried with relief and happiness, but no one saw the weakness.

A very few streets away, Dr Lucille Graham sat over a breakfast of freshly squeezed orange juice, poached eggs on toast, and hot fresh coffee. She read her letters; one from her father from Washington DC:

. . . I plan to see one or two places before I return permanently to Scotland. Once at home with you, my dearest child, I know I shall not want to wander far from my pipe and slippers. I have long wanted to see the Rockies and the deep South. The du Pays have invited me on a little jaunt to Georgia. By the way, you do remember the du Pays? They are incredibly powerful and have the wealth that goes with such power, but there is something about Max that is so innocent, so naïve. I think perhaps he would have found life easier had he been born in a different century . . .

Lucy tried to conjure up a picture of Maximilian du Pay, but it was horses she saw, splendid, perfectly matched horses.

'Well, thank you for being so sweet to my dear father.' She sent the thought-wave three thousand miles and returned to the enjoyment of perfectly made coffee.

'Mr Kier, Doctor.' Isa was at the door and there behind her was Kier.

'Oh, that coffee smells wonderful. May I have some? Lucy, darling, it's worked. She's got a job.'

'Good morning, Kier,' said Lucy repressively and waited while Isa carried a cup and saucer from the sideboard.

'I'll fetch some brown sugar, Mr Kier.'

'Don't bother, Isa. Mr Anderson-Howard wasn't invited for coffee.'

Kier smiled at Lucy and then, meltingly, at Isa. 'She doesn't mean it, Isa. She knows well the rigours of an early ferry from Fife. I am in need of a restorative, no longer being in the first flush of youth as you might say. Lucy, darling, all that is needed to make today perfect is for you to say you'll marry me.' He stopped clowning as if he, like Lucy, was taken by surprise by his levity. 'Please, Lucy. I want to be married. My house is so big and so empty.'

'An excellent reason for marrying,' said Lucy tartly, although her heart was pounding.

He sat down and stirred the sugarless coffee and, not for the first time, Lucy wondered if she had said the wrong thing. 'When is a woman old enough to know when she is saying and doing the right thing?' she thought.

'Father is in Washington. He's having a splendid time with all his old "buddies".'

He leaned across the table and put his strong

brown hand over her equally strong pale fingers. 'Rose graduates today, Lucy. I had hoped you might hire her; you need a junior. You could go on holiday, visit your father, get married.'

There it was again. But was it now a joke?

'Can you come with me to the capping?'

Lucy looked at him in amazement. He had made no secret of his interest in Miss Nesbitt. What had been impossible to gauge was the depth or quality of his interest.

'I have met Miss Nesbitt twice, Kier. She would be extremely surprised to see me there.'

'But Lucy, darling. Think of our graduations. All the old toothless aunties; lovely presents, lashings of food and gallons of champagne. This poor little thing has no family. Her brother, who kept her alive until she was almost old enough to fend for herself, was captain of a whaling vessel which went down with all hands when she was scarcely sixteen. Her half-brother, her only other relative, is in Australia and seldom corresponds. Medical school was hard for you, Lucy, because of the climate of the time. Think of what it was like for her and come to cheer her.'

'I have an afternoon clinic.'

'Just this once, for me, can't you postpone, or get someone to help? Old Bracewell thinks the sun rises and sets on your head. Won't he take your overfed old biddies, just for today?'

Lucy folded her napkin primly, a gesture that should have told him, had he been in a mood to read signals, that she was angry; usually she tossed the napkin beside her plate.

'That was an uncalled-for remark. I can't think why you should think either Miss Nesbitt or myself would be cheered by an afternoon in the other's company.

Now, if you have finished your coffee, I suggest you
leave, so that one of us at least can do a decent
day's work.'

He looked after her. That last had also been an
uncalled-for remark. He was wealthy enough never
to have to work but he worked very hard, not only
in the management of his estate but in every charity
or good cause that she herself laid before him.

'Women,' he muttered under his breath as he stood
watching her furious departure from her elegant
dining room.

Kier could not know, of course, for Lucy had taken
great care that he should not, of the many hours of
correspondence that lay between one Doctor Lucille
Graham and those in charge of the future of his
protégée, Miss Rose – so soon to be Dr Rose –
Nesbitt.

Lucy had thought of offering Rose a job. She
needed a junior; the girl was superbly qualified
and trained. But between them stood Kier. Not for
a second did Lucy think that Kier loved Rose. She had
known him all her life; she had nursed him through
illness and through Camillas, Claires, and Carolines
and sundry other females. Rose was different, she
was so obviously not of his milieu. But Lucy could
not like her and she knew herself well enough to
realize that she liked her less because of Kier.

'Am I a frustrated old woman who doesn't want
him herself but doesn't want anyone else to have him
either? I don't think so. If he loved, really loved, and
was loved in return I could cut the knots, but I'm still
being weak in not taking Miss Nesbitt into my home.
It's not because of Kier; it's because of my patients.
This is my consulting room but it's also my home. I
want to be happy here. I want the atmosphere happy.
I cannot like Miss Nesbitt.'

And then at one of her committee meetings of the Women's Hospital Board, the possibility of the offer of the Chair of Gynaecology had come up.

Lucy had thought long and hard, and eventually rejected the offer. 'I am sensible of the honour, gentlemen, but am forced to admit to you that I have no deep interest in the subject. I would suggest to you that Doctor Wentzell is far more qualified.'

'We thought that, since you are a woman, Doctor Graham . . .'

Lucy smiled. It really was the only thing to do when men pointed out something she had known for nearly thirty years. She spoke boldly, the weight of dear Mrs Dryden's money behind her.

'I have a proposition . . . Lady Donaldson is particularly interested in a young female student . . .'

'Mr Carnegie's protégée? Miss Nesbitt?'

Lucy had not heard of the great philanthropist's interest in Rose, but it proved surely that she was right that Rose was a suitable candidate. She agreed readily enough.

'In 1907 the degree M.D., Doctor of Medicine, will be introduced from this university.' (Oh, that I could take it myself. You can't, Lucy, you can't. Too many depend on you.) 'If the university were to offer the Chair to Doctor Wentzell, who is gaining a world-wide reputation in the field, and a two-year research fellowship to Miss Nesbitt as his assistant . . .'

'Mr Carnegie will be satisfied. We gain a world-renowned professor and, in two years' time, our first female M.D.'

'And I don't feel that, because of Kier, I have to offer a job to Miss Nesbitt,' thought Lucy.

There had been times when Lucy thought of submitting her own name as assistant to Dr Wentzell. She had even thought of offering Rose a partnership

so that she would have time to study for the degree
herself. Lucille Graham, M.D., Lucille Graham, Doctor of Medicine.

'Had it been surgery, you would have jumped,
Lucy Graham,' she told herself. 'But this is ideal.
They say Miss Nesbitt is superbly qualified and
according to her record, she has a particular interest
in obstetrics. She should be the one to assist Doctor
Wentzell.'

Lucy tried not to dwell on the knowledge that
a two-year research scholarship would keep Miss
Nesbitt very busy. By 1907 the world could have
changed. Practices all over Scotland would be lining
up to hire female doctors. Therefore she, Lucille
Graham, would not feel that she had to ask Miss
Nesbitt to join her.

'I could have taken her as a locum and seen
whether or not we could jog along together. Or I
could have taken a holiday, joined Father on his little
jaunt to Georgia or his trek through the Rockies. How
wonderful that would be . . .'

Patients and their well-being came first. The
Rockies would stand until she had time to visit
them.

She did not attend Doctor Nesbitt's graduation,
and so she did not know that the day had been
spoiled for Rose by the action of a half-demented
drunken woman who had begged to be allowed into
the hall where the capping was taking place.

'We're no guid enough fer her noo, but whae
worked in the mills tae keep her ladyship at the
skill. Yer mither wis a hoor, Rosie, bluidy doctor
Nesbitt, same as mine, and don't you forget it.'

Kier saw and heard the woman. He saw Rose, her
face ashen, and then he saw Dr James Robertson
gently lead the woman from the hall.

Rose saw him and felt the sudden bile in her throat. He knew, he knew, he had attended Elsie. Kier would find out, the dream was ended.

Her classmates were at her side, chafing her hands, begging her to take no notice, to remain calm.

'Doctor Robertson says there's an old drunk turns up at almost every graduation in Dundee. Part of the festivities.'

Rose could not enjoy her celebratory meal with Kier. Her trembling hands could not open his gift. Her mind was too full of Donaldina and the action of Dr Robertson. She had seen him often since the night when Elsie had died, and he had been his usual aloof self. Never, in any way, had he referred to the night, the patient, or the disease from which the patient had died. Why not? And once again he had rescued her. Why? What did he want? He had to want something. No one did anything for nothing, did they?

Had there been any phantoms at the capping, phantoms of long-dead lovers who had given everything they had for nothing, surely they would sadly have slipped away.

'Let me,' smiled Kier and he took the jeweller's box from Rose. There was a delicate gold watch inside. 'You see, not a personal gift, just something an old friend can give . . .'

Rose winced at its beauty. 'Rose Nesbitt, M.B., Ch.B.' was engraved in fine script on the back.

'It's lovely,' she said.

'There's just room to add M.D.'

A little colour flowed into Rose's face. 'It all seems like a dream,' she said.

'It's not a dream; it's very real. You're a doctor, Rose. In fact, you're Assistant Professor of Gynaecology at the University of Dundee. Where are you going to live?'

'Live?' The thought had obviously not occurred to her.

'You can't stay in student lodgings. Have they told you there is accommodation at the university? I'm sure there must be.'

'I'm afraid I'm not taking anything in. It's all too wonderful.'

He smiled at her. 'It's going to be even more wonderful. Come along. You're dead on your feet; I'll take you home.' He saw the sudden look of panic in her eyes. 'I must catch the last ferry so I shall dump you out, Doctor Nesbitt, very unceremoniously, on your doorstep.'

She laughed and a few minutes later he did almost exactly that. He had gone before Donaldina staggered out of the bushes in the basement.

'Well, well, Doctor Nesbitt, too good fer yer ain blood.'

'I'm not working yet, Donaldina. I'll give you what I have, but I won't be able to help much for another two years.'

She emptied the shillings in her purse on to her sister's dirty, calloused hand. First thing in the morning, she vowed, first thing, she would find somewhere else to live, and she would leave the university as a forwarding address. She looked down at the dainty gold watch.

'I'm a doctor. I've done it and no one is going to spoil it.'

13

Dundee 1907

DUNDEE HAD MANY philanthropists and among the most generous were the Cairds. In 1899 J.K. Caird, LL.D., together with the Forfarshire Medical Association, had built a maternity hospital in Dundee. The need for maternity beds very quickly outgrew the new facilities, and in 1907 an extension was opened. There were six beautiful new spacious wards, each one holding twenty beds.

Dr Lucille Graham was one of the many doctors at the official opening. Dr Rose Nesbitt, Assistant Professor of Obstetrics and Gynaecology at the university, was the only other practising female medical practitioner present.

The younger woman bowed politely to the slim elegant figure in the soft grey silk gown. Lucy smiled and held out her hand.

'Dr Nesbitt, how very nice to see you. I hoped you would be here; I hear such exciting things about you.'

Rose had learned to school her features but still a little surprise showed, while at the same time she strove to sound sophisticated and blasé. 'You terrify me, Doctor. Surely not from Mr Anderson-Howard?'

'From Professor Wentzell and from other members of the faculty. I have been asked to attend your graduation, and will be most happy to be there.'

'How very kind,' said Rose quietly. She wished she

could have bitten back that stupid remark about Kier. Now Dr Graham would think her guilty of bad taste, and it was so important to make a good impression – even after this, after nearly two years of research. Her findings had been published in the prestigious *British Empire Journal of Obstetrics*, and yet, and yet . . . She smiled at Lucy. Surely it was not too late to make friends.

Lucy made it easy for her. 'You must be very proud of yourself, Doctor. I would give anything to be in your shoes, to be the first female medical graduate of St Andrews University, the first to be able to call herself M.D.'

Rose was surprised out of her usual challenging, defensive mood and, if she only knew it, was for a moment at her likeable best. 'I can't believe it's all happening,' she confessed excitedly. 'I pinch myself sometimes. It's as if, suddenly I'm looking over my own shoulder and I see myself practising medicine, I see someone look at me and take courage from my presence . . .' She stopped and blushed furiously. 'I'm sorry.'

Lucy felt a stirring of genuine liking. 'No, it's like that for me too; it has to be, hasn't it, or it makes everything else, the . . . little sacrifices . . . meaningless.'

Rose looked at her as if she could not see what sacrifices a woman like Lucille Graham could possibly have made. 'Perhaps she's right,' thought Lucy. 'Perhaps I have made no sacrifices. Marriage, children, Kier? Did I really want them? Do I still?'

'Tell me about the graduation, Doctor Nesbitt. I believe it is to be quite splendid?'

'I will find it difficult to be the centre of all eyes, Doctor Graham,' answered Rose truthfully. 'A new hood has had to be designed. It is to be magenta silk lined with white satin. The Department has paid for it – two pounds ten shillings, can you believe!' She laughed at the carefulness of the Department. 'And so they would like it back for the museum.'

Lucy laughed with her and then spoke seriously. 'You have made a mark on the world, Doctor.'

'I never meant to . . . make a mark. I wanted to make a difference . . . to the poor, to my own people . . .' Perhaps she could talk to this elegant, sophisticated woman who never in her life had had to wonder if there would be food on the table, who certainly never had to save for a year for the £10 needed to pay for the degree.

'And Mr Anderson-Howard is to host a dinner-party at the Faculty Club?'

She had to explain. 'He is a good friend, Doctor Graham, so unfailingly kind.' She could not add, 'It's no more than that. I do not want more, I fear more, and he is still confused by you, by the hold your shared memories have over him.'

Perhaps that was not true, completely true, either. The two women sat in nervous silence and, at last, the ceremonies began and they were able to stop thinking, analysing, and to give themselves up to the speeches, the rhetoric, the music, and then the interminable luncheon with more speeches washed down by, to Lucy if not to Rose, indifferent wines.

Lucy left before coffee was served. 'I was unable to get a locum and have had to delay my hospital visits, and then there is my evening surgery.' She held out her hand, now encased in the softest of soft grey leathers to match her exquisitely cut, deceptively simple gown. 'I have enjoyed today, Doctor Nesbitt, and look forward to – what would Kier say? – cheering wildly at your graduation?'

Rose watched her go, saw the heads bow as

she passed, the lanes of frock-coated barrel-chested men separate to make passage for her, respect and admiration in their eyes.

'She did not ask and I could not say, but I must, I must if I am to have a chance of staying here.'

For the truth was that the men who controlled the hospitals, the practices, were no more amenable to Rose Nesbitt, M.D., than they had been to Rose Nesbitt, M.B., Ch.B. Rose, who was about to leave her two-year secondment, had received but two offers of employment. The first was in Rhodesia and the second was in Australia.

'I suppose they are desperate in those countries and will take anything with a qualification,' Kier had said when Rose laughingly told him of her predicament, and she had laughed at his confusion.

'I know, I know you did not mean that I am better than nothing but, Kier, it is so bizarre. I had thought, in all modesty, that all doors would fly open before me at the end of this two years, but we are still as locked in the dark ages as ever we were. The very hospital where I lecture and do my research says there is no place for me in its wards I am even unwanted in gynaecology, my speciality. I have written to every authority in the country and even the inhabitants of the remote isles, it seems, would prefer to die rather than to be treated by a woman.'

'You must speak to Lucy, or let me. She needs a junior desperately.'

She leaned closer to him, and he was aware as always of the slight scent of Erasmic Violet soap that she used, and which he was still able to contrast with that faint musty smell that used to hang on her clothes. This new pleasing scent always made him feel protective.

'Don't, please, Kier. I couldn't bear it. Doctor

Graham hasn't asked me to work with her; she must know I will soon be free.'

'But Lucy wouldn't intrude. She will have assumed you are ploughing your way through offers. You must let her know you are available. There's been so much on her mind this past year.'

Rose thought of Donaldina, whom she had managed to avoid but whom she still expected to pop up suddenly one day to burst her carefully blown-up little bubble. Perhaps it would be good to go to Rhodesia, not Australia where she might encounter Murray, or worse still Nancy, and be made aware again that her career had stolen Nancy's future.

'They say Africa is very hot, and I do like the sun.'

'No.' He was quite adamant and she was surprised at the violence of his reaction. 'You can't go to Africa. My God, I've been there. It's no place for a white woman, and especially a beautiful young one on her own.'

Rose blushed. Beautiful, he thought her beautiful. No, Doctor Graham was beautiful with the kind of looks that stay. She herself was pretty, like an advertisement for soap, all curls and innocence, and neither would last.

'I won't be on my own, Kier. It's a hospital. There are Catholic nuns and priests and at least one grizzled old doctor . . . and his wife.'

'Sounds a heaven on earth,' he said drily. 'Look, can we make a pact? I'll have this little party for you when you're capped and if Lucy hasn't spoken to you before then, you must ask her for at least a temporary contract, you know, to see if you would rub along together. I can't see that you couldn't. She's the dearest thing and as hard-working as you could like. You'd make a perfect partnership.

She hates gynae. and you loathe surgery. Do you know she's talking about putting her name down for a motor-car? The electric tram is a boon, but a car! There was a fellow had a little two-seater in 1899, used to watch him tootle down Reform Street. I'd have given my commission for that car. But anyway, Lucy needs a car. She can't be in two places at once, but a car would make it almost possible. She needs an automobile, but more than that she needs a junior and you are ideal. Will you speak to her?'

Rose thought carefully. Yes, to work for Doctor Graham would be the ideal solution. She could take care of the poorer end of the practice while Lucy dealt with the malingerers among the idle rich, but Lucy hadn't asked her and probably wouldn't ask. She doesn't like me. Oh, Kier, you poor fool. She'll hate us both if you ask her.

'I may approach Doctor Graham if I have received no other offers, but you must promise that you won't ask.'

He had promised and he kept his promise, but Lucy would have had to be extremely stupid not to be aware of the seeds he was planting.

Lucy sat whenever she had a chance to sit and watched the white blossoms drift down from the gean trees outside on the pavements. They were glorious, beautiful trees. In spring they were a mass of flurry, as Donald had called the cherry blossom, in summer they were cool and green, in autumn again they were spectacularly beautiful in their crimson and yellow gowns, and in winter they held their naked branches up against the bleak sky like some examples of primitive sculpture.

'Dr Nesbitt, I find I need a junior.'

'Doctor Nesbitt, if you have not yet accepted an offer, I wonder if you would care to work for me.'

She had to hire a junior. Perhaps it should be a man? Many of her patients' husbands, fathers, sons, still preferred a male practitioner. There were several capable boys graduating this summer. Hire one, check that he could handle the practice and then a three-month holiday, Italy, the Gulf of the Poets . . . You're daydreaming, Lucy. Your practice is 99 per cent female. You will lose them all if you hire a boy and then go off for a . . . she had been about to say 'jaunt' but that was still too painful a word to use. Hire the little Rose and earn Kier's undying gratitude.

'Most men marry for security, for children . . .' The words came back to her and angrily she pushed them away.

'If you love, when you love, really love, then nothing will stop you from marrying, not all the patients in the world.'

Who had said that? When? Oh, it was nothing. She would sleep on the problem. It really was the only thing to do.

14

Dundee 1907

IT WAS SURPRISINGLY easy to sleep once the decision
had been made. Lucy had lain, gritting her teeth,
demanding that sleep come. She had a long day
ahead, consulting hours, home visits, hospital visits,
the paper to prepare on the health of working-class
children in the local schools, and Rose . . . oh, yes,
Rose. Doctor Nesbitt had said that she might call
in, that she had something she wanted to discuss.
Lucy knew the subject of the discussion. She had to
be fully rested and alert to deal with Rose; not only
Rose's life but Lucy's own future hinged on what she
said to her. She had no real choice, only one decision
could be made. Lucy made it and was asleep before
she even had time to feel satified with herself.

Was there even a dent made in her pillow by the
time Isa was there with her morning tea?

'It's half-past five and you said not to let you lie
a minute longer,' said Isa, plumping up the pillows
behind her mistress.

'Oh, I've just closed my eyes,' groaned Lucy. 'How
do you always wake so fresh, Isa?'

'Sleep's a matter of a clear conscience,' said Isa,
pouring the tea. 'You were an awfie time walking up
and down afore you put your head on the pillow.'

If she hoped that her mistress would allow her into
the causes of her insomnia she was disappointed.

'I'll be down in a minute, Isa. I have a visit

to make to the Infirmary before my morning surgery.'

'You'll be the better for a boiled egg. That gives you
three minutes from the time I get down the stair.'

Lucy smiled to herself. 'Oh, Isa, live for ever, and
keep me sane with your boiled eggs,' she whispered
to herself as she scurried around. 'I should definitely
cut you off,' she told her hair as it defiantly swirled
around her head, pushing the hairpins out as if the
hair and the pins had lives over which they alone
were in control, but at last she saw reflected in
the mirror, Lucille Graham, M.B., C.M. If the eyes
were not quite so sparkling as usual and the face
was perhaps a little paler, no one would notice. Dr
Graham was in control.

It was two-thirty before she had time to stop
again.

'You look tired out,' scolded Isa. 'You'll have
chicken soup; it's always good for whatever ails
you, except lack of sleep. Come on, Miss Lucy.
There's time before your evening surgery, and you'll
do your patients no good if you faint from lack of
nourishment.'

Lucy was sitting in solitary state at the top of
her mother's cherished Jacobean dining-room table
when she heard the front door-bell and Isa's voice as
she muttered about the utter selfishness of those folk
who would not leave a poor overworked woman to
get a bite to eat. Lucy smiled and finished her soup.

'It's Doctor Nesbitt, Miss Lucy.' Isa was at the door,
half in, half out.

'I was expecting her, Isa.' True enough. Rose had
had to come, but she had thought tonight, surely,
after her lectures.

'I've put her, them, in the morning room, Doctor.'

Alarmed, Lucy half rose from the table. Isa only

called her Doctor when there were patients within
hearing or if she was seriously disturbed. 'What is it,
Isa? Has Doctor Nesbitt brought a patient, a slum child
to dirty your chairs? You will have to learn to . . .'

'Mr Kier's with her.'

Kier! Lucy's heart rose. How lovely! It had been an
exhausting day; it was only half over but seeing Kier,
letting him hear her decision, that would be a joy.

She hurried past Isa and went to the small morning
room. She had time to wonder at the beauty of the
blossoming gean tree as it filled the window.

'Kier, my dear, how nice of you to bring Rose.' She
went to him, her hands outstretched in welcome.

'Lucy.' He grasped her hands and held her there
at arm's length. 'Lucy,' he said again.

Lucy turned to Rose. How delicate she was, how
dainty. Rose had moved to the window and now
stood, haloed by white blossom – an indescribably
lovely picture. Lucy looked down at her plain black
gown and contrasted it with Rose's pink silk. She
wished she had tidied her hair.

Rose made as if to speak, but Kier caught her hand
and at the look in his eyes, the smile on his face, Lucy
sighed: 'A medical fact, dear Doctor Graham. When
you are about to receive bad news your blood does
indeed run cold,' she told herself.

'I'll tell her, Rose; it's only right. Lucy, my dear, I
found I could not bear the thought of Rose leaving
us for the vast uncharted wastes of Rhodesia. This
morning she has done me the great honour of promising to become my wife.'

It does indeed feel like a sharp blow. Words hurt;
they cut deeply, cleanly. Lucy heard herself utter all
the right things, was aware that she was doing all the
right things.

'You must come back for champagne, after my

evening surgery. I do insist. You see, you now have two things to celebrate. I had planned to offer you a place here, Rose. I need a second good doctor. For Isa's sake if not for mine, you must accept, unless of course your . . . husband would not wish his wife to practise after the wedding.'

Was there a slight look of guilt on the achingly young, lovely, face? It was fleeting, a trick of the light perhaps, as it played among the cherry blossoms.

'Heavens, I thought only to keep Rose from emigration. What do you think, darling? Shall you accept? Shall I become a patient? And which of my two favourite doctors shall attend to my every ache and pain?'

'I have nursed you enough, malingerer.' Lucy was almost able to speak normally. 'When is the wedding to be, Rose? Your family . . . ?'

'My poor Rose is quite alone in the world, Lucy. It was the typhoid epidemic that took your parents, wasn't it, darling?' He did not wait for an answer. 'My mother, as you well know, Lucy, will be only too delighted to have me married as quickly as possible.' He looked at Rose. 'You don't intend to keep me waiting long, do you, my dear?' He turned again to Lucy. 'I shall take her over on the first train. Picture my mother's face, Lucy, when this time I tell her that her dinner guest will stay for ever.'

'After the wedding, Kier dear,' said Rose, a little archly. 'Do you mean it, Doctor Graham, Lucy? Do you want me?'

'There is more than enough work in Dundee for the two of us, Rose.' She could not lie in reply to the second part of the question, but Rose seemed happy enough with her answer. 'And I have promised Isa a holiday. We have lost so much this past year . . .'

'Then I accept and thank you.'

Lucy shook hands with her new partner and all the time her mind raced. 'Could she not have acknowledged our losses? No, Lucy, be kind; she's young and in love and she has just become engaged to be married.' At last, at last they were gone and there was Isa to tell her that her first patient had arrived, had been there for some time in fact. It was Mrs Brady, wife of a local councillor, and as usual she was worried about the condition of her heart. Lucy examined the woman, her face showing no distaste at the smell of unwashed flesh that fled from the tight encasings once Mrs Brady had been persuaded to – modestly – remove the top of her dress.

'Eat less and get a little exercise.' Lucy almost heard herself say the words. The practice had grown a thousandfold since Mrs MacDonald and Mrs Dryden had taken up the new young lady doctor. Now there was more money to enable Lucy to practise in a less salubrious area of the city where the women desperately needed medical attention. Rose would enjoy that part of the practice, the Hilltown, the back streets of central Dundee. Lucy smiled at Mrs Brady, whose money made a partner possible.

'Your heart's sound as a bell, Mrs Brady,' she said and saw the disappointment on the fat face. 'I expect you are allowing yourself to worry too much about your family.' She coated the bitter pill of truth with sugar. 'I'll give you a little something to steady your nerves.'

The woman sighed with gratitude and relief. 'Thank you, Doctor Graham, I knew I could rely on you.'

Lucy showed her out, thinking, 'Be kind, Lucy, be kind. Perhaps there is some dark reason why she haunts your surgery.'

The afternoon wore into evening, and still they

came, and her mind had to deal with real people and real illness, but at last they were gone and she had to go upstairs and dress – to please Isa – for dinner. She had to sit at the table and toy with her glass of wine and face the fact that Kier would never sit at the end of it as her husband and now that it was too late, now that he had promised to marry someone else, Rose, she had to admit that always, always, every day of her life there had been the belief that one day, some day when she had achieved what she needed to achieve, when she had done what needed to be done for her own fulfilment as a woman, as a doctor, he would be there, smiling at her, holding out his arms to her, and she would run into them and . . .

Isa heard the crash of the door and her steps as she fled upstairs.

'Ach, have a bit greet, lassie, and maybe you'll learn what every fisherman kens. There's faur better fish still in the sea than ever came out of it.'

Lucy had herself well in hand when Isa brought the early-morning tea next morning. She had cried – but more, she admitted, for the end of a dream than because her heart was broken. She had cried too because now there was no one in the world to whom she could tell her tale of woe. She could hardly tell Kier how she felt, if she could indeed work out exactly how she felt herself, and Sir John was dead, and Kier's defection had brought that appalling tragedy back. Sir John had gone from his 'jaunt' to the deep South on a 'jaunt' to the Rocky Mountain region of the western states. His last letter postmarked Portland, Oregon, April 10th 1906, had spoken of the majesty of the country, and had said that:

after a tour of San Francisco, where I go tomorrow,

I plan to return to Scotland. I have had enough of
wandering and feel that I will be most happy never
to have to venture farther than Fife. Can you house
a crusty old soldier?

She had not worried when April newspapers spoke
of an earthquake in San Francisco. After all, she
still thought him to be among the magnolias and
gardenias he so admired in Georgia. Max du Pay's
letter had come in a diplomatic bag and so was faster
than her father's last letter.

When we heard of the devastation in San Francisco,
I was able to go at once. We knew Sir John was to
stay there and it distresses me to have to tell you,
Miss Lucy, that the authorities do list as missing,
assumed dead, one Colonel Sir John Graham.
The center of the city was practically razed to
the ground and the chaos from the continuing
explosions from burst gas mains and the ensuing
fires had to be experienced to be believed. Sir
John's hotel was totally destroyed and I will repeat,
verbatim, the story told me by a waiter, a lad of
about fourteen:

'The building just collapsed around us like one
of them card houses the real good gamblers can
make. We were in the dining room and lots
of folk got killed as the chandelier crashed
to the ground. There was dust thicker than a
desert wind and I couldn't see nothing, nor hear
nothing but the screaming of people, me mostly,
I think, and the groaning of timbers. Then this
thing appears, this great tall man comes out of
the dust and he's carrying these two little girls
and he's leading their momma and then, oh God,
it was awful but the floor opened up right under

us. There's this chasm in the floor and there's nothing below, not the laundry rooms which shoulda been there, just nothing but smoke and this dust that got everywhere so you couldn't breathe or see, and it gets wider and wider and then it closes up a little again and then it opens and then it kinda stays in one place. The guy sets down the little kids and he smiles at me and he says – and he talks real funny – "I do believe I can see what must pass for safety on the other side of this ravine," and I says, "That was the smoking room but I think we just made us another garden room." He was smiling so he made you pretend not to be scared, you know. And he looks down at the girls and he says, "Ladies, we are going to have an adventure. I am going to be a bridge and you are going to walk across the bridge to my young friend's new garden room. Can you jump the crater?" he asks me and I say, "Yessir" although I never jumped nothing that wide before, and he says, "Good chap." Good chap. But I can't. I'm no athlete and it's wider than me and he says, "Try the bridge" and he lays down – Blessed Saviour, he lays down with his hands on one side and his feet on the other – and I run across his body, quick and light as I can, and the lady nudges the little girls on his back and she's sorta pushing them from one side and I'm reaching for them from the other and they make it and he calls her to go and she's crying and he says, "Your children" 'cause he can't really speak, and she stands on him and he shifts a bit and then, dear God, it's getting wider and he gasps, "Your children" again and she sorta runs across him and we both turn to reach for him – and he's gone.'

Sir John was the only British resident of the hotel at that time, Miss Lucy, and the actions of that brave man just tell me this was the last deed of your father and my friend.

The letter had gone on to talk about gallantry awards, but Lucy had read it again and again and hugged it to her. She had cried and then she had laughed because Sir John had saved four people and one was a waiter and she could almost hear her mother's voice: 'Your father just does not know how to handle staff.'

His body had never been recovered, and once again there had been a sad little ceremony in the churchyard in Fife. No bodies lay under that hallowed soil.

'I'll be the first,' thought Lucy, and had given herself a shake and told herself not to be morbid but to think of having a nice holiday with Isa who, after all, had lost Donald to pneumonia last winter. 'We'll go somewhere warm, just as soon as they're back from their honeymoon and Rose has proved that she can do justice to my patients.'

Dr Nesbitt did not face the dawn of her wedding morning with any of the feverish excitement experienced by most young girls. She had come to the conclusion during the long night that she had made a grave mistake. Had she waited one more day, just one more, Lucy Graham would have offered her a job. She did not want to marry Kier Anderson-Howard. She did not want to marry anyone, and certainly not now, not just at the beginning of her real career. And it was too late to tell him so. Today she was going to marry him, and tonight she would have to sleep with him. He had been so good, so patient. She did love him, she did, and she would do her best to be a good wife, but his restrained love-making frightened her and what it would be like when his passions were allowed full rein . . . oh God, it did not bear thinking about. All that *stuff* led to babies, no matter that early man had thought it led only to disease, and she wanted no squalling brats around her. She was no Elsie to take them all in her stride, no Leslie to die in her own blood giving birth to them. Oh, Doctor, Doctor, scratch an insecure woman and all the book-learning flows out with the blood.

'I'll get used to it, and it will mean nothing, and anyway, men want only satisfaction and once they have it, and that takes but a few moments, they sleep.' Rose had learned all these inalienable facts in her childhood and in her years of study among the poor and downtrodden – and yes, among the rich too. Men had the best of everything. Damn them all! Had they given her the job she had earned by right, then she would not now be lying in a cold sweat waiting for the dawn she did not wish to see. If only it could be just the way these last few weeks had been, the only cloud the patent dissatisfaction of Kier's mother. Kier was a gentleman and when told that his fiancée had not been brought up to 'indulge' her fiancé's baser instincts, he had coloured furiously and been a perfect angel ever since. Lucy was a splendid, generous and helpful employer. She had encouraged Rose to increase their list of poorer women, but had coaxed her into meeting the richer ones like Mrs MacDonald and her lovely young daughters. They liked having such a pretty new doctor. The oldest daughter, like Doctor Nesbitt was also engaged, but how differently she approached the marriage bed.

'I can hardly wait, Rose. I may call you Rose. Frank and I are modern; we do not expect that I shall be, like my dearest mother, in an *interesting* condition every year. I could not have this conversation with dear Doctor Graham. Ma adores her but, *entre nous*, she is such an old fuddy-duddy.'

Miss MacDonald found that, like Doctor Graham, Doctor Nesbitt too was an old fuddy-duddy. She confessed to knowing all that there was to know about, well, you know . . . making sure that . . .

'Contraception,' Rose had said, taking great pleasure from seeing the effect that calling a spade a spade had on the pert young woman. 'I will be happy to give you the sum total of my knowledge. . . . as soon as you are married.'

'Mother fell with me on her wedding night,' had argued the thoroughly up-to-date young woman.

'A risk all well-brought-up young women have to take. I will see you when you return from your wedding trip.'

'Please, could I not see you before, the day before? Even if I wanted to, I couldn't possibly commit a sin on the night before my wedding. The house will be packed to the ceiling with decaying relatives.'

Rose had promised to see her . . . and the embarrassed Frank.

Oh, yes, she liked being a doctor. She could spend the rest of her life quite happily just doing her job. And Kier? Could she do without Kier?

Kier was sweet; he was gentle, although every now and again she thought she saw a glimpse of steel, and he was kind. He was also very, very rich, and he owned Laverock Rising. Rose was honest enough to admit that she would love to live in that house, that its very name stirred her. As soon as Kier's mother moved out – she had bought a town house in St Andrews, bless her – Lucy would have the house redecorated. Kier wanted her to change everything, to put her own stamp on the place. My God, to go from the Hilltown, to lodgings, to Laverock Rising. If she had to pinch herself to believe she was really a doctor, what would she have to do to convince herself that she owned that house?

Rose groaned and, turning over, buried her head in her pillow. She knew what she would have to do, and she hated the very thought.

15

Venice 1908

AT FIRST VENICE was a disappointment. Where was the light, the colour, the play of the reflections of the buildings on the waters of the canals? It rained the whole of the first day. Lucy sat at the window of her little hotel, La Colombera, and looked out across the waters of the canal to the Jewish quarter.

'I might as well be in Scotland,' she thought as countless tourists must have thought before her. 'At least there I could understand what is going on.'

She rang the bell for the maid and, with much laughter and gesticulation on both sides and referral by both women to Lucy's phrase book, managed to order water for a bath.

La Colombera, she wrote in her diary, for she could not write to Kier, not now that he was married to Rose, has the prettiest name, the prettiest maids and the hottest water in the whole of Italy. Her love affair had begun.

They took a gondola to St Mark's Square.

'You have to come, Isa. Heaven knows what the Italians would think if I travelled about alone.'

Isa had proved an enthusiastic traveller. She had, after all, never been anywhere before, but she had her standards. 'I'm not going in there,' she protested as they approached the doors of the great basilica.

'No one is asking you to convert, but merely to see

the architecture. It's reputed to be quite magnificent inside.'

But Isa would not compromise and stood outside under her umbrella while Lucy explored.

Even in the rain, in early April, the building was busy with worshippers and sightseers. It was very, very dark, and Lucy stood for a while until her eyes became accustomed to it and it was then that she became aware of a low sound, a voice at prayer. At a side altar a priest knelt. Aware only of his God, he was singing, and his voice, Lucy knew in wonder, could have graced any of the world's great stages. He was singing quietly, communicating only with God; his prayer was not meant for the world to hear, but Lucy moved over and stood behind him, listening, and as she listened she was filled with a tremendous feeling of peace and relief. It was as if her sadness and sense of loss were pouring out of her and joining the glorious voice as it rose to heaven. She felt that she could have stayed there for ever.

'Well, as I live and breathe,' said a voice directly behind her and Lucy turned and saw Maximilian du Pay.

He had hardly changed – tall, sun-bronzed, arrogant, his dark eyes smiling down at her.

Her heart leapt, her stomach churned. My God, after all these years, could his very presence have this effect on her?

'Max. What on earth are you doing here?' She did not wait for an answer but went on, 'Oh, Max, how very nice to see you.'

She had never answered his letter that told her of her father's last moments. She had meant to: she had sat, often, pen in hand, but the words had refused to put themselves down on the paper.

He smiled again, the smile that told her that he knew exactly what was going on in her mind.

'Good voice,' he said. 'Wasted, don't you think?'

'How can you say such a thing?' They were back in Washington DC, fighting with one another.

'To make you mad, Miss Lucy, or must I call you Doctor now?'

She blushed at her gaucheness. She had not seen him for, dear God, was it fifteen, sixteen – no, seventeen years! His last act to her had been one of immense kindness and yet she was prepared to squabble.

'Max.' She looked around. There was no one who was obviously with him. 'I can hardly believe that you are really here. Your wife?'

'No wife,' he said. 'Not yet. Foot-loose and fancy-free, Miss Lucy.' In his turn he looked around. 'And you? Married to medicine?'

He did not make it sound attractive. Again she bristled. 'As it happens, that's exactly the situation.'

'It's so easy to make you mad. Where's your group, or shall I be your guide? I know everything about this church, since it has rained every day I've been here and it's the nicest place to shelter. Are you one of the faithful? Not that it matters in St Mark's which isn't really Roman Catholic. That's why that loss to the world of grand opera is singing at a side altar – the centre aisles belong to the Orthodox lot. Five denominations are represented here, even our Jewish brethren round the back.'

'Herr Colner.' For the first time in many years Lucy thought of her old tutor. 'I'd like to see the Jewish part, if it's true.'

'Now, why would I lie? This church wasn't built for the greater glory of God, Lucy' – he had dropped the Miss, but there was no point in saying anything, she knew he would pay no attention – 'but for the greater safety of man. It's a centre of wordly power, a defence against the infidels pouring in from the North. Religion is incidental, but nice, when it's sincere like the boy with the voice over there.'

First Lucy had to marvel at the magnificent marble screen with its statues of the Virgin, St Mark and the Apostles, and to stop, dazzled by the Pala D'Oro, the golden jewel-encrusted altar-piece of the Presbytery. But at last they reached the Jewish part of the great basilica.

'I don't know which way to look. It's all so over-whelming, overpowering, so unbelievably beautiful.'

'Here you are. Say prayers for your Jewish friends here. Basilica means, or was, the Roman centre of administration. Crafty Venetians added the religious element so that they had a place of sanctuary big enough to take the population. Jews were very welcome; they were the money-makers, and Venice even had at least one Jewish Doge. Why have you never married, Lucy?'

She had not remembered that Americans were quite so direct; she found herself answering honestly. 'I was never sure whether I loved the man I loved enough to marry him. And then he married someone else.'

'And are you sad?'

'Sad for me, yes, because time is rushing past, and I'm confused too.'

Even in the semi-darkness of the church she could see that he smiled.

'Then you can dine with me tonight and we'll talk about old times.'

What arrogance! He took her acceptance for granted. He led her through the church and out on to St Mark's Square where Isa still stood under her umbrella.

'Where are you staying? I'm at the Gritti Palace. Say you're there.'

'I'll say it, but it wouldn't be true. We're at a little hotel on one of the side canals, La Colombera.'

'I'll find it.'

'I haven't said I'll come.'

He smiled again. 'You have to take pity on a lonesome old friend. Eight o'clock.'

'Miss Lucy.'

Perhaps it was the note of warning in Isa's voice, but Lucy found herself agreeing.

'I'm not a young girl, Isa,' she justified herself on the way back to the hotel in the gondola, 'and besides, I've known Mr du Pay for years. His father was a good friend of my father. It was Mr du Pay, remember, who wrote to me about Father's death.'

She had nothing festive to wear. Every dress in the wardrobe said 'professional woman'. She threw them on the bed in a despairing heap.

'I need something frivolous to wear when dining with Maximilian du Pay.'

Desperately she took her scissors and unpicked the lace inserted into the neckline of her dark blue silk.

'Miss Lucy?'

Lucy ignored the shocked voice of censure. 'Good heavens, Isa! I could wear this gown at a medical consultation. All Mr du Pay will see is three inches of skin, well, maybe four.' She laughed, the laughter of a young carefree girl. 'I've missed this, Isa, this dressing-up and going out. I didn't realize how much. Whem my father was alive, I dined out almost every night, and danced and listened to beautiful music in lovely rooms full of hothouse flowers.'

She stopped, for suddenly a picture of the very young Lucy Graham had come into her mind. She was in the Russian Embassy in Washington DC, and she was wearing a white lace gown and her first, her only, string of pearls.

'I'm old, Isa. He'll see how changed I am.'

Since the death of her husband in the same month as that of Lucy's father, Isa had become more maternal, more proprietorial. She sprang now to Lucy's defence. 'Nonsense, Miss Lucy. He'll see a beautiful, elegant woman who has dedicated her life to others. He'll be honoured to take you to dinner.'

But Lucy looked at herself in the mirror and could see no shadow of the girl she had been.

'Has it stopped raining yet?' she asked calmly, for what did it matter? She was dining with, . . . she could hardly call him an old friend, someone she had once known and whom she had met by accident and would no doubt never see again.

The rain had stopped and Max had arranged for a private gondola. He helped her in as if she were a piece of exquisitely delicate Venetian glass, and for the first time in her life Lucy felt small and vulnerable.

'I thought it best to dine at the Gritti Palace, Lucy. Should any of your family connections see you, your reputation would come to no harm in such a public place.'

'Good gracious Max. I'm not a young girl.'

He laughed, a full-throated laugh that echoed over the waters of the canal.

'Bravo, Miss Lucy, for a horrible moment I thought you'd changed.'

They smiled and gave their attention to enjoying the journey as they turned into the Grand Canal. Churches and palaces stood shimmering in the waters, lights streaming from every window. The mooring poles for private gondolas stood, their family flags blowing in the evening breeze. Liveried gondoliers handed jewelled women on to sumptuous cushions and, everywhere, there were reflections.

They caught glimpses of inviting little side streets. 'Oh, wouldn't you love to explore up there, Max?'

'I have. The gondolas take so long to get anywhere because the canal twists and turns, but actually it's quite easy to get from here to there if you walk, crossing the bridges. I've found churches with paintings by Canaletto just hanging on the walls, exquisite little gardens. The entire city is a living, breathing art gallery.'

Lucy clapped her hands like a child, her face still turned to the wonders on either side. 'I must take a tour. It's a dream city.'

They arrived at the small dock outside Venice's grandest hotel and the gondolier handed Lucy out. She looked back at the canal.

'It's so ethereal, I almost expect it to disappear.'

'I don't want to disillusion you, but sometimes you might wish it would disappear. They're not always too careful about hygiene.'

'Oh, don't, Max.'

He tucked her gloved hand into his arm as they walked into the hotel. 'Tonight, I promise you, only Venice's glorious surface.'

It was pleasant to bask in the unexpected admiration in a man's eyes.

'You grew up, Miss Lucy,' said Max in his soft Southern voice as Lucy handed over her cape. 'We won't have champagne. Italians, very sensibly, see wine as an accompaniment to good food – the two together, very rarely alone. Shall I order for you?

You would be sensible to have fish; or do you know Italian food?'

The meal was exquisite. Because of her father's career and her own long training, Lucy had travelled extensively and was used to different cuisines, but Italy was new and she revelled in it, protesting only at the array of sweets that finished the meal.

'I can't, Max. I've eaten vegetables, and pasta, and such delicious fish. I've had soup and bread and . . . was that really rice with the fish, and so much wine . . .'

'Let's dance then. I've never danced with a doctor before. I met one once, a lady doctor, that is . . .'

'You make it sound like a bug, Max.' Lucy laughed and deepened her already throaty voice. 'I met one once. Shot it and had it stuffed.'

He held her more tightly and they moved together on the terrace to the sound of violins.

'We could have champagne now, or more wine?'

'Coffee,' said Lucy firmly.

He laughed and led her back to their table. 'Now tell me more about why you haven't combined matrimony with your career?'

It was an impertinent question, but tonight was a special magic night and she answered without thinking.

'It's as I told you, Max – and almost every minute since we last met, I've been studying or working. That doesn't leave much time for love.' How easily she could speak to him. 'Can you understand how important medicine was, is to me? I had to do something with my own life to make things better for those less well-off. Everywhere I went with Father it seemed to me that the poor really had little chance of a decent life, and women almost none at all, and there I sat in my lovely home with my lovely gowns

and everything was so easy and my parents, my
mother, expected that it would go on. I would come
out, marry the right man . . .' Her voice broke a little
and Max squeezed her hand. When had she given
him possession of her hand? '. . . and have the right
number of children, but I couldn't. Oh, Max, if you
could see some of my patients . . .'

'You work with the poor?'

'No, not really. My parents weren't wealthy. I have
no private income and so I have two practices, one
supports the other. My . . . my colleague, to her
credit, works mainly with the poor, but . . . she is
married now, and no doubt things will change. She
will have children . . .'

Her voice wobbled again. Rose would have children, Kier's children. Lucy shivered.

'Let me get your cloak. We'll walk back across the
bridges of Venice, and tomorrow I will take you to
the Bridge of Sighs and I'll show you a church where
paintings by Canaletto hang for everyone to see.'

She was outside, and somehow it seemed right that
he should hold her hand, and she trusted herself to
him completely as he crossed one bridge and walked
past sleeping buildings, and then crossed another
little bridge and they stood and looked at their reflections quivering on those of Venice in the waters.

Did Venice work its magic or was it Max? She
could have walked for ever. She forgot Kier and
Rose and her patients and was, once again, carefree.
They were outside La Colombera, where Lucy lifted
her head to look at the carved doves that flew
permanently among the flowered vines that hung
over the door and Max kissed her, softly, very gently,
on her lips.

'Tomorrow, I'll show you paintings, Veronese,
Tintoretto . . .'

'And Canaletto.'

'Better bring the dragon lady, although I'm quite sure she'll find Veronese's voluptuous women quite decadent.' He kissed her again and this time she lifted one hand, rather tentatively, to his neck.

He smiled. 'Yes, better bring Isa. Good night, little doctor. I've never kissed a doctor before.'

He turned and she stood watching him until he crossed the last little bridge and disappeared up a side street.

An old lady, disapproving like Isa, handed Lucy her key.

'It's only an interlude, a magic interlude,' she told herself as she prepared for bed.

'And so sensible, Isa, to go with Mr du Pay who knows Venice so well,' she told Isa next morning as they ate their delicious breakfast of coffee and warm, crusty bread straight from the oven.

For three days they went everywhere with Max. He was a knowledgeable and charming guide and even Isa relaxed and admitted, somewhat grudgingly, that Venice had its points and only some decent roads could improve it. Rice, however, would always remain something with which to make a pudding and should have absolutely nothing to do with fish or meat.

Max did not kiss Lucy again.

'It was the wine,' she told herself. 'We had too much wine.'

For their last dinner together, she bought a new gown.

Signor Bico, the owner of the little hotel, told her how to get to a shop where she could find a reasonable gown, Italian in design and cut but not Venetian in price. That price still made Lucy gasp, but, oh, she turned this way and that and knew that somehow the dress had been designed for her alone.

She dressed for dinner, put on her pearls and took them off again.

The admiration in Max's eyes was unmistakable. 'You should have rubies with that gown, Lucy. May I buy you rubies, a souvenir of Venice?'

'Don't be silly.'

The dinner was superb and the orchestra in the little restaurant played the same Italian serenades as the musicians in the Gritti had done. They danced and Lucy relaxed in his arms and willed the night to go on for ever.

'Shall we walk back through the streets, one last walk?'

Of course, how silly. It was over. It had to end but she had not expected it to hurt so much. They put Isa into a gondola; she now trusted Max completely and apart from a, 'Don't stay out too late, Miss Lucy,' she said nothing.

'I'm leaving tomorrow, Lucy.' They had reached the little bridge. She looked down into the water and saw his reflection as he moved closer and tilted up her face for her kiss.

'Come with me, Lucy.' His voice was almost desperate. 'I'm going north to Tuscany . . . to paint. There's so much I have to . . . we have to decide.'

He kissed her again.

'It's Venice, it's Venice,' she tried to tell herself as her pulses raced and she pushed herself even closer to him, responding with every fibre of her being.

Drowning in her own senses, she pulled away from him. 'Don't, Max. I can't think.'

'You think too much, Lucy,' he said breathlessly. 'Sometimes it's better just to *do*.'

'No, no, I can't go to Tuscany.'

'You're not a child, Lucy. I won't deny that I have designs on your virtue, but I am, I hope, a gentleman. Bring Isa. I have hired a woman to live in and cook and clean; she has her husband with her to drive the cab. I'll tell her to bring her cousins and aunts if that makes you feel better, but we can't just decide, "that was a real nice little holiday," and go back to everything the way it was before. At least I can't, Lucy. You've come to mean so much. I can't tell at this point if it's love or lust, not with you standing there shimmering in the moonlight. I'm in Italy to decide what I want to do with the rest of my life: I think I want you to be a part of it.'

She heard a small, trembling voice say, 'We'll come.' The voice was stilled by his kiss. She saw Venice reflected in the water and then she could see and hear and feel nothing but Max. He gained control first.

'If your patients could see you now,' he said somewhat shakily. 'Don't change your mind, Lucy of the red dress. You have thinking to do too, I know. Let's think together in Tuscany.'

And that was why she found herself on a train with Isa, a thoroughly disapproving Isa who sat tight-lipped as they crossed one after another of Italy's wonders of engineering.

'Look, a bird's-eye view of Italy,' Lucy would say as she peered out of the window and looked down at the valley hundreds of feet below. She tried hard not to think of what would happen should the train fall off the track.

'It's not my place to say, Doctor . . .' Isa would begin.

'No, it's not.'

'But it's not what Sir John wanted for you.'

Ah, that silenced Lucy's protests.

'It's perfectly correct, Isa. We are going together to stay with a friend. There are servants in the house.'

Lucy sat, pulses racing, feeling a little sick. What had she promised on that magical Venetian night?

'I'm not a child, I'm not a child,' she kept telling herself, 'and Max is a gentleman.'

Just thinking of him seemed to conjure him up in the carriage, although he had gone ahead the day before leaving Lucy perfectly free to change her mind. At the station, before leaving Venice, she had almost done so when she had to telegraph Rose to let her know of the change of plan.

Venice was wonderful. Going on to Tuscany to compare Florence. Returning one week. Lucy.

'I'm insane,' she had chastised herself. 'I'm a respected Dundee doctor; I've worked so hard to be where I am. What am I doing here?'

And all the feelings of hurt and despair came flooding back. She was here because all her life she had loved Kier Anderson-Howard and he had married Rose and for the rest of her life she would have to watch them, day after day, unless, unless . . .

She sent the telegraph but the doubts did not fly away with it. How can I go to one man while I love another? What do I feel for Max? Do my pulses race whenever I see him because I love him, or am I a desperate woman snatching at a chance for happiness, a chance to experience what Rose has experienced? I'm thirty-six years old. Am I flattered because a handsome man desires me? Oh, God, does he desire me, Lucy, or just the body?

Dusty and tired, she climbed from the train when it finally stopped at the station at Aulla, and there was

Max. He shook her hand, friends who were meeting to tour a delightful region of a delightful country.

'Look,' he pointed behind him. 'There's still snow on the mountains but the valleys think the spring is here: Mauro will take your bags, ladies.' An incredibly bent and wrinkled old man, rather like a splendid vine, smiled broadly at Lucy through blackened teeth and, picking up all the bags in one massive sweep, loaded them into the back of the little trap. 'We're heading up there.' Again Max pointed to the mountains. 'Can't you just see why Italy produced Titian and Michelangelo? I've already set up my humble easel in an overgrown orchard.'

He talked and talked and the nervousness fell away; even Isa seemed to succumb again to his charm and more than once pointed out clumps of wild irises waving at them from the roadside.

'You'd pay a penny or two for flowers like that in Dundee,' she said.

'I did explain this was no luxurious villa I've rented?' asked Max anxiously as the sure-footed pony pulled the loaded trap up winding roadways. It's a maze of little rooms added as the family expanded. It was a farmhouse, but as far as I can make out everyone in the village owns a bit of the land now.' He became very quiet as the trap pulled further and further into the mountains and into the village of Montale. To Lucy it seemed as though the streets were too narrow for more than one human being, never mind a trap loaded with four people and luggage, and several times she could have touched the walls or picked flowers from a garden, but at last they stopped. Mauro jumped down and held the pony's head – in case we slip back down the mountain, thought Lucy.

'Welcome to Casata d'Aurora, Lucy.'

The house was long and low and built of white-washed stone. There was a courtyard in front where a yellow cat dozed on a terracotta pot full of blue blossoms that Lucy did not recognize. The courtyard supported several ancient vines which laced together overhead to form a roof.

'In summer, they say, the leaves and grapes give shelter from the sun.'

In late spring the sun chased its own beams through the tracery of bursting young leaves. The house itself was held in the arms of the mountain slopes and seemed to rise out of a cloud of white and pink blossoms.

'Cherries,' said Max, 'and peaches, apples of course, and pears.'

'Casata d'Aurora?' asked Lucy in a voice so quiet that it could not break the spell.

'The little house of the dawn.'

'Ven, ven, ven . . .' The raucous voice disturbed the moment and out of the door burst a little woman as gnarled and wrinkled as Mauro.

'This is Stella, my housekeeper, and she has hot water ready for you to refresh yourselves, and a meal fit for a king.'

16

Tuscany 1908

CHURCH BELLS WOKE Lucy at 5 a.m. She counted them and then smiled and tried to go back to sleep. Almost five minutes later the church on the other side of the Tavernelle told the sleeping village that it was 5 o'clock. Lucy smiled again but gave up all thought of sleep. Five hours was a good night for a doctor. She would lie and rest and wait for the dawn.

It came and, forewarned by bird-song, Lucy sat wrapped in her dressing gown and watched the sun appear over the mountains. Sentinels of pink and gold and blue painted the mountains and the trees and the old churches. They reached the orchard and Lucy saw the blossoms quiver as they saluted the arrival of the Sun God. The valley shimmered in a blue haze. And then Max appeared, a Max that Lucy had never seen before. He wore no collar and his shirt was unbuttoned and, unaware that he was being watched, he stretched his arms above his head as if he too showed obeisance to a deity. How tall he was, and how masculine. The peasant shirt was moulded to his body and Lucy hugged herself, why she did not know. Max set up the easel and after several minutes while he watched the mountains and Lucy watched him, he began to paint. He was totally absorbed in what he was doing. She could not stay and watch him secretly; that was almost like spying. She would dress and go out to him.

Lucy winced as her bare feet touched the tile floor. Quickly she washed, using the cold water in the ewer, and dressed. She thought for a moment of leaving her hair down, but then quickly coiled it and pinned it securely to the top of her head.

So engrossed was Max in what he was doing that he did not hear the swish of her skirts through the long grass of the orchard. He was painting a picture of the mountainside. There was the rough outline of the first church which towered above the house, the trees, even the blossoms.

He had to decide about the rest of his life. Was this the decision that had to be made?

'Are you trying to decide whether or not you have enough talent to become a painter?'

He made as if to stand up and she put her hand on his shoulder to keep him down. 'No, don't get up. I didn't mean to disturb you.' Her fingers stayed lightly on his shoulder and she could feel the strength of him through the thin fabric of the shirt. When she lifted her hand and held it tightly against her, she could still feel the heat in her fingers.

'No.' He answered the question. 'I'm a mere dilettante.'

'Well, now that I have become such an expert on Italian artists, I would go so far as to say that you are very talented.'

'Why, thank you, Ma'am.' He looked at her and smiled, and it was she who dropped her eyes and moved away. Something was happening to her. She could feel Dr Lucille Graham slipping further and further away. It was the magic of Italy, of course, nothing more.

He had followed her. 'I cannot paint the mountain with you standing there against the cherry trees, Lucy.'

'They're quite beautiful, aren't they?'

'Yes, very beautiful.' But he was not looking at the trees.

'Why, there's Stella,' said Lucy almost breathlessly. His size was so overpowering in the small orchard, and yet she was not a small woman.

'She has coffee ready and fresh bread.'

They went back to the dining room with its bare whitewashed walls and heavy oak table.

'What an absolutely divine smell,' said Lucy. 'I'm hungry, would you believe? After that dinner last night, I felt sure I could never eat again.'

The moment of tension was over as they drank large mugs of coffee and ate bread still warm and steaming inside.

'Shall we go to Florence today, or shall we explore the valley?'

'Oh, the valley please, Max. I'm still digesting the magnificence of Venice.'

For the next few days, with Isa, they meandered along winding lanes. Bird-song accompanied them, and the tinkling of the bells worn by goats and sheep and the occasional cow. They met very few people, and those they did meet were shy but friendly.

'They are so poor, Max, and they work so hard, but they seem to have no jealousy. And the children we see look healthy.'

'Country living, Lucy. The back streets of the cities will teem with disease and squalor, just like every place else.'

'I suppose you're right. I must make notes, though. The chestnut flour for bread and their pastas, eggs, goat's milk, and cheese.'

'And a long summer of vine-ripened tomatoes, and countless other vegetables and fruits, but think of this paradise in the winter when the snows come down from the mountains.'

'They must preserve food. I shall ask Stella.'

'That will be an interesting conversation,' laughed Max.

'I meant, you will ask her for me, won't you Max?'

'I am clay in your hands, Lucy, not marble.' He looked towards the mountains. 'Carrara is over there. Carrara, where Michelangelo got his marble. I wonder if we could get there in a day?'

They never got to Carrara; neither did they see Florence.

'I'd like to paint the house from the top of the mountain. Let's take a picnic up there.'

Isa preferred not to go. 'What am I supposed to do with myself while he sits for hours painting flowers and you get lost in a book? I'll stay and work with Stella.'

'Analyse that friendship, Doctor,' laughed Max as he encouraged the pony to trot up the mountain path. 'One speaks not a word of English and the other no Italian, yet they laugh and chatter by the hour together.'

'Perhaps they're saying perfectly dreadful things to one another.'

It was a glorious day, the warmest they had had so far. The air was soft and clean and clear. They reached a glade in the shadow of the ruined church that towered above the valley and unharnessed the pony.

'I hope I can catch the little rascal this afternoon or we'll have a long walk and some explaining to do to Mauro.'

Max set up his easel and Lucy spread a blanket on the grass and sat beside him. She did not read, but closed her eyes to enjoy the feel of the warm sun on her face. The sounds of the valley floated up to join those of the mountain; bird-song, bells, the dull but rhythmic sound of a woodcutter, running water. Lucy slept.

'*Una biquieri di vino rosso, Signora?*' Max's voice disturbed her. He was sitting beside her on the blanket, two glasses of Mauro's raw red wine in his hands. 'You hold the glasses and I'll get the bread and cheese.'

The food tasted as Lucy had never tasted simple bread and cheese before.

'It's the air,' said Max, and then he kissed her and it was the most natural thing in the world. She was lost in his kiss; she knew nothing, thought nothing. All she could do was feel. His hand was on the buttons of her blouse and, for a second, Lucy's eyes flew open and she could have said no. But her senses, so long repressed, were surging and seething and her whole body was on fire with longing. His fingers touched her breast, his lips found her nipples and she moaned with a desire for fulfilment. He moved away from her and she groaned and pulled him closer. She could not bear it; he must not leave her. She was dying.

And then his body blotted out the sun and she knew nothing, nothing but the wonder of Max du Pay . . .

She opened her eyes to a snowfall of white apple blossoms. They were on Max's hair, his back, her breast. She laughed and Max opened his eyes.

'Veronese,' he said and kissed her again.

'Canaletto,' she answered and allowed her hand to slide with proud ownership over his bare broad shoulders. 'But I'm too skinny for a Veronese portrait.'

'You are magnificent,' he said.

Lucy shivered.

'The sun has gone behind a cloud,' he said and helped her to her feet. 'Well, ma'am, I have come to a decision today. I love Lucy Graham and I want to stay here and paint for the rest of our lives.'

Lucy turned away from him as she fastened her skirt. Her mind was racing. Stay here for ever? He loved her. She had to love him. She could not have responded to him so eagerly and fully if she did not. But stay here? What about her patients? Isa?

He smiled down at her, a smile tinged with sadness. Had he expected her to say something? Of course he had. But what could she say?

'Come along, Miss Modesty. Help me catch Generalissimo.'

The pony was only too happy to be harnessed and Max seemed to be totally occupied in harnessing him and loading the little cart. Lucy reached for the picnic basket just as he did and their hands met. He tightened his hold on her fingers and Lucy trembled as the fire that had consumed her began again to glow.

'Oh no, please, Max, don't touch me. I can't think.'

'I know. I don't want you to think, Lucy.'

'It's not fair.'

He bowed; there were still blossoms in his hair and her hand ached to reach out and touch them.

'We'll talk at the table. You at one end, me at the other.'

'We'll have to shout,' said Lucy and he smiled.

Isa and Stella watched them arrive back at the house. Stella smiled and shrugged as if to say, 'Of course, it has happened. They are in love.'

Isa did not shrug with the calm easy acceptance of the Italian. She shook her head and went back to washing the vegetables. Vegetables were the same in Scotland or Italy; they came out of the ground dirty and you washed them.

Lucy wore the red dress at dinner.

It seemed as if Stella had lit every candle she could find in Tuscany and the sombre dining room was bright as day. The candlelight glowed on Lucy's white shoulders; it revealed highlights in her dark hair; it showed her eyes sparkling and shimmering.

Max stood behind her to pour the wine. He did not touch her but still she felt as if his hands caressed her shoulders as they had caressed her body a few hours before. They did not shout, they did not even speak. They sipped the sparkling Italian wine and their eyes talked across the table.

Stella placed the food before them and they made an attempt to eat. Lucy tasted nothing, she did not know what she ate. When Stella came to remove the plates of antipasto Max stood up and Lucy watched him as he came to her. She gave him her hand and he pulled her to him. He did not kiss her but stood for a moment looking down at her, and the desire in her rose to meet his. His arm went around her waist and, unafraid, she went with him.

Stella found the room empty when she returned with the steaming vegetables. She shrugged and smiled.

'Well, well,' she said. 'The chickens will feast tomorrow.'

For three days they lived in a world where nothing mattered but their love. All day they talked and said nothing that was significant, content to live for the moment in the world of their senses. They took huge picnics with them to local beauty spots and while Lucy ate – she could not believe her appetite – Max painted. He painted furiously as if he had already wasted too much time, or perhaps as if he knew that it would be years before he painted again.

All night they loved and Lucy thought of nothing but Max and her need for his hands, his mouth, his body.

On the fourth day they went once more to the orchard above the Casata, and Max painted Lucy as she lay among the blossoms. They returned to the house to find the telegram which had followed him from Venice and lay on the table. All her life Lucy was to hate telegrams.

'They're never good news, are they, Max?' she said.

'It's my father.' His face was grim. 'I have to leave at once, Lucy. I may be too late already.'

Less than an hour later she said 'Goodbye' to him.

'Oh, dear God, if only it wasn't so far,' he groaned into her hair as he held her close.

'You'll write, Max, when you can? I'll wait for your letter.'

She stood in the soft Italian dusk for a long time and watched the progress of the pony and trap as it went off down the mountain. Even after she could no longer see it, she stood on the terrace under the great vine and looked down into the valley.

'*Caffè, Signora?*' Stella was there and Isa, an Isa with eyes full of sadness.

'*Si, Stella. Grazie.*' She took the coffee. How hot it was. How good.

'We'll leave tomorrow, Isa. We really shouldn't have stayed so long. Mrs Anderson-Howard – (somehow the name didn't hurt) – has held the practice together too long on her own.'

They took a cab from the station when they finally arrived in Dundee. Isa was white with exhaustion and Lucy felt guilty. Isa was too old to be trundling around Europe like this.

'I told Donald I'd aye bide with you to look after you, Miss Lucy, and that's what I'm going to do,' she had insisted.

'You can have a good sleep in your own bed tonight, Isa, and a lovely long rest tomorrow.'

'A rest . . . with my kitchen not scrubbed for weeks?' The jute-filled air of Dundee had revived Isa as the clear air of Tuscany had rejuvenated Lucy. For the first time since the telegram, Lucy was able to smile.

'It was sensible to come back before I'd made any irrevocable decisions,' Lucy told herself as she stood in front of her mirror brushing her hair, hair that Max had admired as it tumbled down over her bare shoulders.

'You should always wear blossoms.' She could almost hear his soft warm Southern voice.

She trembled and was suddenly filled with an agonizing sense of loss. 'Max, Max,' her body whispered across the miles. She ached for him. If only, if only. 'Selfish,' she scolded herself and tried to think of Max's father and of Max's unhappiness. Had he really made the decision to stay in Italy? Could she have, would she have stayed with him?

She hardly slept and welcomed the bracing effect of the cold water she splashed over her face and neck next morning. When she had finished dressing she looked again in the mirror. Tall, thin, almost sallow. Brown hair pulled back tightly into a coil. A high-buttoned, plainly cut dark blue dress. This was the woman who had gone to Italy to nurse a broken heart. Of the naked girl in the apple orchard there was no sign.

When Rose arrived for her morning consultations, Lucy was already seated at her desk going through the accumulation of letters and notes on cases that

awaited her. Rose was conscientious and thorough
and her notations were copious and detailed. They
made it easy for Lucy to greet Kier's wife.

'And how is Kier?' she was able to ask as they
finished the coffee Isa brought for them.

'Thoroughly happy,' said Rose. 'He is taking a real
interest in finding us a house in Dundee. This daily
travelling across the Tay is really not very sensible
for me.'

'No, you're right. It does make for a tiring day.
Where are you looking?'

'Kier likes Broughty Ferry, but I think a small flat in
this area. Kier thinks he'll want to stay in town during
the week but really, it would be more sensible for him
to stay at home. We don't need two large houses.'

Lucy looked at her and heard the deliberately light
tone. Six months married, and already Rose was
talking of separate living arrangements. Of course,
it was sensible. She was seeing a problem where none
existed, she told herself as she stood up.

'You have had to work so hard while I was away,
Rose. I don't know how you managed it. Perhaps
you would enjoy a few days at home, or to go
house-hunting?'

'I've loved every minute, Lucy,' protested Rose. 'I
don't mean that I haven't missed you . . . the practice
hasn't missed you, I mean, but I've relished it, being
responsible. At last, at last I am a real doctor and you
trusted me enough to leave me in charge. I hope I
haven't made any mistakes.'

'It's unlikely that the best diagnostician of her year
has made any mistakes,' said Lucy drily, 'but we
ought to start seeing our patients. I have a paper to
write on the health of Dundee school-children, and I
would like to do as many home visits as I can today. If
you'll send in my first patient on your way out . . .'

Eczema, ecthyma, strumous sores, psoriasis, scabies, warts; Mrs Campbell to be assured that her first pregnancy was progressing perfectly naturally; polite and encouraging words to tell Mrs Hartley without offence that there was nothing wrong with her that less rich food and more exercise wouldn't cure; Mrs McLeod to be told that, yes, she had a tubercular disease and that she had allowed it to go too far for there to be much her doctor could do for her except make her more comfortable.

There was no time for lunch, not that day nor the next nor the next. How had Rose managed on her own? Hospital visits had to be made – not many, only to her wealthy patients in their private rooms. Oh, the frustration of not being allowed into the general wards to see the women there, to see anyone, man, woman or child. Overworked, underpaid male doctors struggled along in the wards because too many still believed that women were too delicate and pure to be subjected to the sights they would see in a hospital.

Rose raged. Lucy accepted.

'It's changing, Rose, but things move slowly and we will only hold up the changes that are bound to come if we antagonize everyone in power. You are a doctor. Isn't that enough for now?'

Rose's answer was almost a groan. 'No, no, no. It isn't. I have to admit that I long to change the world.'

Lucy smiled. This was the Rose she liked and admired. 'You have changed it, Doctor. Now go home. You have a husband to look after now too, and I have my paper still to finish.'

'I shall be anxious to see your paper, if I may. Remember I have first-hand experience of both the Harris and the city centre schools.'

Lucy looked up from her notes. Rose was standing in the doorway. Where had she come from, the beautifully groomed and dressed woman who stood there, a diamond and ruby brooch glittering amongst the lace at her throat.

'Rubies, let me buy you rubies.' She heard Max's voice so clearly that she almost answered him again: 'Don't be foolish.' She had packed away the red dress carefully. When would she ever wear it again? Italy. Italy. Just a few days ago I was in Italy in an orchard and Max . . .

'Are you all right, Lucy?' Rose's voice was concerned.

'Tired, as you must be.'

'I'll say good night then. You must tell us all about Italy, Lucy. Kier is anxious to hear all about Venice.'

Venice. Casata d'Aurora. In the busy days that followed Lucy began to feel almost as if it had never happened. She prepared her paper:

I have examined 539 girls. Among these were six mentally defective twelve-year-olds who are being dealt with in the infant classes. They have learned nothing.

There are appalling differences between children from various schools. In good schools, and I mention particularly the Harris Academy, girls and boys seem equal in their intelligence and ability, but in the poorer areas girls are much brighter.

Lucy stopped writing and looked again at her notes. Bodies very dirty. The boy with honeycombed teeth. Rickets. Lice. Enlarged hearts. St Vitus' dance. Bowed legs, flat feet, spinal curvatures, knock-knees, pigeon breasts, rickets, rickets and more rickets, wryneck, cleft palates, anaemia . . . oh, God, would the list of the sufferings of children never end? If they could only get better food; if there could be cleaner air in the classrooms. Surely opening windows would be a good start? Could there be some way that they could remove outdoor clothing indoors? Cloakrooms of some kind? Sometimes it appeared that the ones without shoes and coats were healthier than those well wrapped up. Perhaps it was because wet feet dry much faster than wet shoes.

> In the poorer schools, the older girls are usually quite clean, but the bodies of the smaller children are very dirty and their heads are lousy . . .

It was then that Lucy realized that for the first time since she had begun to menstruate she had missed a flow.

17

Dundee

IT WAS IMPOSSIBLE to expect a letter from Max so soon and yet Lucy found herself feverishly turning the letters on the breakfast table over and over, half hoping that somehow she had missed an envelope with Max's distinctive thick black writing on the front.

'I will not panic,' she told herself a million times a day while she dealt with other women's wanted and unwanted pregnancies.

'Shall I write to him?' She did not. If she wrote she would be forcing him into a decision which he had to make for himself. Instinctively Lucy knew that, if she were to tell Maximilian du Pay that she was expecting his child, he would move mountains to marry her.

'He has to want me, just for me,' Lucy whispered as she lay night after night in sweat-soaked sheets, and tried to work out how long it would take a letter from Max to reach her.

'He needs to write it first, and if his father is ill he will be too worried and too busy, and if his father has died then he will have the funeral to arrange and the family business to re-organize. He will have no time to write to me until everything is settled. It could take months. I must be patient.'

Lucy remembered that Max's father had been a member of the United States Senate, and she tried hard to recall everything her mother had said about the family, but try as she would nothing came back. The young Lucy Graham had been too interested in flirting with a Russian count – or had he been French? She could not remember. He had mattered so little and Max du Pay mattered so much. How had he come to mean so much and in so short a time?

'I didn't even like him,' she told herself in anguish. 'He was so arrogant, so sure of himself.' And then she turned her head into her pillow and wept. 'I must have been so young: too young to realize, to see how really wonderful he was.'

And still no letter came.

'Are you all right, Lucy?'

It would be impossible to hide from the trained eyes of another doctor, a doctor bursting with youth and beauty.

'You have been working so hard since you came back. You must come and dine with us on Saturday,' Rose went on. 'I have made a few changes to the house, just a few, and I would like to hear what you think of them. And then there's Venice. You promised to tell us all about Venice.'

She went to dinner and she sat at the Anderson-Howard table where the young Lucy had sat so often and where she had imagined herself as Kier's wife. She saw the candlelight dancing in Rose's eyes and Kier's mother's diamonds sparkling around Rose's white young neck, and she told them about Venice and Canaletto and Veronese, and she gave them their Venetian glass candlesticks, and she did not mention Maximilian du Pay. She did not tell them about Tuscany either, and certainly said nothing about an orchard and a man and a woman with blossoms in their hair.

Kier was happy. He followed Rose's every movement and listened avidly to everything she said.

'Do you approve of my changes, Lucy?' asked Rose
as they sat in the drawing room after dinner.

Lucy had noticed the different wallpaper and the
new upholstery in Kier's mother's little sitting room.
To her the newness had been like a raw wound, but
she had tried to see it with a stranger's eyes and
she had to admit that the selections of bright new
materials were charming.

'I have no right to approve or disapprove, Rose.'

'Oh, I know that, but you have such excellent
taste and I wanted to know if you agree with my
choices.'

Of course she would need to change the fur-
nishings; she had to stamp her personality on to
this house that had sheltered Charlotte Anderson-
Howard for nearly half a century.

'Mother thinks it lovely, Lucy. She says she was
always much too lazy to change anything,' said
Kier, his eyes noting his wife's skill as she poured
the coffee from the Georgian coffee pot that had
belonged to his great-grandmother.

'It's charming, Rose, and a perfect foil for you.'

That was when the cramp struck and she bit back
a gasp of pain and surprise. She excused herself and
hurried along the corridor to the room set aside for
her use.

'Not in this house,' she prayed. 'Not in this house.'

Another ferocious cramp gripped her stomach and
she felt the warm sticky wetness on the insides of her
thighs, but she was a doctor and had dealt with the
symptoms so often. There was pain and relief mixed
with sadness in the white face that stared back at her
out of the mirror.

'Did you merely hope to be pregnant, Doctor
Graham?' she whispered to herself. 'Travel, change
of food, of climate . . . of living conditions, all upset

the harmony of normal bodily functions. You need never write to Max du Pay. There is nothing he needs to know.' She wanted to get home, to weep for the end of a dream, for the end of a nightmare.

There was still the evening to be got through, and she was glad she had not accepted the invitation to stay for the night.

'Are you unwell, Lucy?' Rose was outside in the corridor.

'No, thank you. Merely "the curse of Eve".'

'Oh, won't you change your mind and stay? Bed and a nice hot-water-bottle on your stomach . . .' Rose blushed. 'How dare I prescribe for you?'

'Dear Rose,' smiled Lucy. 'It sounds delightful, but I'm perfectly well and will catch the Aberdeen train. Isa would worry.'

And when the evening was over and she had said all the right things and admired all Rose's changes, Kier took her to Leuchars and she got on the train and sat down with relief in a first-class carriage where she was the only passenger. She put her hands on her stomach and hated its flatness, its barrenness. 'Poor unconceived little baby,' she thought. 'If you had existed, what price to pay for a marriage that your father surely does not want. For him I was part of the romantic dream of Italy, nothing more.'

There Lucy wronged Max. He had laughed at the young British miss he had watched flirting so admirably with the Russian Count at the Embassy in Washington. He had thought then that she was too young for him. She should have her head for a while; she should be allowed, even encouraged to break the hearts of a dozen Washington beaux, and then when she had reaped the field – and if she had not herself been harvested – he would make his play. Max du

Pay well knew what a catch he was on the marriage market; he had been told often enough.

When circumstances changed and the flibberty-gibbet young socialite had shown the depth of character he had only suspected and remained in Britain to attend a university, he had sighed a little over his wasted opportunity but wished her well. There were, he thought, a thousand Lucy Grahams. But he had never found one . . .

And then he had reached the age when even he told himself that it was time to settle down, time to decide whether politics or managing the family's considerable business interests was to be the life for him, time indeed to marry. But Max was a romantic and wanted to marry a woman he could not possibly live without, and not just one who would be a perfect hostess in the du Pays' magnificent Southern mansion house or who would properly spend a large proportion of the du Pay money.

He had been seeing a great deal of Ammabelle Redmond.

'That girl's chitter-chatter is like water on a stone, Mister Max,' his old nurse, Florrie, told him time and time again. 'If you don't come to a decision, she and her mammy are going to do it for you. They'll wear you down and you'll find yourself hogtied before you can say it don't make no never-mind.'

Max did not at that time appreciate the incredible power of dripping water.

His father wanted him to assume control of du Pay Chemicals and du Pay Engineering, and his mother wanted him to marry Miss Redmond and to stand for the soon-to-be-vacated local Congressional seat. Max could just as easily have done one as the other, and had decided to travel in Europe for a while before deciding. And there in Venice he had met again Lucy

Graham and, being a romantic, had recognized his twin soul, and the intensity of his feelings had almost frightened him and had made him shout out with laughter and relief as he walked back to the Gritti Palace from the little hotel where Lucy was staying.

'What a woman,' he had told a black Venetian cat as it looked at the strange, tall man who was not drunk but who sang out like a drunk across the Venetian waters.

He could have told her of his feelings that first night in Venice but as he had held back in Washington, so he held back now. In Tuscany, in the apple orchard there had been no need to hold anything back for she had held nothing back from him. She was tall and strong; she was a doctor. Yet she had made him feel like a giant whose sole aim in life was to protect her. The telegram, so unexpected as are most of life's blows, had spoiled everything. He had to get back to his father, to his mother who would surely crumble like a building that has lost its foundations should anything happen to Henri Jacques du Pay, 'Senator Hank' as the Southern press called him. They were already publicizing his death when his only son reached Georgia, and his mother, who for years had ruled a huge staff with an iron will, sat crumpled in a chair like a heap of faded flowers and held up a devastated face to her son.

When had he promised to marry Ammabelle? She and her mother had been there in the cool, quiet room with his mother when he arrived. They seemed to have been there every time he turned around since – at the funeral, at the interminable reception afterwards where he had to smile and say all the right things when he wanted to cry like a little boy, on the verandah beside him when he waved goodbye to the last house-guest. His mother said

that he had promised, and that the marriage would
have made his father very happy. The pictures in his
mind of Lucy, shyly smiling at him in the gondola,
devastating in the red dinner gown, naked in the
orchard with apple blossom in her hair and on her
breast, began to fade or at least were superseded
by other more immediate pictures and sounds –
the dull thud of wet mud falling on his father's
coffin, and Ammabelle's soft Southern voice like
dripping honey. He felt tired and listless; he had
no energy. One month since he had left Lucy, two
months, three. Surely she would have written if he
had meant as much to her as she had to him? Surely
she would have expressed regret at the death of his
father? The announcement had to have been in the
British press.

The British press had covered the death of the
eminent Southern politician, but it did not cover
the engagement of his son to Miss Ammabelle
Redmond of Sea Island, Georgia and Philadelphia,
Pennsylvania, nor publicize the society wedding of
the year.

On the morning before his wedding day Max
had left the house at dawn and saddled the tall,
raw-boned horse that was his favourite. He had
ridden until he and the horse were exhausted, and
then he had lain down under a tree and slept. It was
late afternoon when he awakened, and he had sat up
and leaned back against the tree and tried to sort out
his thoughts.

'I am marrying Ammabelle and I love Lucy. This
is crazy. How did it happen? If I told her yes, if I
asked Ammabelle to be my wife, I cannot turn my
back on her. Was I mad with grief? I thought I was
rational. I did everything that had to be done. I talked
to Ammabelle of marriage, at least she talked to me,

but that was before I went to Europe, why I went to Europe, because I could not make up my mind. Or was it just about working for the family? I can't think, I can't think.'

Max beat his fists against the hard ground in frustration and remembered that the last time he had lain on the ground he had lain with Lucy.

'Oh, Lucy, my heart! What have I done?'

His horse stood patiently at his side, reins trailing. He caught them up and vaulted into the saddle, his body and his heart for the first time in months as light as thistledown.

And there on the verandah was his mother, as pale and frail as a moth.

'Oh, Max, my dearest boy,' she whispered in her pale, frail voice. 'I was so worried, you were gone so long. We have to get ready for your bachelor party, my dear.' She clung, light as a burr, to his arm and led him along the verandah to the door of his room. 'Oh, Max, I have always wanted you to marry dear Ammabelle, the daughter of my very dearest friend. You have given me something to live for. Your father would be so proud of you. I wasn't going to tell you this yet, it's a kind of wedding present, but the Party wants you to fill Daddy's place. What a truly good son you have been to me all my life, and especially now in my time of grief. I wanted to die with Daddy, Max, but now you and Ammabelle will fill this sad house with music and laughter again.'

Her hands clung, her voice clung, sweet sweet as honey, till he felt he was drowning. He could not get his head out from under.

18

Dundee 1914–1916

'DON'T BE RIDICULOUS.' Rose was angry but also, and later she would try to analyse why, a little frightened.

She pushed back her chair and stood up. 'I'm going to bed, Kier. Have your coffee here or in the drawing room.'

'But wherever you have it, don't bother me. Is that what you are trying to say, Rose?'

The years had not been so kind to Kier Anderson-Howard as they had been to his wife. He looked his age, although he was fit and healthy and carried no spare weight on his tall, lean frame. Rose was still slim and, to Kier, even more lovely. He had long since forgotten the waif in the too-big dress. No one could possibly recognize Rosie Nesbitt with her rough red hands and the badly bitten fingernails in the delightful creature staring angrily at him from the door.

'You always have to equate everything with sex, don't you, Kier? I would prefer to sleep alone tonight because I have to get up very early tomorrow – Lucy and I have an important consultation at the Infirmary – but I have never denied you and if you must have sex . . .'

'Sex? I might have felt like making love, Rose, but not now. You're quite safe.'

He turned away and reached for the claret jug that still stood, almost full, on the table.

'Perhaps I won't bother with coffee. Good night, Rose. I'll sleep in my dressing room.'

'And you won't do anything silly?'

'As usual you are right, my dear. The British Army wouldn't want such an ancient recruit.'

Rose stood for a moment watching him. She wasn't worried that he would drink too much – no, not Kier. He was as disciplined in his way as she was in hers. Perhaps if he wasn't . . . But at least he was not going to contact old friends at the War Office and ask their help in enlisting. Enlisting? At his age? Blast the Germans! Life was so pleasant, and they were spoiling everything.

The practice had grown. They had even hired a male colleague, and so Lucy had begun to fulfil her dream of taking a further degree at the university. Now the decision as to whether or not she should specialize in surgery was being taken out of her hands. War had been declared and young Doctor Thomson, like too many other young men, was anxious to leave everything for which he had worked so hard, to join the Army. And there too was Kier, Kier who had willingly resigned his commission to take over his estate, aching to 'have a go at the Hun'.

Rose undressed angrily. Men were so stupid! If they were not, if they were as rational and as level-headed as women, there would not be this war that was raging out of control all over Europe. Stupid men with their hearty 'over by Christmas, lads'.

'I can't see it being over until they've all blown one another to bits,' thought Rose, 'and where does that leave me? They wouldn't take him; surely they wouldn't.'

Rose liked being Dr Rose Nesbitt very well. She

admitted too that she liked being Mrs Kier Anderson-Howard very well too. Kier was an attentive, even an adoring husband, although sometimes in the last year or two she had found him looking at her in a questioning way. She knew he was distressed that there had been no children. He did not know that there were no children because Rose was taking great care that there should be none. At the beginning of her marriage she had said, 'In a year or two,' but now, she admitted to herself – and Rose was almost always truthful to herself – that she had no intention of ever having a child. Because she knew more about birth control than probably any other doctor in Britain, it was quite easy for her to adhere to this decision.

'I don't want a child because it would obviously interfere with my career. Kier even complains about having a working wife. If I had a child he would really put his foot down.' She tried not to admit that, even though she was a doctor and had been at countless live births, the thought of having a baby terrified her. She had watched women in labour, women powerless to control what was happening to their own bodies. 'No, no, I must always be in control. I know it's safer now than when my sister died, safer than when my mother was producing rapidly and, in her case, easily, but it's not for me. I'm needed where I am.'

She heard Kier's firm tread as he reached the door of their bedroom and she sighed resignedly and threw down the covers in welcome; she would never deny him. But when the footsteps died away towards his dressing room, she pulled the covers back up and turned over into the pillows. No, he would not change his mind. He had said she would sleep alone and he always kept his word. The sheets were cold. Kier always lay on her side to warm it before he slid

over to his own side. It would have been quite nice
to have had his arms around her. She had not been
home for a week, and before that she had had her
period.

'If he'd just do it and get it over with, I'd call him,'
but of course he wouldn't because for him it wasn't
just sex but love, and he would do his utmost to see
that his wife was pleasured too.

'Damn all men,' thought Mrs Kier Anderson-
Howard, and eventually fell asleep in the cold bed
that could so easily have been warmed.

'I have your anniversary gift at the house, Rose,' Lucy
said next morning as they drove to the hospital in
Lucy's splendid new Bentley.

'Oh, how kind, Lucy,' said Rose. 'After all these
years, you shouldn't have bothered.' But inside she
was realizing why Kier had been just a little difficult
at the weekend. She had forgotten again and this was
the second year in a row. To keep Kier happy she
should have been delivering and receiving unsubtle
hints about gifts, but she found that difficult. Kier
had given her so much in the last seven years that
there was nothing to want, nothing to desire, and
what *he* wanted she could not, would not give.

'Can you and Andy handle surgery tonight, Lucy?
I wanted to surprise Kier by going home for dinner.'
She would do what she could.

It was worth the trouble. He was like a child on
Christmas morning when he came out of the musty
old estate office she never entered and found his
lovely wife sitting in a swirl of yellow silk in her
drawing room.

He stood at the door for a moment, joy leaping in
his eyes. 'Rose, my dear. I hardly hoped . . .'

She stood up gracefully and walked towards him.

'Silly, did you think I would miss our anniversary?'

'Surgery?'

'Lucy and Andy will manage.' She said it lightly, as if he was much more important than the evening consultations. 'Lucy has sent us a gift. You can open it after dinner and come in with me tomorrow, if you're not too busy, to thank her.'

'Tomorrow?'

'I must catch an early train, but I couldn't not be with you on our sixth wedding anniversary.'

'Seventh, darling.'

Rose coloured delicately and raised her lovely face to his. 'Sixth, seventh? I can't remember life before you, you silly old thing. Don't you realize that?'

And it was true, of course. She had become both Rose Nesbitt, M.D., and Mrs Kier Anderson-Howard within the same three months and she had had no time to think of the hard years of struggle before then. If a photograph had existed of Rosie Nesbitt, she would not have recognized her; she would not have *wanted* to recognize her. Sometimes, in the mean bedroom of a simple house, she would find memories tugging. She would look at a wee girl in a patched frock sitting by the side of her mother as the woman struggled for the seventh, eighth, ninth time to bring new life into the world, and she would remember Rosie, more often Elsie, and double, if possible, her attempts to ease and help. Her work done, she would return to her spacious modern flat. She would have a hot bath in her beautifully appointed bathroom; she would make herself some tea and some toast; she would remember Kier and his constant worries over her health, and she would boil an egg, and then she would sit and in the peace and quiet of her home, gather strength again for the next day. Life was good.

There were the odd niggles. Kier's mother had

never really wanted her as a daughter-in-law. She was unfailingly polite, but she had wanted Lucy, poor Lucy who obviously still loved Kier. Clever Lucy, she managed to treat him like a favourite brother but, poor thing, she had made no attempt to find anyone else. The servants, too, made Rose uneasy. They were never insolent, for then Kier would have dismissed them, but there was a certain something, too many . . . 'Mister Kier said . . .' She was 'madam', very rarely even 'Mrs Anderson-Howard'. Kier's mother, in her lovely town house in St Andrews, was Mrs Anderson-Howard. No, this was where she belonged, in this lovely renovated flat, and alone. She was happier alone. She was so tired after a day and sometimes an evening of medicine.

'You're not strong enough for the life of a doctor, Rose.' That was Kier. 'No woman is . . . well, there are exceptions, like Lucy. She's physically strong. But you're such a delicate little woman.'

Remarks like that brought back memories too, memories of running from the Hilltown to the Harris, a fresh bap in her hand, another in her bag for dinner.

'Of course I'm strong, much stronger than I look. I've never been sick a day in my life.'

Andy Thomson enlisted: silly young fool. There was no need for him to enlist; as a doctor he would have been quite safe.

'We'll have a place for you when you get back, Andy,' said Lucy. 'We'll even be thinking of a partnership, won't we, Rose?'

Rose smiled at the joy in the boy's eyes. Yes, he had good reasons for coming back: a partnership, and a young teacher at the High School who was no doubt promising to write.

*   *   *

'You didn't tell me Andy had enlisted. I met Lucy for lunch this morning when I was in town and she told me.'

Rose had not expected to find her husband in her flat when she returned home from the hospital. She liked to keep the flat as a sanctuary, just for herself. 'I didn't think it very important,' she said lightly.

'Rose? Your junior decides to go to war and you don't think that important?'

'Of course it's important, but we don't see one another every day and it wasn't . . . vital. I mean he hasn't gone yet. For heaven's sake, Kier, did you come here to fight? I would have told you when I remembered.'

He came over and put his arms around her. 'I'm sorry, darling.' He kissed her gently, tenderly, softly, until she relaxed against him. 'Do you mind if I stay? I miss you.'

'You own this flat.' Her voice was calm but there was no excited welcome.

He moved away from her. 'Rose, I bought the flat for you. The deeds are in your name.'

She went after him, put her hand on his arm. 'Did you have a decent lunch with Lucy? I have eggs and perhaps some cheese . . .'

His face lit up. He was so sweet, so like a child. 'You can't cook, can you? I thought we might go out.'

'I can't cook, darling, but I can scramble eggs. We could have a light supper here, just the two of us.'

He followed her into the tiny kitchen. 'I have never seen anyone cook anything in my entire life, you clever little thing. Nanny used to make cocoa. My mother doesn't know where the kitchen is.'

Rose tied a sensible apron around her trim waist. 'I'm quite sure she does. Mrs Potter is for ever telling me how much better the real Mrs Anderson-Howard does things.'

He looked ill at ease. 'Old family retainers are . . . difficult, but one word from you and they go, my darling, every one, lock, stock and barrel.'

Rose laughed and handed him a bowl. 'Here, take your vehemence out on these eggs.' She took another apron from the drawer and tied it around his waist. 'Now, aren't we the domesticated old married couple? I understand Mrs Potter. Don't worry. It's difficult for them, I know.'

'Perhaps Mother should have taken the old ones with her to St Andrews. It's just that Laverock Rising is their home.'

'I understand.'

He put down the bowl. 'Lucy, let's go to bed. If you had a baby, if you stayed at home all day, things would be different.'

She turned off the gas burner and went with him. What could she say? 'Even if I did have a baby I would still want to work. I couldn't give up medicine, I couldn't.'

Later, as Kier slept, she poured the beaten eggs into the sink and washed up the dishes. She did everything else she had to do too; there would be no baby. In the bedroom she looked down at her husband. Curious how young and vulnerable he looked while he slept. She felt a rush of almost maternal warmth as she bent down and kissed him lightly, and he smiled and stirred in his sleep.

Andy Thomson went off to the Front, but to his dismay – and much to Lucy's joy – his Front was a hospital near London. Lucy bought him a copy of a book that had just been privately printed and which was setting the literary world afire, James Joyce's

Dubliners, and sent it off in a box with shortbread –
Rose never used her sugar ration and had willingly
handed over a supply for Christmas baking – and
some of Isa's best oatcakes.

The year 1915 started badly with Clydeside arma-
ment workers striking for more pay, and got steadily
worse. In May a train crash at Gretna Green in the
south of Scotland killed 158 people, many of them
soldiers. In July, 200,000 miners in Wales went on
strike, and on December 30th a U-boat sank the liner
Persia with a loss of 400 lives.

In October, the Germans had executed the nurse
Edith Cavell, and not only Kier but Rose herself
began to mutter about 'helping put an end to all this
madness'.

Lucy remained calm and sensible.

'How could they shoot a nurse, Lucy, someone
who was there to help?' Kier Anderson-Howard was
a decent man who could not understand or accept
unreasoning, ferocious brutality.

'To them she was not a nurse; she was merely
someone who broke martial law. It was a particularly
stupid thing to do because they have created a lovely
young martyr for the Allies.'

'Will her death help to end this abominable war?'

'Would yours, Kier? Miss Cavell did what she did
because she knew that, for her, it was the only way
to behave. You have a huge estate to run, an estate
that feeds hundreds. That is viable war work.'

'My grieve can run the farms, Lucy. I am a crack
shot and a trained soldier; perhaps I would be better
employed in the Army in some capacity.'

In the end Kier and Rose decided to turn Laverock
Rising over to the Ministry of Defence for use as a
convalescent home, and Kier moved permanently
into the small flat in Dundee. Their marriage had

been shaky for some time, but while they had maintained the custom of Rose working in town all week and going over to Fife at the weekend, the cracks had not grown or even, to the unobservant, been particularly visible.

'Sometimes I wish he would join the Army,' Rose confessed in exasperation to Lucy one day as they found a few moments to sit and enjoy the soup that Isa had made for them.

'Good gracious, Rose! You can't mean that; he's too old to start all over again.'

Rose sighed. 'Of course I don't really mean it but, Lucy, I can't breathe in the flat with Kier there. He's so big and when I come home at night, he wants me to sit with him, talk to him, listen to music. I want to be alone, to unwind, to rewind. I usually eat a boiled egg, have a bath and go to bed. Kier wants Mrs Kier Anderson-Howard at his beck and call. And that dratted woman is driving me mad.'

Lucy hesitated. She had worried about the marriage for a long time. She had watched Kier change from being the sunniest of men to one who was withdrawn and even moody. He was her oldest friend, but her partner was his wife and she could not take sides.

'It must be difficult with Mrs Potter in such a tiny flat.'

'I seem to be the only one making adjustments. They invade my home . . .' She stopped as if she was aware how odd that must sound. 'I mean, it's the huge meals, every night, dressing for dinner . . . Mrs Potter didn't even pass on a message last week. "Madam is at dinner", says she. I was so angry I could hardly speak.'

'Yes, that was unforgivable, but understandable. Why don't you buy a bigger house?'

'I suggested that but Kier says that it would be wrong. Surely you must have noticed how diffident he is about having so much money, and to spend hundreds of pounds on a new house when people are starving all over Europe . . .'

Lucy could see his point, but she could see Rose's position too. A pity that they had got into the habit of being part-time man and wife.

'Be patient, Rose. Kier will change his mind if he sees how difficult such cramped living is for you.'

But by their eighth wedding anniversary Mr and Mrs Kier Anderson-Howard were barely speaking to one another, and Rose was finding more and more work to do and more and more reasons to stay overnight in the quarters made available to her in the hospital.

19

Dundee 1915–1916

AN OUTRAGED ISA was at the door to meet her. Lucy registered the fact that she was still wearing the old dressing gown that she had first worn all those years ago, that she had even taken to Venice, that had gone to Tuscany. Tuscany . . .

'My God, Isa is old, old and tired.'

'It's Mr Kier; he insists on seeing you. I told him you were out at a confinement and would need your sleep as soon as you got home, but will he listen? And' – and Isa was outraged – 'he's been . . . drinking and he . . .'

'Go to bed, Isa, dear. I'll speak to Mr Kier.'

'I'll go when I've given you your supper and watched you eat it, and not a minute before.'

'Where's your new dressing gown?' asked Lucy, knowing the answer but vainly trying to deflect the old woman's ire.

'Oh, that's far too good for the house. It's for the hospital when my time comes. I'll not have you ashamed of me.' She turned towards the door. 'He's in the morning room and I redded up the fire. If he's not too drunk, he'll have put a log on.'

The firelight danced around the little room as years ago the sunlight had danced through the window, turning Rose into a fairy-tale creature. Now it showed Rose's husband lying in her father's chair by the fire, his long legs stretched out before him. He looked young and vulnerable, fourteen again.

'Oh, dear God, what happened to us?' her heart cried.

She shook him. 'Kier, wake up.'

He groaned and stirred and then opened his eyes and he no longer looked a child. He was a man, a sad unhappy man who, for once in his adult life, had had too much to drink. He stumbled to his feet.

'Lucy, forgive me, what a time to be calling, but I had to tell you. You had to know first.'

Lucy turned up the gas-light and he turned away from her. She went to him. 'What is it, Kier?' She grasped his arm. 'Turn around and face me, man. I've seen and heard worse than you can ever tell me.' She felt a sudden fear. 'Is Rose all right?'

He laughed, a singularly unpleasant sound. 'All right? Rose is always all right.' He was quiet for a moment as he leaned on the black marble mantelpiece and then had to push himself up from it. He obeyed the urging of her arm and turned to face her. 'I raped her, Lucy, raped my own wife, but that's not what I've come to tell you.'

'Your tea, Doctor, and there's coffee for him.'

How much had Isa heard? Her face registered nothing.

'Put it on the table, Isa, and go to bed.' Lucy spoke sharply, more sharply than she had intended, and the old woman walked stiffly from the room.

'I'll worry about her hurt feelings tomorrow,' thought Lucy as she handed Kier a cup of scalding coffee.

'I'm not drunk, Lucy.'

'I know. Sit down and tell me what it is.'

He stopped, the cup poised near his face. The steam hid his eyes. 'I've enlisted in the Black Watch,' he said simply. 'I'm off tomorrow, today. It wasn't over by Christmas, was it?'

Whatever she had expected, it was not this. 'But you're a married man, and you're far too old.'

How like a man: his vanity was offended. 'Good heavens, Lucy. I'm fitter than half these boys they're taking.' He sipped his coffee and smiled at her, the old charming smile that made her heart turn over. 'It's who you know in this insane world.'

Still she said nothing.

'Rose doesn't need me; she's never needed me. You would have given her a job so that she would never have had to emigrate.' So he knew he had been used then, but he was not angry, unless he had worked off his anger. What had he done to Rose? He put the cup down and stood up, his tall, slim frame filling the small room. 'Poor little Rose. We can't realy understand what it was like for her, growing up in poverty. She did, you know. She thought she had hidden it but there was a sister, a half-sister; she got in touch with me and I made her an allowance until she died. I don't blame Rose for being hard. She only wanted to better the conditions of her class, and you can't blame her for that. You'll be kind to her, Lucy, won't you, if anything happens to me? She'll inherit, of course, probably turn it into a children's home after the war. Not a bad idea. I wanted children. So did Rose. If she'd had an easier life, maybe . . . That's all by the by.' He turned away from her. 'I said some hard things and I . . . well, I'm not too pleased with myself. Always felt deep down that Rose didn't really love me. Maybe, when this mess is over, maybe if tonight has cleared the air a bit, we can start again. You will look after her for me? She's not like us, Lucy, not . . . secure . . . yes, that's the word, secure. Every child should be given security. If I'd had a child, I'd have made her feel secure.'

What could she say? To her dismay she found that tears were rolling down her cheeks. A knight in shining armour should not go to war with his heart broken. It unarmed him.

'Oh, what have you done, Kier? Whatever has happened between you and Rose, surely you don't have to run away like this? Go back home and talk to her.'

'I've talked, Lucy. Perhaps too much. I don't want to see Rose again; I can't see her again, not for a while. If there's anything for me to forgive, I forgive her and I hope she'll forgive me for tonight.' He stretched out his hand and imprisoned a tear on the end of a finger. 'She said I'd always loved you, you see,' he said gently, 'and that I'd been unfair to her too. I suppose she's right.' He moved to the door, leaving her standing there with tears streaming unchecked down her face. 'Make it better, Doctor,' he said, and then he was gone and the door had closed behind him, and a moment later she heard the sound of the front door being shut.

Lucy stood there for some time looking at the door. The fire had died down and the room was growing colder, and she began to tremble, but whether from cold or from shock the doctor could not tell. Like an old woman she turned to the fire and put up the guard, not that the few embers in the grate could cause any damage. She turned off the lamps and went softly out, closing the door behind her. Methodically she locked and bolted the front door and then she went upstairs, leaving the hall lights hissing gently on. Isa found them still lit in the morning, sighed for the sinful waste, and said nothing.

Lucy had not slept; she had not even undressed.

She had no energy. It all seemed to have gone with Kier. All night she sat by the window watching countless ghostly phantoms passing in the snowy lamplight below her. Kier at fourteen, ill and fretful; at fifteen, scoffing at her lack of education; at nineteen, telling her for the first time that he loved her. Later, telling her that he was going to marry Rose. She saw Rose too. Rose, at the garden party in the ridiculous dress which had made her look so helpless and vulnerable; Rose, the secret smile of triumph when they had announced their engagement, the look – was it of chagrin? – when she had offered her a post. She saw her, a vision in her wedding dress, and then the older, sophisticated, harder Rose.

Kier said he had raped his wife. He could not have hurt her, not Kier, surely? Rose did not need medical attention, and if she did the last doctor she would want to see would be Dr Lucille Graham. Because she was so tired, Lucy allowed Max to walk out there in the snow, and at the thought of him she cried out in pleasant pain.

'Oh, Max, my love, my love. Everything has gone wrong, for me, for Kier, for Rose . . . for you? But we were right, Rose and I, we were right to fight for our place in the world. We have made a difference to countless others, haven't we, Max? Butterflies in December. Did I ever tell you that my father called me that? No. I told you so little and oh, dear God, what am I supposed to say to Rose in the morning?

Rose herself forestalled everything. She arrived at the office on time and looking just as lovely and untouched as ever. It must all have been a dream; this ethereal creature had never been raped in the early hours of the morning, by her own husband.

She had not lain awake seeing the ghosts of the past, the frightening visions of a desolate future.

'I'd better tell you, Lucy, because you'll have to know sooner or later,' she said, her beautiful soft leather bag held almost defensively in her gloved hands. 'Kier is being absolutely silly; he met some old chum from Sandhurst at a party and the bloody fool has enlisted . . . gone . . . "having a go", he says.' She half turned from Lucy as if she did not really wish to look directly into her eyes and laughed, a bitter unnatural little laugh. 'I'm sure the War Office will send him home with a telling-off about food supplies and being there for our women and children, but . . .' and for a moment her schooled face was bleak '. . . in the meantime he's playing soldier. Black Watch. If he hasn't scuttled home by the weekend . . .' She stopped. 'I'm off. I have a million calls to make.'

She was gone. Lucy sat looking at the door for some time.

'Are you having a surgery or are you not this morning, Doctor? There are children with snotty noses and dirty shoes in my front room.' Isa could always be depended upon.

'Send in my first patient, Isa.'

The morning wore on, and the afternoon, and three weeks, and still Kier had not returned. Had he been accepted? Rose said nothing and Lucy dared not ask. If he had been dismissed would he tell them, tell his wife?

'They've reinstated him and promoted him.' Rose was paler than usual, and was she even thinner? She looked drained, tired. She must, thought Lucy, be under enormous strain. 'Nearly all the young officers are dead. Hardly worth having a child, is it, to watch them grow and see them go off to be blown to bits? Do you think the bullets will know that

Major Anderson-Howard was decorated in the Boer War and is therefore too senior to be obliterated?'

'Sit down, Rose, and I'll have Isa bring us some coffee.'

'No coffee, Lucy. I can't face it these days.' She stopped and for a moment Lucy felt that she was about to say something real, something important. 'It's all such a mess, isn't it?' was all she said, and then she turned and began to walk into her own office.

Lucy jumped up and followed her. 'Rose, please. Where is he? When did you hear? Is he well?' She stopped, angry at her show of emotion. She saw too that Rose had misinterpreted her interest.

Rose laughed, an ugly laugh. 'So we're both spurned, neglected women, are we, Lucy? I was almost sure I'd find him here that morning, you know. I thought he would run to you to tell you what a bad wife I'd been.'

'He came . . . to say goodbye. Never, *ever* has he said one word against you. He was always your champion, Rose.'

'My champion? I never needed a champion. Was he rescuing me? From what? What conceited arrogance, Doctor Graham. I may not have had your advantages growing up, but I certainly needed no knight in shining armour to rescue me from the gutter.' She threw off Lucy's restraining hand. 'I have patients to see. We'll discuss this intolerable situation later.'

20

Dundee 1916

DECISIONS THAT CHANGED one's life were often easy to make in the lonely dark stretches of the night. In the morning the spring sunshine was calling all tired, old, even dead things back to life. The blossoms on Dundee's ethereally beautiful cherry trees seemed to hang dazzled in the air as Rose walked the few streets to Lucy's offices. They called to her highly charged mind, assaulted her quivering senses.

'I'll think about it,' Rose found herself saying. 'My God, I'm having a conversation with a tree. Is this what being pregnant does to you?' But she was almost happy as she reached Shore Terrace and the new day of satisfying work that lay ahead of her.

Lucy did not ask about Kier and Rose found that odd.

'She should ask if I've heard from him. Wouldn't it be normal for an old friend to ask, for my partner to ask about my husband? Unless she has had a letter.'

'I have an address for Kier if you would like to have it,' she said brusquely. 'I heard yesterday.'

Lucy looked up from her desk and, for the first time, Rose was aware of the dark shadows under her eyes, of the fact that Lucy, always slim, was even thinner.

'Oh, I'm so glad, Rose. Is he well? Did he say where he is?'

Rose answered the second question; she did not

know the answer to the first. 'No, and the address doesn't tell anything but I'll give it to you.' She turned to leave the office and then stopped. 'He hasn't written to you, then? Dreadful correspondents, men.'

When the door closed behind her Lucy sighed with relief. 'Dreadful correspondents? Men? Kier?' She thought of all the letters she had received over the years. 'Poor Rose. Poor Kier, but at least he has written. They will work this dreadful thing out. I hope he's not in France. Surely to God, he's too old to be sent to France.'

The telegram waited all day for Rose to return. Mrs Potter put it down on a silver tray and carried it into the drawing room at Laverock Rising. The room was soft and mellow in the warm summer sunshine. As she put the tray down beside a crystal bowl of Rose's favourite yellow roses, she did not notice the teardrop that beaded on the polished wood beside it.

'Thank God she'll find out here. Thank God! Poor lassie.'

Rose waited for the train. She was anxious to get to Fife for the weekend and she desperately needed to loosen her corsets. 'What a fool I am, what an utter fool! I can't go on like this much longer.'

At last she was able to sit down in the first-class carriage and she relaxed. Soon she would be at Leuchars. Someone would be there with the car. She must learn to drive. 'I was right to ask for the use of a flat,' Rose smiled. At Laverock Rising she had come to terms with what had happened to her. She had drifted, like the cherry blossom, until the decision was taken out of her hand. Was it that or a gut feeling that abortion was wrong, that she, who strove so hard to maintain life, should be the last person in the world to end it? Or was it merely a bargaining tool in her battle with Kier? Whatever it was, she was now six months pregnant. 'Why can't I bring myself to tell Lucy? I can't hide it any longer. How have I hidden it from her? Surely she suspects; some doctor!' Rose smiled. Lucy preferred bones to babies. 'Half my patients are making cosy remarks. If I don't get this bloody corset off I won't have to tell her, I'll abort anyway.' And suddenly, suddenly Rose felt cold and very frightened. She put her hands for the first time protectively over her stomach where tight corsets and the fashion of the day had allowed her to conceal the fact that she was most definitely pregnant.

'I'll admit you're there on Monday, little person. I'll need your Aunt Lucy. I certainly don't want your grandmother around.' The relationship with Kier's mother, never good, was now non-existent.

She was home. Laverock Rising. Everything would be all right.

'This came this morning, madam.'

Rose stood still. She did not turn but slowly eased her kid gloves off her long slim fingers, as always having difficulty sliding the material over the huge diamond Kier had given her on their engagement. She knew. She had had that cold feeling in the train. Or was it the housekeeper's tone, the voice low and almost breaking? She laid the gloves down on the polished rosewood table. Ma would have admired that table. The right glove, then the left glove. Turning, she saw the small buff envelope and stretched out a hand that would not be allowed to tremble.

'Thank you, Mrs Potter. That will be all.'

She did not notice that, for the first time ever,

Mrs Potter bobbed a slight curtsey before she withdrew.

How long did letters take to get to the Front, for that was where he had been, some damned place in France. This would be so much easier to bear if she could be certain that he had had the letter, that he had known.

Kier looked through the smoke. What was it? Mars, Flaming God of War. It was not Mars. Surely a God, if there was a God, would be a noble being. If He brought death and destruction, would there not be some beauty in that death, some justice at least?

It was a dragon. He could see it, them. Sweet Jesus, there was more than one. He could see them advancing towards the trench where he stood. He could hear them. Yes, that was the sound he had made all those years ago when he had played St George and the Dragon. Lucy had been better though. Darling Lucy, she had been better at everything. He smiled. Did she know? How happy she would be for him.

Someone was pulling him; voices were screaming at him. He was so tired of noise, interminable noise.

'Bird-song,' he said quite seriously. 'Bird-song is the best sound. I used to think it was the sound of a violin, properly played of course, or a tenor. Yes, a tenor: Caruso. The most beautiful sound in the world.'

'Christ, Major. Them's flame-throwers. The bloody krauts are going to incinerate what they haven't blown to bits.'

Kier looked again. He echoed the soldier. 'Christ,' he said.

He could feel the heat.

'Run,' he yelled. 'Run!'

He shook off the hands and climbed out of the

trench. Which way, which way? Any way but forward. That's where the dragons were making their
slow, deadly and inexorable progress. 'And more
inexorable far, Than empty tigers or the roaring sea.'
Shakespeare; he was quoting Shakespeare. Was it
because part of his mind refused to believe what
his eyes were telling him, that this could not be
happening?

'Major?'

He came to himself, sensible, articulate, trained.

'That way, lads. Run.' He looked around. Easy
enough to find a weapon later if they escaped. The
ground was littered with the debris of the dead.
'Throw away everything that will hold you back.'

A man went up beside him like a bonfire at
Hallowe'en. The screams threatened sanity. No time
to think, to plan. The terrified soldiers ran tossing
rifles, even masks, aside in their mad need to get
away from the advancing horror. The mud grabbed
at their feet, clung to them like a lover, loth to release
them. They slipped, stumbled, fell and, sobbing
desperately for their wives, their mothers, they tried
either to rise or to bury themselves under the mud,
to do anything that would help.

Kier fell and a rat popped up from the mud in
which he lay. He could see its little eyes, terrified,
insane. 'Just like mine,' he thought as the most
excruciating pain enveloped his entire body.

'No, please,' he said and his prayer was answered.
His agony, everything, was blotted out . . .

It was impossible that anyone could be left alive.
Kier regained consciousness to find himself lying
against the wall of the trench into which he had
fallen. Gradually he became aware of silence. When
had the pounding stopped, that relentless pounding
that had gone on and on, and roared around in his

brain until he could do nothing but beg for a respite, beg even for death in order to escape it?

'Am I dead too?'

The air was full of smoke from the flame-throwers but no gas: they hadn't used gas this time. Kier straightened up slowly and that's when the pain started, pain that made him cry out. The sound startled him.

'I'm not dead if I can feel pain,' he said.

'Help me . . . somebody help me.'

There was someone else. Thank God, thank God, he was not alone.

Kier tried desperately to focus his eyes. The voice came again.

'Who's there? Is that you, Joe? Major, is that you?'

He should answer; he was the Major. He knew that, but his tongue refused to obey the commands his brain was sending. The voice stopped and the moaning started.

'I'm here,' he said desperately, but no sound came. He was confused. There was the pain that clawed at him, and the groaning of dying men that was almost as hard to bear as the pain. But from somewhere there was the scent of violets. Who wore violets? Lucy? No, no, it was Rose.

'Rose?' he said but the sound of her name, the smell of her flowers, they were in his head. He tried to smile. 'Rose,' he said it again and this time he could see her. He was in the nursery at Laverock Rising; he was with Rose. The pain ebbed away. There was no moaning, no sound but the sweet Scottish voice.

'Kier,' she said, so clearly that he lifted his head to smile into her lovely, smiling, happy, eyes. 'Kier,' she said again and held out her hands to him.

The officer found them . . . at least he thought that

the blackened remains had once been men. He looked and he retched.

'In the name of the Father,' he began, 'and of the Son, and of . . .' But the prayers refused to come. He tried again. 'Into Thy hands, oh Lord.' The tears were running unchecked down his cheeks.

'Lieutenant? Are you all right?' The boy soldier was very young.

The officer looked at him, at his frightened young face.

'How will the world remember us?' he asked. 'Will they think of Germany and say Goethe, will they say Wagner? Will they say Beethoven . . . or will they say . . . savages?' He looked down at his feet. 'Rest in peace,' he said softly. 'I pray that I could.'

Dr Rose Nesbitt, Mrs Kier Anderson-Howard, widow, was extremely drunk. She was still sober enough to know that she was drunk and she was very ashamed of herself. She had ordered a bottle of Kier's best claret to be sent up from the cellar just because she felt that old Baxter did not really want her to have it. It belonged to Kier, to the master, the laird, and now that he was dead it was to be kept inviolate. Rose had always known that the staff did not like her. She thought it was because they could strip away the veneer of expensive clothes and see the frightened slum lassie underneath.

'Why couldn't they accept me?' she raged. 'I never pretended to be anything other than what I am. I'm proud of my fight out of the gutter.'

Then she remembered all the people who had helped her struggle, especially Frazer and Ma, and she cried maudlin drunken tears.

'Ma would have understood why I would never have introduced her to Kier. I didn't know a thing about my husband. I was never really interested. He was Lucy's, and I took him away from her and made him miserable and I didn't even need to do it. Oh, Lucy, why didn't you ask me to work for you when I first qualified? Why did I have to go through all those applications? Why did I have to threaten to go to Africa? I could have had a practice and you could have had Kier. No, not Lucy's fault. Rosie's. Rosie uses people. She used Frazer and old Wishy and Ma . . . and Lucy and Kier. But I'm being punished now. Oh, God, I'm being punished.'

Rose lurched across the room and violently closed the curtains. Kier's gardens were so beautiful. She did not want to see them

When had she ordered a second bottle? When had she drunk it? She staggered across the room to find the door. When she had negotiated the beautiful oak staircase she found her bedroom, their bedroom, and fell across the bed. Rose slept.

It was dark when she woke up and she was glad. She never wanted to see sunlight again. She would stay in the bedroom for ever and she would draw the curtains to make sure the light stayed out.

Rose moaned as she tried to rise from the bed. Her head was aching and swimming and her stomach . . . she barely managed to reach the bathroom.

When the retching was over she was unable to rise from the floor and lay for some time beside the lavatory. At last the top of her head seemed to have settled itself where it belonged, and she managed to push herself up by holding on to the lavatory and then the hand-basin. She did not recognize the ravaged face that stared back at her with frightened eyes from the mirror.

She splashed cold water on her face and into her mouth and then managed to undress by pulling at

the buttons so skilfully and expensively sewn down
the front. She managed to get back to the bed and
this time to throw off the counterpane and to crawl
tremblingly under the blankets. Rose slept, but the
nightmare was still with her when she woke up.

'Doctor Graham sent a messenger to see how you
are, Mrs Anderson-Howard.' Mrs Potter came in
answer to her bell. 'Baxter told him to say that you
would prefer to be alone, that we would take care
of you.'

'I'd like some tea, please, Mrs Potter.'

'I'll fetch something else as you'll be the better for
it. First we'll get you into a nice fresh nightie.'

Rose tried to protest but found herself, for the first
time in her life, being undressed and tidied up.

'There, doesn't that feel better? I'll be back with
your tea.'

Rose barely had time to realize how much better she felt before her housekeeper returned with
a tray of tea and a bowl of a strangely-smelling
brown liquid.

'It's just a bit of bread and a little Worcester sauce.
I know, smells awful when you're hung over but it'll
cure you. Come on, eat up.'

With a barely suppressed shudder, Rosie put a
morsel of the foul-smelling mess into her mouth.

'There, now. Doesn't that feel better?' Mrs Potter
spoke as if Rose was a child. Was that how she dealt
with her own grief, looking after Kier's . . . widow?
'Here,' her voice was motherly, almost loving, 'have
a nice hot cup of tea. Then you can sleep again and
you'll feel better in the morning.'

But in the morning Kier was still dead and nothing
would make her feel better. How could she feel
better when he would never feel again? He lay dead
somewhere in the mud of a river called the Somme.

They had strolled near there on their honeymoon. The banks of the river had been ablaze with wild flowers; the sky had been reflected with the flowers in the clear water. Kier had pulled her down among the flowers and . . . 'Oh, God, don't let it be the same place. They don't even know, they can't even tell me . . . his mother will never get over this, ever. There's no body, nothing. "The officers made a pact to lie with their men." Was that supposed to make me feel better? Would it make his mother feel better? Would this? I should tell her. Had he known? Was he pleased? Oh, please God, please let him have known.'

She took two days to recover from what Lucy called 'grieving' and Rose knew was merely a hang-over. She returned to the offices on Shore Terrace to find Lucy looking almost worse than she did herself. She had had the extra burden of her own real grief and Rose's patients but, as usual, she angered Rose by being solicitous.

'You shouldn't have come back, Rose. People won't expect you to carry on like this.'

'I want to come back, Lucy.' Rose reached for the file with the names of the patients she was to see that day. 'I need to be back. I'm sorry that you've had extra work.'

'I was happy to do it. It's understandable. You should have taken some time as soon as you heard the news. I feel that perhaps you still need time. Two days . . .'

'For God's sake, Lucy. You always have to see the best in people, don't you? I had a hangover, a simple hangover because I drank too much. I wasn't weeping a widow's tears.'

'We all grieve in our own . . .'

'Oh, no platitudes, Doctor, please. Have you grieved yet? For my husband, your lover?' She hadn't meant to say that, she knew Lucy and Kier had never been lovers. But Lucy had loved him and, oh yes, Kier had really loved Lucy.

'Poor Rose,' said Lucy. 'Poor Kier,' she whispered. 'We were never lovers, Rose. I loved Kier and once, a long long time ago, I thought I was in love with him too, but I wasn't, Rose, and he was never *in love* with me. He loved you, or he would have if you had let him.'

'Oh, excuse me. Now you're the great psychiatrist too. Well, I did let him love me,' said Rose, deliberately misunderstanding the sense of what Lucy was saying, 'so much so that I'm going to have his child.'

There, she had said it. The words hung in the air between them as they stared at one another. Lucy recovered first.

'Oh, Rose, that's wonderful; that's the best of all good news.' She started up from her chair, her hands outstretched.

Rose ignored the gesture and leafed through her file. 'Is it?' She had not meant to be so blunt, so unnecessarily cruel. What devil got into her sometimes? 'I'm glad you're pleased, Lucy. I hope Kier's mother will be . . .'

Lucy stared at her incredulously. 'You haven't told her . . . but this will . . .'

'Make her accept me . . .'

'Make it easier to bear, Rose.'

'I have ambivalent feelings, Lucy. I almost aborted, you know. A baby, the result of . . . Then, I thought, it might help . . . but that's hardly fair to the baby. Let's just say that I left it too long and now it's too late. A child has no real place in my life, my career. How can I go on with my work with a child? Every day I see or hear of more people who need us. I shall have this child . . . but as soon as I am physically able, I shall be back at work.'

She left the room and went to her own office, calling to their receptionist on the way.

As usual the morning passed so quickly that she had no time to think of anything but the needs of others. At lunchtime she found herself walking smartly along the High Street to Draffens where she bought a coat. It was a lovely coat, soft blue wool beautifully cut into a body-skimming line; it was not a widow's coat.

'Would madam like to try it?' asked the puzzled assistant.

'No, thank you. Wrap it, please. I'll take it with me.'

Outside in the street she waited patiently in the line for the tram and, carrying her parcel, made her way to the Hilltown.

She stood in the street outside the closie where Ma and Frazer and Lindsay and Murray and the others had all lived. People looked at her strangely – she was so very well dressed – but passed on. She held on to the coat, Ma's coat, a much better one than the coat Frazer had bought . . . oh, so many years ago. But Ma was dead, dead from too much work and too little food and from damp and, oh yes, from her way of life, but most especially from despair.

A woman approached her. 'Can I help ye, missus?' The voice was quiet and solicitous; obviously the speaker wanted only to help.

Even in the depths of despair Rose recognized the qualities in the voice. 'Typical Dundee,' she thought. 'Why have I abandoned my own people for so long?' She looked at the stranger with a doctor's eyes. 'Yes,' she said. 'Yes, you can help me, you can accept this coat.' The woman looked at her warily. 'I bought it for someone who lived up that closie – Elsie Nesbitt, but she's been dead for years.'

'Elsie?' The woman's face was an artist's study of joy, but still she did not hold out her hands to receive the parcel. 'Hell, I kent Elsie fine. Grand woman. One o' her bairns took to the doctoring, would you believe? There was a big joke wi' Elsie. All her bairns was cried efter the faither, Frazer, Lindsay . . . except for that wan. She was Rose. Never kent why. Maybe Elsie liked roses.'

'Perhaps,' said Rose. 'Will you take this?'

The woman took the parcel. It would probably never be worn by her; it might change hands in a pub up the Hilltown or be sold in a pawnshop – there were plenty of them on the very street where they stood – but that didn't matter. Somehow a little of the debt was paid, but there was still so much to pay and the safe birth of this baby was the first step.

'You had better be a boy,' said Rose as she hailed a cab.

Frazer Lucille Anderson-Howard was born in her godmother's private room at the Dundee Royal Infirmary.

'It's a beautiful name for a beautiful baby,' sighed Lucy as she gazed in rapture at the perfection of the tiny hands. 'Frazer?' She dared not ask, but allowed her voice to rise a little.

Rose lay back against the white pillows. She had been surprised at the powerful feelings that had surged through her when the tiny scrap was put into her arms. Never demonstrative, she had felt an almost uncontrollable desire to cover the tiny face with kisses; almost, but not quite.

'Kier would have wanted a boy,' she said.

Lucy wanted to protest, to say that Kier would

have been delighted with his daughter, but she said nothing.

'Not Frazer,' said Rose.

'Not Lucille, but something nice, a good name to grow up with.'

'Frazer Lucille, on papers, but I'm going to call her . . . Robin.'

Lucy looked down at her face. 'Welcome, Robin,' she said and she held out her hand and touched the tiny infant. To her delight, Miss Anderson-Howard gripped the finger held out to her and, though she did not know it, in that spontaneous action she had forged a bond with Lucy that nothing would ever break.

Rose laughed. 'You look positively maternal, Lucy. You should have had her, not me.'

Lucy's thoughts went back to the awful panic of the days following her Italian holiday. A baby. Max's baby. Kier's baby.

'I would have liked to have had a child,' she admitted. 'I can only hope you will let me share your daughter a little.'

'You may share with pleasure, Godmama, you and her besotted grandmother.' She hesitated, just a fraction. 'I have already engaged a competent nursemaid . . . They'll stay in the flat at Laverock Rising. Kier's mother will be there constantly and we . . . well, there are weekends.'

'Oh, Rose,' Lucy began to protest and then thought better of it. She had no right to tell Rose how to bring up her own child. 'You won't be able to give her up to a nanny, Rose.'

But Rose *was* able. Within the month she was back in her consulting rooms and her daughter was safely ensconced in the light, airy nursery where her father had spent his infancy and where the young Kier

and the young Lucy had forged their friendship.
Lucy asked as often as she dared about the baby's
progress.

'You must visit her for yourself, Lucy. She is, after
all, your god-daughter.'

And so began the Sunday afternoons, the times
that were to become for Lucy the highlight of her
busy week. She took the train from Dundee to
Leuchars where Rose's smart new car met her to
take her to the house. She lunched with Rose in the
dining room where she had so often sat with Kier
and his parents and then Miss Robin was brought
down, starched and laced, to see her adoring public.
It did not seem to Lucy that Rose adored the baby –
she rather laughed at Lucy's infatuation – but Lucy
was content to admire the child and to talk to her and
even sometimes in fine weather to take her out in the
gardens.

Kier's mother was almost always there. She
seemed to have called a truce with her daughter-
in-law, for nothing would keep her from her granddaughter.

'Stupid name, Frazer,' she told Lucy. 'Why Frazer?
If she had to give the child a man's name . . .'

'It's a family name, I think, and really it's not
important, darling.'

'Why not Kier?'

They were silent, and Lucy looked at Kier's mother
and saw that the baby's coming had not worked the
miracle for which she had hoped. She was trying hard
and she adored the baby, but her heart was broken.

'I'm beginning to see him everywhere, Lucy,
especially here. I turn round and he's teasing me
from behind a hedge, or I hear him calling from the
stables. Why did he go? He was too old. Different if
he'd stayed in, but suddenly to enlist like that and

then . . . the Somme, . . . so many, Lucy, so many. You'll see that things are done . . . our way, Kier's way, won't you?'

Lucy was embarrassed. 'Her mother knows what Kier would have wanted, and you'll be here . . .'

'I won't. God knows I want to watch this baby, but I'll never see 1918.'

She caught a cold in October 1917. She had been playing with her granddaughter in the garden, which was so lovely in its autumn colours, so lovely but so cold. The cold developed into pneumonia.

'She didn't even try to fight,' wept old Baxter. 'I never knew an Anderson-Howard that wouldn't fight.'

21

France 1918

ROSE THOUGHT IT might have been easier to bear if Robin had not looked quite so much like Kier. The little girl became more and more like her father as she changed from mewling infant to rounded baby. By the time she was eight months old she was crawling around the floor, lifting a gummy grin to her mother on Rose's infrequent visits, and by her first birthday she was hauling herself upright by whatever means she could and taking brave steps into the unknown. She attempted to use her first Christmas tree, ablaze with flickering candles and bedecked with gaily wrapped parcels, as an aid to walking, but luckily the faithful Sarah was there to rescue and to scold her and to tell Dr Nesbitt, Mrs Anderson-Howard, that they could not possibly have a lit Christmas tree this year, not with Miss Robin trying to walk.

Rose, who had never experienced Christmas until she married Kier, had shocked Sarah by ordering the Christmas tree to be set up instead in her private sitting room where no one and certainly not – and this according to Mrs Anderson-Howard's strict orders – Miss Robin was ever allowed.

Sarah, of course, turned a blind eye to the number of times Dr Nesbitt lifted the sleeping child from her crib in the beautifully appointed nursery and carried her off. It was hardly a nurserymaid's place to reprove her mistress for waking her own child from her sleep. And so Robin's first real Christmas found her sitting, as midnight and Father Christmas approached, on her mother's exquisitely tailored tweed lap in Mummy's sitting room, watching the candlelight dancing on the tree.

'Your father was such an idiot about Christmas,' Rose whispered into the child's black curls. 'He told me he believed in Santa Claus and he said that if I was a good girl I should have everything I asked Santa to bring. I asked for diamond bracelets and they were there, every Christmas, and Daddy asked for a fat little baby with black curls and Santa Claus never brought him his present. But now you're here, Miss Anderson-Howard, and Daddy is singing carols lustily with all the other angels. Can you hear him? He sings so dreadfully, but he played the piano beautifully. Perhaps a nice old angel has taught him to play Christmas carols on a celestial harp. I doubt that even an angel could teach him to sing.'

Robin nuzzled against her mother's blouse and, half asleep and half awake, listened to the soft Scottish voice.

'I was not a good wife to your daddy, little lambie. He really loved Aunt Lucy' – Robin smiled at the only word she recognized – 'but he was so gallant, he thought I was a poor little frail creature to be cherished and he mistook that for love . . . And I? Oh, Robin, did I lose the ability to love in the closies up the Hilltown? No, I loved him. How could I not love someone so good and kind? Your Uncle Frazer was just such a man; he sacrificed everything for me. And then there was this old classics teacher. I called him Wishy. He taught me Latin and Greek and never asked a thing in return, and that's why we're having this wee chat, lambie. I need to pay a debt, Robin, to Daddy and Uncle Frazer and Aunt Lucy – poor Aunt

Lucy. She never married, Robin, because I stole her love. He should have married Aunt Lucy years ago, and they should have had half a dozen bairns to fill this house.'

The baby yawned and then slept and Rose looked down at the little face with the dark curling lashes. 'If I'd known what joy a bairn could bring, I'd have had you long ago, but you did get in the way, Robin. You see, I'm a doctor. I take care of the sick; that's all I ever wanted to do. It was like the visions the knights in armour are supposed to have had, me – wee Rosie Nesbitt from a closie up the Hilltown – caring for the sick. And I did it. I've made a difference. If I died today I could say, "My life made a difference." I'm going away, Robin. There's a horrid war going on. It killed your daddy and it's killing other people every day and every night. There's a lovely old convent in France. Daddy and I went there on our honeymoon. What's left of it is a hospital, and I am going there to work until the war is over. You will stay with Sarah, and Aunt Lucy will come to see you often. Won't that be nice?'

Aunt Lucy did not think so. She was aghast at the thought of a young mother going off to work at the Front.

'How can you leave her, Rose? It's totally unsuitable. A baby needs her mother.'

'Robin needs Sarah, who feeds her and keeps her clean.'

'And loves her? Who could love her like a mother?'

'You, Lucy. And Sarah.'

'Oh, Rose, it's not the same thing.' For the first time she broke her self-imposed rule. 'Kier would never have approved.'

Rose laughed. 'You must feel really strongly. I

have to do it, Lucy, and it's done: I leave for France on Friday. And I'm not an angel of mercy; it's miles from any battlefield, but it's just more immediate help than I'm giving here, more . . .' She wanted to say reparation, but she couldn't say that to Lucy, to anyone but her small daughter who could not understand.

'I signed over the estate to Kier's daughter as soon as she was born,' she went on, 'and so, should anything happen, there will be no problems.' She got up abruptly and began to pace the room. The first flush of enthusiasm was over and the reality of what she had decided to do was making itself felt. She was going into a war zone, she could be killed. 'I want you to take care of Robin if anything goes wrong. Make the decisions for her future that Kier would have made.' She stopped as Lucy made a gesture towards her and she turned away from the desk. 'I see dirt and disease every day. This should not be very much different.'

But it was. Rose had seen mangled bodies before, but usually one at a time. And it had not been huge pieces of flying metal that ripped flesh from bone or limb from body. She had listened before to the groans or screams of injured men, women in advanced stages of difficult delivery, abused children – but this noise, this constant screaming of men, of shells, the staccato drumbeat of death-dealing bullets . . .

'I can't think in this noise,' she said to a French nun, Mère Dolle.

'The silence is more frightening. In the Convent silence was welcome, a chance to offer up the whole mind and heart. Here, if there is silence, I see evil as a huge bat gathering itself up to throw more death

at these poor boys. And they are only boys, Madame
Médecin. Look at this *pauvre bébé* here.'

The soldier was almost no more than a child. Had
a beard ever grown on that almost grey skin?

'Why, he's German,' exclaimed Rose.

'Le bon Dieu looks only at the soul, Madame,'
chided the old nun gently.

'I didn't mean . . .' began Rose and stopped as she
looked into Mère Dolle's eyes. Around her was war
and hatred and fear, and in those eyes was unques-
tioning love and acceptance. Oh, for such serenity,
thought Rose and bent over the German youth.

The boy opened his eyes and, seeing Rose, began
to cry and plead in German.

'What is he saying?' she asked the nun who was
soothing the boy in his own tongue. Not for the first
time, she wished she had had more classes in French
and German.

'He is afraid you will cut off his arm.'

Rose almost fainted at the smell from the wound
as she uncovered it, and she had to turn away for a
moment to discipline her heaving stomach.

'I may have to,' she said when she could speak.
'There's little left to save.'

The boy soldier had lost consciousness and they
worked over him in the poor light.

'I need another nurse, Sister. Is there anyone else?'
She looked at the nun, who was now almost as grey
as the boy. 'Don't faint on me,' she pleaded silently
and, as if she could hear, the nun smiled. 'I am well,
Doctor, only tired.'

They were all tired, hideously tired. How old was
Mère Dolle? Better not to ask. She was not young;
the few wisps of hair that stole out from under the
wimple were quite white. The capable hands were
marked with age spots and yet she stood hour after

hour, day after day, and often long into the night, and did everything that had to be done. Rose had never seen her eat or drink. Once she had been given a mug of hot soup and had turned modestly away to drink it.

'Strange creatures, nuns,' thought Rose, who had never met one before. The older ones were unfailingly cheerful; only the very young occasionally broke down under strain and then, when they had recovered, worked twice as hard as if to expiate the sin of being merely mortal.

'Have you had much medical training, Mère Dolle?' she asked as they finally sat down to rest. A young nun brought them soup. Oh, the power of a bowl of delicious soup! Mère Dolle again turned away so that Rose could not see her but, back to back on the old bench, they chatted.

'None at all, Madame Médecin. I spent my days until the war teaching fat little girls to sing, and playing the chapel organ like that boy there, the German. He is a student of music. That is why he fears the loss of his arm. There is little piano music for a one-handed pianist.'

'Oh, God, war is hell,' said Rose.

'*D'accord*,' said the nun as countless others had agreed before her.

Rose sat drinking her soup and looking at the slim black shape before her: a musician with no medical training, a life of prayer and penitence devoted to the service of God, and yet she did the most intimate and, to some eyes, demeaning things for these men without a murmur or whimper of complaint. Why? How? Too difficult to tell if she had been pretty when she was young. Had she ever had a lover? Had she ever wanted one? She herself would have been content without a lover, except that there was now Robin. Robin . . .

'I have a little girl, Mère Dolle.'

'You miss her?'

'I did not expect to miss her. I have spent very little time with her because medicine always came first.'

'It was Bach with me . . . or Beethoven. I have been blessed because I gave them up to the Saviour and He has given them back to me. Your sacrifice will not go unnoticed, Madame.'

'My husband died in France in 1916. He didn't even know about her.'

'He does now.'

'You really believe that?'

'*Bien sûr*, Madame.'

The strange conversation came to an end as Mère Dolle finished her soup and straightened her back. 'Why don't you have a . . .' she began. Rose was never to know what she had wanted her to have . . . a bath . . . a rest . . . a walk in the Convent gardens?

'We have two more field ambulances coming in, Doctor.' An ambulatory patient had come in to the ward. 'Doctor Mutton wants you in theatre if you're not doing nothing.'

Dr Mouton was an elderly French doctor who headed the medical team at the convent. Like Mère Dolle, he seemed possessed of extraordinary strength. Rose only learned much later that his shame that so many French troops at the Front had mutinied on May 4th had caused him to come out of retirement, leaving his gardens to the weeds he had fought assiduously and successfully for five years. He spoke no English and Rose was only beginning, thanks to Mère Dolle, to really learn any French, but with the nun's help the two doctors understood one another well enough.

At 3 o'clock the next morning Rose fell fully dressed on to her bed and slept. She had been on her feet for twenty-five hours. When she awoke she found that she was dressed in a cool white broderie anglaise nightgown and that she was inside the crisp white sheets. Even her hair was brushed.

'Can I come in, Doctor?'

'Come in, Nurse.'

'Look at this,' said the girl, pointing to the plain white china as if Rose might not recognize the object that sat in the middle of it. 'It's an egg. We've got one each.'

Rose did not look at the egg, welcome stranger though it was. She looked instead at the round cheery face of Nurse Jeanette McDonald. The eyes were twinkling – had she stolen the eggs? – and the perpetual dimples in her cheeks were dancing with suppressed laughter.

'How did I get undressed?'

'Ach, that was me and Mother Dolly. She was worried aboot you, you being such a wee bit thing, and there is nothing of you. Mind you, my mither aye said it was the skinny ones had the strength. You've had twelve hours. Everything's quiet and there are smells coming oot of the kitchen . . . I can hardly wait for my dinner. It's the garlic, Doctor. Did you ever use fancy things in your cooking? I never used onything but a wee bit salt myself, but Sister Anthony Joseph says add an onion, a tomato and garlic and you have a meal fit for a king. Roll on the end of the war. Wait till Glasgow tastes my mince!'

'Have you a big family waiting for you, Nurse?'

The cheery face clouded for a moment and then the sun shone again. 'Not really, no. My mither sort of just gave up and died when wee Jimmy got killed at Verdun. Five boys, and every one deid. No fair, is it, Doctor, but two of them was married with bairns and I'll cook the new mince for them.'

'The young German, Nurse?'

'We've had to send him up to the big hospital at Le Tréport; the arm has to come off if we want to save his life. I doubt he'll even survive the trip. The road's no' there at all now. Well, I'll leave you tae get dressed. Mother Dolly told me tae watch you eat every bite.' She walked to the door as Rosie slipped out of the bed. 'We're going to have a bit sing-song for the laddies the nicht. Have you heard her play a polka? She's fabulous, she can even play "Loch Lomond". You hum it, Mother Dolly'll play it.'

The door closed behind her and, apart from the clack of her heels as she walked quickly along the polished corridor, there was a welcome silence. Rosie hurried to dress. When had Nurse McDonald rested, or Mère Dolle or, even more importantly, Doctor Mouton?

The wards were quiet apart from the moaning of wounded men for whom they did not have enough painkilling medicines. A young nun was washing the floor. The Mother Superior obviously believed in the old dictum that cleanliness is nearest to godliness. In Rose's book it was certainly nearest to 'good chance of survival'.

'Nurse, Nurse, give me something, can't you?'

It was not the first time the mistake had been made and it would not be the last. Rose walked across to the patient and looked first at him and then at his chart.

'I'm sorry,' she said gently. 'There is nothing I can do for you. Your wound is healing nicely.'

'Get the Froggie doctor. He'll give me something.'

Rose tried not to let her distaste show on her face. 'Doctor Mouton is not on the wards at the moment.'

'Get him then . . .'

'Glad to hear you are almost back to normal, Corporal.'

Rosie had not heard the dressing-gowned figure enter the ward.

'I'm Captain Drummond,' he said, 'and you must be Doctor Nesbitt. What an honour to meet you when I'm awake, Doctor.'

Rose laughed and took the hand held out to her. Captain Drummond had been unconscious the last time she had seen him.

'A woman doctor! No bloody wonder I'm still lying here.'

'Mind your tongue if you don't want to be put on a charge, Corporal. It's thanks to Doctor Nesbitt that you're even alive.'

'Thank you, but that's not quite true,' said Rose as they moved away from the bed. 'The corporal's wound is minor compared to some of the injuries, your own for instance. Who gave you permission to get out of bed?' She was a doctor, and as a doctor found it easy to speak naturally to this gaunt young man whose voice and manner told her that he was just such another as Kier.

'I dreamed I was at the Usher Hall with my best girl who looked very like you, if I may be so bold, Doctor, and an angel was playing Bach.'

'It wasn't an angel – or maybe it was: it was Mère Dolle.'

'The old nun? My God, what a waste!'

'She would not agree with you, Captain.'

'Andrew, call me Andrew.'

She smiled. 'Back to bed, Captain Drummond.' 'Oh, Kier, what a lot you taught me,' she found herself thinking, 'or is it just that I now wear a mask labelled Doctor and no one can believe in the lassie from the slums who is still underneath? Or is she still there? Have several years of marriage to a *gentleman* turned me into a *lady*?'

Captain Drummond was not so easily put off by the young doctor's sternness. He had himself wheeled into the recreation room at the Convent where the concert for the invalids was being held and even, against Doctor Mouton's wishes, took a turn on the piano. He did not have Mère Dolle's classical training nor Kier's delicate touch, but he could certainly thump out the rousing choruses the soldiers wanted to hear.

'You will open your wound, Captain Drummond.'

He looked up at her from the piano stool; he was laughing, but the eyes were strained with denied pain.

'If a beautiful Scottish doctor was to say, "Go to bed at once, Andrew", I would probably obey.'

'Captain Drummond,' she began, and then she too laughed and capitulated. 'Andrew, you must give your stitches a chance to heal.'

He got up slowly. 'Has anyone ever told you that you are very beautiful? I can't call you Doctor . . . I won't.' He stood demanding an answer.

'Rose. And yes, my husband, quite often.'

He looked down at her ringless hands.

'I left them for my daughter, just in case; they were heirlooms.'

'Your husband?'

'Good night, Captain Drummond.' She turned as if to leave him there in the middle of the corridor.

'I'm sorry, Rose. You know you can't abandon me, but I promise not to ask any more. It's just so strange. I have a feeling that there is so much to know and so little time left. I was aware of you, you know, through the pain and the anaesthetic . . .'

She interrupted. 'Medical school. Lesson no. 24. Your male patients will all "be aware" of you.'

'Not Corporal Dempsey,' he teased and she had to join in his laughter. When had anyone ever made her laugh so easily?

Thus began two of the happiest months Rose had ever known. When the horrors of daily life became almost too much to bear, there was Andrew with his ready smile and his humour. It was not that he did not take life seriously. He did, but he had an amazing capacity for finding humour in the strangest situations, and he could explain it in his execrable schoolboy French well enough to raise a smile from even Doctor Mouton.

Rose always spent her free time in the Convent garden. She would love to have been allowed to kneel down and work in the soil with the two nuns who seemed to spend their lives weeding and hoeing, but they would not allow it. It would not be suitable, but Madame Médecin was welcome to sit there and watch while they worked. Captain Drummond found her there and often they would sit saying nothing, but allowing the peace of the garden to wash away the stress of the moment. Rose no longer noticed the constant roll of guns from just over the fields; it was Andrew who told her that the war was relentlessly coming closer and closer.

'We are going to have to evacuate our walking wounded, Rose. We're smack in the way of a German retreat. Our lads will follow them but . . .'

She wanted to cry out, 'No,' but she said nothing for she could not tell him what she felt. How could she say that her first thought had been that she would miss him, Andrew Drummond? For the first time ever, she had thought of herself before her patients.

Then she laughed, a wry little laugh. Andrew was a
patient still.

'I will travel with my patients then.'

'I'm trying to decide what would be safer for
you. The nuns will stay, and Monsieur Mouton and
those who cannot be transported. I doubt that they
will be in any real danger from a retreating army.
Mother Superior will be happy to hide you and Miss
McDonald in the cloisters.'

'That's a very funny thought, Andrew. Wee Rosie
Nesbitt from the Hilltown in Dundee hiding in a
convent.'

He turned to her then. 'Oh, Rose, I always felt there
was so litle time. There's so much I want to know
about you . . . important things like, "Do you like
Christmas pudding with custard or brandy sauce?"'

'I hate Christmas pudding.'

'Do you prefer Bach to Beethoven?'

'I'm a Mozart lover.'

'Do you like John Buchan?'

'I don't know him.'

'Shame on you! He's an exciting Scottish writer.'

'I haven't read a real book in . . . a hundred
years.'

'I have some Sassoon in my kit.'

Rose smiled. 'I've read him.' She looked at his
anxious face and laughed. 'I liked the poems. Is that
what you wanted me to say?'

'There, you see; we've got lots in common, apart
from Christmas pudding . . . and I would find myself
with no appetite anyway with you at the table.'

She moved as if to get up, but he grasped her hand
and pulled her down.

'It's too soon, Andrew . . .'

'It's too late, Rose; for me it was too late when I
saw your lovely face through the mists of ether or

whatever it was that put me out.' He saw tears start
in her eyes and impetuously kissed first one and then
the other and she sat unmoving, but trembling, and
the tears slipped down her cheeks. 'What is it, Rose?
Your husband? The professional oath? Asclepius,
ancient God of healing, is that it? He said doctors
can't be kissed by their patients?'

'Hippocrates. He was a doctor.' Rose looked up at
him, at his gaunt face almost wavering before her as
she tried to stem the tears. There was a strange but
pleasant feeling in the pit of her stomach, she felt as
light as a feather. A defeated army was approaching
rapidly and she could not fear, she could not worry,
because of this young man. She forgot Kier; she forgot
Robin. 'Oh, Andrew,' she said and leaned towards
him, and in a second she was in his arms and kissing
him as she had never kissed Kier.

They did not hear the two soldiers approach. The
voice that spoke was educated and apologetic.

'How charming. I am so sorry to put an end
to this idyll . . . for the moment, of course, Captain.'

Rose and Andrew looked up at the two soldiers.
Rose was still dazed from the enormity of what had
just happened to her, and it was a few moments
before she realized that the men were German.

'You are the senior officer here, Captain. I am
Major Heinrich Von Kesserling of the German Army.
I regret that we find ourselves in need of some
supplies.'

Then Rose noticed that both men held guns and
that the weapons were pointing at them. She clutched
Andrew's arm protectively.

'You are in no danger, Nurse. I have some men
who will be grateful for your help perhaps.'

'This lady is a doctor, Major, and you must speak to

Mother Superior if you need supplies. We are merely guests here.'

'Then we must find this lady, Captain. You will take us to her?'

It was couched as a question, but with two guns trained on them there was nothing they could do. The second German soldier said something and the officer answered angrily. Andrew too spoke in German.

'What is it? What is he saying?'

'Nothing,' said Andrew shortly. 'Uncouth fool!'

Rose walked beside him quickly through the gardens towards the Convent. It was unreal, it could not be happening. A few minutes ago the gardens had been the most beautiful place in the world, and now they were contaminated, soiled. As if he sensed her thoughts, Andrew smiled down at her.

'They won't stay, Rose. They are anxious to get away. Our boys have licked them and now they are right behind the retreating glorious army. Isn't that right, Major?'

'We will not impose on the good sisters' hospitality longer than we need, Captain. And please, Captain, it is not wise to try to provoke. Not all my men have had my advantages. No doubt it is the same in the British Army: there are some with, how would you say, a nervous finger on the trigger? Ah, *bon soir, Ma Soeur* . . .'

Mère Dolle had come out of the Convent at their approach. She answered the officer in fluent German and then returned to English . . . 'for the sake of Madame Médecin' and she smiled at Rose.

'This is a house of prayer and peace, Major. I would ask you to put away those weapons.'

'In good time, Sister. I must inspect first. You understand?'

How did it happen? How *did* it happen? For the rest of her life Rose went over and over those few minutes. As Mère Dolle and Major Von Kesserling spoke, the other German soldier moved nearer to her. She made as if to move closer to the nun, and he followed. He grabbed her arm and said something, and then everything happened at once. The nun and the German officer turned and spoke in rapid German, and at the same time Andrew pushed the soldier as hard as he could. He was not strong; he had been badly wounded, and the blow was not severe. A light of madness was lit in the soldier's eyes and he fired once and then turned the gun towards Rose. There was a second shot . . .

Major Von Kesserling put his gun away. 'I regret, Sister,' he began but Rose heard no more. She was on the ground beside Andrew, desperately feeling for a pulse. The German soldier lay spreadeagled beside him.

Happiness is such an ephemeral substance. Rose knelt in helpless anguish on the dusty pathway. Mère Dolle knelt beside her and prayed the prayers for the dead, both English and German, and for the living who had to watch their happiness slip away.

Rose considered returning to Britain after Andrew's death. For a while it seemed to her that everything she had ever touched was doomed to end in disaster. Had her education cost Frazer his life? Even old Wishy had not lived long enough to receive the free medical attention that he had claimed as his payment for the hours and hours of tuition he had given her. She stood in the garden beside the grave that held the mortal remains of Captain Andrew Drummond who had died, not in glorious battle, but because he had objected to what an uneducated lout had said about her.

'I'm sorry, Andrew. We hadn't time to . . .' To do what? To learn from and to accept the lessons of the past . . . to fall in love?

Had he parents? If he had, should she write to them and tell them how their son had lost his life? Would they be proud of how and why he had died? Would they sit in a gracious drawing room somewhere and say, 'We brought the boy up to be a gentleman and he never let us down'? Or would they scream and cry and rail against fate as she wanted to do?

She knelt down in the dust beside the grave. She was so tired, so very tired. The visiting American Congressmen had been exhausting in their kindness, in their repeated reassurances that the war could last only a few more weeks. Were they right? She remembered the tall Southern one: she had liked his soft warm voice. It had made her feel protected – easy to believe what he said.

'Robin. I must get back to Robin, to Kier's daughter. Kier. Oh, Kier, I wish I knew that you had my letter. She is so like you in so many ways.'

More regrets. He had died for her too, in a way.

Doctor Rose Nesbitt pulled herself to her feet. There were still patients to see and the Americans had brought supplies.

'I have a dispensary now,' said Rose and laughed. 'At last I have a dispensary and there's medicine in it.'

Mère Dolle was in the ward.

'You look exhausted, Doctor,' she said. 'Why don't you finish your rounds and go to bed? Do you know the Americans left us a ham? Can you imagine? We shall have a feast, and then I shall go to the chapel and play for you . . . Bach, I think.'

'Bach? Someone once told me that the angels play Bach's music in heaven.'

'A good choice. Go to bed, little doctor. I shall bring you food myself.'

Doctor Nesbitt was asleep when the nun arrived with the tray. Mère Dolle stood looking down at her, at her blonde hair tumbling in damp curls around her face. The skin was so white, and under the eyelids she could see the blue tracings of the veins.

'Sleep is better than food,' she said.

Rose heard the music in her sleep, but she did not recognize it. Kier or Andrew could have told her that it was part of the first Brandenburg Concerto. She sighed, not with grief but with contentment. It was so warm and peaceful, and the faint notes of the organ caressed her wounded spirit. Mère Dolle would have said that music caressed the soul. Rose sank once more into a deep sleep and in the morning, when she did not appear as usual in the wards, it was Mère Dolle who went to find her.

At first she was not too worried. A rest, complete rest, that was surely all that was required. She hurried out, no panic, just efficient speed, and found another nun to help her lift Rose from the bed. Together they changed the sheets, but it was Mère Dolle's loving hands that washed the damp body, replaced the soaking nightgown.

Doctor Mouton diagnosed pneumonia.

'Thanks to the Americans we have medicine, Sister,' he said. 'Our little Rose has exhausted herself in our service.'

'We'll give her round-the-clock care, Doctor.'

Did Mère Dolle sleep at all for the next few days? She was there when the climax came, when Rose's fevered body tossed and turned to try to get away from the heat that was consuming it.

'The fever will break,' the doctor said. In all the cases of pneumonia he had ever treated where the patient was young and well-fed and well-nursed, this had been the pattern.

Mère Dolle replaced the damp cloth with which she was attempting to cool the delirious woman. She held Rose's hot hands and talked to her, sang to her, tried to keep the wandering attention firmly attached to a world which had not treated her too well.

Doctor Nesbitt talked to many people whom she seemed to see around her. Some she smiled and laughed to greet, others made her cry . . . tragic tears which further weakened her. There were Ma and Frazer and Wishy, Lucy, and Kier. Lucy calmed her, and the nun welcomed her presence as if she was indeed there in the darkened room.

Rose lay quiet and Mère Dolle rose to adjust the light. The climax had arrived: the fever was breaking.

'Kier.'

She heard her patient say the name so clearly and the voice was light and happy. Rose was lying on the bed, her eyes were open and she was smiling, a smile of such intense love and beauty that the nun was moved almost to tears.

Rose closed her eyes with a soft sigh.

'Robin,' she whispered, and the voice held regret. 'My little Robin.'

22

Dundee-London 1921

ON THE 15TH of March 1921, an African country called
Ruanda was ceded to the British by the Belgians.
Lucy and Robin did not notice this latest piece
of world news. Robin was too interested in the
mysteries of penmanship as revealed to her at the
High School of Dundee, where she sat every morning
in a grey skirt that she hated but accepted as the
price she had to pay for education. Lucy treasured
Robin's days at school in Dundee and she enjoyed
to the full the job of surrogate mother, for early in
1919 a letter had come from France. The writer was
of course unaware that Lucy was a fluent French
speaker and the letter, in English, was short and
rather stilted. Doctor Nesbitt had caught pneumonia
in the winter and had died of endocarditis. She had
asked to be buried in the Convent grounds beside
allied personnel who had also died as a result of the
conflict. She had been much loved by the Community
and would be greatly mourned.

Endocarditis, a heart disease for which there was
no cure, and which had probably been lying latent,
waiting to strike down Rose's overworked body.
Kier had intuitively worried about the strength of
his wife. Lucy sighed and reapplied herself to caring
for their child.

Robin had not grieved, as she did not grieve for
her father, but Auntie Lucy worked hard to paint a

picture of her parents for the little girl. At five years of age, however, all that was real to Robin was Lucy and Sarah, weekly visits to Laverock Rising, and now the world unfolded by education. Lucy watched her as she sat hunched over the table, a strand of curly hair and her pencil clenched between her teeth, and she sighed for all too soon she was going to send the little girl to the boarding school in the south of England which was to have been the scene of her own formative years. Robin accepted the news of her future departure as she accepted twice-yearly visits to the dentist or hot baths in front of the nursery fire every Wednesday and Saturday whether she was dirty or not. She was always dirty on Saturday. Saturday they went to Laverock Rising, and Robin gloried in her pony and the dogs and, in season, the lambs and the calves, for Lucy was determined that the young laird should grow up familiar with her home and known by her tenants. She knew many of them too well and was spoiled atrociously. Every baker in that beloved corner of Fife outdid herself to provide home baking, 'in case Miss Robin should stop by'. And Miss Robin did. She rode her pony, not only over the huge estate which she had inherited from her father but over the surrounding countryside, and she stayed longest with those who had known her father or her grandparents. Unfortunately, as far as Aunt Lucy was concerned, many of these old acquaintances vied with one another for the little girl's favour, and she had to be very strict about Robin's diet during the week. Apart from writing and reading and a weekly piano lesson, Robin hated weekdays.

Another important reason for Lucy – who, as the daughter of a diplomat, would have been intensely interested – to miss the Ruanda news was the announcement – with much invective – that a

Doctor Marie Stopes had opened a birth control clinic in London.

'Good heavens,' she exclaimed as she sat at breakfast, 'she's only forty and she's making such a mark. Rose would have welcomed her. I must visit.'

She wrote to Doctor Stopes and was invited down to see the clinic. Doctor Hendry agreed to give emergency care and Lucy planned her visit carefully.

'We will go to London together soon, Robin,' she told the little girl as she towelled her dry – on Wednesday – 'and we will see the Tower of London . . .'

'And Wendy's home?'

'Oh, yes, of course, dear.' Robin, like every other child in Britain, knew all about Wendy Darling and her friend Peter Pan who had been delighting children since 1904.

It was not of Peter Pan or Wendy or even the Lost Boys – although probably they were nearer her heart than the very secure Wendy and Peter – that Lucy was thinking as she checked into the brand-new home of the Overseas Club, Vernon House on Park Place, just off St James's Street. As always, when she travelled, Sir John and his terrifying but heroic death were on her mind. She had joined the Overseas Club, now the Overseas League, almost in memory of her father. Like that other more famous John, John Evelyn Wrench, who had founded the Overseas League, Lucy's father had believed in a 'world society', a brotherhood of widely different men and women in every corner of the globe. She looked around the lobby on this, her first visit, and admired the Edwardian panelling which lined the lovely wooden stair-well. She did not see the man who was descending that very stair.

'Why, as I live and breathe. Lucy?' The voice was hesitant, doubtful of its welcome, but recognizable.

Lucy concentrated on writing her address to give herself time and then turned, nothing on her schooled face showing the unutterable consternation raging inside her. Once before he had appeared in her life after years of mutual neglect, and he had turned her carefully developed existence into glorious chaos. He would never ever know how much she had loved him, how much she had mourned him and their never-to-be-born child, how much she had suffered at his too casual rejection of her. 'Max, good heavens, the proverbial bad penny; you do get around. I can't say that it's a joy to see you.'

He was older, of course he was. The hair was grey but still thick, and the eyes were as keen and full of humour as ever. He was so obviously American that she wondered why she had never noticed that about him before.

'Because he means nothing,' her head said, while her blood told her something very different.

'One meets every foreign acquaintance one has ever made at the Overseas Club, eventually,' she said, more for the benefit of the interested clerk than to hurt Max.

He was gazing at her as if he had been struck by a vision. 'My God, Lucy.' He pulled her almost fiercely away from the desk. 'Of course you must hate me, but give me a chance to explain,' he whispered. 'Take tea with me, Lucy, please,' he asked pleasantly, again for the benefit of the clerk. 'You must be ready for tea. Aren't the British always ready to drink tea after a journey?'

'I need to go to my room and unpack.'

'After a cup of tea. Oh, take pity on . . . an old

acquaintance. There's so much I want to say, need to say.'

Lucy was in full control of herself. 'I don't think there's anything for us to say, Max. Now, if you'll excuse me . . .'

'Dad, would you believe, there's a box for the . . .' The boy stopped talking as he saw Lucy. 'I'm so sorry, ma'am,' he went on. 'I didn't see you there.'

'This is Doctor Graham, Brook, one of the very first lady doctors in Scotland and an old and dear friend. Lucy, my son, Brook.'

The sight and sound of the boy hit her like the killing blow of a sledgehammer. She felt almost faint, a mist clouded her eyes.

'Ma'am,' the boy said anxiously, 'are you OK?' There was no way of avoiding the du Pay men. Their charm, their personality, their sheer size made it impossible for Lucy, herself a tall woman, to do anything other than be guided by Max to a table in an alcove.

'Come join us for tea, Brook. Doctor Graham needs tea after her long journey, and Mother's . . . resting.'

'She'a always resting,' said the boy in a matter-of-fact tone, 'but she'll be thrilled about the ballet. Do you like ballet, ma'am . . . I mean . . . Doctor?'

Years of discipline came to her aid. 'Yes, I like it very much, Brook,' Lucy said as she watched the boy's face and listened to his voice, so like his father's. 'I prefer Grand Opera, though.'

'Crikey, no way! All those Italians screaming at one another.' He laughed and Lucy smiled at him. How assured well-brought-up American children were, friendly but not forward. She liked it.

'You can come with us if you like, ma'am. I got the whole box, Dad; I didn't quite understand what I was buying.'

They all laughed and Max looked at her, a question in his eyes.

'I couldn't, Brook. I'm sorry. I'm here on business and brought no clothes suitable for the theatre.'

'Why, you look just fine to me. Wow, look at all these tea-cakes. Wasn't I right, Dad? You have to try everything a country has to offer, don't you, Doctor? Sadler's Wells. Afternoon tea.'

There was something so infectiously likeable about the American boy – How old was he? He was tall, but oh so young, twelve, perhaps? – that Lucy found the tea-party almost enjoyable. She devoted herself to introducing Brook to the intricacies of scones with cream and jam, to crumpets – which she assured him ought really to be hot – and to the wonders of shortbread. Because he was so open she discovered that his mother was an invalid – 'I don't remember her ever being well, poor Mother' – and that they were on a trip to some of the spas in Germany so that she could take the waters.

'One day, if Mother gets a little bit stronger, Dad and I are going to tour all the art galleries in Europe. I want to study art in London, you have such fine schools here. But when I finish school I have to go to Yale first, to please Mother.' He blushed as if he was ashamed that he might have sounded just a little disloyal. 'I mean, I want to go. I think she's so right. Everyone should have a really broad education, don't you agree, Doctor?'

'Yes, of course, Brook.' What a lovely and unusual name. He could be mine; he *should* be mine. She could bear no more.

'I really must go and unpack. I have an early appointment.'

They stood up. 'You're still practising, Lucy?'

Max did not ask about marriage; he had seen her ringless hands.

'Oh, I could never give up medicine, Max,' she answered lightly. 'You know that it always meant everything to me.' There, she had told him he meant nothing. 'Enjoy the ballet, Brook, and the rest of your stay in London.'

She managed to get across the foyer and into the lift, aware that they stood watching her as she walked away from them. She found her room and sat down on the edge of the bed to steady her legs. His voice, his eyes, his hands. How had she ever told herself that she had forgotten the feel of his hands, the demands of his lips?

She waited until they would have left for the theatre before she went down for dinner, and felt quite sure that she would have breakfasted and gone to her meeting before they were even awake in the morning . . .

Max was waiting in a car as she stepped out into the early spring sunshine.

'Why call a cab when I can easily drive you, Lucy?'

'I have ordered a taxi. Here it is now.'

'Sorry, the lady made a mistake,' said Max and handed the taxi driver a note which earned him a, 'Crikey, ta very much, sir.'

'You had no right to do that,' Lucy said stiffly as, aware of the doorman, she allowed Max to hand her into the beautiful car.

'We have to talk . . .'

'There is nothing to talk about. We had, what, a passing affair fourteen years ago? You must have an incredible conceit about your charms, Senator.'

'I love you, Lucy. I have never stopped loving you, and I have thought of you with longing every day of my life.'

Lucy looked down at her clenched hands where the knuckles strove to push themselves up through the soft kid of her gloves. 'Stop this car and let me out. How dare you! If you think for one moment that you can come back into my life after abandoning me . . .' She turned to look at him, her face showing for the first time in years the despair that had tortured her. 'I thought, I prayed that I might be pregnant. I waited for letters . . . and nothing, *nothing*. Let me out or I shall start screaming . . .'

'Please, Lucy. I apologize if I have insulted and embarrassed you, but you can't get out in the middle of the street. I'll say no more but I'll drop you off . . . where?'

'The Marie Stopes Clinic. It's on . . .'

'I know. I helped . . . family money helped . . . fund it. What a wonderful woman she is. You know of the pioneering work on birth control by . . .'

The awkwardness over, he drove surely and safely to the clinic and let her out. 'I won't offer to come in with you; I was here yesterday. You know how we Americans like to know we're getting value for money. I can't offer to come back either; I'm taking Brook to the Tate.'

'He's a nice boy, Max.'

He smiled, that remembered smile that lit up his face from the inside. 'He's about the only thing in my . . .' he began. 'We must talk again before I leave, Lucy. Please?'

'Thanks for the lift,' she said and walked into the clinic. Her heart was pounding and she doubted that she could speak rationally to the doctors. His wife was an invalid. No doubt an ailing woman found *that* side of marriage tiring. Lucy could name a dozen such invalids, real or imagined, from her own practice. He could not still love her. Had he ever loved her? He was a virile man and the intimate side of marriage would be important to him. For years she had told herself that in those, to her, idyllic days in Italy, he had wanted only sexual release. She had taught herself to dislike him, to forget – no, never to forget, to ignore the memories, the longings, and here he was overturning her carefully nurtured life as easily as he had done all those years ago. 'No, no, Senator, no willing frustrated woman to toy with as an extra on your London jaunt.' Was there one in Paris, in Rome? Why had they not visited Venice? What had the boy said? 'Dad says the lagoon waters would be bad for Mother's health.' She was talking to Doctor Stopes; was she herself making any sense? Would she remember one word of this conversation? Lucy took herself firmly in hand and thrust Maximilian du Pay back into her subconscious.

He was not so easy to dispose of physically however. Having spent the day in the clinic, Lucy returned late to the Overseas Club. She could see his long legs stretched out in the foyer as she came through the entrance. He was not alone; a woman like a decaying flower sat across from him in a pink chair that could just have been chosen to suit her soft fragility.

'Doctor Graham, if you're not too tired, my wife would love the honour of meeting you.'

He had no right to do this. He should get out of her life. He had his wife and the boy. She had Robin; it was enough. But she could not ignore him without being deliberately rude.

She avoided his outstretched hand and went over to his wife.

'How do you do, Mrs du Pay.'

'Doctor,' Ammabelle du Pay raised a languid

hand, 'I am honoured to meet you. Had I had
a tenth of your strength' – immediately Lucy felt
like a veritable Amazon – 'I should have liked to
do something for my fellow man. As it is, I give
of my money and my time, I do admit, to many
charitable causes, and none dearer to me than birth
control. Max, the champagne. You British have your
afternoon tea, but I have one glass of champagne; it
refreshes me and gives me strength for my evening
duties. You will join us, Doctor Graham, or may I too
call you Lucy? Such a charming name.'

She stopped for a second while Lucy murmured all
the polite things and wondered why Max and Brook
were not the exhausted ones. Surely that clinging
voice would suck the very life-blood from anyone
on whom it fastened? She looked with trained eyes
at the woman in front of her. 'One glass in public,' she
thought. 'How much in private?' She looked at Max,
who seemed unable to meet her eyes, and sadness
for all the wasted lives overwhelmed her. 'Poor Max,'
she thought.

The champagne came and Max himself opened it
expertly. He would be an expert, supposed Lucy, if
he had opened a bottle every single afternoon for the
last fourteen years.

'Come the recession, I can get a job as a wine
waiter.' He laughed as he poured.

'A recession? Surely America is leading the world.'

'There's a great big bubble blowing in the States,
Lucy, and bubbles burst.'

'Don't be silly, Max,' said Ammabelle shortly.

'Does she always dismiss her husband so readily,
and in public?' thought Lucy, but she smiled as Max's
wife turned to her.

'He's made millions, Lucy. He's every bit as fine a
businessman as even my dear late father was. And,

would you believe, we had to coax him to take his father's Senate seat.'

'But you don't go into the Senate to make money, do you?' Lucy asked before she could stop herself.

'Touché,' laughed Max and his eyes smiled at her across the rim of the glass.

Mrs du Pay, Ammabelle, was annoyed. 'Of course not. I just meant that we need men with brains in government and Max has brains.'

'Government needs men with hearts too, Mother, and that's why Daddy's successful.'

'I've ordered you some fruit juice, son,' said Max quickly.

Was there an undertone there? The boy said nothing but poured himself a glass of juice. Silently and solemnly he toasted the adults and then he flopped down beside Lucy, almost spilling her drink.

'Gosh, I'm sorry, ma'am,' said Brook, but he was looking at his mother. 'Sometimes I can't handle my legs – like a colt, you know, all legs and no body.'

'You just need to think of others, Brook,' said Mrs du Pay, 'and don't interrupt. His father spoils him abominably, Lucy. You were telling us all about your visit to Dr Stopes' clinic?'

'Was I?' thought Lucy.

'There are no clinics such as this anywhere else in Britain at the moment,' she said. 'I shall be pleased to learn more from Doctor Stopes and to pass the information on to my patients.'

'Bravo, Lucy. What men fail to understand is that a child not only drains a woman's body of all strength and vigour for nine months, but continues to make demands of his poor mother every minute of every day and often night, too, until he is quite grown up. If only the agonies were over with the birth pangs.'

'What an unutterably selfish woman,' thought
Lucy as she looked at Brook's young, fresh face. It
registered nothing. Had he heard it so often before
that he no longer listened or no longer minded?
Max's lean brown hand was on the boy's knee.

'I've never had the joys or the pains of a child
myself, Ammabelle, and so I can't really agree or
disagree, but even the poorest of my patients in the
meanest of circumstances seems to feel that the joys
of motherhood far outweigh the pain.'

'Even those with nine, ten or even more children
whom they cannot afford to feed or clothe?'

'Well, they don't want them when they're carrying
them, and too many resort to unbelievable methods
to rid themselves of unwanted pregnancies, but once
that child is in their arms . . .' She stopped and looked
at the boy, and the bleakest moment of her entire life
came back to her. It was not the day she realized
that she had lost Max, but that awful moment in
Rose's bathroom when she knew that there was to
be no baby, no baby to grow into this beautiful,
sensitive boy. 'He should be mine . . .' her thoughts
repeated.

'What are your professional feelings about legal-
ized abortion, Lucy?' asked Max across the darkness
and she was glad to answer.

'I went into medicine to save life, and so to deliberately take life would hardly be acceptable, but there
have been cases, even in my experience, where it is
necessary to think of the greater good, to sacrifice the
child to save the mother. I welcome Doctor Stopes
and her teaching. To prevent conception is surely the
answer, for the duchess or the mill-girl.'

'Bravo, Lucy! You are a shining light in your
profession. Too many doctors mumble platitudes
about woman's natural function. Let them try it.'

Ammabelle stood up. 'Now I hope you will take pity on my family and dine with them. I was dragged to the ballet last night when all I really needed was rest, and today I have trailed all over London looking at pictures, some of them quite ghastly, and I shall go to bed and have a little toast and soup. I am exhausted. No, don't come with me, Max. I want you and Brook to have a nice evening and I am too tired to be gay.'

She held up her cheek to be kissed, gave Lucy a hand that felt like paper, and drifted away to the stairs.

'Will you dine with us, Doctor Lucy?'

Brook sounded as if he really wanted her company and she wanted to be with them, just once. 'I'd love to dine with you, Brook,' she said; Max was not to think she wanted to be with him. She followed Ammabelle upstairs and washed and changed as quickly as possible. As always, she found herself remembering the dress she had bought in Venice. She had never had another occasion to wear it and now, of course, it was a museum piece. 'Face it, Lucy. You are an old woman and life has passed you by. You are not going down there to pretend you are a family.' But still she had to admit that she was glad, glad that Ammabelle had been too . . . *tired* to dine with her husband and son.

'But there's no need for me to be quite so dowdy,' she decided as she walked downstairs in a service-able wool dress that she had brightened up with pearls and her grandmother's amethyst brooch.

Max and his son greeted her with obvious pleasure. 'Americans are so polite,' thought Lucy, not for the first time. 'They would never let me know they think they're dining with a frumpy old maid.'

'I thought the Dorchester,' said Max, taking Lucy's arm and leading her outside. 'We can dance after dinner the way . . . well, we can remember our youth.'

'You don't dance, Dad,' said Brook. 'You and Mother sit out all the time back home. But I learned to do the waltz at school, Doctor Lucy . . .' The boy blushed at his audacity and subsided into silence.

'How can you refuse such a charming invitation, Lucy? I will hobble in after Rudolph Valentino here, and maybe if you have a pill I could use if it all gets too exciting for me . . .'

'Aw, Dad.' The boy was embarrassed and suddenly looked his age. 'Doctor Lucy knows what I mean.'

'Of course I do, Brook, my dear, and if you're sure you would like to dance, I would be honoured to be your partner.'

'I don't really want to,' the boy answered honestly, 'but I have to at home, at family parties and such. Everybody wants to dance with me, but they know Dad's a Senator and they know he's rich and I sometimes think I could be bowlegged and have adenoids . . . you know. Things like that never seemed to bother Dad.'

Lucy remembered the young Max. No, it would never have occurred to him that he was popular because he was rich, but this boy was a more sensitive soul.

Max was smiling. He understood his son more than the boy knew, and that he loved him was so obvious. No, she must not find herself wishing, wishing . . .

'I feel guilty eating all this wonderful food while Ammabelle eats toast alone,' she said later as a sumptuous dessert was placed reverently before her. Did Max and his son look at one another quickly before laughing off the remark and devoting themselves to their own puddings?

Later, they sat drinking coffee and watching the dancers. Brook excused himself and went off to find the gentlemen's room.

And then Max said, 'This feels good, Lucy, feels right.'

'Please, Max. If you say anything, I'll leave.'

'You won't run out on the boy. He likes you.'

'He's a puppy; he likes everyone.'

'No, he doesn't like everyone.' His voice was cold and tired and he leaned across the table, his face inches from her own. She could not get away from him, she had to hear his explanation and she wanted to hear it, no matter how much she told herself that it did not matter to her. 'I couldn't write at first, Lucy. My father had already died when I reached home, and I spent every moment arranging the funeral, comforting my mother and dealing with all the business affairs. It was to escape . . . it was to make up my mind about marriage and career that I went to Europe, and there I found you again.' He laughed, for a moment as young as his son. 'I should have hauled you off on a white charger that night at the Russian Embassy, but I had this fool idea I had to let you grow a little, experiment a little. God, you were lovely, and you didn't know it, or at least acted like you didn't – and that was so refreshing, and then I was so much older.'

'Please, Max. I can't listen to this.'

'I loved you, love you more than I have ever loved any woman. Even now in that silly old-lady frock. Hell, Lucy, are you forty yet?'

'I'm fifty, as you well know. I must go, Max,' She half rose from her chair and he stood beside her, and she was as aware of him as she had ever been. She could smell his strength, his vulnerability – God help her, his masculinity. Knees weak, she sank back into her chair and with trembling hands sipped at the glass of champagne that stood, all its bubbles long gone, beside her coffee.

'When my father died I was devastated.' That was all he would ever say to excuse himself, but Lucy had met many women like Ammabelle du Pay. She was only too aware of the fragile ropes that bind the strongest men, the unvoiced blackmail, the feelings of unwarranted guilt. There had been one tonight. 'Why, you all go and enjoy yourselves and poor little exhausted me (exhausted from the birth of one child twelve years before) will just stay here with a little hot soup.' But still she must not listen.

'I don't know when I asked Ammabelle to honour me by becoming my wife, but I must have done and I could not back out and embarrass her and her family and hurt my own sorely grieving mother. She died happy, just after Brook was born.'

He believed all this, he really believed it. There was nothing devious about Max du Pay. He was just a century behind his time. Lucy could just hear the weak echoes of those soft Southern voices that had trapped him in a loveless marriage. No, she must stop this thinking. He was an international statesman, a world traveller. She knew enough to know that a sexual relationship went on in marriages where there was no real affection. And if Ammabelle du Pay pleaded exhaustion, no doubt her husband found physical consolation outside the bonds of holy matrimony. She thought of Isa: 'You've made your bed, noo lie on it.' By marrying Ammabelle he had effectively made Lucy's bed too, and she was quite happy. She had medicine and she had Robin, and she could not live without either.

'You could have written, Max, to explain, just even to let me know that you were alive.'

He bowed his head in shame. 'I have no excuse. But you didn't write either, Lucy. I hoped and prayed, and then decided your first love had won.'

'Well, it did win and I have Robin.'

'Robin?'

'My god-daughter. Her parents both died in the war; her mother was my partner.'

'Were you bombed? I didn't think Dundee, the bridge maybe . . .'

'She went to France to work in a hospital, really a convent where she and Kier had spent part of their honeymoon. Why, what's wrong?'

'This is unbelievable, but I must have met her. As you know, we didn't come in to the war until near the end, April 1917. We lost a lot of men around the Argonne area, and in 1918 the President asked several of us – Senators, Congressmen – to tour the war zones, see our boys had supplies. We found the Convent near this little town called Le Tréport just a day or two after some Germans had arrived. There was an old French doctor, and a young Scotch girl who looked like a Georgia breeze would blow her away. We gave them supplies – heck, they had everybody's walking wounded in there, Brits, Canadians, French, Germans, and not so much as an aspirin. I asked this old nun what language they communicated in and she said, "The language of love." Pretty soppy, maybe, but old nuns can get away with stuff like that. But you say your partner died there? What a waste! They thought the world of her.'

'I'm glad. I'll tell her daughter.'

He was gazing at her with such intensity that she stopped. 'What is it, Max?'

'I was so close to you. I could have spoken about you and I didn't even know.'

'And Rose? We know so little of her last days.' Speak about Rose, about anything except themselves, except the longing to hold him in her arms, to be held by him.

'Like I said . . . looked like a puff of wind would blow her over, but she worked all the hours God gave her and then some.'

'Her daughter will want to know.'

'Well, she looked happy. They all did. There was this incredible atmosphere there, you could just feel it.'

They sat quietly. Anyone watching would have thought them absorbed in the music, but they were each thinking of Rose Nesbitt, Max with nostalgia and Lucy with a mixture of sadness and love.

Brook came back and Lucy and Max laughed as he tried to stifle a yawn.

'I think we should go?' suggested Lucy.

Brook looked relieved; he would not have to dance. It was impossible to read the expression on Max's face.

The doorman summoned a cab and they sat in silence as the famous buildings of the world's most famous city slipped by in the moonlight.

'You go on up to your room, Brook,' said Max at the door of the club. 'I think we'll walk a while.'

Lucy could not speak. She was not tired and she wanted to walk with him through the starlit streets of London, just once, just once.

They did not talk but walked companionably for a while. Lucy had no real idea of where she was but it did not matter, nothing really mattered. After a while he felt for her hand, and she tensed a little and then relaxed. Was there any harm, just once, in pretending that there was no Ammabelle, no Brook, no Robin?

They were on a bridge crossing the river. Above

them they could see the carved front of the Abbey soaring into the heavens.

'A beautiful sight,' said Max and his voice was husky. It was inevitable: Lucy turned into his arms with a sigh and for a while they stood and she relaxed against his heart, at ease, at home. When he bent his head she turned her face to him like a flower to the sun that gives it life. Her heart soared higher than the façade of the beautiful building behind them. She was a girl again, on a bridge over the Grand Canal. No, no, she was not. Feverishly she pulled herself away.

'Max, no, this is madness.'

He stopped her protestations with his lips and for a moment she fought, and then gave herself up to the feelings that were overwhelming her, feelings that had not abated in fourteen years but had lain, disciplined, just under her control. This time it was Max who stopped.

'Oh, God, Lucy, what a bloody mess I have made of everything.'

'We made it together.'

'Let's walk some more or, so help me, I won't be responsible.'

'I can't lose you again, Lucy,' he went on. 'I fought the yearning for fourteen years and one sight of you at that desk with that silly little hat . . . You're wearing it again; it's a doctory little hat!'

She unpinned the hat and threw it into the Thames and then she unpinned her hair and let the pins fall unheeded to the ground.

'My God, don't do that.' His voice was harsh and rough. 'You're such an innnocent, Doctor Lucy, or is that something they teach in medical school – "Let down your hair when you want to entice a man."'

'No, but they do teach how to blow out the fire if it's started.'

He laughed and hugged her, the spontaneous gesture of a brother, not a lover.

'Time to get a cab. Come on.' He tucked her arm into his and they walked towards a busier street. 'I can't divorce my wife, Lucy. I wish I could. It's not that she loves me . . . you see, she's . . .' He stopped; he would not be even more disloyal. 'Can we, at least, write one another, even maybe call when they get these transatlantic lines in, see one another when I'm in Europe? I could send the boy to school here; I could come over every year . . .'

She said nothing, for she could not speak. Her heart was breaking for the despair and anguish in his voice. She wished they had not met . . . No, she didn't. Oh God, oh God, it was an impossibility. What good could come of it? Better to make a clean break, to cut out the heartache.'

She heard her voice. 'I'll write, as a friend, at Christmas time.'

He had hailed a cab and, to her surprise, handed her in and gave the driver the address and the fare.

His voice was calm but his eyes were unutterably sad.

'Until Christmas, friend of my heart,' he said and stepped back into the shadows.

23

Dundee 1921

LUCY LEFT EARLY next morning, or that morning, for Dundee, and therefore did not see Max or any member of his family again. She had not slept but had packed her few clothes and the toys bought for Robin into her small overnight bag and then, fully dressed, had lain down on the bed to wait for her early morning tea. Over and over again she had relived those moments with Max by the river. Her feelings for him had not died as, for fourteen years, she had fought to convince herself that they had. Instead they had grown and matured like the fine wines of which he was fond, but he would not divorce his wife and Lucy would not – when she was rational and the blood was not raging through her fevered veins – have wanted him to take such a drastic step.

By the time the chambermaid arrived with the tray, she was going over and over the things she had learned in Doctor Stopes' clinic, and which she intended to utilize as soon as she returned to her practice. There was a parcel on the tray – from one of London's finest jewellers, and beautifully wrapped. Max's card, in a small envelope, was beside it.

The box contained a small gold brooch in the shape of an exquisitely formed butterfly; the body of the butterfly was a perfect ruby.

'Merry Christmas past' was the inscription on the card.

'I can't accept jewellery from a man,' said Lucy to herself as she pinned the brooch to the front of her dress.

An hour later she was on the train north.

Robin was sitting on the dining-room table when Isa welcomed Lucy home. She jumped from the table into Lucy's arms.

'Ladies do not sit on dining-room tables,' said Lucy, kissing the child's tumbled curls.

'Isa has told me all day that I am not a lady.'

'And so, you decided to prove that she was right. You are a naughty girl and should not be given the parcel that's at the bottom of my bag.'

It was good to be home. Already it felt as if she had never been away.

The brooch caught in Robin's hair as she slid out of Lucy's arms.

'Pretty,' she said.

'Robin, I almost forgot. The friend who gave me this brooch knew Mummy in the war. He said she was beautiful and brave and saved the lives of lots and lots of soldiers.'

Robin forgot about the parcel waiting for her in Lucy's bag while she heard over and over again about the meeting of Dr Rose Nesbitt and an American senator. Some things Lucy had to realistically invent. 'What was Mummy wearing? How many British soldiers did she save? Did she save German soldiers too? I hope she didn't.'

'But of course she did, Robin, for Mummy was a doctor and the poor German soldiers didn't want to fight any more than the Scottish ones did.'

'That's stupid. If no one wanted to fight, then why was there a war?'

Lucy looked down at the five-year-old child who

had lost both her parents to a war neither had wanted. She did not know the answer and so avoided the question. 'It was so awful, Robin, that there will never ever be a war again.'

'Good. Did you bring me a book?'

'I thought little girls liked dolls.'

'Not so much as books.'

'Wherever I go from now on, I shall buy you a book.'

Robin nodded emphatically. 'Good.'

'Time for bed. I'll bath you.'

'I haven't done my homework and you haven't sharpened my pencils. Get a scalpel. Mine have to be the very, very sharpest. Miss Blair likes Fiona best 'cause she has the best pencils.'

Lucy sighed. Robin adored her teacher, an iron-clad maiden lady, and wanted to please her in every way. Miss Blair demanded four sharp pencils every day, and so every evening they went through the ritual of sharpening Robin's pencils to danger point.

'You are trying to make me forget that you have not yet done your homework, madam.'

'It's just to read, Aunt Lucy, and to learn three words and I already know them anyway, but if you hear me say them, then you can sign my jotter and Miss Blair will love me as much as she loves Fiona.'

Was it her lack of parents that made Robin so insecure, or did all little girls want to be loved by their first teacher? Lucy could not remember, but vowed to have a word with the, to her, formidable Miss Blair. She listened to Robin read, signed the jotter to show that BELL, WELL, and SPELL could be correctly spelled by Miss Anderson-Howard, and an hour later managed to sit down to go over the accumulated letters.

'A doctor should ken not to read while she's

eating,' fussed Isa. 'It's very bad for the digestion and not a good example for Miss Robin.'

'She's sound asleep, Isa, and this halibut is wonderful.'

Somewhat mollified, Isa went off and Lucy finished her meal and went through her letters. She went into her office and began to go through her notes on birth control and then somehow, all by itself, the pencil wrote 'Merry Christmas past'. She had promised to write to him, once a year, at Christmas. She would send it once a year, but there could be no harm in writing little bits all year round. Having no real idea of the length of time it would take for a letter posted in Dundee to reach Washington DC, she posted her first letter to Max on the 1st of October 1921.

Max laughed with pleasure when the strange letter arrived a full month before Christmas and sat down to answer it immediately. He had never been to Dundee and he had certainly never seen her home, but he imagined her fairly accurately as she sat before a roaring fire in her elegantly furnished sitting room, scribbling away everything except what was really in her heart. He took his tone from her letter. Brook was a joy. Ammabelle was rather unwell – he did not give her illness a name and Lucy sighed for him. He had hoped that the trip to Europe, new sights, new sounds, would help, but if anything it seemed to have made things worse. She could not bear to have Brook near her and was somewhat less fond of his father.

I refuse to leave her though, for I feel that she does draw some strength from my presence although she denies it and says my very size tires her. The doctors agree with me but suggest I do send Brook to a board school. It is not merely with my own interests at heart that I have decided on one of your fine Scottish institutions.

In August 1922 Brook du Pay arrived at Lucy's front door just as she drove up with Robin. Lucy's heart leapt like a spawning salmon trying to jump up a waterfall and then settled somewhere at the bottom of her stomach. At thirteen the boy was tall and slim; it was Max she saw there, Max. 'Brook,' she whispered and then recovered. 'Brook!' Her voice was much stronger. 'How lovely to see you.'

'I guess the letter didn't reach you.' His voice had changed in a year; low and strong, it uncannily resembled the mellow tones of his father. 'Dad sent me over with a tutor. Mother is . . . well, she's kinda sick, Doctor Lucy, and I really get in her hair.' He broke off and looked at Robin who was staring at them with both her eyes and mouth wide. Lucy laughed. 'Brook, this is my god-daughter Robin Anderson-Howard.'

'How do you do, Miss Robin Anderson-Howard,' said Brook and held out his hand.

Robin shook hands formally and Lucy was proud of her training. Then the child spoiled the effect by adding, 'You are a very pretty boy.'

'Robin, "how do you do" is enough.'

'Heck no, Doctor Lucy, no one ever told me I was pretty before.'

'Where are your cases,' – no, what did Americans say? – 'your bags, Brook?'

'Oh, we checked into a hotel and Mr Van Doeren let me take a cab over. We're only here a few days. I have to get to Edinburgh to buy the outfit.'

Isa had opened the door and was standing waiting. 'Are you coming in or are you going to stay out there all night?'

'We have a guest for tea, Isa.' For the moment Lucy
had forgotten that Isa had been with her in Venice,
with her in Tuscany.

'Oh, no,' breathed Isa as she looked at the boy's
face, so like that of his father. 'It can't be.'

'This is Brook du Pay, Isa.'

'I'll get the tea,' Isa muttered, ignoring Brook's
outstretched hands.

'Please forgive her, Brook,' said Lucy angrily.
'She's a rude, bad-tempered old woman.'

'She isn't usually,' said Robin, 'but it doesn't
matter. She makes lovely biscuits.'

There was no opportunity to talk to Brook until he
was seated beside her in the car driving back to his
hotel. Robin had demanded his full attention to her
school-books and Lucy had enjoyed watching them.
They were very alike, tall for their ages, slender and
dark-haired, 'almost brother and sister', she thought
and tore her mind away from that path.

'I'm sorry that your mother is no better, Brook.'
She did not want to pry, to make the boy unhappy
by forcing him to face a situation that his father
had obviously encouraged him, in public at least,
to avoid.

'She's never been very strong, Doctor Lucy, and
she gets real exhausted when there's any kind of
pressure, I guess you'd say. She used to love our
house in Washington and all the parties, but now
she never goes and Dad has to go himself . . . but
this year he has decided to stay in Georgia, just until
she gets a little better.'

'And he has decided to send his much-loved son
away from him,' thought Lucy. She had been a doctor
for a long time; she had many patients who shared
Ammabelle's symptoms, but she could not tell the
fragile boy that she knew. She muttered something

encouraging and then talked of the adventure of going to a new school in a new country.

'And you can come to me for exeats, Brook. You must never stay in school when you have permission to have a weekend away.'

Later, in her bedroom as she sat at the mirror, she regretted those words.

'Oh, Max, am I to be content with being a surrogate mother for your child as well as Kier's? I should be content; my child-bearing years are over. I should have forgotten the anticipation, the uncontrollable leaping passion. I should have forgotten Italy, forgotten those desperate words in London. Better far to say you never meant it, to hate you, to put you out of my mind. Better not to encourage your son, Ammabelle's son, to make himself welcome in my retreat. This house is for Robin. And it's a doctor's house, a place where people come to get well, to find hope and joy and courage in despair.'

She glared in the mirror at the dark eyes, the tumbling brown hair that had – yes, it did – flecks of grey. 'You're too old to still want Max, too old to have your heart dance with joy at the sound of his name, at a glance from his son that reminds you of Washington and, oh, dear God, how he reminds you of Tuscany. Why do I torture myself with longing? Max belongs to Ammabelle and I can't hope, can't . . . must not pray.'

24

1923

ALTHOUGH LUCY HAD sent her yearly letter, she received no Christmas letter from Max, but in early December a card arrived from Brook. He was on his way home for Christmas: he hoped to resume his studies in the New Year. What did it mean? Lucy refused to speculate – she could not, must not. A few days later a small packet arrived for Miss Anderson-Howard and, when opened on Christmas morning, was found to contain a silver propelling pencil . . . 'to make your jotters tidier . . .' Robin practised all day.

'When he comes he'll see I'm neater than Fiona.'

Lucy tried delicately to prepare her to be hurt. 'He might not be able to come back for a while. America is a long way away.'

Robin wrote a superbly beautiful 'B' on her paper. She decorated it with flowers. 'He'll be back, Auntie Lucy.'

The New Year came. The spring followed, but there was no communication from Georgia or Washington DC. Lucy accepted an invitation to a conference in Paris.

'Paris? Can I come?'

'Not this time, Robin. I'm working. One day, I promise.'

'But you will go, won't you? You'll go to see my father's grave?'

Lucy faced that that was what had been in the back of her mind since she heard about the conference. The first war graves had been officially prepared in 1920. Why had she not gone then? 'Robin was too small,' she answered herself. Now there was no excuse, no excuse not to find and visit both graves.

'I'll go, sweetheart, and I'll put some flowers there.'

'I'll pay for them,' said Robin, and fished a rather sticky sixpence out of the pocket in her knickers.

The conference in Paris went very well. On the first Friday evening Lucy took the train to Amiens, which was relatively close to everywhere she wanted to go and where she could at least find taxis, if not a car for hire. It was late and dark when she arrived, and so she went straight to her hotel. Even on the trains she had been aware of the cemeteries; it was impossible not to be aware of them. They stretched, in silent witness to the stupidity of man, for miles into the distance. She had Robin's sixpence. Tomorrow she would take the equivalent amount in francs and see what flowers a little girl could buy for the father she had never known and who had probably never even known of her existence.

The hotel was comfortable and clean and, thanks both to Herr Colner and to her year in Rouen, she was able to order a delicious meal.

'I'll bring Robin here one day,' she thought.

There were few other guests in the hotel, and the others in the dining room were obviously local people who appreciated Madame Viseux's superb cooking. Madame took pity on her foreign guest – perhaps because that foreigner had enough sense to try the local speciality of Queues de Boeufs aux Olives Noirs and not to stick to the familiar Coq au

Vin that all other foreigners ordered – and stood beside her while she drank her second cup of excellent coffee.

'You are on holiday, Madame?'

'No. I was in Paris on business . . .'

Madame Viseux was interested. A woman alone and on business.

'Business, Madame?'

'I am a doctor and I am attending a conference.' Lucy realized there was no reason not to tell her; the woman was interested, not nosy.

'Médecin. This is undoubtedly an honour, Madame.'

'You are a superb cook, Madame.' It was time to share the glory.

Madame was complacent. She shrugged, a typically Gallic shrug, and Lucy smiled to see it. 'We all use the talents le bon Dieu gives us, Madame Médecin. You have come for the graves?'

'Yes.'

'Few come but we are thinking, Jean Luc and I, we are thinking that a trickle is becoming a tide and we should expand our hotel.'

'Very wise, Madame.'

'The good food eases the heartache, no?'

'Indeed.'

'Your husband, Madame?'

'A friend.'

Well satisfied, Madame Viseux took herself off to the kitchen where Lucy became a woman who had lost her lover to war and who had become a doctor to cure the ills of the surviving world. Unaware of the halo she was wearing, Lucy went to her comfortable room to write to Robin and to sleep.

. . . Now I am in Amiens and tomorrow I will find

Daddy's grave in Louvencourt. The War Graves
Commission have worked so hard to make a list
of where every brave soldier is buried. It is very
beautiful and peaceful. I have your sixpence, dear
Robin, and I am sure I will find some lovely
flowers.

This hotel is small, very comfortable, and the
food is, you will be glad to hear, absolutely superb.
It is a perfect place for a little girl to practise her
French, and one day soon, we shall have a holiday,
a *vacance*, here.

The next morning a solicitous and sympathetic maid
brought croissants light as air and the coffee Lucy
had ordered although she had been offered tea.
The tea in Paris had cured her of ever making that
mistake again.

'No doubt Madame could make a decent cup of tea,
but in Rome etc etc,' she told herself. 'Who knows,
tomorrow I may be brave enough to try chocolate in
the morning.' She could imagine Annie as clearly as if
she were in the room. 'Chocolate, for breakfast? You
have your cocoa afore you go to your bed.'

But Annie was dead, had been dead for years. Lucy
shivered. She had not thought much about it before
but, apart from Isa, only Robin was left, a tiny thread
connecting her to everyone who had gone before.

She left the hotel and her taxi driver escorted her
to the cemeteries.

'You should have seen them just a few years ago,
Madame: wild flowers everywhere, scarlet poppies,
blue cornflowers, white camomile, perfect for French
and English dead, no? But, like you English we
French are good gardeners and we have worked
hard to grow the flowers of the countries these
children left behind. Unfortunately the giant maples

of Canada do not grow well here, or some of the flowers of India. You have forget-me-nots for your husband, Madame?'

'No.'

'Your King came in 1922 . . . to Passchendaele. At Étaples he asked the gardener to take him to a grave, not one of the ones he was being shown. The King of England, Madame, he stood by this little grave and he took an envelope from his pocket. There were forget-me-nots in it, sent by the soldier's mother, a simple woman, to the Queen. He bent over the grave and carefully put the little bouquet upon it. Then he turned to the gardener: "See you keep them watered as long as possible," he said. I hope his maman knows how hard we try.'

Her heart too full for speech, Lucy lay back and watched the rows and rows of headstones go by. How many mothers would be unable to put flowers on these graves? They reached Louvencourt and she asked the driver to wait. She would not be long.

She had already contacted the authorities and knew the number of the cross and the line it was in. Her arms were full of the flowers for which France was justly famous. She stopped on a path and looked around and remembered Wordsworth's poem about the daffodils. But it was not gaily dancing flowers that stretched as far as the eye could see here, but little headstones marching in solemn witness towards Blomfield's magnificent cross of remembrance. The silence crushed her eardrums, her brain. Thousands and thousands of mute appeals. Lucy knew the figures. She had read them every day in the newspapers but eight thousand, eleven thousand, nineteen thousand in one day meant nothing, nothing until now.

Her eyes misty with unshed tears, she started walking again to the section that sheltered Major Kier

Anderson-Howard. Private ——— aged nineteen; Gunner ——— aged seventeen, Fusilier ——— aged nineteen. 'My God, they are children. We fought a war with children.'

No, not all were children. Here lay husbands and fathers. How many, like Kier, had never known that they were to live on in the gift of an unborn child?

Her feet had found his grave, but her knees refused to support her legs and she sank down on the neatly mown grass.

Almost four years. Did it make it easier to accept death if one could take part in its rituals? Had she really realized the finality of death? 'The War Office regrets . . .' Had they really accepted it? Now she saw with painful lucidity that it had taken seeing this plain little white stone with his name and rank and the simple cross carved on it and the date of his death. She looked around again. How many of the wives, mothers, sweethearts of all the men buried under these crosses could ever afford the luxury of seeing the grave, of attending it as she was doing, of putting a floral tribute on the sad mound? The war was not over – the fighting perhaps, but for too many women the war would never end.

Lucy looked in her handbag and found her nail-file; it was all she could find with a sharp point. She began to dig, and when she had a little hole she dropped Robin's sixpence in it and covered it up.

'She's giving you all she had, Kier. You would love her; she's very like you, in looks but in nature too. I'll have to watch her as she gets older, make sure no one tries to take advantage of her soft heart. You should see her on her pony, fearless, but unlike you she is too interested in food and I have to watch her like a hawk. We don't want a fat child, do we? I can't understand where that comes from. Rose ate next to nothing.' Suddenly she made up her mind. 'I wasn't going to, but if the conference finishes early I'll try to see Rosie for you too, Kier, and for Robin.'

That night she finished her letter to Kier's daughter.

The graves are very peaceful. There is an atmosphere – a feeling, a peacefulness. I gave Daddy your flowers and I have taken a photograph. (*She was no expert with the unfamiliar equipment and prayed it would turn out.*) There are gardeners, old soldiers, who drive around in a dreadful old car but they keep everything quite beautiful. There are flowers all year. The French are so good at flowers, and Daddy did love the gardens at Laverock Rising. I go back to Paris tomorrow and I shall buy you a new frock – and a book . . . in French!

I may be a day or two late – I will send a telegram – but I will have lots to tell you when I meet you in London.

Lots of love,
Aunt Lucy

The next morning, after a second visit to the cemetery, she went back to Paris. On the train she looked at and revised the notes she had made for her paper on community welfare and found herself drafting a letter to Colin Dryden, still a valued friend, who might just start a fund that would allow impoverished relatives to visit, at least once, the graves of their dead. She would call it the Anderson-Howard Memorial Fund. Did not both of the Anderson-Howards lie in graves in rural France marked only by small white stones? Four days later, her paper delivered and well received –

the French had Madame Curie after all; they easily accepted a woman – she was on a train to Ste Antoine sur Somme. No lines of crosses here. She hoped there would be an hotel, and made enquiries.

'There are fine hotels at Le Tréport, Madame, or Dieppe itself,' she was told, 'but the Convent sometimes takes guests. At least they used to, before the war.'

The Mother Superior welcomed her with coffee in a room that should have been gloomy but was not. The heavy oak furniture was lovingly polished and there was a glorious arrangement of roses in a silver bowl set in the middle of a round table. Reverend Mother spoke excellent English.

'We have not had an English guest for some time, Madame. The coming of the motor car . . .' She shrugged her shoulders. No one needed to stop at the Convent now.

Lucy, who found her Bentley a necessary and welcome replacement for her old pony and trap at home, commiserated with her.

'But we must not stand in the way of progress, Sister.' She bit into a biscuit that dissolved like snow on a child's tongue. 'The new idea is to advertise. These biscuits would bring hungry guests from all over Britain.'

Reverend Mother laughed and threw up her hands in mock horror.

'What a truly terrifying thought! We are a contemplative order, Madame. Our hospitality was originally a gesture of good will, charity if you like, to the benighted traveller. But you have come deliberately to see us, Sister Antoine says.' Her voice rose a little, questioningly. She would never ask outright, but if Madame chose to honour her with a confidence . . .

'I am not Madame Graham, Sister, but Doctor

Graham. I wrote to the Convent in 1918 . . .' She stopped. As soon as she had said the word Doctor, a warmth had come into the old nun's eyes. 'Did I write to you, Sister?'

'No, Madame. I was not Superior then, but I was told about your letter. You have come about La Petite, the little doctor?'

'Yes. Doctor Nesbitt was my partner, and I am guardian of her daughter.'

'You will wish to see her grave. It is marked like the others and I tend it myself. Unfortunately, it is too dark now, but tomorrow morning . . .'

'Then I may stay for a day or two?'

'But of course, and now you are doubly welcome.' Reaching behind her, she took a photograph in a silver frame from the bookshelf and handed it to Lucy. It was a group picture and the photographer had not been very skilled. The figures were blurred, but she recognized Rose. She had changed from the elegant and sophisticated woman who had gone to France. Always slight, she was almost emaciated, but even the poor quality of the photograph could not hide the happiness in the face.

'She was happy here, Sister. I am so glad. She had not been happy for some time.'

'Ah, the death of her husband. I understand. We worked together. There are sisters here and even people in the village who remember her with gratitude; she was a good doctor.'

The old nun's hand was held out. Lucy was embarrassed that she had stared so long at the photograph, at Rose surrounded by recovering patients, she supposed, and one or two nuns.

She handed it back. 'You are not in the photograph, Sister?'

'She liked music, La Petite, and so did Captain

Drummond.' She pointed at a tall, thin soldier beside Rose. 'When we were not too busy I played the piano. The patients liked to hear it when they rested in the garden.'

'It's a lovely garden.'

'Ah, tomorrow you will see. It is back to the splendour of before the war. The other doctor, Doctor Mouton, weeded when he had the chance. Not much opportunity to garden in a war and, besides, it is well known that the soil of the Somme is heavy with chalk, is it not?'

'Rose stayed here on her honeymoon in 1907, Sister.'

'I wondered, but I was not here until the war and we never knew her married name.'

'Anderson-Howard.'

'Come in, Sister.' Lucy had not heard the soft footsteps.

'Sister Antoine will show you to your room, Madame. Dinner will be served to you there. If there is anything at all that you want, please ask.' She hesitated. 'You speak French very well, I think.'

'I studied in Rouen for a year.'

'Forgive me, Madame. Usually the British . . .'

'I am rusty, Sister, and will enjoy being oiled by conversation with Sister Antoine.'

'And if I may continue to practise my English . . .'

Lucy smiled. The nun's English was stilted but very good.

The guest room was simply furnished and reminded Lucy with a pang of her bedroom at Casata d'Aurora. In the morning she found that the view was not of mountains but of the garden, and as soon as she was ready she hurried out to see it in all its glory. She walked briskly down a path, trying to see everything as Rose had seen it, and came to a small gate. The graveyard: so unlike the serried rows in Louvencourt and Le Tréport. There were a few stones to commemorate members of the community who had died and then, against a wall of pear trees, the graves of the Allied servicemen, and of the Scottish and French doctors who had died as a result of the war.

'You wish to change the inscription?' The Reverend Mother had joined her from another pathway.

Lucy shook her head. 'I don't think so. One day her daughter will decide, but as Rose Anderson-Howard she is commemorated on her husband's family crypt. I like "Rose Nesbitt, Médecin".'

'We had begun to pray that she might find new happiness with the young officer. He died saving her, you know, from a German. He lies here too, the German, but in another part. His commander shot him. They were not all bad, the Germans.'

Lucy had wondered about the serenity in Rose's face in the photograph, and had decided to ask no questions about Captain Drummond.

'Were you taken by the Germans, Sister?'

'No, they were retreating and wanted only food. The Americans came after them – a day or two, no more – but one day too late to save the gallant captain.'

'And Rose?'

'She worked too hard and, I think – though perhaps you will say I am a romantic old woman living vicariously – I think she lost heart.'

Perhaps she did, thought Lucy, but the photograph had told her that Rose, as she had expected, was already ill.

'I nursed her myself as well as I could. We had no trained medical personnel at all by that time. Our recovering patients returned to their armies and, her job done, La Petite released her hold on life.'

'Did she speak about her daughter?' She could not tell Robin that her mother had seemed to have forgotten about her completely.

'She did not speak very much at all, Madame. I knew she had a child – she told me, but she was a very private person. She liked birds, though; she was very fond of birds.'

'Birds?'

'Ah, the ubiquitous little robin. Madame's mind wandered at the end and always she said, "My robin, my lovely little robin."'

25

1923

IT WAS RAINING when Lucy arrived in London. After the sunny skies of France that fact should have been guaranteed to dampen the spirits, but for some reason she felt happy. She would see Robin; she would tell her about her mother and about the bravery of Captain Andrew Drummond. She would not tell the child that at last her mother had been falling really in love, but she would tell her Rose's last soft words. Looking out of the taxi windows at the sheets of rain, she became more practical. It would be very nice if the rain would go before morning. Tomorrow they were shopping.

The Overseas League was as warm and as welcoming as ever. Lucy signed in and looked automatically for Robin's name. She and Isa should have arrived yesterday:

Miss Anderson-Howard
Mrs Isa Murray

There was another name written in large, proud letters at the top of the page, just above Robin's. Lucy gazed at it, her heart doing remarkable, very unmedical things inside her body.

Maximilian du Pay

She should not be surprised. Thousands of people

used the Club as a home from home. He was an
international statesman, and the Overseas League
was more intimate than a hotel; probably he was here
on Senate business, and was not even going to tell
her. Well, she would dine in her room. Robin would
like that. They would make it a party; she need not
even see Max.

He was alone. Ammabelle? Brook? Yes, Ammabelle
was better and he had decided to see his son's school
for himself. That was all.

'He doesn't mean to see you, Lucy, to raise hopes.
Oh, stop your heart leaping, the way it leapt all those
years . . . all those wasted years . . . It should be
schooled by now. The fires should be dead.'

She turned to the porter. 'Send up some tea, please,
and milk for my ward.'

'There's a note, ma'am – I'd almost forgotten. Mrs
Bell has taken the children to the opera.'

How dare he? Isa would never have contemplated
such a thing. He had sent them off to leave the way
clear . . . for what?

She smiled at the porter. 'Tea for one, then, please,'
and went off up the lovely wood staircase to her
room.

There were roses in her bedroom; their scent filled
the air. They were everywhere: on the table by the
window, in the fireplace, on the bedside table. Lucy's
heart leapt again. No, no, it was stupid. This was the
action of a romantic young man. She had been given
the wrong room, a honeymooner's room. She would
complain at once . . . her hand reached for the bell to
summon a chambermaid.

It was Max who stood there when she opened the
door. She could say nothing, do nothing.

'I couldn't quite match your red dress,' he said at
last, and then she was in his arms. There were tears

on her face. Were they hers? Were they his? She could not see him through the haze. There was nothing and no one in the whole world but Max du Pay . . . another woman's husband. She wrenched herself out of his arms, turned away from him and stepped back into her room.

He stood in the corridor and waited. A thousand thoughts were rushing through Lucy's head. She was a young girl again and she had no idea what to do or what to say.

'We Southerners don't compromise our women,' said Max from the safety of the corridor, and she turned and saw that he was laughing at her gently, understandingly. 'I guess the red dress is long gone?'

She nodded.

'We'll buy a new one tomorrow. Tonight, you look just beautiful the way you are. Will you have dinner here in the restaurant with an old friend?'

Why did she hesitate?

'We have to talk, Lucy.'

She was filled with panic. 'I've ordered tea . . . I'm tired, Max . . . the conference . . . the boat-train.'

'I cancelled your dratted tea.'

He straightened his shoulders and she looked at him. He had changed, he looked like a man who had . . . suffered.

'Ammabelle is gone, Lucy,' he said quietly, 'and I deeply regret any part I played in her death. She had cancer of the liver; too many years of too much champagne, maybe because a rich husband who didn't really love her wasn't enough for her. I'm fifty-five years old, Lucy. I've wasted half my life, more. I don't regret it all; there's Brook, and I think I can be proud of some of the work I've done . . .'

He stopped as an interested chambermaid hurried

past the open door. Lucy laughed and pulled him inside. 'I'm too old to be compromised,' she said and, without thinking, she put her arms around his neck.

Max bent his head, but he did not kiss her. He held her gently as if she was a butterfly that must not be crushed, and buried his face in her hair. As they stood together without speaking, in a silence that said more than a thousand conversations, Lucy felt all the doubts and worries and regrets of thirty-four years grow lighter and lighter and eventually fly away.

'We'll have dinner,' he said at last, his mouth still against her hair, 'and we'll talk. Come with me now, because if I leave you here you'll start thinking about age and your patients and Robin . . .'

'And the fact that you live on one continent and I on another . . .'

'Little things, little things,' he said. 'Come on, before I change my mind.'

She laughed and they went downstairs hand-in-hand, but said nothing until they were at a table in the dining room. Words did not seem to be necessary. The waiters came and Max ordered for them both.

When the wine steward had poured the glasses of champagne, Max lifted his glass and toasted her silently. Then he spoke.

'I wish I could say I loved you from the moment I first saw you, Lucy. I sure . . . fell in like with you . . . that evening in Washington . . . you flitted like a butterfly among all those old iron-clad people.' He stopped for a moment, remembering. 'And then, when I was drifting so aimlessly, I found you again . . . in Venice. Venice and the Casata d'Aurora . . .'

He stopped and they looked at one another, and the lost years of pain melted away.

She blushed. 'It must be changed,' she said to hide her confusion.

'No,' he said, 'nothing's changed. I bought it that winter, you see – for us, Lucy. One of Mauro's sons looks after it for me. His kids play in the orchard where I still see you . . . the blossoms in your hair . . . on your breast. I've carried that picture in my head all these years . . . He stopped and Lucy smiled at the look on his face. 'You're wearing my brooch.'

'Every day,' she told him.

He stretched out his hand and lightly touched the brooch and then her mouth.

'I've got it all worked out,' he said at last. 'I've resigned my Senate seat. The businesses have good managers. You want to keep on working, I'll . . .'

One day you'll meet a man and you'll know. Nothing else will be important.'

'I do,' she said. 'You've never asked, Max, but I do. I love you, and nothing else is important.' She hesitated. 'Well, that's not quite true. I can't leave Robin. Otherwise I would go with you tonight, anywhere, to Washington, to Georgia, to Italy . . .'

'You'll go nowhere until you're married, you hussy,' he said and his voice was low with suppressed passion.

Married? Married? How? There was Robin, and there was Brook, and there were patients – always, always her patients.

'You will marry me?' he asked anxiously. The obstacles disappeared. How could he doubt?

'Yes,' she said simply and her hand reached for his across the table, and all the years fell away and they were young again.

'I'll establish residency,' he said, his voice choked with emotion. 'December?' he suggested.

'December,' she said.

'Women like you are rare, Lucy, like butterflies in December.'

Walnut Shell Days

For Ian Sommerville

Acknowledgements

Thank you to all the writers who share so much, especially Hugh Rae, Sheila Lewis and Elizabeth Sutherland.

Prologue

Paris, 24th May 1900

HE HAD LEFT THE WINDOW open and the sound of the fruit sellers' carts, as they rattled along the cobblestones, woke him. The early-morning scents of Paris – baking bread and cold, damp, sickly-sweet river water – drifted through the windows and mixed with Genevieve's perfume, the bouquet of the remainder of that second bottle of very good claret and the pleasing, masculine smell of an excellent cigar.

He smiled and stretched, remembering the assorted pleasures of the night. France was a most civilized country. Great food, fine wine, wonderfully seductive and enchanting women; too much to expect the cigars to be French. He should buy a box or two before he caught the boat train: couldn't get tobacco like that at home.

Genevieve woke, her glorious eyes focusing slowly.

'Jean,' she breathed, in that so French way she had of caressing his very ordinary Scottish name, the way that turned his legs to water. 'Jean,' she said again, and she stretched out her white hand with the scarlet fingernails towards him and he almost yielded.

'Must go, my darling,' he said, kissing her lightly but keeping out of the way of those nails, nails that could caress so softly but could scratch so deeply. 'I have to catch the steamer train.'

'Oh no,' she said, her hands gripping him. 'You said two whole days in Paris.'

He laughed. 'It has been two days, *ma belle*, the most beautiful two days . . .'

'Of our lives, my Jean.'

She was so desirable; he had never met a woman like her. He groaned and forced himself to move away from the rumpled bed. How easy it would be, and how very, very pleasurable, to slip back into the warm bed, into Genevieve's arms. 'I have something to attend to in Scotland, Genevieve. I'll come back just as soon as I can.'

Genevieve was not a woman to beg. She shrugged a shoulder in a very French way. *Très bien*, her shoulders said. Who cares? I am just as content if you go. What does it matter?

For a moment he looked down at her creamy back and toyed with the idea of making her change her mind. He could do it. They were all the same, *n'est-ce pas*? And then he remembered Scotland and his responsibilities. He echoed her shrug and began to dress.

Less than half an hour later, he was whistling merrily as he sauntered down the plushly carpeted staircase to the foyer, where two maids were already angrily scrubbing and polishing unseen dirt. He strolled past them and reached the door.

'Monsieur, Monsieur, the bill?'

John Cameron tipped his hat lightly back on his handsome head. He stared boldly at the hotel manager out of his grey-blue eyes and laughed.

'Don't fret, my man. Madame will take care of it.' And, once more whistling gaily, he was gone.

Priory Farm, Angus, 24th May 1900

Pain gripped Catriona. It tore at her angrily, as if punishing her for some unknown crime. Sweat broke out on her forehead and she tried desperately not to scream. She had never believed it would be like this, never. Was she not the daughter of farmers? Had she not seen birth a dozen times a year – a thing done privately, causing as little trouble as possible.

'Ach, lassie, let it oot. There's nane tae hear but me and auld Jock oot there and he'd bear it for ye, gin he could.' The voice was that of Maggie, employed by Jock Cameron as dairy maid and now midwife.

Catriona's scream tore through the air and died to a gasping whimper. Maggie held her hand and outside Jock stopped his pacing and listened.

'Dear God, help the lassie, as I've never been able to help.' She was quiet. Was that it? Was it over? Was he a grandfather?

There was another scream, cut short by the simple expedient of biting as hard as Catriona could on the rolled-up towel that old Maggie had put into her open mouth. Catriona's eyes rolled in agony; there was a name she wanted to call out, but she would not. She would not beg and she would not hurt the old man any more by having him hear it.

The pain receded and she took the towel away. 'It's cold for May, Maggie, so cold.'

The midwife looked at the girl for a moment. Cold? It was a perfect May day. This morning the sweat had been rolling down between her ample breasts as she had sat milking in the parlour, and now her newly washed cotton frock was damp with perspiration. But the lassie was cold. 'Dear Lord, shock.' She ran to the airing cupboard for clean, warm blankets. Everything was to hand, meticulously prepared by Catriona herself.

'Let me hap you up a bit mare, lassie: you've lost a wheen too much blood but it'll soon be over. In a moment, the next push will bring us the head and your bonnie wee bairn will slip oot like a boat bein' launched intae the Tay.'

Catriona could hear Maggie's voice but she could not

make out the words. She seemed to be floating. It was such a lovely feeling. She had been suddenly so cold, and now she was happed up the way her own mother had happed her up against the cold of an Angus winter. So safe, so secure. Nothing hurt, nothing mattered – nothing, nothing. She would drift away, oh so slowly, like a leaf tossed into a quiet stream.

But Maggie would not let her slip away into that peace and contentment. She shook the girl, she cajoled, she wheedled. 'Catriona, Catriona, fight, lassie, fight. The bairn's crowning. He's coming, lass. I can see his heed. Whit a crown of dark hair, jist like his daddy.'

His daddy. John. John with his grey-blue eyes, his devastating smile, his hands that could . . . For a moment she struggled but no, it was so warm here, so peaceful – no pain, no tears, no wondering why. She would stay here where it was warm, where nothing hurt, where sound was blurred and hazy and soft. 'Oh, John, why?' Had she said the words or just thought them? She had no time to wonder, for the pain struck again and instinct took over her exhausted body.

'Work with the pains, lassie, dinnae fight them. That's it, that's it. Jist a wee breath there, a wee rest tae get ready for the next one.'

In the passageway outside, Jock Cameron still paced as he waited. It was his fault, all of it. That lassie had been in there for fourteen hours trying to birth her baby, and the man who should have been here, either by himself or marching side by side with Jock, was God alone knew where.

'I spoilt him, Mattie,' he told his long-dead wife. 'He was that bonnie and winning though, and aye minded me of you. I couldnae hit you, Mattie, that's whit it would have felt like and he knew it, the wee rascal, but he's a grown man now, Mattie. I'll never forgive him for this and if the good Lord spares me my daughter-in-law and my grandchild, I'll make it up to them.'

He walked on, backwards and forwards, sometimes praying to the Almighty, at other times justifying himself to his Mattie. Then he would work out how best to reward Catriona for her patience, her friendliness, her charm. He would bypass John, hurt him in his pocket – that would teach him. He would see the lawyer fellow and write the laddie in and John out.

The door of the best bedroom opened and Maggie stood there, drying her hands on one of Catriona's best towels. She was smiling – well, as near as auld Maggie could get to a smile for a man. 'You can stop your tramping, Jock Cameron. You've near worn a hole in that good rug and it's the mistress will have to be on her knees darning it, and her with more than enough to do.'

'Catriona? The bairn?' He could barely speak, so anxious was he.

'Mistress Cameron's fine. A bit tired, and who's to wonder at that after what she's been through. The bairn's a bonnie fechter. She'll lead you a dance, you auld fool.'

'A lassie?' The relief was so great that he felt his knees buckle and he forced them to stay straight. A wee girl. What a comfort to an auld man a wee lassie would be. He felt humble and grateful.

'Can I see them?' he asked.

She stood back to let him enter the dark, low-roofed room. Catriona, her face pale in the cloud of her red hair, was lying back against the pillows, but she opened her eyes as if she sensed his presence and smiled tiredly at him. In her arms rested a tiny shawl-wrapped bundle, no bigger, he thought, than one of her own clootie dumplings.

'I'm sorry it's no a laddie, Faither.'

'A laddie?' His heart swelled within him with love and he put out a hard, calloused, work-worn finger and gently touched the bundle. 'Ach, Catriona Cameron, was it not a lassie like you and my Mattie that this house needed?'

The baby lay snug in her mother's arms, and as her

grandfather leaned over she yawned heartily in his face. Then she opened her eyes and stared at him measuringly, as if she found him wanting. He was captivated.

'You'll have thought of a name, lass.'

Catriona was quiet, as if summoning up her strength. She had been through so much, one way and another, in the past nine months. At last she said, 'I prayed for a boy, another John.'

Mattie, he thought, it should be Mattie. Then he turned from his study of the baby's face and looked at the serene expression of his daughter-in-law, after all she had been through. Women were amazing creatures. He would never understand them.

'Do you know what day it is today, lass? It's the auld Queen's birthday. Can you believe she's eighty-one years old and most of that spent on the throne? Victoria. Is that no a name for a bonnie fechter?'

'Victoria. It's perfect. Welcome, Victoria Cameron.'

Miss Cameron yawned again and thus dismissed her court.

'I'll leave you to sleep, lass. I'm sorry my son's no at your side where he belongs, Catriona. If I could change him I would, but I promise you this, lass. Everything I have is yours and the bairn's and I'll no allow John to gie you ony more pain.'

She tried to argue, to talk, to tell him that a halfpenny-worth of love from John Cameron was worth more to her than anything.

'It has to be my fault,' she tried to say. But how can you tell your father-in-law that in some essential way you must have failed his son? Otherwise John would be here, wouldn't he? She knew well that they did no real business in France. John's business trips to see stock, to see crops – she forced herself to admit that he had to be seeing other women. 'But dear God, dear God, I have no pride. I want him. I need him.'

She closed her eyes and the old man tiptoed out and left her to sleep.

John Cameron arrived home from his latest business trip in France to be met by the barrel of his father's shotgun.

'You shouldnae hae dismissed your cabbie, lad. It's a long walk tae the toon in your fancy shoes.'

'Faither, are you crazy, man? It's me, John.' He made to move closer to the house, but the rock-steady hands of the old man gestured backwards with the gun – the gun that John knew could be used to deadly effect against foxes and other predators. Jock Cameron never wasted a shot. He would not waste any now.

'I ken fine who you are. Isn't it me that's ashamed of fathering you.'

'Come on, Faither, it was business. Wasn't I looking at French cattle? I want tae see my wife and my bairn. You cannae deny me my ain child. A boy, it'll be – a grand, healthy John Cameron tae carry on the farm.'

'And whit do you care aboot the child or the farm? Whit were you doing the nicht your wife lay in there near bleeding tae death tae bring your daughter intae the world? You're nae good, John. Ye never were, and for your mother's sake I wouldnae let myself admit whit I saw, but that's over. I should hae belted ye years ago, and as God's my witness, ye come one step nearer this hoos and I'll blaw yer head aff and swing fer you.'

John started to shout then. 'Ye crazy auld fool. I'll get the bobbies in. Catriona, Catriona, come out here and tell that auld devil tae let me in my ain hoos.'

'It's my hoos, John Cameron,' old Jock said, 'and one day it'll be the lassie's. Take yersell back tae yer French whoor, and see if she'll keep ye warm when she finds oot the landed gentleman has lost his land. Not a penny mair dae ye get from me. I'll be at Boatman's office first thing in the morning tae change my will.'

He wouldn't shoot him, he wouldn't. John moved closer and the gun spoke. John jumped as the dust flew from the ground exactly in front of his right foot.

'You're crazy, you old fool.' He was crying with fear and anger, and with fatigue. 'Catriona,' he called out desperately, 'Catriona.' But he did not see the weeping figure at the window, and he turned from the gun and stumbled blindly into the night.

1

1910

IT HAS BEEN SAID BEFORE, and will, no doubt, be said again, that the time before the Great War was very special.

Certainly it was for Victoria Cameron. She was a most important small person, at least in the eyes of Grampa, for whom she could do no wrong. Mamma was firmer, but that was the way, Victoria knew, of both mothers and grand-fathers. She loved them both fiercely, and she loved the old stone farmhouse with its magic kingdom of the walled farmyard, where Grampa would groom the Clydesdales. There were always six huge, broad, gentle beasts with noble names – Scottish Maid, Glentanar, Thermopylae, Stornoway, Queensberry and, of course, the Cutty Sark. Grampa never used these grand names; to him the horses were always 'hen', 'lass', or 'ma wee laddie'.

To the end of her life, Victoria could recall him as he polished their coats before hitching them up to the carriages, which local children took on their annual Sunday school picnics.

'That's it, hen, guid lass; aye, that's ma ain guid lass.'

Sometimes he would hoist Victoria up and put her sitting on the broad back of a large horse. She would clutch the mane with her little hands and look down, down from the broad, gleaming shoulders of the horse to the ground so far, so very far below; and she would look into Jock's whiskered face and she would laugh. Fear? She did not know the meaning of the word, not with Grampa there, with his strong brown hands.

Did the sun always shine in the years before the war? There must have been rain and snow, but Victoria's memories were full of sun-filled days, days when she would wander out of the farmyard and follow one of the drystane dykes to the burn. There were two stiles between the house and the burn. Years later she could still feel the sense of adventure that she experienced each time she climbed a stile and wandered farther away from her mother. She never went too far, though, for in later years she recalled that she had always been able to see the house.

Her mother worked the whole day long. Everything in the house, including Victoria, was scrubbed to within an inch of its life. Like the linens, Victoria was also starched and ironed.

Mamma baked, preserved, cured and dressed, and in the evenings she sewed and mended, knitted beautiful woollens for the three of them and somehow found time to do exquisite embroidery.

Her day of rest was Sunday, and so Sunday was Victoria's favourite day of the week. Jock would hitch two of the Clydesdales to the carriage, and everyone, masters and maids, stiff and starched in their Sunday best, would set off for their beautiful little country church.

But it was the time after the traditional huge Sunday midday dinner that Victoria relished. It was then that she and Grampa would escape. For this truancy they had a beautiful little phaeton, which was always pulled by the Scottish Maid, the lightest of the Clydesdales, and off they would go, Grampa in his black frock-coat and hat and the child stiff and starched in her pinafore and best Leghorn hat.

There was not a nook or cranny in Angus that they left undiscovered. The old man was never loquacious, but their silences were companionable. Every now and again he would say, 'Whoa, Maid. Whoa, ma lass,' and together old man and young child would sit and drink in the view. Wherever it was, there were always trees somewhere in the landscape.

'Breathe deep, Victoria,' he would say, 'there's no air in the world to match this. It's a perfect walnut shell day.'

The little girl looked up at him with those clear, grey-blue eyes – Mattie's eyes. It was bearable to think of them as Mattie's eyes.

'What's a walnut shell day, Grampa?'

'A day that's beautiful because you're with the person you love most in all the world. Everything is so perfect that you want to keep it for ever, so you put it in a walnut shell and save it for the days when nothing is good. Then, my wee Victoria, you take it out and all the joy and peace is there just as you remembered it. Oh, my wee Victoria, is life not fell hard at times, and does that not make these walnut shell days a' the mair precious?'

He looked gently down at the much-loved child and knew that she did not really understand.

Momentarily his heart sank – for Jock Cameron knew that, in time, God love her, she would know only too well what he meant.

'Let there be plenty of walnut shell days for her, Lord,' he prayed, and for months afterwards he would save walnut shells for Victoria to attempt to fill.

Memories of past picnics were enclosed in them. Wrapped in a clean, white linen napkin would be their shivery bite. They would sit on their tartan rug in the shadow of a ruined abbey and eat their scones and talk of the holy men who had lived there, and of how they must have enjoyed just the same trees, 'but, never the same scones, Victoria.' Grampa would laugh, for everyone in Angus knew that there was no finer baker than Catriona Cameron.

*   *   *

Victoria Cameron was so used to being the centre of attention that it came as rather a shock to find herself ostracized at the local primary school. Only the other social outcast, Nellie Bains, who wore ragged clothes, smelled and had a constantly dripping nose, wanted to play with her. And Victoria, who had been brought up to know her own worth, did not want to be anywhere near a dirty, ragged child like Nellie Bains. When she was small, Victoria saw only the rags, the tangled hair, the runny nose. She did not see the smile of pure friendship; she was too young and self-centred to glimpse the reflection of a loving heart.

'Nobody plays with me, Mamma,' Victoria complained. She did not mention Nellie, who was a nobody and therefore did not exist.

Catriona's eyes filled with tears. How dare they make her child suffer? She hugged her daughter so hard that the little girl pushed herself away. She put her balled-up handkerchief into the front pocket of her hand-embroidered apron and tossed back her dark hair.

'Nellie Bains said a bad word, a really, really bad word. She said I was one and none of the nice girls is allowed to play with me.' She leaned towards her mother and whispered the offending word so quietly into her ear that Catriona, taken by surprise, asked her to repeat it, and was then both shocked and mortified that her little daughter had ever uttered such a word.

'You are not,' said Catriona angrily. 'Shallow minds, with not enough to do but make up stories. Just never you mind, Victoria. Some day a really nice little girl will want to play with you.'

'Why some day? And what does that bad word mean, Mamma?'

But Catriona refused to tell her, saying that well brought-up children should not know such words. Victoria was looking both upset and slightly mutinous. Catriona desperately tried to find a solution and then she found one, but one

that frightened her, for she was not used to confrontation.
'I know, Victoria. I'll come into the school and have a word
with Miss Spencer.'

But the word with Miss Spencer did not mend matters,
for Miss Spencer looked down her educated nose and told
Catriona that it was all highly irregular and she could not
control what the children learned in their own homes.

Catriona had never disliked anyone in her entire life.
Even her philandering husband had received no criticism
from her, but this was different: this concerned her child.

Narrow spinster, thought Catriona angrily. No wonder
no man's wanted her. Thirty years old, if she's a day, and
trying to look like a lassie.

But she was no match for the contempt of the other
woman. Besides, Catriona had been brought up to think
teachers superior to ordinary mortals. Were they not full
of book learning? Some had even been to a place called the
university. That inbred feeling of inferiority, however, was
warring with her own very justifiable anger.

'Just make sure you control what they learn here, Miss,'
she said furiously and, head up in defeat, she walked
away.

And then Nellie, angry that her offers of friendship were
constantly being spurned, took matters into her own rather
grubby little hands and told Victoria exactly what the bad
word meant.

'Ye've nae pa, ye stuck up wee chiel, and yer ma's nae
better nor she should be.'

Victoria looked at Nellie, at her dirty face and her snotty
nose. She was not quite sure what Nellie was saying, but she
recognized the vindictiveness with which it was said. She
slapped Nellie hard across her wizened wee face. Then she
turned and ran crying from the playground, and she did not
stop running until she reached the haven of the farmhouse.

'Where is my faither?' she blurted out as soon as she
could draw breath.

Catriona, who had felt the heart stop beating in her body as her distraught daughter almost fell in through the door, sat down on a kitchen chair, something she seldom did during the day. She took a deep breath and tried to steady the wild clamour of her heart. It had to come, of course. Faither had warned her that she should have spoken of John, so that the bairn could grow up accepting his absence. But it was hard, so hard, to admit her failure. She took the angry, distressed child on her lap.

'Your father was not a very good . . . not a very dependable family-type of man, Victoria, not like Grampa; but I loved him very much . . . Maybe I still do,' she added sadly. 'He had charm, you see, like Grampa, but he was never meant to be a farmer – more a man of the world. He has gone away: he went away before you were even born. He was Grampa's son, but we don't speak of him.'

'Where is he? Didn't he like me? Grampa likes me.'

Catriona looked at her daughter. Which question to answer? The memory of that awful evening when John had turned up at the farmhouse, only to find the door barred and his father standing there with a double-barrelled shotgun in his hands, made her wince. She could almost hear the angry voices. At first John had cajoled, in the way he usually did, to worm his way back into his wife's or his father's affections.

'Faither,' Catriona had begged. 'He's sorry. He's Victoria's father. I cannae deny my bairn her father.'

'I'll see Boatman aboot mair than my will the morn, Catriona. Lassie, ye cannae still love him efter the way he's treated you.'

'I don't know. Sometimes I hate him . . . sometimes . . .'

Jock had looked down at her compassionately. 'That goes, lassie, believe me. You're better aff without John. He'll break yer heart.' He had turned back to the window and pushed the barrel of the shotgun through the opening. The blast had shattered the silence and caused the sleeping baby to awake, screaming.

Catriona had stared at her father-in-law and the blood had receded from her cheeks. 'John,' she had gasped on the point of fainting.

'Lassie, lassie, away tae the bairn. It was only a rat that was sunning itself at my very byre door. I wis wantin tae mind John on who it was that taught him tae shoot.'

And now Catriona turned to her daughter. 'He never knew you, sweetheart. When he did come home after you were born, Grampa wouldn't let him in the house. He left us, sweetheart, but I will never leave you, never.'

Victoria had stopped sobbing. Still she shuddered, but now she was calmer.

'And I will never leave you, Mamma, never.'

There was an earnestness in the young voice that almost frightened Catriona as the child added, 'That's a really truly promise, Mamma.'

2

1913

THE SEASONS CONTINUED IN all their varying splendour and the world moved just as steadily towards madness. Victoria finished at the little local school and went, every day, in the horse bus to the Harris Academy in nearby Dundee.

Grampa and Catriona, but not Victoria, had had many discussions about the form that the young girl's further education should take. It was a momentous decision to make. After all, no one on either side of the family had ever gone beyond an elementary education.

'Our lassie has a brain, Catriona,' murmured Grampa in awe. He himself had had to leave school, where he had not been known for perfect attendance, just after his twelfth birthday. 'Third prize and a special certificate for music. Clever *and* musical.'

Catriona was not sure that an ability to thump out marching tunes for the Boys' Brigade on the old upright piano in the parlour could be classed as musical, but she, as well as her father-in-law, was quietly pleased with Victoria's achievements.

She was, however, full of doubts about this new stage in her daughter's development. 'I wouldnae want to push, Faither. Victoria's never talked about staying on at school. It's no as if she's always said she wanted tae be a teacher, or a missionary or anything. Just happy to spend her days reading books and walking around the farm.'

'I'm talking about a university education for my wee lassie, Catriona. So it'll be the Harris Academy. I've met some fine people that got their schooling there. We don't want tae send her tae the High School. I've walked by there some days when I'm in at the bank and, I'm sorry, but some of those bairns get a bit above theirselves. I wouldnae want anything rubbing off on our wee lassie, but you're her mother. If you want her at the High School, I'll be more than happy tae find the money, you know that, and I'll rely on your good sense tae keep her feet on the ground.'

Privately, Catriona thought there would be obstreperous children in every school, but Victoria herself had shuddered at the idea of going all the way into the city centre to Dundee High School. One or two of the friends she had eventually made at Birkie would be at the Harris. She wanted to be with them.

As it happened, her best friend at the Harris Academy was to be a girl she met on her first day. Elsie Morrison was the only girl in a large family and she fascinated Victoria. Her life, surrounded by parents and grandparents, brothers, aunts and uncles and cousins, was so different from Victoria's own rather narrow existence. Every spare minute that the girls had they spent together, for while Victoria loved being exposed to the rough and tumble of Elsie's overcrowded life, Elsie loved the peace and quiet of Priory Farm. In the evenings they would sit in the comfortably upholstered farm parlour (or sitting room, as Elsie insisted on calling it) and play the piano and sing, or wind up the old Victrola, put on a record and dance. Elsie knew all the latest dance steps; she had seven brothers, after all.

On Sundays after church, when Grampa was too tired or too busy, Victoria and Elsie would go rambling all over the countryside. Sometimes they took a tram and then walked to a well-known beauty spot, or they would pack a picnic tea into their saddle-bags and venture farther afield on their bicycles. It was during one of these rambles that Victoria met Robert.

It was one of those September days when the world was warm and golden. The trees were just beginning to turn, and green, yellow, scarlet and brown leaves danced, it seemed, on the same branches; brambles hung fat and juicy on the hedgerows, and rowans and rosehips vied with each other in colour and number; the friendly smell of wood smoke from a hundred cottage gardens hung on the air. It was a walnut shell day.

The girls, like countless other Dundonians, took the ferry across the Tay to the village of Newport, in the Kingdom of Fife. They left the others happy to laze on the Newport Braes, those pleasant grassy slopes, and were soon deep in woods near the estuary of the great river. Rowan, oak, pine, birch, beeches – everything that was beautiful – was growing in those woods and the girls were going to sketch them. At least Elsie was. Victoria played with her charcoal and then wandered off.

She sat down on a mossy bank, trying to memorize the colours and, as always, feeling inadequate. She could not possibly paint the autumnal tints, let alone the sighs that the boughs made when a breeze moved them or the rustle, like golden coins, as they fell.

'Quite something,' said a voice beside her.

His voice was what Grampa termed 'county'. It belonged to the crested carriages that occasionally came to the wee village church. Normally Victoria would have curtsied quickly and moved away, but there was a power in the golden day that made her stay.

'Quite lovely,' she agreed, and looked up at him as he stood silhouetted against the pale autumn sun.

Her heart seemed to stop beating. He was the most beautiful boy she had ever seen – tall and slender; an aquiline profile with deep blue eyes and hair the colour of a raven's wing, blue where the sun struck it. And how the sun was shining that day in September 1913.

She was suddenly breathless, and fought for control of her heart, which was beating so rapidly that her blood seemed to be rushing around her veins in the strangest, and yet most pleasant, way. 'I was trying to sketch it,' she managed at last, holding up her sketchpad with its virgin pages.

He looked at it measuringly, as once she had seen her art teacher do when the First Year Art Appreciation class had walked into the Dundee Art Gallery to view its master-pieces. 'You sketch as well as I do,' he said laughing, and they laughed together.

He helped her up, and at the touch of his hand her whole body seemed to burst into flame. She was afraid that her normally pale skin had turned red – so unattractive – but he appeared not to have noticed, and she turned away to pick up her drawing materials. Somehow it seemed right that he should stay beside her as she continued her walk. They talked easily of the beauty of the woods. The splendid boy (what was his name? Oh surely, surely, Hector or Lysander – something poetic) pointed out some especially fine speci-mens and Victoria wondered at a boy who could speak so easily and serenely about nature. Grampa might say that he liked flowers, but he was old. She could not imagine Elsie's brothers admitting to a fondness for flowers.

They talked too of the ugliness of war, for the boy said that his father knew someone who said that there were evil people in the world, who would stop at nothing to force their views on others. Then, too soon, because the tides of the River Tay wait for no man, and certainly for no wee lassie who has just met her Sir Lancelot, it was time for Victoria to go home.

He watched her walk off through the great bushes of rhododendrons and then, as she reached the turning that would take her out of sight, he called, 'What's your name?' She turned and saw him again, outlined against the sun as if he were not quite real, and she knew that this moment and this boy were important and had changed her for ever. She called back, 'Victoria.'

'I'm Robert.'

'Robert.' Not the name of a knight in a picture book. 'Robert.' Such an ordinary name for such an extraordinary boy. No, it was right, perfect. She had never met anyone who wore their name so well. She whispered *Robert* over and over again on the long journey back to Dundee. She wondered where he lived, and where he went to school, and whether she would ever see him again. For Robert's face was the one she had given every knight and hero she had ever read about, and Robert's slenderness and grace were theirs too. She did not say 'I am in love' because she was only thirteen years old, but wherever she went after that she looked for Robert, and each time she returned to the enchanted woods she felt a dull ache of disappointment that Robert was not there.

Not, that is, until Easter 1914. Victoria and Elsie were looking for spring flowers, and *Robert*'s woods were full of them. Elsie sat on a fallen log, happily sketching primroses while Victoria wandered off, as usual.

'Hello, Victoria,' said a voice, and there he was.

He was taller and thinner and even more beautiful than she remembered.

'Hello,' she said as calmly as possible, for her heart was beating so loudly that she felt he must hear it.

'No sketching today?'

She gestured back to where Elsie was sitting. 'I was, but I'm no better at sketching now than I was in September, so I decided to walk a little.'

He fell in beside her and they began to pick up where they had left off in that golden autumn.

'There will be real trouble soon, Victoria, you'll see,' said Robert. 'Lots of chaps at school are joining up. I wish I were old enough. I'd go, and we'd soon rout those Huns.'

The Huns. Everyone talked about them, but no one talked
with relish, not in the the way Robert was talking, as if what
was happening was a great game. Tam Menmuir, Grampa's
best worker, had sons, and Victoria had heard them talk
about these people called Huns. They talked with sorrow,
with anger, with despair. They worried that if these Huns
were not controlled, there would be trouble. Then they went
on to talk about record harvests and yields, and about the
things that really mattered.

Suddenly Victoria felt older than Robert, older than
Catriona, older than Grampa. 'How old are you, Robert?'
she asked.

'Sixteen – almost – but I'm tall enough for sixteen, don't
you think?'

He grabbed her hands and whirled her round in a mad
dance. 'That's what I'll do. I'll lie about my age.'

How could he look so happy at the prospect of going to
war? Victoria fought down a rush of fear. She hated the
very idea.

Her scarf had slipped down from her neck and he bent
to retrieve it from the carpet of leaves.

'I shall keep this, Victoria, as a favour from a lady.
Perhaps I shall tie it round my rifle.'

Again he bent, but this time he picked two perfect
primroses. 'Take these in exchange.'

'These are private grounds. It's against the law to pick
flowers here,' said Victoria primly, although she took them.

Robert laughed. What a joyous laugh he had. 'They'll
forgive a knight going off to the Crusades.'

Perhaps many of the boys and men who went to the
carnage that was the Great War thought of themselves as
Crusaders – knights in shining armour, fighting evil. Right
was on their side and they would win. But at what cost?

'I must get back to my friend,' Victoria replied conscientiously, instead of expressing all the sensible things she
wanted to say about the futility of war.

'Wait,' he said. 'Victoria, may I write, if I get in, I mean? And you could write to me, about home fires and all that rot. Here,' he snatched her sketchpad and tore a sheet from it. 'Write your name and address and I'll write mine.'

She scribbled them down, then they swapped papers and she blushed furiously when she saw his name. Of course he could pick the primroses on his own father's land.

'*Au revoir*, Victoire,' he said grandly, and, taking her hand, he raised it, in what she thought of as a very Gallic gesture, to his lips.

'Goodbye, Robert,' she answered softly and another blush swept over her cheeks.

She returned to Elsie and very carefully put the primroses between the pages of her sketchpad. Later that night she gently pressed them between the pages of *Mansfield Park*. Her Bible, she thought, would have been a worthier repository, but she used it often and the primroses would have been sure to fall out.

Europe went mad and the glorious harvests of 1914 and 1915 were obliterated by marching feet and tanks, and by all the other implements of mass destruction. Not in the Angus glens, though, where Jock Cameron stood sucking his empty pipe contentedly, as he watched the final gathering of his most successful harvest. Victoria, her hat falling from her tangled hair and her skirts kirtled up about her legs – best make sure Catriona did not catch her ewe lamb looking like that – waved to him from Glentanar's back.

'I've eaten all the brambles I was supposed to collect for jam, Grampa.'

He laughed. She had no need to tell him. Was her face not stained with the evidence?

'Best slip doon and tidy yourself afore your mother catches you, young lady,' he said in mock seriousness, but Victoria did as she was bid.

When she had dismounted from the gentle giant she ran

to his side, shaking down her dress. 'Oh, Grampa, was there ever such a walnut shell day. It's the best ever.'

For a moment she almost took that back, for was not yesterday the best day ever, because a scrap of paper had arrived from *Somewhere on the Front*.

No, she could not share that even with Grampa. It was too new, too precious, too achingly sweet.

They went back to the farmhouse. Catriona took one look at her hoyden of a daughter and began to fill a bathtub with boiling water from the kettles on the gleaming range.

'I do not know which of the two of you is the greater child, Faither,' she said crossly. 'I'll never get her fit for the harvest dance.'

But she did, and three hours later a model of propriety stood with tapping foot beside her grandfather. Catriona and Bessie Menmuir, wife of Grampa's senior stockman, had laboured for hours the previous night, after Victoria had gone to bed, to make a dress fit for this first dance. No couturier ballgown this, but still a hand-sewn work of art. Where had they found the material? The dress was, in fact, made from tartan tablecloths that Jock's wife, Mattie, had made long before the turn of the century, and which had been discovered by Bessie in a trunk in the attic. The neck was cut lower than Catriona could permit, so she had ripped cream-coloured lace from her late mother-in-law's one and only evening-gown and filled the neck with that. There were lace bows at the cuffs of the sleeves, which sat just below the girl's sun-browned, dimpled elbows, and more lace disguised the hem of the swirling skirt, where one tablecloth had had to be tacked to the other.

Conscious that she had the most beautiful dress in the room, Victoria sparkled with a young girl's joy as she waited impatiently while her grandfather welcomed neighbours and workers alike to his home. Oh, if only there was some way to capture her image in her lovely dress and send it to *Somewhere on the Front* to warm the heart of

a soldier boy. Victoria smiled and looked at the tables
sagging under the weight of the pies that Catriona and
her helpers had spent days preparing. When the dancing
started, whisky and ale would flow more readily than the
water in the parched Tay. Would it be in poor taste to write
a description to Robert, who was existing 'somewhere' on
meagre rations?

It was the most joyous evening. Victoria danced with
everyone, young and old alike: Tam Menmuir, Davie (his
oldest son, home on leave from the war), ploughmen and
cattlemen, Bessie, Catriona, Elsie, and finally she forced her
Grampa away from his whisky and his cronies.

'A dance, Grampa, come on. Sandy's away to play "Strip
the Willow".'

Surely only a man with shoes nailed to the floor could
have resisted the fiddle that night. Jock Cameron whirled
his granddaughter round as if she were no heavier than the
small treasure he held tight between his gnarled fingers.
One of Elsie's brothers, the only one of the seven not already
in the Forces, his eyes almost blinded by the mad sweep
of Victoria's lacy petticoats as she whirled past him in her
grandfather's arms, stood waiting to snatch the girl for the
next dance.

Suddenly Jock stopped his mad dervish whirl. He looked
across the smoke- and dust-filled room at his daughter-
in-law.

'Forgive me, Catriona,' he said. 'I always meant to put it
in the lassie's name,' and he fell forward. The walnut shell
he had been clasping slipped from his fingers and rolled to
the feet of the girl, who stood like a statue frozen in stone.
It was then that she screamed.

Jock would have enjoyed his funeral – the biggest in Angus
for many a long day. Crested carriages and farm carts
jostled for room and, even in her grief, Victoria could see
how much he had been loved. Although her eyes were

swollen and red, she did not cry in public. Nor did her mother and yet her grief was as great as, if not greater than, the girl's. And to that grief was added worry for the future, for in her head were echoing the words: 'I always meant to put it in the lassie's name.'

A few weeks after the funeral, Victoria came back from school to find an unfamiliar pony and trap in the farmyard. Old Tam had been watching for her and he came out of the stable, comb in hand.

'Away ben tae the scullery fer yer tea, Victoria. The mistress has yon lawyer fella with her.'

In the scullery, perched on a scrubbed stool, Victoria ate scones with jam and drank hot, sweet tea and tried to taste them. 'The best baker in Angus.' Was that not what Grampa had said about her mother? Grampa? She felt again the hot tears squeezing up and she struggled to force them back. Would she ever, ever be able to think of him without crying?

'Oh, Grampa, Grampa,' she sobbed to herself. 'Why did you leave me?'

Later, Catriona came into the scullery while Victoria was at her homework, and sat down at the table beside her.

'Victoria, my dear,' she said. 'The time has come to talk, a little, about your father.'

Victoria looked at her expectantly, but with misgivings. Her father? She cared nothing about her father. It was Grampa she cared about.

Catriona understood what was going through her daughter's mind and ached to be able to spare her pain. She began to speak in a clipped, almost cold voice – emotionless. How else could she cope?

'Your father, my husband, was . . . is, as you know, your grandfather's son. I . . . I . . . divorced him ten years ago.' Once again Catriona thought with gratitude of the love and care of the old man, who had insisted that she be freed from his own son. Thank heaven, he had always said, that Scots

law was light years ahead of English law. All Catriona had
had to do was prove that John had deserted her. And since
he had never been seen in Angus since the day that his
father had thrown him out, desertion had been cited as the
just cause. She had found out later about the fees old Jock
had had to pay, first to Arbuthnott Boatman and then to the
very competent Edinburgh advocate, whom the canny Scots
lawyer had recommended to handle the case. But, however
much it had cost, he had paid them willingly.

Catriona continued. 'Since then I have been housekeeper
here for Grampa. He always meant to make a new will,
in your favour, Victoria, but he never got round to it.
However, he – without my knowledge, needless to say –
has paid me an extremely generous wage all these years,
and it has accumulated at a good rate of interest. We
will be able to cope, but we must leave the farm. It now
belongs to . . . Grampa's son. As yet we do not know
where he is, but Mr Boatman will find him. Lawyers are
very clever, Victoria. Anyway, I want to leave as quickly
as possible. I will not be here when . . . It is better to
make a clean break. Do you understand, Victoria? Mr
Boatman is arranging to buy a house in Dundee for us,
on Blackness Road.' She stopped, and in her mind's eye
she saw once again the house she intended to buy. So
different, so very different. She went on, 'It's a respectable
area. You will be able to continue at the Harris Academy, Victoria, and so all your friends will remain the
same.'

She stopped and looked at her daughter expectantly but,
in the depths of her own grief, Victoria was too numb to
think. Nothing registered, but that awful moment of silence
when Grampa had stood there staring at Catriona, clutching
at his heart, his voice gasping. What had he said? What did
it matter? He was dead.

'I don't care where we live,' she said and Catriona
winced, but she knew the child was putting up her defence

mechanisms just as she, with her cold, unfeeling voice, had done.

Victoria always wondered how her mother managed to be out of the farmhouse within the three days that followed the signing of the contracts between Catriona and the lawyers of the late owner. She must surely have stayed up all night, for the following Saturday found them ready to leave Priory Farm.

Had the farm ever looked lovelier as it sat nestled among its carefully tended gardens? Redcurrants that Catriona had been unable to put up were still hanging like rubies on the bushes. The sun sparkled on the early-morning spider's webs strewn across the hedges. Already, smoke from the fires in the tied cottages was drifting out of the chimneypots and Victoria could tell which of Grampa's workers were already up and ready for the day.

I can't bear the pain, thought Victoria. I can't leave here. I'll die, away from this air, these scents.

She said nothing of her agonies as they spent the day carrying out their last duties, for Catriona was determined that the new owner would find no trace of the previous occupants. At last it was time to eat one final meal and, for the very last time, climb into the old phaeton that Victoria and Grampa had used for their forays. She could still, she was sure, smell his familiar, much-loved presence. She did not look round as Tam bowled them out of the farm and along the road to Dundee.

'It's a nice area, Victoria,' said Catriona desperately. 'Near Elsie and the Harris. We'll make it work.'

Victoria said nothing as they raced along the road, past Templeton Woods and into Dundee. Had the river ever looked more beautiful, stretching for miles like a long, silver ribbon? Had the sun ever burnished the leaves on the trees to such splendour? No one in the phaeton noticed the beauty of the road; no one cared.

'Keep going, keep going for ever and ever until we

run off the edge of the world,' Victoria silently told the horse.

But eventually it stopped and the two passengers looked at what was to be their new home.

'Ach, Mistress,' Tam said, before he remembered that he was only a servant, 'ye cannae bide here. It's nae better nor a slum.'

Victoria looked up and saw a three-storey stone house almost buried beneath its overgrown garden. The gate was hanging on its hinges and all the ground-floor windows were broken.

'It's not as bad as it looks, Victoria,' said Catriona, desperately trying to reach inside the unblinking statue that her daughter had become.

Victoria climbed like an old woman from the phaeton. She helped Tam unload, much against his wishes, since he had strict ideas about what was right for masters and what was expected of men, and she carried some baskets into the house. Catriona had gone ahead to light some lamps and set a match to the fire she had laid earlier in the week. She did not light all the lamps – lamplight is flattering and welcoming, but better perhaps to keep the real state of their new home from Victoria until the girl had slept.

Victoria said nothing as she put baskets in the kitchen and wicker hampers of clothes in the bedrooms. Catriona carried a small leather steamer-trunk, which really belonged to John, but which he had given her for their wedding trip. Most of the labels had peeled off over the years, but one still said Hôtel St-Etienne, Paris. Had she realized it was there, Catriona would have scraped it off too.

'We'll make some cocoa afore you go back, Tam,' she said as he put down the biggest and heaviest of the boxes.

'Mistress, come on back tae the Priory. We'll think on something. This is no right, and it's no whit he would hae wantit. We can talk tae the new boss.'

'I've made my bed and I mun lie on it, Tam. We'll be fine,

Victoria and me. We'll manage, you'll see. Whit was it Jock used tae say, when we complained about anything? *Pull yoursel thegither, laddie. Ye've never deid a winter yet.* Well, we're not going to die this winter either, Tam. We're going to manage.'

Victoria stood at the dirty window and looked out on to the darkened street. How strange to see houses, side by side, some with soft lamplight glowing, most in darkness.

'Oh, dear Grampa,' she whispered, 'definitely not a walnut shell day.'

3

AN ARTIST WAS BUSY OUTSIDE her bedroom window. The huge beech trees were just struggling into their green spring coats – how many tints and shades there were. Mother Nature never ceased to astound her. Soft green shoots were bravely pushing up their heads, like so many watchful sentinels, out of the ground, away from the weakening grip of winter and towards the young sun. She could see two – no, three – of Jock's beloved Clydesdales in the far field, their heads bent as they grazed. Suddenly one, his particular favourite, The Cutty Sark, threw up her tail and her heels and went skittering away across the field. Catriona peered to see what had excited the horse.

It was Jock, his hands full of carrots, his pockets full of apples. He looked up, but his face disappeared and in its place Catriona saw . . . horror! She woke up with a start, and at her anguished cry the rat that had been chewing the wainscotting in the corner whisked out of sight behind the wardrobe.

Victoria, beside her mother in the big bed, moaned softly in her sleep. Catriona leaned over, as she had done so many times over the years, to soothe her child.

Victoria fell quiet and Catriona lay back again and tried, as she had always done before rising, to make a list of all the tasks she hoped to accomplish during the day. First thing was to light a fire. At least Victoria would be warm. She slipped out of bed, pulled on her dressing gown and crept quietly down to the kitchen.

The table was a seething mass of mice. They were every-where. Already they had eaten their way into the bags of flour and sugar, the packages of good farm butter, the loaves of yesterday's bread. Some of them jumped from the table at Catriona's arrival, but the bigger and bolder ones looked at her with their malevolent, beady eyes and went on chewing.

It was too much . . . to be brought to this. All her life, every day, every moment, Catriona had worked and cleaned, and tried to keep up the standards instilled in her by her mother. Now . . . to come to this.

I always meant to put it in the lassie's name.

Dear God, would the words always be there to haunt her, to poison her love for the old man, to tarnish his memory? She could bear no more. For the first time since Jock's sudden death, Catriona began to cry. Great choking sobs were wrenched from her and scalding tears chased one another down her cheeks.

'Oh, why, Faither, why? I cannae thole this; I cannae deal with sich dirt and damp, and neglect.'

A mouse, startled by her cry, ran across her foot on its way to its hole and the delicate touch was the final straw. Catriona screamed and screamed and screamed. The vermin ran to their holes and Victoria, terrified out of her sleep by her mother's distress, jumped from the big double bed and, without waiting to put on dressing gown or slippers, rushed down the stairs and into the kitchen.

She was nearly fifteen years old and suddenly she grew up. She threw her arms around the wailing woman and Catriona felt their strength.

'It's all right, Mother,' soothed the girl. Never before, no matter what had happened, even on that dreadful night when Grampa had died at her very feet, had Victoria seen her mother unable to cope. She held her mother and was no longer a child; she would never again be a child. At the sight of her mother's distress Victoria had stopped thinking

only of herself. She had grown up. She felt a million years
old. 'We'll cope. We will. We'll make it work, together. I'll
help. Don't cry, don't cry.'

She pushed her mother down into the chair beside the
range and, putting her arms around Catriona's waist, laid
her head in her mother's lap, but still she was the comforter,
not the comforted.

'We'll cope, Mother. A cup of tea. I'll make you a nice
hot cup of tea and then we'll start.' She looked around and
repressed a shudder. 'It's only dirt. Dirt has no respect for
anyone, rich or poor, but boiling water and good carbolic
soap'll sort it. You'll see. You won't recognize this place
when we're finished with it.'

She looked fearfully at the wainscotting and observed the
tell-tale holes. She had seen the mice rushing away from her
mother's screams. No mouse or rat had dared to disturb the
peace of Priory Farm. Had they done so, they would have
met a timely end. Victoria took a deep breath.

'We need a good mouser and we'll get one, but first we
need tea. That was what Grampa used to say, Mother, do
you remember? 'I can handle anything, if I get a decent cup
of tea. Nane of your holy water here.' Do you remember,
Mother, how he loved his tea?'

She got up and Catriona, calmed by her daughter's
strength, watched her at work. The set of the head on the
thin, young shoulders was John's; the flashing grey-blue
eyes that had vowed to do battle with dirt and poverty
were John's; but, oh dear God, thank you, the courage and
character were Jock's. That they were also hers did not occur
to Catriona Cameron.

'Tam will tell us how to deal with vermin, Mother,' said
Victoria later, as she held the teacup so that her shaking
mother could drink the reviving brew. Oh, so nearly had
she said, 'Grampa will tell us.' Sometimes her grandfather
seemed still to be alive. She could almost hear his voice,
almost smell his pipe. But here she could smell only damp

and a strange, rotting smell that had to be the mice. Tam would know how to deal with mice. And might there be rats too? Victoria shuddered and tried to smile at her mother. Had Grampa still been alive, of course, there would have been no need to learn how to cope with such horrors.

'Now, Mother,' said Victoria as Catriona made no move, 'have some more tea and I will find something for us to eat.'

Catriona retched. 'No, child, there were mice in everything. Everything's contaminated. We can't eat.' Her voice rose hysterically and Victoria heard the warning signs of distress and tried to deal with them.

'We *must* eat, Mother. We have a great deal of work to do. See, the eggs are untouched. Wasn't that nice? The mice left the eggs to have as their second course and now they've lost them. I'll make something nourishing. You go upstairs and wash and dress. Here, there is water in the kettle. We'll get this range cleaned and then it will stay lit twenty-four hours a day and there will be water, lovely hot water. And in two shakes of a lamb's tail there won't be a germ anywhere.'

To Victoria's delight, her mother tried to smile.

'I'm fine now, lass. It was just—'

'I know, but we'll survive, Mamma, and we'll do more than that. Just think. It's the two of us against the world. Does the world have a chance? No.'

Victoria found a bag of flour that the mice – she refused to think any more about the possibility of rats – had left inviolate and soon there were scones browning on the griddle iron.

'I'm making up the whole bag,' she said as Catriona, washed and dressed, re-entered the kitchen. 'I hope I remembered your recipe properly. I should, since I've watched you bake often enough. We'll have scrambled eggs and scones for breakfast, and boiled eggs and scones for dinner. We have plenty of vegetables for soup, and you can make that, Mother, while I start cleaning. Unfortunately, we've no bone for stock.'

'There's a wee grocer's just round the corner.'

'No.' Victoria was in control. 'We'll be pioneers today and use only what we have. There isn't time to go to the shops, and by the look of this place we'll be too dirty to go anywhere. Here, Mother, doesn't a scrambled egg scone taste wonderful?' Catriona had to agree that it did.

After breakfast Victoria went to dress while Catriona washed their few dishes, and then they started to clean. Everything the vermin had contaminated was taken out into the back garden and burned. The dirty paper that had lined all the shelves in the kitchen followed the foodstuffs on to the fire. The floors were swept and scrubbed, and after the floors came the walls and the shelves, even the doors. Soon the smell of dirt and decay was replaced by the healthy and not too unpleasant smell of carbolic.

'Once we start polishing there'll be a fresh smell of lemon in here and then we'll get some apple logs for the fire. Won't that be nice?'

'I'll do the privy,' offered Catriona, anxious to make up for her weakness of the morning, 'and you can get started on the front room.'

Victoria dropped into a chair by the fire. 'The front room? Mercy, Mother. Would you look at the time. It's nearly four and we've been at it since before nine this morning. If I don't eat I . . . I . . . don't know what I'll do.'

'You're right, lass. Look, I'll start making the soup and it can be simmering while we finish. I'm glad we brought these oil lamps from the farm. They're homely, aren't they?'

Victoria turned away. She was not ready for talk of the farm, and certainly not ready for odious comparison. 'I'll boil these last two eggs, Mother, to go with our soup. Or will it just be mixed vegetables, since there's no stock for flavour? Doesn't matter. Tomorrow we'll investigate the wee shop.'

Did Arbuthnott Boatman deliberately choose an extremely wet day on which to take the new owner of Priory Farm around his property?

John Cameron had spent the night very comfortably at the nearby Birkhill Inn. His handsome face and figure and the cut of his London clothes had endeared him to the barmaid, and his generous tip had won the heart of the groom who was to convey Mr Cameron the two miles to the farm. Sammy Taylor was not the brightest employee of the inn, but he knew horses and he knew farms. He looked at the hand-made leather shoes, at the polish and the fine tooling with something approaching anguish.

'Ye'll no hae a pair o' galluses, Maister?'

John shuddered at the thought of squeezing his beautiful shoes into a pair of ugly, but no doubt practical, galoshes. 'Wore my last pair some years ago.'

'There'll be a puckle mud at the fairm.'

'Which I shall be more than happy to wipe from my feet, laddie,' said John grandly.

He would go, as his father's lawyer wished, to the farm and he would see the inventory, and then he would take the wind from Arbuthnott Boatman's sails by telling him to sell up. He could hardly wait to change that pained, prune-faced look to one of surprise.

Arbuthnott Boatman, in a sensible hooded driving cape and with his best-quality rubber galoshes pulled carefully over his second-best pair of shoes, waited at the once sparkling mullioned windows of the front room of Priory Farm. Catriona had been gone only a few days but already the house seemed to sag into itself, as if ashamed that it was not as immaculate as it had always been. Boatman saw, with some pleasure, the look of irritation on his new client's face as he stepped from his cab into a puddle, which immediately oozed over the top of his shoes and ran down inside his silk-socked ankles. He hid his smile and walked out briskly, an expression of welcome painted on his face.

'Mr Cameron, I'd have known you anywhere. You have the look of your father about you.'

John avoided the outstretched hand. There was no need for pretence with this man. They did not like one another, but what did that matter? He, John Cameron, owned every mucky inch of this place, every wisp of hay, every hen – even, he supposed, every mouse that lurked in the warm barns. His father could hardly have shot them all, he decided with a quick flash of irritation. The other man was his employee. It was a good feeling.

'It was always dinned into me that I resembled my mother,' John said coldly. 'Now, if you don't mind, can we sign whatever we have to sign? I'm thinking of heading for Mexico. This damned war has ruined France, but with the proceeds from the sale of this little lot I should be able to live like a king in Baja California. And there's America just over the border, if I feel the need for what passes there as civilization. Ever been to France, Boatman?' He did not wait for an answer. 'France is the country, Boatman. Such wine, such women, such food. I'll miss French wines, but Mexican *señoritas* and excellent cigars should compensate. And they say there's the odd vineyard, and lobsters, of course, jumping straight out of the sea into the pot.'

'Sounds delightful,' said Boatman drily. 'But what of the farm? And, by the way, Cameron,' he added, knowing full well that it was not only unprofessional, but none of his business, 'you haven't forgotten that you still have a daughter?'

Did John flinch for a second at the word 'daughter'? Had he missed holding his own child? Did he regret not hearing her first, lisping words?

'Neither means a damn thing. The farm never has: sometimes I even wondered if I was my father's son. As for the girl, I came back from business – important business – in Paris at considerable discomfort to be there within hours of her birth and they turfed me out. Never even saw her. I owe the girl nothing.'

'I take it you want me to find a suitable tenant?' The lawyer's mind was working furiously. Could Catriona lease the farm? With Tam to help, really to run the place . . .

John looked at him, his face a caricature of incredulity. 'A tenant? You must be out of your mind, man. When I shed the mud from these shoes, I want to do it in every way possible. There's a war on, in case you hadn't noticed. I don't intend to stay guarding the ancestral acres while waiting to be conscripted. Mind you, if all else failed, I'd be a farmer before I'd be gun-fodder, and I suppose if I made a show of farming, they'd give me a dispensation.' He thought for a minute, obviously weighing up the advantages of a safe haven for the rest of the damned war against the lure of exotic places. Mexico. What did he know of it? He looked over at the barn and saw the short, broad shape of Bessie Menmuir carrying peelings to the chickens. He could find nothing alluring in the sight. But Spanish *señoritas*. Sunshine . . . 'Show me where to sign. Sell, and sell now.' He looked around him at the carefully tended farmsteading. 'It should make a nice tidy sum.'

The two men looked at one another and, for once, the lawyer's guard dropped and his dislike of his client showed in his eyes. John Cameron blushed with embarrassment. Well, let them all hate me. What do I care? I am going to sell.

'Shall I quote you the full legal terms of your father's will, which is essentially the same as his father's, or do you want it in plain English?' Boatman waited, childishly and unprofessionally relishing the other man's discomfort. How had a son of the soil like Jock Cameron ever fathered a wastrel like this?

'Get on with it, man. Spit out your legal jargon.'

'No legal jargon, Mr Cameron. The farm can't be sold.

It's yours for your lifetime, Cameron, and then it goes to Victoria.'

'Victoria?'

'Your daughter.'

'My daughter? You mean he left the farm to the girl? A girl I've never laid eyes on.'

'She is your child.'

John laughed. 'Either that or an immaculate conception, man. You wouldn't catch Catriona in the barn with the ploughman. More's the pity,' he added under his breath. 'She might have been more fun.'

Boatman looked at him dispassionately.

'Your late father made his will when you married in 1899. He left everything to you for your lifetime. Anything except the house and the land can be disposed of as you see fit, but it wouldn't be wise to dispose of animals or machinery; you'll get little rent for a farm without them. The farmhouse and the land become the property of your surviving legitimate children on your death. Victoria's.'

'What's she like, the girl?'

Arbuthnott Boatman considered both the question and his answer. Had John asked because he had a man's normal interest in a child he had fathered? Perhaps there was a nice John Cameron under all the antagonism. 'She's a pretty wee thing. Very like you,' he added honestly.

John tried to picture a girl with his hair and eyes, his features, but all he could conjure up was a picture of himself just after his mother had died. He saw a pale, drawn face, shadowed blue-grey eyes that were used to smiling and were now wet with tears that he would not shed. He supposed the girl must be pretty.

'Well, she'll catch herself a man in no time, if she plays her cards right. Let's hope she can keep him. Depends what her mother has taught her. There's more to marriage than well-cooked meals, Boatman.'

'Indeed, and as the Merry Monarch, Charles the Second, told us, there's more to marriage than four legs in a bed.'

John turned away in anger. What was the dratted lawyer trying to say, with his Charles II nonsense? All John knew was that, even in death, his father had thwarted him. He had tied him to this damned place. Well, he would *not* be tied.

I'm off to Mexico, he thought. They can send me the money there. 'Get the best rent you can for the place, Boatman. Shouldn't be difficult in wartime, with people anxious for security and the Government keen to make the country as self-sufficient as possible. I'm sure there's an account at the bank that I'll be able to draw on from overseas. Your firm must be big enough to have overseas clients. My grandfather dealt with your grandfather, or so my father was always fond of telling me. Old established firm. Anyway, he had some way of making sure that I was always able to get funds in France.'

'Of course.' Boatman would not say 'Mr Cameron'. 'We have several agreements with the Bank of Scotland and I'm sure we can have the necessary paperwork drawn up before you leave. Have you a sailing date?'

'Need to get myself a tenant first. How long should all this take?'

'Who knows? I'll advertise locally and nationally. Or maybe one of your father's men would like the opportunity? They're good workers and they know the land, the animals and the people. Perhaps Mrs Cameron . . .' he began tentatively.

John did not even have to think before rejecting that hare-brained idea. Catriona, his former wife, living in his home. 'Don't talk rubbish, man. What would a woman know about running a farm? She'd ruin it, and me, within a year. Besides, it's poetic justice, isn't it? She threw me out. Now the boot is on the other foot.'

John looked down at his hand-made shoes and did

not see the look of dislike thrown at him by Boatman. His anger still simmering, he ignored his ruined shoes and walked boldly through the mud away from the lawyer. 'Do what you can, as quickly as you can,' he shouted. 'There's more than the mud of Angus that I want to brush from my shoes.'

'Good day to you,' said Arbuthnott Boatman, but the words went unheard – or ignored.

4

IT WAS THE FIRST TIME in her life that Victoria Cameron had
ever walked to the kirk. Every Sunday, for as long as she
could remember, she had gone in a carriage with Grampa
and the folk from the farm. Summer or winter, rain or shine,
he had insisted on using his own father's carriage, and
Victoria had sat squeezed between him and the window
and had looked across at the unfamiliar Sunday face of
her mother. Catriona, her red hair firmly pinned down
under her hat – which was anchored, but surely not to her
scalp, with huge pins ending in improbable diamonds – her
ruffled blouse buttoned up to and beyond her chin, had sat
unsmiling as she in turn had examined her daughter for
any speck of dirt or dust that had gone undetected.

But their world had changed. Now there was a new
church in a new town and they were alone, just the two of
them. When the minister raised his hand for the final blessing, Victoria's hand sought her mother's and she squeezed
the leather-gloved fingers gently. With God's blessing and
their own hard work, they would manage.

The minister welcomed them at the door, introduced
himself and said that he would call on them. He knew,
as well as they, what a visit from the minister of the established kirk would do for their standing in the community.

'You've taken on quite a job with old Mrs Thomson's
house, Mistress Cameron. It stood empty quite a while.
Family wrangling, I believe, and no doubt a bit of legal
wrangling, too. There'll be a job of work to get it in order,
I expect, but there was always a nice garden there – some

grand gooseberry bushes at the bottom, if I remember properly.'

Catriona had had little leisure in which to inspect the garden. All her time was taken up with making the house a fit place in which to live.

'We had hoped soap and water and some new windows would cure its ills, Mr Brown, but I'm afraid neglect and some vandalism have caused major problems.'

The minister shook his head in disbelief. 'Vandalism . . . on Blackness Road, and you not too far from that nice private hospital for women. What is the world coming to? It's the war, of course, not the militant suffragettes, I'm happy to say. Everything that is going wrong can now be laid at the feet of this unholy war.'

'So no doubt everything that went wrong in Dundee before the war was caused by the suffragettes.' Thus Victoria dispensed with the militant women. What is a holy war? she thought. The two words don't seem to go together. Surely all war is unholy. But she hid her thoughts and smiled at the minister.

'Well, if there's anything I can do,' he said, and he meant it, 'you have only to ask. And I shall certainly drop in to see you both later this week. You'll have met your neighbours – such good people, pillars of the kirk and the community.'

Catriona mumbled something innocuous and they moved on.

'Good neighbours who have done nothing but inspect us through their lace curtains, Mother,' said Victoria as they walked off together.

'Aye, but Mr Brown visiting can only help us, Victoria, and he knows that.'

The streets of Dundee were quiet, the only people abroad being those on their way to or from their local church. Catriona and Victoria, chastely buttoned up to their chins in their best Sunday black, nodded and bowed to the people they passed, but no one stopped to chat to them, no one dropped into step beside them as they walked home.

'It'll be different when we know people, Mother,' consoled Victoria, 'when we're accepted.'

Catriona noted again the use of the formal 'Mother' and sighed for Victoria's lost childhood, but she said nothing. They walked along, admiring the trees and talking of how lovely they would be in the spring. Suddenly Catriona stopped in the middle of the pavement and her heart, dead with grief for the past few weeks, began to swell and burst with renewed love and hope.

'Look, Victoria, oh look.'

The road outside their house was awash with people, and with carts laden with tools. Victoria, forgetting her new-found adulthood, kirtled up her skirts and ran, calling as she did, 'Tam, Nellie, Bessie,' and then, 'Flash.' It was Jock's collie who had stayed at the farm with Tam Menmuir.

Tears of happiness were in Catriona's eyes as she greeted her former servants – now, in her eyes at least, her equals.

'We'd hae been afore, Mistress, but had tae wait for a free day,' said Bessie Menmuir. 'We're here tae gie a bit hand, like.'

'But it's Sunday, Bessie.'

'Did the auld meenister, bless his heart, no haud an early service the day, and he'll be here hissel as soon as he's had his soup. Martha Livingstone wouldnae let him oot of the Manse without he had his denner. Noo, you and wee Victoria go and get oot of your kirk finery, and in twa shacks of a ram's tail we'll hae this place redded up. The laddies are in the garden. You'll no mind that they took the liberty. Oor Davie's no a lad for wasting his time and he's aff tae his regiment again the morn. Tam'll get tae yer roof – it's no looking sound – and I'll pit some soup on and some tatties. We brought you some tatties and some neeps for your pantry. They'll rot in this rain if we dinnae use them up.'

An hour later, Catriona went out to call in the Menmuir 'laddies' – grown men all. The wilderness at the back of the house was beginning to resemble a garden.

'It was no that much work, Mistress,' said Davie Menmuir, a tall, strapping Black Watch sergeant, just finishing his leave from the Front. Married and widowed in the same year as Catriona's own marriage, he had become quiet and introspective, but never surly. 'The beds had been well laid oot and a guid gardener had known fine what he was doing. We had naethin to do, like, but just tidy up and get it under control a bit.'

Catriona looked at what had, a few hours before, been an impenetrable jungle. 'Oh Davie, it's like a different place. Thank you.' She said nothing about the gooseberries that might or might not be growing at the bottom of the wilderness.

Davie blushed with the embarrassment of the countryman who sees no need for thanks for giving a little help to a neighbour. Had not Catriona Cameron spent near sixteen years at Priory Farm helping its workers in a hundred different ways?

'I'll leave my brothers tae finish off here, Mistress, and I'll fix those windows afore we go. Sam has gone tae cut glass for them. You should be watertight afore night.'

The tears once again threatened to overwhelm Catriona and she turned from him and stumbled back to the kitchen. At least she could help Bessie dish up hearty plates of the good broth she had brought with her and had heated up on the iron range.

'I don't know how to thank you all, Bessie,' she began.

'Ach, Mistress, is friendship no like the land? You only get out of it whit ye've put in. Now, if you take that meat out of the soup pot we can serve it with tatties and neeps, and then I've a tart we can enjoy with a guid cup of tea afore we get back tae work. Where's wee Victoria? She was supposed to be setting the table.'

Victoria had finished the table. The last time she had helped to set a table for so many had been the night of the harvest dance and she was determined not to cry at the memory, but to rejoice in once more being with her people. But it was too hard, and she could not keep back the choking tears. She heard a footstep outside and, so as not to be caught crying, whisked herself under the table. Davie Menmuir caught a glimpse of woollen tartan skirt as he entered. He knelt down beside the table and fished a little bundle out from inside his shirt.

'Ma was thinking that you'd take this wee fellow, Miss Victoria,' he said to the skirts of the tablecloth. 'He's his mother's son and already jumping on anything that moves. Faither'll take care of the holes and he's put some stuff down for . . . well, anything that shouldnae be here. But when this fellow grows he'll make sure there's nothing living in this house that you and your mam don't invite. Faither's leaving you Flash as well.' Davie stopped and smiled as he heard the excited rush of indrawn breath. 'He's an auld dog, too old to take to a new master, and deserving a bit of retirement. A grand house-dog for the people he knows well. There's nobody will cross this threshold without an invitation.'

The tablecloth moved, a tear-stained face smiled up at Davie and a hand reached for the kitten.

Victoria looked into the kitten's soft little face. 'I should call him Ginger, Davie, but maybe there's too many ginger toms around. I'll call him Priory.' She held the mewing bundle against her cheek. 'He's a bit of it, after all.'

She crawled out from under the table. 'Don't tell Mother I was crying. It just all reminded me of Grampa.'

'But that's good, lass. Enjoy your memories of him.'

'He always told me to remember good days, Davie, and to put the memories in walnut shells for the bad days.' She laughed and removed the kitten, who had shown his adventurous spirit by digging his little claws into the fabric of her dress as he climbed up on to her shoulder. 'I think this is a good day.'

Davie thought with some trepidation of what the morrow would bring for him. 'It's the season for walnuts, lassie. Maybe I'll take one with me.'

She looked up at him, suddenly remembering that Davie Menmuir had been a soldier for almost as long as she had known him.

'I have . . . a friend . . . at the Front, Davie. He's in the Black Watch too. He's only sixteen. His name is Robert.'

Davie looked at her. Had his wife lived, had the bairn had a chance to grow and develop in her womb, he too might have had a daughter exactly this child's age. Already she was walking out, was she? A lad in the Black Watch, somewhere on the Front. Thank God she obviously had no idea of what the word 'Front' meant. 'If I come across him, lassie, I'll try to mind him for you. Now let's tell your mam we can have our dinner.'

Much much later Catriona and Victoria sat before a roaring fire, with Flash curled up on the rag rug, one that Catriona had made and brought from the farm, and Priory asleep in Victoria's lap. For once there were no scuffling, scuttling sounds and the curtains no longer moved with the winds that battled furiously outside, unable to gain entrance.

'Our friends are coming back next Sunday to help repaint the house,' said Catriona. 'Maybe the war will be over in the spring and Davie will help Tam do the outside. What a fine, good man Davie Menmuir is. Your grandfather aye liked him the best of all the Menmuir laddies, and they're all grand men. He'd have made a good farmer if he hadn't joined the army to get away from all his memories. I was that surprised to see him today, working away.'

Good, thought Victoria. This was perfect, a natural lead-in to what had been on her mind for some time.

'Mother, talking about helping . . . We can't depend on

the Menmuirs and the others too much. We are going to have to earn some money.'

'I know, lassie, and I have it all thought out. Listen, Victoria, it's not what either of us was brought up to, but once the inside is painted I'll make some nice new curtains and I'll find some decent bits of furniture from a roup-sale, then . . .' Catriona stopped. How on earth would her daughter accept what she was going to say? She finished off in a rush, 'I'm going to take in some boarders.'

Victoria's answer surprised her and showed her that the girl had been doing her own heart-searching and thinking over the past few weeks.

'Good, Mother, you'll be wonderful at that. But in the meantime I think I should look for a job.'

'Oh, no, lassie. You have such a good brain, Victoria. Grampa was so proud when you won the scholarship to the Harris. Do you know he even said to me once at a prize-giving, "I wouldnae be a bit surprised if our Victoria was the first Cameron ever tae go to the university." Think of that, lass.'

Victoria had thought. She had dreamed of a university education; she had seen it within her grasp. She had discussed it with Elsie, who was to go to a training college for teachers. She had even written about it to Robert, who talked grandly of *going up to Oxford when this little show is over*. But in the cold light of day Victoria was clever enough to see that there was no way she could remain a financial burden to her mother for the next seven to ten years. With the optimism of youth, she rewrote the scenario. She would work for a while at any job she could find, then, when the house was as habitable as its neighbours', Catriona would take in lodgers and, relieved of her burden, Victoria could pick up her education where she had left off. This wasn't the Middle Ages, after all. Heavens, it was the twentieth century. There were night schools where one could learn secretarial skills. Nothing should spoil this walnut shell day. From now on, life was going to get better.

The next morning, full of enthusiasm, Victoria took the tram into town. She had taken the trams to the Harris when they had lived at the farm, and she had had to hold her nose against the overwhelming smell of jute. The jute workers rode the trams, loud and raucous in the mornings as they saw old friends not seen since the night before, quiet and white with fatigue in the evenings as they headed home for their bacon busters, their chips and their good hot soup. Deliberately, Victoria now took her handkerchief with its delicate edging of white lace away from her face. She would get used to the smell of jute: she was going to be a part of it, and there was no time like the present to start.

There was a crowd outside the factory gates. Baxters were hiring. Jute had always been a job for women. Men demanded too much money: better by far that they should stay at home and mind the bairns, while their wives worked for half the money that the owners would have had to pay the men. Now both women and men were finding well-paid jobs due to the insatiable appetite of the war machine.

Victoria had scoured the employment columns in the *Courier and Advertiser*. Good, plain cooks were wanted. Strong, willing boys were wanted. Message boys . . . girl to work in dairy . . . Nothing for which Victoria Cameron was suited. Grampa had never let her soil her hands with farmwork and Catriona had taught Victoria few domestic skills, preferring her to devote her time to academic study. But the hungry maw of the jute mills would not care that Victoria could write a tolerable essay or could tot up a column of figures faster than any boy in her class.

A voice hailed her from the open door of the factory.

'Victoria? It's never you, Victoria Cameron.'

Victoria looked at the grey figure in front of her. She could tell it was a woman because of the skirts, but as for her age, she had no idea. The woman could have been anything between fourteen and fifty, so pale and drawn was her face, so thin her body, so grey with dust her indiscriminate hair. Only the eyes shone out as merrily and cheeky as ever.

'Nellie, Nellie Bains?'

'Aye, it's me. Whit are you dain here? I haven't seen you since I left the school at Liff.'

'I need a job, Nellie.'

Nellie looked at her in disbelief. 'Victoria Cameron at a jute mill. Ye'll be gan intae the office fer a secretary.'

'No. I have no skills, Nellie. It's the mill for me too.'

Nellie looked at her compassionately. She saw well-tended skin and hair, good well-cut clothes carefully cleaned and pressed. She could bet the nails hidden by those gloves were well manicured, and certainly not bitten to the quick like her own.

'Ye'll never thole it, lassie. It's back-breaking work and the jute gets in yer eyes and yer mouth, and up yer nose. And you cannae dress like that and be a mill lassie; it's only the weavers that wear a hat and gloves to work, tae show that they're better than a'body. Ye'll get the claes pulled from your back and the hat and the hair from your head. I wouldnae wish the mills on my worst enemy and you were never that. A wee bit stuck up, with yer bonnie frocks and ribbons, but you and yer ma always gave good parcels tae the Bains.'

Victoria thought with shame of the many times she had refused to sit beside Nellie because she smelled. It was easy to give away outgrown clothes and extra food from a well-stocked larder. Real kindness was harder. Nellie obviously had it. Victoria resolved to try for more of that virtue.

'That was nothing, Nellie,' she said seriously. 'And now I need a job and I'd be grateful if you would tell me what to do. And if I do look a bit odd to the rest of the workers, they'll get used to me.' She tried to laugh and managed a half-smile. 'I dare say, if I don't tell my mother, I can stop wearing a hat and gloves.'

'My lad's a tenter, Victoria. Maist of them are right bastards – they're fell important, you see – but Tam's a decent laddie and will maybe gie you a job. Ah cannae see onybody else takin you on.'

Victoria had no idea what Nellie was talking about, and Nellie saw the incomprehension and she sighed. 'Tenters recruit workers. They look efter aboot twenty machines each and every machine needs its workers. You'll maybe get a job as a shifter, and God in heaven I hope you're strong enough for it. All you have to do is take the filled bobbin off the frame and put an empty one there. You'll get so many machines tae look efter and, since they'll all run oot at different times, you'll aye be chasing your tail. You have tae watch out for the shifting mistress; the auld bitch has a strap, but I think she'll no use it on you, just on the weans – the half-timers, ye ken.'

'That's children who work part-time and go to school part-time?'

'Right. Now come on, I've jist missed my breakfast with talking to you, but I'll tak you to Tam afore you get thrown oot. I'm a weaver's apprentice – informal like, but it beats shifting, and I'll get my own machine one day, especially since my lad's the gaffer.'

Two hours later Victoria stood with Nellie before a frighteningly huge machine that deafened her with its noise and blinded her with the bits of flying ooze from the jute. Wordlessly she did as she was told, over and over again. The noise beat her head and body, the incessant rattle of the enormous machines made the very teeth in her head shake. She would never get used to it, never. Where now the scholarship-winner to the Harris Academy? Here she was the lowest of the low – a shifter, not even a spinner, and certainly not a lordly weaver. At last, when she thought she would fall down from exhaustion, a hooter sounded and they all poured out into the yard to eat their lunch. Victoria was incapable of thought. She stood wordlessly while the others walked and talked around her. Inside the mills a sign-language had developed, for no word at all could be heard above the machines, and now the women (for it was mostly women) talked as if they would never stop, would never tire of hearing the sound of a human voice. Not so Victoria. She just wanted to lie down and sleep.

'I thought it was time to go home,' she almost sobbed to Nellie.

'We're bare stertit, Victoria. We wis late sterting this morning, wi having tae learn you everything.'

Humbled, Victoria tried to swallow the bread she had brought with her, but it stuck in her dry throat and refused to go down.

'It'll get better, hen,' said Nellie, putting a calloused hand on Victoria's soft white hands.

The hooter deafened them yet again.

'I hate that sound,' said Victoria.

'Ach, it's only in the morning when I'm warm in my wee bed that I cannae thole it, Victoria. Jist think, the next time ye hear it, ye'll be on yer way hame tae yer ma.' She stopped awkwardly, as if unsure about whether or not to proceed. 'We heard . . . aboot you and yer ma gettin thrown oot. We're a sorry. Ye'll tell yer ma.'

Victoria looked at her. This was much, much worse than she had imagined. To be the subject of talk among the likes of the feckless Bains . . . 'Thank you, Nellie. It was kind of your family to worry. We're fine.'

Five hours later she stumbled back to the tram stop with an undaunted Nellie.

'Ach, dinnae let it fleg you, Victoria. You'll get the hang of it in no time. I'm away tae the pictures with Tam when I've had my tea. The one and only Charlie Chaplin in *Charlie at the Bank*. Want tae come?'

Victoria did not have the strength to tell her that all she

wanted to do for the rest of her life was sleep. She fell fast asleep on the tram and overshot her stop and had to walk back through the dark, unknown streets. Catriona had been out with an old lamp from the farm several times to look for her and was so relieved to see her exhausted daughter stumbling along that she managed not to scold her until she was safe in the big chair by the fire, a mug of soup in her hands, with Priory in her lap and Flash on the floor at her feet.

'You're not to go back, Victoria. I always wanted better for you even than I had. Your Grampa wanted to see you a teacher, maybe a doctor even.' She shook that ridiculous thought away. 'Well, at least a teacher. Never, never the mills, Victoria. That's for, for—'

'People who are desperate to feed their families, Mother,' answered Victoria more fiercely than she had meant to.

'But you have a good brain,' Catriona almost wept.

'And so do too many of the women in that mill, Mother, and in other mills all over Dundee.' She sat up, revived by the soup. 'And I'm learning there. We've always taken the mills for granted, but it's quite exciting being there.' She crossed her fingers in her lap, hoping that God would forgive her for that dreadful lie. There was nothing exciting; it was soul-destroying. She went on, 'It's hard work and the noise is almost unbearable, but the jute itself comes all the way from India, halfway across the world. Women in India break their backs to pick it and we break our backs spinning and weaving it. We're connected, Mother, a girl near Calcutta and me. Maybe one day . . .' She stopped for a minute and her pale face was suddenly aflame with enthusiasm and the glow from the fire. 'Wouldn't it be wonderful to go to India, Mother, to see the Rajahs on their golden thrones, with emeralds as big as eggs for buttons, to walk along the banks of the Hooghli and see those graceful Indian girls.'

She laughed at the expression on her mother's face. 'Life

is what you make it, Mother, and if I have to work in a mill, I'm going to learn as much as I can while I'm there.'

'Come to the table and eat your tea. I'm not having you sit at the fire, like . . . some I could mention. We'll keep up our standards, Victoria, and you'll get out of that mill just as soon as it can be managed.'

But it was the evidence of Victoria's growing wanderlust that was terrifying Catriona. Was that why John had not stayed beside her? Had he too felt the call of exotic places? Was there more of him in his daughter than she, Catriona, wanted there to be? She had to get the girl out of that mill, and the first step was to finish the house so that her way to becoming a landlady was clear.

It took a whole year, a year that saw Victoria change from a fresh-faced country girl to a thin, grey-faced town woman. There was little enthusiasm left for learning of the wonders of the mysterious East after a day in a jute mill. All Victoria wanted to do was lie on her bed in her clean, quiet room and look at the trees from her window and pretend that she was at the Priory. She had no energy even to write to Robert and had forgotten who had written the last letter. Sometimes those few hours with him in the woods seemed like a dream, a fairytale to tell to children. The Prince had come, had awakened the Princess with a kiss, but her waking eyes now saw only dirt and oil, and noisy machines that invaded her mind as the jute invaded her body. When she did manage to think of Robert, she could not keep him in the beauty of the woods: he refused to stay there but stood, with her scarf around his rifle in a mud-filled hole, which was even noisier and more horrifying than the one into which she had so willingly flung herself.

Catriona watched her daughter grow old and redoubled her efforts to restore the house. Priory grew from playful kitten chasing his own or Flash's tail into the terror of four-footed vermin. Elsie, preparing for her own safe studies in

Edinburgh, had taken one look at the house on Blackness
Road, at Victoria's once-immaculate fingernails, and had
decided that 'pressure of academic work' meant that she
could not visit – 'just until my exams are over, Victoria.'

In the autumn of 1916 two advertisements appeared on
the same day in the Dundee *Courier and Advertiser*. One was
for a 'Deplenish Sale of House Goods from the Home of a
Lady' and the other stated 'Parlour and Bedroom wanted by
Professional Lady'. Catriona went to the first and answered
the second, and the result was that in October of that year
Miss 'Doctor' Currie moved into the newly decorated front
parlour and best bedroom of the scoured, mended and
repainted house on Blackness Road. She had liked the
comfortable settee in the parlour and the highly polished
oak table, which was just the right height for her work.
If she had known they had come from the home of a
'Lady' and been purchased at a bargain price through
Catriona's haggling, she would have said, 'Well done.'
She had frightened the life out of Catriona by arriving
in a very noisy and unbelievably fast little car, driven
by herself. Never in her life had Catriona been so close
to someone so elegant and, as soon as the doctor spoke,
Catriona realized that Dr Currie was not only a woman but
was herself a 'lady'.

What was someone who had so obviously been born with
all the advantages of life doing working for a living and in
such a profession? Grampa might have thought doctoring
suitable for his beloved grandchild, but he had known
nothing at all about the daily grind of a doctor's life and
had in his mind an idealized picture of an immaculately
dressed, starched Florence Nightingale. What would he
have made of Dr Currie, who was even now stubbing out
a cigarette in the ashtray of her motor car?

Dr Currie had correctly interpreted Catriona's look of
shock. Had she not seen it a thousand times before? 'I'm
gynae, Mrs Cameron,' she had explained, 'and you can't

tell an unborn baby to wait for the number twenty-seven bus. Now, I like the rooms and – not that it's important – I like you. I'll arrange to have a telephone put in, but don't worry, I'll pay for everything myself. You'll find it a boon, believe me. What a great time the twentieth century is.'

Although Dr Currie was supposed to look after herself, Catriona soon found herself setting an extra place at the table for her and, although the doctor paid extra for her meals, it would have been worth while just to have her there to help Victoria. She brought a gale of educated fact and opinion into the house, and her very presence seemed to have medicinal value. She also gave some interesting unmedical advice.

'Buy a bottle of Abdine, Mrs Cameron, and give Victoria a restoring glass every morning. Good for the stomach and very good for the complexion. At least, she'll think it's good for her – the advertisements tell her so – and therefore it will be.'

To Dr Currie, who occasionally gave her a lift into Dundee, Victoria revealed all about Robert and her hopes for further education.

'I thought I could go to night school after the mill, Doctor, but I'm too tired. My friend Nellie had a baby . . . without being married,' she added delicately, 'and she laughed and said it was the easiest way out of the mill, and she's only sixteen. Her . . . friend, the baby's father, left to join the army. He gets lots more money and he sends her some regularly. She has a room up the Hilltown.'

Dr Currie sighed. 'She's changed one life of drudgery for another, Victoria, but at least she'll have a little love.'

Love. Victoria was rather shocked at the easy way in which the doctor spoke of something that normal people never mentioned in the course of conversation. She was heady with excitement, with the car, the conversation, this amazing woman in a man's world.

'May I ask what brought you to Dundee, Dr Currie?'

Flora Currie inhaled deeply and then blew the smoke out into the confined space, but Victoria was used to filling her lungs with jute. The tobacco smoke she found more pleasant.

'The war,' said Dr Currie. 'Surgeons and doctors are being begged to enlist. That left jobs for second-class citizens. Women, my dear,' she explained. 'I had to work in Africa for two years and I got home as fast as I could when the war started.'

Victoria gasped in awe. 'You've been to Africa?' She wanted this journey and this conversation to go on and on. Unfortunately they had reached the turn-off to the infirmary and Victoria had to get out and walk the last part – her mind, for once, full of adventure: Africa . . . King Solomon's mines . . . diamonds and lions . . . the Victoria Falls.

I know very little about Africa, Victoria castigated herself. Mary Slessor, David Livingstone, I presume. I'll get books from the library and I'll try to talk to Dr Currie.

She walked happily to the mill, her footsteps light.

At home, Catriona was awaiting a second lodger. A Mr Dundas was to call and Catriona had spring-cleaned the already spruce best back bedroom and had opened the windows to let the cold, fresh air sweep any stale air away. It would be nice to have a man about, for safety's sake. Flash was grand, and Dr Currie added even more security, but there was a war on and there were, according to Tam Menmuir, unsavoury characters in plenty who would be only too willing to take advantage of lone women.

She put a shepherd's pie, top-heavy with potatoes, into the oven for Victoria's supper and went to answer the demanding doorbell.

She looked up and her welcoming smile froze. Her heart plummeted into the pit of her stomach and for a second she felt faint. Then she stiffened her backbone.

'What are you doing here?'

Her visitor swept the hat from his still-black locks and bowed to her mockingly. 'I find myself in need of temporary accommodation, and I must confess that after all these years I was curious. May I come in?'

'There's no welcome for you here.' Catriona tried to close the door, but he had already stepped part-way into the hall.

He smiled, the smile that had so easily charmed the heart from her body. Was it working now, still?

'My God, but you're a handsome woman, Catriona, and by the smell of supper, as good a cook as ever you were.' He pushed her easily aside and closed the door, thereby confining them together in the tiny hallway. 'A man could do a lot worse. Come on, lass, let's give one another mutual aid. And then, of course, there's my daughter . . .'

She slapped him as hard as she could across the face and he shouted with anger and grabbed her arms. He did not hit her but just held her, unable to move, to breathe, in his arms. Then he bent his head and kissed her. She stood unmoving and, slightly embarrassed, he let her go.

'You threw me out, Catriona, you and my sanctimonious, self-righteous father, so don't accuse me of having no interest in the girl.'

'You managed to pull yourself out of some French . . .' She could not bring herself to say the word which sat on the edge of her tongue. Aware of her difficulty, he laughed again.

'Trollop's bed, were you going to say, Mistress Cameron?'

'You knew our baby was coming – *our* baby, John Cameron – and you left me for her. I near died giving birth to *my* daughter and then, bold as brass, you turn up. I needed you, John. I cried for you, and who was there? Your father. *He* walked the floor, not you. He held my hand, not you. He heard Victoria's first cry, not you. And did you once write to ask forgiveness? Did you once try to make amends? No. You waited like a vulture till he was dead, and now you come back for what you can get.'

'It's mine. He left it to me.'

'He meant to leave it to Victoria,' she said vindictively. Oh, she wanted to hurt him, as he had hurt her. To let him know that his father had intended to change the will, but just had not found the time or energy to do so. 'Those were his last words, John. *I always meant to put it in the lassie's name.* So enjoy your inheritance, but you won't enjoy it here. Anyway, why should you want to? The farm is yours.'

'Like Hell it is. It's tied up and pays me almost nothing. At the moment I find I'm a little short of cash: just until the next quarter-day. Come on, Catriona. Let me stay. I'll pay my way, and maybe I can get to know the girl and you again, and we can make our peace. At least give me a chance. You were always fair, lass.'

'Aye, and where did my fairness get me?'

At that very moment they heard someone at the front gate and Victoria, still keyed-up and excited by her talk that morning with Dr Currie, hurried up the pathway and opened the door. She stopped short, aware of the tension, of unease. Her mother and Mr Dundas, she assumed, were standing so close, so very close together.

'Mother? Hello, Mr Dundas. Do you like the room?' She looked at him with interest. He reminded her of someone. Who? She smiled at him. 'Next to Miss Dr Currie's, it's the best in the house.'

He smiled at her, sensing easy prey. 'Oh, I'm sure I'll love it, my dear. Why don't you show it to me? Your mother was just about to do so.'

He looked at Catriona. His eyes, so like her daughter's, gazed so charmingly, so straightly into hers. She had fought so hard to get him out of her heart. Had it all been for nothing? I will not be soft-talked again, she thought. I must remember, I must remember that this man is a swine.

'Victoria, this is not Mr Dundas, and he is not—'

'Catriona, my dear, let me introduce myself to this beautiful young woman.'

John turned away from Catriona and smiled his melting smile at Victoria, who, immediately captivated by his charm and his strange familiarity, smiled back. 'Let me take your coat, my dear, and hang it up for you. There must be a lobby-press. Your mother was always proud of her lobby-press. Every boot and shoe in its appointed place.'

Victoria stared at him, mesmerized, and he smiled again. 'My name is Cameron, Vicky, John Cameron, and I'm your long-lost father.'

5

IT WAS NOTHING LIKE HIS dreams of glory. It was dirt and squalor, and blood and fear – and more: it was smells, the sickly smell of earth soaked by rain and blood, the palpable smell of raw terror, but even worse, above everything else, it was noise. Shrieks, from men and machines, the booming or cracking of guns, whinnies or squeals from wounded horses, shouted orders, muttered prayers to God, to the generals, to mothers – and somewhere, at all times of the day or night, the sound of sobbing. Robert Fotheringham pulled one foot out of the clinging mud that invaded everything and then, with an almost unbearable effort, the other foot, and turned round so that he could lean his head against the wall of the trench. Tomorrow, just a few hours away, there was to be a big offensive, but first there was something he had to do. Yes, he wanted to write to Victoria. If he tried hard he could just remember what she looked like, and if he tried really hard he could smell her – clean, sweet, fresh – although that lovely scent made him hungry for something that he did not really understand and was becoming more and more elusive. It could not cope here: it was too lovely, too innocent, too pure to exist in this charnel-house. He looked out across the no-man's-land where death and destruction waited in hungry anticipation and he saw not miles of smoke-blackened French farmland that had once been fertile, but his home, his beloved Inchmarnock, and red rowan berries blazing on the trees and great copper beeches raising their mighty arms to the skies above the Kingdom of Fife, and below them drifts of purple autumn crocuses and among them Victoria, her empty sketchbook in her hand. She raised it to him and she laughed.

'I was trying to sketch it,' she said, and the autumn sun shone on her dark hair and Robert reached out to touch her, to put her between him and the insanity to which he had willingly, happily, proudly bondaged himself – but she was not there.

He felt in the pocket of his battle-dress and pulled out the little gold pencil that Pa had given him for his fourteenth birthday. Paper? What could he write on? Pa's letter was there, with its message of fondest love from Ma. Ma? He saw her too easily. He sighed. He would write on the back of Pa's letter.

My dearest Victoria,

Tomorrow we're going over the top. Isn't that a silly expression for a major offensive? But a humble private, even one with an Honourable stuck in front of his name, doesn't tell the High Command what he thinks. He just does.

It's not as I saw it . . .

No, he could not tell her what it was really like. He could not say, 'It's so awful that grown men are blubbing like babies and I am so scared, not that I will die, but that I will be hurt so badly that I will cry too, and I just couldn't bear to lose face like that.' He could not say, 'I have never been hurt before,' because only the people one loves are capable of inflicting real pain.

It's different, it's real. I find that if I remember the woods and you, and the way the sun makes your hair shine, and how stern you were when I picked Pa's primroses, then somehow I remember why I am here, why I must stay and do the right thing, why we must never, ever allow this monstrous insanity to happen again . . .

'Fotheringham, stop mooning there, laddie. Did ye no hear the pipes?'

The pipes. Pipes, bugles, shouted orders. Fall in, fall out, fall in, fall out. How in the name of God were they expected to fall in when this ghastly mud gripped the boots so that merely to lift them was an effort? He folded up the letter, scribbled Victoria's name and address on the grimy envelope and stuffed it back into his pocket. His rifle – oh, dear Lord, where was his rifle? The sergeant would kill him if he'd let it slip into the mud. Kill him, that was funny. Robert Fotheringham was laughing as he followed his platoon over the top. But he was not laughing while utter chaos and bedlam broke out all around him, when he could see nothing but smoke and occasional flashes of fire. Where was the sergeant? Where was the enemy? They were everywhere and they were nowhere. He could see and hear nothing that made any sense, so he was certainly not laughing when the shell exploded and sent his cloth bonnet flying into the air like a partridge; sent him, bleeding, back down into the welcoming embrace of the mud.

'France, the only civilized country in the world, Victoria. I loved it there.' John Cameron stopped walking and turned to look at his daughter. She was his flesh and blood, good lines there – peasant stock no doubt, the aristos would say, but good stock for all that. 'We should go there, together. A decent dress, your hair . . . Wait till you see the restaurants, the little sidewalk cafés. Every woman looks like one of those mannequins in the tea-room at Draffen's: such elegance. And the countryside.' He kissed his fingers with a very Gallic *moue* and Victoria laughed up at him.

'You are funny, Father,' she said and she smiled, because really, did any girl in Dundee have a more handsome, elegant and cosmopolitan father than hers? He even spoke some French, learned, he explained, on business trips.

'Like the one I was on when you were expected, lass. I

rushed from Paris – rushed, Victoria – to get home and what happened? They turfed me out. My own wife in league with my father against me, as if I were responsible for the vagaries of French timetables, for the appalling weather in the English Channel.'

'It was May,' said Victoria shortly. How often had she heard that soft May discussed and described: never better blossoms on the flowering cherries, never a finer crop of spring flowers.

'Aha. There speaks the non-sailor. The English Channel, my dear, is like a woman and has a mind of its own, which it's constantly changing, and always without warning.'

She smiled. She wanted to believe him. It would just be so wonderful if he and Catriona could make up, but even though Victoria had persuaded her mother to give 'Mr Dundas' a temporary welcome, she saw no thinning of her mother's antagonism, even though Victoria had explained that the 'Mr Dundas' charade was so clever really, if only one was prepared to listen. 'He wanted to see you, Mother, and me. Isn't that romantic?'

Now Victoria said, 'It's a shame Mother couldn't rent the Priory, Father. I wish you would live in it. I'm so glad you didn't sell.'

'Sell? Victoria! Would I sell my only child's birthright?' His eyes were wide-open and honest.

'Mother would have made a good farmer.'

'Your mother is a grand housekeeper, lass, always was, but the truth is she couldn't run a business. The men would have taken advantage of her.' He stopped, sensing that Victoria felt allegiance to the farm folk and he didn't want to alienate her, not when the next rent from the farm was six months away. Besides, Catriona was a good cook, almost as good as some French women he'd known. And she was attractive. If Menmuir wasn't so old and doddery, John might have thought there was something besides fellowship in his constant 'dropping in wi some tatties'. *My* tatties, thought John, although he could hardly complain, since they were being given to his wife – ex-wife – and his daughter, and he himself ate one or two. That potato soufflé she'd made last night, for example . . .

'When this blasted war is over, Victoria, I'll take you to France. We'll go and see some of those marvellous *châteaux*, and Paris. The sights, the sounds, the smells . . .'

'But I like all the sounds and sights and smells here, Father,' said Victoria, sweeping out her arm to encompass the view, which stretched across acres of fertile farmland to the banks of the great River Tay. 'Grampa and I used to explore every nook and cranny of the farm and then, when I was bigger, we would go out into the countryside. We'd take scones wrapped up in cloths to eat, and a jug of sweet milk to drink, and he'd tell me about all the people who had lived here, and why our farm is called the Priory. It's built from stones from an old abbey. Did you know that?'

John forgot that when he was a child his father had been a working farmer with no time for stories. 'No, he was always on at me about lessons and chores. No wonder I hated farming – muck and glaur from morning to night. Do you know what glaur is, Victoria? It's mud that seeps everywhere and won't let you get yourself clean.'

Victoria recognized the bitterness in his voice and was distressed. She fished in the pocket of her dress. 'Look, Father.' She held up two perfect halves of a walnut shell.

He took the shells from her with a pitying look. 'No, don't tell me, that nonsense about the walnut shell. "Put your nice day in here, wee John, and when the cauld wind blows, bring it oot and it'll warm ye." Silly notion, Victoria. It's good hot coal and fine foods and wines that warm ye, and coats and boots with fur linings. And you won't get those by struggling away in this patch of mud, till they cart you off dead to throw you into more Angus mud.'

Desperately she tried to repair the day. 'No, Father, it's a lovely idea. This could be our first walnut shell day – yours and mine. We're here together; we have had our picnic.' She looked up at him with those eyes so like his own and smiled shyly at him. She really was a fetching wee thing. 'I always wanted to know you, you know. I used to worry so much that you didn't want me. Maybe,' she began tentatively, 'we could really get to know one another.'

He smiled at her, his well-practised, devastating smile that never failed. It didn't fail him now. She tucked her arm into his and sighed happily.

'Don't hang on to idle dreams, lass. Life is tough and you have to fight for what you want. Come on, we had better be getting back. I'm out of cigarettes. Eight pence they asked me for ten State Express yesterday. I had to have Black Cat at fourpence-halfpenny.'

Without thinking he stopped and swung his arm, and Victoria saw her grandfather's walnut shell sail in an arc through the air and land far out in the silvery waters of the Tay. She choked back a sob. She guessed that he would not appreciate tears. Tears were for babies, not modern young women. It wasn't his fault. She had not told him that that particular shell had actually been given to her by her beloved grandfather. He didn't understand, but she would make him understand. Like so many women before her, Victoria forgave him. She stifled her fears and vowed to change him. She could do it, she just knew she could, and how happy Catriona would be.

That same afternoon Dr Currie threw her car through the wonderful wrought-iron gates of Professor Dobson's home on Perth Road, narrowly missing two Italian flowerpots, a gardener, who swore under his breath with amazing fluency, and two of Dundee's matrons, who had had to walk to the soirée and were therefore doubly annoyed.

They could not, of course, let their ire show. Not only was Dr Currie Dundee's leading female medical practitioner but, gossip had it, she was related to several of

the finest families, not in Scotland – insular, surely – but
in England, and her little eccentricities like motoring and
smoking cigarettes were therefore to be tolerated. The good
doctor knew exactly what was going on in their minds and
despised them for it, while at the same time she admired
such virtues as they undoubtedly possessed.

'Got more than enough patients, Maudie,' she yelled to
Mrs Lionel Brewster, who was in jam. 'Never hit anyone
I didn't want to yet,' she added to Mrs Samuel Taylor,
who was in jute. She forced the car to a halt just the right
side of her host's prized rose garden, jumped out with an
amazing show of well-shaped and expensively stockinged
leg and swept the bewildered ladies before her down the
fairly steep driveway to the door, where several attendants
waited to take their wraps.

'Price of sugar must be playing hell with jam-making,'
she went on for no apparent reason, except perhaps to
add to their shock with her use of the common word
for the Kingdom of Beelzebub. The huge entrance hall
was already full of all the local dignitaries, whom the
university's professor of music and his wife, Jessie, had
gathered together at an extortionate two shillings a head
to drink tea and listen to a little music, all in aid of the
Boxes for Jocks campaign.

'I hope to God if I have to listen to music, Archie,' said Dr
Currie as she kissed her old friend, 'that it's you playing the
piano and not some ghastly soprano screeching away.'

'Both, except that she doesn't screech.'

'Spare me, Archie, you old liar. Every soprano screeches
– the only bearable human voice is a basso profundo. Well,
I'll park myself in the back row so that I can escape if it's
unbearable. Being a doctor does have some advantages. If
I leave, no one will know whether I'm on an errand of
mercy or merely bored out of my tiny mind.' She knew
perfectly well that her host would not be insulted by her
pre-performance criticism of his entertainment and turned

to his wife. 'You've done wonders with this hall, Jessie, and those stained-glass windows are a delight.'

She moved away and joined a group of local businessmen and their wives, who were all bemoaning the atrocious rise in prices.

'Do you know, I told Jessie I would make her some egg salad sandwiches. Three shillings a dozen for local eggs. Can you believe it? Still, I've done my bit.'

'It's not just the prices,' said Alistair Smart, owner of a local jute mill. 'It's the shortage of manpower. I can't get an office boy for love nor money. Three weeks I've advertised in the *Courier*, but nothing but the halt, the lame and the lazy have turned up. And no, don't tell me I shouldn't turn away someone who's lame – the poor man didn't have any of the skills I need. I did give him a chance, but every time he added up a row of figures, and it took him all day, he got a different answer and none of them right.'

Dr Currie moved closer. 'What else does your office boy have to do, Alistair?' she asked.

'Well, adding up accurately is vital. Then he mustn't be afraid of the new telephone system – up-to-the-minute my firm is – a neat hand, of course, and an ability to look a customer in the eye without being shy or bold. Impossible to find.' He looked at her hopefully. 'Don't tell me you know a boy with all those talents, Flora?'

Dr Currie smiled at him and slipped her arm through his. 'I may just have the answer to your prayers, Alistair. Let's slip out before the singing . . .'

They wandered out into the lovely garden, which sloped down towards the Tay. Flora led her reluctant escort down to a seat under some gnarled old apple trees.

'This had better be good, Flora. Archie and Jessie always have the best musicians.'

'It's a soprano, Alistair,' replied Dr Currie, as if that explained everything. 'Don't fret. We'll hear her down here and with less damage to our eardrums. Now, this job. I just happen to know someone who is young, smart, intelligent, able to use the telephone, very good at figures and with a fine, legible hand.'

'And why isn't this paragon in the army?'

Flora Currie held up her cigarette for him to light and gave him a straight answer. 'Because she's a girl.'

'A girl. I've never heard of an office girl. How old is she?'

'Sixteen. She's my landlady's daughter – really university material, but the family fell on hard times. Give her a chance. I think the only thing she can't do is make tea.'

He laughed. 'Miss Jessop makes my tea. It will be hard enough having another female around the place, without having one who might usurp her rights.'

'Good. Come on, there's your soprano. I'm going to stay down here to smoke. When may I bring Victoria in?'

'Just an interview: I'm not promising. If Miss Jessop objects . . . Very well. Tell her to come tomorrow at eleven.'

Dr Currie smiled and lit her cigarette. She had done her part. It was up to Victoria to win round the formidable tea-making Miss Jessop.

Victoria was too tired to eat that night when she came home from the mill. Catriona had made a rabbit stew, with two rabbits that Tam Menmuir had brought her, together with some carrots that 'will nae last the winter, Missus' and an earthenware bowl containing eggs that had been preserved in glass water. Catriona had wept over the simple goodness of her friends, who had little themselves but were always ready to share. But even the enticing smell of the stew could not tempt Victoria's appetite.

Catriona looked at her. The girl was too thin. My bairn is fading away in front of my very eyes, she thought. She's gone from wee lassie to auld woman, and what can I do to stop it?

She heard the sound of the front door opening. Dr Currie

was home. That should encourage Victoria to make a pretence of eating.

The doctor came in. 'Come along, Catriona,' she ordered, as she saw the state of apathy in which the girl sat. 'Major surgery required. Put that wonderful stew to the back of the boiler, pour me a cup of tea to hold me and then – we are going to give Madame Victoria here a bath.'

Victoria jumped up. It was years since she had had to be bathed. She looked at her mother in alarm, but Catriona looked just as puzzled as she.

'I'm clean, Dr Currie. I'll have a bath on Saturday night for the kirk.'

'You'll have a bath tonight, my dear, for the office.'

She laughed at their expressions and told them of Victoria's opportunity and, as she had known, Victoria brightened up and, her fatigue forgotten, became once again an excited sixteen-year-old.

'Now, you haven't got the job yet, but he's fairly desperate. Gosh, how rude! I didn't mean that to come out the way it sounded, but Mr Smart has a secretary, a formidable elderly spinster, whom he inherited from his father, and she's the hurdle over which you, my dear, will have to jump. As far as I can gather, she won't mind how much office work you do, just so long as you don't run round after Mr Smart. She likes to do that herself. She is also unbelievably efficient and may make you wish you were back in the mill. She is, although you are to pretend you don't know, a teeny weeny bit afraid of the telephone.'

Victoria clasped her thin, reddened hands together. 'And I'm not, thanks to you, Dr Currie.'

'If I needed an office girl, I would hire you myself, Victoria. But now we need to get the smell and stour of jute out of that lovely hair of yours, and out from under your fingernails.'

'And out of my nose, Dr Currie. Oh, just think, Mamma, if I get this job, I may never sneeze again. Did you know,

Dr Currie, that lots of the mill lasses take snuff to clear their nostrils?'

'Well, it's a blessing that's a bad habit you never developed.'

An hour later a very sweet-smelling, happy girl with a rediscovered appetite sat down to eat. Victoria looked at her mother and at their lodger, who in such a short time had become such a part of their family. What could she say? What could she do to let them know how much they meant to her?

Dr Currie looked at her and smiled softly. 'Don't fret, Victoria. Words aren't always necessary between people who care for one another.'

6

THE BRITISH ARMY LOST 60,000 men in 1916, 19,000 on the first day of the Battle of the Somme. Almost everyone had someone 'out there' or knew someone whose brother, uncle, father or sometimes, God forbid, all three were there. Davie Menmuir came back to Angus with lungs blackened by smoke and his mother told Catriona a little of the horrors he had experienced. Catriona listened with sympathy and patience, but tried to shoo Victoria away. She had the same argument with herself over Dr Currie's vast learning and was in a quandary – on one hand approving of the pursuit of knowledge, but on the other disapproving of most of the knowledge that the lady doctor had.

'It's not fitting that Victoria should hear such things,' she had explained diffidently at the dinner table, and now she certainly did not want her daughter to hear, almost at first hand, of the horrors of war.

But Victoria was fascinated, for Robert was out there, wasn't he? She had told him of her new job. He had said in one of his letters that it was so wonderful to hear of everyday things. She had told him of her interview with Mr Smart, and of the much more frightening Miss Jessop.

But I got the job, probably because there was no one else, and there is so much work and I love every minute. Miss Jessop is really very sweet and thinks I should go to a business college to learn shorthand . . .

But Robert did not write back to say how pleased he

was that she was out of the mill – he had hated, he had written in one letter, to think of her in a jute mill, but her being there had helped him, in a way, to be accepted by the rank and file. With his accent, his education and that Honourable before his name (which a sergeant had discovered and used, not unkindly, but in fun) Robert should have been an officer and at first the men hadn't accepted him. But his girl worked in a mill – everybody's girl worked in a mill – so Robert became one of the boys. But he did not write, although Victoria refused to believe that anything was wrong. She wrote again, telling him that she had actually written a letter to Calcutta, India.

And then, in late April, when she had almost given up hope, there came a letter of beautiful parchment quality, so stiff that it crackled in her hands.

'It's from London,' she breathed in awe, looking at the envelope and the postmark but making no attempt to open the letter. 'Who do I know in London?'

'Open it and find out, girl,' said Dr Currie with her usual cool common sense, and Victoria did so. A small blood-stained piece of paper fell out as she withdrew the letter from its beautiful envelope. She bent to pick it up and then, recognizing the almost indecipherable spidery writing, held it against her breast as she read the other letter.

Dear Miss Cameron,

The enclosed letter was found in my son's battle-dress at the military hospital in France some time ago, but I only now find myself able to deal with it. The news of course was so appalling that, if you can understand a mother's love, I was quite unable to cope . . .

'It's from Robert's mother,' Victoria whispered, lifting a white, drained face to Dr Currie. Her mind leaped swiftly to the obvious conclusion. 'He's dead,' she moaned, as the awful reality of the dried blood forced itself on her consciousness, 'killed, in France.'

'Oh, my dear,' said Dr Currie, but Victoria had gone back to the letter. She read on.

'I don't understand. No, wait . . .'

The sight of my beautiful baby, his face swathed in bandages, his sensitive hands smashed . . . I can't bear to see him and, for his sake as well as my own, I have left him with his father at the hospital at Craiglockhart in Edinburgh. I felt, although I am at a loss to understand how you can even have met one another, that a visit from you might cheer him up. I enclose, together with his letter to you, a banker's draft to cover any expenses you might incur.

Julia, Lady Inchmarnock

Victoria sat in a crumpled heap in the chair by the fire, where Dr Currie had unceremoniously planted her with her head between her knees, and she handed Dr Currie the letter. The blood-stained paper she kept to herself to read later on, if she could decipher the words. Had he been writing to her when he was hit? Had he been carrying the letter when they had gone into action? It did not matter. Recently, when she had almost believed that he had forgotten her, Robert had been thinking of her and writing to her.

'Never did see what Sandy saw in that empty head,' said the doctor of Lady Inchmarnock as she finished the letter. 'Well, you'll go, Victoria?'

To Edinburgh? Going to Fife was an adventure. Victoria tried to remember what Robert looked like. How often had she met him? How often had they written? She still clutched the blood-stained piece of paper with the half-written letter. She took a deep breath. 'Yes, of course I'll go. But, oh, Dr Currie, I'll be so scared.'

'We'll go together.' Dr Currie also made instant decisions but, unlike Victoria, she had years of experience of doing so. 'I'd quite like to see how they're handling things at Craiglockhart – should be jolly interesting. It was a spa, you know, before the war, a fearfully expensive watering hole for the idle rich who ate or drank too much. We'll stay the night, Victoria, and make a holiday of it. I have a cousin who'll put us up. We'll have an adventure. I wonder if your mother would come . . . a ladies' day out? Afternoon tea at The George. We all deserve some fun. Work, work, work – ruins more than just your lily-white hands, Victoria. It would be good for our absent friend to look after himself for one night.'

By the time Dr Currie had finished talking, Victoria no longer looked as if she was going to be violently ill. 'He's alive, Dr Currie. Robert's alive.'

'Yes, dear,' was all the doctor said.

Catriona could not possibly go to Edinburgh. With two of them out of the house, it would be a good chance for a thorough spring-clean. The house pleased her now: she no longer felt as if she did not belong and, although everything was in pristine condition, she would enjoy re-establishing her old tradition. The Priory had been spring-cleaned every year. It would be the same with Blackness Road. Catriona smiled quietly to herself at the thought of the pleasures in store.

She tried not to show her hurt that Victoria had been corresponding with a young man and had never even told her own mother. 'It is the twentieth century,' she reminded herself. 'Things are different from how they were in my young day.'

Instead of scolding Victoria for deceit, she did everything in her power to make sure that her daughter enjoyed this first exciting train journey as much as possible. Even though Catriona was quite sure that sandwiches made with her own bread would be infinitely superior to anything the railway company could manage, she gave in to Dr Currie's plea that Victoria should be allowed to be her guest for the day. The banker's draft had been sent back to London, with a short note signifying that it might better be used for one of the many war charities – Catriona was embarrassed and angry that anyone should think her daughter could not afford to travel.

Victoria slept not a wink the night before the impending journey. She took out her few letters from Robert and read them, desperately trying to remember him. They had been children, and it had all been so long ago. When she did conjure up a picture of him, he appeared dressed in silver armour like an illustration by Alma-Tadema, and with a halo of light around his beautiful head.

It was a groggy Victoria who boarded the Edinburgh train the next morning. Even the lovely new Border tweed costume that Catriona had bought for her from D. M. Brown's in Dundee, at the unforgivable price of five whole carefully saved guineas, failed to cheer her. She had never been in a hospital; she had never seen anyone hurt or injured; and the lovely old spa was said to be full of terribly injured young men. What would she do if she started to cry, or ran screaming from the place at her first sight of horror or pain? More terrifying still was the nightmare thought: what if she did not recognize Robert? She had met him only twice, and his mother had said that his head was bandaged.

'You merely ask the nurse, dear,' said Dr Currie calmly, and then she smiled an absolutely devastating smile, which included more than a hint of wickedness. 'Besides . . . I know his father.'

Victoria could not eat, but drank three cups of hot, sweet tea between Dundee and Edinburgh, which meant an embarrassed muttering to Dr Currie before they got a taxicab. She saw the solid bulk of the castle and tried to fix it in her mind to describe to Catriona, for she knew that later her mother would be thrilled that she had seen it. In

spite of her tension, she marvelled at the city's skyline as
they bumped and jolted their way up Lothian Road, around
Tollcross and out to Craiglockhart.

They got out of the taxi and looked up at the massive
stone building, with its welcoming open doors. Several
young men, some with slings or crutches, were draped
picturesquely on park benches, on the lawn itself and on
the wide stone steps that led down to the grass tennis
courts. Victoria cheered up. They didn't look too awful.
One even shouted, 'Looking for me, darling?' She laughed
and waved.

And then they were inside, and the atmosphere changed.
It was cool and quiet, and everything in sight was clinically
scrubbed and polished. A nurse in a starched blue dress,
and with starched white wings flying from her head, directed them up the wide marble staircase to the second floor.
Robert was in a little room that held nothing but an iron
bed, a chair and a small wardrobe. There was a lovely
watercolour on the wall, of an old-fashioned boy with
softly waving, long blond hair, a brown smock and blue
stockings, standing in a wood full of bluebells. It imprinted
itself on Victoria's mind and never left her. A tall, slender,
distinguished-looking man was sitting by the bed reading a
book, and he got up when they entered. His face went quite
white as Dr Currie held out her hands, which he gripped
painfully.

'By Jove, Flora, what a sight for sore eyes,' he said and
hugged her to him.

Victoria took all this in and then her attention focused on
the bed. There was a long, painfully thin body lying under
the white sheet and rough grey blanket, but whether it was
that of a man or a woman . . .

'Robert?' she whispered and reached for the bandaged
hands. The thing lying on the bed winced and drew them
painfully away.

'I'm sorry,' she whispered, aware that somewhere behind

her Dr Currie (Flora – strange to realize that Dr Currie had a first name) and Robert's father were talking softly, happily, like old friends.

There were slits in the bandages and she could see his eyes staring at her, alight as if with fever.

'Victoria?' It came from the grotesque slit that allowed his father to spoon soup into him and the nurses to administer oral medication. 'Victoria,' he said again, and this time the voice was more human, less tortured. 'I prayed you'd come. They thought I was going to die, but I knew, Victoria, if I could get back to you, to the woods . . . I'll get well in our woods, Victoria, won't I?'

'Yes,' she whispered while the tears ran unchecked down her face. She could say no more.

Dr Currie was at her side, lifting her up. 'Victoria, I think that's enough for now: speaking tires him.' She turned back to Lord Inchmarnock, who had moved to the other side of the bed and had one hand resting gently on Robert's shoulder. 'I'll take her to Charlie's flat, Sandy, to freshen up. Then we'll come back after tea.'

Victoria must have shaken hands with Robert's father, for ever afterwards she had the memory of a very kind face, but she felt nothing and cried helplessly all the way to Dr Currie's cousin's flat in Heriot Row. Even the fact that Charlie was an unmarried man who lived alone did not occur to her until they were on their way back to Dundee, and Catriona's questions. She did recover though, after a bath and a lovely meal in the most beautiful room she had ever seen in her entire life. Charlie had been introduced – a gentle, stooping, scholarly man – but Victoria could not remember his name and afterwards she could not even remember his face. He had been solicitous during the meal, a charming and generous host, and then he had left them.

'Not leaving to smoke, my dear,' he had said to Victoria. 'Cousin Flora has all the bad habits in our family. She smokes, as no doubt you know, but I like neither cigarettes nor coffee, both of which you will be offered now.'

He excused himself and Victoria sat back in the beautiful chair and relaxed. 'This is class, isn't it, Dr Currie,' she said, looking at the light furniture, the Chinese rugs, the etchings, the exquisite lamps.

'Well, it's good taste, dear, which isn't always the same thing. Old Tam Menmuir has class – a real gentleman. Sandy has it and so does Charlie, who also has good taste. I think that Grampa of yours probably had it too.'

Victoria smiled. 'You mean class is more what a person's like inside?'

'Exactly. Never pay attention to labels, Victoria. Examine the merchandise for yourself.'

'Is Robert going to get well?' Victoria asked abruptly.

'It's too early to tell. We'll go back for another visit.'

Victoria rested by the fire and drew strength from the atmosphere of peace and beauty in the lovely room. Then, when Dr Currie felt that Victoria was ready, they returned to Craiglockhart.

Robert was alone. His eyes were closed and his body was very still. Victoria looked down at him and in her heart she heard his laugh, as he had picked the primroses. The knight had gone to the Crusades and had come home battered, while the battles still raged. An overwhelming anger filled her and, as if he felt her passion, his eyes opened and slowly focused on her. They crinkled as if, under those bandages, he was trying to smile.

'I thought you were a dream,' he whispered. 'I kept seeing you among the trees, and sometimes there were primroses and sometimes autumn colours. But when I tried to touch you, you dissolved, like a will-o'-the-wisp.'

'No, I'm very real.'

'Never leave me, Victoria. Promise you'll never leave me.'

Again she heard an echo from the past – a little girl's voice saying, *I will never leave you, Mamma, never.*

'Promise.'

'I promise, Robert. I'll never leave you.'

She sat beside the bed, his bandaged hand resting in hers, until Dr Currie told her that he was asleep.

'Write him a letter, Victoria, to say that we'll come back just as soon as we can. Sandy will read it to him.'

'I promised him. I said I'd stay.'

'No, you said you wouldn't leave him, dear. That's not the same thing. His father will stay by his side. We have responsibilities in Dundee. Our work. Your mother.'

In Dundee, Catriona had finished her labours and had made herself a nice pot of tea. Wickedly she spread real butter on the heel of a loaf. She had worked so hard cleaning the rooms. Even John had been out all day. Where he got to she did not know, nor what he did with his time, and, she told herself, she did not care to know what he did. But today he hadn't even come in for tea, so the fish pie could be heated up tomorrow. It was hard to get a nice bit of fish and she'd managed to fill this one out with some dried eggs.

Oh, the taste of real butter. Imagine, some children born in the past few years had never eaten anything but margarine. Well, Maypole wasn't bad, and only elevenpence a pound, but butter . . .

Catriona was almost content. She lay back on the settee and looked around her, her eye catching the Wally Dug that Tam and Bessie had brought on their last visit. She really didn't care for china animals, but it made her think of the farm and it cheered Victoria. Thanks to Dr Currie, Victoria had that lovely office job at Smart's, and Mr Smart was talking about sending her for secretarial classes one day a week. If she could just get rid of John . . . But, honestly, did she want to get rid of him? Yes. No. She didn't know.

'Goodness,' Catriona laughed at her fancies and put

another log on the fire. What strange roads eating a pat of precious butter sent one down. She caught a glimpse of herself in the mirror before sitting down again. She was quite a well-looking woman, considering, and although she had become scrawny and haggard after Jock's death, she was beginning to relax and fill out again. And this scrape of butter will help that along, she thought and then she sighed. Where had she gone wrong? What had she not been able to give John that would have kept him beside her? By rights they should be out there at the Priory – solid Angus farmers, with a brood of children round the table of an evening. In the early days it had all been so wonderful.

Alone now, she allowed herself to indulge in happy memories. She had hardly been able to believe it when John first asked her to walk out with him. Her father was a farm labourer, but John's father actually owned his land. John could have had any woman in the district, and the talk was that he had had many of them. But he had wooed her honourably, and their first days of marriage had been everything that any young bride could have dreamed about – sun-filled days of hard work, and nights . . . oh, the nights, of learning, seeking, loving. She arched her back slowly and stretched, yearning, remembering. 'Oh John, where did it all go wrong?' Did she ask the question out loud?

She looked up out of memory-filled eyes and he was standing there on the rug in front of her. She had been so busy with her thoughts and, oh yes, her achingly sweet memories that she had not heard him come in. She had not lit the gas, and the firelight flickered, sending shadows over his handsome face. He knelt down beside her and she tensed, but he turned sideways so that he was looking at the fire and held his hands to the flames, as if for warmth. She relaxed again. For some time they were quiet, enjoying the peace and the warmth.

'You're still a fine-looking woman, Catriona,' John said into the fire. 'I came back to you, you know. I left her in Paris and came back to you and the lassie, to the blasted farm.'

So he had been with a woman. But how good, how noble of him to admit it, after all these years. She had known and had forgiven him long since.

When had he turned to imprison her work-worn hands? His head was on her knee: she could feel the warmth of his mouth against the thin stuff of her dress. She wanted to move, to break the spell, but she dared not, could not. His mouth, warm and soft, still against her thigh, his hands moving softly, gently, teasingly. Oh God, oh God, how sweet, how achingly sweet.

'Do you remember yon Hallowe'en sociable, Catriona?' His voice was as gentle and loving as his hands. 'You had a yellow dress and a ribbon to match threaded through your curls.' He could feel her relaxing and he smiled inwardly and let his hands continue to do their work. 'You were as light as thistledown on your feet and I wanted to imprison you in my hands, in case someone else stole you away. I could hardly bear to wait for you until we were wed. You didn't know your own power, did you, lass? You still have it, Catriona.'

He was up and beside her on the settee.

How good his arms felt. It had been so long. She allowed him to rest her head against him and to stroke her hair and cheek. The flames danced before her eyes and it was so warm and cosy. She sighed and his hands strayed lower, and she tensed again, but he knew the ways to make the old magic work and she gave herself up to him.

'Catriona,' he moaned softly and kissed her very gently on her lips. 'Catriona,' he said again, and he pushed her back against the cushions and his hands moved and his lips demanded. His hands were inside her blouse; they found her nipples, swollen and erect.

Dear God, what was she doing? With all her strength she pushed him away. Had she gone mad? This man had

left her and her unborn child to spend his money on some
floozie. For months now he had been playing with Victoria's
innocence, watching Catriona struggle out of the gutter that
he had landed her in – and now this. No, no, no! She came
back from the brink of insanity, or whatever this feeling
was, and fought him with all the strength she possessed.
And she begged.

'No, John, please, I don't want this. No.'

But if he heard, he paid no attention. Catriona struggled
and cried out, but she was no match for him. Behind them
the fire burned fiercely, like John's passion, and then died
low in the well-blackened grate.

Eventually John too was still. He lay heavy on top of
her for a few moments, then he stood up and righted his
clothing.

'Christ, you never were any bloody good in bed. I must
have been desperate for it. At least you were cheaper
than the Dock Street whores, Catriona, but not nearly so
much fun.'

She did not hear the words; she was barely aware that he
had moved away from her. She did not hear the door close
or the front door slam. She lay where he had discarded her
and then, as the fire died and the room became cold, cold
as her heart, she pulled herself up and sat rocking herself
as she wept.

DR CURRIE DROPPED VICTORIA AT the door of Smart's office and drove on to the Blackness Road house. She had enjoyed her short break; if she was honest with herself, she would admit that it had been especially good to see Sandy Inchmarnock again. He was one of those men who look better as they age, unlike his son, who had been a particularly lovely boy. She refused to admit to any feelings at all, besides pity, for her old friend. It would be a long time, if ever, before the boy recovered and there was obviously no consolation to be found for either Lord or Lady Inchmarnock in their marriage. The thought: What if he had married me, as everyone expected him to do? popped briefly into her head and she snorted in a most unfeminine fashion. All those years ago, none of their set had been able to see anyone else when Julia was in the room. It had been a competition, and Sandy had won the prize. Dr Currie banished the images of privileged Victorian youth and turned her attention to her driving.

It was she who had suggested that Victoria go into the office to begin catching up with the work that would have accumulated during their two days in Edinburgh. The girl had been quiet on the train, withdrawn and worried. Now that she was away from the boy, she had time to realize what she had seen in the last few days, to wonder about what she was expected to do now and to pray that she could cope.

'Go to the office for the afternoon, Victoria. Mr Smart isn't expecting you until tomorrow but he'll be delighted to have you.' She did not add, 'Hard work will take your mind off your young man and his troubles.'

She thought about Victoria and young Robert, and about the conversations she had had with Lord Inchmarnock and the doctors attending the boy, all the way home. Her mood was as melancholy as Victoria's as she stepped out of her little car and into the lovely May sunshine. What a delightful month it was in Dundee, with some trees still in glorious blossom and others unfurling their fragile green leaves tentatively to the sun.

The curtains at the house on Blackness Road were still drawn. How unlike Catriona, the most fastidious and conscientious of housewives, not to have the blinds drawn up and the windows open to allow the wind to blow away the bad night air. The doctor trod firmly, but without undue speed, up the path and opened the unlocked front door. She heard Flash barking from Victoria's room, where he and Priory had no doubt decided to sleep during their mistress's absence. She called out reassuringly to him and the dog fell quiet. So too was the rest of the house – deathly quiet. Dr Currie began to feel the first twinge of unease. At this time of day Catriona should have been cooking or ironing, and she could smell neither activity.

She found Catriona huddled on the settee in the living room. Her hair had escaped from its neat pins and her dress was torn and disarranged. Her knees were drawn up and she had her arms wrapped round them, and she was rocking herself back and forward and moaning, moaning, moaning. Dr Currie, who had seen such sights too often before and who realized without asking the cause of Catriona's distress, went over to her quickly.

'It's all right, Catriona. I'm here. Everything is going to be all right.'

'Victoria?' It was a tortured, pleading gasp.

'I sent her to work.'

The mother relaxed and allowed the doctor to help her from the room and upstairs.

Quickly and methodically Dr Currie stripped and examined her landlady, now so horrifyingly her patient. There was little external damage. The scratches and slight bruising would heal quickly. The real wounds, which were internal, would take time to mend.

An unforgivable invasion of her self, thought the doctor angrily as she worked.

Later, her patient finally sleeping peacefully, Dr Currie went to release the animals. Flash had contained himself, but not Priory.

'If life isn't one mess, it's another,' said the doctor, disobeying Catriona's strict instructions and lighting up a cigarette before beginning her second clean-up operation.

She opened Victoria's window to allow the cigarette smoke and animal odours to drift away together, then she set the living room to rights. Only then did she make tea for herself and her patient. She forced Catriona to drink and to eat a little bread and butter, while she sat by the side of the bed and listened to the distressed woman going over the sordid little story again and again.

'It was my fault, Doctor, my fault. He always was a . . . loving . . . man, and I led him on. I—'

'For heaven's sake,' said Dr Currie, when she had listened to the story for the umpteenth time. 'When will you stop blaming yourself for John Cameron? He's no good, Catriona – never was – and it has absolutely nothing to do with you.'

Catriona looked at her. She did not believe her. She did not really believe that an unmarried woman could possibly understand what had happened. But Catriona had been brought up to look upon doctors, ministers, and teachers as almost God-like creatures, with whom one never argued. 'I don't want Victoria to know,' she said finally. 'I've sheltered her from everything sordid.'

'Catriona, Victoria has just spent two days at the bedside of a gently reared young boy who, for reasons known only to the powers that be, has spent the last several months fighting for his life in a rat-infested hell-hole known as a trench. He has been hideously disfigured and is now fighting a second, even tougher, battle. Victoria was calm and supportive. She will not see what has happened to you as the end of the world.'

'What are you talking about, Dr Currie? What has happened?' Victoria was standing in the doorway, the hat and gloves that an office girl could wear with impunity grasped unceremoniously in her hands, her eyes anxious.

They had not heard her come in.

Ignoring Catriona's protestations, Dr Currie told Victoria truthfully and simply what had happened.

Victoria went white and then red, first with shock and then with barely suppressed anger. Sex . . . Violation . . . She had never given either one much thought. Sex was something that married people did occasionally. It had to be done, of course, or there would be no children, but to think of it in terms of her mother and her new-found father. No, it could not be. There was some horrible mistake. She looked at her mother, grown old and frail again in the space of a night, and Victoria went to her and, as she had done on the very first morning in the house, took the older woman in her arms. 'How could he, how could he?' she seethed. 'It's my fault, Mamma. I forced you to take him in. I should have been here to protect you.'

'Enough,' said Dr Currie. 'What a pair for overloading yourselves with guilt and responsibility. John Cameron is responsible for this, and no one else.'

'Can we have him arrested for assault, Doctor?' Victoria could see only the need to punish someone for her mother's pain. She was ready to rush to the nearest police station.

The two older women exchanged glances over her bowed head. A divorced woman who takes in her former husband as a lodger, and then claims that she has been assaulted, might not be dealt with too sympathetically.

Dr Currie, more sophisticated and worldly wise than Catriona, tried to answer as diplomatically as possible. 'It would be too unpleasant for your mother, Victoria. He was her husband . . .'

'They are divorced,' Victoria reminded her, and felt her mother wince even at the sound of that shameful word.

'He was living here, Victoria. Some people might find that fact . . . interesting.'

'I could explain that it was for my sake, that I wanted to get to know him, that I hoped . . .' Victoria's voice trailed off. What had she hoped? Was she a child who believed in fairy stories?

All three women were silent while unpleasant thoughts chased around in their heads.

'Where has he gone anyway?' asked Victoria at last. 'He needs money. He never paid for his lodgings and the next rent from the farm isn't due until the September quarter-day. I'll check his room.' She jumped up and hurried out.

Dr Currie leaned over her patient and adjusted her coverings. 'Excuse me for a moment too, Catriona. I'll heat up that fish pie . . . No, I'm perfectly capable of seeing that it doesn't burn.'

But the doctor did not go to the kitchen. With a heart beating faster than it had done for some time, and a feeling of disaster threatening to overcome her, she hurried downstairs to her own quarters. She closed the door behind her and leaned against it while she tried to calm her heart. He had, oh dear God, he had. Several times in the past few months she had felt that someone besides Catriona had been in her room. A ten-shilling note had been removed from her purse, but never all the money, so that a busy woman might think she had spent it; or a shilling had disappeared from the pile she kept on her dressing table for emergencies. She had decided to say nothing to Catriona, in the hope that she and Victoria would soon see the true worth of John Cameron. But now this.

Like an old woman, she stumbled to her bed and looked at the small space beside her pillow, where the exquisite gold half-hunter watch with the words *Sandy loves Flora* picked out in diamonds had kept her brave for twenty lonely years.

Oh, they could have a warrant made out for his arrest now. But would it bring back her watch, her carefree girlhood?

For the first time in those twenty years Flora Currie sat down on her bed and allowed the tears to roll down her cheeks. A few hours ago she had been remembering with pleasure the days of her girlhood, the days when young Sandy Fotheringham had spent every minute he could in her home; she had remembered fondly the excuses he had made to find himself beside her at a tennis party or a ball. Every day for twenty years she had seen the watch he had given her on her eighteenth birthday, just a few days before Julia swept through London society like a comet. And now it was gone. And to think that its sale would line the pockets of a wastrel like John Cameron. Feeling that she too had been violated, Dr Currie sniffed loudly, blew her nose soundly and, after washing her face, went back upstairs to comfort her patient.

And who is to comfort me? she thought. I cannot add to Catriona's guilt, and if I tell her she will blame herself. There must be something I can do. Or must I let him get away with it?

Nellie Bains sometimes wondered if she had been right to exchange the drudgery of the jute mills for the somewhat dubious pleasures of motherhood. Wee Jimmy was quite a handful for a lassie not yet eighteen years of age, and now that Tam was away in Flanders with the Black Watch, the cramped room and kitchen up the stairs in the Hilltown was often a lonely place.

Perhaps she should have married Tam, then at least there would have been some money coming in. He had promised to arrange things and at first there had been a few shillings regularly every week, but since he had been away, she supposed that he had been too busy marching and saluting officers to worry about his family. That was all he had done, he said, during his three-week training period. He had learned to salute his superiors, and heaven knows but it seemed that everyone was more important than eighteen-year-old Tam Sinclair; and he had learned to slope arms, whatever that meant. He had not yet seen a machine-gun and he had never fired a rifle, but now he was off defending the Empire and Nellie was left behind to look after his son. She decided to take him for a walk in the lovely June weather. They would walk down the High Street and look in the windows of all the posh shops.

Victoria saw Nellie as she left the office for her lunch break and called out to her.

Nellie was surprised, but delighted to be hailed by her one-time schoolmate. She only wished that any one of her neighbours was there to see her well-dressed friend.

'Well, Victoria, that costume definitely says: I work in a nice clean office.'

'Oh, I know, Nellie. I'm so lucky. I love the work and I go to Bruce's College one day a week for shorthand and typing. But what about you?' Victoria looked down and was rather disconcerted to find herself being grinned at by a very gummy little face. 'Is this your wee boy?'

'He's teething,' explained Nellie, wiping the child's cheeks with a far from clean handkerchief cut from an old sheet. Nellie looked at her son through the eyes of this well-fed, sophisticated friend from her childhood. 'He's a bit washed-out looking, isn't he?' she said critically but honestly. 'I wish

I could get him out to Birkie, Victoria. The air was different out there, wasn't it?'

Victoria smiled. Even to think of the air of Birkhill cheered her. 'Nothing like it anywhere, Nellie. A tonic for what ails you, my grandfather used to say.' For a moment she thought of her mother, still unable to cope fully with what had happened to her barely a month ago. She smiled brightly at Nellie again. 'Can't you move in with your mother while your . . . man is at the war?'

'Move in with my ma and seven other weans, and two of them with bairns, in one room and a kitchen? You must be kidding. I have a room just for the two of us . . . and Tam, when he's hame. I like my independence and my privacy.'

Victoria looked at Nellie. The snotty-nosed ragamuffin had grown into a handsome woman. Her clothes were well pressed and mended, and it was only the child's face and the over-used hankie that were dirty.

She spoke spontaneously. 'Let's take the bairn to Lamb's for coffee, Nellie. My treat.'

'Goodness, are the waitresses there no as stuck up as the clientele, Victoria? They'll no be happy to see me in there, especially wi wee Jimmy. I read in the paper once that Mrs Pankhurst – you know, *the* Mrs Pankhurst, the votes-for-women lady – she ate at Lamb's. They'll think they've come doon in the world serving me and wee Jimmy.'

'You have as much right in there as anybody else. Besides, he looks like a well-behaved wee laddie.'

Nellie hoisted her son on to her hip, where he settled contentedly. 'Oh, he's grand, jist greets a bit when the pain's bad, but a wee nip of whisky soothes the gums.'

Victoria looked at Nellie in horror as she ushered her charges across the tramlines. 'The bone of a lamb chop is better, Nellie, and has nourishment in it, too . . . So the doctor that lodges with my mother tells her patients.'

'Aye, well whisky's easier tae get, Victoria. My, isn't this a bonny place?'

They had arrived at Lamb's and were shown to a table that Victoria could not help but notice was hardly the best seat in the restaurant. Should I make a fuss? Am I brave enough to ask for a better table? Nellie and the baby seemed perfectly happy, so Victoria sat down. Since she had no experience of small children, she was interested to see how the boy accepted being in a different environment. He accepted it as he accepted everything. He stared around at the green plants, the tables with their starched white cloths and the waitresses in their starched white aprons, and he grinned cheerfully at anyone who looked at him.

'He's a happy baby, Nellie,' said Victoria with a tinge of jealousy in her voice.

'Och aye, he's a nice bairn, and my family is great with him. Granny, my ma, my sisters . . . everybody helps.' Nellie deposited her son on the floor at her feet, helped herself to a cream-filled cake and leaned across conspiratorially.

'You'll never guess what I did the other day? The wean had a hen: you know, we were all told to have hens and eggs to help the war effort. Well, we got this tough old hen from the Priory – don't ask how, Victoria – and we put it in a pen on the drying green. I gave it tattie peelings and scrapings from the porridge pot, and it laid three lovely brown eggs, no all on the same day, but then the thrawn old thing stopped laying and just ate me out of house and home. So, says I tae myself: We'll hae a good bowl of soup. I wrang its neck, but wee Jimmy saw it before I had the thing plucked, and you'll never guess what I tellt him.' She leaned across the table, her eyes sparkling with humour and pleasure at being in such a nice place with a friend.

Victoria humoured her. 'I hardly dare think, Nellie Bains.'

'I tellt him the Germans got it. We buried it on the drying green, with a cross and everything, and when I'd put him down for a sleep, I went to dig it up to cook it.' She stopped talking and started laughing uproariously.

'Nellie,' said Victoria. 'You didn't eat the child's pet, especially after you had buried it in the ground?'

Nellie wiped her eyes with the same cloth she had been using for Jimmy's nose, and for his wet and now cream-covered cheeks, before answering. 'I would have done, but old Maggie Thomson up our close had dug it up as soon as my back was turned. I made her give me the carcase for soup.'

Nellie held no grudge towards the neighbour who had stolen her dinner: she would probably have done just the same herself. Victoria thought again how well Nellie handled hardship. Sometimes, in the years since her grandfather's death, she had felt that the Camerons had hit rock-bottom, but they had never yet had to dig up a dead hen. Nellie had nothing . . . except happiness.

'And how are you all, Victoria? Yer mam?'

'Oh, you wouldn't recognize the house, Nellie.' Victoria could not tell her the truth; she could not say that Catriona was a shadow who floated around the house or sat dully, staring into space, and who started at any sound, especially the noise of an opening door. 'We have a lady doctor living with us, but you knew that. She's wonderful. You wouldn't believe the hours she works. She has a motor car and she smokes cigarettes but, it's funny, Nellie, she's still a lady.'

'I've seen her. Don't get in her road if she's heading for the Dundee Royal,' said Nellie feelingly. 'Must be great tae know a real live doctor, even if it's a woman. Dae ye get free medical care?'

Victoria thought of the care and attention her mother was receiving. 'Me, Nellie? I'm as healthy as one of Grampa's Clydesdales.'

'Oh, I loved tae see him sitting up there on a Sunday in his tall hat and his frock-coat. Whae has the horses now?'

'One or two were sold off when Grampa died, but

Glentanar and the Cutty Sark still work the farm. Tam
Menmuir loves them just as much as my grandfather did.
It's almost like seeing Grampa. He speaks to them in the
same way. I'll need to go, Nellie. You wouldn't believe
the demands for jute with this war going on and on. I'll
be lucky if I get all the letters and bills typed in time to
catch my tram.'

Victoria paid the bill, said Goodbye to Nellie and hurried
back to the office. She loved being there. She loved the
dark wallpaper, the heavy polished wood, the feeling of
usefulness and especially of accomplishment at the end of
the day. If only everything in life was as easy as neatly
typing a column of figures.

8

LORD INCHMARNOCK SAT BESIDE HIS son's bed and waited
for the surgeon. They were going to take off the bandages
that had been applied after the first of many operations that
they had told him Robert would have to undergo. He was
not expecting much. Unlike his wife, he had sat there day
after day while Robert, his face an unrecognizable mass of
bone and bloody tissue, waited to heal sufficiently and grow
strong enough to endure surgery. Lord Inchmarnock knew
what lay under the bandages. If it even looked a little better
than it had done; even, please God, just a little better . . .

From which ancestor had the boy's beauty come? He
looked like his mother, but stronger, and he looked like
his father, but finer. He resembled the seventeenth-century
portrait of a dilettante Inchmarnock, but there was nothing
dissolute about Robert's finely carved features or about his
character. What a lovely, happy little boy he had been. His
father looked at the still figure in front of him, and his
mind filled with pictures of an ethereal child in a sailor
suit, running to him across the great lawns of Inchmarnock
House, filling his life with love and joy.

There had been precious little joy during the last few
months: there had been that first, almost unbearable joy
when he had heard that his son, although wounded, was
alive, but now the boy did not want to go on, had to be
coaxed, cajoled and convinced that life could still be sweet.
For me it's sweet, to have you here alive, my son.

'Beauty is only skin-deep, Robert.' To his abject horror, he
heard himself mouthing platitudes and he tried to repair the

damage. 'I mean, dear boy, the people who love you won't care . . . It's you, laddie, the essential you that matters, and you're still there, Robert. And, in time, you'll feel better and . . .'

Did the slit in the bandaged mask move? The voice was a snarl.

'Don't talk rot, Father. It may not matter to you . . .' The bandaged hand reached towards his father and the voice grew gentler, no longer the horrible caricature of Robert's well-modulated tones. 'No, Pa, it doesn't matter to you.' The wounded boy-soldier sighed softly and stopped to gather his strength. 'But it sure as hell matters to me,' he said, and the anger and pain in his voice made his father wince.

'Robert, Mummy—'

'Can't even bear to look at me. What girl is going to look at me, Pa, if my own mother finds me so abhorrent?'

Lord Inchmarnock did not try to defend his wife. The boy had gone through too much already. Besides, try as he might, he could not forgive Julia for running away, for that was what she had done. It was not Robert she had been considering, but herself. Safely in London, she could pretend that all was well.

'There are nice girls . . .'

'Who won't mind being seen with a horror?'

'It's only the first operation, laddie. Each time it will get better.'

His whole body moved as Robert sighed deeply. 'It hurts,' he said simply. 'And I wonder how many operations I can take, Pa, and for what?' He stopped and there was silence for a time, while Sandy sat and tried to will his own strength into the broken body of his child. Then the voice came again. 'Is it the cricket season yet? If I'd stayed at Eton, I could have been captain. Winterton joined up – bought it, poor devil – and Nash and Thomson-Smythe. Not a decent batsman left in the side.' Again silence fell, and the father sat with his heart breaking. 'Has Victoria come back?' Robert asked after a time.

'She's a working girl.' Lord Inchmarnock tried to sound as calm and reasonable as possible. 'She'll come again as soon as she has a chance. Jolly decent girl. I've never met anyone who has worked in a factory before. Very educational experience. Good for the likes of us to meet real people, laddie. Puts a different perspective on life, don't you think? Flora Currie – you remember Auntie Flora?—She's like your Victoria. Brought up to believe that the sun rose and set on her head, and look at the work she does now.'

'Yes,' said Robert bitterly. 'She's a doctor. Horrid job for a decent woman, isn't it, dealing with all that ugliness and misery, and death.'

'And wonder, miracles and birth, laddie. She'll bring Victoria back just as soon as she can.'

'But I could feel her hands shaking, and she hadn't even seen my face. Her letters said I was like a knight in shining armour, Father. You must bring me a helmet from the staircase – to hide her hero's face.'

'She seemed like a nice girl, Robert,' said his father desperately. 'Flora thinks highly of her, and she always was a splendid judge of character: I mean, she adored me when we were youngsters.' He tried to laugh, but even to himself it sounded hollow.

'Victoria won't throw me over, Father. Were you there? *I won't leave you, Robert.* She is prepared to stick with me, but I have decided that I just couldn't bear to have any woman look at me with pity. And that's all it will be, you know. I don't want pity.' Robert stopped talking, exhausted by the effort, and Lord Inchmarnock hoped that he had fallen asleep. He stood up to fold the sheet more comfortably over his son's bandaged chest. And then the voice, despairing and hopeless, came again. 'Oh, dear God in heaven, Daddy, why won't they let me die?'

*   *   *

Arbuthnott Boatman enjoyed looking at fields of ripe grain. It was a comfortable feeling. For one thing, he admitted happily, it represented the back-breaking labour of other men, and all that grain meant food for the winter and, therefore, money in the bank. He patted his well-fed stomach happily.

'What do you see when you look at a grand field like that, Tam?'

'Ripe grain,' said the new tenant-farmer drily.

'Ah, you have no poetry in your soul, man. It should make you feel the warmth of coal fires for the winter; you should smell loaves baking in the oven.'

'Aye, and see money flowing into John Cameron's pocket. He's ages with my Davie, Mr Boatman, and there's one man ruining his health for the King and another living off the fat of the land.'

The lawyer sighed expansively. 'No more, Tam. There's a warrant out for his arrest . . .'

The farmer started up from the fence that had been supporting his thin frame. 'Land's sake, no: you can't do that. You can't drag the Mistress through the courts. A decent woman couldnae hold up her head in the kirk after the talk that would flee about.'

'I have no idea what you are talking about, Tam,' Mr Boatman lied beautifully. 'A Dr Fiona Currie – you may well have met her, splendid woman – has complained to the police that a one-time lodger in the home of her respectable landlady has stolen a very valuable gold pocket-watch set with diamonds. He will be brought to justice.'

Tam looked at the lawyer measuringly. 'Jock Cameron was the finest man that ever walked behind a plough, Mr Boatman. His son, I cannae take it in, tae be stealing from defenceless women, and noo tae be had up in court. Mind you, they'll need tae find him. He'll no stay in the country waiting for the rap on the door. That lazy layabout is guy fond of foreign travel.'

'Even better – though you did not hear me say that, Tam.
If the rightful owner of the farm is, as they say, of *unknown
address*, then it is, of course, impossible to forward the rent
to him. A fund would have to be established and in the
course of time the rightful, or shall we say legal, owner, not
returning to claim such funds in the time designated by the
law, then they would naturally become the property of the
next in line.'

'The lassie?'

'Aye, the lassie.'

The rock-hewn expression on Tam's face creased into a
smile at last. 'Well, the lads will no mind working for
Victoria. Got the best of her mam and her grandfaither
in her, that lassie.' He removed his pipe from the side of
his mouth and knocked the dead ash out on the sole of
his hob-nailed boot. 'Now, I'd best get back to work, Mr
Boatman. There's a wheen mair tae fermin than jist leanin
on a fence admiring the crops.'

'Ach, who knows, Tam. I always stand taller when somebody tells me I'm a grand figure of a man: maybe the crops
grow better too, for a wee bit of praise.'

Tam looked at him sceptically. He was never sure how
to deal with the lawyer's odd sense of humour. But if Mr
Boatman had nothing better to do than lean over a fence
and waste the best part of the day, Tam would not join
him. He had promised to be back at the cottage in time
to see that Davie had a decent dinner before he went off
to Dundee to the doctors.

'You'll hae a cup of tea with us, Mr Boatman?'

'No, Tam, I thank you. I have another client to look in
on, out this way.'

The two men shook hands and separated. Tam made his
way back to the cottage, only to find that his son had eaten
his dinner and gone off to catch the bus to the tram terminal.
Miss that bus and there was a long walk before him.

*   *   *

Davie Menmuir did catch the bus and he did get to his appointment. Mind you, he was there far too early and had to sit in the waiting room twiddling his thumbs, while he waited for the doctor to see him. The alternative, however, was to be too late. It would never have occurred to him to point out the difficulties of arranging transport into Dundee. He was just grateful for the medical attention that was slowly, slowly making him feel almost whole again. He was so euphoric about the congratulations of the very pretty nurse at the hospital that, on leaving, he got on the wrong tram and ended up in Dock Street. The last time he had been near a harbour had been when the ship bringing him back from France had docked at Southampton, and then he had been in no fit state to appreciate his surroundings. Now he felt like a new man. That nice doctor at the infirmary had told Davie that, although he would never really be fit for labouring and was certainly unable to return to the army, the condition of his lungs was better than he or his doctors had any right to expect. With a little light work and plenty of fresh air, he could expect to live a productive life.

I'll have a wee walk along the river, thought Davie, who was wrestling with another problem. For Davie was in love, although he himself would never have used such a picturesque phrase. When his young wife had died within a day of their baby, Davie had believed that he would never love again. But over the years another woman's strength and kindness had caused him to be aware once again of the blood that flowed in his veins. He had never approached her – how could he? But now, now things had changed, and surely she needed him as much as he needed her.

Davie stopped for a rest and, with his back to the wall that paralleled Dock Street, looked up towards the Law, the ancient extinct volcano that now watched benignly over Dundee. A man came out of an alleyway and, with his hat pulled well down over his face, began to make his way up the street towards the Wellgate.

An expletive that he would not have wanted his mother to hear burst from Davie's lips and he began to run after the retreating figure.

John Cameron hardly knew what hit him. He heard a voice calling his name and began to run. He had no reason to suppose that the owner of the voice would be friendly towards him, and he was right. Davie forgot the doctor's warnings about *taking things easy*. Instead he remembered Victoria breaking down in his mother's arms when they had called with the surplus of the first strawberries. Anger lent speed to his legs and breath to his tortured lungs. He made a flying tackle, caught his arms around his quarry's legs and brought him down. There was no breath left for speech. The two men fought with every weapon at their disposal: Davie, a trained soldier, had the advantage of skill, while John had the advantage of good health. Back and forwards they rolled on the pavement, while passers-by berated them and sped on their way so as not to become involved. At last, when his strength had almost left him, Davie found himself on top, with his hands around the throat of his childhood friend. The terrified eyes looked up at him beseechingly, but Davie saw only Catriona and Victoria and, with the last ounce of his strength, squeezed. Sanity returned almost at once.

'Dear God in heaven, what am I doing?' He rolled off his opponent and lay for a moment with his eyes closed, while he desperately tried to suck in some refreshing and life-giving air. He felt sick, but whether his nausea was caused by the exertion or the awareness that he had come perilously close to taking the life of another man, Davie did not know. This was not Flanders. This was Dundee and he was a law-abiding man.

I must get a policeman, he thought. Maybe I've killed him. He struggled to his feet and, leaving John lying quiet on the pavement, he began to stumble towards the Wellgate, where he would be sure to find an officer of the law.

Ten minutes later, after he had haltingly and breathlessly
convinced the constable on the beat that he had not only
apprehended a wanted man but had probably strangled
him, Davie returned to the spot where he had had his
desperate fight.

There was no sign of John Cameron. Only a few spots of
blood, probably his own, showed Davie that the fight had
in fact taken place.

'He was here, Constable, lying right here.'

'Oh, I'm sure he was, but you didnae hit him as hard as
ye thought ye did.'

'I near strangled him,' said Davie simply. He looked
around at the warren of small alleyways running up and
down the street. 'What would he be doing down here?'

'There's several pawnshops in this area would no think
twice about handling stolen goods, so your man was probably getting rid of his booty.' The policeman gestured to
the busy harbour. 'A wheen o ships in the day as well, Mr
Menmuir.'

'You don't think . . .'

'He's wanted for theft; he's probably avoided conscription.
He knows you were away to find the polis. He'll no hang
aboot Dundee waiting for us.'

'Can't you do something?'

'What? Go down tae the docks and ask tae search every
vessel? They'd find me floating in the Tay as weel, come
the next high tide. Naw, I'll report this, Mr Menmuir,
and I'll be glad tae take yer statement . . .' The bobby
looked with compassion at the white, drawn face of the
man beside him. 'And we'll get you a nice hot cup of tea
afore ye fall doon but, if you ask me, it's guid riddance tae
bad rubbish.'

Davie looked at the teeming docks, at the closed doors
and drawn curtains of the tenements around him. He
would have liked to go to Catriona like a conquering
hero, having fought for her honour and found the treasure

that was lost, but, he thought wearily, he had achieved nothing. He had driven John Cameron farther into that underworld. Would Catriona thank him or hate him? Only time would tell.

VICTORIA LOVED EVERYTHING ABOUT Alistair Smart's office. She loved the dark-panelled walls, with here and there a watercolour bought on one of his trips to the mills in India. She loved the heavy leather armchairs and the worn carpet which he could easily afford to replace but never would. Each day, during all the months she had been working here, she found that she liked the funny beeswax smell of his highly polished, mahogany rolltop desk, with its collection of pens and pipes and its meticulously arranged papers. The sole offering to modernity was the black telephone, which stood at the very edge of his desk, as though he did not really want it there but had been persuaded to endure its undoubted convenience. Victoria, standing in for the irreplaceable Miss Jessop, who was recuperating from a bout of flu, treated the instrument firmly and without fear.

She looked up now from her notebook and caught her employer's eye. Each was so surprised at being caught looking at the other that they smiled and went back to their work – one dictating and the other taking notes.

'You'll have those ready for me by lunchtime, Victoria?' said Mr Smart, unaware that it was already quarter to eleven.

'Of course, Mr Smart.' She smiled and went out to the outer office, where she had a desk beside that of Euan Gordon, the company bookkeeper.

Euan loved to watch Victoria at work. Everything had to be just so before she started and then, once she had her equipment arranged the way she wanted it, her fingers would fly over the carriage of the typewriter. He was right in assuming that she loved the process just as much as, or even more than, he did. Now he watched her arrange herself as if preparing for a long day.

'He's not wanting them done before dinner, is he, lass? You know, you can easily talk to him. He does listen. Miss Jessop takes no nonsense from him.'

'Oh, I'll send Peter down to Lamb's to get me a sandwich, Mr Gordon. I'd rather work through the dinner break than be late home.' She stopped delicately. One day soon she would have to tell everyone, or would she? Could they keep their horrible mess a secret for ever? 'My mother isn't too well at the moment, so I want to get the five o'clock tram.'

She went out to the main office to see the office boy, just as Mr Smart came in to ask her to add a rider to one of the documents.

'She's away to get the laddie to pick her up a sandwich, Mr Alistair. She's a good worker, that lassie, as hard working as she's pretty.' Mr Gordon had worked in Smart's office since he was fourteen years old and he was now almost fifty-nine. He could take his younger employer to task.

'Shame on you, Euan, a grandfather noting the charms of a female employee. You should be telling me about her typing speeds.' Alistair Smart smiled at his old friend and did not say that he needed no one to point out Miss Cameron's charms to him. Perhaps he was old enough to be her father, but he was neither blind nor uninterested.

'You know, Mr Alistair, I was that surprised when you hired a lassie.' Like most of the employees, Euan found Miss Jessop completely sexless – neither male nor female, just Miss Jessop. 'And I have to confess I thought you had gone too far with this "*Let's get ourselves firmly into the twentieth century*" business, but the girl has proved me wrong. She's bright and friendly without being forward. She works hard and she does her work well.' He stopped, remembering that Victoria had cheerfully decided to work through the firm's dinner break. 'She deserves to go far, Mr Alistair.'

Alistair Smart looked at his chief clerk. 'And so she will, Euan.' He put the paper down on Victoria's typewriter and turned to go back into his own office. 'We're well into this brave new century of ours. There's even talk of air travel. Can you imagine? One day, when Miss Jessop has retired of course, Miss Cameron might fly to India on company business. I can't see it in my lifetime, mind you,' he added honestly. 'I can see her going to India, though. She'd be extremely useful to me, to the firm. But flying? What kind of fuel could they use to keep a machine in the air between Dundee and Calcutta? I have to think carefully about fuel when driving my motor between Dundee and Edinburgh. They'll never construct a flying machine that could go all that way without stopping.'

'What a dreadful idea, Mr Alistair. I hope never to see it. Can you imagine the confusion up there, although I suppose there is plenty of space. Anyway, that lassie will be married with a family long before the boffins have such an invention on their drawing boards.'

'Of course she will,' said Alistair Smart lightly, and he was surprised to find that he did not much like the idea of his efficient assistant being married.

Back in his office Alistair Smart pulled out the sheaf of letters from his mills in India. 'Blast this war.' In one way, it was good for business, which had never been better. But he had always liked a hands-on approach to business and had visited India once every three years since entering his father's firm at the age of sixteen, twenty-five years ago. His next visit was overdue and, although the managers in Calcutta were sound people, they too appreciated a visit from Head Office. As well as the very necessary business discussions and apportioning praise or blame, it meant more parties in an already frenetic social round, new dresses for the wives and, more importantly, new conversation.

'If only this dratted war would just come to an end, thought Alistair, I could sail to India. And then into his head came a blissful picture – himself in white tropical gear strolling along a moonlit deck with a girl . . . Any girl? Certainly not Miss Jessop. How wonderful to take Miss Cameron. She is so well organised and . . . He stopped his wayward thoughts. Take a seventeen-year-old girl to India? My God, if he was not arrested, he would certainly be laughed at by his colleagues. No, Miss Jessop – the wonderful, sexless, but efficient Miss Jessop – should go to India. If Miss Jessop will forget her fear of creepy-crawlies, I will take her again, and the wonderful— No, he would not describe Miss Cameron, even to himself. Miss Cameron could easily run this office. They're all eating out of her hand already. Pity she's so young (he refused to add 'and attractive') because it would be quite fun to show her India. I bet she wouldn't ask for three-minute boiled eggs at the hotel.'

He remembered his secretary's first visit to India and the incredible patience with which the Indian staff had dealt with her mounting paranoia. She would not eat any curried dishes.

'Don't put that in your stomach, Mr Smart. I have ordered some poached chicken. Those spices merely cover up bad meat. Everybody knows that.'

She had almost been pleased when he had contracted dysentery. She, with her poached chicken and her three-minute eggs, had sailed through everything. In India she had eaten exactly what she ate in Dundee, prepared and cooked in exactly the same way as her elderly mother cooked it, and she had proved her theory. Maybe so, my dear Miss Jessop, but how narrow your life is, he thought.

No. Taking Victoria Cameron to visit the East could be a very enjoyable experience indeed.

Victoria was too busy thinking of her mother and Robert to daydream about the mysterious East. Dr Currie had taken another day off from her duties at the hospital and had gone to Edinburgh.

'I'll see Robert for you, my dear, and tell him that you will visit some weekend soon. Write him a note if you like, and his father will read it to him – or I will, if you'd rather.'

'I wish I could send something nice.'

'His father takes care of everything material, Victoria. It's a message from a friend that Robert needs.'

And so Victoria, mindful that other eyes would read her note, had written a stilted little message and given it to Dr Currie, before she lost her nerve and tore it up.

'I shall see Robert's father at the hospital,' said Dr Currie. 'He spends every moment he can there.'

But on the telephone Lord Inchmarnock had asked her to dine.

There was no harm, she decided, in meeting an old friend for dinner, even though the friend had been married for nearly twenty years to someone else. It was quite acceptable. After all, was she not a doctor and was the friend's son not very ill? To explain what the busy doctors in the hospital had no time to explain, in detail, to an anxious father was surely a kindness.

Flora took an early train to Edinburgh so that she could have a shampoo and wave, and she wore her soft blue woollen dress. It was a colour made world-famous by a young American socialite who gave it her name, Alice. And, like Alice Roosevelt, Flora knew what suited her.

They met in the dining room of the Overseas Club, and it pleased Flora that the comforting bulk of Edinburgh Castle filled the window where they sat. It had stood there for hundreds of years and had seen both comedy and tragedy enacted, often under its very roof, and still it stood there, calm, dignified, comforting.

Even the stress and worry over his son's condition had not detracted too much from Sandy Fotheringham's good looks and soldierly bearing, and his manners were as perfect as they had been all those years ago, when they had walked and hunted and danced their young lives away in an endless round of social engagements.

Why didn't I marry him when I had the chance? Flora thought to herself, as he held the chair out for her to sit down at the table. Or did I ever really have a chance? Did I even put up a fight after Julia appeared? Was I so used to being handed everything I wanted on a golden plate? Well, my dear Flora, those days are gone and, no doubt, that is a good thing.

She smiled up at Sandy as she sat down, and the smile revealed nothing of her inner turmoil. He returned the smile and there was one of those precious moments when time stands still and all worries disappear – little moments that are given to everyone, and which the wise snatch and keep safe. Victoria would have put the intimate smile in a walnut shell, but Flora knew nothing of walnut shells.

'They have some decent wine, Flora. I ordered this morning in order to save time – I hope you don't mind. I knew you would understand the lateness of our engagement, but I must spend as much time as possible at the hospital.' He tried to laugh. 'But don't worry. I remembered your sweet tooth and I've ordered a pudding.'

He was quiet as the waiter poured the wine and Flora felt that the interruption was giving him a chance to shape his next sentence. 'He's stopped asking for his mother, you know,' Sandy said when the waiter had gone.

Dr Currie's first impulse was to reassure him. 'Some people cannot take the sounds and smells of illness, Sandy, and to see a dearly beloved only child . . .' Dr Currie knew that they both knew she was lying, and she stopped.

'A less selfish woman would put the boy's needs first,' said Lord Inchmarnock angrily, then he remembered that he was discussing his wife. Bad form to discuss one's wife. Unforgivable to censure her behaviour. 'Forgive me,

I didn't come here to air my own mistakes, especially to you. Delicious pâté.' He forced a smile. 'I wish you liked it. I always wanted to share everything with you, you know.'

'Friends,' said Flora, with perhaps a little undue stress on the word, 'don't need to share everything. They can appreciate their differences. Remember the hours and hours I spent watching you play cricket? Dear Lord,' – she laughed, a genuine laugh – 'what a soul-destroying game. Only thing that made it bearable was reading, when you couldn't see me. I went through several of the classics. Some might consider that to be two punishments in the same afternoon,' she finished lightly.

He reached across the table and touched her hand, and she let it lie there until he smiled and let go. And then he frowned. 'You're not wearing your watch. You used to wear it all the time, but, now that I think about it, you weren't wearing it that first time you came to see my laddie. Is that a message for me?'

She thought for a moment and almost lied, but he deserved the truth. 'It was stolen.' Her eyes filled with tears as she relived the moment when she had gone into her bedroom to check. 'My landlady's ex-husband. What an absolute cad he is, Sandy, and she is well rid of him. Unfortunately he seems to have disappeared. Perhaps he's gone abroad, I certainly hope so. He never was the slightest bit of good to them. You know the type of man, all charm and no substance.'

'Yes, my dear, I know the type, and this one took your watch?'

She nodded. 'I reported the theft to the police.'

Suddenly he was angry. Flora Currie in a boarding house in Dundee. She could afford better. 'I can't understand why you're living like that anyway, Flora. What would your father have had to say about it?'

'Catriona's house is clean and convenient. She does everything for me, even washes my clothes. I'm unbelievably undomesticated, Sandy, or just lazy. And it is difficult, especially since the war, to get decent help.'

'If only you had chosen me, instead of medicine, Flora . . .'

She could hardly breathe. Chosen him, instead of medicine. Oh, you fool, Sandy Inchmarnock. What need would I have had for a career if your love had survived the test, but it hadn't. It had dissolved, just as the patterns Jack Frost leaves on the windows dissolve as soon as the first rays of the sun appear. That sun was Julia, and her rays had burned through everything. Flora tried to laugh, to be nonchalant and sophisticated.

'Oh, darling Sandy, you know you were knocked for six when Julia appeared like a comet, cutting a path through all you young men.'

They looked at one another, each surely seeing the other as they had been all those years ago. He looked away first, bowing his head in acknowledgement of the truth. He had been insane, with an insanity that had, unfortunately, lasted only a few years.

'Well, what was it my father's old coachman used to say? Ye mun drie yer ain wierd, and I have and I will. But my boy, Flora? What future is there for my boy?'

Instantly she was the consummate professional. 'He can live a full life, Sandy. They'll do wonders rebuilding his face, and the rest of his injuries will repair with time. Robert's main problem is what we call the will to live. His spirit will take longer to recover.'

'Will it ever recover? Will he laugh again? Will he enjoy life?'

'With you there to love him, and his mother . . . She must be there to support him.'

'And the girl? She's a brave little thing. I see her refuse to flinch when she looks at him. Will she come back?'

'Oh, yes, Sandy. Victoria will come back. Some women are faithful, you know, against all the odds.'

She looked at him across the candlelit table and she could

see the warmth, even the love, in his eyes. She prayed that
he could see their reflection in her own. Was that all life held
for them – reflections of what might have been?

'Julia's coming up at last,' he said, when he could bear the
tension no longer. 'I'm taking the boy to Inchmarnock. He'll
get better there, in his mind anyway.'

'That's nine-tenths of the battle.' Flora too was relieved
that the spell was broken. 'I shall look forward to seeing
Julia again. It will remind me to have a manicure. I can't
remember when I last applied any polish.'

Julia Fotheringham, Lady Inchmarnock, unaware that her
very presence could cause such a change in the lifestyle
of her husband's old friend, did make the long journey
from London to Edinburgh after Robert's operations: not
immediately, so that Sandy might feel he had the upper
hand, and not so long after the operation that her 'set'
might think her unfeeling. Robert's face, her husband
told her, was decently hidden by bandages so, thought
Julia, she could bear to see her beloved son again. Robert
understood her feelings, even if her husband did not. But
then, Julia thought, Robert had always been much more
sympathetic and sensitive than his father, and she was
coming for him, not because Sandy had almost ordered
her to come.

She could also visit society's most controversial young
poet, Siegfried Sassoon, who was, so a particularly dear
friend had told her, recuperating in the very same hospital.
This knowledge, naturally, had in no way influenced Julia's
decision to steel herself to visit her son. She prayed that
she would not break down and weep over Robert, and
she prayed too that she would be able to lie convincingly
and tell him that his hideously disfiguring injuries would
make no difference at all to the feelings of those who loved
him. It certainly had in no way changed hers. She would
suggest that young Sassoon visited Robert with her. When

she returned to London *everyone* would be thrilled to hear
of her meeting with the poet.

Lady Inchmarnock was, therefore, not too happy to arrive
at the George Hotel to find her husband in possession of the
suite she had booked.

'Don't unpack, Julia,' he said. 'I've opened Inchmarnock.
We're taking the boy home tomorrow.'

'Home?' The ready tears welled up in her eyes. 'Oh,
Sandy, a mother's prayers have been answered. He's better.
Our boy is better.'

Lord Inchmarnock looked at her beautiful face. What
was it he had accidentally overheard an old friend say?
Julia Fotheringham's face has never been lived in. My God,
how true it was.

'The lad is being sent home to recuperate from this
operation, Julia, and to build up his strength for the next
one. We're taking him to Inchmarnock, which he loves
and where he may be happier. With both of us there to
reassure him, he'll get well. He said a funny thing to me
today: "*Inchmarnock's a walnut shell place.*"'

Lady Inchmarnock clutched at her husband's sleeve. 'Oh,
Sandy, is his mind affected? There are no walnut trees at
Inchmarnock.'

Patiently, but firmly, he removed the clutching hand from
his well-tailored suit.

'I've hired a motor and a driver for tomorrow, Julia. The
boy will be more comfortable and more at ease than on
a train.'

'But the ferry . . . ?'

'He likes the ferry. And the sea air will be good for him.
I've ordered lunch to be sent up to you later on. I assume you
are too exhausted from travelling to face the dining room.'

'I didn't sleep a wink on the train, Sandy, and had
intended to take a little nap before dinner.' She stopped
and looked around, but could see no real evidence of her
husband's cohabitation.

He saw the frown of worry between her beautifully plucked eyebrows and smiled grimly. 'Rest easy, Julia. I'm bunking with old Charlie. Your sleep will not be violated. You have until three, and then I will fetch you in a cab and we'll go together to see Robert. Try to pretend that you are a loving mother.'

He was gone before she could throw something at him, or even think of anything devastating to say. It was grossly unfair. No one understood. How could she make Sandy appreciate the very real pain she felt when she saw their son – pain for the boy and for his ruined life, his destroyed hopes, not pain for herself. Oh, how dare he, how dare he? He could not understand her feelings. He had not carried the child as she had, in her very body for nine whole months. How could she have persuaded herself that he was a sensitive, loving man? He was a boor. She threw herself on the bed and enjoyed the indulgence of a good cry.

Three days later the Fotheringhams were comfortably resettled in their country home and Lady Inchmarnock found that it was not too painful to look at her son and to contemplate his future. She had had a wonderful idea that would make everything bearable. To this end she had sent Sandy's motor with its uniformed driver to fetch Miss Victoria Cameron. She felt that Miss Cameron could not possibly refuse to return with the driver. Who could reject an anguished mother's plea? What a lovely surprise it would be for Robert, who was now sitting happily in a shaded part of the terrace. Lady Inchmarnock rose as she heard the door bell and walked quickly to her beautifully appointed rose drawing room. The private motor, then tea with a *real* lady in such surroundings. Oh, yes, her plan was so perfect.

'Victoria, my dear,' she said as the maid announced Miss Cameron. 'How very sweet of you to come at such short notice. I may call you Victoria? We're going to be such friends, I can feel it. I'm terribly sensitive, you know. It's such a handicap sometimes. India or China?' she asked so suddenly that Victoria was somewhat disconcerted, until she saw her hostess gesture to the ornate silver tray with its tea service.

'India, please, Lady Inchmarnock,' she said quietly.

Victoria had been surprised by the summons and had been in two minds over whether or not to jump when her ladyship called, but there was Robert to think of. If this afternoon tea had something to do with Robert, then she had no choice but to give up her one free afternoon and go. She wished that Dr Currie was at home so that she could discuss it with her, but since she was not, Victoria had made light of the summons when the chauffeur-driven Bentley stopped outside the modest house on Blackness Road. She was aware that the house and its occupants had been the subject of much speculation recently in the neighbourhood, and now here was more fuel for the flame of gossip. Still, she dressed in her new suit, worn only once since her first visit to Robert's bedside, and she sprayed a modest amount of eau-de-Cologne over her hair. The light perfume gave her courage.

'Should you not take a gift?' Catriona had asked. 'We always took eggs, or a nice boiling fowl, when we called on folk.'

'Flowers maybe, Mother, to the aristocracy, but she has plenty of those. Don't worry. I won't let you down. You put your feet up and have a rest this afternoon.'

Now here she was with Robert's mother, who was offering her sandwiches no bigger than her thumb and a cup and saucer finer than anything she had seen outside the walls of a museum.

'And how is Robert, m' Lady?' she asked. Victoria was not going to be bullied by Lady Inchmarnock and she wanted to find out immediately the purpose of the visit.

Robert's mother looked at her measuringly for a moment.

'Do you know, Victoria, a pale-green Chinese silk blouse would be adorable with that suit,' she said. Then she added, 'He is so well, my dear. His father and I have every expectation that he will live a completely normal life.'

Victoria smiled at the words and visibly relaxed. She swallowed the tiny sandwich she had been holding in her hand and sipped from her cup. 'I'm so glad,' she replied. 'You said in your note that he was temporarily at home. That must be beneficial: you know how he loves Inchmarnock.'

Julia bristled. She did not need some upstart working-class office girl telling her whether or not her only son liked his home, but she forced herself to return Victoria's smile. 'Pearls are really the only suitable jewels for a young unmarried woman, but that suit does cry out for a discreet diamond brooch, don't you think? Sandy, Lord Inchmarnock, and I are so glad that you and Robert became friends, my dear,' she lied easily. 'In fact, that is why I asked you to come.'

Victoria rose. 'Do you want me to visit him, Lady Inchmarnock? Is he in his room? I'm sure my mother will have no objection, since you are here.'

Oh God, thought Julia, how distressingly working-class. What on earth did the mother think would happen if she were *not* there? Such dirty minds. 'Later, dear. Do sit down, Victoria. Robert is resting in the garden, on the terrace – it's such a lovely afternoon. More tea? No. Then I'll get to the point, shall I?'

Victoria sat down, her heart beating uncomfortably. She knew that she was not going to enjoy what she was about to hear. Surely Robert had not been discharged from the hospital in order to die at home. He had come through the operation well, Dr Currie had assured her.

'In some ways Robert will make a complete recovery. He can walk. His broken bones have healed. The damage to his internal organs will incapacitate him to a certain degree, but then, as I'm sure you know,' she added spitefully, 'he does not have to earn a living. It is his face, Victoria, and his spirit.' Julia stopped and tried hard to conjure up a picture of Robert's face. 'He's like me,' she said. 'He looks like me. Dark hair and eyes, beautiful eyes.' She laughed and blushed like a girl. 'I'm describing my boy, y'know – a sensitive mouth, but there's no femininity in his. A straight nose. The mouth so beautifully . . .' The picture just would not come. 'His face will never be rebuilt as it was. He will always be . . .' She stopped and pulled a handkerchief from her skirt pocket and dabbed delicately at her eyes, which were swimming with unshed tears. 'Oh, Victoria, can you understand a little of a mother's anguish?' she asked and began to weep softly.

Victoria sat, horrified. Had it been Catriona or even Dr Currie, she could have moved, done something, said something to offer comfort. What did one say? Anything would sound like a platitude, and she could not console this woman because she could not reach her in any way. 'I'm so sorry,' she said at last, 'but surely, surely we can make him see that his looks don't matter?'

Robert's mother blew her nose. It was the most incredibly refined and ladylike action and only succeeded in making Victoria feel worse than she had done before.

'I knew you would say that, Victoria, but all girls are not like you. Robert will feel like a pariah in society, my dear. Every time I see him, I am reminded of the obscenity of war, and I am his mother. I love him and I can't bear for him to suffer any more. What will be the attitude of some empty-headed débutante? I feel – I'm sure his father does too – that there is little real future for Robert in the world into which he was born.'

To Victoria's horror she leaned across the rosewood table and grasped her hand, and Victoria had to steel herself not to snatch it away.

'But you, Victoria. Even as he is, Robert can offer you more than you could ever imagine. Was it not pleasant to arrive exactly at your destination in a chauffeur-driven motor? Would it not be pleasant to throw that dreadful suit away, to wear pure silk against your skin, to put diamonds around your neck and in your ears, to live here, Victoria, as mistress of this house, to change this room and every other in this house as you see fit? I do not expect you to love him, my dear, and I'm sure that his health is such that he would not be a . . .' She stopped, while she searched her mind for the right adjective, and Victoria held her breath and prayed for the courage not to slap the beautiful, insensitive face. '. . . demanding husband. You would be rich, Victoria, secure for the rest of your life. There is even a cottage in the grounds where your mother would be quite comfortable. After all, it's not as if you and Robert will entertain.'

Victoria sprang to her feet and in one swift movement went to stand behind the chair on which she had been sitting. She clenched her hands on the rose silk and stared across the chair and the little table, with the remains of their elegant afternoon tea.

'How dare you?' she almost screamed. 'You are, without a doubt, the most insensitive and selfish person I have ever met in my life.' She stopped for a second as a picture of another selfish human being rose in her mind – that of her father – and that made her even angrier. 'You can't begin to understand, but I could never be bribed into marrying your son. I liked a boy I met twice, twice . . . when we were children. To me he was St George or Sir Lancelot. I could have loved him, had I been given a chance, and perhaps he could have loved me – and wealth and power, and whether or not he is hideously disfigured would not have entered the equation. And nothing will ever get me to part with this *dreadful* suit – perhaps it's not *haute couture* and needs a little silk something here, and a teeny-weeny diamond something there, to make it bearable to a fine lady like you, but to me it's elegant and lovely, and a joy to wear, because someone who loves me and all my faults gave it to me, and you can't understand that either. I'm sorry for you, Julia Fotheringham, and my pity is another thing you can't understand. If Robert wants me to visit him in hospital I will go gladly, but I hope with all my heart that I never see you again.'

Victoria turned and fled from the room. Lady Inchmarnock stood, shaking, as she watched the flight of the only person in the world who had ever shouted at her. Neither of them saw the bowed figure of Robert turn from the window, where he had been standing for five of the most miserable minutes that he had ever lived through.

10

Robert watched Victoria leave the room, then he made his way slowly along the terrace until he reached the windows of his father's study. How he had loved, as a small boy, to creep along here and then to jump in at the french windows. Each time his father had shrieked with fear. How old had he been before he had realized that Pa had expected the intrusion, had waited for it, lovingly. Dear Pa, thought Robert, dear old Pa.

He smiled a twisted smile at the memory and entered the study through those selfsame french windows. He went to the desk and sat down for a moment to rest. How he loved this room. How it spoke to him of his father. He ran his scarred hands along the top of the highly polished mahogany desk, along the oak case of his grandfather's favourite guns, and he breathed deeply, taking in that special smell of cigars and horses, books and Knight's Castile soap, which spoke so eloquently of Lord Inchmarnock.

How peaceful it was. He had always been safe here. As a small boy he had hidden – with Pa's connivance – from Nanny and bedtime, under the knee-hole desk. Could I curl up there again, with Teddy under one arm and Pa sitting there, looking so patently honest? 'Gosh, Nanny, has that scamp gone missing again? Try the kitchens. They absolutely ruin him there. I'll speak firmly to Cook, I promise you I will.' And Nanny had looked at him with a look that told him that she knew perfectly well that he knew that the much-maligned Cook had nothing to do with little

Robert's transgressions. Now Robert smiled at the panelled walls, as if they could see him and accept him – as he had been, and as he was now.

. He opened a drawer in the desk and took out some of his father's heavy vellum, crested notepaper. He fished in his pocket for his handkerchief and his trembling fingers encircled something. A walnut shell. He brought it out and struggled to open it. Even his fingers disobeyed him these days, trembling, trembling, like old Granny Inchmarnock's. But she was eighty, he thought, and I am just nineteen. How he had hated her trembling hands: they had frightened the boy Robert.

He had the shell open now and he smiled. She was right. Victoria was so very right. He could see the woods, first in their spring glories, then in their autumn dress, and always among the trees was a girl, a young girl, innocent, unaware. She smiled at him.

'These are private grounds,' she said primly, but with a dimple in her cheek, a dimple he had been able to see, almost to touch, in the bad days. 'It's against the law to pick flowers here.'

'They'll forgive a knight . . .'

He glanced up quickly from the walnut shell and his own face looked back at him. Photographs, photographs in silver frames, everywhere. Robert, a plump baby beside the Christmas tree with its breathtaking array of candles; Robert so solemn and unafraid on his first pony; Robert, even more aware of the weight on his young shoulders in his cricket whites, when he made the team; Robert, terrified, expectant, reluctant, in his first dinner jacket at his first dance.

He picked up a paperweight and smashed the shell, and the days of childhood and innocence disappeared and other days came flooding in. The Somme. The guns. The smell. The noise. The pain . . . The pain, and then Mother, Mother . . . buying him a wife.

'You're so right, Mamma,' he whispered, touching his scarred face with trembling fingers. 'No one could love this . . . except Pa. Oh, Pa, I'm sorry, I'm so very sorry.'

For a few moments he bent and wrote quickly on the expensive paper. He finished with a flourish, *Goodbye, Robert*, and then threw the pen from him, so that several of the pictures were splattered with ink.

In the hall the 'tweenies wondered whether or not they should try to *do* the study. They had finished everything else, but Jarvis, the butler, had said as how Master Robert had gone into the room, and he did so hate for the maids to see him.

'Poor lamb, he should get used to us being around,' said Milly solicitously to her friend Bess. 'Then he'd know we only see a hero what has suffered for our freedom.'

'It'll take—' began Bess but she never finished, for just then the silence of the great house was shattered by the blast of a shotgun. It was only too obvious that the soul-destroying sound had come from behind the closed door of Lord Inchmarnock's study.

The butler had met Victoria in her flight and calmly, as if every day of the week a guest rushed headlong from the house, he arranged to find Madame's coat, Madame's car.

'I prefer to take a bus,' said Victoria. 'Please, I would enjoy the walk down the driveway to the road.'

'As you wish, Madame, but his Lordship . . .'

'Can think what he likes,' wept Victoria. 'Please, I have to go, please.'

He opened the great door and she hurried down the steps. A path wandered off and hid itself among the rhododendrons and Victoria took it. She did not want the watching house to witness her flight. She ran and soon found herself at a pond, where a weeping willow bent over to admire its own reflection.

'Oh, dear God, this is the place. I've been here before.'

She stopped and looked around. Yes, it was the same spot where the boy Robert had met the girl Victoria. The great trees stood even taller now and once more their branches were visions of red and gold, yellow and brown. Under the trees, purple autumn crocuses were spreading themselves.

With eyes full of tears, she stood and looked at the archway created by the towering beeches. An autumn sun shone hazily through the leaves and she thought she saw a figure appear on the path – a boy, tall and slender. He shimmered and dissolved, and she blinked against the tears and the sunlight, and there he was again. 'They'll forgive a knight going off to the Crusades,' he said and he held out his hand. It was autumn, but in his hand he held a posy of small yellow flowers.

'Robert, Robert, my dear, where did you get those primroses?' And then suddenly birds rose up in alarm from every tree, and the sky was dark with their wings and the air was full of their cries, and the boy was gone.

Her soul full of an unbearable knowledge, Victoria stood for a long time looking at the spot where the boy had stood, this moment and a lifetime ago. Then, chilled and unbearably anguished, she turned and, with head held high and tears streaming unchecked down her face, she walked down the path to the road.

She did not wait for a bus but walked along the river to the ferry. How calm, how peaceful, how beautiful it was. It was possible to believe that there was no evil in the world, no sadness, no madness, when one watched a great river. The sunlight rested on top of the still water and the underlying currents teased the rays and pulled them this way and that.

Victoria bent down and picked up a stone. She hurled it into the water to break that deceptive air of calm. There was too much evil in the world hiding just under the surface.

Get it out, get it out and deal with it. The Tay was beautiful, smiling in the sunlight, but it was a treacherous river.

She felt slightly calmer after throwing the stone and continued to the ferry terminal, where she scrubbed her face dry with her handkerchief. She sat, until the ferry left, staring into space and, if she had but known it, her eyes were so full of unimaginable horror that two other passengers could not bear to sit near her.

She did not wait for a tram at the other side, but walked up to the Perth Road and out, farther and farther, until she came to Blackness Road. When she saw the dim light shining from the window of the room where Catriona waited, Victoria cried again and, heedless of the shock to her neighbours' sensibilities, ran until she was safe in her mother's arms.

Catriona rocked her and wisely asked nothing until Victoria was quiet.

'He's dead, Mother. I saw him in the wood, but he wasn't there. He was himself again, the way I want to remember him. Oh, his poor parents, his father.'

> '*Soldiers are citizens of death's grey land,*
> *Drawing no dividend from time's tomorrows . . .*'

Sandy Fotheringham, Lord Inchmarnock, held the slim little book that the other young soldier had given him at the hospital and he read the words from the last poem his son ever heard. The poet, Siegfried Sassoon, had himself read it to Robert. Now his father read it over the boy's open grave. The weather underscored his grief. It was a cold and raw day. The great trees in the churchyard held their bare arms up in supplication as he intoned his prayer. He had wept. Dear God, how he had wept. Not at first; not for some time after the remains of what had been the person he loved more than anything, or anyone, in the whole world had been tidied up and taken away. Only then had he raged like a wounded lion through the beautiful rooms of the house they had both loved, and which he never wanted to see again. Memories of Robert were everywhere in the great house, but too often the picture of what had been left of his son superimposed itself on the father's precious pictures: Robert in his baby clothes smiling up at his father; Robert, a plump toddler in his embroidered nightshirt running, squealing, up and down the corridors, evading capture and the inevitable bedtime, Robert, Robert, Robert . . .

Did anyone guess Sandy's agony as they saw his erect and proud bearing, his aristocratic head bent over the little book of poems as, in his well-modulated voice, he read the words of the soldier-poet who, better than anyone, exposed the futility of war.

> '. . . *Soldiers are sworn to action; they must win*
> *Some flaming, fatal climax with their lives . . .'*

Oh, sweet Lord, what was the flaming climax to my boy's life?

Julia Fotheringham too had read the sombre words. She would not talk of Sassoon when she returned to London's drawing rooms: he was for ever bound up with the horror that was Robert's final action.

> *Soldiers are dreamers; when the guns begin*
> *They think of firelit homes . . .*

An elegant, even beautiful figure in her black high-necked gown, she sat in her firelit home, winding the jet mourning beads round and round in her beringed fingers.

He's dead. My baby, my child, my son. So beautiful, so loving and kind, and he's dead. Dear God, what did I say to make him do this terrible thing? It wasn't me, it wasn't my fault. Oh, please, dear God in heaven, don't let it have been my fault. I couldn't bear that, and I have had so much to bear.

She crushed the letter yet again between trembling fingers, the letter that started *Dear Pa*, as if his last thoughts were only for Sandy: Robert didn't even want her to know what he was thinking. He had shut her out at the end. Why? Dear God in heaven, why? Didn't he understand that I couldn't bear for him to be unhappy, not like me . . . He didn't know how empty our marriage has become. He was the priceless pearl, the only common unit that we loved, the precious chain that held us together – our son, our joy.

> *I see them in foul dug-outs, gnawed by rats,*
> *And in the ruined trenches, lashed with rain,*

The letter she had received from the boy-soldier slipped from Victoria's trembling fingers. She sat on her bed, looking out at the garden but seeing, through eyes swimming with tears, other trees.

What a waste! She wished from somewhere she could find stronger words, words that would express what Robert's loss – his terrible, dreadful way of ending his life – really meant. He had been so beautiful and so good. If he had grown up, he would have become a truly fine man, a good man. And his was not the only tragedy. In homes all over Europe girls were sitting on beds weeping for lost loves; mothers and fathers were asking Why? For what has our child paid the ultimate sacrifice? Although Robert Fotheringham had taken his own life, he was as much a war casualty as any boy lost in battle. Would he have been a poet, a painter. . . ? In spite of her numbing grief, Victoria laughed, a painful, croaking laugh. No, not a painter. He could paint no better than she. A teacher, perhaps. A man of vision. How many men of vision had died, together with the dreams they had not begun to realize? How many pieces of soul-soothing music would never be written? How many cures for diseases of the mind and body had died unborn, with their discoverers, in the Flanders mud? Why did they die? For Truth, Freedom, Justice, Right?

Oh, dear God, wept Victoria and she hugged herself for comfort against the almost unbearable pain. Don't let those words become trite platitudes. Let there be an end to war. Is there no great writer out there somewhere, no great statesman who can make the oppressors realize that their way is wrong, that every man has rights, that every man has a place in the great scheme of things? When will there be peace, so that we can mourn for the unachieved flowering of a generation's genius?

Victoria bowed her head again over Robert's last letter and sobbed. Could she have said something to change his mind from its dreadful course? Should she have visited him more often? Had he felt her first, involuntary withdrawal at the sight of his ravaged face? Oh, Robert, Robert, it did not matter, and I soon learned not to mind it. Did you hear me talk so cruelly to your mother? Did you misunderstand what I said? I did not say that I would not, could not marry you. I said I could not be bought.

She got up suddenly from the bed and went over to her bookcase. *Mansfield Park* still stood in its accustomed place and it immediately yielded up its secret: the petals of a flower so silver and fragile with age that she was afraid to touch them, for fear that they would disintegrate at the slightest touch. She bent her head and tried to breathe in their fragrance, but she smelled only a book that had lain too long unread on its shelf.

'I will keep them all my life, Robert, and I will remember you as you were. If I failed you, I am sorry. Rest in peace. Rest in peace.'

*   *   *

'. . . *Dreaming of things they did with balls and bats,*
And mocked by hopeless longing to regain
Bank holidays, and picture shows, and spats,
And going to the office in the train.'

Lord Inchmarnock finished and stood, with head bowed, as he prayed for his son and for all the other sons. And then his silent prayer was joined by that most poignant of sounds – the lone pipes. Where in the world, thought Sandy, had that eerie, mournful pibroch not sounded? The lament faded away and Sandy stooped and gathered a handful of good Fife soil. With his other hand he reached into his pocket and took out the walnut shell that Victoria had sent him by Flora.

'I'll try to remember only the walnut shell days, Robert, my heart,' he said as he threw, together into the open grave, the walnut shell and the handful of Inchmarnock soil.

He started to rub his hands together to wipe the clinging bits of dirt from them. Then he looked into the grave and saw the wooden box, and he stuffed his hands with their light traces of soil into his pockets. Would that I never had to wash them again, he thought. Would that I could keep this final, tentative connection with the boy-soldier who was the last in a proud line. He raised his head. He was almost alone. The many mourners were moving away towards their carriages and motor cars and, he was happy to note, their farm carts – his tenants, obviously.

'They're all to come to the house, Simon,' he said to his grieve, who was standing respectfully a little way off. He watched the man hurry after the tenants and sighed. Thank God that is over, he thought. I lived for Robert. Perhaps Julia did too. Where will we find the strength to go on? Well, we'll start with the mourners. One duty after another. Perhaps that's all life is, a series of duties.

11

As WINTER APPROACHED, CATRIONA PUT her mind to the household tasks. If her mind was busy with the house and its welfare, there was less time to think of herself and her problems. She worked so hard every day that when she finally fell on to her bed at night, she slept like one dead, one who no longer had to think. In this way life became bearable. Victoria and Dr Currie watched her cope and each, in her own way, tried to help. If she would only speak about it. But since that night when, in her own mind, she had given way to weakness and had cried in her daughter's arms, she had shut herself away and brooked no argument.

'You can help me best by allowing me to go on with life as best I can,' she said.

Davie Menmuir was always there to help, too. He rarely spoke, but for some reason Catriona tolerated his presence and seemed to draw some comfort from his being there.

'I should hae a look at the gutters, Mistress,' he said. 'There's already a wheen leaves come down and we'll no want the rones blocked.'

Catriona looked at him and sighed. If only she didn't always feel so tired these days, she could cope better. It was just tiredness that prevented her from climbing up that ladder herself and attending to the gutters.

'I'll hold the ladder for you, Davie,' she said, conscious as always of his emaciated figure. What a fine lad he had been, when she had first come to Priory Farm. But better not to think of those – what would Victoria call them? – walnut shell days.

Davie, for his part, hated to admit that he now needed a woman to help him do a simple chore. He began to reject her offer, but then thought better of it. That would give birth to the thought they were all avoiding. They might just have to mention why Catriona should not be holding heavy ladders.

They worked companionably and quietly together until Davie had been all the way around the house.

'Well, that's a grand job done, Mistress. I'll wash up at the pump and be on my way home.'

So easy to let him go, to take his help for granted. But old habits of hospitality die hard.

'I've a rabbit stew in the oven, Davie. You'll take your tea with me afore you head out for the bus?'

He washed at the pump in the back garden, then went into the kitchen, where the table was now laid for two. How companionable it all looked: the coals glowing in the grate, the cat snoozing on the rag rug with old Flash curled up beside him, the dog's eyes wide open and following the path of his mistress as she moved slowly – not quickly and sharply as she usually did – from stove to table, from table to sink.

Davie sighed.

'You're tired, Davie,' said Catriona, misreading the sigh. 'Here, have some bread, I baked it this morning.'

'Bread dipped in rabbit gravy,' said Davie contentedly. 'I wouldn't call the King my brother, with a meal like this in front of me.'

She smiled at him and cut another slice. 'Davie,' she began tentatively, 'I've been meaning to say thank you. You know, for that day in the town. Yon policeman told me how you hammered John.'

He blushed and stammered something incoherent.

'You're a good man, Davie Menmuir,' said Catriona.

Then, afraid that she had said too much, and more than she had meant, she busied herself refilling his plate.

'I wonder where he's gone,' she said as she sat down. She neither knew nor cared where John had gone, but she had to make conversation, for Davie never would and they would just sit there, eating stew and avoiding what would one day have to be acknowledged. 'It was aye France he was off to before, but they'd no welcome him in the middle of this, would they?'

'There was two ships in the harbour that day, the policeman told me. One had come from India with a load of jute for the mills. The other was going to Mexico. Mexico,' Davie savoured the name. 'Have you ever heard of a place called Mexico?'

'Mexico?' Catriona thought for a moment. 'Is that one of thae places in Europe where they're aye having revolutions? I'm sure I've read the name in the *Courier*. Part of Spain, is it? I'll fetch Victoria's atlas. She was good at the geography.'

She got up from the table and went to the dresser, and eventually she unearthed a heavy green-bound book, which she carried back to the table and laid in front of Davie. 'Do you mind the geography lessons we had when we were at the school? Capitals and rivers.' Catriona laughed, the laugh of a carefree young girl, and he laughed with her.

'For a minute there you looked just like you looked the first day I saw you at the farm,' he said. And she saw admiration in his eyes and tensed.

'That was a lifetime ago,' she replied, 'and we're different people now.' She riffled quickly through the pages. 'K . . . L . . . M . . . Mexico. Goodness, it's half a world away. It's nowhere near Spain. That's the United States. Goodness, Davie, it's a place stuck on to the bottom of the United States of America. How could you ever get all the way to a place like that? And what language would they speak? They'd never speak English there, would they, Davie?' She held the atlas, and as he looked down at the huge green and brown mass that was Mexico, she saw his strong brown hands on her starched clean tablecloth. Those hands have never willingly hurt anything in their life, she thought. His wife should have lived. He should have had children. She felt a slight fluttering in her insides and sat down quickly. Davie jumped to his feet.

'Catriona, lass, you're unwell. What can I do?'

She ignored his use of her given name. She ignored the almost overwhelming impulse to break down and cry, and have him take care of everything as easily as he had rid her gutters of leaves.

'You can eat your stew, Davie Menmuir, and I will eat mine.' She closed the book and put it back in the drawer. 'Talking of jute ships minds me on Victoria. She loves her new job. I don't know how to thank Dr Currie for everything she has done for this family. Victoria would still be in that mill. Sometimes I have nightmares about it. Jock would have given heaven and earth to keep her out of the mills. Look at Nellie Bains. She took a way out of the mills, didn't she? Maybe more misery before her than behind her, though. An illigitimate child! Dear God, Davie. Can you imagine the shame of having an illegitimate child? And my Victoria took up with her again – even took her out to tea. I've nothing against Nellie, but I'm not Christian enough to want my Victoria associating with her.'

Completely unaware that she was causing Catriona Cameron such heartache, Nellie Bains was tackling her number one enemy – dirt. She was being helped or hindered by her son, Jimmy, who, perhaps because he was immersed totally in water only every Saturday evening, was fascinated by the lovely liquid slopping around in his mother's pail and kept getting in her way.

'If you put yer hands in that bucket again, I'll clout yer ear. Ye've dirty watter up tae yer elbows.' Nellie glared at her son, who grinned back at her with that engaging smile that turned her knees to water. 'I mean it this time, ye wee toe-rag.'

'That wean's got ye wrapped roon his pinkie, Nellie.' The voice came from up the stairs and Nellie lifted her head and looked up through the wrought-iron banisters.

She sighed. 'The dirtier that watter, the happier the wee rogue is, Mrs Dow.'

'Ach, I'll come doon and mind him fer ye.' Mrs Dow removed her ample bosom from where it had been resting on the banister and followed it down to the landing that Nellie was scrubbing. 'Tell ye what, Nellie. It's a braw day. I'll tak the wean doon tae the drying green and gie him a wee push on the swing.'

Nellie looked at the girth of her neighbour and at the swiftly moving lightning bolt that was her son. 'Are ye sure? He's a richt wee handful,' she said, pushing her damp hair back from her forehead, but Mrs Dow gathered the baby up in her arms and he buried his dirty face in her neck quite cheerfully.

Nellie smiled. 'Thanks, Mrs Dow. You're a grand neighbour.'

'Lassie, lassie, it wid be a poor world if we couldnae help one another.'

Mrs Dow set Jimmy back on his feet again. It was safer to walk hand-in-hand with him down the stairs. She held on to the banister with one hand, Jimmy with the other, and Nellie watched their progress, Jimmy's feet touching, at the most, every third stair.

Ach, he'll be safe enough wi Mrs Dow, thought Nellie, She's never drapped a bairn yet. And she knelt down to get on with her once-every-five-weeks job of washing the stairs, the landings and the stairwell.

It had been a rainy month and there was an amazing amount of mud on the stairs, hence the dirty water. Still, without wee Jimmy's help, she got on more quickly.

Two urchins took delight in running up part of the

stairs that she had just scrubbed and then, with an almost believable 'Sorry, Missus', ran back down again. At the third attempt Nellie collared one of them. 'Run doon my clean stair again and I'll skite ye both aff that wall,' she said. After that they contented themselves with making occasional rude noises at her from the mouth of the close.

'Wee toe-rags,' said the good-natured Nellie. 'My Jimmy'll no behave like that when he's big. Mind you, if I get what I'm wantin, there'll be nae stair heid for him tae play in.'

That thought cheered her up and she bent to her scrubbing with renewed energy. The stairs would be dirty again before nightfall, but for a few perfect hours they would be as clean as Nellie Bains could make them. She fought the dirt as fiercely as her man was fighting his enemy, *somewhere on the Front*. Eventually she finished and stood, with aching back, watching her son squealing in delight as he soared through the air on the makeshift swing. It was good to rest after her hard work and Nellie took satisfaction from the sight of her child and the knowledge of the clean stairs behind her. She should take him upstairs and feed him his tea. There was some broth left and, if she soaked a slice of stale bread in it, the baby would be perfectly content.

Seems a shame to dirty my clean stairs right away, though, she thought and went over to the green to play with Jimmy. Mrs Dow cheerfully surrendered her charge and Nellie gave herself up to one of the real pleasures of motherhood.

'Wheee,' she yelled, as she pushed the wooden swing into the air.

'Wheee,' answered Jimmy, as well as he could while the wind tried to blow the breath from his little body.

Nellie stood pushing until she was exhausted and, finally refusing the repeated entreaties of 'More', she climbed happily back up her already dirty stairs.

Five hours later she was back downstairs with the three-legged milking stool that had been one of her legacies from her family's tied cottage at Birky. It had been too rickety for the dairy maid and so it had been deemed good enough *fer a wee bit lass like Nellie*. Nellie had been savouring the last of her plate of deep-fried chipped potatoes, liberally sprinkled with salt and vinegar, when Mr Flett from across the stairs had knocked on the door to remind her that she was also supposed to renew the gas mantle. It had got broken in what he had called a *stramash* when the next-door pub closed its doors the previous Saturday night.

'And here's me, on my ain withoot a man, going oot to a dark closie at this time of the night. Do you no think that self-righteous bugger could hae done it hissel and told me how wonderful he was the morn's morning?' She checked that Jimmy was asleep, left the door unlocked so that she could get back in and hurried down the dark stairs. She eyed the broken mantle and she eyed the stool. Since Jimmy's birth she had not been quite the slip of a girl that she had been when she had inherited the stool. She sighed, but decided that life would be easier for everyone if there was light in the close. She positioned the stool and balanced tentatively on it.

'Tak care noo,' a male voice boomed out of the darkness and Nellie dropped the shade with fright. How often had her mother told her not to get herself into such situations?

Nellie took a deep breath and peered into the poorly illuminated close, where the figure of a man loomed. And then her generous heart began to beat, but not with fear – with anticipation. It was a soldier: from her precarious perch on the stool she could smell the dirt and sweat that no doubt he himself no longer noticed. She placed her hands on her hips and swayed provocatively towards him.

'They've nae baths at the Front?' she asked pertly.

'Naw, Nellie lass. There's an affie lot Dundee could teach the French. I'll no be too dirty for a wee kiss?'

Too dirty! Too dirty! Nellie threw herself off the stool and into his arms and for a few blessed moments the ill-lit stairwell was the most beautiful place in the world. At last the soldier pulled himself away.

'I'm lousy tae, Nellie. The wee buggers are in my hair and under my arms and places I'll no mention, but gin I'm scrubbed you're gan tae see them for yourself.'

'I cannae wait, Tam Sinclair,' said Nellie boldly and almost pulled him to the stairs.

He laughed. 'Away, ye bold lass. Ye'll need tae boil everything, including me.'

'Pity I wore my brush oot on the stairs,' she laughed, close to tears. 'For it'll tak mair than water tae get the dirt aff you. And the smell of you. Can you no smell yourself?'

'Ach, I'm past smelling, or feeling, or even hearing, Nellie. We've had that much of everything, we notice nothing now.'

'Is the war over then, lad?'

'Naw. I finally got some leave, and if God is as good as you're always teling me He is, then it'll be over afore the end of my furlow.'

'Furlow. Noo there's a word for the wean.'

'How is he, Nellie? Is he well? Does he remember me?'

Their arms around one another, they had reached the door of their tiny home. Nellie opened it and Tam saw a welcoming fire, polished linoleum and the crib. He tiptoed, in his great mud-caked boots, over to where his son lay. They looked down at the child, who lay like a reluctant angel on the pillow. His thumb was in his mouth and his dark eyelashes fanned his plump cheeks.

Tam stretched a filthy finger down to his son and gently touched the small head. 'This is real, Nellie. I never knew it till now, but this,' he gestured at the child, 'was whit we've all been fighting for these last years. I've seen deid bairns, Nellie, and I suppose I prayed tae hold mine in my arms.'

'Well, we'll get ye clean first,' said the practical Nellie, who could scarcely contain herself at hearing words like that from her Tam. She wanted to cry, she was so happy, so she took refuge in making herself busy. 'I'll boil some water and you get out of those clothes. Pit them in the sink at the stairhead. I'm no having any of your lodgers crawling along my settee.'

'Nellie. How can I get tae the stairhead withoot my clothes?' demanded the modest Tam.

Nellie put her hands on her ample waist and laughed with joy into her man's dirty bearded face. 'This close has seen worse, Tam my lad, a lot worse,' she said and turned away, so that he could not see the tears of joy in her eyes. 'Wrap yoursel in a blanket aff the bed, ye daft gowk, and I'll meet you at the door and take it back along tae the sink.'

Tam tiptoed out on to the landing and quickly began to undress. The top half was easy, but once he had wrapped the thin, clean blanket around his shoulders, getting his lower half undone without dropping his covering was difficult. He was reminded of the days of childhood, modestly trying to preserve his dignity behind a threadbare towel at family picnics.

'Cover yourself, oor Tam,' his mother's voice came back to him. Not a voice with which to argue. He had become so used to taking orders that it had never occurred to him to argue with Nellie.

'Yes, sir. No, sir.' How many more times would he say those words? And later there would be a job in this brave new land for which they were fighting and dying, and he would be back to saying, 'Yes, sir. No, sir.' But at least he'd be living. Sometimes the dying was the cleanest part of it. 'Dear God, don't let me tell Nellie any of the real truth of the glory. Glory!' He stood at the sink and the tears for his lost innocence made tracks in the dirt on his tired face. Oh, he was fell tired. Oh, to hold Nellie's warm, clean body, to lose himself and his memories in her, to be reborn, the old Tam, who had never stolen, never lied, never killed.

'Tam Sinclair, if you don't come back in this hoos, I'll be forced tae dae something I tellt my mother I'd never dae up a closie in Dundee.'

He laughed. 'Nellie, Nellie. I'll no lay a finger on you till I'm clean.'

'Well, stop standing there like a tumshie in a field, Tam. Come on.' Her arms were round him and her breath was warm on his neck. He could feel her warmth through his towel. Her voice was no longer bold, but the real voice of the real Nellie. 'I want tae make the most of every moment we've got thegither. First we'll get you clean and then I've some soup, Tam. Then, well, you know what we'll do, and then we'll sleep, stuck thegither like two spoons in a drawer. But ye'd better get a move on, for that son of yours is up with the birds and he's oot of the cot and in my bed.'

Tam saw the picture in his mind and it was a lovely picture. 'Ach, Nellie,' he said as he thrust the blanket into the sink and began to sprint, as naked as the day he was born, for the haven of his home, 'that would never never do.'

Her laughter and then her lovely self followed him, and he heard the bolt shoot home in the door.

12

Las Estrellas, Mexico

CONSIDERING THAT SOME OF the battles of the bloody civil war had raged very close to them, the tiny village of Las Estrellas looked quite lovely in the sunlight. The bunting, hung everywhere to celebrate the end of the civil war, added to the air of festival. Ragged, barefoot children ran shrieking around in the dirt, sending clouds of red dust scurrying into the air. The dust immediately draped itself on the nearest object – dog, or peasant, or sidewalk table. For the children it was good to run for the sheer joy of being alive. For years they had run – from bullets, from machetes, from plunging horses – and they had run quietly, their eyes staring in horror, soundless mouths wide open, too terrified to scream. Now they ran and yelled in the hot sunshine and their elders sat at the rickety wooden tables and washed the dust down into their stomachs with warm beer or fiery tequila, distilled from the Mezquite that grew everywhere in this otherwise almost barren land. A hairless dog chased its own tail until it was exhausted and then it too lay down in the dust.

John Cameron, brown as a nut from his months with the guerrillas, sat at a table on the verandah where there was some shade and sipped the raw red wine that was produced in the area. Now that this blasted war was at last over, maybe the peons could get back to tending their grape vines, most of which had withered and died in the past few years. He laughed at himself for his bad luck in running away from one war, only to be caught up in another one, and for his good luck in managing to make money – even though he was unsure as to the value of pesetas in real terms – out of that war. Gun-running was extremely profitable, and here in Mexico there was money to be made if one had a brain and no conscience.

'Madre de Dios,' he said and sat straight up in his chair. One of the sons of the local *Padrón*, Don Alejandro Alcantarilla Medina, was riding past on a magnificent stallion. But it was not the horseflesh – superb though that was – or even the dignified, aristocratic bearing, the almost insolent arrogance and self-confidence of young Don José Luis, the *Padrón*'s eldest son, that drew his eye. The young *hidalgo* had his sister with him. She was riding, as aristocratic Spanish girls often did, behind her brother, her arms around his slim waist: she had no fear of the strength of the dancing horse, for was not José Luis in complete control? *La dama* Lucia, sixteen years old, and home from her convent school for the first time in months, was wearing riding dress: a wide, blue skirt exquisitely embroidered around the wide hem, which fanned over the rump of the horse: a matching short blue jacket that was also embroidered with – could it be?—gold thread, over a man's-style ruffled shirt, of a whiteness that almost blinded John's eyes. Her black curls were trapped against their will under a severe *gaucho* hat, and her dark eyes twinkled with excitement, even more brightly than the diamonds screwed into her perfect little earlobes.

Don Alejandro had locked his precious only daughter away for her own safety as the war had raged around his ancestral acres. So today, at last, she was happy to be free, to be with José Luis, to be . . . admired. She knew that the *gringo* at the table admired her. Had she not seen his eyes almost start from his head as she and her brother made their stately way along the dusty main street? It would be fun to tease him, especially since José Luis could not see her naughtiness. She forgot everything that dear Mother Mercedes had taught her about the wicked, lustful ways of men and she devastated John Cameron with her smile.

'Ay, *caray*,' breathed John Cameron in his newly learned Mexican Spanish, 'did you ever see a plum so ripe and ready to fall from the tree?'

Pedro Robles looked around, fearful that the very dust might listen and report the insolence of this foreigner to the *Padrón*.

'Sh! How you are stupid, Señor, even to look on the face of Don Alejandro's daughter. He would whip the skin from your back. And *la dama*? She would spit in your face.'

John laughed. No woman – not even Catriona when he had bid her farewell – had done that. 'Yours, I'll grant you, Pedro, and who could blame her. But, believe me, *amigo mio*, the lady who can resist the charms of John Cameron hasn't yet been born.'

'You have learned much of our language, Señor Juan,' said his companion, a shifty-eyed *paysan* in dust-caked jeans, 'but not enough of our culture. You might as well touch the moon as the daughter of *el Padrón*. Just to look at her with bold eyes could cause her father or her brothers to cut out your heart. Men disappear in Mexico and no one who is wise asks questions. And who will ask for you? Be on your guard: you are not safe here. You have no nation: you could just disappear. And who would mourn?'

John upturned the wine bottle to find that it was indeed empty and reached for his other drink. He threw rough salt on to the back of his left hand, picked up the roughly cut lime in his right, licked the salt from his hand and squirted the lime juice into his mouth, as he had seen Pedro and the others do, before draining his glass of tequila. He winced; not a drink for a gentleman. He gestured for a second bottle of wine, his gaze still on the straight little back of Lucia Alcantarilla Medina. It was doubtful that he had even heard his friend's warning. Perhaps it was the masculine, but yet so feminine, riding habit. Or perhaps it was six lonely months under cold Mexican stars. But he longed to see the girl's face again, to hear her speak. Her voice, he knew without hearing it, would be as beautiful as her smile.

He would go to what passed for a hotel and pay for a hot bath and a shave. 'Learn from a master, my friend. All I need in order to have that rich young beauty eating out of my hand is time: time and a little Scottish cunning.'

He stood up, picked up the rather dirty bottle of wine and threw some thin coins on the tabletop. He looked down at Pedro and smiled inwardly. 'And I have plenty of both.'

For days he waited, starting from his chair at the sound of any horse's hooves, but no bloodstock pranced down the dusty streets of Las Estrellas. John rented a horse and rode out to the Alcantarilla ranch but he was turned away by well-armed, well-fed, well-clothed guards.

'Private land,' they said. 'No road this way.'

Or this way or that way. God in heaven, did the Don own the whole of Mexico? If Mexico had suffered during the civil war, the Alcantarillas had not. Herds of fat cattle grazed on the land guarded by a veritable army of well-mounted men.

'You can ride for three days, Señor Juan, and not get to the end of *el Padrón*'s land. Give up this foolish idea,' advised Pedro. And John, unused to horses or leather saddles, rode back to town and soaked his sore bones in tepid, dirty water and dreamed of black curls and flashing Spanish eyes.

And then there was the *corrida*, the bullfight. And the best bullfighters in Mexico came at the invitation of *el Padrón* to fight his best bulls in the ring: a celebration of peace. Afterwards there would be dancing in the streets to the music of a *mariachi* group, who were coming all the way from Cuernavaca to play for the *fiesta*.

'*Mariachi*?' asked John, without too much interest.

'It is from the French, Señor, *le mariage*. We were ruled by the French, you know, and they left us much of their food and their customs. The *mariachi* was music for the marriage, and now it is just music for pleasure, for joy. Now it is Mexico.'

'And what is happening?'

'In two days there will be the bullfight. Then everyone will eat too much, and drink too much and love too much.' He laughed, the laugh of an experienced man. 'And it will be *la Navidad* before we find relief from the headache, and maybe some of us will never find relief, for there will be more mouths to feed next spring, and there will be angry fathers and brothers.'

John went into the hotel and he washed his one good shirt and polished the silver points on the end of his string tie. If everyone was coming to the *corrida*, he would see *la dama*.

She came in state, like a queen, her father silver-haired and ramrod-straight beside her, her brothers riding beside the carriage, they and their magnificent horses looking as if they had been carved from the selfsame pieces of fluid metal. Lucia threw roses in the dirt at the feet of the Mexican women, who cheered her and wondered at her milky-white skin, her dress of silk and lace, her jewels.

It was the first time John Cameron had seen a heavy cream-coloured lace mantilla arranged on shining curls of the bluest black.

'Every woman should dress like that, Pedro,' he said. 'She's beautiful, innocent and yet provocative.'

'She's danger, Señor.' But John did not know enough Spanish to realize that Pedro had used the noun, danger, instead of the adjective, and perhaps he was not clever (or wise) enough to understand the subtle difference.

He made his way through the crowds to a spot where he could run in the street beside the rose-filled carriage like the peasants. He picked up one of Lucia's discarded roses and, when he saw that she saw him, he kissed the rose and threw it back into the carriage. She looked at the dusty rose on the immaculate cream lace of her skirt and she picked it up.

She's hooked, he thought. She'll keep it.

But Lucia Pilar Francesca Alcantarilla Medina knew who and what she was, and she looked saucily into John's eyes as he ran beside her carriage, and she dropped the rose into the dust and turned a haughty cream shoulder to the man who had almost fallen under the hooves of her brothers' horses to throw it to her.

'Bitch,' he snarled. Then he laughed, for it was a game, and the game was no good unless both could play. And in the flower of the Alcantarillas he had met a worthy adversary.

He made a point of walking near the flower-filled box with its green and red bunting. Then, when he saw that the girl had spotted him, John stared at her indifferently and turned away, and when he turned again she was talking animatedly with her brothers and fanning herself furiously with her exquisite ivory fan.

For weeks he teased her. She did not know that he watched the dusty road out of Las Estrellas to see the clouds of dust that told him she might be condescending to visit the town. When he saw her, he looked at her coolly, although the blood was leaping through his veins. He turned away as her carriage passed through the streets and went into the nearest shop, as if his business was so much more important than the sight of a young girl. At last, one day, she avoided her *duenna* and tricked the youngest of her brothers into riding with her into town.

'Go, Alvaro,' she ordered imperiously. 'See if there are messages for Papa at the telegraph office. I will wait here and drink a glass of water.' And the owner of the bar scrubbed a tabletop with his best towel and washed and cleaned a glass until it shone, then, reverently, he filled it with water and handed it to the *Padrón*'s daughter.

'Lucia,' began Don Alvaro.

'Who will hurt the daughter of *el Padrón*, Alvaro? Go.'

The young man shrugged his shoulders and went. Don Alejandro could forbid his daughter nothing. He would scold her for sitting in a café, but it would be her brother who would feel the real weight of his anger.

And who will hurt her? thought the young man, who had not seen the *gringo* gun-runner sitting in the shade.

John did not understand every word Lucia had spoken. He was lost in the musical notes of her voice. He watched her sip the water, and then he noticed her scarf slip from the shoulders of her shirt and fall to the floor. Such an old ploy. He laughed and she pouted, and after he had made her wait just long enough, he moved forward and picked it up.

'*Gracias*, Señor,' she said, her voice and her eyes kept low. Her little hand was held out for the scarf, but John bowed low and then pushed the scarf into the pocket of his tough denim trousers.

She did not know what to do. She was so young, he thought. Then, unbidden, came the picture of another girl of about the same age. His daughter, Victoria.

Angus

Rain was beating down on the streets of Dundee.

'It's the stotting kind,' old Euan Gordon told Victoria, and he traced the rain's passage with his hand. 'It comes down and then it goes back up.'

'We need it,' said the daughter of the farm. 'If it just lasts the right time and gets everything well watered. But, have you noticed, Mr Gordon, that rain either lasts far too long and floods everything or it doesn't last nearly long enough. Very perverse thing, rain.'

Mr Gordon was quite taken aback. The climate was his favourite subject of conversation, but he was not used to having the discussion taken seriously. Miss Jessop would merely have said, as she always did, 'so it does, Mr Gordon, so it does.'

He was so disturbed that he almost forgot to tell Victoria that she was required in Mr Smart's office. When he did remember, she grabbed her notebook and her pencil, smoothed her hair – how like a woman, thought Mr Gordon – and hurried into the office.

Alistair Smart was standing at the window watching the rain, the stotting kind. 'Ah, Victoria, thank you for coming in.' He gestured to the rain. 'You should see it in India – so heavy sometimes that it could knock a wee thing like you clean off your feet.' He pulled out a chair. 'I have a proposal to put to you. Sit down, my dear.'

Alistair Smart had been standing behind his massive desk when she had entered, clutching her notebook. Today's departure from the norm made Victoria nervous. Usually, because he was a very courteous man, he stood up when she entered the room, but he never came out from behind his desk. What on earth could he be going to say? She hoped she was not to be dismissed. With so many men coming back from the war looking for work, it would be inevitable that some women lost their jobs.

She was so caught up in her own feelings that she did not notice that her employer was as nervous as she herself was.

'I'll get right to the point, Victoria,' he said and she braced herself for disappointment. 'I would like you to come out to the Calcutta office with me.'

He said it as if he was saying nothing more significant than 'I would like you to run out and pick up a *Courier*.'

She said nothing. Calcutta . . . India . . . The mystical East. He had actually said he wanted her to accompany him to Calcutta.

'I can see you are somewhat taken aback, Victoria. Let me explain. It's obvious that the war will be over in a few months. I must see what has been going on at the mills out there. Usually we have someone on home leave every year, and although we have had several written reports there is nothing quite like seeing for one's self. Don't you agree? And the admirable Miss Jessop says that her one trip to India has cured her for ever of wishing to travel. She says that if she sails as far as the Isle of Arran on her summer holidays she will have spent as much time in a boat as she wishes. I cannot do without a secretary, Victoria, and Miss Jessop herself has suggested that you should accompany me. I have given the matter a great deal of thought. You are very young, but we have worked together for some time now. Dr Currie encouraged me to ask you and, since she is, as it were, your reference, I have decided to ask you. You would be perfectly safe and all the conventions would be followed. I am sure you need have no worries on that score. If, however, you feel that you are too young, that your mother would worry about you on such a long voyage, I will understand, but I will have to find someone else.'

He stopped and Victoria nodded vigorously. Her mouth had gone dry and she could not speak. Calcutta . . . to go to Calcutta . . . the Straits of Gibraltar, Suez, Port Said . . . Bombay, overland to Calcutta. Oh, yes, oh, yes. She could almost feel the heat between her shoulder blades; she could smell the spices, the exotic flowers. She could hear the temple bells, the call to prayer. She came back to earth with a bump.

She could see her mother struggling bravely against the tragedy that had overwhelmed her, trying desperately to pretend that it was not happening. She could hear a young girl's voice promising, 'I will never leave you, Mamma, never.' But she had never believed that promise would mean that she would lose an opportunity like this. What an incredible chance. To work in this lovely office had been the answer to her prayers. But now this, to travel under her employer's protection, to be paid a wage, for she would be working, and yet, at the same time, to see sights that most men never saw. She had to go; she *had* to go. It was too cruel.

The colour drained from her face so rapidly that Alistair Smart thought she was about to fall.

'I can't, Mr Smart,' she blurted out. 'I would love to go, and I can't tell you what it means to me that you asked me, but . . . I can't leave my mother.'

She turned, groping at the same time for her handkerchief, and hurried from the room.

Alistair Smart stood for some time just looking at the closed door. She had said no. He could hardly believe it. He had thought that she would jump at the opportunity of safe, escorted travel. He had seen the initial joy and excitement in her face and he had been sure that she would accept. In fact, it had never occurred to him that she would refuse. He sat down wearily in his chair. He was . . . disappointed. No, it was more than that. He was hurt. She had said no. She did not want to travel across the world with him. Was she afraid? No. She knew that she was safe. Good heavens, he was her employer, and old enough to be her father.

Why, in the name of heaven, you old fool, does it matter to you? he asked himself. Why do you suddenly feel bereft, as if all the lights have gone out? It can't be, no, it can't be that . . .

He thrust the thought away and, drawing a ledger towards him, began to work.

Victoria took refuge in the lady's room – a facility added by old Mr Smart upon the hiring of Miss Jessop, and which should now, more properly, be called the ladies' room. Mr Smart, Senior, had had very Victorian notions of the sensibilities of females and, besides the usual offices, there was an enormous *chaise-longue* – possibly for combating fainting fits or the attacks of hysteria from which all decent women, he was sure, suffered. In its thirty-year occupation of the little room at the end of the executive corridor, nothing more weighty than Christmas parcels had rested upon it. Now Victoria threw herself down on it and christened it with her tears.

I have to get over this disappointment before I go home, she thought. I could not bear poor Mother to know how very much I want to go and oh, please God, don't let me resent my promise to her. I can't leave her now. I *want* to be with her. Her dreadful situation is partly my fault. Oh, John Cameron, what a cruel charmer you are. I hope there is nothing of you in me, and I pray that you never ever hurt anyone else.

She sat up, feeling melodramatic and slightly silly. Where are you, John Cameron? Oh, dear God, forgive me, but I wish he were dead.

Then, since that was an appalling thing to say about anyone, and doubly wicked about one's own father, Victoria Cameron knelt down and rested her head on the *chaise-longue* and prayed for forgiveness.

13

DAVIE MENMUIR WRESTLED BOTH WITH the root and with his inclinations. The root was causing serious plumbing problems in the Blackness Road house and was proving the very devil to haul out. Four years ago, before this bloody war had started, he would have had that root out and the garden tidied long since, but he wasn't the man he had been: there wasn't the strength in the injured body that there once was. Despite his efforts to control it, Davie began to cough and wheeze and, fearful that Catriona would look out of her window and see him, he stumbled behind the resurrected gooseberry bushes and lay there until the spasm had passed. What he thought best for Catriona had ruled his life for years now, and he had spent so much time battling with his own feelings and desires that trying to do what he thought Catriona wanted came second nature to him. But, at the same time, sense and practicality told Davie that something had to be done – and soon. How long could Catriona pretend, or perhaps deny her condition?

'The hale street knows, lassie,' he told the root, when he went back to the fight, 'and I'll no have them lace-curtained wifies condemning you. The god Respectability hides some fell queer goings-on.'

As if as a sign to him, the root finally yielded up the battle and capitulated, sending both victor and vanquished backwards into the bushes. Davie swore, picked himself up, and hauled the rest of the monster out of the pipe. Then he carried it, waving over his shoulder like a giant serpent, down to the bottom of the garden, where he put it on the bonfire with all the other garden rubbish he had been accumulating all afternoon. He watched the roots writhing in the flames and then, when all danger from the fire had gone, he washed his hands at the standpipe and went in to do battle with Catriona.

She looked surprised to see Davie enter without knocking, but there was a faint smile of pleasure in her tired eyes.

Ach, lassie, lassie, he thought, can you not give someone else a share in your burden? What joy it would be to help you. But he had had too many years of not expressing himself and stood tongue-tied looking at her.

Catriona looked back at him and, as if she sensed his feelings, she put her hands protectively over the voluminous apron she had taken to wearing.

'You know then, Davie?'

'Aye.'

'And yet you don't condemn.'

At this Davie forgot his habits of taciturnity and grabbed her hands. 'Lassie, lassie, could I have killed him for you, I would have.'

Abruptly Catriona sat down and he pulled out one of the wooden chairs from the table and sat near her, almost close enough to touch her, if he could summon up the courage to do so.

For some time they sat without speaking, Catriona with her head bowed, apparently looking at the work-worn hands in her aproned lap, and Davie looking tenderly at her red-gold head with its streaks of silver. At last Catriona began to speak, haltingly.

'I was so ashamed, Davie, and afraid that you . . . that everyone would think I had . . .' She could not continue.

He leaned forward but he did not touch her. 'Naebody that kens you could think you would encourage him, Catriona.' There, he had said her name, but if she noticed she gave no sign.

'I did not fight at first, Davie.' She looked up at him

unflinchingly, straightforwardly. 'You have to know that. It was like a dream, and then I realized what was going to happen, what was happening, and I fought but . . . it was soon over. And I prayed, really for Victoria, that nothing would come of it, that I could just forget it, put it away like a horrible nightmare. Dr Currie forced me to accept what had happened to me, what was happening. I was terrified, so ashamed, and I thought of the shame to Victoria, her embarrassment when people found out. After . . . after that night, perhaps I worked too hard to try to let nature take a natural course, but then I thought: poor wee soul, it's not your fault that you are coming so unwelcomed into the world. I'm having John's baby, Davie, and although in the beginning I would have done almost anything to get rid of it, later sometimes I was almost glad. When he moved, Davie, when he told me he was alive and growing . . . my heart melted.

'When John left – well, when his father wouldn't allow him back – and he never tried, not once, to contact me or even to see Victoria, I still thought of myself as his wife. Even after the divorce went through, I never thought of remarriage. I loved John so much; it took a long time to tear him out of my heart. And when he came here, well, he was Victoria's father, and then I've always been a very practical woman, and I talked myself into thinking that he really would pay his way, that maybe we could come to some sort of civilized relationship.'

She looked down at her lap again. 'Divorced, with a daughter; how I have prayed and thanked God that my mother never lived to see me divorced. The shame of it, Davie, but I was brought up to endure what must be endured. To many, maybe myself included, I was beyond the pale of respectability. I decided to devote myself to Victoria, to do my best to give her a decent home. And when John came and I saw him work his charm on her . . . But I thought he might truly come to love his own child.

That would be natural, wouldn't it? So I felt that I had no right to stop them loving one another. And now this . . .'

She smiled at him tentatively. 'Am I making any sense? The neighbours, some of them, began to avoid me and I lost my nerve. I haven't been outside the door in weeks, not even to the kirk. The shame of divorce is nothing to the shame of this. Victoria is my comfort, and then there's Dr Currie. I thought she would find new lodgings – and who would blame her? – but there's two of them prepared to fight for me.'

'There's three, lass, if you'll let me.' Davie laughed aloud with joy. For weeks he had been trying to find the words and now, when he had not even been thinking, the right ones had popped out by themselves.

Catriona looked at him. She did not understand his laughter. 'What are you saying, Davie Menmuir?'

'I'm saying that I've admired you half my life, Catriona Cameron. I'm saying that I've learned to respect you even more these last few years. I'm saying that when I was a lad, I fell in love with a lass and we had a good marriage, and I wouldn't want a moment of that changed, but I'm saying that it's no an untried lad, but a man, that loves and wants you, Catriona Cameron, as he has never wanted any other woman.'

As if surprised by his words, Davie fell quiet.

'But Davie, I'm soiled and you . . .'

Soiled? Soiled? How could she think that of herself? Anger swelled inside him until he thought he might start to cough again. He fought his illness more strenuously than he had fought the root in her plumbing and interrupted her.

'I have little to offer you, lass, but my name and my heart. I can't bring you riches, or even a regular wage, but when I'm well I'll work all the hours God gives me, and I could do a lot round here for you. Did you know I've become a grand cook? Isn't it my mother herself who says nobody makes better pastry.'

Catriona smiled. 'But the baby, Davie?'

'Is more mine than his. Was he not here only for the begetting? I'll love him, Catriona. Och, lassie, the birth of an innocent baby is a reason for joy in this sorry world! That young laird that was buried – did wee Victoria love him? Will a marriage and a new wee brother or sister not help to heal her wounds and all?'

Catriona stood up and went to the range. She lifted the lid from the pot that stood there and mouth-watering smells filled the small kitchen. Davie felt his tastebuds quiver in anticipation.

'I don't know what she felt about the poor laddie,' said Catriona as she stirred. 'I'm not sure that she knows herself. And lately she's been so busy helping me and sustaining me. You should see her walk to the tram with her head held high. I'm so proud of her, Davie.'

'And so you should be. She's Jock Cameron through and through, is she not? And she's her mother's daughter too, Catriona Cameron. You never give yourself credit for that girl. When she did well at the school it was because she was her grampa's girl. You, and only you, should get the credit that she's turned out such a nice lass. And another thing you don't seem to want to admit is that she's no a wee lassie any mair: she's a grown woman. Victoria deserves her own life, Catriona. For her sake, if not for yours or mine, marry me.'

There, he had said it. Marry me. That was it. He wanted to marry her. She thought she was shop-soiled goods, and he knew that he was only half a man, but his loving heart was intact. He could love her and work for her and protect her, if only she would give him that right.

Catriona moved away from the range and put her hands on the strong back of one of the kitchen chairs. She gripped it hard. He could see her knuckles standing out.

'Oh, Davie, it's not right to marry just to give the baby a name, to save what little reputation I have left, to release

Victoria – although Victoria mustn't be made to feel that she has to stay. I want her to go out, to meet young people, both boys and girls. This great love of hers – how could it be love, Davie? They were bairns, and she must get over his death and open her heart again.' She stopped and they looked at one another. Was Victoria the only one who was to open her heart to a new love? Catriona took refuge in stirring her soup again and then she turned back to him, standing there so anxious, so caring. 'And I never suspected . . . I couldn't bear to be married out of pity. You do pity me, Davie. No, let me finish. You're a kind and loving man, a decent man and maybe you're mistaking pity for something else. Maybe you're just giving it another name.' She looked up and met his gaze squarely, unflinchingly. 'Besides, don't misunderstand me – and, oh, God knows, Davie Menmuir, that I don't want to hurt you or throw your gift back in your face – but I don't know what I feel about you. I know I've come to rely on you. I know it makes me happy when you are here. But is that enough?'

'It's enough for me.'

Catriona looked at him, at his honest, fine-boned face with the lines of both pain and laughter etched deeply into the skin. He had been a soldier for a long time, but he still had a farmer's eyes, keen and clear. He saw birth and death as equal partners in the game, each with its rightful place. He was a good man. A woman would be proud and lucky to have such a husband. But was it fair to him?

What have I to give him at my time of life? I'm forty-one years old. I have a daughter a step away from her eighteenth birthday, and . . .'

Whatever else she thought she had was lost in an unbelievable pain that ripped through her. It was so sudden and so intense that nature controlled her intellect and Catriona moaned and clutched her middle. Sweat broke out on her forehead and she stumbled forward and gripped the table for support. Cloth, dishes and cutlery fell unheeded to the floor.

'Oh, God, Davie, the baby,' she said and this time she screamed as another searing pain struck her.

Davie had his arms around her. They were strong. 'There, there, my lass,' he said, automatically using the words and the tone that he had adopted naturally with his master's animals in like circumstances. 'There, there.'

'Use the telephone, Davie,' gasped Catriona. 'It's easy. Lift the receiver and ask for Dr Currie's office.'

The telephone. He couldn't deal with that new-fangled machine. He would run down the road and get a cab, and perhaps a policeman.

'The telephone, Davie. Please,' groaned Catriona. 'You'll see, Davie lad, it's easy.'

He looked at her, lying moaning in the chair. The telephone. If a lassie like Victoria could handle it, so too could Sergeant Davie Menmuir, late of the Black Watch. Davie gritted his teeth, straightened his shoulders and hurried out into the hall.

Nearly five hours later Davie sought comfort in his mother's kitchen. He sat in the big chair before the fire, stretched his stockinged feet out to the brass fender, lay back on her cross-stitched cushions and let the heat soak into his cold bones. 'I had to leave her,' he said in a voice harrowed by pain. 'It's no human.'

'Ach, Davie lad, there's nae place for a man at a birthing. Thae hospital doctors know fine what they're doing. Catriona's in good hands.'

Davie looked up at his mother and took the mug of hot soup from her. He needed both its warmth and its sustenance.

'It was jist, they knew I had nae business there, nae right.' His tone was so despondent that his parents looked at one another over his bowed head. Was he thinking of his young

wife, so cruelly dead before her baby was even big enough
to be born?

'Catriona's a strong woman,' said Bessie Menmuir firmly.
'It'll be different this time.'

'Aye,' said Davie sadly, 'and me as much use as I was
the last time I was near a birthing.'

If their widowed son's obvious interest in their former mistress was not one they would welcome, the older
Menmuirs gave no sign. They were country people, accepting birth and death as one accepts the changing seasons –
perhaps not always to be welcomed but, in their words, to
be *tholed*, or accepted.

'The land's looking grand, Faither,' said Davie, trying
to cheer up his parents and himself. There was nothing
they could do for Catriona and it would be better to
think of something – anything – to keep his mind off
the swift pace of events after his first, quavering use of
the telephone. 'That trust fund must be growing like the
winter wheat,' he went on, as if he had nothing else on
his mind.

'Aye, lad,' agreed old Tam, as he bent towards the fire to
light a taper for his nightly indulgence of a good pipe. 'Mr
Boatman is a very astute fellow, and as honest as the day
is long, and him a lawyer,' he added, as if the two were not
naturally compatible. 'Tae let yon English school teacher
rent the house, and have me and my own men do the work
the way we always did it for old Jock, was inspired thinking.
Do you not think so, Bessie?'

Bessie Menmuir was not in the habit of handing out
praise. She avoided the opportunity again. She ignored
the talk of lawyers and trust funds, neither of which she
knew a thing about, and went straight to the real issue.

'Well, what *was* inspired thinking was for our Davie tae
take the tram hame. A good meal and a good sleep in your
own bed, Davie.'

'Aye,' agreed his father. 'Mistress Cameron will need her

friends more than ever when this is over, and you'll be little use tae her gin you're sick.'

Davie looked up. Had his father stressed the word 'friends'? There was no time to question him though, for from the yard came the sound of a hooting car horn. Who would come calling at Priory Farm who also owned a motor car?

All three Menmuirs rushed to the door and threw it open.

Outside, a fraction of an inch from the heavy iron gate of the steading, stood a car, and climbing out of it were Dr Currie and Victoria. Victoria ran to Mrs Menmuir.

'It's a boy, a bonnie wee boy, and my mother is fine.'

'Over already?' breathed Davie. 'And she's fine – and a wee laddie.' He looked up at Dr Currie and took over from his father, who was obviously too overcome to act the host. 'You'll come in, Dr Currie, and wet the bairn's head?'

Dr Currie bent to enter the little cottage and its warmth reached out to her. 'I'd be delighted, Davie, and Victoria assured me of a good tea, Mistress Menmuir, if we can impose.'

'Impose, impose, what a word for a cup of tea and a bit scone.' Davie's mother bustled around, thought Victoria, like one of her own hens. Bessie had never entertained a lady doctor before, but she was serenely at ease. Everyone who came to the Menmuir door would receive the same welcome: what we have we share.

The whisky was passed around and Victoria took a cautious sip. Then she put the glass aside and gave herself up to enjoying being back in this cottage, which she had visited a thousand times as a child. Dr Currie was giving the Menmuirs an abridged account of Catriona's labour and delivery and, Victoria saw with delight, was appreciating her whisky as much as Davie and Tam.

'I'll have her moved to a private room, Mrs Menmuir,' the doctor was saying. 'That way there is a little more freedom for visitors. And if you can convince Matron that you know what you are doing, who knows, she just might let you hold . . . Victoria's wee brother.'

'Oh, how wonderful,' said Victoria. 'You know, I never really thought until you said those words, Dr Currie, but I have a brother – and one day this farm will be his. Don't you think Grampa would have loved to have had a grandson?'

The four older people looked at one another and then looked away again.

'It's a grand, clear night, Victoria. Hap yourself up against the cold and see that nowt has changed,' said Davie. 'We'll hae oor drink and then it's me that will help with the tea.'

Victoria smiled at the gentle man who was coming to mean so much to them. And, after wrapping her shawl warmly around her shoulders, she went out into the crisp night air.

She laughed again as she saw how nearly Dr Currie had missed the gate and then she stood and looked up at the sky. The stars were so bright she felt that she could almost touch them. And as she stood holding her breath, as she had done all those years ago in this selfsame spot, a streak of silver flashed across the sky and disappeared into nothingness.

A shooting star. A baby is born and a star has died: nature's balance. Will I be the first to tell you of shooting stars, little brother, and of walnut shells? I'll fill one tonight and I'll put your birth in it, and Dr Currie and the Menmuirs, and the shooting star and the lovely sound the cattle make there in the steading as they stand together to keep warm.

She walked across to the gate and looked over the top at the milling beef stirks. One stayed near the fence and did not flinch from her hand as she touched his soft, warm nose. 'And I'll put your courage in, little stirk, and this starry sky, and the joy of seeing lighted windows and knowing that people you love are in there, waiting.' She breathed in the smells of the farm, the wood smoke from the cottage fire, the warm breath of the animals. 'This is me and this is mine. It will always be home – no matter where life takes me.'

The door of the farmhouse opened and a river of light spilled out into the darkness. Then the light was broken by the dark figure of a man.

'Tea's on, lass,' came Davie's voice. 'Come in afore the cold gets you.'

And Victoria had a feeling that she would often stand there in the years to come, and that Davie's voice would call to her across the darkness, as would another voice, that she had not yet heard but for which she was prepared to wait.

'I'm coming, Davie,' she said and he heard the smile in her voice.

14

DAVIE MENMUIR'S STARCHED COLLAR THREATENED to rub a line on his neck. He stuck his calloused fingers inside it to try to ease the stiffness. That was better. It was the Sunday tie; how he wished he could take it off. He had his Sunday suit on, too, and he was carrying a parcel and, quite frankly, he felt a bit of a fool.

There was a surprising number of men visiting the Dundee Hospital for Women, but only a few were there to see new babies, as most babies were born at home. Davie moved across the antiseptic waiting room to position himself beside another man. That way, he thought, he could blend in better. He hated the antiseptic smell. It made him remember the trenches and the military hospital. It made him remember pain and, more importantly, fear, and he did not want to be reminded of the fear. It was strange to think that the selfsame smell could be associated with birth.

The other man held up his parcel to Davie. 'Wallace's pie for the Missus,' he said. 'She hates the food here. She's dying for a beer too, but I was scared tae risk it.'

The door opened before Davie had an opportunity to explain the contents of his own brown-paper parcel, and the nurse appeared. She was as starched from head to toe as Davie was around his neck and he stood awkwardly, his bonnet in his hand. How clean she looked, how efficient. Perhaps she wouldn't let him in.

The nurse did not smile. She looked them over one by one, and each expectant visitor was left feeling inadequate in some way.

'Dae ye think she's starched underneath as weel?' whispered the man next to Davie. 'If this is the nurse, God helps us all when the Matron sees us dirtying up her nice clean hospital.'

'This is a hospital,' said the nurse, glaring at them both, 'not a variety hall.' Suddenly she stopped as a loud 'atchoo' split the frozen air. 'Who sneezed? No one with a cold may come in. How old are you, Miss?' She swooped on a girl who stood with her mother.

'Thirteen, Miss.'

'Too young. Come, the rest of you. No more than two to a bed and do not, I repeat, do *not* touch the beds at all. When the bell rings, do not dawdle. Leave at once.'

'Righto, Sergeant,' said the happy-go-lucky man beside Davie. Davie admired his bravery. The nurse did not.

'Mr Menmuir?'

Davie clutched his parcel. She was looking out for him. Why?

'Yes, Nurse,' he said.

She smiled graciously. 'Mrs Cameron has been moved out of the general ward to the room that Dr Currie reserves for her private and special patients. If you will follow me.'

Thankful that he had asked his mother to put a crease in his trousers, Davie followed the starched back down a long corridor, through some swinging doors and into yet another corridor.

'Mrs Cameron is in room B. She may have her young man with her . . .'

Davie held out his hands for inspection, as he had done all those years ago at school, and the nurse smiled gently. 'It never occurred to me that your hands would be dirty, Mr Menmuir. I was just going to ask you if you were the one who sneezed. We don't want our young man catching a bad cold, do we? No? Then in you go. I think Miss Cameron is there too.'

Victoria was indeed in the room but Davie had eyes for

no one but Catriona. She was lying back against the pillows and, to him, she looked like the young girl who had come to Priory Farm twenty years before. He felt awkward. He had never seen her with her hair down, and he had certainly never seen her in a nightgown. He blushed and she smiled at him and held out her hand.

'Well, Davie, have you come to see the bairn?'

'Aye, and your guid self.' Somewhat nervously he handed her the parcel. 'The lady at Draffens said it was quite respectable and fitting tae buy this.'

Catriona had undone the string and opened the parcel. In her hands she held a fine, knitted shawl. It had cost Davie a princely 14s 11d and he had swithered between the shawl and a lovely bedjacket at the same price, but had decided, in the end, that the jacket was too intimate a gift.

Catriona held the soft wool between her fingers and did not look up.

He panicked. 'It's tae put round yer shoulders, but if ye don't like it . . .'

She looked up and he saw that her eyes were filled with tears. 'It's the finest shawl I've ever had, Davie, and I'm proud tae put it round my shoulders.'

Victoria smiled as she thought of the drawer full of Catriona's own exquisite hand-knitted creations.

'And what about this young man,?' she asked Davie, who was still gazing in a tongue-tied way at Catriona. 'Have you no time for him?'

For the first time Davie noticed the little crib near the window.

'Isn't Dr Currie wonderful?' Victoria went on. 'Mother gets to have Baby . . .' She stopped and laughed with delight. 'We can't keep calling him Baby. We will have to choose a name for him. Think, Mother. Will you call him after one of the royal princes?'

Catriona shook her head. She had had plenty of time to think of a name for her baby. 'Andrew, I thought,' she said. 'A good, strong Scottish name and all his own, no one else's.'

Victoria leaned over the crib. 'Hello, Andrew,' she said softly and picked up the tiny shawl-wrapped bundle. 'Here, Davie, do you want a shot? He won't break, you know,' she added, as she saw the look of mingled hope and dismay on Davie's face.

'Pretend he's a lamb, Davie,' said Catriona.

'What, and throw the pair wee soul over my shoulder? No, I'm no feart tae touch him, jist amazed at the wholeness if him. Wad ye look at the fingernails.'

'Mrs Cameron. I'm sorry to disturb at visiting hours but there are forms to be filled in.' It was the nurse again. She read off Catriona's name, address and date of birth. 'The father's details aren't down here, Mrs Cameron. I take it our gallant soldier is still at the Front.'

Catriona and Victoria looked at one another.

'No, he's not at the Front, Nurse, he's . . .'

'My wee brother and I have no father, Nurse,' said Victoria firmly. 'You may just leave that bit blank.'

Catriona looked at Davie, and she saw the love and tenderness in his eyes as he held the infant in his arms and gently soothed him. He looked up and smiled at her, and Victoria saw the look that passed between them.

'Mother?' she questioned.

'Maybe you're wrong, Victoria,' said Catriona, although she still gazed at Davie. 'Maybe wee Andrew is going to have a daddy, after all.'

The nurse was becoming impatient. She could sense the atmosphere in the room, but she had too much work to do to wait while these people ironed out their lives.

'That's all very nice,' she said, 'but there's still a space on my form.'

'Menmuir,' said Davie, but the beaming smile on his face was directed at Catriona. 'David Menmuir, Esquire.'

15

Las Estrellas, Mexico

JOHN CAMERON HAD NOT FULLY appreciated the difficulties he would encounter in trying to form a relationship with the daughter of Don Alejandro. The girl was escorted everywhere by one or other of her brothers. There was always a stout Mexican matron in heavy black silk with her in the coach, or in the motor car when the *Padrón* wanted to show the villagers that their sleepy part of Mexico had moved firmly into the twentieth century. And there were always servants running behind and beside her to pick up anything she might drop, or to anticipate her slightest wish – to pick that flower, to hold and soothe that baby, to visit that church.

La dama Lucia became very devout in the weeks after the *corrida*. 'I have not done all the things my dear Mother Mercedes asked me to do, Papa,' she said demurely. 'I have not prayed novenas or visited the sick and so, from now on, I will visit the mission regularly and light a candle at the statue of the Virgin.'

Don Alejandro could deny her nothing. Besides, he knew that none of the men in the village would dare to raise their eyes to stare at his daughter. If he knew of the *gringo* gun-runner – and he must have known, for he was informed of every single thing that happened in his village – it never occurred to him that his gently reared and cosseted Lucia would find the bold stare of those blue-grey eyes a challenge.

John contrived that they should meet in the garden at the

mission, and there he fell in love with her halting English as much as with her beautiful dark eyes. She, for her part, loved to hear about that wild, beautiful country far across the world, where there was grass all year round, and rain, and soft, delicate flowers so unlike their own strident, exotic reds and oranges.

'Stay here and pray enough for both of us, Inez,' she ordered her *duenna*. 'I was allowed to walk alone in the gardens at the convent. What harm can come to me here? Besides, I must be a little free sometimes, to walk, to pray, to dream.'

And John Cameron watched her enter the garden and set out deliberately to seduce her. For him it was a game. He had never known anyone like her.

He did not listen to Pedro's warnings. He laughed at them. He thought Pedro's fears and grim forebodings of swift and frightening restitution were the result of too much tequila, too much raw red wine.

'This is not the Middle Ages, Pedro. Good heavens, I'm only talking to the girl. I'm helping her improve her English. She's quite good – learned it from some old nun in a convent – but it's stilted, book English. Her father should be paying me.'

'He will, Señor Juan,' said Pedro seriously. 'I beg you to be careful.'

And since neither Lucia nor John liked to be told what to do, they enjoyed their rebellion, and what had begun as a game became much more serious.

Lucia told John how to get on to Alcantarilla property without being seen by the guards, who were really there to look for stray cows and did not expect stray adventurers. One night, after she had been sent to bed while her father and her brothers remained smoking their cigars and drinking their imported brandy, she let herself out of a side door and made her way to a dried-up creek some distance from the great house and hidden from it by some sage brush and stunted bushes.

And there Lucia Alcantarilla was kissed for the first time by a man who was not related to her, and she liked the experience very much indeed.

My God, she's so ready, thought John as the soft, white hands caressed his sunburned neck and the soft, red lips parted under his.

He thrust her away. 'Lucy, no,' he said and wondered at the words he heard being spoken in his own voice.

'Don't you like kissing me, Juan?' she asked. 'Me, I like it very much.'

John looked down into the dark eyes, where the tears sparkled as brightly as the jewels in her ears, and he was almost lost.

'Lucy, you don't know what you're doing, but I do. I'd best go now – before it's too late.'

She wanted to cling to him, but she remembered her noble birth. An Alcantarilla would never beg: they did not have to do so. 'You will come again, Juan,' was all she said, 'to tell me of this Scotland and your estate.'

'We'll meet at the mission,' he replied, and that was what he meant. It was foolish to trespass on her family's land and yet more foolish to dally with an innocent young girl, who did not really understand the forces at her command, even if she pretended to. But John was lonely and Lucia Alcantarilla was very beautiful, very desirable and very rich, qualities that he had always admired in a woman. He found that he could not keep away from her. And several times he rode out to the ranch, where he waited alone and cold by the creek, and Lucia did not come.

Then one night he heard a soft footfall and there she stood in the moonlight and he thought he had never seen anything so lovely. He kissed her and the blood leapt in her veins, to pulse with the blood that was leaping in his. Much later she struggled only a little when he began to undo the buttons of her gown.

Lucia had been told little of the real ways of men and

nothing at all of the desires of women. She did not know what was happening, but the sensations clamouring in her body made her breathless. She could not bear it, but she did not know what it was that she could not bear. She clung to John as tightly as he clung to her, and she went where he guided her, and she screamed at him for ease of this torment. Then at last there was a wonderful explosion of release and Lucia lay back, exhausted, exhilarated.

John lay against her for a few minutes and then came terrifyingly to his senses.

God in heaven, what had he done? He pulled himself away and began to tidy his clothes. He did not look at her. He did not want to see her again. Would there be a look in her face, in those great eyes, that would tell the world – and especially her father – what they had done? He shivered.

'Is that what men and women do together, my Juan?' she asked wonderingly. 'Well, I like it very much, and Inez was wrong. It did not hurt at all.'

'You must go back to the house, Lucia.'

She twined her soft arms around his neck. 'When will you come again, my Juan?'

He pulled the arms away, but gently. 'Lucia, I must go, and you must go back quietly to the house and . . . and have a good hot bath. The ground is dirty. Look at your dress.'

She shrugged. When had Lucia Alcantarilla Medina needed to consider her dress? 'It is nothing. I will give it to one of the maids. Tomorrow, you will come tomorrow.' And he promised that he would, so that she would turn and run back to her house.

He had to get away, to get out of the state and then out of the country. He would like to run tonight, but he was waiting for a bank draft from . . . a client. Too much money to lose. Oh, but the girl had been sweet. Wonderful . . . He would like to go back, again and again, but that way spelled madness. He was not as fearful of *el Padrón* as the peasant, Pedro, but he knew that no man would like his daughter's virtue taken before her wedding. John smiled to himself. 'Some Mexican aristocrat is in for a surprise. He'll thank me for waking her so gently.' He hoped Lucia's husband would see her initiation in that light. But now he had to make his arrangements, he had to get away.

My John, my Jean, my Juan. He was tired of them all, these clinging women. Why could they not love lightly, as he loved, and not seek to own him? Much against his will, he stayed in the village of Las Estrellas and went every day to the telegraph office and he waited, and while he waited he sat in the *cantina* and drank young red wine, and the wine warmed his blood and he thought of Lucia. He had to see her again.

Did the wine cloud his judgement? He was not quite so careful this time as he rode to the Alcantarilla ranch. Lucia was sitting on a tree stump by the creek and for perhaps the first time in his life, John Cameron felt some regret when he saw her. She was beautiful – even more beautiful than she had been just a few weeks ago – but she was pale and the great, dark Spanish eyes were sad.

'Lucia,' he said softly.

She looked up and saw him, and what man could have resisted the joy that he saw springing into her eyes?

'Juan, oh Juan. I thought you didn't love me any more.'

'Love you?' He rushed to her and knelt at her feet and put his head against her legs. 'Love you? Oh, Madonna, I adore you, as I have never loved any other woman. But, Lucia, I'm not worthy of you.' For once John Cameron spoke the truth, but the girl was too young, too innocent to realize this.

She was not so young that she did not understand the danger in which they stood.

'You are a crazy man to come here in the day, my Juan. My brothers have such feudal ideas, especially José Luis. He is a medieval man, my brother, and thinks to marry me to one like him. You must go away . . .' She saw the disappointment in his face and smiled. 'Only a little distance into the hills, *mi corazon*,' she said coaxingly. 'There is a hut. See, I will draw it for you in the sand. The *vaqueros* use it, but not at this season. I will come when I can.'

He held her close. 'Come now,' he begged.

'Oh, Juan, you will never understand. Trust me: we have to go so slowly. To my brothers and Papa you are as nothing. We have to think, to talk . . . Go.'

He got up from the ground at her feet and thought that he would ride back to town. But then he looked down into her eyes and decided that it would be as well to wait in a hut as to wait in the dusty, dilapidated heap of clapboard structures that was Las Estrellas.

She came that night, bringing bread and wine, but they did not talk and they did not think. And for two weeks John hid in the hut and waited for Lucia Alcantarilla Medina. And he was as drunk with her young freshness as he was with the raw Mexican wine.

'I must go into town soon, Lucia,' he whispered one night as he kissed her goodbye. 'My money will be here and I can't risk losing it, especially if I am going to prove to Don Alejandro that I can support his daughter.'

'Soon, Juan. Maybe next week. It's not easy for me to get away. That's why I was so late tonight. Alvaro insisted that I play cards and I could not say no, or my father would have been suspicious. Alvaro is my favourite and I love to play cards with him. Or at least I did, before I met you.'

'We should take a break, *querida*. I will go into town to wait for my money and you can be a loving daughter, just for a few days. Now, don't be careless.'

But Lucia had been careless. She had not seen her brother as he stood by the creek and wondered who had drawn a map in the sand to a *vaqueros'* hut, and why. She did not see the trembling and the ready tears in the eyes of her maids, as they prepared her for bed each night, for she was too anxious for them to be gone so that she could throw on some riding clothes and steal from her father's house. She was in love with love, and with the power she had over this foreigner. She was half-frightened and half-exhilarated by the efforts she had to make to outwit her *duenna* and her brothers and father, and by all the restrictions that had pinned her, like a butterfly to a collector's board, since the day she was born.

John left the hut reluctantly, but the money was too important to lose. He took up his place at the table in the little *cantina* and it was there that Don José Luis Alcantarilla found him.

John Cameron had never been so near the aristocratic figure of José Luis and he found himself wishing that he was not quite so close now. The young man's powerful figure in his beautifully cut clothes, his very air of supreme assurance and arrogance thrust the near-squalor of the room into stark relief. José Luis Alcantarilla Medina was sublimely indifferent to the effect he had on other people, but he was not unaware of it. He smiled now at John Cameron, but it was a smile that did not reach those beautiful, dark Spanish eyes, eyes so like those of his enchanting sister.

John returned the smile. He had seen the young don several times from a safe distance, had seen the respect and, yes, the fear in the eyes of the Mexican peasants when the don and his younger brothers passed. Now Don José Luis was standing there in front of the rickety table at which John and Pedro sat, and the power emanating from him was almost palpable. Pedro, who had managed to combine grovelling with jumping to his feet, was already sweating with fear, but John would not sweat. He would bluff his way through this encounter as he had done through many others. It was obvious that his relationship with the girl had been discovered – or was it? Why the wait of several days? Surely, if the don knew, then he, John Cameron, would now be lying bleeding in the dirt.

Everything depended on Lucia. How much had she said? To what had she confessed? God, that Mexican moon had

driven him mad. Otherwise he would not have, not have
. . . He looked into the young man's cold eyes. Did he know
what John had done with his sister? A shiver of fear passed
down his spine, but he would not abase himself here.

'Don José Luis,' he said, rising to his feet. 'This is an
honour, sir. May I offer you a drink? Though I regret to
say that this *cantina* does not serve the vintages that men
like you and I usually enjoy.'

'It is a *cantina* for peasants, Mr Cameron,' said the young
man, 'and the wine is good enough. It comes, after all, from
my father's vineyards.' Don José Luis watched the flush of
embarrassment travel up from the *gringo*'s neck, and again
he smiled. It was not a pleasant smile. 'It is of my father that
I wish to speak. His Excellency wishes you to join him for
dinner. You will come too.' He gestured to the cowering
Pedro and, without waiting for a reply, turned and left
the room.

'When does he mean?' began John.

'Now.' Pedro was almost in tears. 'He expects us to follow
them. I do not like this, Señor Juan. No way would the don
and his family eat with me. He has found out that you are a
nuisance to *la dama*.'

'Stop grovelling,' snapped John. 'If the don has heard
of a little dalliance, he has sensibly decided to become
acquainted with the one his daughter favours. This is the
twentieth century, man, not the middle ages.'

'No, Señor Juan. This is Mexico, and *el Padrón* is King. He
will never accept you into his blood, and he will banish *la
señorita* Lucia to a convent before he allows her to sully her
bloodline.'

In spite of his bravado, John was more than a little concerned by his henchman's obvious fear. 'It will be different
when he finds out that I too am a landlord, Pedro, that I
too have acres of fertile farmland.' Mentally he thanked
the ill-luck that had made him unable to sell the Priory. It
would perhaps be necessary to *exaggerate* a little, but since

he had no intention of returning to Scotland, it was highly unlikely that any of the Alcantarillas would compare the actual acreage with his description. For the rest of the long ride to the *hacienda* he sharpened up his descriptive skills.

The house came as a surprise. He had been some distance from it on his visits to the creek and had not expected anything quite so grand. It was long and low, all on one level, and lights spilled from every one of the many windows. They had ridden for miles into the desert, but before the house there was a green lawn, a fountain surrounded by blooming flowerbeds and some strange but lovely bushes with bright red leaves.

His host, looking like a portrait from an old schoolbook, was on the verandah to meet John. Like his sons, *el Padrón* was tall and slender, with the incredibly straight carriage of the lifelong horseman. He was dressed in black, but they were the evening clothes of a Spanish grandee, not the riding dress usually favoured by his sons. There was no smile on his cold face as he greeted his guests.

He dismissed Pedro to the servants' quarters with a gesture and preceeded John into the house. His two younger sons stood before a fireplace of Moorish tiles imported from Spain. Of *la dama* Lucia and Don José Luis there was no sign.

'You would like to wash the dust away, Mr Cameron. My son is doing the same in his room, and Soledad will show you where you can ready yourself.'

An elderly woman in stiff black silk smiled graciously at John and showed him into a well-furnished bedroom. The air was full of the scent of the white lilylike flowers that stood in a bowl on the table, and John saw a basin, a pitcher of water and a soft, clean towel arranged beside the flowers. Soledad gestured to the silver-backed brushes on the dressing table and then withdrew slowly, closing the door behind her.

John almost rubbed his hands together. 'God, what

class,' he said, 'what style, and in a God-forsaken place like Mexico.'

Quickly he washed his face and hands in the scented water, brushed his hair and tried to remove at least the top layer of dust from his clothes. Satisfied with his appearance, he took the towel and wiped it across the toes of his boots, reflecting, when he saw the dirt transferred to the towel, that only a servant would see it and the servant's opinion of her master's honoured guest did not matter. He dropped the towel on the floor and returned to the large hall, to find the tableau hardly changed since he had left it. A peasant woman in a richly embroidered blouse and skirt brought him a glass of sherry. The glass was of fine crystal, and the sherry was subtler and smoother than anything he had ever drunk.

'My daughter will join us when her brother is ready, Mr Cameron,' said the don in his perfect English. 'She is a very silly little girl and I should beat her – so say her brothers. Well, except for Alvaro, who takes her side always.'

John met the measuring glance of the youngest of the brothers, but his smile was not returned. Don Alvaro's softness was reserved for his sister.

'Your daughter is enchanting, *Padrón*.'

'And very foolish. My first thought when Jaime' – he gestured to his second son – 'told me of her indiscretions was to send her back to her convent. I kept her here because I am an old man, and I had sorely missed her laughter for three long years.'

'You were right, Don Alejandro,' said John.

'I was wrong, Mr Cameron,' said the old man and his voice bit with the accuracy of a rattlesnake, 'but I do not make the same mistake twice. My daughter is spoiled and headstrong.' John almost winced at the contempt in the voice as he continued. 'She says she will marry you, Señor Cameron. I have brought you here to renounce her within her hearing, and before me and my sons.'

Before John could answer, there was a flutter of skirts and
a sound of running footsteps, like castanets, on the cold tiles
of the floor. Lucia freed herself from her brother's arm and
threw herself at John.

'No, Papa, I will not give him up. You may do as you
wish.'

'Foolish child,' said the don coldly. 'But come, Mr Cameron,
we are civilized people, and José Luis tells me you are a
connoisseur of fine wines. We will dine. Remember your
breeding, Lucia, or Jaime will be forced to take you upstairs
to your nurse.'

Lucia flounced over to her brother Alvaro and pouted at
Jaime and José Luis. Her father smiled.

'She is a child pretending to be an adult, Mr Cameron, and
not yet worth the regard of any real man. And no real man,
of course, would dally with a young girl in the grounds of a
mission, and assuredly not on her father's land – and never
against her father's wishes.'

John coloured furiously. Damn these aristocrats. What
made his daughter so special? All women were the same,
everywhere. How much did the don know? I could tell you
a thing or two about your precious, innocent little daughter,
my oh-so-patronizing señor. Wisely, however, John decided
to say nothing, but to follow his host into a large dining
room where a huge, carved wooden table stood flanked
by twenty superbly carved chairs. There was fine plate on
the table and the glasses at each place were of the finest
crystal.

'We have selected a French meal in your honour, Mr
Cameron. I am told that you have spent some time in
France and, as you no doubt know, France and Mexico
share a cultural heritage.'

John smiled, man to man – naturally he, as a man of the
world, was familiar with Mexico's history. No need for the
don to know that it was a chance conversation with Pedro
that had taught him all he knew. What did trouble John was

the fact that his past seemed to be an open book to his host. What else had this haughty man learned?

The meal was superb and the wines that accompanied each course better than any John had ever tasted. As one glass followed another, John relaxed. What a set-up. Thank God that his late lamented father had insisted on a divorce. If the old fool could see me now, thought John, a grandee among grandees. I hope you're looking on with envy, he said to the memory of Jock Cameron.

Don Alejandro's cold voice cut through John's warm thoughts. 'It is time to banish Lucia to her *duenna*, Señor, so that we may enjoy our cigars, like the men of the world we are.' He stood up and walked to his daughter's chair. 'I ask you now, in her hearing, to say that you have realized that the gulf between you – of culture, education and breeding – is too large to be bridged.'

John choked on his wine. What had gone wrong? A few seconds ago everything had been going swimmingly. He recovered and looked up. Lucia was staring at him, her eyes wide in terror. How beautiful she was. He remembered her boldness tempered by her innocence and shyness, her sweetness, her passionate response. A few weeks ago he had been praying that he would soon be out of her life for ever. Now he felt that he could not give her up. Perhaps it was time to settle down again.

'I cannot, Don Alejandro. Your daughter has entered my blood like a drug.'

Don José Luis sprang to his feet, a knife in his hand. 'Easy to let her out, *gringo*.'

'No, no!' It was Lucia. She jumped to her feet, her yellow skirts flying around her ankles like a host of exotic butterflies. She threw herself at her brother's chest and he held her easily and gently, as he would have trapped the butterflies.

'Little vixen,' he said. 'This foreigner is not worth your little finger. I will cut his fingers off, one by one, and give them to you to play with.'

'Silence.' The cold voice cut through the excited cries.
'Such melodrama, José Luis. We do not wish to frighten Mr
Cameron. Listen to me, Señor. Never will I give permission
for my daughter to marry you. I would rather return her to
her convent and have her take the veil.'

'No, Papa, no,' cried Lucia. 'I must marry him. I have . . .
we have . . .' She stopped, confused, unable to meet her
father's eyes.

'I know what you have done, Lucia,' said the don and his
voice was like ice.

Lucia looked at him and at John, then she put both of her
beautiful little hands on her stomach.

'No, Papa. It's too late.'

Don Alejandro stood up and for just one fatal moment
he looked like a very old man. Then the colour returned to
his face. He took his daughter from her brother's arms and
looked at her very gently.

'Is this true, Lucia, or a story?' But he could not doubt
what the girl was too terrified to tell him. 'So,' he said sadly
and he turned away. Lucia relaxed against her brother, who
held her again. The *Padrón* walked to his high, carved chair
and sat down and for some time no one spoke.

Then at last Don Alejandro looked up and a wordless
communication passed between him and his eldest son. 'So,'
he said, 'I thought we were to have a funeral tonight, but
instead we are to have a wedding. Jaime, go to the mission
for a priest. Alvaro, take your sister to her *duenna* and have
her dressed in her prettiest gown. And José Luis, take Mr
Cameron upstairs and find him something decent to wear
. . . for his wedding clothes. I will stay here and make the
arrangements.'

John smiled. He had not expected the don to capitulate
quite so quickly. He was to marry Lucia. He had never really
believed in his wildest dreams that he would be allowed to
marry her. He was not quite sure that he did in fact want to
marry her; she was so young. Another young girl's face

came into his head and he dismissed it. So, what if Lucia was even younger than his own daughter? He banished the thought. She was beautiful and very, very wealthy. He would be a faithful husband, at least until she became fat like the peasant women who had waited at table. He smiled and followed the silent figure of Don José Luis.

He did not see the look of hatred and calculating cruelty on the face of the man who had just ordered his wedding.

This time José Luis led John up one flight of stairs to another bedroom, even more ornately furnished than the first one. It felt as if someone lived there and since the wardrobe, when opened, revealed rows of hanging clothes, John decided that it was probably José Luis's own room. The young don rifled through the suits and eventually selected one, which he threw on the bed. He went to the dresser and found shirt, tie and cufflinks, and then from another wardrobe he withdrew a pair of hand-made leather shoes.

'Try these,' he said coldly. 'I will wait outside, unless you would like me to play valet.'

John decided correctly that the last remark was facetious, and he laughed and began to peel off his clothes.

The shirt and suit fitted surprisingly well, but the shoes, although beautifully soft, were perhaps a little too narrow for perfect comfort.

'Their cobbler will soon get my size right,' he said to himself, as he took one last, admiring look at himself in the mirror.

Then he went out and joined the young man who was about to become his brother-in-law and together they walked down the wide staircase.

John Cameron had never seen anyone more beautiful than Lucia Alcantarilla in her wedding gown. It was a high-necked white lace gown that contoured her young figure so perfectly that it could have been sewn upon her form. A necklace of pearls the size of pheasant's eggs hung around her neck, and there were more pearls in her ears and entwined in her glossy black curls. In her hand she held a crucifix formed of yet more pearls and tiny, perfect diamonds. Through the exquisite matching lace mantilla that covered her head John could see her eyes shining like the diamonds in her hands.

'I have no ring,' he had gasped to his prospective brother-in-law, who had wordlessly handed him a thick gold band set with dark-green emeralds.

'Her mother's,' said Don José Luis and his eyes had glittered, not like the diamonds, but like the eyes of a snake.

I am not young Joseph's favourite relative, thought John, trying to shake off the cold feeling at the nape of his neck.

It was not the happiest of weddings. Only the bride was smiling. The priest from the mission conducted the service as if he could not wait to get back to his cell to fall upon his knees in prayer. Don Alejandro was grim-faced as he gave his daughter in holy matrimony, and his sons knelt with bowed heads and made automatic responses to the prayers.

'You will wish to change, Lucia,' said Don Alejandro at the end of the service. 'The cooks are preparing a feast: you have plenty of time. José Luis will take Juan to his room to rest until you are ready. José. You have the room arranged, with everything as I ordered?'

'*Si*, Papa. Everything is perfect for him.'

Don Alejandro took his daughter's hands in his and looked down at the winking emeralds on her finger. 'Go with your nurse and take off your mama's dress. You look very beautiful, Ninita, almost as pretty as Mama.'

Lucia pouted, threw her brand-new husband a kiss, lifted her lace skirts and hurried up the staircase, the lace mantilla floating around her shoulders.

'Juan,' said Don José Luis and pointed to the staircase.

John went with the young don and the two men walked side by side to the first turn of the stairs. They stopped and looked back. The *Padrón* was standing, his other sons beside him, motionless, silent.

John shrugged. It would take time, but he would win them round.

Don José Luis led him down another corridor to a room with magnificently carved double doors.

'My father keeps this room for very special guests, Juan,' said José Luis. 'I trust you will be comfortable.'

'Is this the bridal suite? Will my wife join me here?' John refused to be intimidated.

'Dona Lucia's rooms are on the other side of the house. Please, allow me to open the door for you. See, it is a beautiful room, no?'

John stepped inside the door, and immediately José Luis closed it behind him and John was alone. The room was sombrely furnished with heavy Spanish furniture, but there was an embroidered red satin cover on the huge bed and coiled in the middle of the bedspread . . .

John gasped and turned desperately, his hands clawing at the door handle but although it turned, the door did not open. He had been locked in.

'José, Don José Luis, for God's sake,' he whimpered as he turned again to look at the bed. 'For Lucia's sake. Help me.'

'It is for *la dama*'s sake, swine,' came the cold voice from the other side of the door. 'You think to despoil the jewel of the Alcantarillas. May you rot in hell.'

There was the sound of scuffling, a strange rattling, then silence followed by a scream that soared around the wooden rafters and died away, as Don José Luis unlocked the door and, without even looking in, turned and walked away.

16

AT ELEVEN O'CLOCK ON 11TH November 1918 Tam Sinclair was still with his regiment in France. His heart was, however, in a wee flat up a close in one of the less salubrious areas of Dundee.

'It's over, Nellie, it's over,' his heart sang across the miles, 'and gin somebody tells the laddies over there who are still shooting at yours truly to stop, I'll be coming back to you, to you and wee Jimmy.'

There was a defiant hail of bullets over his head and he ducked automatically to avoid them.

'Haven't you got a home to go to, Fritz?' he yelled, as soon as he could stand up again, across the mud. 'I've a girl and a bairn waitin' for me.'

Dear God, I'm no the laddie you met at the mill, Nellie, I'm a man sure, and I'm coming home to marry you and tae be a faither tae wee Jimmy.

'You should see my lassie, Fritz,' he yelled again. 'That clean and wholesome I can smell her from here, sae sweet the breath stops in my throat with the longing for her. Have you got a lassie?'

'Sure, Jock.' To his surprise a voice came back. 'Is Helga und two babies, girls.'

'Mine's a boy,' shouted Tam. Then he realized that he was having a conversation with a German, the enemy, and in English. The wonder of it amazed him for a moment. 'Where did you learn tae speak the King's English?'

'In the school, Jock. You learn German?'

'I never learned nothing. All my learning I did here,' he

yelled and then he added softly, 'or in Nellie's arms.' He shouted across the mud, 'Are you married?'

'Of course,' came the reply.

This German was that good at his English that he did not even think before replying. Wait till Nellie hears about this.

'In the church,' the soldier went on. 'You too, Jock?'

'No, but it's the first thing I'll dae, Fritz. I'll marry my Nellie in the kirk and I'll take them oot o' the toon and into the country, where Nellie wants tae be. I'm gan tae learn farmin'.'

'Farming? Such hard life, Jock. Me, I like the city. I work in a bank, nice and clean. You come one day to Germany. Is so beautiful a country and the people are good, Jock.'

The people are good, Jock. Tam looked around at the desolation. Three-quarters of a million dead on the British side. One and a half million injured. Who knew how many the Germans had lost. But the people were good.

'You're right, Fritz. The people are good. Anytime you're in Scotland . . .'

'The people there are good?'

'Och, aye, Fritz. The people there are good.'

And then 'Jock' and 'Fritz' realized together that there was silence around them. No guns pounded, nothing crashed or erupted in flames, no one screamed. They had not shouted their last sentences at one another.

'Hey, Fritz, dae you think your officers have finally got the message?'

'I think so, Jock. Excuse, please, I am crying like a baby. Are we at peace?'

'Well, I've been at peace for a few minutes, Fritz. It's your lot what's been doing the shooting.'

'Funny, Jock, but I am more frightened now than I was before. Four years, Jock, four wasted years.'

'Ach, it wasnae wasted, Fritz. We've learned oor lessons.

Nae mair wars. Your lassies and my wee laddie will grow up in peace.'

'Please God, Jock.'

'I doot He's got much tae dae with it, Fritz.' Tam had never learned much about the deity. There had been a bit of hellfire and brimstone on the one or two occasions he'd been forced to go to Sunday school, but he could not say or think God and war in the same breath, as it were. War certainly existed, but did God? 'Kiss your Helga for me.'

'And you too, Jock. Kiss Nellie for me.'

Tam laughed. He could just imagine Nellie's response if he was to tell her that he was kissing her for a German soldier he hadn't even met, but whom he would remember for ever. He found himself praying, though, that the war was really over, that there had not been some terrible mistake and that the first moment he lifted his head it would not be shot off by his friend Fritz. But, his head still whole and entire on his shoulders, he duly sailed for home, and Nellie.

'Wash your mouth out wi' soap, Tam Sinclair,' was what Nellie said, when Tam finally arrived home and told her *This kiss is from my good friend Fritz.* 'Thae Germans started this hale thing.'

'Nellie, Nellie,' laughed Tam, as he held both her and Jimmy in his arms, planting kisses on each of them wherever he could. 'The people dinnae start wars. It's the high heid yins, and Fritz was jist like me, wearying tae get hame tae his wife and his wee lassies.'

'His *wife*, you say,' said Nellie archly.

'Aye, lass. Nellie Bains, will you – and wee Jimmy – marry me?'

'We will, Tam,' replied Nellie softly.

'And we'll ask your freen Victoria tae help me get a job on a ferm. I haven't a notion what tae dae, but I'll give it a shot. I've it all worked oot, Nellie. First, get oorselves married, then a job on a ferm and a nice, wee tied cottage where we can raise Jimmy in good, clean, fresh air.'

'If that's what you want, oor Tam,' said Nellie, who had dreamed of nothing but a cottage in the country since the day she had started work in the Dundee mills, 'that's what we'll do.'

Catriona and Davie were to be married on Saturday, 21st December 1918. Victoria was at work, making lists of all the things that had to be done, for the wedding and for the holiday celebrations. She should have been typing letters for Mr Smart, but her mind was firmly on the exciting events to take place on Blackness Road and on the heart-to-heart conversation that she had had with her mother.

Now that the house was in good shape, with a new tenant joining Dr Currie in January and Davie there to help, Catriona had tried to persuade Victoria to think again about further education.

'You're eighteen, Victoria, and you've been the best daughter any woman could ever have wanted, but maybe it's time for you to move on, to think about your own future. I'm that happy I can scarce believe it, but I don't want to hold you back any longer.'

'I made a promise, Mother, to stay with you for ever.' Victoria had smiled teasingly at her mother, who was blushing like a young bride. 'Am I supposed to believe that I will be in the way and will be cast aside now that you have found Davie?'

Catriona had looked as if she did not know whether to laugh or to cry, and Victoria had put her out of her misery. She'd placed the little box containing two hand-embroidered pillow slips – a wedding present from an elderly neighbour – down on the pile of similiar boxes all waiting to be acknowledged and had sat down on the floor at her mother's feet, in the way she had often sat as a little girl.

'I'm so happy for you, Mother, you know that. I've always liked Davie and you love him, and that's wonderful. I have been doing a lot of thinking, and part of that thinking says that a newly wed couple shouldn't have to have a great girl underfoot all the time.'

Catriona had stroked the shining, dark hair. 'You're my daughter, Victoria, you'll always belong here. Your grampa always wanted you to go to the university—'

'It's too late, Mother,' Victoria had interrupted. 'I've thought about it, but I don't have entrance qualifications and I don't want to go back to some cramming school to get them. I really love working at Smart's. It's interesting. I'm learning a lot and I'm skilled, Mother, and getting better all the time. I can't think what I'd want to study now if I went to a university. I don't think I ever really thought too much about it.'

'But you'll live here at home with me and Davie, and wee Andrew?'

'For a while, Mother. Who knows? Maybe one of these days I'll get a chance to travel the world.' She would never tell her mother that she had been offered the chance to travel in luxury to India, but had rejected the opportunity in order to stay with her. 'And somebody who's never been farther from Dundee than Edinburgh would surely jump at the chance to do that.'

Now, Victoria dragged her thoughts back from the happy little family in Blackness Road to concentrate her mind on invoices, bills of lading and various letters to type for Mr Smart. She worked steadily for almost an hour until the quiet hum of activity in the office was shattered by Euan Gordon.

'How on earth am I supposed to do that?'

At the interruption Victoria looked up from the work she was trying desperately to finish. 'What's the problem, Mr Gordon? Can I help you?'

'It's Mr Alistair's trip to India, Victoria. It's on again, now that the war is definitely over, but everything has to be done so quickly. He's taking presents – Keillor's Marmalade, if I can get any. Does he not remember there was a war on, no sugar and even fewer oranges?'

'You'll manage something,' began Victoria, but she bent her head over her typewriter again as Mr Smart himself came in from his office.

'And could you make sure that the shipping company has the tickets sent here, rather than to the house, Euan?'

'Yes, Mr Alistair.'

Victoria's heart was beating in a strange way. India . . . India. She was aware that her employer had stopped at her desk, but she refused to look up. If she had, she might have seen the wistful expression in the man's sad brown eyes. 'What a pity you can't accompany me, Victoria. What an opportunity, what a chance for advancement, and of course, speaking quite selfishly, I can't imagine how I am to manage.'

Victoria's heart began to sing. She could hardly believe it, but it looked as if she was going to be given a second chance. Oh yes, oh yes, she would grasp the opportunity. She looked up and Alistair Smart saw the flush on her cheeks and the brightness in her eyes. 'Well, actually, Mr Smart, now that Mother is to be married again, she has actually encouraged me to think of my career.'

'Do you mean that you will be able to accompany me after all, Victoria? I won't have to try to break in some stranger to my ways? Splendid, simply splendid. Arrange it, Euan.' And having dropped his bombshell so casually, he turned and went quickly into his office, leaving his two employees gazing after him.

He closed the door and leaned back against it, his heart racing. Why this euphoria, you stupid old fool? So you are to have a secretary after all. It's relief you should feel, not this . . . this . . . Oh, what is this joy that makes me want to caper like a child on Christmas morning? Yes, yes, to have a competent secretary will make life so much easier. That's all it is.

Behind him, in the general ofice, Victoria wondered how she could ever handle the events of the next few months competently. She was going to India, to India. But first, first, there was the wedding.

It was as perfect as they could make it. Catriona and Davie were married in the Register Office. Victoria and Tam Menmuir were the witnesses.

Did either Catriona or Davie think back all those years to when, at different times in the same wee Angus kirk, they had stood happily making the same promises? They had vowed then to be faithful and to do their best and each had kept faith. Now they stood and promised to love, honour and cherish one another.

Victoria cried. This time it would work out. These two lovely people, who meant so much to her, deserved to be happy. She prayed for their future.

She turned and saw Davie's mother, tears of joy running down her cheeks, her lips moving in silent, impassioned prayer. Victoria tried to send her a message. It will be all right: this time, for both of them it will be all right.

It would not be the fault of their friends if anything went wrong. After the simple wedding they all went back to the house on Blackness Road and Victoria was amazed by the number of well-wishers who crowded into the little house. Arbuthnott Boatman was there with champagne that he must have bought before the war. Bessie Menmuir and Catriona had, from austerity rations and generous gifts of produce from the farms, created a meal that many a guest would talk about for years.

Tam Sinclair and his wee Jimmy, each scrubbed and polished as clean as only Nellie could get them, stood gaping at the sight of a spread that surpassed their wildest dreams.

'Well I tell you, oor Nellie,' said Tam, as he held his family close against his side, 'if these are farming folk and this is the way they eat, I'm glad I've got my name doon for a job out at Birkie.'

'They're no all farming fowk, Tam. That thin, kinda elegant woman is a real lady doctor. She's taking wee Andra while Mrs Cameron's away . . . No, wait, it's Mistress Menmuir noo.' Nellie sneezed as the bubbles of the first champagne she had ever drunk in her life went up her nose. Then she laughed and drank Tam's, because she had drunk hers too fast and had barely tasted it.

Poor Tam was quite happy to hand it over. 'Don't tell them I dinnae fancy it, Nellie,' he said and smiled with real pleasure as the new man of the house handed him 'a dram, Tam? A real drink?'

'See that toff wi the doctor,' giggled Nellie. 'I hear he's a real live lord. Victoria says he's been twice tae the hoos tae see the doctor, and the net curtains the length of the street have been twitchin' like naebody's business. He's a married man, but the rich are no like you and me.'

Tam watched the expression on the face of the real live lord as he talked to the lady doctor.

'Oh, aye they are, lassie,' he said. 'They jist wear better clothes.'

'There's Victoria's boss,' said Nellie and she waved enthusiastically at Alistair Smart who, with great good humour, waved back. 'He lives in Broughty Ferry. Did ye ken everybody that bides there's a millionaire. He's lending Catriona and Davie his gate-hoos for the weekend. Can ye believe that? A hoos for a man that does nout but open the gate.' She was silent for a moment. Even the champagne had no strength here. 'He's dead, that man, in the war.' The champagne was playing havoc with Nellie's train of thought. 'You're aboot the only one here that came back in the one piece, Tam. Some of them never came back . . .

Davie's brother, the auld minister's laddie, half the farm
laddies . . .'

'Here, Nellie, hold oor Jimmy while I get you a nice cup
of tea. That fancy wine's gone tae yer head.'

Tam went off and was nearest the front door when there
was a knock. He opened the door to Catriona's former
minister.

'How could I not come, Catriona, and you too, Davie,
to wish you well in your new life together and to say a
blessing on this marriage of yours.'

For the second time that day Victoria watched Bessie
Menmuir weeping tears of joy. The old woman held the
baby, who had wakened up to join in the party, and her
tears mingled with his as he cried for his supper.

'I'll give him his bottle,' said Victoria and she whisked
him off to the kitchen.

Alistair Smart followed her there and jiggled wee Andrew
up and down while Victoria warmed his milk. Then he stood
and watched her as she held the child.

'There is something so powerful in the image of a woman
feeding a baby,' he told her. 'Men look . . .' He stopped,
because he could find no words.

'Sweet,' Victoria finished for him. 'Men look sweet. Except
men like Davie, who are used to looking after small things.
He looks just right.'

Alistair looked down on her bent head as she attended
to her small brother. You look so right too, Victoria, he said
to himself, so very, very right.

'I'd best go back to the party, my dear,' he said, suddenly conscious of the intimacy of the moment. He was
disappointed that Victoria did not even look up from her
all-important task as he left the room.

Sandy, the fiddler from Priory Farm, had driven the
minister to Dundee, and wee Andrew stopped sucking on
his bottle when the new sound danced into the kitchen.

'So you're a music lover, are you, my wee man?' Victoria

asked her brother as she burped him. 'Well, let's change your nappy and then I'll take you back and dance a reel with you.'

In the corridor she met Dr Currie and Lord Inchmarnock. Their set faces showed Victoria that these two were the only unhappy guests at the party. Victoria smiled shyly at Sandy Inchmarnock: she could never really be at ease with him. He was Robert's father and Robert was dead, and Victoria had never been able to find the right words of consolation for him. Are there any words to help deal with things that are unbearable? Is it enough to say, 'I'm sorry. I wished I had known what to do, to say. I wish I could help.'

She turned sideways now, with the baby in her arms, to let them pass her in the narrow passageway.

'There's no one in the kitchen, Dr Flora,' she said. 'If you were to start making the tea, you could have the place to yourselves for a wee while.'

'Bless you, Victoria. Try to get us ten minutes of peace and quiet,' said Dr Currie and she led Sandy into the kitchen. 'Have you any idea how to make tea, Sandy?' she asked lightly as she saw him look round in amazement. The entire house was smaller than his kitchens at Inchmarnock. 'Sit down, my dear. Perhaps it will be easier for you to explain if you don't have to look at me.'

'I want to look at you, Flora. I want to spend the rest of my life looking at you.'

Flora Currie wanted desperately to hear those words. They were sweet, as soothing as any medicine she had ever been able to prescribe for a patient, and as healing. But she could not listen: she had no right to hear them.

'Well, you can't, Sandy,' she said almost jovially, 'so do stop being silly.'

'We talked about divorce,' he said baldly. 'I'm going to divorce Julia or, at least, I'll see to it that she can divorce me.'

The words thundered out against the sounds of merriment from the front room.

Flora almost fell down on the three-legged stool by the stove. 'Oh, my very dear,' she began, her hands held out in supplication. 'You can't. Julia would be a pariah. She would no longer fit in the nice little mould she has made for herself. You can't do that to her. You're a man – all the chaps at your club will laugh heartily and say, "Heard about Inchmarnock, the old dog", and they'll continue to ask you to dine and shoot. But Julia will be ostracized. She won't be allowed at court. Sandy, you can't do that. She'll shrivel and die. Hasn't this year been hard enough?'

'It was Robert's letter, Flora. Have you any idea how the boy's words haunted me in the middle of the night – night after night? We talked. Julia and I have talked more since . . . since Robert died than in our entire married life. She as good as told a shocked, traumatized child that he was incapable of inspiring real and lasting love. She tried to buy your Victoria for him.'

'Oh, God, he heard that?' Victoria had told Dr Currie of the events leading up to Robert's suicide, of her horror and her own feelings of guilt that, at the one time it counted, she had not said the right thing.

'She said she couldn't be bought—'

'She meant only that money wasn't necessary, Sandy. Victoria liked Robert. If she had—'

It was his turn to interrupt. 'I know, Flora. The children might have made a go of at least friendship, if they had been left to get on with it. But Julia pushed before either of them was ready.'

'She meant well, Sandy. Oh, dear God, you have lost your only child. Don't lose your wife too.'

'The boy I have in my heart and soul,' he said sadly. 'My wife I lost a long time ago. How like you to think of her, Flora, but she wants a divorce too. She has a . . . friend. I'll give her the grounds; it's quite easy to do, you know. Some people make a nice little living out of, shall we say, indelicate photographs. At least Julia won't have the trauma of being the one divorced. She can divorce me and, as for money, even after this damn war that's not a problem. I'll sell the estates up here, the stuff that's not entailed – I couldn't bear to be in Scotland without my laddie – and Julia can take the proceeds and live abroad. She's actually talking about the United States. Titles still count there, even with some of their top society people. It's too soon, of course – maybe in a year or two – but I wanted to ask you . . . Will you wait for me, Flora?'

Flora leaned forward on her three-legged stool. She put her arms around his neck, as she had done twenty years before, and she kissed him lightly on the lips.

'I'd wait for you for ever,' she replied softly.

It was unfortunate that Agnes Johnstone, Catriona's next-door neighbour, should choose just that moment to come into the kitchen to see what on earth was happening to the long-promised pots of tea.

17

VICTORIA THOUGHT SHE MIGHT BE sick with excitement. She was not; but she was very sick with the motion of the great liner as it sailed across a stormy Bay of Biscay.

Her first thought, when she could stand up again without wanting to die, was that she should have been working. This was not a pleasure cruise; she was a working woman. The stirrings of joy began to defeat the qualms of nausea. She was going to India. She staggered up on deck to look for her employer.

Alistair was standing by the rail, wrapped in a long fur coat, deep in conversation with another traveller, but he hurried across the deck as soon as he saw her. 'My dear Victoria,' he said with evident relief. 'How nice to see you above decks. Come, stand by the rail and enjoy the sea breeze. Or would you prefer a chair out of the wind? There will be quite a change in the heat in a day or two. Would you believe you shall soon have to guard your complexion?'

Victoria, who had heard from the medical officer that her employer had asked for her constantly and had ordered several delicacies to tempt her palate, smiled at him warmly. 'I have wasted enough time already, Mr Smart. I am quite ready to take dictation.'

'My dear girl, get yourself well. Enjoy the voyage. There's dancing every night, and as soon as the sun comes out we shall have deck games. I hope I have not lost my skill at quoits. There is to be a treasure hunt too, and although you have missed your first opportunity to dine with the captain, we have been asked to cocktails. I have no idea what a cocktail is – some new craze from America, I suppose – but I am assured we will enjoy the experience.'

'Sounds fun.'

Fun. That was not a word that had figured too much in Alistair Smart's vocabulary. He usually preferred a good book. The ship's library possessed the latest John Buchan and he had put his name down for it. He took a deep breath and told his secretary of the fancy-dress party that was to take place. It was only right that she should enjoy such frivolity.

By the time they were approaching Egypt, Victoria had forgotten her appalling sea-sickness. The ship was full of young army officers and their wives, young men who were going out to work in the jute industry, civil servants. Victoria soon found herself an accepted part of a lifestyle she had previously only seen from the outside. The army, however, preferred to keep to its haughty self.

'Their loss,' laughed Victoria, who quite forgot her employer for long hours of every day, as she walked and talked, and ate delicious food and danced away the glorious starlit nights. She met Mr Smart at mealtimes and, after dinner, he would ask her for one dance. Then he would retire to his cabin.

'We haven't done any work, Mr Smart,' Victoria would remind him every few days.

'Plenty of time for work, my dear. Enjoy yourself.'

And Victoria did.

And then there was the treasure hunt. The clues did not seem, to Victoria, too difficult. She worked them out, one after the other, and ranged over the ship in search of the next clue. So did Captain Edward Welborn. They met behind the second lifeboat from the right.

Eddie Welborn was quite happy to find himself behind the lifeboats with Miss Cameron. He had wanted to speak to her since she had first appeared on deck, but too many constraints had got in the way. First, as an officer raised from the ranks, he felt insecure as a member of this august ruling class of officers and gentlemen. He had been told that Victoria was 'trade, m'boy, and you don't mix with shopkeepers, not if you want to wear a gong one day'.

Eddie was not sure that he wanted to become a general. He wasn't even sure that he wanted to stay in the army. He had gone in because there was a war on, and his father's little Lake District farm could not support three sons. He had become an officer because, he said, 'everyone else bought it'. The general who had recommended his promotion remarked, 'best foot soldier I've seen since the Boer War.' Eddie was going out to India to see if he might like to leave the army and take a good job in jute. But he knew he would hate the sun: it had already blistered his skin. How he could bear three years of it, in or out of uniform, he simply could not imagine. He had sat in the shade with a book for two weeks and listened to Victoria's laughter, wishing that he had enough courage to defy the rules, as he had once defied the German army.

'So she's a shopkeeper,' he had argued with himself, 'and you, Edward Welborn, are a sheep farmer in funny clothes.' But until he had found himself behind the life-boats he had not plucked up the courage required to defy convention.

The two young people looked at one another and at the hiding place contained in the clue. Who would reach for it first?

'You go,' said Eddie.

Victoria looked at his honest, freckled face and the clear blue eyes and she smiled. 'No, you go,' she replied. 'If I'm totally honest, I have to say you were here first.'

Eddie looked at her and thought that she was even prettier than he had believed and that her simple flower-patterned evening frock was much more becoming than all the expensive creations that the officers' wives were

wearing. 'Shall we work together on it?' he asked now.
'After all, either you will follow me around or I will most
certainly follow you.'

'Sounds good,' said Victoria and blushed. 'I mean, the
working together bit.'

'Come along then. Twice I heard giggling. There are
others looking for our clue.' Boldly he took her hand and
Victoria shyly allowed it to rest in his. His skin was not so
soft as she had thought it would be. After all, he was an
army officer. She wasn't sure what they did, but she was
sure it involved delegating, rather than doing.

'Your skin's quite hard for a gentleman,' she said and
blushed again furiously at her boldness.

Eddie looked down at his hand. 'It's masquerading,' he
laughed. 'It's a farmer's skin and it's taken four years of
war to soften it.'

A farmer. In seconds their shyness was gone, like snow
in summer, and Victoria heard all about the difficulties of
sheep farming in the Lake District. In return Eddie was told
a little about the Priory, and about Grampa and old Tam
Menmuir, but nothing about John Cameron.

Hand in hand they continued the hunt and two hours
later, to their great surprise but even greater joy, found
themselves the winners.

'The prize is a bottle of bubbly,' said the ship's captain,
'and you shall receive it at the ball on the last night. I take
it you'll be partners.'

They looked at one another. Victoria knew perfectly well
what the military said about the others on board. Civil
servants might be tolerated. Trade was anathema, unless
they were owners of the firms – and even then they were
suspect. She also had to think of her employer.

'We shall certainly be there, Captain,' said Eddie boldly,
'and I shall ask the young lady to have the last waltz
with me.'

'Yes, please,' said Victoria and blushed again, for surely

sophisticated world travellers did not say such naïve things to young men.

Eddie seemed to see nothing amiss. 'Would you care for some tea before . . . retiring, Miss Cameron?'

Miss Cameron would care. They sat in one of the ship's lounges and drank tea and ate delicious little butter biscuits. And they talked and talked until Victoria felt that there was nothing she did not know about the Welborn family. She in turn told Eddie almost everything about her own family. But she could not bring herself to speak about her father, so she skirted over Andrew's birth.

Eddie, for his part, had heard about the baby's birth and the marriage some weeks later of Victoria's mother and stepfather, and he had reached his own wrong conclusions. But he had never before judged anyone without seeing for himself and he did not start now.

It was after two in the morning when Eddie, with a soldierly salute, left Victoria at the door of her cabin, but it was some time before she fell into a deep, untroubled sleep. She sat watching the moon on the water from her porthole and thinking that really life aboard ship was romantic and Eddie Welborn was the nicest young man. Catriona would like him. But how would she meet him? Catriona lived in Dundee and Eddie Welborn was going to India and might well stay there. Victoria smiled at the moon.

'What's for me will no go by me,' she told it and, happier than she had been for some time, Victoria Cameron slipped into bed and was soon sound asleep.

'I won the treasure hunt,' Victoria told Alistair the next morning at breakfast.

'I know, my dear, with a Captain Edward Welborn.' He held up the daily newspaper that was printed on board. 'Well done you. I hope you have saved your prettiest frock for the ball. I shall certainly come to see you receive your prize.'

'You won't mind if I give it to Eddie. I slowed him down a bit.'

'Not at all. Now, perhaps we could make a few notes about letters to send back upon arrival in India.'

He watched Victoria as she bent conscientiously over her notebook. Eddie, she had called him Eddie, and they had only just met.

But that's as it should be, he told himself. You are her employer, Alistair, and she is young enough to be your daughter.

Unbidden, the ghost of another young girl came into his mind. It was an old memory and had been locked firmly away, so it was rather hazy. No, Victoria is nothing like Mabel. Mabel was fair and frail and . . . But there is something in the tilt of the head, in the clear, untroubled look in the eyes. Almost enjoying the pain, Alistair remembered.

'Where's your pride, Alistair? She's an office girl. She'll never command respect.'

He should never have listened to his father. He should have married his Mabel. They could have had a year before the dreaded tuberculosis took her. No point in wondering whether money could have helped keep the killer at bay.

The remainder of the voyage was not enjoyed by Alistair Smart. Victoria and young Welborn were soon inseparable and, as if to rub salt into a wound that he could not know was gaping, Eddie came every day to ask punctiliously for Alistair's permission to take Victoria away – to dance, to play deck tennis, to swim, to walk in the moonlight, hand in hand, around the deck. Alistair watched them and he tried to be happy for Victoria. And, because he was a thoroughly decent man, he made no excuses about pressure of work to keep the girl by his side.

'This is as it should be,' he said. 'Every young girl should have a shipboard romance. Good heavens, what would it be like to go back to Dundee and not to have flirted madly with a gay young blade?' And he almost convinced himself that it was he who had begun the whole thing and that he was quite proud of himself.

Victoria, for her part, was experiencing thoughts and sensations that she had never before encountered. Robert had been a dream, a fairytale and, like too many other fairytales, it had ended in horror. She had not been in that lovely library with the boy when he pulled the trigger, but too often in the night she had awakened with a cry, sure that her sleep had been disturbed by the blast of a shotgun. She had been able to tell Eddie about Robert and he, who had seen more horror than Victoria could ever imagine, had held her hand tightly and prayed for the courage to hold her in his arms and to kiss away the nightmares.

And all too soon they were approaching Bombay.

The noise, the smell, the heat, the crowd – it was all overwhelming.

Victoria and Alistair disembarked at Bombay, the gateway to India since Charles II had been given it as a wedding present from the father of his Portuguese wife. They were to stay in a hotel suggested by the firm for a few days, before setting off on the long, dusty train journey across the subcontinent to Calcutta. Victoria's earliest childhood memories were awakened by the sight of the overworked horses that pulled the Indian taxis. Oh, Grampa would have laid about him with a whip, had he seen his own animals so badly abused. Her anger helped her tolerate the amazing smells of India as they trotted towards the hotel.

Alistair Smart was not so lucky, and the smell of urine and dung, and dirt and incense, and . . . and . . . stuck in his throat and tortured his eyes. He was made even more unhappy when he saw that the unattached soldiers from the ship were also unloading their baggage at the hotel. He had watched Victoria floating around the deck in the arms of Edward Welborn and had forced himself to smile with everyone else at the attractiveness of the young couple. And he had consoled himself that the army was off to Delhi, while he and Victoria were bound for Calcutta.

Two nights after their arrival he sat in his white dinner jacket among the palms of the hotel foyer and watched Victoria and Edward dance with each other again.

He's holding her too close for decency, he raged, and then he scolded himself for being an old fuddy-duddy. 'Tomorrow we're off. By the spring that boy will be nothing but a memory.'

The music stopped, but Victoria and Edward did not. They continued to waltz out of the ballroom and into the fan-cooled foyer.

Alistair could do nothing but sit quietly and pretend to be engrossed in the week-old *Times*, while Victoria and Edward stopped and gazed at one another.

It was like one of those dreadful Hollywood films, except that the piano player was no longer playing. Edward was not much taller than Victoria. Alistair watched him bend his head and kiss her. He watched as her arms stole up around his sunburned neck.

'I hope that hurts,' Alistair said viciously under his breath. Then, because he was a good man, he tried again to find the answer to the crossword clues. I should have said . . . But I couldn't . . . She is in my employ. She is young enough to be my daughter. We are going to Calcutta tomorrow. She will forget him. Please God, let her forget him. But why? Why should she forget him? Because he is an army officer, Smart, and you think he will go away and forget her, and she will be hurt.

Once again he buried his head in the newspaper and, oblivious to everyone and everything, Victoria and Eddie wandered out on to the verandah.

'I love you, you know, Victoria.'

'I know.'

Eddie looked at her. He was not experienced at telling

young women that he loved them, but he had a suspicion
that 'I know' was not exactly the answer he had expected.

'And?'

'Oh, Eddie, I'm confused. I don't know what love is. I love
my mother and my wee brother. I loved my grandfather.
I don't know what I felt for Robert, but it's not the same
as I feel for you. I always saw him as a knight in shining
silver armour . . .' She fell silent, ready almost to burst into
tears. She knew that this conversation was probably the
most momentous of her whole life and she did not want
to spoil it.

'I'd look stupid in armour, Victoria, and I hate horses.
Well, they hate me. They always want to stand on my feet.
I'm no god. I'm a normal man, and I want to see you every
day for the rest of my life. Now that, to me, is love.'

'It would be nice to see you every day too, Eddie,' said
Victoria simply. And she smiled shyly at him and he held
her hand again.

'Now, you're going to be in Calcutta for three months and
then back to Scotland.' He was once again the experienced
army officer – capable, in charge. 'I must go to Delhi with
the regiment, but I can be demobbed almost at any time,
Victoria. And I want to go back to the Lake District and try
to find a tenancy somewhere. I know a lot about sheep. We
could write to one another. There's a bus or a train from
Scotland that passes quite near us, so it must go back the
other way as well. We could see one another. My mother
would be happy to meet you.'

'Yes, Eddie, and my mother would like to meet you.
My stepfather's father still lives on my Grampa's farm.
It would be interesting for you, wouldn't it, to see a
Scottish farm?'

'Yes, it would. Victoria, I'm rather tired of talking. I'd
quite like to kiss you again, if you don't mind.'

Victoria did not mind, and by the time she went to
bed that night she had quite decided that life would be

insupportable if she was not to see Eddie Welborn every day of her life. How she would live through the next few months she could hardly imagine.

18

WHILE VICTORIA PLAYED DECK TENNIS and quoits in the sun, Priory Farm trembled under the weight of a deluge.

Tam Sinclair stood in a ditch up to his knees in muddy water. He stretched his aching back, whacked his freezing hands against himself to try to restore the circulation, and laughed.

'Better than crying, Tam me lad,' he told himself. 'Only difference between this and Flanders is that no one is shooting at you.'

He bent again to his task. He had to clear the ditch or the water would pile up in the fields, and then the topsoil and the seed would run on to the roads. Up down, up down. He shovelled and threw the piles of rotting vegetation over his shoulder. Then he came across the small heap of bones and the bile rose in his throat, so that he retched. For a horrible moment he could smell death again and he could hear the whining of the shells, the dull thud of the guns, the screaming of the horses and men.

For a long moment he leaned all his weight on his shovel. 'Hold it, Tam lad. It's nout but a wee rabbit eaten by a stoat: a wee Scottish rabbit eaten by a wee Scottish weasel.'

Almost tenderly he laid the bones on the side of the ditch and put his raw hands into the mud to pull out more.

'Well, that was stuck in one overflow pipe,' he congratulated himself, as the water began to run more fiercely and the level went down. If only the wind would stop, or the stinging rain that lashed his cheeks. It was impossible to see what he was doing. He worked on blindly, and where the tears of cold stopped and the raindrops began he did not know.

'They can stuff this bit of farming,' he told himself, as he wiped his wet nose with an ever wetter hand.

The one constant joy of farming was that the sun dictated the hours. Tam worked on until he was in danger of cutting off his legs in the dark, then he pulled himself out of the ditch, shouldered his spade and his axe, and set off for the cottage where he and Nellie had set up home after their ne'erday wedding in the wee kirk. One family's tragedy was another wee family's good luck. There were tied cottages available, and work for man and wife to go with them. Nellie cleaned twice a week for the school teacher, who did not mind Jimmy as long as he neither heard nor saw him; and Tam struggled along at Tam Menmuir's side and tried to learn and love an alien way of life.

The curtains were open so that the firelight danced out to meet him. Nellie would draw the curtains only once her man had found his way home. Tam shivered as the icy water ran down his neck and his frozen feet squelched in the pools lying in the soles of his boots, but he kept his eyes on the glow from his home.

He opened the door and there was Nellie.

'Och, Tam love, ye're frozen. Come ben tae the fire. Jings, man, look at yer hands: they're bleedin with the cold.'

Tam closed the door to shut out the rain and leaned against it, as he eased off his sodden boots. The warmth from the fire hurt his hands and the wood smoke caught in his throat and eyes. Jimmy appeared from the kitchen, his nightgown trailing the ground and his fat little arms holding some protesting kittens, who were mostly upside-down.

'Put the kitties doon, laddie, afore they scratch you. No, don't come tae Daddy till I'm dry. And whit have you and Mammy done the day?'

'Ach, we've had a lovely day at hame jist the two of us,

Tam, while you were out there in that. Can ye smell that stew? There's rabbit in that, and a pigeon.'

Tam sat and watched the steam rise from his socks and he laughed at Nellie as she laboured over his poor, calloused hands.

'Them's a working man's hands, Nellie Bains Sinclair, no a fancy school teacher's lily-whites. They're perfect for dandling wee laddies and cuddling big lassies.'

'You be sure it's only the one lassie, Tam Sinclair,' said Nellie, putting away the ointment. 'Noo, is that no better? How are you feelin, love?'

Tam smelled the stew and the fire, and he looked round the front room with its box bed and its dresser containing Nellie's granny's best plates. He saw his son rolling among the kittens on the rag rug and he saw the love in Nellie's eyes.

'Will I tell you what I feel, Mistress Sinclair? I feel something I thought I had lost for ever in the hell-holes of France. I found it in the hell-holes of Angus: wasnae there mair than enough watter to float it back tae me? I feel happy, Nellie, jist plain happy.'

Nellie lifted Jimmy, who had twice rolled against the fireguard, and he protested loudly.

'Jimmy Sinclair, you'll bring this hoos aboot oor ears. Time he had a brither, Tam Sinclair,' she suggested archly. 'He's wasted. Mrs Menmuir's got him as fat as a Christmas pig with her baking, and here's you thinkin the sun rises and sets on his heid.'

'Brawest sight in the world, Nellie lass, a healthy, happy bairn. Mind you, twa healthy, happy bairns would tak a lot of beatin'. We'll jist have tae grin and bear it, lassie, until we're sure his brother is well stertit.'

'Let's get you warm and dry and fed, Tam Sinclair, afore ye stert your grinnin' or ocht else.'

In the West End of Dundee Mrs Murray Gow, née Emily

Simpson, was feeling very happy too. Her star was in the ascendant. Murray, her husband of eleven months, two weeks and three days, who had shone at the Harris Academy, had been promoted to manager of the bank and had also become an Elder of the kirk. Only this morning he had told her that he thought they might move in a year or two to Barnhill. Barnhill! A detached house would need at least two maids and a gardener – Murray could not dig potatoes after a day spent sorting Dundee's finances. She would ask Pa – discreetly – to get them the latest in sanitary conveniences. If Murray continued to do well, Pa might even be able to move his own plumbing business from the Hilltown. Not that there was anything wrong with the Hilltown – fine people, all of them.

She sat in the waiting room to see dear Dr Braithwaite. She was not quite ready to announce that she and Murray were to be blessed . . . So difficult – everyone would know that she and Murray, well . . . It was an act sanctioned by the church, but better that no one knew just yet. Better that the neighbours dwelt on the sterling work that she and Murray had done during the war and on the wonderful fund-raising she was doing for those poor soldiers who had given their all, or nearly their all – they were coming back, after all. And she was there twice a week with solid half-crowns, clean boots and changes of clothes. That nasty man who had yelled that he didn't need charity, he needed a job, had been so misguided. But she had forgiven him, and had smiled understandingly as she had picked up the half-crown from the corner where it had rolled. She returned it to the pile, waiting for the next unemployed veteran – and the next, and the next.

'Mrs Gow, Doctor will see you now.'

The starched nurse knew who she was. Emily bowed at her slightly and rose to follow her into Dr Braithwaite's consulting room.

'Wait a minute. This isn't the way to the doctor's rooms.'

The nurse turned. 'Dr Braithwaite has an emergency at the Royal, Mrs Gow. He asked Dr Currie to see you.'

Emily stood quite still where all the waiting patients could see and hear her.

'Currie? Not Dr Flora Currie?'

'Yes, Mrs Gow, but Dr Currie is even more qualified in obstetrics than Dr Braithwaite. That was one of the many reasons why he hired her.'

Emily could not believe her ears. Obstetrics – the nurse had given her business away. How mortifying! Not only that, but she was to be seen by a woman doctor, *and* one whose name featured in the less salubrious papers. Should she make a stand now? Was it time to show Dundee that Emily Gow was not like other women? Yes, it was. It would be painful to make a scene, but one had one's principles. 'Make me another appointment,' she said rather too loudly and a teeny bit squeakily, because she was not, at heart, a fighter. 'I have, after all, another six months to go. Quite frankly, Nurse, I'm surprised that dear Dr Braithwaite hasn't fired that . . . that scarlet woman.'

The nurse was angry. 'Mrs Gow, please!'

'I did not want the dear doctor to hire a woman doctor. How unfeminine to wish to be a medical person – so unladylike. But that he continues to sponsor someone who figures so luridly in the less professional press shocks me.'

The other patients were beginning to look embarrassed, worried or angry, and Flora had come out of her office to see what was causing the delay.

Emily saw her and, although she would have preferred to have attacked without her victim's knowledge, did not draw back.

'I'm sorry, Dr Currie, but everyone is talking about it. I know the papers say that dear Lord and Lady Inchmarnock are not to divorce, but I have heard it from a friend of mine who saw you last Christmas at a very – well, quite frankly – a very working class party.' She stopped for a second in embarrassment. What was her friend doing at such a party? 'It was a function that my friend attended mainly to keep on pleasant terms with all her neighbours, and you were seen, deny it if you dare, kissing Lord Inchmarnock.'

Flora stared at her in horror. Should she deny it? Should she say that she and Sandy were childhood friends? Should she ignore it? The papers speculated constantly about the Inchmarnocks. *Grief-stricken peer seeks solace* had been one rather kind headline. What would they be like when the divorce actually came through . . . ? Even in the twentieth century divorce was looked upon as almost more abhorrent than murder. Sometimes excuses were found for murderers.

'I shall find another physician,' finished Emily grandly and she swept out.

Flora watched as two, then three other patients rose. 'I'm sorry, Doctor,' said one as she passed. 'I just can't afford to be associated with anything not quite nice.'

Me neither, thought Flora as, with her heart plummeting into her expensive leather shoes, she ushered in her last remaining patient. No man and no career either, if things continue like this.

'Come on, Dr Currie,' whispered her patient. 'I think you're the best doctor in Dundee and I need you to help me birth a live baby this time.'

Flora smiled down at the girl who had suffered three miscarriages in as many years.

'That's what's important, Sarah, my dear. And we'll do it this time, together.'

After she had examined young Mrs Black and sent her happily on her way home, Flora had time to sit down and write to Sandy Fotheringham, but she did not mention the problems with her patients. Poor old Sandy, she felt, had more than enough problems of his own. He was determined to be a free man and had gone off promising to let her know the outcome of his attempts to give his wife due cause for divorce. It all seemed so sordid and hopeless, and sometimes Flora wondered if it was worthwhile. She loved Sandy, she always had, but she had lived without him for a long time. She was no longer a giddy young thing. She had her work and the ache in her heart no longer bothered her. At least, she was very little aware of it.

She posted her letter on the way back to Blackness Road and then waited patiently for a reply. Sandy did not write or telephone. He arrived himself and they went out to a hotel for dinner.

'It was so sordid, Flora. The woman reeked of cheap perfume and the room . . . peeling wallpaper, damp patches, cigarette burns and such tawdry finery.'

He looked at Flora, so clean, so elegant somehow, even though he could see she never really made an effort. It was just Flora, just the way her bones allowed the clothes to drape themselves over her as if they had been made there, her hair going grey and being allowed to show its dignity. He thought of his wife and of how much time she spent adorning her face and her person. The results were beautiful, but contrived. Here was a real woman. Not like that ghastly woman in the hotel. She had had the audacity to laugh at him – not out loud, but he had known she was laughing.

'This is all dreadfully embarrassing.' How stupid he had felt saying that, but the words had burst out before he could control them.

Sandy Fotheringham, Lord Inchmarnock, had looked around the hotel bedroom and had barely repressed a grimace of distaste. It was a hotel that had never before known his patronage and certainly never would again. He could hardly believe the seediness of the décor or the rank atmosphere.

'What do you want me to do?' God, what a fool he felt. He had absolutely no idea of what steps one took.

The lady in the scarlet and black négligé pouted at him. 'Come on, darlin', you've surely been to bed with a woman before.'

That was not the kind of flippant remark that was calculated to endear her to her unwilling customer. 'Please, let's not make this any more distasteful than it has to be.'

'Sorry, love,' said the woman. What was her name? Miss Lulu-Belle de Chastelaine. In other circumstances he might have laughed. 'Look, it's a job. You want a divorce, or your lady wife wants one. I need the money. Slip off your dressing gown and get into bed. For pity's sake, I won't bite. I get in beside you, snuggle up, make it look a bit compromising. Bob takes the pic, gives it to your wife, who weeps over it and shows it to your nice expensive lawyers – and that's it. D.I.V.O.R.C.E. and you free to marry. Couldn't be easier.'

Sandy did as he was bid. It was all so sordid. Why could they not end the marriage in a dignified and civilized manner? Hadn't he come across an anthropological record somewhere that said divorce was achieved by saying three times, 'I divorce thee, I divorce thee, I divorce thee'? That seemed eminently civilized to him.

Miss de Chastelaine slipped into the bed beside him and manoeuvred her not inconsiderable weight closer to Sandy. She looked at him adoringly, the door burst open and there was a loud flash, the smell of powder and the door closed again.

Sandy threw off the girl. 'That wasn't how it was supposed to be. That wasn't the photographer I met earlier.'

Lulu-Belle lay back on the pillows and reached for her cigarettes. She lit one, inhaled heavily and blew smoke at him through her mascara-laden eyelashes. 'Sorry, darlin', but a girl's got to think of herself. You're the answer to a prayer, you are. That picture, which will appear in all the papers tomorrow, is my passport to at least six months on the West End – well, just off, near as makes no difference.

You'll still get your divorce, of course – or at least her ladyship will. We looked you up, *Mr Fotheringham*. You know what they say about need, ours being greater than yours and all. No hard feelings?'

In the elegant Dundee hotel dining room Flora looked at him and smiled. Poor Sandy. She saw seediness and tawdriness every day. He had got off lightly, but still, he had been fooled and cheated. He had not known that Miss de Chastelaine was a third-rate actress: but he should have known, with a name like that.

She removed one of the pile of newspapers from the table in front of her. 'Some of my patients have been bringing these tabloids in. This one says, "The beautiful Bella" – and she is lovely, Sandy—'

'Good heavens, Flora, how can you say that? So, so . . .' He was lost for words.

Flora ignored the interruption. '. . . has a contract at the Variety, but has vowed never to open her heart about your affair. How noble of her!'

He had had enough of jokes at his expense, even from Flora. 'Dash it, Flora, I never set eyes on her before that day.'

'I know,' she said simply and she smiled at him. Then her face changed and became sad and Sandy did not like what he saw.

'But you have to face that this changes things, Sandy my dear, for both of us. You've become a dashing blade and I've become a notorious woman. Everyone knows it's a set-up, but they think it was done because we are . . . involved.'

'But that's nonsense.'

'I know it. You know it. But please try to think rationally. Forget your wounded pride and the humiliation, and think clearly. My reputation has to be whiter than white, Sandy. My authority depends on it. My patients don't want to be treated by a scarlet woman.'

He stood up angrily and walked over to the window. Outside, the garden was full of Michaelmas daisies and chrysanthemums, serviceable flowers but no less lovely for that. For a moment a picture of the scarlet, brown and yellow colours that the house at Inchmarnock wore in the autumn blotted out the Dundee streets and the pain gripped him, as it always did.

He turned again to look at her and held out his hands. Flora went to him and they leaned close together, each taking comfort from the presence of the other. The small private dining room was empty but for themselves, but their need for each other was so great that, had it been full of other diners, it is doubtful they would even have noticed.

'I've thought and thought, my darling, and it seems to me that Fate, in the person of the delectable Miss Lulu-Belle, has stepped in. There is no reason to wait now. Julia can divorce me as quickly as she likes. She will have everyone's sympathy. "Heartless bounder, not enough that she has to lose her child, but old Sandy gets himself involved in a scandal." We can move away, Flora. Even with the proceeds of the house sale going to Julia, I have far too much money.' He held her away from him and looked into her compassionate, understanding eyes. 'Some would say the war was good to me; there's irony for you. You don't need your patients, Flora. Marry me and you'll never have to work again. You can snap your fingers at all the narrow little minds that revel in the misery of others.'

'That doesn't describe my patients, Sandy. Oh, some of them have been quick to judge, but I'm never surprised by human nature. I want to marry you. This . . . unpleasantness won't make me change my mind, but . . . Oh, darling Sandy, I never really thought about the commitment I am making to you. I'm a doctor, and there are people who depend on me. Please, dear, don't interrupt. I know there are other doctors, but patients don't see things that way when they are frightened. There are people I have to help through things – birth, death . . . I can't just abandon them, not without warning. Give me some time. Give us both some time – for you to be divorced, to finish the sale, for this appalling nonsense to die a natural death. I'm asking you to go away, Sandy . . .'

He could hardly believe what he was hearing. To go away. She wanted him to go away. Where could he go without Robert, without her, that would not plunge him into everlasting misery? His son, his bright little boy, was horribly dead, and Sandy had climbed out of his grief, taking comfort in the knowledge of Flora's friendship and then her love. And now . . .'

'Flora, please. I've lost Robert, must you . . . No, no, forget I said that. I make you sound like the prize I get if I'm good, like Nanny in the nursery. "Eat all your toast soldiers and you shall have a chocolate biscuit." Forgive me, I'm not myself. It's all so . . . galling, mortifying. Of course I understand. You need time, space. We both do. I'll go to town and help Julia. There are things she must want from Inchmarnock, Robert's things. We must go through the treasures together. Some of Inchmarnock is entailed, you know, the house itself. My cousin or his son will inherit.' He stopped as the memory of the boy who would not inherit intruded on his present grief. 'I shall write you often and, when you are ready to see me, even just for dinner . . . I'll stay at my club, I think. That would be best, it's so impersonal.'

Oh God, oh God, he thought, please help me to get through this added misery without breaking down. Quick and sure is the best way. Like putting down a beloved old dog. Have to do it oneself. Less pain that way. He reached into his breast-pocket and took out a little gold-wrapped packet. 'Not an engagement gift. You see, dearest, I will never presume. Just a . . .' He handed her the packet. 'I won't even kiss you, Flora. I do, in my heart and soul, every minute of every day. Goodbye, best beloved.' And he was gone, and Flora saw the door swing shut behind him, and she heard him running down the great stone stairs. She knew that she could have called him back and he would have come, and he would never have left her and she wanted that so badly, so desperately. And she bit her lips to stop herself calling out his name.

She held the packet against her cheek for a moment, feeling the warmth of his fingers, and then she opened it slowly. A watch, almost the image of the one that John Cameron had stolen, lay on a bed of velvet. She took it out and, through her tears, read the inscription picked out in diamonds on the back. Twice she rubbed her eyes. No, it was not exactly the same.

Sandy loves Flora – always.

19

Victoria spent most of the voyage back to Britain
writing letters to Eddie. When she worked with Alistair
Smart, or sat with him in the ship's dining room, she did not
notice that he had changed subtly from the kind, thoughtful
man who had sailed to India just a few months before. He
was still kind and still thoughtful, and therefore seemed to
Victoria to be just the same nice, old Mr Smart. But he no
longer waited after dinner for one dance and, since Victoria
spent the evenings walking around the deck looking at the
moon, and wondering if Eddie was seeing the same moon,
she failed to notice.

They arrived back in Dundee in a downpour and Victoria
laughed with joy.

'Yes, my dear,' smiled Alistair Smart rather sadly, 'some
things never change.'

Catriona, Davie and wee Andrew were at the station to
meet them, and after Mr Smart had greeted the family, he
was taken off in his chauffeur-driven motor car while Davie
loaded Victoria's bags into a hired taxicab. She had acquired
so many souvenirs that another bag had had to be bought –
'They are so cheap. Mother, you won't believe the prices.
Wait till you see the brass plate I've brought you for the
front hall, from Tibet.'

'This seems like money for jam, Catriona,' said Davie, as
they squashed together in the back of the cab, 'money for
taking folk home from the station.'

Normally Catriona would have agreed, saying that when
the good Lord gave folk legs, He expected them to use

them. But today she could think of nothing but the elegant woman who sat beside her, hugging wee Andrew, who in turn looked up wonderingly at the almost brown face above him, from his big blue eyes.

'You're that brown, Victoria, and you're taller and thinner. You're not a wee girl any more,' said Catriona, when they arrived at Blackness Road.

'She's been round the world and back, Catriona, and here's me thought I was a big man, with my free trips to France.'

Victoria laughed. 'India's not around the world, but it's a long way away. Mr Smart bought me a camera, Mother, and I've got some lovely snaps. I'll show you an elephant, Andrew, a great big elephant with a big, long trunk and funny teeth that stick out of his jaw.'

For a few minutes she was the young, silly Victoria as she pretended for her brother that she had a trunk and big ears. Andrew, however, who had never even seen a picture of the strange animal that his sister was trying to portray, was singularly unimpressed.

When they looked at the photographs Catriona noticed, but did not mention, that there were more than a few snapshots with the same young man in them. In one, a rather indistinct picture of a young woman standing under a huge arch that appeared to be formed of carved elephants, the same young man was standing with his arm casually around the girl's waist. Victoria looked at it for a long time, rather dewy-eyed, but apart from a dismissive 'Well, that's Eddie Welborn. I told you about him in my letters', she said no more.

Before she went back to work, Victoria had three days at home to rest and tell her family all about her experiences. They sat up night after night, exclaiming over the picture postcards, the Chinese porcelain, the embroidered blouses, the sandalwood boxes and, for Andrew, the carved wooden dolls that Catriona showed him and then put away on a shelf above his head, before they ended their short lives in his mouth. Victoria seemed to have remembered every meal consumed, not only on both voyages, but in the luxurious hotels in which she had stayed. And so well did she recount her experiences that Davie felt he could almost smell the curries and taste the fruits with their wonderful names. How much more exciting 'papaya' sounded than 'apple'.

'I shall try to prepare a curried meal, Mother,' said the new, sophisticated Victoria. 'I have brought packets of spices with me.' And Catriona and Davie looked at one another and wondered anxiously if their Scottish digestions were a match for the exotic East.

Victoria saw the looks and laughed. 'Don't worry. Here's me that can barely boil an egg properly talking about oriental cookery. It'll just be a wee sauce on your mince, Davie, just to give you an idea. Some of it I just couldn't eat, but Eddie has a digestion that a horse would envy.'

Had she any idea how many times the word 'Eddie' came into her conversation, or how her voice dropped and her eyes softened at his very name?

After three days Victoria went back to work and it was amazing how quickly the little house got back to normal, except that every morning Victoria was the first to rush to the front door to see if the postman had left any letters, especially thin blue ones. It was some weeks, of course, before he did and every day that he did not, Victoria retreated angrily upstairs to get ready for work. And as she worked she blamed the blameless postman for not delivering her letters.

'It cannae be that you are expecting a letter, lassie?' laughed Davie, and at the twinkle in his eye Victoria laughed herself out of her ill-humour.

'Waiting's so hard, Davie,' she said.

Davie smiled and there was a lifetime of experience written in his smile for those who could read. 'There's me could write a book about waiting, lassie.' He leaned forward and gently touched her hand, so softly and quickly that she felt she could almost have imagined the intimate gesture. 'It's aye worth it, though, lass, aye worth it.'

Victoria smiled at him fondly and tried to be patient. And the days went on, and eventually two or three blue letters came all at once, and then again there was a wait.

Victoria went on working for Mr Smart, and she continued to write her own letters after tea in the room that looked out on to the garden so carefully tended by her stepfather. She set herself to helping her mother, and she loved and appreciated the time that she had been given to get to know her little brother.

Most days she stayed at the office at lunchtime and ate a sandwich, but on the days when it was just possible that a letter might arrive, she hurried home at noon, and Catriona treasured those days.

One warm day Catriona greeted Victoria at the door. 'You will never guess who I met in Muirhead this morning?'

Victoria took Andrew in her arms and was rewarded with a very wet kiss on the cheek. 'Tora,' he said rapturously and then immediately struggled to be put down.

'Who, Mother?'

'You are so brown, Victoria,' said Catriona, ignoring the question for a moment. She had still not got used to having her daughter home after almost a year away in India, and she never tired of her daughter's stories. 'It's actually becoming. Oh, what was I saying? Elsie, Elsie Morrison. You remember Elsie?'

How could Victoria not remember Elsie, her first real friend. But had she been a real friend, for she had never been a recipient of the secret of Victoria's first love? Only *Mansfield Park* knew that whole story.

Unware that her daughter's attention had wandered, Catriona went on. 'She was fascinated to hear about your travelling. She's left Glasgow and is back at home. She is, would you believe, one of these dreadful "votes for women" feminists. She is actually, behind the scenes, I should add, going to work for one of these ardent reformers. What's the expression, dear, the Power behind the Throne? Locally, of course, in the first instance and then, who knows?'

Victoria obligingly set up some skittles for her small brother and watched his pleasure as he immediately knocked them down. She pictured Elsie, her one-time best friend, who had accompanied her on so many rambles, who had been there every time she had met Robert, who had dumped her when the Camerons had fallen on hard times.

'Perhaps with a view to becoming a councillor, Mother, or even, one day, Member of Parliament?' asked Victoria drily.

Catriona, an ardent believer in the natural order of things (man first, woman a long way behind), laughed at her daughter's nonsense. 'Away with you. What will you say next? Anyway, she is quite anxious to hear your views on votes for women, suffragettes and suffragists. According to Madame Elsie, she absorbed these notions practically at the breast. Her own mother went to all those dreadful meetings which the suffragettes held in Dundee before the war and, since Elsie was one girl among all those boys, her mother took her along too. Goodness, my poor mind was spinning with all the stories and the new ideas. She's sure that now you are travelled, you will agree with her. She's a great fan of Neddy Scrymgeour and thinks that his bad luck has run out . . .'

Even in India, Victoria had kept abreast of local Dundee politics and she knew the name Edwin Scrymgeour, the prohibitionist candidate and vociferous critic of what he saw as a corrupt city corporation, who had fought and lost every election since 1908.

'What bad luck?' she asked. 'I never heard of anything unpleasant happening to that family.'

'Well, it's surely bad luck to lose so many elections, dear – embarrassing too, I should think. Anyway, Elsie says his share of the vote in Dundee has crept up to twenty-eight percent and she thinks that he'll defeat that dreadful Churchill at the next election. You know, that man isn't really interested in Dundee. He just sees us as a safe seat. I think Elsie wants you to help her to help Neddy Scrymgeour kick him out. I did hint, delicately, that perhaps you might be rather too busy next year, but she asked if she might drop in. I was delighted to tell her that we have a telephone and that she should try ringing you first.'

'She's teaching, I suppose?'

'Oh, aye, at a primary school along the Perth Road. Primary Four she has, forty-three eight-year-olds. You could forgive anybody anything who has to suffer that day in, day out.'

Victoria was not so sure. 'If she rings while I'm at work, you could ask her to the harvest dance.' She looked up at her mother. 'I've not thought about it for a long time, but she was at that awful dance when Grampa died. All her brothers were in the Forces – no, one was still at home. I still miss Grampa, Mother, There are so many things I want him to share.' Victoria heard her favourite sound and stood up. 'Quick, Mother, watch Andrew, that's the dinner-time postie.'

'Well, I was sure you weren't coming home these dinner hours for my cooking,' said Catriona fondly as she carried Andrew into the kitchen and tied him into his chair.

Victoria hurried out into the hall and saw a thin blue letter on the rug at the front door. She carefully teased it open and read it three times, before following her mother into the kitchen. She was blushing as she saw her mother's happy, knowing look.

'He's coming home, Mother. He's had enough of the army and hates the thought of an office job. He's coming back to Britain. He'll go first to see his family and then, oh, Mother, he's coming here. There's a question he has to ask me.'

'And what will you say, love?'

Victoria smiled, but did not answer the question directly. 'It'll mean that I'll go away again, Mother. You know that, don't you? He hopes to have saved enough at least to get a tenancy somewhere. The Lake District, perhaps.'

Catriona removed too big a piece of bread from her son's mouth. 'I wouldn't have it any other way, Victoria. I left my mother. She left hers. Besides, if we all learn to drive one of these dreadful machines like Dr Flora, we can see one another often. The twentieth century is a grand time to live in, don't you think?'

'It is indeed,' agreed Victoria, but she was thinking of Eddie Welborn and of the very exciting developments in her personal and public life, certainly not of politics, or of the real place of women in their new society. 'Now I'll need to eat this up quickly and get back to work. Mr Smart's up in the air a bit just now. We've been asked to join a conglomerate of all the big jute industries. It's all very exciting, but nerve-wracking. Cox's, Gilroy's, Kyd's, oh, all the big companies want to form a textile conglomerate. This was a good year for jute, but things are looking a wee bit shaky now. Calcutta's beginning to undercut Dundee. Luckily Mr Smart has his own family mills in Calcutta, but it's still . . .' She stopped and laughed as she saw the look on Catriona's face. 'Marriage and motherhood have changed you, Mother. You were always so interested in business.'

'Oh, I still am, dear, but you'll find that marriage changes your perspective on things. Right now, Davie's lungs, Andrew's teeth and your happiness are the most important things in my life and so whether your boss – nice and generous as he is – makes two million pounds' profit this year or twenty million isn't really top of my list.'

'Marriage, if I get married,' Victoria said as archly as only a girl who has had a written proposal of marriage can, 'won't change my interests, Mother. I think I'll phone Elsie when I get home and go along to one of her suffrage meetings. Eddie wouldn't want a wife who knew nothing but the price of potatoes.'

'Sixpence halfpenny a stone,' said Catriona immediately and they both laughed, well pleased with one another and the shape their lives were taking.

Dr Currie drove them all out to Priory Farm for the harvest dance. She had the night off, but refused to participate in the festivities. Some brightness seemed to have gone out of her since Lord Inchmarnock had sold as much of his Scottish estates as was not entailed and had gone away. She was still as hard working as ever, if not even more so, but her laughter was not heard so often, and her car was driven more sedately and rarely came screaming to a halt just inches from disaster.

'I have letters to write and case notes to make, Catriona. I'll come back for you all later.'

She drove off and the family was soon caught up in greeting old friends, who admired Victoria's sophistication and Andrew's new tooth with equal enthusiasm.

Because of several nights of working late before the formation of Jute Industries Ltd, Victoria had been unable to attend one of Elsie's meetings, so they met for the first time in many years at the harvest dance. Victoria wondered if she would even recognize her old friend. Had she herself changed beyond recognition? Victoria stood at the door, where she had stood with Grampa, and waited for Elsie – Elsie who had taught her to dance, Elsie who had suggested that they go sketching in those enchanted woods, Elsie who had not wanted to dirty her expensive shoes in the unrestored Blackness Road house. Forgive and forget. Elsie had lost five brothers in the Great War. Maybe such an experience would have turned Victoria too into a fighter.

She saw Elsie arrive and it was as if it was all those years ago, although this time Elsie arrived without her usual fraternal escort. The two surviving brothers obviously preferred to be with their own families. The women looked at one another, burst into tears and, with their arms around one another's waists, went and sat in a corner, as it seemed for hours, talking about their lives since they had last seen one another. For Elsie those years had been mainly at university, where she had first become interested in politics. Now she was back in Dundee in her first year of teaching.

'But you've done so much, Victoria. It's hard to believe you won't be twenty till next year.'

'I've never really thought about it, Elsie. I was usually far too busy to think about what I was doing, what with school and Grampa's death and the mills. I'm glad that's over, but I don't regret working there.'

Elsie gave a delicate shudder of distaste. 'You can't mean it, Victoria. When I think of how you were raised. Your grampa worshipped you. We were sure he'd leave you the farm. My mother thinks there was maybe some funny business with lawyers there.'

Victoria thought of their dealings over the years with Arbuthnott Boatman. 'Nonsense, Elsie,' she said sharply. 'Grampa just never got round to changing his will. Perhaps he couldn't bring himself to change it, to write his only child out. Anyway, I assure you that Mother and I are delighted with the house and the way things have worked out. She has a lady lodger from the Harris, now, a classics teacher, Miss Davis. Can you imagine if we'd had the boarding house when we were at the Harris?'

'You could have had old Smelly Socks to board. You'd have got one hundred percent in everything,' laughed Elsie.

'If we hadn't been closed as a health hazard.'

Tensions were forgotten for a moment as they laughed like young girls instead of the sophisticated young ladies they now were.

'And I hear Dr Currie boards with you as well. Now

there is someone I admire, Victoria, and would love to meet sometime, if it could be arranged. What integrity. A woman in a man's job and she carries on with such courage when mud is thrown.'

'There's no dirt would stick to our Dr Flora,' responded Victoria, ready to fly to Dr Currie's defence, but Elsie was totally on her side.

'I'm so jealous of your life, Victoria,' she said. 'I have been no farther than Glasgow, and you have sailed all the way to India and lived there.'

'Your bairnie's greetin',' said a wee voice at her elbow and there stood Jimmy Sinclair. 'We're gettin another yin, are we no, Mammy?'

Victoria laughed and so did Tam, who had come up with his wife to claim their son. 'There's Mammy's wee surprise ruined.'

Victoria introduced them to Elsie, who seemed rather surprised at the obviously intimate terms between Camerons and Sinclairs.

'I'll away and get Andrew. He's heard the fiddles and is furious at being shut away from the fun,' said Victoria. 'I'm so thrilled at your news, Nellie, and I'll hear—'

What she expected to hear was cut off by an excited cry from Catriona. 'Victoria, Victoria. Look who's here.'

Victoria looked past her mother to the door. There stood a beaming Davie, Dr Currie and . . . Victoria jumped up from her chair and ran.

'Eddie, oh, Eddie,' she said, her heart in her eyes and, oblivious to the crowds around them, Eddie folded her in his arms.

He did not seem to be in the slightest bit embarrassed by the loud cheer that went up as he kissed her vigorously.

'Come on,' he said, grabbing her by the hand and pulling her to the door. They went out into the starlight, accompanied by a great many catcalls, whistles and cheers.

'These farmers are just like the ones at home. They'll be telling me what to say next.'

'You're so sunburned, Eddie,' said Victoria, suddenly overcome by the actual presence of someone she had been dreaming about for so long. Dreams are usually easier to deal with than real live human beings. 'I've got some marvellous ointment Mother makes from elderflowers.'

'My mother makes wine from elderflowers,' said Eddie. 'They can swap recipes.'

They did not notice that the barn had gone quiet behind them and that more than one person was making an excuse to take a little fresh air.

'I didn't take a train from Tilbury to talk about flowers, Victoria. It's all clear in my mind now. I was a good soldier while there was a war on, but I'm not cut out for army life, not as an officer anyway, and working in an office would bore me to distraction. I'm a farmer and I can't change that. I want a farm of my own – just a wee place would be fine, a place where a man can breathe, where he's not falling over his neighbours all the time, like in India. God, but that's a soul-destroying place, Victoria. I've travelled as much as I ever want to travel. I know you enjoyed it, but the road from Scotland to England is about all the distance I want to travel now. Now, you got my letter, I know, and I wrote everything but the actual words. But you know what I was trying to say. I've talked to your mother and to Mr Menmuir, and now I'm asking you. Victoria Cameron, will you marry me?'

In later years Victoria was to tease Eddie that she had never really accepted his proposal. If she did answer, then her reply was lost in the cry of joy from the host of well-oiled folk standing in the doorway. The fiddlers began to play for the young couple, enabling them to waltz as they had waltzed on the night they had first met.

Elsie sat watching them and, although she had decided that marriage was not the only fulfilment available to women in the twentieth century, she had to admit that they did indeed look very right together and she sighed. Dr Currie watched them with tears in her eyes. Were the tears for her own situation, or were they tears of happiness for Victoria? Catriona's were tears of joy. 'He's such a fine-looking boy,' she told Davie for the tenth time. 'What a pity he has to go all the way to England for a farm. You master that car, Davie, and we won't have to rely on the bus.' She sighed with happiness at the thought of all the pleasurable preparations she would be called upon to make. 'Davie, do you mind old Jock? Do you mind what he would have said about this party?'

'I know fine what he is saying, Catriona Menmuir. He's saying, "What a lovely walnut shell day!"'

20

IT WAS DAVIE WHO BROUGHT Catriona the letter. He had looked at the stamp but could not decipher the smudged writing. He didn't think it was an Indian stamp; he had got used to those while Victoria was abroad. He stood in the garden, where he had been when the postie had given him the fragile letter with its blue and red markings and its strange stamp, and he almost wished that it had not come. Why, he could not understand.

Catriona was making something special to try to tempt Dr Currie's never robust appetite. 'This'll bring a gleam to her eyes, will it not, Davie?' she asked. 'She never did much mind what was set in front of her, not like Miss Davis now, who likes her food. Still, these days I feel I could put old rope on Flora's plate and she wouldn't notice. That letter must be for her,' she added, rejecting the envelope that Davie held out. 'Or maybe it's for Miss Davis. Who would send me an airmail letter?'

'It's got your name on it.'

Catriona took the letter and looked at it suspiciously. 'Mistress Cameron,' she read. 'How very old-fashioned. Goodness, Davie, haven't I been *Mistress* Menmuir for near two years. Who would be writing to Catriona Cameron and not know that she was Mrs Menmuir?'

Davie laughed as he watched her study the writing. He had had a few letters from his parents during the war and he had ripped them open within seconds of receiving them into his dirty, muddy hands. How could she stand there and look and question, and never ever think to open the envelope to unravel the mystery? 'Better open it, love, and find out.'

Since the unopened letter would certainly yield up no secrets, Catriona took a sharp knife from the kitchen drawer and slit the tissue, like paper. She read it carefully for a few minutes, then she gasped and Davie, to his horror, saw the colour literally drain from her face. He ran to her and helped her into a chair.

'What is it, love? Bad news?'

'Yes. No. Oh, Davie, it's John. There have been times when I did not wish him well, but this . . . He's dead.' She gestured with the flimsy paper to Davie, but he shook his head. He wanted to read nothing about John Cameron. Catriona took a strengthening breath and went on. 'There was a terrible accident.' She looked at the letter again and then in anguish at her husband. 'Near a year ago now, Davie. You would think they would have sent one of them Marconigrams, but well, maybe John didn't tell them about us. It doesn't say how they knew to write to me. He'd never have me still down as his next-of-kin, do you think, Davie?' Poor Davie was becoming so frustrated by his wife's dallying that she bent her head again and finished the letter. 'He was staying with friends in Mexico. Mexico? This is from their lawyers. Why didn't they write themselves? The guest rooms – what a fancy house, Davie, to have special rooms for guests, not just a spare bed, but a separate room. Anyway, they are far away from the family living area of the house and John was alone in his bedroom. It was a rattlesnake, Davie. Somehow it got into the house and he must have surprised it, they think. He was bitten several times and no one heard him. The man of the house, someone called the padron, went upstairs when John did not appear for some kind of late party they were holding, some celebration or other, maybe to do with the end of the war. They were all waiting for him downstairs. This man, the padron, shot the snake, but it was too late to help John.

What kind of a country is Mexico, Davie, where a man walks around his own house with a gun? Oh dear God, Davie, what a dreadful way to die.'

Catriona began to cry for John, her once-loving husband; for old Jock, who had died at odds with his only child; for Victoria, who had never really known her father and whose memories of him were unhappy ones. Like Davie, Catriona had quite forgotten that wee Andrew was also John's child.

Davie held her and let her weep. She should mourn. It was natural, but as he held her a feeling almost of exaltation filled him. He too could have prayed for an easier death for his enemy, but John was dead and his heir was Victoria.

Catriona was too stunned to realize what John's death meant, but Davie and his father had talked of old Jock's real wishes many times. And the old man's wishes were finally, in this dreadful way, being carried out. The realization could only cheer Catriona.

'Sweetheart,' Davie whispered into her hair. 'Do you see what this means? The Priory belongs to Victoria. Your daughter won't have to leave you after all.'

At his words Catriona began to wail.

Arbuthnott Boatman was a contented man. He poured coffee from his mother's second-best Georgian silver tea-pot into one of her second-best Minton coffee cups and handed the cup, resting on its equally lovely saucer, to his newest client.

'Your grandfather would have been very happy to see you at the Priory, Victoria. He always meant to make a will in your favour. I reminded him several times, but I don't think he could bring himself to face the fact that John was a waster.' Suddenly conscious of the fact that he was talking about his client's late father, the lawyer coughed as if needing to clear his throat. 'Too bad about John. Perhaps if his mother had lived . . .' He changed the subject. 'I do hope your mother is well. It's been so difficult for her.'

'She has Davie and wee Andrew, Mr Boatman. No one could have wished . . . my . . . father such a death. The Mexican family was so sorry; they did and said everything right – through their lawyers, of course. Perhaps they speak no English. I would like to have known more: what my father was doing in that strange country, for instance. Still, they explained the circumstances of his death. He surprised the snake, which was nesting in an unused guest room. It's an arid country and sometimes snakes do come inside, as in India.'

Mr Boatman coughed. He led the topic of conversation away from the horror and sadness. 'You do understand that the farm and the trust fund are solely yours, Victoria. Your brother is—'

'To have half of everything, Mr Boatman,' said Victoria firmly. She had had plenty of time to think since her mother had broken the news of John's death. 'Andrew is not to blame for the circumstances of his birth. But that will be between us. My mother and stepfather love Andrew and think of him as their child. I have written to my fiancé. Naturally I am hoping that we will make our home here: he is a farmer too, and it would be good for the Priory to have an owner-occupier who loves the place. Edward could certainly come to love this area. But he is a proud man and may prefer a tenancy in England to living on my land.'

My land. Oh, what beautiful words. Until the lawyer had actually spoken, Victoria had not really let herself think about her new status. She owned outright every stick and stone of the Priory – every flower, every tree – and she loved everything about it: the burns that rippled through the meadows, even the very leaves that fell from the trees in autumn. Edward had to be prepared to love it too. Edward, however, did have some initial doubts.

*   *   *

'Come on, Eddie lad.' It was his father who convinced him. 'It's the twentieth century. Marriage is a partnership, you know, and you're a farmer born and raised. You'll be equal partners with Victoria. She may own the land but it's your brain and your sweat as will make a living from it. From what you tell us, your lass hasn't lived on the farm for years, and even then she did no labour . . .'

In his tiny room under the eaves Eddie read and re-read the letter from Victoria.

I can't mourn him, Eddie, although I hate to think of anyone dying such an awful death.

The farm is mine, because Andrew is illegitimate, but I have to share it with him. I know you will understand. There's room too for my mother and Davie and the bairn, but they want to stay in Blackness Road and make a go of the boarding house. Mother thinks newly weds should be on their own. Besides, she has come to enjoy being self-supporting, and now with Davie as a partner . . .

I have thought and thought and prayed too for guidance and I can see that a proud man might not want to start married life in his wife's home. I cannot sell the farm, but I am prepared to leave a manager in it and to go with you wherever you want. In India I realized that I can only be happy on the land, but I will be blissfully happy wherever you are.

Eddie sighed with sheer happiness. What a woman! She was prepared to give up her beloved home for him. No. When they were married, he would work all the hours God gave him to make her farm the best in the county. On that first visit to Angus, when he had asked Victoria to marry him, they had wandered hand-in-hand around Priory Farm and his trained eye had seen areas that could be improved, low hills where nothing was growing, which would be ideal for sheep-grazing. He knew nothing of soft fruits, but Victoria had told him there was a great summer trade and plenty of workers from nearby Dundee to help with the abundance of raspberries, strawberries, and redcurrants, which hung like rubies from the bushes every harvest. And Eddie would learn. He rolled off his bed and went to the table in the window to write to his Victoria. He was much more romantic, or perhaps more expressive, in his writing than she.

My dearest wife-to-be, he began and filled a page with sweet nothings that Victoria carried close to her heart until the next letter arrived.

Victoria had, of course, given in her notice to Mr Smart and had spoken to him about the advisability of having her train her own replacement. But although he said that he would advertise for a new assistant, he seemed reluctant.

'He hates change,' pronounced Miss Jessop. 'It's a shame you are to marry, Victoria, although I don't mean that in a nasty way, because I had hoped to see you in my place. Goodness knows what he will do when we both leave him. Men are such useless creatures, you know. They may talk about widening the Empire, but that's all it is, talk. Your Eddie will be the same, you'll see. Just start the way you mean to go on. Tell him what to do, congratulate him when he's done it and let him believe he thought of it for himself.'

'How that dried-up old stick, who's never got near a man except the two of us in all the time I've known her, can pass herself off as an expert on holy matrimony, I can't imagine,' sniffed Mr Gordon, once Miss Jessop was safely installed in Mr Smart's office.

Victoria smiled as Euan proceeded to tell her how to make her marriage a success. That was what she had heard everywhere since her engagement had been announced. The only two people who had not spoken to her of the dos and don'ts were the two people to whom she would have listened, her mother and Dr Currie. Both seemed strangely reluctant to offer advice.

'It's a meal on the table, clean clothes, and a bit of peace and quiet to read the paper, Victoria. That's all a man needs, and as for women, get your Eddie to take you to the pictures every Saturday night without fail. A bit of a canoodle in the one-and-nines and a choc-ice at the interval, maybe fish and chips on the way home.'

'Thanks, Mr Gordon. You can tell him yourself at the wedding.'

'And well I may, my girl. Forty-two years I've been married, man and boy.'

Catriona prepared for the wedding with a joy that knew no bounds. Victoria was to marry a young man whom she loved, and who loved her, and she was to live in the home that her beloved grandfather had always wanted her to have. *I always meant to put it in the lassie's name.*

How often those words had come back across the years to disturb Catriona's rest. But everything was going to be wonderful. John was gone and the farm belonged to Victoria. Everything had turned out well. She had Davie – dear, kind, hard-working Davie. A few weeks before the wedding, when she should have been deep in preparations and thank-you notes, and possibly even pre-wedding nerves, Victoria, with the aid of Dr Currie, had taken Catriona and Davie into Dundee. And there Victoria had presented them with a motor car.

'It's a second anniversary present, or a gift to celebrate my wedding. Call it what you like.'

Catriona and Davie had stared in fascination at the little black car.

'Lassie, lassie, brides don't give presents, they get them,' said Davie, as he wiped away a tear.

'The look on your face is my wedding present, Davie

Menmuir,' laughed Victoria. 'No, seriously, it's to say thank you to the two of you for everything.'

'This is not the way to begin married life, Victoria Cameron,' said Catriona sternly, but her gloved hand was already protectively rubbing imaginary dust off the mirror. 'You shouldn't be spending your trust fund on presents.'

'I have only bought one present, Mother, and if you're going to mention Eddie, he knows and he thinks it's a great idea.'

'And I shall give you driving lessons, Davie, and you too, if you'd like, Catriona,' volunteered Dr Currie.

Catriona managed not to shudder at that terrifying prospect, but privately vowed that Davie should learn to drive properly, in spite of dear Dr Flora's efforts to help. He was already talking of hiring himself out as a private taxi service. So much quicker than the horse buses or those draughty, uncomfortable motor buses that now clanked their way up and down Reform Street and the High Street. They would keep the telephone when, and if, Dr Flora left – she had said nothing about Lord Inchmarnock for some time, but Catriona had noticed the new watch and the long telephone calls. The telephone machine would be very convenient for her other lady guests and for those who needed a private hire car.

Wedding gifts for Victoria were pouring in from all sides. Mr Smart had given her a chest of sterling silverwear, each piece engraved with a flamboyant W. Dr Currie had given them a Crown Derby dinner service. Davie's mother had hand-embroidered an Irish linen tablecloth and twelve napkins. Where had she ever found the time, and how had those hands that could milk cows, cut wheat, clean brasses and sort potatoes ever been able to do do such delicate work? The stitches, Catriona admitted, for she was always honest, were better than her own. There were humbler gifts aplenty too, but each one would be treasured.

Thank-you notes were being written as the gifts arrived and posted back to the generous givers.

'We'll not need to buy a thing, Mother,' said Victoria as she unpacked a second copper jelly pan. 'That means that what's left of the fund can be used to improve the farm. Oh, Eddie is so clever and has such plans. If only Mr Smart . . .'

She stopped talking, but Catriona pressed her. 'Mr Smart what, dear?'

Victoria looked perplexed. 'He hasn't been himself since we came back from India and he hasn't done a thing about replacing me. I'm worried about him. I hope he didn't pick up some germ there.'

Catriona could imagine just what illness ailed Mr Smart. She had seen his eyes as he watched her daughter, and she ached for the man, but that was the way of the world. Victoria was far too young for Alistair Smart, and Catriona hoped he would soon realize it and put his foolishness behind him. He had been so generous and always so unfailingly courteous. Well, the young ones would soon be married and busy on their farm with their new life. An advertisement for secretarial assistance should go into the pages of the *Courier* soon, and the sooner the better, thought Catriona, giving her already scrupulously clean sink another wipe.

And Elsie had taken Victoria to a meeting in the Caird Hall. This votes business was another nonsense that Catriona could well do without. The sooner Victoria was married and away from the sphere of Elsie's influence, the better. Elsie had taken to popping in once or twice a week during the school dinner hour, and Victoria was certainly enjoying having a friend to talk with again. Better when they were discussing dresses and petticoats, though, rather than women's rights. Catriona rubbed her kettle until she could see her face in it. This war had done no good to anyone and had merely, as far as she could see, turned the world on its head.

'And when you're standing on your head,' said Catriona as she attacked the dust that had dared settle on her clean floor, 'you're no use tae man nor beast.'

'Who is standing on his head?' It was Davie at the door, looking for his dinner.

Catriona laughed. 'There's nothing like getting angry for getting brasses clean. Away and lift the bairn, Davie, and we'll maybe have peace to eat our dinner. I'm glad Elsie has classes this afternoon, for Victoria has another fitting at Draffen's and, according to Miss Morrison, yours truly has no eye for the latest fashion. She'd have Victoria walking up the aisle like a dressmaker's dummy, if I wasn't there to say No. Victoria's mooning over Eddie's letters all the time: I don't think she knows what she's doing half the time.'

'Don't underestimate my lassie, Catriona Menmuir. Remember she's been all the way tae India and back again, and run a big office full of men that say "Yes, Miss Cameron" and "What do you think of this, Miss Cameron?" She'll let Elsie talk, but I've yet to see her pay attention to anything she's said.'

'Except this suffrage nonsense.'

Davie took his undisputed courage in both hands. 'Maybe the lassies are in the right of it, Mistress Menmuir,' said he and ran off up the stairs to fetch Andrew.

21

Las Estrellas, Mexico

AFTER THE CRUEL TWIST OF fate that had left her a widow, Lucia Alcantarilla Cameron had passed the long, hot days in prayer. At least, she had tried to pray, but for what? Mother Mercedes told her that she should pray for the repose of the soul of her husband, so cruelly killed on their very wedding day, but Lucia did not want to pray for a dead man. She wanted to pray that it was all a horrible mistake and that the accident had not happened and the snake had not killed Juan. She wanted to pray that one day, perhaps today or surely tomorrow, her father would come to the convent and he would say, 'Ninita, you are forgiven. I have come to take you home, so that you may have your baby in the luxury and comfort into which an Alcantarilla-Medina-Cameron should be born. As far as we can, we will put these awful months behind us.'

But he had not come.

Sitting under the jacaranda trees, Lucia had remembered the discussions between her father and her brothers, when it became obvious that the child-widow was about to become a child-mother.

'We will take her to Mexico City. Surely a doctor can be found there who will abort this child.' That was Alvaro.

And then the shocked tones of José Luis. 'Cut out your tongue in shame, brother. To abort a child is a sin against God's law.'

Abortion was, to the religious José Luis, a sin. Those who whispered, therefore, that he had known of the snake in the unused guest chamber were wrong. For surely if to kill an unwanted baby was murder, then conniving at the death of a man who had seriously embarrassed one's family must also be murder and just as much against the laws of God.

'No reputable doctor will do it.' This from Jaime. 'We should take her to the United States, Papa. There you can pay for anything.'

But to *el Padrón* also, abortion was a sin. He would have none of it. 'My daughter will return to the convent of the good sisters. When this child is born, they can find a home for it and my little girl will come home and be herself again. We will find her a suitable husband and she will forget this madness.'

But no one asked the girl, who could never again be as she had been before. She had loved a man and she agreed with her father and brothers that she had sinned, but she was a married woman with her mother's rings upon her slender fingers and there was no need to hide her away in shame. The baby was her compensation for the loss of all her dreams, and so she would change those dreams. Papa would see the baby, his first grandchild, and he would love him. But Don Alejandro did not even say *adios* to his daughter, as she left to hide her mistake away in the cloisters, and Lucia did not understand that it broke his heart to banish his treasure and that he did it only because, after hours of prayer and thought, he had come to the conclusion that what he was doing was best for her.

José Luis had accompanied her. 'Everything is going to be all right, Ninita. This man took advantage of you, but the sisters will never tell and no one, except your future husband, need ever know. It is a bad dream, Lucia, but all dreams, good and bad, come to an end. See, I have bought for you some dream-stealers.'

He handed her the jeweller's box and, when she would

not take it, he opened the box. As if she were a child who could be humoured into taking her present, he showed her the beautiful silver earrings shaped like delicate spider's webs, from which dangled a tiny silver eagle's feather. In the centre of each fragile web hung a small turquoise. The indigenous peoples of the Americas believed that if they hung a representation of a spider's web above their baby's cradle, any bad dream flying through the air would become trapped in the web and would not disturb the child's slumbers. Clever jewellers had taken the legend and turned it into money.

José Luis had bought her the pretty baubles because he loved her, and he was sorry that he had had to make her cry. The old Lucia would have delighted in them, and would have thrown her loving arms around her brother's neck and kissed him. The new, mature Lucia had turned her head away and looked out of the dusty windows of the car.

'Lucia,' pleaded José Luis, 'try to understand. The blood of hundreds of years of Spanish history flows in your veins. It must not be mixed and weakened. You have had a shock and, unfortunately, you are to have a child. But you will never see the baby and therefore will not love it. It will be as if this year had never happened. Papa talks of taking you to Europe. Think, Lucia. Paris, Rome, Seville, the city of your ancestors. You will come home and there will be celebrations and a real marriage, to someone who is worthy of alliance with you. There will be other babies. Wear your earrings, Ninita, and let the bad dream go away.'

But Lucia did not wear her dream-stealers and she did not answer her brother.

And she did not speak much to Sister Mercedes, who loved Lucia and who did not judge and wonder how it could be that there was to be a baby and there had been no wedding night.

They walked in the convent gardens and the nun described

the great cities of Europe, which another young Mexican girl of good family had seen years before.

'It is strange, Lucia – and you must write to me and tell me if it is the same with you – but everywhere in Seville I saw and heard Beethoven, who was not of course a Spaniard.'

But the nun looked at the stricken face of the child beside her and stopped speaking of Beethoven, who had written so powerfully of the rights of man. What, she wondered, of the rights of women and of this unborn baby, condemned even before his birth by the very people who should have loved him most?

'Mozart, too, set operatic work in Seville, Lucia.' The nun tried again, but she fell quiet at the realization that perhaps *Don Giovanni* was not the best opera to discuss with a girl who, according to her father, had been violated.

Lucia saw her difficulties and smiled politely. 'I prefer Beethoven, *Madre*,' was all she said.

For the months of her confinement Lucia was biddable. She rose each morning and went to the chapel and seemed to pray. She ate a little of everything that was presented to her, but only smiled when coaxed to eat and reminded that she was eating for two. Every day she walked in the shade of the gardens and sat reading in the cool of the evening. Twice Don Alvaro arrived in secret and she awoke to his presence like a flower to the sun.

'Don't let them take my baby away, Alvaro,' she begged.

'I don't know how to defy our father, Lucia. If he knew I was here . . . We must pray for time, little sister. Papa loves you.'

Her delicate hands gestured that thought away.

'He does, Lucia, but I think perhaps he does not know how to love. He mourns for you as if you were dead. He truly believes that this is the right thing to do, and maybe it *is* best.'

She stood up imperiously. 'Leave me, Alvaro.'

'Please, Lucia, listen. To deal with Papa you must be as devious as he. Wait. The sisters have been asked to give your baby away. I will know where he is, sister, and I will keep my eye on him and his well-being until we can convince Papa that he should return to his family.'

She would not ask the only question she wanted to ask: Did my father murder my husband? She smiled at her brother. Poor Alvaro. He knew how to love.

'I hope you find someone worthy of your love one day, *mi hermano*,' she said.

'I love you, Lucia, and Papa too when I am not afraid of him, and even José Luis.'

'He is a cruel man, Alvaro.'

'No. He is, as he sees it, just, Lucia. How unfortunate to be born the oldest son of Don Alejandro. I am forgiven much, because no life or death decisions depend on my competence.'

'There must be more than competence. There must be feeling.'

'Papa feels, little sister, and so too does our brother.'

'So they banish me with my sin to the convent and they will take my child away, an Alcantarilla Medina to be raised by some peasant.'

'You will change them. Papa can deny you nothing. How he missed you during the civil war. "Is she safer with the sisters than with me?" he would ask. "The war rages close. Should I bring the rose of the Alcantarillas here, where I can defend her honour with my blood?" And, yet, despite his care, it was in his house that . . . well, you know, Lucia. And he blames himself.'

'Was it so great a sin to love a man who is not of our people?'

Alvaro thought of the man, John Cameron, but he could not say to her, 'Only that man, Lucia, for he knew you were only a child.' So he took his sister's hand and wondered that the hand of a pregnant woman should grow so thin. And he promised that he would help her and he walked with her in the garden.

Then Alvaro went home and dared his father's wrath by admitting that he had visited his sister. And his father smiled sadly. 'Do you think one blade of grass grows on my acres that I do not know about, Alvaro? I am doing what is right, *ninito*, for all of you. I am arranging a great alliance in Spain for your sister. She will thank me when she sits at her table with many fine sons around her. But not the child of Cameron, Alvaro. The man was a cheat and a liar and he seduced a sixteen-year-old child. The snake was too good for him. Visit your sister when you must, but do not come whining and confessing your trangressions to me. And, for the sake of peace in my unhappy home, keep out of your brother's way, for he does not have my forbearance.'

A few months later Alvaro stood by the altar as his oldest brother took a wife. And when José Luis was safely on his wedding journey, Alvaro went back to the convent and what he saw there made him send his groom back immediately for Don Alejandro.

The child comes before its time and my sister does not try to help. You must come and tell Lucia that she is loved and that you will bring her and her baby home.

And Don Alejandro drove through the night to the convent and found the door to his daughter's rooms barred to him.

Inside the room, the girl lay on the narrow white bed and held in her hand the jewelled crucifix she had held on her wedding day. The pains gripped her tired body, and at last she could bear no more and cried out. The old nun who sat by her bed stood up and went to the door.

'It is time, *Padrón*,' she said to the tall man who knelt at the prie-dieu in the corridor.

'If I could suffer her pain for her, I would,' said Don Alejandro. 'Do your best for her, Sister.'

'You should not have put her here, Father,' whispered Don Alvaro. 'She is a flower, and flowers die without sun. There was no sun for my sister without the love of her family.'

Don Alejandro stared blankly at his youngest son and wondered why he did not strike him for his insolence. Sun! There had been no sun for him either, for the last nine months, but soon it would be over and Lucia would come home and forget all her troubles. New clothes, jewels, travel, new friends – the girl whom José Luis had just married would be a perfect companion for his beloved daughter. Soon the baby that had ruined Lucia's life would be born and she could come home and be his little girl again. He willed it to be so.

Three hours later the sobbing nuns held out the squalling baby to him. 'She did not try, *Padrón*,' they wailed. 'Her heart was broken.'

He ignored the wailing child: he felt no love, no pity, for it. He ignored his youngest son, who wept quietly by the bed. He knelt and kissed his daughter's clasped hands. Gently he removed the heavy emerald-encrusted wedding band and the jewelled crucifix. They had been his wife's jewels and then, for so short a time, his Lucia's. He handed them to the nun who held the baby.

'Get rid of it,' he said coldly. 'I never want to hear from you again. Go outside until you can behave like a man, Alvaro,' he ordered, as he pulled the young man to his feet and thrust him into the corridor.

He waited until they had gone, sobbing, from the room and then Don Alejandro knelt down on the bare floor beside the body of his child and began, very quietly, to weep.

22

LORD INCHMARNOCK TOO WAS A man who was having to adjust to circumstances. He had been taken by complete surprise when his Flora had told him that she would find it difficult to choose between him and medicine. His upbringing had not really prepared him for a strong, capable and yet intensely feminine woman. Everything he had been brought up to believe in was as much under fire as the men in the trenches during the war.

'I love you dearly, Sandy,' she had said and he could not doubt the sincerity in her voice, 'but I have accustomed myself to living without your love. I am a doctor, and I find that I cannot give that up while I am still useful. Don't make me choose between you.' She had stood up then and moved away from him, and Sandy had looked at Flora and seen that she had never been more beautiful, or more desirable, and he had wondered at this mysterious chemistry, for to most she would have looked tired and even gaunt. She had turned back to him and put out her arms, as if to hold him, then she had dropped her hands by her sides. And she had spoken eloquently about her calling and her patients.

He cast his mind back all those years and saw the young Flora – Flora, whose every unexpressed wish had been answered by an army of faithful servants. She tore a flounce on her dress and somehow it was mended. She soiled her gloves and they were returned to her clean. She was hungry and every dish that could tempt her appetite was prepared in case Miss Flora should prefer . . . That dratted war had changed things – and not all of them for the better. Women who had been brought up to expect that there would always be servants to do things for them had dirtied their hands for the first time, and had enjoyed the experience, and his Flora more than most. He had jilted her for the flighty Julia, and Flora had squared her delicate shoulders and become a doctor: she had been present at births, at deaths and at every human condition in between. Now he wanted to take her away from it all and make life as sheltered and charmed as it had once been, but she did not want that. She wanted him, but she wanted her life of service too.

Was Britain ready for them both yet? He could no longer stay in Scotland, because in that beautiful country he had been too happy and then too sad. Perhaps after several years had passed he would not see Robert everywhere, would not turn with a start because the set of the shoulders of a young man who had just entered the room made him think, 'Robert'. One day he would surrender to the knowledge that Robert would not return.

England, then? No, not yet.

Australia. That was the place. As soon as the divorce was final he would go to Australia and buy some land. He and Flora would marry and no one there would care that he was divorced. Flora could practise medicine. From what the Ambassador had told him, she would be welcomed with open arms. Pity he didn't know a thing about sheep – but he could learn, *would* learn. If that laddie Sinclair could step out of a jute mill in Dundee and take to farming like the proverbial duck to water, then how much easier for him, who had grown up on the land. With Flora beside him, he could do anything.

Again the searing pain of his loss tore through him.

'Oh, Robert, laddie, how can I even begin to think that I might get over losing you. But, oh dear God, I pray to be able to think of you without pain.'

Sandy sat down to write to his love and, like Eddie Welborn, he had no trouble saying what was in his heart.

Dr Currie laughed and cried when she read the letter. Australia. If they went there, it was tantamount to saying goodbye to everything and everyone she held dear: Catriona, Victoria, wee Andrew, Davie, her colleagues, her patients. And here was Victoria in the middle of preparations for a summer wedding, and Flora did not want to miss that. And did she even want to go to Australia? She looked into her heart and answered the question herself. If she had Sandy Fotheringham and her work, she would go anywhere – even to the other side of the world, away from everyone and everything she knew.

Darling Sandy,

Of course I will go with you to Australia. I would walk beside you and, with you, brave any hardship. It's going to be such an adventure, but we must go together.

I shall begin to wind up my affairs here, but there are one or two patients who still need me and who will need me for the next few months. After that, your Flora will go anywhere with you.

Victoria and her Eddie are to marry and to live at the farm. He is a very sensible young man and it is obvious that he is deeply in love with Victoria. She, of course, is walking around deliriously happy and getting in Catriona's way. The wedding is to be at Priory Farm and I should like to be here for that. Then there is Nellie's second confinement.

Wee Jimmy arrived with the help of his granny, but Jimmy's sibling is to have all 'modern conveniences'. You see, I am as welcome as the latest in plumbing. No doubt I will be valued in like fashion in the great outdoors.

And do you really intend to become a sheep farmer? Since your wife-to-be is determined to work, are you determined to labour too? Thank you for understanding my needs.

The next part made her write and tear up the first few
drafts. She was, after all, forty-two years old and had,
many years before (the year in fact that Julia had drifted
down the aisle to marry Sandy Inchmarnock) given up all
thought of having a child of her own. But, maybe, just
maybe she was not too old. Should she say something that
might raise hopes of a bereaved father? Yes. No. She wrote
and discarded, then took refuge in being enigmatic.

*And remember, my dearest, that my health has always been
good. Perhaps one day I shall have other things to occupy
me – and I do not mean 'good works', like Victoria's friend,
Elsie. I shall miss day-to-day knowledge of Elsie's career,
but I am sure even Australia shall one day hear of her.
She has determined that the vote is not enough and that
women are also entitled to representation. A female Member
of Parliament! Can you think what my dear father would
have had to say about that? Perhaps it is as well that you
propose to take me halfway across the world, for the notion
of joining the martial Elsie has occurred to me, and I fear
I have already blotted my family copybook enough. I see
that Julia is to be a member of a committee that will raise
funds for war relief. It is an excellent way for her to begin
to reinstate herself in her circle. I could not be happy, Sandy,
at the expense of her suffering. She sent me a sweet note to
wish us well, and I pray that she too will eventually find
some happiness.*

*Can you come North for the wedding? Then we too can
be married quietly and make that incredible journey to the
Antipodes together. See how bold the modern woman has
become!*

*I wear your watch every day and take comfort from its
inscription.*

Dr Currie delivered Miss Mary (after Her Majesty the
Queen) Flora (after the lady doctor) Bains-Sinclair two days

before Miss Victoria Cameron married Mr Edward Welborn at the wee church at Liff, where both Miss Cameron and Mrs Sinclair had been christened. Miss Cameron was given in marriage by her stepfather, Mr David Menmuir. And since her chosen attendant was necessarily unavailable, she was attended rather amusingly by Master James Sinclair, who ate the flowers in his posy all the way down the aisle, and by her brother Andrew, who abandoned both sister and posy in the middle of the aisle, when he discovered his Menmuir grampa trying to hide from him in a side pew. Miss Elsie Morrison was heard to mutter that she could hardly wait to get both little boys to the Harris Academy for 'sorting', but even she was seen to wipe a tear from her eye at the look in Eddie Welborn's face when he turned and saw the ethereal figure of his bride coming down the aisle on the proud arm of Davie Menmuir. Neither wee boy would stand still for the obligatory wedding picture, so Victoria held one and Eddie the other. But even the stiff result of modern photography could not hide the happiness in the eyes of the new Mr and Mrs Edward Welborn. The young couple, who had both travelled extensively, went off for a week's holiday to Pitlochry, where Eddie began to teach Victoria to play golf and Victoria taught Eddie the new dance steps learned from Elsie, that arbiter of fashion, in the days before the wedding. Then they had a week in the Lake District with Eddie's parents and, during lovely long walks, began to think seriously about the changes they might make at their own farm.

'I can still hardly believe that the Priory is ours, Eddie,' said Victoria, as she sat very decorously beside her new husband on the train journey back to Dundee.

Boldly Eddie took her hand with the shiny, new gold ring and held it in his. 'Yours and Andie's, Victoria.'

'We're partners, Eddie, in everything,' smiled Victoria. Then she blushed furiously at the thought that Eddie might think her remark bold.

Davie met them at the station and, after a quick visit to Catriona at Blackness Road, he drove the Welborns to their own home.

'We're having a telephone put in, Davie,' said Eddie, 'and as soon as my wife is ready, she will ring you two and invite you to dinner.'

Davie was delighted. He had never before been formally invited to 'Take yer dinner with us, Davie', and he drove off happily to tell Catriona of the delights in store. But it was three weeks later before Victoria felt confident enough in her housewifely abilities to contemplate having guests for dinner. Nellie Sinclair was anxious to get back to work and seemed to see no problem at all in working for her old school friend. Still, Victoria wanted to tidy her new house all by herself and to cook her very first dinner for company without any help. Because Catriona had always washed the best dishes before and after every use, Victoria spent a lovely day washing her new china and setting the table in her grandfather's panelled dining room. She looked at the beautifully embroidered cloth, the fine silverware and the exquisite china, and she smiled with brand-new housewifely pride.

'The food won't be as good as Mother's,' she whispered to whatever happy spirits hovered around her, as she went about her self-appointed tasks, 'but there's a surprise after dinner and it's especially for you, Grampa.'

The Scotch broth was a little too salty, the roast beef rather well done, and the sherry for the trifle had been poured with rather too liberal a hand. But the errors were all ones that would mend, and the guests, Catriona, Davie and wee Andrew, were lavish with their compliments, although Andrew made a terrible face when he tried his trifle and demanded to get down, in a tone that brooked no argument.

'Don't let him outside, Davie,' whispered Victoria. 'We don't want him falling in our hole.'

At last the time had come for her surprise. Davie captured Andrew and kept him happy rolling nuts along the table, while Victoria told Eddie about walnut shell days.

'And because we are so happy, darling Eddie, and our life is going to be full of walnut shell days, we are going to have our very own walnut tree. Outside, everyone.'

They went outside to the small lawn that ran from the house down to the brook. A few days before the party Tam and Davie had dug a fine hole in the middle of the lawn, and sitting lopsidedly beside it was a small sapling.

'That's our walnut tree, Eddie, for our tomorrows are going to be full of walnut shell days, just like today.'

She stood still suddenly as from the past a well-loved voice came to her. *It's a day that's beautiful because you are with the person you love most in all the world* . . . Victoria listened to the beloved voice and smiled mistily at her husband. 'Now, Eddie, if you and Davie lift it and put it in, Mother and I will finish planting it.'

Catriona said nothing, but her eyes were wet with tears as she watched her husband, her son and her new son-in-law manoeuvre the walnut tree into its new home. The men walked off to the brook to sail leaf boats for Andrew, and Victoria and her mother were left alone.

'This is for Grampa, Mother, and for you, and for dear Davie who has brought so much happiness into our lives.' And Victoria knelt down on the grass and firmed the soil around the tree's roots with her hands. She laughed as the good Angus earth dulled her tiny diamond, and she brushed her ring clean on her skirt.

Catriona knelt beside her and took handfuls of soil which she patted into place around the base of the sapling. 'And it's for dear Flora, who will soon be the new Lady Inchmarnock, and for Nellie and her family, and for your Eddie, Victoria, and for all the people who will belong here after us, and especially for you. I couldn't have wished for a better daughter.'

They were Angus farm folk. They were unused to the kisses on the cheeks that other people used, often with little meaning, but their hearts were full. And there on the ground they leaned towards one another and Catriona held her daughter in her arms, as she had done when she was a child, and Victoria held her mother, and together they thought of all the people they had mentioned.

'And it's for all the others who mean so much to us, Mother. Mr Smart and all the Menmuirs, and even Arbuthnott Boatman and Lord Inchmarnock. Do you think they're too grand to want to be in a walnut shell?'

'Och, lassie,' said Catriona, getting up rather stiffly from the ground. 'Is there a person in the world who doesn't need the memory of a walnut shell day? Be happy here, lassie, with your Eddie, all the days of your life.'